FIRST AMONG E~

Jeffrey Archer is a master storyteller, the author of ten novels which have all been worldwide bestsellers. *Not a Penny More, Not a Penny Less* was his first book, and it achieved instant success. Next came the tense and terrifying thriller *Shall We Tell the President?*, followed by his triumphant bestseller *Kane and Abel*. His first collection of short stories, *A Quiver Full of Arrows*, came next, and then *The Prodigal Daughter*, the superb sequel to *Kane and Abel*. This was followed by *First Among Equals*, considered by the *Scotsman* to be the finest novel about parliament since Trollope, the thrilling chase story *A Matter of Honour*, his second collection of stories, *A Twist in the Tale*, and the novels *As the Crow Flies* and *Honour Among Thieves*. *Twelve Red Herrings*, his third collection of stories, was followed by the novels *The Fourth Estate* and *The Eleventh Commandment*. A collected edition of his short stories was published in 1997, followed by another collection, *To Cut a Long Story Short*.

Jeffrey Archer was born in 1940 and educated at Wellington School, Somerset and Brasenose College, Oxford. He represented Great Britain in the 100 metres in the early sixties, and entered the House of Commons when he won the by-election at Louth in 1969. He wrote his first novel, *Not a Penny More, Not a Penny Less*, in 1974. From September 1985 to October 1986 he was Deputy Chairman of the Conservative Party, and he was created a Life Peer in the Queen's Birthday Honours of 1992.

JEFFREY ARCHER

FIRST AMONG EQUALS

THE ELEVENTH COMMANDMENT

Grafton

Political cartoons by Charles Griffin

This omnibus edition published in 2003 by
HarperCollins*Publishers*
77-85 Fulham Palace Road,
Hammersmith, London W6 8JB

www.**fire**and**water**.com

First Among Equals
Copyright © Jeffrey Archer 1984

The Eleventh Commandment
Copyright © Jeffrey Archer 1998

The Author asserts the moral right to
be identified as the author of this work

ISBN 0 00 768315 4

Set in Baskerville

Printed and bound in Great Britain by
Mackays of Chatham Ltd, Chatham, Kent

To Alan and Eddie

Raymond Gould

Simon Kerslake

Charles Seymour

Andrew Fraser

PROLOGUE

WEDNESDAY 10 APRIL 1931

If Charles Gurney Seymour had been born nine minutes earlier he would have become an earl, inherited a castle in Scotland, 22,000 acres in Somerset, and a thriving merchant bank in the City of London.

It was to be several years before young Charles worked out the full significance of coming second in life's first race.

His twin brother, Rupert, only just came through the ordeal, and in the years that followed contracted not only the usual childhood illnesses but managed to add scarlet fever, diphtheria and meningitis, causing his mother, Lady Seymour, to fear for his survival.

Charles, on the other hand, *was* a survivor, and had inherited enough Seymour ambition for both his brother and himself. Only a few years passed before those who came into contact with the brothers for the first time mistakenly assumed Charles was the heir to the earldom.

As the years passed Charles's father tried desperately to discover something at which Rupert might triumph over his brother – and failed. When they were eight the two boys were sent away to Summer Fields where generations of Seymours had been prepared for the rigours of Eton. During his first month at the Oxford prep school Charles was voted form captain and no one hindered his advance *en route* to becoming head boy at the age of twelve, by which time Rupert was looked upon as Seymour Minor. Both boys proceeded to Eton, where in their first half Charles beat

Rupert at every subject in the classroom, outrowed him on the river and nearly killed him in the boxing ring.

When in 1947 their grandfather, the thirteenth Earl of Bridgwater, finally expired, the sixteen-year-old Rupert became Viscount Seymour while Charles inherited a meaningless prefix.

The Hon Charles Seymour felt angry every time he heard his brother deferentially addressed by strangers as 'My Lord'.

At Eton, Charles continued to excel and ended his schooldays as President of Pop before being offered a place at Christ Church, Oxford, to read History. Rupert covered the same years without over-burdening the examiners, internal or external. At the age of eighteen the young viscount returned to the family estate in Somerset to pass the rest of his days as a landowner. No one destined to inherit 22,000 acres could be described as a farmer.

At Oxford, Charles, free of Rupert's shadow, progressed with the air of a man who found the university something of an anticlimax. He would spend his weekdays reading the history of his relations and the weekends at house parties or riding to hounds. As no one had suggested for one moment that Rupert should enter the world of high finance, it was assumed once Charles had left Oxford that he would succeed his father at Seymour's Bank: first as a director and then in time as its chairman: although it would be Rupert who would eventually inherit the family shareholding.

This 'best laid plan' changed, however, when one evening the Hon Charles Seymour was dragged off to the Oxford Union by a nubile undergraduate from Somerville, who demanded he should listen to the Eights Week motion, 'I would rather be a commoner than a lord'. The President of the Union had achieved the unique coup of having the motion proposed by the Prime Minister, Sir Winston Churchill.

Charles sat at the back of a hall packed with eager students mesmerised by the elder statesman's performance. Never once did he take his eyes off the great war leader during his witty and powerful speech, although what kept flashing across his mind was the realisation that, but for an accident of birth, Churchill would have been the ninth Duke of Marlborough. Here was a man who had dominated the world stage for three decades and then turned down every hereditary honour a grateful nation could offer, including the title of Duke of London.

From that moment Charles never allowed himself to be referred to as 'the Hon' again: his ultimate ambition was now above mere titles.

Another undergraduate who listened to Churchill that night was also considering his future. But he did not view proceedings crammed between his fellow students at the back of the crowded hall. The tall young man dressed in white tie and tails sat alone in a large chair on a raised platform, for such was his right as President of the Oxford Union.

Although Simon Kerslake *was* the first-born, he had otherwise few of Charles Seymour's advantages. The only son of a family solicitor, he had come to appreciate how much his father had denied himself to ensure that his son should remain at the local public school. Simon's father had died during his son's last year at Lancing College, leaving his widow a small annuity and a magnificent MacKinley grandfather clock. Simon's mother sold the clock a week after the funeral in order that her son could complete his final year with all the 'extras' the other boys took for granted. She also hoped that it would give Simon a better chance of going on to university.

From the first day he could walk Simon had always wanted to outdistance his rivals. The Americans would have described him as 'an achiever', while many of his contemporaries thought of him as pushy, or even arrogant, according to their aptitude for jealousy. During his last term at Lancing Simon was passed over for head of school and he still found himself unable to forgive the headmaster his lack of foresight. Later that year, some weeks after he had completed his S-levels and been interviewed by Magdalen, a circular letter informed him that he would not be offered a place at Oxford; it was a decision Simon was unwilling to accept.

In the same mail Durham University offered him a scholarship, which he rejected by return of post. "Future Prime Ministers aren't educated at Durham," he informed his mother.

"How about Cambridge?" she enquired, continuing to wipe the dishes.

"No political tradition," replied Simon.

"But if there is no chance of being offered a place at Oxford, surely –?"

"That's not what I said, Mother," replied the young man. "I shall be an undergraduate at Oxford by the first day of term."

After eighteen years of forty-yard goals Mrs Kerslake had learned to stop asking her son, "How will you manage that?"

Some fourteen days before the start of the Michaelmas Term at Oxford Simon booked himself into a small guest house just off the Iffley Road. On a trestle table in the corner of lodgings he intended to make permanent he wrote out a list of all the colleges, then divided them into five columns, planning to visit three each morning and three each afternoon until his question had been answered positively by a resident Tutor for Admissions: "Have you accepted any freshmen for this year who are now unable to take up their places?"

It was on the fourth afternoon, just as doubt was beginning to set in and Simon was wondering if after all he would have to travel to Cambridge the following week, that he received the first affirmative reply.

The Tutor for Admissions at Worcester College removed the glasses from the end of his nose and stared at the tall young man with a mop of dark hair falling over his forehead. Alan Brown was the twenty-second don Kerslake had visited in four days.

"Yes," he replied. "It so happens that a young man from Nottingham High School, who had been offered a place here, was tragically killed in a motor cycle accident last month."

"What course – what subject was he going to read?" Simon's words were unusually faltering. He prayed it wasn't Chemistry, Anthropology or Classics. Alan Brown flicked through a rotary index on his desk, obviously enjoying the little cross-examination. He peered at the card in front of him. "History," he announced.

Simon's heartbeat reached 120. "I just missed a place at Magdalen to read Politics, Philosophy and Economics," he said. "Would you consider me for the vacancy?"

The older man was unable to hide a smile. He had never in twenty-four years come across such a request.

"Full name?" he said, replacing his glasses as if the serious business of the meeting had now begun.

"Simon John Kerslake."

Dr Brown picked up the telephone by his side and dialled a number. "Nigel?" he said. "It's Alan Brown here. Did you ever consider offering a man called Kerslake a place at Magdalen?"

Mrs Kerslake was not surprised when her son went on to be President of the Oxford Union. After all, she teased, wasn't it just another stepping stone on the path to Prime Minister – Gladstone, Asquith . . . Kerslake?

Ray Gould was born in a tiny, windowless room above his father's butcher's shop in Leeds. For the first nine years of his life he shared that room with his ailing grandmother until she died at the age of sixty-one.

Ray's close proximity to the old woman who had lost her husband in the Great War at first appeared romantic to him. He would listen enraptured as she told him stories of her hero husband in his smart khaki uniform – a uniform now folded neatly in her bottom drawer, but still displayed in the fading sepia photograph at the side of her bed. Soon, however, his grandmother's stories filled Ray with sadness, as he became aware that she had been a widow for nearly thirty years. Finally she seemed a tragic figure as he realised how little she had experienced of the world beyond that cramped room in which she was surrounded by all her possessions and a yellowed envelope containing 500 irredeemable war bonds.

There had been no purpose in Ray's grandmother making a will, for all he inherited was the room. Overnight it became his study – full of ever-changing library and school books, the former often returned late, using up Ray's meagre pocket money in fines. But as each school report was brought home it became increasingly apparent to Ray's father that he would not be extending the sign above the butcher's shop to proclaim 'Gould and Son'.

Shortly after his eleventh birthday Ray won the top scholarship to Roundhay School. Wearing his first pair of long trousers – turned up several inches by his mother – and hornrimmed spectacles that didn't quite fit, he set off for the opening day at his new school. Ray's mother hoped there were other boys as thin and spotty as her son, and that his wavy red hair would not cause him to be continually teased.

By the end of his first term Ray was surprised to find he was far ahead of his classmates, so far in fact that the headmaster considered it prudent to put him up a form – "to stretch the lad a little", as he explained to Ray's parents.

By the end of that year, one spent mainly in the classroom, Ray managed to come third in the form, and top in Latin and English. Only when it came to selecting teams for any sport did Ray find he came bottom in anything. However brilliant his mind might have been, it never seemed to co-ordinate with his body. His single greatest academic achievement during the year, though, was to be the youngest winner of the prize essay competition in the school's history.

Each year the winner of the essay was required to read his entry to the assembled pupils and parents on Speech Day. Even before he handed in his entry Ray rehearsed his efforts out loud several times in the privacy of his study-bedroom, fearing he would not be properly prepared if he waited until the winner was announced.

Ray's form master had told all his pupils that the subject of the essay could be of their own choosing, but that they should try to recall some experience that had been unique to them. Thirty-seven entries arrived on his desk by nine o'clock on the closing date six weeks later. After reading Ray's account of his grandmother's life in the little room above the butcher's shop the form master had no inclination to pick up another script. When he had dutifully struggled through the remainder he did not hesitate in recommending Gould's essay for the prize. The only reservation, he admitted to its author, was the choice of title. Ray thanked him for the advice but the title remained intact.

On the morning of Speech Day the school hall was packed with 700 pupils and their parents. After the headmaster had delivered his speech and the applause had died down, he announced, "I shall now call upon the winner of the prize essay competition to deliver his entry: Ray Gould."

Ray left his place in the hall and marched confidently up on to the stage. He stared down at the 2,000 expectant faces but showed no sign of apprehension, partly because he found it difficult to see beyond the third row. When he announced the title of his essay some of the younger children began to snigger, causing Ray to stumble through his first few lines. But by the time he had reached the last page the packed hall was still, and after he had completed the final paragraph he received the first standing ovation of his career.

Twelve-year-old Ray Gould left the stage to rejoin his parents in the body of the hall. His mother's head was bowed but he could still see tears trickling down her cheeks. His father was trying not to look too proud. Even when Ray was seated the applause continued, so he too lowered his head to stare at the title of his prize-winning essay: 'The first changes I will make when I become Prime Minister'.

Andrew Fraser attended his first political meeting in a pram. True, he was left in the corridor while his parents sat on the stage inside another draughty hall, but he quickly learned that applause signalled his mother would soon be returning. What Andrew did not know was that his father, who had made his name as Scotland's finest scrum-half since the Great War, had delivered yet another speech to the citizens of Edinburgh Carlton in his efforts to capture a marginal seat on the City Council. At that time few believed Duncan Fraser was more than a rugby hero, and consequently he failed to win the seat for the Conservatives, if only by a few hundred votes. Three years later Andrew, a sturdy four-year-old, was allowed to sit at the back of several sparsely filled halls as once again he and his mother trailed round the city to support their candidate. This time Duncan Fraser's speeches were almost as impressive as his long pass, and he won his place on the City Council by 207 votes.

Hard work and consistent results on behalf of his constituents ensured that the marginal seat remained in the hands of Councillor Fraser for the next nine years. By the age of thirteen, Andrew, a stocky wee lad with straight black hair and a grin that no one seemed to be able to remove from his face, had learned enough about local politics to help his father organise a fifth campaign, by which time neither party considered Edinburgh Carlton a marginal seat.

At the Edinburgh Academy it came as no surprise to his fellow pupils that Andrew was chosen to captain the school debating society; however, they were impressed when under his leadership the team went on to win the Scottish Schools debating trophy. Although Andrew was destined to be no taller than five-foot-nine it was also widely accepted that he was the most complete scrum-half the Academy had produced since his father had captained the school side in 1919.

On matriculating from the Academy Andrew took up a place at Edinburgh University to read Politics, and by his third year he had been elected President of the Union and captain of rugby.

When Duncan Fraser became Lord Provost of Edinburgh he made one of his rare visits to London, to receive a knighthood from the Queen. Andrew had just completed his final exams and, along with his mother, attended the investiture at Buckingham Palace. After the ceremony Sir Duncan travelled on to the House of Commons to fulfil an engagement with his local member, Ainslie Munro. Over lunch Munro informed Sir Duncan that he had contested the Edinburgh Carlton seat for the last time, so they had better start looking for a new candidate. Sir Duncan's eyes lit up as he savoured the thought of his son succeeding Munro as his Member of Parliament.

After Andrew had been awarded an honours degree at Edinburgh, he remained at the university to complete a thesis entitled 'The history of the Conservative party in Scotland'. He planned to wait for his father to complete the statutory three years as Lord Provost before he informed him of the most significant outcome the research for his doctorate had produced. But when Ainslie Munro announced officially that he would not be contesting the next election Andrew knew he could no longer hide his true feelings if he wanted to be considered for the seat.

'Like father, like son,' read the headline in the centre-page of the *Edinburgh Evening News*, who considered that Andrew Fraser was the obvious candidate if the Conservatives hoped to hold on to the marginal seat. Sir Duncan, fearing the local burghers would consider Andrew too young, reminded them at the first selection meeting that eight Scots had been Prime Ministers and every one had been in the House before the age of thirty. He was pleased to find members nodding their agreement. When Sir Duncan returned home that night he phoned his son and suggested that they should have lunch at the New Club the following day to discuss a plan of campaign.

"Think of it," said Sir Duncan, after he had ordered a second whisky. "Father and son representing the same constituency. It will be a great day for the Edinburgh Conservative party."

"Not to mention the Labour party," said Andrew, looking his father in the eye.

"I am not sure I take your meaning," said the Lord Provost.

"Precisely that, Father. I do not intend to contest the seat as a Conservative. I hope to be selected as the Labour candidate – if they'll adopt me."

Sir Duncan looked disbelieving. "But you've been a Conservative all your life," he declared, his voice rising with every word.

"No, Father," replied Andrew quietly. "It's you who have been a Conservative all my life."

BOOK ONE

1964·1966

THE BACK BENCHES

CHAPTER
ONE

THURSDAY 10 DECEMBER 1964

Mr Speaker rose and surveyed the Commons. He tugged at his long black silk gown, then nervously tweaked the full-bottomed wig that covered his balding head. The House had almost got out of control during a particularly rowdy session of Prime Minister's questions, and he was delighted to see the clock reach three-thirty. Time to pass on to the next business of the day.

He stood shifting from foot to foot waiting for the 500-odd members present to settle down before he intoned solemnly, "Members desiring to take the oath." The packed assembly switched its gaze from the Speaker to the far end of the Chamber, like a crowd watching a tennis match. There, standing at the bar of the Commons, was the victor of the first by-election since the Labour party had taken office some two months before.

The new member, flanked by his proposer and seconder, took four paces forward. Like well-drilled guardsmen, they stopped and bowed. The stranger stood at six-foot-four. He looked like a man born with the Tory party in mind, his patrician head set on an aristocratic frame, a mane of fair hair combed meticulously into place. Dressed in a dark grey, double-breasted suit and wearing a Guards' tie of maroon and blue, he advanced once again towards the long table that stood in front of the Speaker's chair between the two front benches which faced each other a mere sword's length apart.

Leaving his sponsors in his wake, he passed down the Government side, stepping over the legs of the Prime

Minister and Foreign Secretary before being handed the oath by the Clerk of the House.

He held the little card in his right hand and pronounced the words as firmly as if they had been his marriage vows.

"I, Charles Seymour, do swear that I will be faithful, and bear true allegiance to Her Majesty Queen Elizabeth, her heirs and successors according to law, so help me God."

"Hear, hear," rose from his colleagues on the benches opposite as the new MP leaned over to subscribe the Test Roll, a parchment folded into book-shape. Charles was introduced to the Speaker by the Clerk. The new member then proceeded towards the chair where he stopped and bowed.

"Welcome to the House, Mr Seymour," said the Speaker, shaking his hand. "I hope you will serve this place for many years to come."

"Thank you, Mr Speaker," said Charles, and bowed for a final time before continuing on behind the Speaker's chair. He had carried out the little ceremony exactly as the Tory Chief Whip had rehearsed it with him in the long corridor outside his office.

Waiting for him behind the Speaker's chair and out of sight of the other members was the leader of the Opposition, Sir Alec Douglas-Home, who also shook him warmly by the hand.

"Congratulations on your splendid victory, Charles. I know you have a great deal to offer to our party and indeed your country."

"Thank you," replied the new MP, who after waiting for Sir Alec to return to take his place on the Opposition front bench made his way up the steps of the side gangway to find a place in the back row of the long green benches.

For the next two hours Charles Seymour followed the proceedings of the House with a mixture of awe and excitement. For the first time in his life he had found something that wasn't his by right or by effortless conquest. Glancing up at the Strangers' Gallery he saw his wife Fiona, his father the fourteenth Earl of Bridgwater and his brother, the Viscount Seymour, peering down at him with pride. Charles settled back on the first rung of the ladder. He smiled to himself: only six weeks ago he had feared it would be many more years before he could hope to take a seat in the House of Commons.

At the general election a mere two months before, Charles had contested a South Wales mining seat with an impregnable Labour majority. "Good for the experience, not to mention the soul," the vice-chairman in charge of candidates at Conservative Central Office had assured him. He had proved to be right on both counts, for Charles had relished the contest and brought the Labour majority down from 22,300 to 20,100. His wife had aptly described it as a 'dent', but it had turned out to be enough of a dent for the party to put Charles's name forward for the Sussex Downs seat when Sir Eric Koops had died of a heart attack only a few days after Parliament had assembled. Six weeks later Charles Seymour sat in the Commons with a 20,000 majority of his own.

Charles listened to one more speech before leaving the Chamber. He stood alone in the Members' Lobby not quite certain where to begin. Another young member strode purposefully towards him. "Allow me to introduce myself," the stranger said, sounding to Charles every bit like a fellow Conservative. "My name is Andrew Fraser. I'm the Labour member for Edinburgh Carlton and I was hoping you hadn't yet found yourself a pair." Charles admitted that so far he hadn't found much more than the Chamber. The Tory Chief Whip had already explained to him that most members paired with someone from the opposite party for voting purposes, and that it would be wise for him to select someone of his own age. When there was a debate on less crucial issues a two-line whip came into operation: pairing made it possible for members to miss the vote and return home to their wife and family before midnight. However, no member was allowed to miss the vote when there was a three-line whip.

"I'd be delighted to pair with you," continued Charles. "Am I expected to do anything official?"

"No," said Andrew, looking up at him. "I'll just drop you a line confirming the arrangement. If you'd be kind enough to reply letting me have all the phone numbers where you can be contacted we'll just take it from there. Any time you need to miss a vote just let me know."

"Sounds a sensible arrangement to me," said Charles as a rotund figure wearing a light grey three-piece suit, blue shirt and a pink-spotted bow tie trundled over towards them.

"Welcome to the club, Charles," said Alec Pimkin. "Care to join me for a drink in the smoking room and I'll brief you on how this bloody place works."

"Thank you," said Charles, relieved to see someone he knew. Andrew smiled when he heard Pimkin add, "It's just like being back at school, old chum," as the two Tories retreated in the direction of the smoking room. Andrew suspected that it wouldn't be long before Charles Seymour was showing his 'old school chum' just how the bloody place really worked.

Andrew also left the Members' Lobby but not in search of a drink. He had to attend a meeting of the Parliamentary Labour party at which the following week's business was due to be discussed. He hurried away.

Andrew had been duly selected as the Labour candidate for Edinburgh Carlton and had gone on to capture the seat from the Conservatives by a majority of 3,419 votes. Sir Duncan, having completed his term as Lord Provost, continued to represent the same seat on the City Council. In six weeks Andrew – the baby of the House – had quickly made a name for himself and many of the older members found it hard to believe that it was his first Parliament.

When Andrew arrived at the party meeting on the second floor of the Commons he found an empty seat near the back of the large committee room and settled down to listen to the Government Chief Whip go over the business for the following week. Once again it seemed to consist of nothing but three-line whips. He glanced down at the piece of paper in front of him. The debates scheduled for Tuesday, Wednesday and Thursday all had three thick lines drawn under them: only Monday and Friday had two-liners which at least after his agreement with Charles Seymour he could arrange to miss. The Labour party might have returned to power after thirteen years but, with a majority of only four and a full legislative programme, it was proving almost impossible for members to get to bed much before midnight during the week.

As the Chief Whip sat down the first person to jump to his feet was Tom Carson, the new member for Liverpool Dockside. He launched into a tirade of abuse against the Government, complaining that they were looking more like Tories every day. The under-the-breath remarks and coughing that continued during his speech showed how little support there was for his views. Tom Carson had also made a name for himself in a very short time, for he had openly attacked his own party from the first day he had arrived.

"Enfant terrible," muttered the man sitting on the right of Andrew.

"Those aren't the words I'd use to describe him," muttered Andrew. "Altogether too many letters." The man with wavy red hair smiled as they listened to Carson ranting on.

If Raymond Gould had acquired any reputation during those first six weeks it was as one of the party's intellectuals, and for that reason older members were immediately suspicious of him, although few doubted he would be among the first from the new intake to be promoted to the front bench. Not many of them had really got to know Raymond as the north-countryman appeared remarkably reserved for someone who had chosen a career in public life. But with a majority of over 10,000 in his Leeds constituency he looked destined for a long career.

Leeds North had chosen Raymond to be their candidate from a field of thirty-seven, when he showed himself to be so much better informed than a local trade-union official whom the press had tipped as favourite for the seat. Yorkshire folk like people who stay at home and Raymond had been quick to point out to the selection committee – in an exaggerated Yorkshire accent – that he had been educated at Roundhay School on the fringes of the constituency. But what really tipped the vote in his favour had been Raymond's refusal of an open scholarship to Cambridge. He had preferred to continue his education at Leeds University, he explained.

Raymond took a first-class honours degree in Law at

Leeds before moving to London to complete his studies for
the bar at Lincoln's Inn. At the end of his two-year course
Raymond joined a fashionable London chambers to become
a much sought-after junior counsel. From that moment he
rarely mentioned his family background to his carefully
cultivated circle of Home Counties friends, and those comrades who addressed him as Ray received a sharp 'Raymond'
for their familiarity.

When the last question had been asked, the party meeting
broke up, and Raymond and Andrew made their way out of
the committee room – Andrew for his tiny office on the
second floor to finish off the day's mail, Raymond to return to
the Chamber as he hoped to deliver his maiden speech that
day. He had waited patiently for the right moment to express
his views to the House on the subject of widows' pensions and
the redemption of war bonds, and the debate in progress on
the economy was an obvious opportunity. The Speaker had
dropped Raymond a note earlier in the day saying he
expected to call him some time that evening.

Raymond had spent many hours in the Chamber, carefully studying the techniques demanded by the House and
noting how they differed from those of the law courts. F. E.
Smith had been right in his assessment of his colleagues when
he had described the Commons as nothing more than a noisy
courtroom with over 600 jurors and absolutely no sign of a
judge. Raymond was dreading the ordeal of his maiden
speech; the dispassionate logic of his arguments had always
proved more appealing to judges than to juries.

As he approached the Chamber an attendant handed him
a note from his wife Joyce. She had just arrived at the
Commons and had been found a seat in the Strangers'
Gallery so that she could be present for his speech. After only
a cursory glance Raymond scrunched up the note, dropped it
into the nearest waste-paper basket and hurried on towards
the Chamber.

The door was held open for him by a Conservative member who was on his way out.

"Thank you," said Raymond. Simon Kerslake smiled
back, trying in vain to recall the man's name. Once Simon

was in the Members' Lobby he checked the message board to see if the light under his name was lit up. It wasn't, so he continued on through the swing doors to the right of the lobby on his way down past the cloisters to the Members' Car Park. Once he had found his car he headed off in the direction of St Mary's, Paddington, to pick up his wife. They had seen little of each other during Simon's first six weeks in Parliament which made the thought of tonight even more enjoyable. Simon couldn't see any easing of the pressure until there was another general election and one party had gained a sensible working majority. But what he feared most – having won his seat by the slimmest of margins – was that such a working majority would not include him and he might end up with one of the shortest political careers on record. After such a prolonged stretch of Tory rule the new Labour Government was looking fresh, idealistic and certain to increase their numbers whenever the Prime Minister chose to go to the country.

Once Simon had reached Hyde Park Corner he headed on up towards Marble Arch thinking back over how he had become a member. On leaving Oxford he had completed two years' national service with the Sussex Yeomanry, finishing his military days as a second lieutenant. After a short holiday he had joined the BBC as a general trainee. He spent five years moving from drama, to sport, to current affairs before being appointed a producer on 'Panorama'. During those early days in London he had rented a small flat in Earl's Court and continued his interest in politics by becoming a member of the Tory Bow Group. When he became the Group's secretary he helped to organise meetings, and had then progressed to writing pamphlets and speaking at weekend conferences before being invited to work at Central Office as personal assistant to the chairman during the 1959 election campaign.

Two years later Simon met Elizabeth Drummond when 'Panorama' carried out an investigation into the National Health Service and she had been invited to be a participant. Over drinks before the programme Elizabeth made it perfectly clear to Simon that she distrusted media men and detested politicians. They were married a year later. Elizabeth had since given birth to two sons, and with only a small break on each occasion she had continued her career as a doctor.

Simon had left the BBC somewhat abruptly when, in the summer of 1964, he had been offered the chance to defend the marginal constituency of Coventry Central. He held on to the seat at the general election by a majority of 918.

Simon drove up to the gates of St Mary's and checked his watch. He was a few minutes early. He pushed back the mop of brown hair from his forehead and thought about the evening ahead. He was taking Elizabeth out to celebrate their fourth wedding anniversary, and had prepared one or two surprises for her. Dinner at Mario & Franco, followed by dancing at the Establishment Club, and then home together for the first time in weeks.

"Um," he said, savouring the thought.

"Hi, stranger," said the lady who jumped in beside him and gave him a kiss. Simon stared at the woman with a perfect smile and long fair hair that turned up at the shoulder. He had stared at her when she had first arrived at the 'Panorama' studio that night nearly five years before and he had hardly stopped staring since.

He switched on the ignition. "Want to hear some good news?" he asked, and answered his own question before she could reply. "I'm paired for tonight. That means dinner at Mario & Franco, dancing at the Establishment, home and . . ."

"Do you want to hear the bad news?" asked Elizabeth, also not waiting for a reply. "There's a shortage of staff because of the flu epidemic. I have to be back on duty by ten o'clock."

Simon switched off the ignition. "Well, which would you prefer?" he asked. "Dinner, dancing or straight home?"

Elizabeth laughed. "We've got three hours," she said. "So we might even find time for dinner."

CHAPTER
TWO

Raymond Gould stared down at the invitation. He had never seen the inside of No. 10 Downing Street. During the last thirteen years few Socialists had. He passed the embossed card across the breakfast table to his wife.

"Should I accept or refuse, Ray?" she asked in her broad Yorkshire accent.

She was the only person who still called him Ray, and even her attempts at humour now annoyed him. The Greek tragedians had based their drama on 'the fatal flaw', and he had no doubt what his had been.

He had met Joyce at a dance given by the nurses of Leeds General Infirmary. He hadn't wanted to go but a second-year undergraduate friend from Roundhay convinced him it would make an amusing break. At school he had shown little interest in girls as his mother kept reminding him that there would be occasion enough for that sort of thing once he had taken his degree. By the time he graduated he felt certain that he was the only virgin left at the university.

He had ended up sitting on his own in the corner of a room decorated with wilting balloons and Day-glo orange crêpe paper. He sucked disconsolately at a shandy through a bent straw. Whenever his school friend turned round from the dance floor – each time with a different partner – Raymond would smile broadly back. With his National Health spectacles tucked away in an inside pocket, he couldn't always be certain he was smiling at the right person. He began contemplating at what hour he could possibly leave without having to admit the evening had been a total disaster. He wouldn't even have answered her question if it hadn't been for that familiar accent.

"You at the university as well?"

"As well as what?" he asked, without looking directly at her.

"As well as your friend," she said.

"Yes," he replied, looking up at a girl he guessed was about his age.

"I'm from Bradford."

"I'm from Leeds," he admitted, aware he was going redder by the second.

"My name is Joyce," she volunteered.

"Mine's Ray – Raymond," he said.

"Like to dance?"

He wanted to tell her that he had rarely been on a dance floor before in his life but he didn't have the courage. Like a puppet he found himself standing up and being guided by her towards the jivers. So much for his assumption that he was one of nature's leaders.

Once they were on the dance floor he looked at her properly for the first time. She wasn't half bad, any normal Yorkshire boy might have admitted. She was about five-foot-seven, and her auburn hair was tied up in a pony-tail, matching the dark brown eyes that had a little too much make-up round them. She wore pink lipstick, the same colour as her short skirt from which emerged two very attractive legs. They looked even more attractive when she twirled to the music of the four-piece student band. Raymond discovered that if he twirled Joyce very fast he could see the tops of her stockings, and he remained on the dance floor for longer than he would ever have thought possible. After the quartet had put their instruments away Joyce kissed him goodnight. He walked slowly back to his small room above the butcher's shop.

The following Sunday, in an attempt to gain the upper hand, he took Joyce rowing on the Aire, but his performance was no better than his dancing, and everything on the river overtook him including a hardy swimmer. He watched out of the side of his eyes for a mocking laugh but Joyce only smiled and chatted about missing Bradford and wanting to return home to nurse. After only a few weeks at university Raymond knew he wanted to get away from Leeds, but he didn't admit it to anyone. When he eventually returned the boat Joyce invited him back to her digs for tea. He went scarlet as they passed her landlady. Joyce hustled him up the worn stone staircase to her room.

Raymond sat on the end of the narrow bed while Joyce made two milkless mugs of tea. After they had both pretended to drink she sat beside him, her hands in her lap. He found himself listening intently to an ambulance siren as it faded away in the distance. She leaned over and kissed him, taking one of his hands and placing it on her knee.

She parted his lips and their tongues touched: he found it a peculiar sensation, an arousing one; his eyes remained closed as she gently led him through each new experience, until he was unable to stop himself committing what he felt sure his mother had once described as a mortal sin.

"It will be easier next time," she said shyly, manoeuvring herself from the narrow bed to sort out the crumpled clothes spread across the floor. She was right: he wanted her again in less than an hour, and this time his eyes remained wide open.

It was another six months before Joyce talked about their future and by then Raymond was bored with her and had his sights set on a bright little mathematician in her final year. The mathematician hailed from Surrey.

Just at the time Raymond was summoning up enough courage to let her know the affair was over Joyce told him she was pregnant. His father would have taken a meat axe to him had he suggested an illegal abortion. His mother was only relieved that she was a Yorkshire girl; like the county cricket selection committee, Mrs Gould did not approve of outsiders.

Raymond and Joyce were married at St Mary's in Bradford during the long vacation. When the wedding photos were developed Raymond looked so distressed and Joyce so happy they resembled father and daughter rather than husband and wife. After a reception given at the church hall the newly-married couple travelled down to Dover to catch the night ferry. Their first night as Mr and Mrs Gould was a disaster. Raymond turned out to be a particularly bad sailor. Joyce only hoped that Paris would prove to be memorable – and it was. She had a miscarriage on the second night of their honeymoon.

"Probably caused by all the excitement," his mother said on their return. "Still, you can always have another, can't you? And this time folk won't be able to call it a little . . ." She checked herself.

Raymond showed no interest in having another. Ten years had passed since that memorable honeymoon; he had escaped to London and become a barrister, but had long since accepted that he was tethered to her for life. Although Joyce was only thirty-two she already needed to cover those once-slim legs that had first so attracted him. How could he be so punished for such a pathetic mistake? Raymond wanted to ask the gods. How mature he had thought he was: how immature he had turned out to be. Divorce made sense, but it would have meant the end of his political ambitions: Yorkshire folk would not have considered selecting a divorced man. To be fair, it hadn't all been a disaster: he had to admit that the locals adored her, and his parents seemed every bit as proud of Joyce as they did of their son. She mixed with the trade unionists and their frightful wives far better than he ever managed. He also had to acknowledge that Joyce had been a major factor in his winning the seat by over 10,000 votes. He wondered how she could sound so sincere the whole time: it never occurred to him that it was natural.

"Why don't you buy yourself a new dress for Downing Street?" Raymond said as they rose from the breakfast table. She smiled: he had not volunteered such a suggestion for as long as she could remember. Joyce had been left with no illusions about her husband and his feelings for her, but hoped that eventually he would realise she could help him achieve his unspoken ambition.

On the night of the reception at Downing Street Joyce made every effort to look her best. She had spent the morning at

Harvey Nichols searching for an outfit appropriate for the occasion, finally returning to a suit she had liked the moment she had walked in to the store. It was not the perfect fit but the sales assistant assured Joyce that "Modom looked quite sensational in it". She only hoped that Raymond's remarks would be half as flattering. By the time she reached home she realised she had nothing to match the unusual colour.

Raymond was late returning from the Commons and was pleased to find Joyce ready when he leaped out of the bath. He bit back a remark about the incongruity of her shoes and new suit. As they drove towards Westminster he rehearsed the names of every member of the Cabinet with her, making Joyce repeat them as if she were a child.

The air was cool and crisp that night so Raymond parked his Sunbeam in New Palace Yard and they strolled across Whitehall together to No. 10. A solitary policeman stood guard at the door. Seeing Raymond approach, the officer banged the brass knocker once and the door was opened for the young member and his wife.

Raymond and Joyce stood awkwardly in the hall as if they were waiting outside a headmaster's study. Eventually they were directed to the first floor. They walked slowly up the staircase, which turned out to be less grand than Raymond had anticipated, passing photographs of former Prime Ministers. "Too many Tories," muttered Raymond as he passed Chamberlain, Churchill, Eden, Macmillan and Home, with Attlee the only framed compensation.

At the top of the stairs stood Harold Wilson, pipe in mouth, waiting to welcome his guests. Raymond was about to introduce his wife when the Prime Minister said, "How are you, Joyce? I'm so glad you could make it."

"Make it? I've been looking forward to the occasion all week." Her frankness made Raymond wince; he failed to notice that it made Wilson chuckle.

Raymond chatted to the Prime Minister's wife about the difficulty of getting poetry published until she turned away to greet the next guest. He then moved off into the drawing-room and was soon talking to Cabinet ministers, trade union leaders and their wives, always keeping a wary eye on Joyce, who seemed engrossed in conversation with the General Secretary of the Trades Union Congress.

Raymond moved on to the American Ambassador, who was telling Andrew Fraser how much he had enjoyed the Edinburgh Festival that summer. Raymond envied Fraser his relaxed clubbable manner and had already worked out that the Scotsman would be a formidable rival among his contemporaries.

"Good evening, Raymond," said Andrew. "Do you know David Bruce?" he asked, as if they were old friends.

"No," Raymond replied, rubbing his palm on his trousers before shaking hands. "Good evening, Your Excellency," he said, glad to see Andrew slipping away. "I was interested to read Johnson's latest communiqué on Vietnam and I must confess the escalation . . ."

Andrew had spotted the Minister of State for Scotland arriving and went over to chat to him.

"How are you, Andrew?" Hugh McKenzie asked.

"Never better."

"And your father?"

"In great form."

"I'm sorry to hear that," said the minister, grinning. "He's giving me a lot of trouble over the Highlands and Islands Development Board."

"He's a sound chap basically," said Andrew, "even if his views are a little misguided." They both laughed as a slight, attractive woman with long brown hair came up to the minister's side. She wore a white silk blouse and a McKenzie tartan skirt.

"Do you know my daughter Alison?"

"No," Andrew said, holding out his hand. "I've not had that pleasure."

"I know who you are," she said, in a slight lowland accent, her eyes flashing. "Andrew Fraser, the man who makes Campbells look trustworthy. The Tories' secret mole."

"It can't be much of a secret if the Scottish Office know about it," said Andrew.

A waiter, wearing the smartest dinner-jacket in the room,

approached them carrying a silver tray of thinly-cut sandwiches.

"Would you care for a smoked salmon sandwich?" Alison asked mockingly.

"No, thank you. I gave them up with my Tory background. But beware – if you eat too many you won't appreciate your dinner tonight."

"I wasn't thinking of having dinner."

"Oh, I thought you might enjoy a bite at Sigie's," teased Andrew.

Alison hesitated, then said, "It'll be the first time anyone's picked me up at No. 10."

"I hate to break with tradition," said Andrew. "But why don't I book a table for eight?"

"Is Sigie's one of your aristocratic haunts?"

"Good heavens no, it's far too good for that lot. Why don't we leave in about fifteen minutes? I must have a word with one or two people first."

"I'll bet." She grinned as she watched Fraser comb the room. His years as a Tory party fellow-traveller had taught Andrew all he needed to know about how to make the best use of a cocktail party. His trade union colleagues would never understand that it was not in pursuit of endless smoked salmon sandwiches drowned by whisky. When he arrived back at Alison McKenzie's side she was chatting to Raymond Gould about Johnson's landslide victory at the polls.

"Are you trying to pick up my date?" asked Andrew.

Raymond laughed nervously and pushed his spectacles back up his nose. A moment later Andrew was guiding Alison towards the door to say their farewells, and Raymond watching them, wondered if he would ever learn to be that relaxed. He looked around for Joyce: it might be wise not to be the last to leave.

Andrew was ushered discreetly to a corner table at Sigie's Club and it became quickly evident to Alison that he had been there several times before. The waiters ran around him as if he were a Tory Cabinet minister, and she had to admit to herself that she enjoyed the experience. After an excellent

dinner of roast beef that wasn't burnt and a *crème brûlée* that
was they strolled over to Annabel's where they danced until
the early morning. Andrew drove Alison back to her Chelsea
flat a little after two a.m.

"Care for a nightcap?" she asked casually.

"Daren't," he replied. "I'm making my maiden speech
tomorrow."

"So this maiden is to be rejected," she said to his retreating
back.

The House of Commons was well attended at five o'clock the
following afternoon when Andrew rose to address his fellow
members. The Speaker had allowed him to follow the front-
bench contributions, an honour Andrew would not be
granted again for some considerable time. His father and
mother looked down over the railings from the Strangers'
Gallery as he informed the commoners that the Lord Provost
of Edinburgh had spent a lifetime teaching him all he knew
about the constituency he was now proud to represent. The
Labour party chuckled at the Opposition's obvious discomfort, but they abided by tradition and made no interruption
during a maiden speech.

Andrew had chosen as his subject the question of whether
Scotland should remain part of the United Kingdom despite
the recent oil discoveries. He delivered a well-argued case,
assuring members that he saw no future for his country as a
tiny independent state. His rhetoric, and his relaxed turn of
phrase, had members laughing on both sides of the House.
When he came to the end of his argument, never having once
referred to a note, he sat down to loud cheers from his own
benches and generous acknowledgement from the Tory side.
In his moment of glory he glanced up towards the Strangers'
Gallery. His father was leaning forward, following every
word. To his surprise sitting in front of his mother on the
benches reserved for distinguished visitors was Alison
McKenzie, her arms folded on the balcony. He smiled.

Andrew's success was considerably enhanced when later
that afternoon another member from the Labour benches
rose to address the House for the first time. Tom Carson

cared nothing for convention and even less for keeping to tradition and made no attempt to avoid controversy in his maiden speech. He began with an attack on what he described as "the Establishment conspiracy", pointing an accusing finger as much at the ministers on his own front bench as at those opposite him, describing them all as "puppets of the capitalist system".

Members present in the Chamber restrained themselves from interrupting the scowling Liverpudlian, but the Speaker stirred several times as the accusing finger appeared to cross his path as well. He was painfully aware that the member from Liverpool Dockside was going to cause all sorts of problems if this was the way he intended to conduct himself in the House.

When Andrew left the Chamber three speeches later he went to look for Alison, but she had already left; so he took the members' lift up to the Public Gallery and invited his parents to join him for tea in the Harcourt Rooms.

"The last time I had tea here was with Ainslie Munro . . ." Sir Duncan began.

"Then it may be a very long time before you're invited again," Andrew interrupted.

"That may depend on whom we select as Tory candidate to oppose you at the next election," retorted his father.

Several members from both sides of the House came up one by one to congratulate Andrew on his speech. He thanked them all individually but kept glancing hopefully over his father's shoulder; but Alison McKenzie did not appear.

After his parents had finally left to catch the last flight back to Edinburgh Andrew returned to the Chamber to hear Alison's father summing up the debate on behalf of the Government. The Minister of State described Andrew's contribution as one of the finest maiden speeches the House had heard in years. "Maiden it may have been but virginal it was not," concluded Hugh McKenzie.

Once the debate was over and the usual ten o'clock division had been declared by the tellers Andrew left the Chamber. One final vote on a prayer detained members for a further forty-five minutes and Andrew found the tea room — the traditional haunt of the Labour party — as crowded as it had been earlier in the afternoon.

Members jostled for the remains of unappetising-looking lettuce leaves that any self-respecting rabbit would have rejected accompanied by blobs of plastic-covered sweating cheese, described optimistically on the bill board as salad. Andrew contented himself with a cup of Nescafé.

Raymond Gould sat alone, slumped in an armchair in the far corner of the tea room, apparently engrossed in a week-old copy of the *New Statesman*. He stared impassively as several of his colleagues went over to Andrew to congratulate him. His own maiden speech the previous week had not been as well received and he knew it. He believed just as passionately about war widows' pensions as Andrew did about the future of Scotland but reading from a prepared manuscript he had been unable to make members hang on his every word. He consoled himself with the thought that Andrew would have to choose the subject for his next speech very carefully as the Opposition would no longer treat him with kid gloves.

Andrew was not concerning himself with such thoughts as he slipped into one of the many internal telephone booths and after checking in his diary dialled a London number. Alison was at home, washing her hair.

"Will it be dry by the time I arrive?"

"It's very long," she reminded him.

"Then I'll have to drive slowly."

When Andrew appeared on the Chelsea doorstep he was greeted by Alison in a housecoat, her newly-dry hair falling down well below shoulder level.

"The victor come to claim his spoils?"

"No, only last night's coffee," he said.

"But won't that keep you awake?"

"I certainly hope so."

By the time Andrew left Alison's home at eight the next morning he had already decided he wanted to see a lot more of Hugh McKenzie's daughter. He returned to his own flat in

Cheyne Walk, showered and changed before making breakfast for himself and going over his mail. There were several
more messages of congratulations including one from the
Secretary of State for Scotland, while *The Times* and the
Guardian carried brief but favourable comments.

Before leaving for the Commons Andrew checked over an
amendment he wanted to move in committee that morning.
When he had reworded his efforts several times he picked up
his papers and headed off towards Westminster.

Arriving a little early for the ten-thirty committee meeting,
Andrew found time to collect his mail from the Members'
Post Office just off the Central Lobby. He set off, head
down, along the corridor towards the library, flicking
through the envelopes to see if he recognised any familiar
hand or official-looking missive that demanded to be opened
immediately.

As he turned the corner he was surprised to find the House
ticker-tape machine surrounded by Conservative members,
including the man who had agreed to be his 'pair' for voting
purposes.

Andrew stared up at the tall figure of Charles Seymour,
who, although standing on the fringe of the crowd, still found
it possible to read the tapped-out message on the telex
machine.

"What's causing so much interest?" he asked, prodding
Seymour's elbow.

"Sir Alec has just announced the timetable that'll be
followed when we select the new Tory leader."

"We all await with baited breath," said Andrew.

"As well you might," said Charles, ignoring the sarcasm,
"since the next announcement will undoubtedly be his resignation. Then the real politics will begin."

"Be sure you back the winner," said Andrew, grinning.

Charles Seymour smiled knowingly but made no comment.

CHAPTER
THREE

Charles Seymour drove his Daimler from the Commons to his father's bank in the City. He still thought of Seymour's of Cheapside as his father's bank although for two generations the family had been only minority shareholders, with Charles himself in possession of a mere two per cent of the stock. Nevertheless as his brother Rupert showed no desire in representing the family interests the two per cent guaranteed Charles a place on the board and an income sufficient to ensure that his paltry parliamentary salary of £1,750 a year was adequately supplemented.

From the day Charles had first taken his place on the board of Seymour's he had no doubt that the new chairman, Derek Spencer, considered him a dangerous rival. Spencer had lobbied to have Rupert replace his father on retirement and only because of Charles's insistence had Spencer failed to move the old earl to his way of thinking.

When Charles went on to take his seat in Parliament Spencer at once raised the problem of his burdensome responsibilities at the House preventing him from carrying out his day-to-day duties for the board. However, Charles was able to convince a majority of his fellow directors of the advantages of having someone on the board at Westminster, although he knew that would cease if he was ever invited to be a minister.

As Charles left the Daimler in Seymour's courtyard it amused him to consider that his parking space was worth twenty times the value of the car. The area at the front of Seymour's was a relic of his great-grandfather's day. The

twelfth Earl of Bridgwater had insisted on an entrance large
enough to allow a complete sweep for his coach and four.
That conveyance had long disappeared, to be replaced by
twelve car spaces for Seymour directors. The bank's new
management-conscious chairman, despite all his grammar
school virtues, had never suggested the land be used for any
other purpose.

The young girl seated at the reception desk abruptly
stopped polishing her nails in time to say "Good morning,
Mr Charles," as he came through the revolving doors and
disappeared into a waiting lift. A few moments later Charles
was seated behind a desk in his small oak-panelled office, a
clean white memo pad in front of him. He pressed a button on
the intercom and told his secretary that he did not want to be
disturbed during the next hour.

Sixty minutes later the white pad had twelve names
pencilled on it, but ten already had lines drawn through
them. Only the names of Reginald Maudling and Edward
Heath remained.

Charles tore off the piece of paper and the indented sheet
underneath and put them both through the shredder by the
side of his desk. He tried to summon up some interest in the
agenda for the bank's weekly board meeting; only one item,
item seven, seemed to be of any importance. Just before
eleven, he gathered up his papers and headed towards the
boardroom. Most of his colleagues were already seated when
Derek Spencer called item number one as the boardroom
clock chimed the hour.

During the ensuing predictable discussion on bank rates,
the movement in metal prices, Eurobonds and client investment policy Charles's mind kept wandering back to the
forthcoming leadership election and the importance of backing the winner if he were to be quickly promoted from the
back benches.

By the time they reached item seven on the agenda Charles
had made up his mind. Derek Spencer opened a discussion
on the proposed loans to Mexico and Poland, and most of the
board members agreed with him that the bank should
participate in one but not risk both.

Charles's thoughts, however, were not in Mexico City or Warsaw. They were far nearer home and when the chairman called for a vote, Charles didn't register.

"Mexico or Poland, Charles. Which of the two do you favour?"

"Heath," he replied.

"I beg your pardon," said Derek Spencer.

Charles snapped back from Westminster to Cheapside to find everyone around the boardroom table staring at him. With the air of a man who had been giving the matter considerable thought Charles said firmly, "Mexico", and added, "The great difference between the two countries can best be gauged by their attitudes to repayment. Mexico might not want to repay, but Poland won't be able to, so why not limit our risks and back Mexico? If it comes to litigation I'd prefer to be against someone who won't pay rather than someone who can't." The older members round the table nodded in agreement; the right son of Bridgwater was sitting on the board.

When the meeting was over Charles joined his colleagues for lunch in the directors' dining-room. On the walls hung two Hogarths, a Brueghel, a Goya and a Rembrandt that could distract even the most indulgent gourmet: just another reminder of his great-grandfather's ability to select winners. Charles did not wait to make a decision between the Cheddar and the Stilton as he wanted to be back in the Commons for question time.

On arrival at the House he immediately made his way to the smoking room, long regarded by the Tories as their preserve. There in the deep leather armchairs and cigar-laden atmosphere the talk was entirely of who would be Sir Alec's successor.

Charles could not avoid overhearing Pimkin's high-pitched voice. "As Edward Heath is Shadow Chancellor while we debate the Finance Bill on the floor of the House, it is he who is bound to be the centre of attention."

Later that afternoon Charles returned to the Commons Chamber. He wanted to observe Heath and his Shadow team deal with the Government's amendments one by one.

He was about to leave the Chamber when Raymond Gould rose to move an amendment. Charles listened with grudging admiration as Raymond's intellectual grasp and force of argument easily compensated for his lack of oratorial skill. Although Gould was a cut above the rest of his intake on the Labour benches he didn't frighten Charles. Twelve generations of shrewd business acumen had kept large parts of Leeds in the hands of the Bridgwater family without the likes of Raymond Gould even being aware of it.

Charles took supper in the Members' Dining-room that night and sat at the large table in the centre of the room frequented by Tory back-benchers. There was only one topic of conversation and as the same two names kept emerging it was obvious that it was going to be a very close run thing.

When Charles arrived back at his Eaton Square home after the ten o'clock division Fiona was already tucked up in bed reading Philip Larkin's *The Whitsun Weddings*.

"They let you out early tonight."

"Not too bad," said Charles, and began regaling her with how he had spent his day, before disappearing into the bathroom.

If Charles imagined he was cunning, his wife, Lady Fiona, only daughter of the Duke of Falkirk, was in a different league. She and Charles had been selected for each other at an early age and neither had questioned or doubted the wisdom of the choice. Although Charles had squired numerous girl-friends before their marriage in between he had always assumed he would return to Fiona. Charles's grandfather always maintained that the aristocracy was becoming far too lax and sentimental about marriage. "Women," he declared, "are for bearing children and ensuring a continuation of the male line." The old earl became even more staid in his convictions when he was made aware that Rupert showed little interest in the opposite sex, and was rarely to be found in the company of women. Fiona would never have dreamed of disagreeing with the old man to his face as she was determined that it would be a son of hers that would inherit the earldom. But despite enthusiastic and then contrived efforts Charles seemed unable to sire an heir. Fiona was later

assured by a Harley Street physician that there was no
reason *she* could not bear children. The specialist had suggested that perhaps her husband pay the clinic a visit. She
shook her head, knowing Charles would dismiss such an idea
out of hand, and never mentioned the subject to anyone
again.

Fiona spent a considerable amount of her spare time in
their Sussex Downs constituency furthering Charles's political career. She had learned to live with the fact that theirs
was not destined to be a romantic marriage and resigned
herself to its other advantages. Although many men con-
fessed covertly and overtly that they found the tall elegant
lady desirable she either ignored their overtures or pretended
not to notice them.

By the time Charles returned from the bathroom in his
blue silk pyjamas Fiona had formed a plan, but first she
needed some questions answered.

"Whom do you favour?"

"I'd like Sir Alec to carry on: after all, the Homes have
been friends of our two families for over 400 years."

"But that's a non-starter," said Fiona. "Everyone knows
Alec is on the way out."

"I agree, and that's exactly why I spent the entire afternoon observing the worthwhile candidates."

"Did you come to any serious conclusions?" Fiona asked.

"Heath and Maudling are out on their own, though to be
honest I've never had a conversation with either of them that
lasted for more than five minutes."

"In that case we must turn a disadvantage into an advantage."

"What do you mean, old girl?" Charles asked as he
climbed into bed beside his wife.

"Think back. When you were President of Pop at Eton,
could you have put a name to any of the first-year boys?"

"Certainly not," said Charles.

"Exactly. And I'd be willing to bet that neither Heath nor
Maudling could put a name to twenty of the new intake on
the Tory benches."

"Where are you leading me, Lady Macbeth?"

"No bloody hands will be needed for this killing. Simply, having chosen your Duncan you volunteer to organise the new intake for him. If he becomes leader, he's bound to feel it would be appropriate to select one or two new faces for his team."

"You could be right."

"Well, let's sleep on it," said Fiona, turning out the light on her side of the bed.

Charles didn't sleep on it but lay restless most of the night turning over in his mind what she had said. When Fiona awoke the next morning she carried on the conversation as if there had been no break in between. "Do you have to be rushed into a decision?"

"No, but if I let it drift I could be accused of jumping on the bandwagon and then I would have lost my chance to be seen as a leader among the new intake."

"Better still," she continued, "before the man you choose announces he is a candidate, demand that he stand on behalf of the new members."

"Clever," said Charles.

"Whom have you decided on?"

"Heath," Charles replied without hesitation.

"I'll back your political judgement," said Fiona. "Just trust me when it comes to tactics. First, we compose a letter."

In dressing-gowns, on the floor at the end of the bed, the two elegant figures drafted and redrafted a note to Edward Heath. At nine-thirty it was finally composed and sent round by hand to his rooms in Albany.

The next morning Charles was invited to the small, bachelor flat for coffee. They talked for over an hour and later, as the two men stood below a Piper landscape in the drawing-room, the deal was struck.

Charles thought Sir Alec would announce his resignation in the late summer which would give him eight to ten weeks to carry out a campaign. Fiona typed out a list of all the new members and during the next eight weeks every one of them was invited to their Eaton Square flat for drinks. Fiona was subtle enough to see that members of the Lower House were outnumbered by other guests, often from the House of Lords. Heath managed to escape from his front-bench duties on the Finance Bill to spend at least an hour with the Seymours once a week. As the day of Sir Alec Douglas-Home's resignation drew nearer Charles realised the leadership result could be almost as important to him as it would be to Heath, but he also remained confident that he had carried out his plan in a subtle and discreet way. He would have been willing to place a wager that no one other than Edward Heath had worked out how deeply he was involved.

One man who attended the second of Fiona's soirées saw exactly what was going on. While many of the guests spent their time admiring the Seymour art collection Simon Kerslake kept a wary eye on his host and hostess. Kerslake was not convinced that Edward Heath would win the forthcoming election and felt confident that Reginald Maudling would turn out to be the party's natural choice. Maudling was, after all, Shadow Foreign Secretary, a former Chancellor and far senior to Heath. More important, he was a married man. Simon doubted the Tories would ever pick a bachelor to lead them.

As soon as Kerslake had left the Seymours he jumped into a taxi and returned immediately to the Commons. He found Reginald Maudling in the Members' Dining-room seated at the table frequented only by the Shadow Cabinet. He waited until Maudling had finished his meal before asking if they could have a few moments alone. The tall shambling figure – not altogether certain of the name of the new member – leaned over and invited Simon to join him for a drink in his room.

Maudling listened intently to all the enthusiastic young man had to say and accepted the judgement of the well-informed member without question. It was agreed that Simon should try to counter the Seymour campaign and report back his results twice a week.

While Seymour could call on all the powers and influence of his Etonian background, Kerslake could rely on the knowledge and arm-twisting skills gained from his time as

President of the Oxford Union. Simon weighed up the advantages and disadvantages he possessed. He did not own a palatial home in Eaton Square in which Turners, Constables and Holbeins were not to be found in books but on the walls. He also lacked a glamorous society wife. Simon lived in a small house in Beaufort Street in Chelsea and Elizabeth was a gynaecologist at St Mary's Hospital, Paddington. Although Elizabeth gave Simon's political aspirations her full backing she still considered her own career every bit as important, an opinion with which Simon concurred. The local Coventry press had on several occasions recalled in their columns how Elizabeth had left her three-day-old child to help perform a Caesarian section on a mother in the adjoining ward and, two years later, had to be dragged off night duty just as she went into labour with their second child.

This independence of character was one of the reasons Simon had admired Elizabeth when they first met, but he realised she was no match for Lady Fiona Seymour as a hostess and he never wanted her to be. He despised pushy political wives.

Simon spent the following days trying to work out the certain Maudling and certain Heath supporters, although many members claimed they would favour both candidates, according to who asked them. These he listed as doubtfuls. When Enoch Powell threw his cap into the ring Simon could not find a single new member other than Alec Pimkin who openly supported him. That left forty members from the new intake who still had to be followed up. He estimated twelve certain Heath, eleven certain Maudling and one Powell, leaving sixteen undecided. As the day of the election drew nearer it became obvious that few of the remaining sixteen actually knew either candidate well, and were still not sure for whom they should vote.

Simon realised that he could not invite them all round to Beaufort Street between Elizabeth's ward duties, so he would have to go to them. During the last eight weeks he accompanied his chosen leader as he addressed the party faithfuls in twenty-three new members' constituencies. Simon travelled from Bodmin to Glasgow, from Penrith to Great Yarmouth, briefing Maudling studiously before every meeting.

Gradually it became obvious to everyone that Charles Seymour and Simon Kerslake were the chosen lieutenants among the new intake. Some members resented the whispered confidences at the Eaton Square cocktail parties, or the discovery that Simon Kerslake had visited their constituencies under false pretences, while others were simply envious of the reward that would inevitably be heaped on the victor.

"But why do you support Maudling?" Elizabeth had asked him one evening over dinner.

"Reggie has a great deal more experience of Government than Heath – and in any case he's more caring about those around him."

"But Heath appears to be so much more professional," Elizabeth insisted, pouring her husband a glass of wine.

"That may well be the case, but the British have always preferred good amateurs to preside over their affairs."

"If you believe all that stuff about amateurs why become so involved yourself?"

Simon considered her question for some time before answering. "Because I don't come from the type of background that automatically commands the centre of the Tory stage," he admitted.

"Neither does Heath," commented Elizabeth dryly.

Although everyone inside and outside of Parliament knew it could not be long before Sir Alec formally announced his resignation it did not become official until 22 July 1965, when he addressed the 1922 Committee of Tory back-benchers.

The date chosen for the leadership election was just five days later. During that time Simon Kerslake and Charles Seymour worked almost round the clock but, despite many national papers' commissioned polls, columns of newsprint offering statistics and opinions, no one seemed certain of the outcome, other than to predict that Powell would come third.

Charles and Simon began avoiding each other and Fiona started referring to Kerslake, first in private then in public, as "that pushy self-made man". She stopped using the expression when Alec Pimkin asked in all innocence whether she was referring to Edward Heath.

On the morning of the secret ballot Simon and Charles voted early and spent the rest of the day pacing the corridors of the Commons trying to assess the result. By lunchtime they were both outwardly exuberant, while inwardly despondent.

At two-fifteen they were seated in the large committee room to hear the chairman of the 1922 Committee make the historic announcement:

"The result of the first election for leader of the Conservative parliamentary party," said Sir William Anstruther-Gray, "is as follows:

Edward Heath	150 votes
Reginald Maudling	133 votes
Enoch Powell	15 votes."

An hour later Reginald Maudling, who had been lunching in the City, telephoned Heath to say he would be happy to serve under him as the new leader. Charles and Fiona opened a bottle of Krug while Simon took Elizabeth to the Old Vic to see *The Royal Hunt of the Sun*. He slept the entire way through Robert Stephens' brilliant performance, before Elizabeth drove him home.

"How come you didn't fall asleep? After all, you've been just as busy as I have the last few weeks," Simon asked.

Elizabeth smiled. "It was my turn to want to be involved with what was happening on the centre of the stage."

Two weeks later, on 4 August, Edward Heath announced his Shadow team. Reggie Maudling was to be deputy leader. Sir Alec accepted the Foreign Office brief while Powell went to Defence. Charles Seymour received an invitation to join the Housing and Local Government team as its junior spokesman, thus becoming the first of the new intake to be given front-bench responsibilities.

Simon Kerslake received a handwritten letter from Reggie Maudling thanking him for his valiant efforts.

BOOK TWO
1966-1974
JUNIOR OFFICE

CHAPTER
FOUR

When Alison McKenzie moved into Andrew Fraser's Cheyne Walk flat everyone, including her father, the Minister of State for Scotland, assumed they would soon announce their engagement.

For the previous three months Andrew had had his head down in committee helping out with the public bills relating exclusively to Scotland which were referred to the committee from the House itself. He found much of the committee work boring, as so many members repeated the views of their colleagues, less and less articulately, and for some time only his doodling improved. Even so, Andrew's energy and charm made him a popular companion through the long summer months and he quickly gained enough confidence to suggest first minor and later major changes to amendments considered by the committee. The disparity between penalties under English and Scottish law had long worried him, and he pressed hard for changes that would bring the two systems closer together. He soon discovered that the Scottish Labour members were more traditional and clannish than even the most hide-bound of Tories.

When the session came to an end Andrew invited Alison to spend a long weekend with his parents at their country home in Stirling at the end of the recess.

"Do you expect me to sleep under the same roof as a former Conservative Lord Provost of Edinburgh?" she demanded.

"Why not? You've been sleeping with his son for the past six months."

"Well, the same roof perhaps, but there's one weekend we won't be able to sleep in the same bed."

"Why not? The Tories may be snobs but they're not hypocrites."

Alison didn't want to admit that she was actually quite nervous about spending the weekend with Andrew's father, as she had heard him continually maligned at her parents' breakfast table for over twenty years.

When she did meet 'Old Dungheap', as her father referred to the former Lord Provost, Alison liked him immediately. He reminded her so much of her own father, while Lady Fraser was not at all the snobbish little battle-axe her mother had prepared her for.

It was immediately agreed that during the weekend nobody would talk politics. Andrew and Alison spent most of the Friday afternoon walking through the heather-covered hills and discussing in detail how they saw their future. On the Saturday morning the minister telephoned Sir Duncan and invited them over to Bute House – the official residence of the Secretary of State for Scotland – for dinner.

After so many years of opposing each other both families were nervous of the social get-together, but it seemed the children were to bridge the political gap they had failed to build for themselves. The McKenzies had invited two other Edinburgh families to dinner in the hope that it would ease the tension of the occasion, a branch of the Forsyths who owned the departmental store in Princes Street, and the Menzies, who ran the largest chain of newsagents in the country.

Andrew had decided to use the gathering to make an announcement at the end of dinner, and having spent longer shopping than he originally intended was the last to arrive at Bute House.

After they had all found their place cards around the long dining-room table the fourteen guests remained silent as a lone piper played a lament before the chef entered carrying a silver salver which bore on it a large haggis for the minister's inspection. Sir Duncan's opinion was sought: "Warm – reekin rich!" he declared. It was the first occasion the two men had wholeheartedly agreed on anything.

Andrew did not eat as much as the others because he

couldn't take his eyes off the guest who had been placed
opposite him. She didn't pay much attention to Andrew, but
seemed always to be smiling or laughing, making those
around her enjoy her company. When Andrew had last seen
Louise Forsyth it had been scoring goals on a hockey pitch.
She had been a dumpy little girl with long pigtails and a
tendency to go for one's ankles rather than for the ball. Now
the jet black hair was short and curly, while the body had
become slim and graceful. After dinner Andrew mixed
among the guests and it was well after one o'clock when the
party broke up: he never managed a moment alone with her.
Andrew was relieved to discover that Alison wanted to spend
the night with her parents at Bute House while the Frasers
travelled back to their home in Stirling.

"You're very silent for a Socialist," his father said, in the
car on the way home.

"He's in love," said his mother fondly.

Andrew made no reply.

The next morning he rose early and travelled into Edin-
burgh to see his agent. The minister had caught the first
flight back to London but had left a message asking if
Andrew would be kind enough to see him at ten o'clock in
Dover House, the London headquarters of the Scottish
Office, the following day, 'on an official matter'.

Andrew was delighted but it didn't change his attitude.

Having answered his local post and dealt with some
constituents' problems he left his office and made his way
over to the New Club to make a private phone call. He was
relieved to find her still at home. She reluctantly agreed to
join him for lunch. Andrew sat alone for forty minutes,
checking the grandfather clock every few moments while
pretending to read the *Scotsman*. When she was eventually
ushered in by the steward, Andrew knew this was the woman
with whom he wanted to spend the rest of his life. He would
have laughed, if he had been told – before the previous
evening – that he could change his well-ordered plans on
what was nothing more than a casual meeting. But then he
had never met anyone like Louise before and was already
convinced he never would again.

"Miss Forsyth," said the man wearing the green livery uniform of the Club. He inclined his head slightly and left them alone.

Louise smiled and Andrew guided her to a table in the corner.

"It was kind of you to come at such short notice," he said nervously.

"No," she said. "It was very stupid of me."

Over a lunch which he ordered but didn't eat Andrew learned that Louise Forsyth was engaged to an old friend of his from university days and that they planned to be married the following spring. By the end of lunch he had convinced her they should at least meet again.

Andrew caught the five-ten flight back to London and sat alone in his flat and waited. Alison returned a little after nine o'clock and asked why he hadn't travelled down from Scotland with her or at least phoned. Andrew immediately told her the truth. She burst into tears while he stood helplessly by. Within the hour she had moved all her possessions out of Andrew's flat and left.

At ten-thirty he phoned Louise again.

The next morning Andrew dropped into the Commons to collect his mail from the Members' Post Office, and to check with the Whips' office as to what time they were anticipating the votes that day.

"One at six and two at ten," shouted a junior Whip from behind his desk. "And we could lose the second so be certain you're not far away if we need you."

Andrew nodded and turned to leave.

"By the way, congratulations."

"On what?" queried Andrew.

"Oh hell, another indiscretion to start the week on. It's pencilled in on the morning sheet," said the Whip, tapping a piece of paper in front of him.

"What is?" asked Andrew impatiently.

"Your appointment as Parliamentary Private Secretary to Hugh McKenzie. For pity's sake don't let him know I told you."

"I won't," promised Andrew, breathing a sigh of relief. He

checked his watch: perfect timing to stroll over to Dover House and keep his appointment with the minister.

He whistled as he walked down Whitehall and the doorman saluted as he entered the ministry. They had obviously been briefed as well. He tried not to show too much anticipation. He was met at the top of the stone steps by the minister's secretary.

"Good morning," Andrew said, trying to sound as if he had no idea what was in store for him.

"Good morning, Mr Fraser," replied the secretary. "The minister has asked me to apologise for not being available to see you, but he has been called away to a Cabinet committee to discuss the new IMF standby credit."

"I see," said Andrew. "Has the minister rearranged my appointment?"

"Well, no, he hasn't," replied the secretary, sounding a little surprised. "He simply said that it was no longer important, and he was sorry to have wasted your time."

Charles Seymour was enjoying the challenge of his new appointment as a junior Opposition spokesman. Even if he was not actually making decisions on future policy he was listening to them, and at least he felt he was near the centre of affairs. Whenever a debate on housing took place in the Commons he was allowed to sit on the front bench along with the rest of the team. He had already caused the defeat of two amendments on the Town and Country Planning Bill in standing committee, and had added one of his own, relating to the protection of trees, during the report stage of the bill on the floor of the House. "It isn't preventing a world war," he admitted to Fiona, "but in its own way it's quite important because if we win the election I'm confident of being offered junior office and then I'll have a real chance to shape policy."

Fiona continued to play her part, hosting monthly dinner parties at their Eaton Square house. By the end of the year every member of the Shadow Cabinet had dined with the Seymours at least once and Fiona never wore the same dress twice or allowed a menu to be repeated.

When the parliamentary year began again in October

Charles was one of the names continually dropped by the political pundits. Here was someone to watch. "He makes things happen," was the sentiment that was expressed again and again. He could barely cross the Members' Lobby without a correspondent trying to solicit his views on everything from butter mountains to rape. Fiona cut out of the papers every mention of her husband and couldn't help noticing that, if any new member was receiving more press coverage than Charles, it was a young Socialist from Leeds called Raymond Gould.

Raymond's name began to disappear from political columns soon after his success on the budget debate; his colleagues assumed it was because he was busy building a career at the bar. Had they passed his room at the Temple they would have heard the continual tap of a typewriter and been unable to contact him on his off-the-hook phone.

Each night Raymond could be found in chambers writing page after page, checking then rechecking his proofs, and often referring to the piles of books that cluttered his desk. When his *Full Employment at any Cost? Reflections of a worker educated after the Thirties* was published it caused an immediate sensation. The suggestion that the unions would become impotent and the Labour party would need to be more radical to capture the young vote was never likely to endear him to the party activists. Raymond had anticipated that it would provoke a storm of abuse from union leaders, and even among some of his more left-wing colleagues. But A. J. P. Taylor suggested in *The Times* that it was the most profound and realistic look at the Labour party since Anthony Crosland's *The Future of Socialism*, and had given the country a politician of rare honesty and courage. Raymond soon became aware that his strategy and hard work was paying dividends. He found himself a regular topic of conversation at political dinner-parties in London.

Joyce thought the book a magnificent piece of scholarship and she spent a considerable time trying to convince trade unionists who had only read out-of-context quotations from it in the *Sun* or *Daily Mirror* that it in fact showed a passionate concern for the trade union movement, while at the same time realistically considering the Labour party's future in the next decade.

The Labour Chief Whip took Raymond on one side and told him, "You've caused a right stir, lad. Now keep your head down for a few months and you'll probably find every Cabinet member quoting you as if it was party policy."

Raymond took the Chief Whip's advice, but he did not have to wait months. Just three weeks after the book's publication the Prime Minister quoted a whole passage at the Durham Miners' Rally. A few weeks later Raymond received a missive from No. 10 requesting him to check over the Prime Minister's speech to the TUC conference and add any suggestions he might have.

Simon Kerslake had sulked for about twenty-four hours after Maudling's defeat for the leadership. He then decided to turn his anger and energy towards the Government benches. It hadn't taken him long to work out that there was a fifteen-minute period twice a week when someone with his skills of oratory could command notice. At the beginning of a new session each week he would carefully study the order paper and in particular the first five questions listed for the Prime Minister on the Tuesday and Thursday. Every Monday morning he would prepare a supplementary for at least three of them. These he worded, then reworded, so that they were biting and witty and always likely to embarrass the Government. Although preparation of such supplementary questions could take several hours Simon would make them sound as though they had been jotted down on the back of the order paper during question time – and in fact would even do so. Elizabeth teased him about how long he took on something she considered trivial. He reminded her of Churchill's comment after being praised for a brilliant rejoinder, "All my best off-the-cuff remarks had been worked on days before."

Even so Simon was surprised at how quickly the House took it for granted that he would be there on the attack, probing, demanding, harrying the Prime Minister's every move. Whenever he rose from his seat the party perked up in anticipation, and many of his interruptions reached the political column of the daily newspapers the following day.

Unemployment was the subject of that day's question. Simon was on his feet leaning forward jabbing a finger in the direction of the Government front bench.

"With the appointment of four extra Secretaries of State this week the Prime Minister can at least claim he has full employment – in the Cabinet."

The Prime Minister sank lower into his seat, looking forward to the recess.

CHAPTER
FIVE

When the Queen opened Parliament the talk was not of the contents of her speech, which traditionally lists the aims of the Government of the day, but of how much of the legislation could possibly be carried out while the Labour party retained a majority of only four. Any contentious legislation was likely to be defeated at the committee stage and everyone knew it. The Conservatives were convinced they could win the forthcoming election whatever date the Prime Minister chose until the by-election held in Hull increased the Labour majority from 1,100 to 5,350. The Prime Minister couldn't believe the result and asked the Queen to dissolve Parliament immediately and to call a general election. The date announced from Buckingham Palace was 31 March.

Simon Kerslake began spending most of his spare time in his Coventry constituency. The local people seemed pleased with the apprenticeship of their new member, but the disinterested statisticians pointed out that a swing of less than one per cent would remove him from the House for another five years. By then his rivals would be on the second rung of the ladder.

The Tory Chief Whip advised Simon to stay put in Coventry and not to participate in any further parliamentary business. "There'll be no more three-line whips between now and the election," he assured him. "The most worthwhile thing you can do is pick up votes in Coventry, not give them in Westminster."

Elizabeth could only manage two weeks' leave of absence from St Mary's, and yet between the two of them they covered the entire constituency before election day. Simon's opponent was the former member, Alf Abbott, who became progressively confident of victory as the national swing to Labour accelerated during the campaign. The slogan 'You know Labour Government works' was sounding convincing after only eighteen months in power. The Liberals fielded a third candidate, Nigel Bainbridge, but he admitted openly that he only hoped to save his deposit.

Alf Abbott felt assured enough to challenge Simon to a public debate. Although it was usual for the sitting member to refuse to be drawn on such occasions Simon jumped at his opponent's challenge and prepared for the encounter with his usual diligence. Seven days before the election Simon and Elizabeth stood in the wings behind the stage of Coventry town hall with Alf Abbott, Nigel Bainbridge and their wives. The three men made stilted conversation while the women eyed each other's outfits critically. The political correspondent of the *Coventry Evening Telegraph*, acting as chairman, introduced each of the protagonists as they walked on to the stage, to whipped-up applause from different sections of the hall. Simon spoke first and held the attention of the large audience for over twenty minutes. Those who tried to heckle him ended up regretting having brought attention to themselves. Without once referring to his notes, he quoted figures and clauses from Government bills with an ease that impressed even Elizabeth. Abbott followed him and made a bitter attack on the Tories, accusing them of still wanting to tread down the workers at any cost, and was greeted by large cheers from his section of the audience. Bainbridge claimed that neither understood the real issues and went into an involved dissertation on the problem of the local sewers. During the questions that followed Simon once again proved to be far better informed than Abbott or Bainbridge, but he was aware that the packed hall only held 700 that cold March evening while elsewhere in Coventry were 50,000 more voters, most of them glued to 'Coronation Street'.

Although the local press proclaimed Simon the victor of a one-sided debate he remained downcast by the national dailies which were now predicting a landslide for Labour.

On election morning Simon and Elizabeth were up by six and among the first to cast their votes at the local primary school. They spent the rest of the day travelling from polling station to committee room to party checking posts, trying to keep up the morale of their supporters. Everywhere they went the committed believed in his victory but Simon knew that the national swing would be impossible to ignore. A senior Conservative back-bencher had once told him that an outstanding member could be worth a thousand personal votes and a weak opponent might sacrifice another thousand. It wasn't going to be enough.

By nine o'clock the last polling station had been locked and Simon and Elizabeth collapsed into a local pub and ordered two halves of bitter. They sat and watched the television above the bar. The commentator was saying that during the day a straw poll had been taken outside six constituencies in London and from those figures they were predicting a Labour majority of sixty to seventy seats. Up on the screen flashed the seventy seats most vulnerable to siege by Labour. Ninth on the list was Coventry Central: Simon ordered the other half.

"We should be off to watch the count soon," said Elizabeth.

"There's no hurry."

"Don't be such a wimp, Simon. And remember you're still the member," she said, surprisingly sharply. "You owe it to your supporters to remain confident after all the work they've put in."

In the town hall black boxes were being delivered by police vehicles from every ward in the constituency. Their contents were tipped on to trestle tables which made up three sides of a square on the vast cleared floor. The town clerk and his personal staff stood alone in the well made by the tables, while council workers sat around the outside carefully stacking up the votes into little piles of a hundred. These in turn were checked by party scrutineers who hovered over them, hawk-like, often demanding that a particular hundred be rechecked.

The little piles grew into large stacks which were then

placed next to each other, and as the hours passed it became obvious even to a casual observer that the outcome was going to be extremely close.

The tension on the floor mounted as each hundred, then each thousand, was handed over to the clerk. Rumours that began at one end of the room had been puffed up like *soufflés* long before they had reached the waiting crowd standing in a chill wind outside the hall. By midnight, several constituencies' results around the country had been declared. The national swing seemed to be much as predicted, around three per cent to Labour, which would give them the promised majority of seventy or over.

At twelve-twenty-one the Coventry town clerk invited all three candidates to join him in the centre of the room. He told them the result of the count.

A recount was immediately demanded. The town clerk agreed, and each pile of voting slips was returned to the tables and checked over again.

An hour later the town clerk called the three candidates together again and briefed them on the result of the recount; it had changed by only three votes.

Another recount was requested and the town clerk reluctantly acquiesced. By two o'clock in the morning Elizabeth felt she had no nails left. Another hour passed, during which Heath conceded defeat while Wilson gave an extended interview to ITN spelling out his programme for the new Parliament.

At two-twenty-seven the town clerk called the three candidates together for the last time and they all accepted the result. The town clerk walked up on to the stage accompanied by the rivals. He tapped the microphone to check the speaker was working, cleared his throat and said:

"I, the undersigned, being the acting returning officer for the constituency of Coventry Central, hereby announce the total number of votes cast for each candidate to be as follows:

Alf Abbot	19,716
Nigel Bainbridge	7,002
Simon Kerslake	19,731

I therefore declare Simon Kerslake to be the duly elected Member of Parliament for the constituency of Coventry Central."

Even though the Labour party ended up with an overall majority in the House of ninety-seven, Simon had still won by fifteen votes.

Raymond Gould increased his majority to 12,413 in line with the national swing, and Joyce was ready for a week's rest.

Andrew Fraser improved his vote by 2,468 and announced his engagement to Louise Forsyth on the night after the election.

Charles Seymour could never recall accurately the size of his majority because, as Fiona explained to the old earl the following morning, "They don't count the Conservative vote in Sussex Downs, darling, they weigh it."

CHAPTER SIX

In most democratic countries a newly elected leader enjoys a transitional period during which he is able to announce the policies he intends to pursue and whom he has selected to implement them. In Britain MPs sit by their phones and wait for forty-eight hours immediately after the election result has been declared. If a call comes in the first twelve hours they will be asked to join the Cabinet, the second twelve given a position as a Minister of State, the third twelve made an Under-Secretary of State, and the last twelve a Parliamentary Private Secretary to a Cabinet minister. If the phone hasn't rung by then, they remain on the back benches.

Andrew Fraser had not bothered to be anywhere near a phone when the BBC midday news announced that Hugh McKenzie had been promoted from Minister of State to Secretary of State for Scotland, with a seat in the Cabinet. Andrew and Louise Forsyth decided to spend a quiet weekend at Aviemore, he to relax and climb other mountains before returning to the House, she to make plans for their forthcoming wedding.

It had taken Andrew countless trips to Edinburgh to convince Louise what had happened to him at Bute House that night had not been mere infatuation that would soon pass, but held long-term conviction. When the one weekend he couldn't travel to the Scottish capital and she came down to London he knew she no longer doubted his resolve. Andrew had found in the past that once the conquest was achieved interest soon waned. For him, though, his love for 'the wee slip of a thing', as his mother had come to describe Louise, grew and grew.

Although Louise was only five foot three she was so slim she appeared far taller, and her short black hair, blue eyes and laughing smile had many tall men bending down to take a closer look.

"You eat like a pig and look like a rake. I don't know how you manage it," grumbled Andrew over dinner one night. He played regular games of squash and swam three times a week to keep his own heavy frame in trim. He stared in admiration and not a little envy as Louise's eyes twinkled mischievously before she devoured another portion of Black Forest gâteau.

Although she had been brought up in a strict Calvinist household in which politics were never discussed Louise quickly learnt about the machinery of Government and soon found herself debating long into the night with Sir Duncan. At first he scored points off her with ease, but it was not long before he had to answer her demands with more and more reasoned arguments, and sometimes even that was not enough.

By the time the election had taken place Louise had become a total convert to Andrew's views. The squalor in some of the parts of the Edinburgh Carlton constituency, which she had never set foot in before, made her sick at heart. Like all converts, she became zealous and began by trying to reform the entire Forsyth clan. She even paid twelve shillings to join the Scottish Labour party.

"Why did you do that?" asked Andrew, trying not to show his pleasure.

"I'm against mixed marriages," she replied.

Andrew was delighted and surprised by the interest she took, and the local constituency suspicions of 'the wealthy lady' soon turned to affection.

"Your future husband will be Secretary of State for Scotland one day," many of them shouted, as she walked down the narrow cobbled streets.

"It's Downing Street, not Bute House, that I want to live in," he had once confided to her. "And in any case I've still got to become a junior minister."

"That could change in the very near future."

"Not while Hugh McKenzie is Secretary of State," he said, not under his breath.

"To hell with McKenzie," she said. "Surely one of his Cabinet colleagues has the guts to offer you the chance to be his PPS?" But despite Louise's sentiments the phone did not ring that weekend.

Raymond Gould returned from Leeds the moment the count was over, leaving Joyce to carry out the traditional 'thank you' drive around the constituency.

When he wasn't sitting by the phone the following day he was walking around it, nervously pushing his glasses back up his nose. The first call came from his mother who had rung to congratulate him.

"On what?" he asked. "Have you heard something?"

"No, love," she said, "I just rang to say how pleased I was about your increased majority."

"Oh."

"And to add how sorry we were not to see you before you left the constituency, especially as you have to pass the shop on the way to the A1."

Not again, Mother, he wanted to say.

The second call was from a colleague inquiring if Raymond had been offered a job.

"Nothing so far," he said before learning of his contemporary's promotion.

The third call was from one of Joyce's friends.

"When will she be back?" another Yorkshire accent enquired.

"I've no idea," said Raymond, desperate to get the caller off the line.

"I'll call again this afternoon, then."

"Fine," said Raymond, putting the phone down quickly.

He went into the kitchen to make himself a cheese sandwich, but there wasn't any cheese, so he ate stale bread smeared with three-week-old butter. He was half-way through a second slice when the phone rang.

"Raymond?"

He held his breath.

"Noel Brewster."

He exhaled in exasperation as he recognised the vicar's voice.

"Can you read the second lesson when you're next up in Leeds? We had rather hoped you would read it this morning – your dear wife . . ."

"Yes," he promised. "The first weekend I am back in Leeds." The phone rang again as soon as he placed it back on the receiver.

"Raymond Gould?" said an anonymous voice.

"Speaking," he said.

"The Prime Minister will be with you in one moment."

Raymond waited. The front door opened and another voice shouted, "It's only me. I don't suppose you found anything to eat, poor love." Joyce joined Raymond in the drawing-room.

Without looking at his wife he waved his hand at her to keep quiet.

"Ray," said a voice on the other end of the line.

"Good afternoon, Prime Minister," he replied, rather formally in response to the more pronounced Yorkshire accent.

"I was hoping you would feel able to join the new team as Under-Secretary for Employment?"

Raymond breathed a sigh of relief. It was exactly what he'd hoped for. "I'd be delighted, Prime Minister."

"Good, that will give the trade union leaders something new to think about." The phone went dead.

Raymond Gould, Under-Secretary of State at the Department of Employment, sat motionless on the third rung of the ladder.

As Raymond left the house the next morning he was greeted by a driver standing next to a gleaming black Austin Westminster. Unlike his second-hand Sunbeam, it glowed in the morning light. The rear door was opened and Raymond climbed in to be driven off to the department. Thank God he knows where my office is, thought Raymond as he sat alone in the back. By his side on the back seat was a red leather box the size of a very thick briefcase with gold lettering running along the edge: 'Under-Secretary of State for Employment'. Raymond turned the small key, knowing what Alice must have felt like on her way down the rabbit hole. The inside was crammed with buff files. He opened the first to see, 'A five-point plan for discussion by Cabinet on how to keep unemployment under one million'. He immediately started to read the closely-typed documents.

When Charles Seymour returned to the Commons on the Tuesday there was a note from the Whips' office waiting for him on the Members' Letter-board. One of the Housing and Local Government team had lost his seat in the general election and Charles had been promoted to number two on the Opposition bench. "No more preservation of trees. You'll be on to higher things now," chuckled the Chief Whip. "Pollution, water shortage and exhaust fumes . . ."

Charles smiled with pleasure as he walked through the Commons, acknowledging old colleagues and noticing a considerable number of new faces. He didn't stop and talk to any of the newcomers as he could not be certain if they were Labour or Conservative and, given the election result, most of them had to be Socialist. A doorkeeper in white tie and black tail-jacket handed him a message to say that a constituent was waiting to see him in the Central Lobby. He hurried off to find out what the problem was, passing some of his older colleagues who wore forlorn looks on their faces. For some it would be a considerable time before they were offered the chance of office again, while others knew they had served as ministers for the last time. As Macmillan had proclaimed, even the most glittering political career always ends in tears.

But at thirty-five Charles dismissed such thoughts as he marched towards the waiting constituent. He turned out to be a red-faced Master of Hounds who had travelled up to London to grumble about the proposed private member's bill banning hare coursing. Charles listened to a fifteen-minute monologue before assuring his constituent that any such bill was doomed through lack of parliamentary time. The Master of Hounds went away happy and Charles returned to his room to check over the constituency mail.

Fiona had reminded him of the 800 letters of thanks to the party workers that had been franked but still needed topping and tailing after every election. He groaned.

"Mrs Blenkinsop, the chairman of Sussex Ladies' Luncheon Club, wants you to be their guest speaker this year," his secretary told him once he had settled.

"Reply yes – what's the date?" asked Charles, reaching for his diary.

"16 June."

"Stupid woman, that's Ladies Day at Ascot. Tell her that I'm delivering a speech at a Housing Conference, but I'll be certain to make myself free for the function next year."

The secretary looked up anxiously.

"Don't fuss, she'll never know any better."

She moved on to the next letter. "Mr Heath wonders if you can join him for a drink on Thursday, six o'clock?"

Simon Kerslake also knew it was going to be a long slog. He was aware the Tories would not change their leader until Heath had been given a second chance at the polls, and that could take every day of five years with a Government which had a ninety-seven majority.

He began writing articles for the *Spectator* and for the *Sunday Express* centre pages, in the hope of building a reputation outside the House while at the same time supplementing his parliamentary salary of £3,400. Even with Elizabeth's income as a consultant he was finding it difficult to make ends meet, and soon their two young sons would have reached prep school age. He envied the Charles Seymours of this world who did not have to give a second thought about their next pay cheque. Simon wondered if the damn man had any problems at all. He ran a finger down his own bank account: as usual there was a figure around £500 in the right-hand margin, and as usual it was in red. Many of his Oxford contemporaries had already established themselves in the City or at the bar and on a Friday evening could be seen being driven to large houses in the country. Simon laughed whenever he read that people went into politics to make money.

He pressed on with demanding questions to the Prime Minister, and tried not to show how frustrated he was by the expectations of his colleagues whenever he rose each Tuesday and Thursday. Even after it became routine he prepared himself thoroughly, and on one occasion he even elicited praise from his normally taciturn leader. But as the weeks passed he found that his thoughts continually returned to money – or to his lack of it.

That was before he met Ronnie Nethercote.

Andrew Fraser had often read that the anger or jealousy of one man could block the advance of a political career but he still found it hard to accept that it could apply to him. What annoyed him even more was that Hugh McKenzie's tentacles seemed to have spread through every other department.

Andrew's marriage to Louise Forsyth had been expansively covered in the national papers and the absence of the Secretary of State at the wedding did not escape the notice of the *Daily Express*'s William Hickey. They even published an out-of-date photograph of Alison McKenzie looking sorrowful.

Sir Duncan reminded his son that politics was for long-distance runners, not sprinters, and that he still had a few more laps to complete yet. "An unfortunate analogy," considered Andrew as he had been a member of the Edinburgh University 4×110 relay team. Nevertheless he prepared himself for the marathon.

"Don't forget, Harold Macmillan spent fourteen years on the back benches before holding office," Sir Duncan added.

Louise accompanied Andrew all over the country for his speeches 'of major importance', usually to an audience of less than twenty; she only stopped travelling to Scotland every week when she discovered she was pregnant.

To Louise's surprise, Andrew turned out to be a keen anticipatory father, determined his son would not think of him only as a politician. Single-handed, he converted one of the upstairs bedrooms in Cheyne Walk into a nursery and sought her approval for a variety of blue decorative schemes.

Louise was anxious that Andrew should extend the same feelings to their unborn child, if they had a daughter.

Raymond Gould quickly gained a reputation at the Department of Employment. He was thought of as extremely bright, demanding, hard working and, not that it was ever reported to him, arrogant. His ability to cut a junior civil servant off in mid-sentence or to correct his principal Private Secretary on matters of detail did not endear him even to his closest staff, who always want to be loyal to their master.

Raymond's work load was prodigious and even the Permanent Secretary experienced Gould's unrelenting 'Don't make excuses' when he tried to trim one of the minister's private schemes. Soon senior civil servants were talking of when, not whether, he would be promoted. His Secretary of State, like all men who were expected to be in six places at once, often asked Raymond to stand in for him, but even Raymond was surprised when he was invited to represent the department as guest of honour at the annual CBI dinner.

Joyce checked to see that her husband's dinner-jacket was well brushed, his shirt spotless and his shoes shining like a guards officer's. His carefully worded speech – a combination of civil-servant draughtsmanship and a few more forceful phrases of his own to prove to the assembled capitalists that not every member of the Labour party was a 'raving commie' – was safely lodged in his inside pocket. His driver ferried him from his Lansdowne Road home towards the West End.

Raymond enjoyed the occasion; although he was nervous when he rose to represent the Government in reply to the toast of the guests. By the time he had resumed his seat he felt it had been one of his better efforts. The ovation that followed was certainly more than polite from what had to be classified as a naturally hostile audience.

"That speech was dryer than the Chablis," one guest whispered in the chairman's ear but he had to agree that, with men like Gould in high office, it was going to be a lot easier to live with the Socialists.

The man on Simon Kerslake's left was far more blunt in

voicing his opinion of Gould. "Bloody man thinks like a Tory, talks like a Tory, so why isn't he a Tory?" he demanded.

Simon grinned at the prematurely balding man who had been expressing his equally vivid views throughout dinner. Corpulent and ruddy-faced, Ronnie Nethercote looked as if he was trying to escape from every part of his bulging dinner-jacket.

"I expect," said Simon in reply, "that Gould would have found it hard to join the Young Conservatives, born in the thirties and living in Leeds."

"Balls," said Ronnie. "I managed it and I was born in the East End of London without any of his advantages. Now tell me, Mr Kerslake, what do you do when you're not wasting your time in the House of Commons?"

Raymond stayed on after dinner and chatted for some time to the captains of industry. A little after eleven he left to return to Lansdowne Road.

As his chauffeur drove slowly away from Grosvenor House down Park Lane, the Under-Secretary waved expansively back to his host. Someone else waved in reply. At first Raymond only glanced across, assuming it was another dinner guest, until he saw her legs. Standing on the corner outside the petrol station on Park Lane stood a young girl smiling at him invitingly, her white leather mini skirt so short it might have been better described as a handkerchief. Her long legs reminded him of Joyce ten years before except that they were black. Her finely curled hair and the set of her hips remained firmly implanted in Raymond's mind all the way home.

When they reached Lansdowne Road Raymond climbed out of the official car and said "Goodnight" to his driver before walking slowly towards his front door, but he did not take out his latch key. He waited until he was sure the driver had turned the corner before looking up and checking the bedroom window. All the lights were out. Joyce must be asleep.

He crept down the path and back on to the pavement, then

looked up and down the road, finally spotting the space where Joyce had parked the Sunbeam. He checked the spare key was on his key-ring and fumbled about, feeling like a car thief. It took three attempts before the car spluttered into life, and Raymond wondered if he would wake up the whole road as he moved off and headed back to Park Lane, not certain what to expect. When he reached Marble Arch he travelled slowly down in the centre stream of traffic. A few dinner guests in evening dress were still spilling out of Grosvenor House. He passed the petrol station: she hadn't moved. She smiled again and he accelerated, nearly running into the car in front of him. Raymond travelled back up to Marble Arch but, instead of turning towards home, he drove down Park Lane again, this time not as quickly and on the inside lane. He took his foot off the accelerator as he approached the petrol station and she waved again. He returned to Marble Arch before repeating his detour down Park Lane, this time even more slowly. As he passed Grosvenor House for a third time he checked to be sure that there were no stragglers still chatting on the pavement. It was clear. He touched the brakes and his car came to a stop just beyond the petrol station. He waited.

The girl looked up and down the street before strolling over to the car, opening the passenger door and taking a seat next to the Under-Secretary of State for Employment.

"Looking for business?"

"What do you mean?" asked Raymond hoarsely.

"Come on, darling. You can't imagine I was standing out there hoping to get a sun tan."

Raymond turned to look at the girl more carefully and wanted to touch her despite the aura of cheap perfume. Her black blouse had three buttons undone; a fourth would have left nothing to the imagination.

"It's ten pounds at my place."

"Where's your place?" he heard himself say.

"I use a hotel in Paddington."

"How do we get there?" he asked, putting his hand nervously through his red hair.

"Just head up to Marble Arch and I'll direct you."

Raymond pulled out and went off towards Hyde Park Corner, and drove round before travelling on up towards Marble Arch once again.

"I'm Mandy," she said, "what's your name?"

Raymond hesitated. "Malcolm."

"And what do you do, Malcolm, in these hard times?"

"I . . . I sell second-hand cars."

"Haven't picked out a very good one for yourself, have you?" She laughed.

Raymond made no comment. It didn't stop Mandy.

"What's a second-hand car salesman doing dressed up like a toff, then?"

Raymond had quite forgotten he was still in evening dress.

"I've . . . just been to a convention . . . at the . . . Hilton Hotel."

"Lucky for some," she said, and lit a cigarette. "I've been standing outside Grosvenor House all night in the hope of getting some rich feller from that posh party." Raymond's cheeks nearly turned the colour of his hair. "Slow down and take the second on the left."

He followed her instructions until they pulled up outside a small dingy hotel. "I'll get out first, then you," she said. "Just walk straight through reception and follow me up the stairs." As she got out of the car he nearly drove off and might have done so if his eye hadn't caught the sway of her hips as she walked back towards the hotel.

He obeyed her instructions and climbed several flights of narrow stairs until he reached the top floor. As he approached the landing, a large bosomy blonde passed him on the way down.

"Hi, Mandy," she shouted back at her friend.

"Hi, Sylv. Is the room free?"

"Just," said the blonde sourly.

Mandy pushed open the door and Raymond followed her in. The room was small and narrow. In one corner stood a tiny bed and a threadbare carpet. The faded yellow wallpaper was peeling in several places. There was a wash basin attached to the wall; a dripping tap had left a brown stain on the enamel.

Mandy put her hand out, and waited.

"Ah, yes, of course," said Raymond, taking out his wallet to find he only had nine pounds on him.

She scowled. "Not going to get overtime tonight, am I, darling?" she said, tucking the money carefully away in the corner of her bag before matter-of-factly taking off all her clothes.

Although the act of undressing had been totally sexless he was still amazed by the beauty of her body. Raymond felt somehow detached from the real world. He watched, eager to feel the texture of her skin, but made no move. She lay down on the bed.

"Let's get on with it, darling. I've got a living to earn."

The minister undressed quickly, keeping his back to the bed. He folded his clothes in a neat pile on the floor as there was no chair. Then he lay down on top of her. It was all over in a few minutes.

"Come quickly, don't you, darling?" said Mandy, grinning.

Raymond turned away from her and started washing himself as best he could in the little basin. He dressed hurriedly, realising he must get out of the place as rapidly as possible.

"Can you drop me back at the petrol station?" Mandy asked.

"It's exactly the opposite direction for me," he said, trying not to sound anxious as he made a bolt for the door. He passed Sylv on the stairs accompanied by a man. She stared at him more closely the second time. Raymond was back in his car a few moments later. He drove home quickly but not before unwinding the windows in an attempt to get rid of the smell of stale tobacco and cheap perfume.

Back in Lansdowne Road he had a long shower before creeping into bed next to Joyce; she stirred only slightly.

CHAPTER
SEVEN

Charles drove his wife down to Ascot early to be sure to avoid the bumper-to-bumper traffic that always developed later in the day. With his height and bearing, Charles Seymour was made for tails and a topper and Fiona wore a hat which on anyone less self-assured would have looked ridiculous. They had been invited to join the McFarlands for the afternoon and when they arrived they found Sir Robert awaiting them in his private box.

"You must have left home early," said Charles.

"About thirty minutes ago," he said, laughing. Fiona looked politely incredulous.

"I always come here by helicopter," he explained.

They lunched on lobster and strawberries accompanied by a fine vintage champagne which the waiter kept pouring and pouring. Charles might not have drunk quite as much had he not picked the winners of the first three races. He spent the fifth race slumped in a chair in the corner of the box and only the noise of the crowd kept him from nodding off.

If they hadn't waited for a farewell drink after the last race Charles might have got away with it. He had forgotten that his host was returning by helicopter.

The long tail of cars across Windsor Great Park all the way back to the M4 made Charles very short-tempered. When he eventually reached the motorway he put his Daimler into fourth gear. He didn't notice the police car until the siren sounded and he was directed to pull over.

"Do be sensible, Charles," whispered Fiona.

"Don't worry, old girl, I know exactly how to deal with the

law," he said, and wound down his window to address the policeman who stood by the car. "Do you realise who I am, officer?"

"No, sir, but I would like you to accompany me –"

"Certainly not, officer, I am a Member of . . ."

"Do be quiet," said Fiona, "and stop making such a fool of yourself."

". . . Parliament and I will not be treated . . ."

"Have you any idea how pompous you sound, Charles?"

"Perhaps you will be kind enough to accompany me to the station, sir?"

"I want to speak to my solicitor."

"Of course, sir. As soon as we reach the station."

When Charles arrived at the constabulary he proved quite incapable of walking in a straight line and refused to provide a blood sample.

"I am the Conservative MP for Sussex Downs."

Which will not help you, Fiona thought, but he was past listening and only demanded that she phone the family solicitor at Speechly, Bircham and Soames.

After Ian Kimmins had spoken first gently, then firmly to Charles his client eventually co-operated with the police.

Once Charles had completed his written statement Fiona drove him home, praying that his stupidity would pass unnoticed by the press the following day.

Andrew even bought a football but hid it from Louise.

As the months passed Louise's slight frame expanded alarmingly. Andrew would rest his head on the bulge and listen for the heartbeat. "It's a scrum-half," he declared.

"Perhaps she's a centre forward," Louise suggested, "and will want to emulate the distaff side of the family."

"If he has to be a centre forward he will play for Hearts," Andrew assured her.

"Male chauvinist pig," she called to his back as he headed off to the Commons that morning. Andrew toyed with the names of Jamie, Robert, Hector and Iain and had settled on Robert before he had reached Westminster. On arrival at

New Palace Yard he hailed the policeman on the gate and was surprised to see the familiar figure immediately rush towards him.

Andrew wound down the window. "What's the problem, officer?"

"Your wife's been taken to St Mary's, Paddington, sir. Emergency wing."

Andrew would have broken the speed limit all the way to Marble Arch if it hadn't been for the traffic. He kept praying he would be there in time, but he couldn't help remembering that Louise was only six months pregnant. When he arrived the doctor on duty would not allow him to see her.

"How is Louise?" were Andrew's first words.

The young doctor hesitated, then said, "Your wife's fine, but I'm afraid she's lost the baby."

Andrew felt his whole body go limp. "Thank God she's all right," he said.

"I'm afraid I can't let you see her until she has come out of sedation."

"Of course, Doctor," said Andrew, glancing at the lapel badge on her white coat.

"But I can see no reason why you shouldn't have more children in the future," she added gently, before he had the chance to ask the quesion.

Andrew smiled with relief and began pacing up and down the corridor, unaware of the passing of time, until the doctor returned and said it would now be all right for him to see his wife.

"I hope you're not too disappointed?" were Louise's first words when eventually he was allowed to see her.

"Don't be silly — we'll have a dozen before we're through," he said, taking her hand.

She tried to laugh. "Do you know my doctor's husband?"

"Not that I'm aware of," said Andrew.

"Simon Kerslake."

"Good heavens, yes. Very capable fellow. Look aye, lass," said Andrew, putting on a deep brogue, "you'll be a new woman after a couple of days' rest, I'll guarantee it."

"And if I'm not?"

"I'll stick with the old one. And I'll tell you what: as soon as they let you out of this place we'll go down to the South of France for the weekend."

"You don't like him because he comes from the East End," said Simon, after she had read the letter.

"That's not true," replied Elizabeth. "I don't like him because I don't trust him."

"But you've only met him twice."

"Once would have been quite enough."

"Well, I can tell you I'm impressed by the not inconsiderable empire he's built up over the last ten years, and frankly it's an offer I can't refuse," said Simon, pocketing the letter.

"I know we could do with a little more money," said Elizabeth, "but surely not at any cost."

"I won't be offered many chances like this," continued Simon, "and frankly we could use the money. The belief people have that every Tory MP has some lucrative sinecure and two or three non-executive directorships is plain baloney and you know it. Not one other serious proposition has been put to me since I've been in the House, and another £2,000 a year for a monthly board meeting would come in very handy."

"And what else?"

"What do you mean, what else?"

"What else does Mr Nethercote expect for his £2,000? Don't be naive, Simon, he's not offering you that kind of money on a plate unless he's hoping to receive some scraps back."

"Well, maybe I have a few contacts and a little influence with one or two people . . ."

"I'll bet."

"You've just taken against him, Elizabeth."

"I'm against anything that might in the long term harm your career, Simon. Struggle on but never sacrifice your integrity, as you're so fond of reminding the people of Coventry."

On Friday morning, two weeks later, Andrew and Louise set out for London airport with one suitcase between them. As Andrew locked the front door the phone rang.

"No one's in," he shouted at the door knob, "but we'll be back on Monday."

He had booked a suite at the Colombe d'Or nestled in the hills of St Paul in the south of France. He was determined to prise Louise away from London and see she had some sun and rest.

The famous old hotel was everything the brochure had promised. On the walls hung paintings by Picasso, Monet, Manet, Utrillo – all of which the patroness, Madame Reux, had accepted many years before in place of payment from artists who needed lodging and a square meal. On the way up the winding staircase Louise was nearly knocked out by a Calder mobile and a Courbet hung above the bed in their room. But it was the bed itself, a sixteenth-century four-poster, that they both coveted. They were soon to discover it possessed a mattress so comfortable that visitors always overslept.

The food was memorable and they walked through the green hills each day to be sure they could tackle another full dinner at night. Three days of no radio, no television, no papers and no telephone ensured that by Monday morning they were ready to face London. They swore they would return again soon.

Once their plane had landed at Heathrow they were made aware that the holiday was over. Twenty minutes passed before someone pushed the waiting steps up to the Vanguard's door. Then a crowded bus to the terminal that seemed miles away was followed by a route-march to customs. Despite their first-class tickets their bags were among the last off. By the time the taxi had crawled through the morning rush hour to their front door in Cheyne Walk all Louise could say was, "I need another holiday." As Andrew put his latch key in the door the telephone started ringing.

"I hope they haven't been trying all weekend," Louise said.

Andrew put the phone to his ear as it went dead.

"Just missed whoever it was," said Andrew, picking up several brown envelopes from the floor. "France already seems about a week ago." He kissed his wife. "Must get changed and be off to the House," he said, checking his watch.

"How has the nation managed to survive without you?" mocked Louise.

When the phone rang again Andrew was just stepping out of the bath.

"Can you take it, Louise?" he shouted. A moment later he heard her rushing up the stairs.

"Andrew, it's the Prime Minister's office."

He ran dripping and naked to the bedroom phone and picked up the extension.

"Andrew Fraser," he said.

"This is No. 10," said an official-sounding voice, "the Prime Minister has been wanting to contact you since Friday morning."

"I'm sorry, I took my wife to Provence for the weekend."

"Really, sir?" said the voice, not sounding at all interested. "May I tell the Prime Minister you are now free to speak to him?"

"Of course," said Andrew, frowning at his nude reflection in the mirror. He must have put on half a stone; it would have to be four games of squash this week and no more wine at lunch.

"Andrew."

"Good morning, Prime Minister."

"Sad news about Hugh McKenzie."

"Yes, sir," said Andrew, automatically.

"They warned me about his heart before the last election but he insisted he wanted to carry on. I've asked Bruce to be the new Secretary of State and Angus to take his place as minister. They both want you to be the new Under-Secretary — how do you feel about it?"

"I'd be delighted, Prime Minister," Andrew stammered, trying to take in the news.

"Good. And by the way, Andrew, when you open your first red box you won't find any tickets for Colombe d'Or, so I do hope Louise is fully recovered." The phone clicked.

They had tracked him down, but the Prime Minister had left him in peace.

The first official function Andrew Fraser attended as Her Majesty's Under-Secretary of State at the Scottish Office was Hugh McKenzie's funeral.

"Think about it, Simon," said Ronnie, as they reached the boardroom door. "Two thousand pounds a year may be helpful but if you take shares in my property company it would give you a chance to make some capital."

"What did you have in mind?" asked Simon, doing up the middle button of his blazer and trying not to sound too excited.

"Well, you've proved damned useful to me. Some of those people who you bring to lunch wouldn't have allowed me past their front doors. I'd let you buy in cheap . . . you could get hold of 50,000 shares at one pound so when we go public you'll make a killing."

"Raising £50,000 won't be that easy, Ronnie."

"When your bank manager has checked over my books he'll be only too happy to lend you the money, you see."

After the Midland Bank had studied the authorised accounts of Nethercote and Company and the area manager had interviewed Simon, they agreed to his request, on the condition that Simon lodge the shares with the bank.

How wrong Elizabeth was proving to be, Simon thought, and when Nethercote and Company went on to double their profits for the year he brought home a copy of the annual report for his wife to study.

"Looks good," she had to admit. "But that still doesn't mean I have to trust Ronnie Nethercote."

When Charles Seymour's drink-driving charge came up in front of the Reading Bench he listed himself as C. G. Seymour – no mention of MP. Under profession he entered 'Banker'.

He came sixth in the list that morning, and on behalf of his absent client Ian Kimmins apologised to the Reading magistrates and assured them it would not happen again. Charles received a fifty-pound fine and was banned from driving for six months. The whole case was over in four minutes.

When Charles was told the news by telephone later that day he was appreciative of Kimmins's sensible advice and felt he had escaped lightly. He couldn't help remembering how many column inches George Brown, the Labour Foreign Secretary, had endured after a similar incident outside the Hilton Hotel.

Fiona kept her own counsel.

At the time Fleet Street was in the middle of 'the silly season', that period in the summer when the press are desperate for news. There had only been one cub reporter in the court when Charles's case came up, and even he was surprised by the interest the nationals took in his little scoop. The pictures of Charles taken so discreetly outside the Seymours' country home were now glaring from the pages the following morning. Headlines ranged from 'Six months' ban for drink-drive son of earl' to 'MP's Ascot binge ends in heavy fine'. Even *The Times* mentioned the case on its home news page.

By lunchtime the same day every Fleet Street newspaper had tried to contact Charles – and so had the Chief Whip. When he did track Charles down his advice was short and to the point. A junior Shadow minister can survive that sort of publicity once, not twice.

"Whatever you do, don't drive a car during the next six months and don't ever drink and drive again."

Charles concurred, and after a quiet weekend hoped he had heard the last of the case. Then he caught the headline on the front page of the *Sussex Gazette*, 'Member faces no confidence motion': Mrs Blenkinsop, the chairman of the Ladies' Luncheon Club, was proposing the motion – not for the drunken driving but for deliberately misleading her about why he had been unable to fulfil a speaking engagement at their annual luncheon.

Raymond had become so used to receiving files marked 'Strictly Private', 'Top Secret', or even 'For Your Eyes Only' in his position as a Government Under-Secretary that he didn't give a second thought to a letter marked 'Confidential and Personal' even though it was written in a scrawled hand. He opened it while Joyce was boiling his eggs.

"Four minutes and forty-five seconds, just the way you like them," she said as she returned from the kitchen and placed two eggs in front of him. "Are you all right, dear? You're white as a sheet."

Raymond recovered quickly, pushing the letter into a pocket before checking his watch. "Haven't the time for the other egg," he said. "I'm already late for Cabinet committee, I must dash."

Strange, thought Joyce, as her husband hurried to the door. Cabinet committees didn't usually meet until ten and he hadn't even cracked open his first egg. She sat down and slowly ate her husband's breakfast, wondering why he had left all his post behind.

Once he was in the back of his official car Raymond read the letter again. It didn't take long.

> Dear 'Malcolm',
>   I enjoid our little get together the other evening and five hundrud pounds would help me to forget it once and for all.
> Love, Mandy.
> PS. I'll be in touch again soon.

He read the letter once more and tried to compose his thoughts. There was no address on the top of the notebook paper. Neither letter nor envelope gave any clue as to where they had come from.

After he had arrived outside the Department of Employment Raymond remained in the back seat for several moments.

"Are you feeling all right, sir?" his driver asked.

"Fine, thank you," he replied, and jumped out of the car and ran all the way up to his office. As he passed his secretary's desk he barked at her, "No interruptions."

"You won't forget Cabinet committee at ten o'clock, will you, Minister?"

"No," replied Raymond sharply and slammed his office door. Once at his desk he tried to calm himself and recall what he would have done had he been approached by a client as a barrister at the bar: first instruct a good solicitor. Raymond considered the two most capable lawyers in England to be Arnold Goodman and Sir Roger Pelham. Goodman was getting too high a profile for Raymond's liking whereas Pelham was just as sound but virtually unknown to the general public. He called Pelham's office and made an appointment to see him that afternoon.

Raymond hardly spoke in Cabinet committee, but as most of his colleagues wanted to express their own views nobody noticed. As soon as the meeting was over Raymond hurried out and took a taxi to High Holborn.

Sir Roger Pelham rose from behind his large Victorian desk to greet the junior minister.

"I know you're a busy man, Gould," Pelham said as he fell back into his black leather chair, "so I shan't waste your time. Tell me what I can do for you."

"It was kind of you to see me at such short notice," Raymond began and without further word handed the letter over.

"Thank you," the solicitor said courteously and, pushing his half-moon spectacles higher up his nose he read the note three times before he made any comment.

"Blackmail is something we all detest," he began, "but it will be necessary for you to tell me the whole truth, and don't miss out any details. Please remember I am on your side. You'll recall only too well from your days at the bar what a disadvantage one labours under when one is in possession of only half the facts."

The tips of Pelham's fingers touched, forming a small roof in front of his nose as he listened intently to Raymond's account of what had happened that night.

"Could anyone else have seen you?" was Pelham's first question.

Raymond thought back and then nodded. "Yes," he said. "Yes, I'm afraid there was another girl who passed me on the stairs."

Pelham read the letter once more. "My immediate advice," he said, looking Raymond in the eye and speaking slowly and deliberately, "and you won't like it, is to do nothing."

"But what do I say if she contacts the press?"

"She will probably get in touch with someone from Fleet Street anyway, even if you pay the £500, or however many other £500s you can afford. Don't imagine you're the first minister to be blackmailed, Mr Gould. Every homosexual in the House lives in daily fear of it. It's a game of hide and seek. Very few people other than saints have nothing to *hide*, and the problem with public life is that a lot of busybodies want to *seek*." Raymond remained silent, trying not to show his anxiety. "Phone me on my private line immediately the next letter arrives," said Pelham, scribbling a number on a piece of paper.

"Thank you," said Raymond, at least relieved that his secret was now shared with someone else. Pelham rose from behind his desk and accompanied Raymond to the door. "You'll be glad to see Yorkshire back as county champions," said the solicitor as he walked down the long passage with the minister. Raymond did not reply. When they reached the outer door they shook hands formally. "I'll wait to hear from you," said Pelham. A pity that the man showed no interest in cricket.

Raymond left the solicitor's office feeling better, but he found it hard to concentrate on his work the rest of that day and slept only in fits and starts during the night. When he read the morning papers he was horrified to see how much space was being given to Charles Seymour's peccadillo. What a field day they would be able to have with him. When the post came, he searched anxiously for the scrawled handwriting. It was hidden under an American Express circular. He tore it open. The same hand was this time demanding that the £500 should be deposited at a newsagent in Pimlico. Sir Roger Pelham saw the minister one hour later.

Despite the renewed demand the solicitor's advice remained the same.

Andrew Fraser never stopped moving from one city to another because the Scottish Office had to show a presence in Edinburgh and Glasgow as well as in London. Louise did not complain; she had never seen her husband so happy. The only moment of light relief during his first three months as a minister came when Andrew found it necessary to send a letter to his father addressed, "Dear Sir Duncan," which went on to explain why he had to reject his offered advice on a Highlands and Islands Board project. Andrew was particularly pleased with the line, "I have for some considerable time listened to both sides of the argument."

Once he had settled in his favourite chair that night with a large whisky in his hand Louise told him she was pregnant again. "When did I find the time?" he asked, taking her in his arms.

"Maybe the half-hour between your meeting with the Norwegian Fishing Minister and the address to the Oil Conference in Aberdeen?"

When the AGM of the Sussex Downs Conservative Association came round in October Charles was pleased to learn that Mrs Blenkinsop's 'no confidence' motion had been withdrawn. The local press tried to build up the story but the nationals were full of the Aberfan coal-tip disaster, in which 116 schoolchildren had lost their lives. No editor could find space for Sussex Downs.

Charles delivered a thoughtful speech to his association which was well received. During question time he was relieved to find no embarrassing questions directed at him.

When the Seymours finally said goodnight, Charles took the chairman to one side and enquired: "How did you manage it?"

"I explained to Mrs Blenkinsop," replied the chairman, "that if her motion of no confidence was discussed at the AGM it would be awfully hard for the member to back my recommendation that she should receive an OBE in the New Year's Honours for service to the party. That shouldn't be too hard for you to pull off, should it, Charles?"

Every time the phone rang Raymond assumed it would be
the press asking him if he knew someone called Mandy.
Often it was a journalist, but all that was needed was a
quotable remark on the latest unemployment figures, or a
statement of where the minister stood on devaluation of the
pound.

It was Mike Molloy, a reporter from the *Daily Mirror*, who
was the first to ask Raymond what he had to say about a
statement phoned in to his office by a girl with a West Indian
accent called Mandy Page.

"I have nothing to say on the subject. Please speak to my
solicitor, Sir Roger Pelham," was the Under-Secretary's
succinct reply. The moment he put the phone down he felt
queasy.

A few minutes later when the phone rang again Raymond
still hadn't moved. He picked up the receiver, his hand still
shaking. Pelham confirmed that Molloy had been in touch
with him.

"I presume you made no comment," said Raymond.

"On the contrary," replied Pelham. "I told him the
truth."

"What?" exploded Raymond.

"Be thankful she hit on a fair journalist because I expect
he'll let this one go. Fleet Street are not quite the bunch of
shits everyone imagines them to be," Pelham said uncharacteristically, and added, "they also detest two things, bent
policemen and blackmailers. I don't think you'll see anything in the press tomorrow."

Sir Roger Pelham was wrong.

Raymond was standing outside his local newsagent the
next morning when it opened at five-thirty and he surprised
the proprietor by asking for a copy of the *Daily Mirror*.
Raymond Gould was plastered all over page five saying,
"Devaluation is not a course I can support while the unemployment figures remain so high." The photograph by the
side of the article was unusually flattering.

Simon Kerslake read a more detailed account of what the
minister had said on devaluation in *The Times*, and noted

Raymond Gould's firm stand against what was beginning to look like inevitable Government policy.

Simon looked up from his paper and started to consider a ploy that might trap Gould. If he could make the minister commit himself again and again on devaluation in front of the whole House he knew that when the inevitable happened Gould would be left with no choice but to resign. Simon pencilled a question on the top of the paper before returning to the political columns.

The devaluation news had caused a Tory lead in the opinion polls of eight per cent, and despite a majority of ninety-five in the Commons the Government had actually lost a vote on the floor of the House the previous day. Nevertheless, Simon still could not envisage a general election for at least another two years.

On the business front Simon had advised Ronnie Nethercote not to allow his company shares to be traded on the Stock Exchange until the Tories returned to power. "The climate," he assured Ronnie, "should be much easier then."

Charles Seymour was glad to be behind the wheel again after his driving ban had been completed, and he had the grace to smile when Fiona showed him the photograph of the happy Mrs Blenkinsop displaying her OBE outside Buckingham Palace to a reporter from the *Sussex Gazette*.

It was six months to the day of his first meeting with Sir Roger Pelham that Raymond Gould received an account from the solicitor for services rendered — £500. He sent the cheque by return of post in a parcel that also contained a copy of the recently published edition of *Wisden*.

CHAPTER
EIGHT

Andrew had been warned by his ministerial colleagues that the first day answering questions at the dispatch box would be an experience he was unlikely to forget.

Questions for the Scottish Office appear on the order paper on a Wednesday once every four or five weeks, and each minister answers on behalf of his own department between two-thirty-five and three-twenty. There are usually four or five ministers of the Crown, not including the law officer available to represent each great department of state. During the forty-minute to one-hour period the ministers would expect to reply to about twenty-five questions, but it is rarely the questions that are the problem; it is the supplementaries.

Any member can place a question through the table office to any minister, and can word it in a seemingly innocuous way. "When does the minister hope next to visit Aberdeen?" to which the minister concerned may reply anything from "next week" to "I have no plans to do so in the foreseeable future" – but when the member who put down the question rises from his seat to ask his supplementary he can change the subject completely. "Does the minister realise that Aberdeen has the highest rate of unemployment in the United Kingdom, and what new ideas does his department have to deal with this problem?" The hapless minister must then come up with a convincing reply on the spot.

In an attempt to see that a minister is adequately briefed, his department will spend the morning scrutinising each tabled question and looking for pitfalls he might encounter. A variety of possible supplementaries will be placed in his brief with appropriate answers. Ministers can, of course, always ask colleagues on their own side what they are hoping to find out from their tabled questions, but Opposition members use question time to test a minister in the hope of discovering some weakness in his armoury, thus making the Government appear incompetent.

Andrew spent a considerable time in preparation for his first encounter at the dispatch box although the more senior and experienced ministers in the Scottish Office had agreed to handle any questions that looked hostile.

He ended up having to respond to only one question from the Opposition benches, while fielding four from his own. Added to which, the timing was such that question number twenty-three from the Opposition member seemed unlikely to be reached by three-twenty, when the Solicitor General for Scotland would have to start answering questions himself.

Andrew's first four answers to questions numbers five, nine, eleven and fourteen, went smoothly enough. He opened his dark blue file and was pleased to confirm the well-prepared briefs to everything that was thrown at him. By three-fifteen, when question number nineteen was being answered, Andrew sat back on the front bench and began to relax for the first time that day.

The Solicitor General for Scotland entered a now packed Commons and, moving alongside the table in the centre of the Chamber, he crouched slightly to be sure he did not obscure the Speaker's view of the Government benches on his right. The Prime Minister had been left a place between the Chancellor and the Foreign Secretary and waited for the clock to reach three-twenty.

The Speaker called question number twenty-one but the member was not present. He called number twenty-two and once again the member was absent. Each had obviously considered that their question had little chance of being reached before three-twenty. At three-eighteen the Speaker called question twenty-three – Andrew's heart sank – which read on the order paper, "Had the minister been invited to visit the Kinross Nursing Home?"

Andrew rose, opened his folder and said, "No, sir."

"No one in the House will be surprised by the minister's reply," said George Younger, the member for Ayr, "because the nursing home has forty-nine occupants, forty-seven of whom have their own television sets and yet the minister demands forty-seven separate licence fees. If they were to congregate in one room, he would expect only one fee. Is this another example of the Labour party's 'Care for the Aged' programme that we hear so much about nowadays?"

Andrew rose to the dispatch box to cries of "Answer, answer," from the Opposition benches. He had checked his crib sheet while sitting on the edge of his seat. Andrew had a prepared answer for medical facilities, old-age pensions, supplementary benefits, food allowances, medical charges – but nothing on TV licences. As he stood stranded at the dispatch box he was aware for the first time of the pitfalls that a minister encounters when he is not fully prepared. Such a system might appear wonderfully democratic to onlookers, he thought, until you are the Christian facing the 300 hungry lions.

A handwritten note was quickly passed along the front bench to him from one of the civil servants who sit in the official box to the left behind the Speaker's chair. With no time to consider its implications Andrew crossed his fingers and read the note out to the House.

"This was a decision taken by the last administration, of which the Honourable Gentleman was a member. We have seen no reason to reverse that decision," he read, thinking how much like a parrot he sounded. He sat down to polite Government murmurs and some considerable relief.

Mr Younger rose again and was allowed a second supplementary.

"Mr Speaker, this is the sort of inaccuracy we have grown to expect from this Government. The decision he refers to was made by his Right Honourable friend, the Secretary of State, only last year, and I think the minister will find, if he does his research more fastidiously, that his party was in power at the time." The Opposition howled their delight.

Andrew rose again and gripped the sides of the dispatch box to avoid anyone seeing that he was shaking in fear.

Several members of the Government front bench had their heads bowed. The Opposition had drawn blood and were baying in triumph. Lord Attlee's words came back to Andrew. "When you are caught out by the House admit it, apologise, and sit down."

Andrew waited for the noise to subside before he replied. "The Secretary of State warned me that a new minister will never forget his first question time and I feel bound to agree with him." Andrew, who knew how the atmosphere in the House can change in a moment, felt such a moment now, and before it could turn back added, "On the question of television licences in the Kinross Nursing Home, I apologise to the Honourable Gentleman for Ayr for my mistake and I will look into the case immediately and send him a written reply within twenty-four hours." "Hear, hears" could now be heard from his own benches and the Opposition benches were quietened. Mr Younger was trying to interrupt again but as Andrew didn't give way he had to resume his seat, knowing the Speaker would not call on him again once the clock had passed three-nineteen. Andrew waited for silence before adding, "And I blame my grandmother for this who, as President of the Kinross Nursing Home and a staunch Conservative, has always believed in increasing old-age pensions rather than looking for false subsidies that can never be fair to everyone." By now the Labour members were laughing and all the heads on the front bench were looking towards the new minister, who remained at the dispatch box until the House was silent again. "My grandmother would be delighted to learn that this administration has raised that old-age pension by fifty per cent in the three years since we have taken office." The Labour back-benchers were now cheering and waving their order papers as Andrew resumed his seat, while the Opposition were silent and glum.

The hands of the clock touched three-twenty and the Speaker said, "The Solicitor General's questions."

Andrew Fraser had made a political reputation, and as the laughter echoed round the House the intense figure sitting on the end of the front bench put a hand through his red hair and wondered if he could ever match Andrew's skill at the

dispatch box. On the Opposition back benches Simon Kerslake made a mental note to be cautious if he ever thought of
putting a sharp question to Andrew Fraser.

As soon as the Solicitor General's questions were over
Simon left the House and drove himself to Whitechapel
Road. He arrived a few minutes after the four o'clock board
meeting of Nethercote and Company had begun, quietly took
his seat and listened to Ronnie Nethercote describing
another coup.

Ronnie had signed a contract that morning to take over a
major city block at a cost of fifteen million pounds with a
guaranteed rental income of over 1.1 million per annum for
the first seven years of a twenty-one year lease with seven-
year rent reviews.

Simon formally congratulated him and asked if this made
any difference to the company's timing for going public.

"Why do you ask?" said Ronnie.

"Because I still feel it might be wise to wait until we know
the result of the next general election. If the Conservatives
return to power, as the opinion polls forecast, that could
change the whole atmosphere for launching a new company."

"If they don't, I shan't hold up going public much longer."

"I wouldn't disagree with that decision either, Mr Chairman," said Simon.

When the meeting was over he joined Nethercote in his
office for a drink.

"I want to thank you," Ronnie said, "for that introduction
to Harold Samuel and Louis Freedman. It made the deal go
through much more smoothly."

"Does that mean you'll allow me to purchase some more
shares?"

Ronnie hesitated. "Why not? You've earned them. But
only another 10,000. Don't get ahead of yourself, Simon, or
the other directors may become jealous."

In the car on the way to pick up Elizabeth Simon decided
to take a second mortgage out on the house in Beaufort Street
to raise the extra cash needed for the new shares. He thought
it might be wise not to trouble her with the details. He
savoured the prospect of the Conservatives winning the next

election, perhaps being given office in the Government and selling his shares for a sum that would make it possible for him to stop the continual worries of how he would finance his children's education. Perhaps he could even give Elizabeth that holiday in Venice she had talked about so often.

When he drove up to the hospital Elizabeth was waiting outside the gates. "We won't be late, will we?" were her first words.

"No," said Simon, checking the clock on the dashboard as he turned the car round in the direction of Beaufort Street.

They arrived at the hall five minutes before the curtain was due to rise. The occasion was their sons' pantomime, and both Peter and Michael had assured their parents that they had major parts. It was Charles Kingsley's *The Water Babies*, and Michael turned out to be a crab, who although he never left the stage lay on his stomach throughout the entire performance and never uttered a word. Peter, who had spent the week learning his words off by heart, was an unconvincing water baby standing at the end of a row of twelve. His speaking part turned out to be one sentence: "If grown-ups go on eating all the fish in the sea there will be none left for me." King Neptune fixed his imperial eye on Peter and said, "Don't blame us, it's your father who's the MP," upon which Peter bowed his head and blushed, though not as deeply as Elizabeth when the audience in front of them turned round and smiled at Simon, who felt more embarrassed than if he had been in the centre of a raging debate in the Commons.

At coffee afterwards the headmaster admitted that the sentence had been added without the approval of the late Charles Kingsley. When Simon and Elizabeth took the children home that night they insisted on repeating Peter's one line again and again.

"If the Government did an about-turn and devalued the pound, would the Under-Secretary find it possible to remain in office?"

Raymond Gould stiffened when he heard Simon Kerslake's question. His grasp of the law and his background knowledge of the subject made all except the extremely articulate or highly experienced wary of taking him on. Nevertheless Raymond had one Achilles' heel arising from his firmly stated views in *Full Employment at any Cost?*: any suggestion that the Government would devalue. Time and again eager back-benchers would seek to tackle him on the subject but once more it was Simon Kerslake who felled his opponent.

Andrew, sitting on the front bench, composed in his mind a sharp reply about his colleagues' collective responsibility, but Raymond Gould said rather ponderously: "The policy of Her Majesty's Government is one hundred per cent against devaluation, and therefore the question does not arise."

"Wait and see," shouted Kerslake.

"Order," said the Speaker, rising from his seat and turning towards Simon as Raymond sat down. "The Honourable member knows all too well he must not address the House from a sedentary position. The Under-Secretary of State."

Raymond rose again. "This Government believes in a strong pound, which still remains our best hope for keeping unemployment figures down."

"But what would you do if Cabinet does go ahead and devalue?" Joyce asked him when she read her husband's reply to Kerslake's question reported in *The Times* the next morning.

Raymond was already facing the fact that devaluation looked more likely every day. A strong dollar causing imports to reach record levels coupled with a run of strikes during the summer of sixty-seven was causing foreign bankers to ask when, not if.

"I'd have to resign," he said in reply to Joyce's question.

"Why? No other minister will."

"I'm afraid Kerslake is right. I'm on the record and he's made sure everybody knows it. Don't worry, Harold will never devalue. He's assured me of that many times."

"He only has to change his mind once."

Pressure on the pound increased during the following weeks and Raymond began to fear that Joyce might turn out to be right.

Andrew Fraser had read *Full Employment at any Cost?* and considered it a succinctly argued case although he did not agree with all the small print. He personally was in favour of devaluation but felt it should have been pushed through in the Labour party's first week in office, so that the blame could be left at the door of the Tories. After three years and a second election victory any such suggestion would rightly be considered outrageous.

As Louise's time of delivery approached she was getting larger by the day. Andrew helped to take pressure off her as much as he could, but this time he did not prepare so obviously for the birth, as he felt his unbridled enthusiasm might have contributed to her previous anxiety. He tried as often as possible to bring the red boxes home each night, but it remained an exception if he returned to Cheyne Walk before eleven o'clock.

"Voting every night at ten o'clock and sometimes on through the night into the next day is one system the rest of the world has *not* considered worth emulating," Andrew had told Louise after one particularly gruelling session. He couldn't even remember what he had been voting on – although he didn't admit that to her. "But as no Government of whatever party has ever seriously considered the idea of limiting the time for ending business 'the troops', as backbenchers are known, go on charging through the lobbies day in and day out. That's why the press refer to us as 'lobby fodder'."

"More like a bunch of unruly children," she chided.

When Louise went into hospital one week early Elizabeth Kerslake assured her there was nothing to be worried about, and two days later Louise gave birth to a beautiful girl.

Andrew was in a departmental meeting discussing Glasgow's high-rise housing programme when the hospital staff nurse rang to congratulate him. He went straight to his fridge and took out the bottle of champagne his father had sent him the day he joined the Scottish Office. He poured a plastic mug of Krug for each of his team of advisers.

"Just better than drinking it out of the bottle," he suggested as he left his civil servants to go to the hospital.

On arrival at St Mary's Andrew was relieved to find Elizabeth Kerslake was on duty. She warned him that his wife was still under sedation after a particularly complicated Caesarian delivery. Elizabeth took him to see his daughter who remained under observation in an isolation unit.

"Nothing to fret about," Elizabeth assured him. "We always take this precaution after any Caesarian birth as there are a number of routine tests we still have to carry out."

She left Andrew to stare at his daughter's large blue eyes. Although he knew it might change in time the soft down on the crown of her head was already dark.

He slipped out an hour later when she had fallen asleep to return to Dover House, where he had a second celebration in the Secretary of State's office, but this time the champagne was served in crystal glasses.

When Andrew climbed into bed that night the champagne helped him fall into a deep sleep with the only problem on his mind being what they should call their daughter. Claire had always been the name Louise favoured.

The phone had rung several times before he answered it and as soon as he had replaced the receiver he dressed and drove to the hospital as quickly as possible. He parked the car and ran to the now-familiar ward. Elizabeth Kerslake was standing waiting by the door. She looked tired and dishevelled, and even with all her training and experience she found it hard to explain to Andrew what had happened.

"Your daughter died forty minutes ago when her heart stopped beating. Believe me, we tried everything."

Andrew collapsed on the bench in the corridor and didn't speak for several moments. "How's Louise?" was all he could eventually manage.

"She hasn't been told yet. She's still under sedation. Be thankful she never saw the baby."

Andrew thumped his leg until it was numb. He stopped suddenly. "I'll tell her myself," he said quietly and remained on the bench, tears coursing down his cheeks. Elizabeth sat down beside him but didn't speak. When she left it was only to check that Mrs Fraser was ready to see her husband.

Louise knew the moment Andrew walked in. It was over an hour before she managed to speak.

"I bet Alison McKenzie would have given you a dozen sons," she said, trying to make him smile.

"No doubt about that," said Andrew, "but they would have all been ugly and stupid."

"I agree with you," said Louise. "But that wouldn't have been her fault."

They both tried to laugh.

Andrew returned to Cheyne Walk a little after four o'clock, but he didn't sleep again that night.

The great orator Iain Macleod once remarked that it was the first two minutes of a speech that decided one's fate. One either grasps the House and commands it or dithers, and loses it, and once the House is lost it can rarely be brought to heel. When Charles Seymour was invited to present the winding-up speech for the Opposition during the Economic debate, he felt he had prepared himself well, and although he knew he could not expect to convert Government back-benchers to his argument he hoped the press would acknowledge the following day that he had won the argument and embarrassed the Government. The Administration was already rocking over daily rumours of devaluation and economic trouble, and Charles was confident that this was the chance to make his name.

Full parliamentary debates usually start at three-thirty, after question time, but can be delayed if there are ministerial statements to be made. The senior minister in the department concerned makes the opening speech for approximately thirty minutes and then the Opposition spokesman addresses the House for the same period of time. Between four-thirty and nine the debate is thrown open to the floor and the Speaker tries to be scrupulously fair in calling a cross-section of back-benchers who have demonstrated an interest in the subject, as well as preserving a party and regional balance. These back-bencher speeches are frowned on if they last for more than fifteen minutes. Some of the most memorable speeches delivered in the House have lasted eight or nine minutes, some of the worst over thirty.

At nine o'clock the Opposition spokesman makes his final comments, and at nine-thirty a Government minister winds up.

When Charles rose and stood at the dispatch box he intended to press home the Tory case on the Government's economic record, the fatal consequences of devaluation, the record inflation, coupled with record borrowing and a lack of confidence in Britain unknown in any member's lifetime.

He stood his full height and stared down belligerently at the Government benches.

"Mr Speaker," he began, "I can't think . . ."

"Then don't bother to speak," someone shouted from the Labour benches. Laughter broke out as Charles tried to compose himself, cursing his initial over-confidence. He began again.

"I can't imagine . . ."

"No imagination either," came another voice. "Typical Tory."

". . . why this motion was ever put before the House."

"Certainly not for you to give us a lesson in public speaking."

"Order," growled the Speaker, but it was too late.

The House was lost and Charles stumbled through thirty minutes of embarrassment until no one but the Speaker was listening to a word he said. Several members of his own front bench had their feet up on the table and their eyes closed. Back-benchers on either side sat chattering amongst themselves waiting for the ten o'clock division: the ultimate humiliation the House affords to its worst debaters. The Speaker had to call for order several times during Charles's speech, once rising to rebuke noisy members, "The House does its reputation no service by behaving in this way." But his plea fell on deaf ears as the conversations continued. At nine-thirty Charles sat down in a cold sweat. A few of his own back-benchers managed to raise an unconvincing "Hear, hear."

When the Government minister opened his speech by

describing Charles's offering as among the most pathetic he
had heard in a long political career he may well have been
exaggerating, but from the expressions on the Tory front
benches not many Opposition members were going to disagree with him.

CHAPTER
NINE

The decision was finally made by the inner Cabinet of twelve on Thursday 16 November 1967. By Friday every bank clerk in Tokyo was privy to the inner Cabinet's closest secret, and by the time the Prime Minister made the announcement official on Saturday afternoon the Bank of England had lost 600 million dollars of reserves on the foreign exchange market.

At the time of the Prime Minister's statement Raymond was in Leeds conducting one of his fortnightly constituency 'surgeries'. He was in the process of explaining the new housing bill to a young married couple when Fred Padgett, his agent, burst into the room.

"Raymond, sorry to interrupt you, but I thought you'd want to know immediately. No. 10 have just announced that the pound has been devalued from two dollars eighty to two dollars forty." The sitting member was momentarily stunned, the local housing problem driven from his mind. He stared blankly across the table at the two constituents who had come to seek his advice.

"Will you please excuse me for a moment, Mr Higginbottom," Raymond asked courteously, "but I must make a phone call." The moment turned out to be fifteen minutes, in which time Raymond had made contact with a senior civil servant from the Treasury and had all the details confirmed. He called Joyce and told her not to answer the phone until he arrived back home. It was several minutes before he felt composed enough to put his head round the office door.

"How many people are still waiting to see me, Fred?" he asked.

"After the Higginbottoms there's only the mad major, still convinced that Martians are about to land on the roof of Leeds town hall."

"Why would they want to come to Leeds first?" asked Raymond, trying to hide his anxiety with false humour.

"Once they've captured Yorkshire, the rest would be easy."

"Hard to find fault with that argument. Nevertheless, tell the major I'm deeply concerned but I need to study his claim in more detail and to seek further advice from the Ministry of Defence. Make an appointment for him to see me at the next surgery and by then I should have a strategic plan ready for him."

Fred Padgett grinned. "That will give him something to tell his friends about for at least two weeks."

Raymond returned to Mr and Mrs Higginbottom and assured them he would have their housing problem sorted out within a few days. He made a note on his file to ring the Leeds Council Housing Officer.

"What an afternoon," exclaimed Raymond after the door had closed behind them. "One wife-beating, one electricity turned off by the YEB with four children under ten in the house, one pollution of the Aire river and one appalling housing problem – never forgetting the mad major and his itinerant Martians. And on top of all of that the devaluation news."

"How can you remain so calm?" asked Fred Padgett.

"Because I can't afford to let anyone know how I really feel."

After his surgery Raymond would normally have gone round to the local pub for a pint and an obligatory natter with the locals. This always gave him the chance to catch up on what had been happening in Leeds during the past fortnight. But on this occasion he bypassed the pub and returned quickly to his parents' home.

Joyce told him that the phone had rung so often that she had finally taken it off the hook, without letting his mother know the real reason.

"Very sensible," said Raymond.

"What are you going to do?" she asked.

"I shall resign, of course."

"Why do that, Raymond? It will only harm your career."

"You may turn out to be right, but that won't stop me going."

"But you're only just beginning to get on top of your work."

"Joyce, without trying to sound pompous, I know I have many failings but I'm not a coward and I'm certainly not so self-seeking as totally to desert any principles I might have."

"You know, you just sounded like a man who is destined to become Prime Minister."

"A moment ago you said it would harm my chances. Make up your mind."

"I have," she said.

Raymond smiled wanly before retreating to his study to write a short handwritten letter.

> Saturday, 18 November 1967
>
> Dear Prime Minister,
>
> After your announcement this afternoon on devaluation and the stand I have continually taken on the issue I am left with no choice but to resign my position as Under-Secretary of State at the Department of Employment.
>
> I would like to thank you for having given me the opportunity to serve in your administration. Be assured that I shall continue to support the Government on all other issues from the back benches.
>
> Yours,
>
> Raymond Gould.

When the red box arrived at the house that Saturday night Raymond instructed the messenger to deliver the letter to No. 10 immediately. As he opened the box for the last time he reflected that his department was answering questions on employment in the House that Monday. He wondered who would take his place.

Because of the paraphernalia surrounding devaluation, the Prime Minister did not get round to reading Raymond's letter until late Sunday morning. The Goulds' phone was still off the hook when an anxious Fred Padgett was heard knocking on the front door later that day.

"Don't answer it," said Raymond. "It's bound to be another journalist."

"No, it's not, it's only Fred," said Joyce, peeping through an opening in the curtain.

She opened the door. "Where the hell's Raymond?" were Fred's first words.

"Right here," said Raymond, appearing from the kitchen holding the Sunday newspapers.

"The Prime Minister has been trying to contact you all morning." Raymond turned round and replaced the phone on the hook, picked it up a few seconds later and checked the tone before dialling London WHI 4433. The Prime Minister was on the line in moments. He sounded calm enough, thought Raymond.

"Have you issued any statement to the press, Ray?"

"No, I wanted to be sure you had received my letter first."

"Good. Please don't mention your resignation to anyone until we've met. Could you be at Downing Street by eight o'clock?"

"Yes, Prime Minister."

"Remember, not a word to the press."

Raymond heard the phone click.

Within the hour he was on his way to London, and arrived at his house in Lansdowne Road a little after seven. The phone was ringing again. He wanted to ignore the insistent *burr-burr* but thought it might be Downing Street.

He picked the phone up. "Hello."

"Is that Raymond Gould?" said a voice.

"Who's speaking?" asked Raymond.

"Walter Terry, *Daily Mail*."

"I am not going to say anything," said Raymond.

"Do you feel the Prime Minister was right to devalue?"

"I said nothing, Walter."

"Does that mean you are going to resign?"

"Walter, nothing."

"Is it true you have already handed in your resignation?"

Raymond hesitated.

"I thought so," said Terry.

"I said nothing," spluttered Raymond and slammed down the phone – before lifting it back off the hook.

He quickly washed and changed his shirt before leaving the house. He nearly missed the note that was lying on the doormat, and he wouldn't have stopped to open it had the envelope not been embossed with large black letters across the left-hand corner – 'Prime Minister'. Raymond ripped it open. The handwritten note from a secretary asked him on his arrival to come by the rear entrance of Downing Street and not the front door. A small map was enclosed. Raymond was becoming weary of the whole exercise.

Two more journalists were waiting by the gate and followed him to his car.

"Have you resigned, Minister?" asked the first.

"No comment."

"Are you on your way to see the Prime Minister?"

Raymond did not reply and leaped into his car. He drove off so quickly that the pursuing journalists were left with no chance of catching him.

Twelve minutes later, at five to eight, he was seated in the ante-room of No. 10 Downing Street. As eight struck he was taken through to Harold Wilson's study. He was surprised to find the Secretary of State for Employment seated in the corner of the room.

"Ray," said the Prime Minister. "How are you?"

"I'm well, thank you, Prime Minister."

"I was sorry to receive your letter and thoroughly understand the position you are in, but I hope perhaps we can work something out."

"Work something out?" Raymond repeated, puzzled.

"Well, we all realise devaluation is a problem for you after *Full Employment at any Cost?* but I felt perhaps a move to the Foreign Office as Minister of State might be a palatable way out of the dilemma. It's a promotion you've well earned."

Raymond hesitated. The Prime Minister continued. "It may interest you to know that the Chancellor of the

Exchequer has also resigned, but will be moving to the Home Office."

"I am surprised," said Raymond.

"What with the problems we are about to tackle in Rhodesia and Europe your legal skills would come in very useful."

Raymond remained silent as he listened to the Prime Minister; he knew what decision he must now make.

Monday usually gets off to a quiet start in the Commons. The Whips never plan for any contentious business to be debated, remembering that members are still arriving back from their constituencies all over the country. The House is seldom full before the early evening. But the knowledge that the Chancellor of the Exchequer would be making a statement on devaluation at three-thirty ensured that the Commons would be packed long before that hour.

The green benches, accommodating just 427 members, had deliberately been restored as they were after the Germans had bombed the Palace of Westminster on 10 May 1941. The intimate theatrical atmosphere of the House had remained intact. Sir Giles Gilbert Scott could not resist highlighting some of the Gothic décor of Barry, but he concurred with Churchill's view that to enlarge the Chamber would only destroy the packed atmosphere of great occasions.

The Commons filled up quickly, and by two-forty-five there was not a seat to be found. Members huddled up on the steps by the Speaker's canopied chair and around the legs of the chairs of the clerks at the table. One or two even perched like unfed sparrows on the empty petition bag behind the Speaker's chair. The galleries to the side and above the Chamber, which normally resembled empty benches at the Oval on a rainy day, had taken on the look of a crucial last Test match against Australia.

The chief doorkeeper checked his supply of snuff that it had been his office to keep since those days when 'unpleasant odours' wafted through London.

Raymond Gould rose to answer question number seven on

the order paper, an innocent enough inquiry concerning supplementary benefits for women. As soon as he reached the dispatch box the first cries of "Resign" came from the Tory benches. Raymond couldn't hide his embarrassment. Even those seated on the back benches could see he had gone scarlet. It didn't help that he hadn't slept the previous night following the agreement he had come to with the Prime Minister. He answered the question, but the calls for his resignation did not subside. The Opposition fell silent as he sat down, only waiting for him to rise for a further question.

The next question on the order paper for Raymond to answer was from Simon Kerslake; it came a few minutes after three. "What analysis has been made by his department of the special factors contributing to increasing unemployment in the Midlands?"

Raymond checked his brief before replying. "The closure of two large factories in the area, one in the Honourable member's constituency, has exacerbated local unemployment. Both of these factories specialised in car components which have suffered from the Leyland strike."

Simon Kerslake rose slowly from his place to put his supplementary. The Opposition benches waited in eager anticipation. "But surely the minister remembers informing the House, in reply to my adjournment debate last April, that devaluation would drastically increase unemployment in the Midlands, indeed in the whole country. If the Honourable Gentleman's words are to carry any conviction, why hasn't he resigned?" Simon sat down as the Tory benches demanded, "Why, why, why?"

"My speech to the House on that occasion is being quoted out of context, and the circumstances have since changed."

"They certainly have," shouted a number of Conservatives and the benches opposite Raymond exploded with demands that he give up his office.

"Order, order," shouted the Speaker into the tide of noise.

Simon rose again, while everyone on the Conservative benches remained seated to ensure no one else was called. They were now hunting as a pack. Everyone's eyes switched back and forth between the two men, watching the dark,

assured figure of Kerslake once again jabbing his forefinger
at the bowed head of Raymond Gould who was now only
praying for the clock to reach three-thirty.

"Mr Speaker, during the debate, which he now seems
happy to orphan, the Honourable Gentleman was only
echoing the views he so lucidly expressed in his book *Full
Employment at any Cost?* Can those views have altered so
radically in three years, or is his desire to remain a minister so
great that he now realises that *his* employment can be
retained at any cost?"

"This question has nothing to do with what I said to the
House on that occasion," retorted Raymond angrily. His
last few words were lost in Opposition shouts of "Resign,
resign!"

Simon was up in a flash and the Speaker called him for a
third time.

"Is the Honourable Gentleman telling the House that he
has one set of moral standards when he speaks, and yet
another when he writes?"

The House was now in total uproar and few members
heard Raymond say, "No, sir, I try to be consistent."

The Speaker rose and the noise subsided slightly. He
looked about him with an aggrieved frown. "I realise the
House feels strongly on these matters, but I must ask the
Honourable member for Coventry Central to withdraw his
remark suggesting that the minister has behaved dishonour-
ably."

Simon rose and retracted his statement at once, but the
damage had been done. Nor did it stop members from calling
"Resign" until Raymond left the Chamber a few minutes
later.

Simon sat back smugly as Gould left the Chamber. Conservative members turned to nod their acknowledgement of
his professional demolition of the Government's Under-
Secretary of State. The Chancellor of the Exchequer rose to
deliver his prepared statement on devaluation. Simon felt
sick as he listened with horror to the Chancellor's opening
words. "The Honourable member for Leeds North handed
in his resignation to the Prime Minister on Saturday evening

but graciously agreed not to make this public until I had had an opportunity to address the House."

The Chancellor went on to praise Raymond for his work in the Department of Employment, and to wish him well on the back benches.

Andrew visited Raymond in his room immediately after the Chancellor had finished answering questions. He found him slumped at his desk, a vacant look on his face. Andrew had never considered Raymond a natural friend but he wanted to express his admiration for the way he had conducted himself.

"It's kind of you," said Raymond, who was still shaking from the experience. "Particularly as you would have demolished the lot of them."

"Well, they're all demolished now," said Andrew. "Simon Kerslake must feel the biggest shit in town."

"There's no way he could have known," said Raymond. "He'd certainly done his homework and the questions were spot on. I suspect we would have approached the situation in much the same way given the circumstances."

Several other members dropped in to commiserate with Raymond after which he returned to his old department to say farewell to his team before he went home to spend a quiet evening with Joyce. There was a long silence before the Permanent Secretary ventured an opinion: "I hope, sir, it will not be long before you return to Government. You have certainly made our lives hard but for those you ultimately serve you have undoubtedly made life easier." The sincerity of the statement touched Raymond, especially as the civil servant was already serving a new master.

It felt strange to sit down and watch television, read a book, even go for a walk and not be perpetually surrounded by red boxes and ringing phones. Within forty-eight hours he missed it all.

He was to receive over a hundred letters from colleagues in the House but he kept only one.

Monday, 20 November 1967

Dear Gould,

I owe you a profound apology. We all in our political life make monumental mistakes about people and I certainly made one today.

I believe that most members of the House have a genuine desire to serve the country, and there can be no more honourable way of proving it than by resigning when one feels one's party has taken a wrong course.

I envy the respect in which the whole House now holds you.

Yours sincerely,
Simon Kerslake.

When Raymond returned to the Commons that afternoon, he was cheered by the members of both sides from the moment he entered the Chamber. The minister who had been in the middle of addressing the House at the time had no choice but to wait until Raymond had taken his seat on the back benches.

CHAPTER
TEN

Simon had already left when Edward Heath called his home. It was another hour before Elizabeth was able to pass on the message that the party leader wanted to see him at two-thirty.

Charles was at the bank when the Chief Whip called, asking if they could meet at two-thirty that afternoon before Commons business began. Charles felt like a schoolboy who had been told the headmaster expected him to be in his study after lunch. The last time the Chief Whip had phoned was to ask him to make the winding-up speech and they had hardly spoken since. Charles remained apprehensive; he always preferred to be told what a problem was immediately.

He decided to skip lunch at the bank and join his colleagues in the House, to be certain he wouldn't be late for the afternoon appointment.

Charles did not enjoy eating at the House as the food, with the exception of the *hors d'oeuvres* trolley, was only a little better than Paddington station and rather worse than London airport.

He joined some of his colleagues at the large table in the centre of the Members' Dining-room and took the only seat available, next to Simon Kerslake. The two men had not really been on good terms since the Heath–Maudling leadership contest. Charles did not care much for Kerslake: he had once told Fiona that he was one of the new breed of Tories who tried a little too hard and he had not been displeased to see him embarrassed over the Gould resignation. Not that he allowed anyone other than Fiona to know his true feelings.

Simon watched Charles sit down and wondered how much longer the party could go on electing Etonian guardsmen who spent more time making money in the City and spending it at Ascot than they did working in the House – not that it was an opinion he would have expressed to anyone but his closest friend. The discussion over lunch centred on the remarkable run of by-election results the Tories had had at Acton, Meriden and Dudley. It was obvious that most of those around the table could not wait for a general election, although the Prime Minister did not have to call one for at least another three years.

Neither Charles nor Simon ordered coffee.

At two-twenty-five Charles watched the Chief Whip leave his private table in the corner of the room and turn to walk towards his office. Charles checked his watch and waited a moment before leaving his colleagues to begin a heated discussion about entry into the Common Market.

He strolled past the smoking room before turning left at the entrance to the library. Then he continued down the old Ways and Means corridor, passed through the swing doors and entered the Members' Lobby which he crossed to reach the Government Whips' office. He put his head round the secretary's door. Miss Norse OBE, the Chief's invaluable secretary, stopped typing.

"I have an appointment with the Chief Whip," said Charles.

"Yes, Mr Seymour, he is expecting you. Please go through." The typing recommenced immediately.

Charles walked on down the corridor and found the Chief Whip blocking his own doorway.

"Come on in, Charles. Can I offer you a drink?"

"No, thank you," replied Charles, not wanting to delay the news any longer.

The Chief Whip poured himself a gin and tonic before sitting down.

"I hope what I'm about to tell you will be looked upon as good news." The Chief Whip paused and took a gulp of his drink. "The leader thinks you might benefit from a spell in the Whips' office, and I must say I would be delighted if you felt able to join us . . ."

Charles wanted to protest but checked himself. "And give up my Housing and Local Government post?"

"Oh yes, and more of course, because Mr Heath expects all Whips to forgo outside commitments. Working in this office is not a part-time occupation."

Charles needed a moment to compose his thoughts. "And if I turn it down, will I keep my post at Housing and Local Government?"

"That's not for me to decide," said the Chief Whip, "but it is no secret that Ted Heath is planning several changes in the run-up to the election."

"How long do I have to consider the offer?"

"Perhaps you could let me know your decision by question time tomorrow."

"Yes, of course. Thank you," said Charles. He left the Chief Whip's office and drove to Eaton Square.

Simon arrived at two-twenty-five, five minutes before his meeting with the party leader. He had tried not to speculate as to why Heath wanted to see him, in case the meeting only resulted in disappointment. Douglas Hurd, the head of the private office, ushered him straight through to the Conservative leader.

"Simon, how would you like to join the Housing and Local Government team in the run-up to the election?" It was typical of Heath not to waste any time on small talk and the suddenness of the offer stunned Simon. He recovered quickly.

"Thank you very much," he said. "I mean er . . . yes . . . thank you."

"Good, let's see you put your back into it, and be sure the results at the dispatch box are as effective as they have been from the back benches."

The door was opened once again by the private secretary; the interview was clearly over. Simon found himself back in the corridor at two-thirty-three. It was several moments before the offer sank in. Then he suddenly felt elated and made a dash for the nearest phone. He dialled the St Mary's switchboard and asked if he could be put through to Dr Kerslake. As he spoke, his voice was almost drowned by the sound of the division bells, signalling the start of the day's business at two-thirty-five following prayers. A woman's voice came on the line.

"Is that you, darling?" asked Simon above the din.

"No, sir. It's the switchboard operator. Dr Kerslake's in the operating theatre."

"Is there any hope of getting her out?"

"Not unless you're expecting a baby, sir."

"What brings you home so early?" asked Fiona as Charles came charging through the front door.

"I need to talk to someone." Fiona could never be sure if she ought to be flattered, but she didn't express any opinion as it was all too rare these days to have his company at all.

Charles repeated to his wife as nearly verbatim as possible his conversation with the Chief Whip. Fiona remained silent when Charles had come to the end of his monologue. "Well, what's your opinion?" he asked anxiously.

"All because of one bad speech from the dispatch box," Fiona commented wryly.

"I agree," said Charles, "but nothing can be gained by tramping over that ground again."

"We'll miss the salary you earn as a director of the bank," said Fiona. "The tax on my private income has made the amount I now receive derisory."

"I know, but if I turn it down, and we win the next election . . . ?"

"You'll be left out in the cold."

"More to the point, stranded on the back benches."

"Charles, politics has always been your first love," said Fiona, touching him gently on the cheek. "So I don't see that you have a choice, and if that means some sacrifices you'll never hear me complain."

Charles rose from his chair saying, "Thank you. I'd better go and see Derek Spencer immediately."

As Charles turned to leave, Fiona added, "And don't

forget, Ted Heath became leader of the party via the Whips' office."

Charles smiled for the first time that day.

"A quiet dinner at home tonight?" suggested Fiona.

"Can't," said Charles. "I've got a late vote."

Fiona sat alone wondering if she would spend the rest of her life cohabiting with three-line whips.

At last they put him through.

"Let's have a celebration dinner tonight."

"Why?" asked Elizabeth.

"Because I've been invited to join the front-bench team to cover Housing and Local Government."

"Congratulations, darling, but what does Housing and Local Government consist of?"

"Housing, urban land, transport, devolution, water, historic buildings, Stansted or Maplin airport, the Channel tunnel, royal parks . . ."

"Have they left anything for anyone else to do?"

"That's only half of it, if it's out of doors it's mine. I'll tell you the rest over dinner."

"Oh, hell, I don't think I can get away until eight tonight, and we'd still have to get a baby-sitter. Does that come under Housing and Local Government, Simon?"

"Sure does," he said, laughing. "I'll fix it and book a table at the Grange for eight-thirty."

"Have you got a ten o'clock vote?"

"Afraid so."

"I see, coffee with the baby-sitter," she said. She paused. "Simon."

"Yes, darling?"

"I'm very proud of you."

Derek Spencer sat behind his massive partner's desk in Cheapside and listened intently to what Charles had to say.

"You will be a great loss to the bank," were the chairman's first words. "But no one here would want to hold up your political career, least of all me."

Charles noticed that Spencer could not look him in the eye as he spoke.

"Can I assume that I would be invited back on the board if for any reason my situation changed at the Commons?"

"Of course," said Spencer. "There was no need for you to ask such a question."

"That's kind of you," said Charles, genuinely relieved. He stood up, leaned forward and shook hands rather stiffly.

"Good luck, Charles," were Spencer's parting words.

"Does that mean you can no longer remain on the board?" asked Ronnie Nethercote when he heard Simon's news.

"No, not while I'm in Opposition and only a Shadow spokesman. Only the Chief Whip receives a salary and is therefore disqualified, but if we win the next election and I'm offered a job in Government I would have to resign immediately."

"So I've got your services for another three years?"

"Unless the Prime Minister goes earlier, or we lose the next election."

"No fear of the latter," said Ronnie. "I knew I'd picked a winner the day I met you, and I don't think you'll ever regret joining my board."

Over the months that followed Charles was surprised to find how much he enjoyed working in the Whips' office, although he had been unable to hide from Fiona his anger at Kerslake taking over his shadow post at Housing and Local Government. The order, discipline and *camaraderie* of the job brought back memories of his days in the Grenadier Guards. His duties were manifold and ranged from checking that members were all present in their committees to sitting on the front bench in the Commons and picking out the salient points members made in their speeches to the House. He also had to keep an eye out for any signs of dissension or rebellion on his own benches while remaining abreast of what was happening on the other side of the House. In addition he had fifty of his own members from the Midlands area to shepherd, and had to be certain that they never missed a vote unless paired, and only then when the Whips' office had been informed.

As Whips are never called on to make speeches in the House at any time Charles seemed to have discovered a role for which he was best cut out. Fiona reminded him once again that Ted Heath had a spell in the Whips' office on his way to becoming Shadow Chancellor. She was delighted to see how involved her husband had become with Commons life but still hated going to bed alone each night and regularly falling asleep before he had even arrived home.

Simon also enjoyed his new appointment from the first moment. As the junior member of the Housing and Local Government team he was given transport as his special subject. During the first year he read books, studied pamphlets, held meetings with national transport chairmen from air, sea and rail and frequently worked long into the night trying to master his new brief. Simon was one of those rare members who, after only a few weeks, looked as if he had always been on the front bench.

Both parties were surprised by the fourteen per cent swing to the Conservatives at the Louth by-election towards the end of 1969. It began to look as if the Labour party did not have enough time to recover before they had to call an election. But in March 1970 the Labour party had a surprisingly good result in the Ayrshire South by-election; it caused the press to speculate that the Prime Minister might go to the country early. The May local elections in England and Wales showed a further swing to Labour, which was contrary to every other political trend of the previous two years. Talk of a general election was suddenly in the air.

When the following month's opinion polls confirmed the swing to Labour Harold Wilson visited the Queen at Buckingham Palace and asked her to dissolve Parliament. The date of the general election was set for 18 June 1970.

The press were convinced that Wilson had got it right again, and would lead his party to victory for the third time in a row, a feat no man in political history had managed. Every

Conservative knew that would spell the end of Edward Heath's leadership of his party.

Andrew and Louise returned to Edinburgh as soon as the Queen had made the announcement. Parliament went into a limbo period while members dispersed all over the country only in order to try and return to Westminster.

Andrew found his local committee had been taken by surprise by the PM's announcement, and realised he only had a matter of days to prepare himself.

The evening he arrived back in Edinburgh he called his General Purposes Committee together and over coffee and sandwiches mapped out a demanding three-week timetable which would allow him to reach every part of the constituency not once but several times. Street cards were pinned on to an old trestle table, soon to be filled in with crayon of various colours according to the canvassing returns: a red line through a definite Labour vote, a blue line through a Conservative one, a yellow through a Liberal and a black line through the growing Scottish Nationalist party.

Andrew began each day of the campaign with a press conference at which he discussed local matters that affected his constituents, answered criticisms made by the other candidates and dealt with any national issues that had arisen during the previous twenty-four hours. He then spent the rest of the morning touring the constituency with a loudspeaker van, entreating people to "Send Fraser back to Westminster". He and Louise would fit in a pub lunch together before the dreaded door-to-door canvassing began.

"You'll enjoy this," said Andrew as they walked up to the first door on a cold Monday morning. The street list of names was on a card in his pocket. Andrew pressed the door bell, and a little jingle could be heard. A woman still in her dressing-gown answered it a few moments later.

"Good morning, Mrs Foster," he began. "My name is Andrew Fraser. I'm your Labour candidate."

"Oh, how nice to meet you. I have so much I need to discuss with you – won't you come in and have a cup of tea?"

"It's kind of you, Mrs Foster, but I have rather a lot of

ground to cover during the next few days." When the door closed, Andrew put a blue line through her name on his card.

"How can you be sure she's Conservative?" demanded Louise, "she seemed so friendly."

"The Conservatives are trained to ask all the other candidates in for tea and waste their time. Your own side will always say, 'You have my vote, don't spend your time with me,' and let you get on to those who are genuinely uncommitted."

"I always vote for Fraser," said Mrs Foster's next-door neighbour. "Labour for parliament, Tory for the local council."

"But don't you feel Sir Duncan should be removed from the council?" asked Andrew, grinning.

"Certainly not, and that's what I told him when he suggested I shouldn't vote for you."

Andrew put a red line through the name and knocked on the next door.

"My name is Andrew Fraser and I —"

"I know who you are, young man, and I'll have none of your politics, or your father's for that matter."

"May I ask who you will be voting for?" asked Andrew.

"Scottish Nationalist."

"Why?" asked Louise.

"Because the oil belongs to us, not those bloody Sassenachs."

"Surely it's better for the United Kingdom to remain as one body?" suggested Andrew. "At least that way —"

"Never. The Act of 1707 was a disgrace to our nation."

"But —" began Louise enthusiastically. Andrew put a hand on her arm. "Thank you, sir, for your time," and prodded his wife gently down the path.

"Sorry, Louise," said Andrew, when they were back on the pavement. "Once they mention the 1707 Act of Union we have no chance; some Scots have remarkably long memories."

He knocked on the next door. A fat man answered it, a dog lead in his hand.

"My name is Andrew Fraser, I —"

"Get lost, creep," came back the reply.

"Who are you calling creep?" Louise retaliated as the door was slammed in their faces. "Charming man."

"Don't be offended, darling. He was referring to me, not you."

"What will you put by his name?"

"A question mark. No way of telling who he votes for. Probably abstains."

He tried the next door.

"Hello, Andrew," said a lady before he could open his mouth. "Don't waste your time on me, I always vote for you."

"Thank you, Mrs Irvine," said Andrew, checking his house list. "What about your next-door neighbour?" he asked, pointing back.

"Ah, he's an irritable old basket, but I'll see he gets to the polls on the day and puts his cross in the right box. He'd better, or I'll stop keeping an eye on his greyhound for him when he's out."

"Thank you very much, Mrs Irvine," said Andrew, laughing.

"One more red," he told Louise as they returned to the pavement.

"And you might even pick up the greyhound vote."

They covered four streets during the next three hours, and Andrew put red lines through those names he was certain would support him on polling day.

"Why do you have to be so sure?" asked Louise.

"Because when we pick them up to vote on election day we don't want to remind the opposition, let alone arrange a lift for someone who then takes pleasure in voting Tory."

Louise laughed. "Politics is so dishonest."

"Be relieved you're not married to an American senator," said Andrew, putting a red line through the last name in the street. "At least we don't have to be millionaires to stand. Time for a quick bite before the evening meeting," he added, taking his wife's hand. On their way back to their headquarters they came across their Conservative opponent, but Andrew didn't respond when Hector McGregor tried to engage him in conversation, again holding him up.

Louise never joined her husband again on these sessions, deciding she could be of more use working back in the Committee Rooms.

In the public meetings held each evening, Andrew made the same speech thirty-two times in twenty-four days with only slight variations to account for national developments. Louise sat loyally through every one of them, always laughing at his punch lines and starting the clapping whenever he made a telling point. Somehow she managed to remain fresh and lively even at the end of the day when she drove her husband home.

By the eve of the election all the press were predicting a clear majority for Labour, but Andrew observed the gleam in his father's eye when he passed him in the street canvassing for McGregor.

At five-thirty on the morning of the election Louise woke Andrew with a cup of tea. He didn't see another cup that day. To his relief the sun was shining when he pulled back the curtains after he had had his bath: bad weather invariably helped the Tories with their never-ending pool of cars, ferrying voters to the polling booths. He returned to the bedroom to find his wife pinning to the lapel of his jacket a vast red rosette bearing the exhortation, 'Send Fraser back to Westminster'.

He was strolling through the streets of Edinburgh shaking hands, chatting to well-wishers, trying to convince last-minute 'don't knows' when he spotted his father heading towards him. They ended up facing each other in the middle of the street.

"It's going to be a close-run thing," said Sir Duncan.

"Then I'll know who to blame if I lose by one vote," said Andrew.

Sir Duncan looked conspiratorially about him, then lowered his voice. "If you win by one vote you'll have me to thank, laddie." He marched away entreating the citizens of Edinburgh to remove the turncoat Fraser.

The next time father and son met was at the count that evening. As the little piles of votes began to grow it became obvious that Andrew would be returned to Parliament, and Hector McGregor was soon shaking his head in disappointment.

But when the first result was announced in Guildford and showed a four per cent swing to the Tories all the previous predictions of a strong Labour victory began to look unrealistic. As each return was announced from town hall platforms all over the country it became progressively more obvious that the Tories were going to end up with a large enough majority to govern.

"I would have thought," Sir Duncan said to his son as the trend was confirmed across the nation, "that you'll be in for a wee spell of Opposition."

"Wee is the important word," was all that Andrew replied.

Andrew retained his seat, keeping the swing against him down to one per cent and his majority a safe 4,009. Scotland wasn't as sure about Heath as the rest of the country, which showed an average swing against Labour of 4.7 per cent.

Simon Kerslake managed a four-figure majority for the first time when he won Coventry Central by 2,118.

When Fiona was asked by the old earl how many votes Charles had won by, she said she couldn't be certain but she did recall Charles telling a journalist it was more than the other candidates put together.

Raymond Gould suffered an adverse swing of only two per cent and was returned with a 10,416 majority. The people of Leeds admire independence in a member, especially when it comes to a matter of principle.

The Conservatives captured Parliament with an overall majority of thirty. Her Majesty the Queen called for Edward Heath and asked him to form a Government. He kissed the hands of his sovereign and accepted her commission.

CHAPTER
ELEVEN

When Simon awoke on the morning after the election he felt both exhausted and exhilarated. He lay in bed trying to imagine how those Labour ministers, who only the previous day had assumed they would be returning to their departments, would be feeling now.

Elizabeth stirred, let out a small sleep-filled sigh. Simon stared down at his wife. In the seven years of their marriage she had lost none of her attraction for him, but he still took pleasure in just looking at her sleeping form. Her long fair hair rested on her shoulders and her slim, firm figure curved gently beneath the silk nightgown. He started stroking her back and watched her slowly come out of sleep. When she finally awoke she turned over and he took her in his arms.

"I admire your energy," she said. "If you're still fit after three weeks on the trail I can hardly claim to have a headache."

He smiled, delighted to catch a moment of privacy between the seeming lunacy of electioneering and the anticipation of office. No voter was going to interrupt this rare moment of pleasure.

"Mum," said a voice, and Simon quickly turned over to see Peter standing at the door in his pyjamas. "I'm hungry."

On the way back to London in the car Elizabeth asked, "What do you think he'll offer you?"

"Daren't anticipate anything," said Simon. "But I would hope – Under-Secretary of State for Housing and Local Government."

"But you're still not certain to be offered a post?"

"Not at all. One can never know what permutations and pressures a new Prime Minister has to consider."

"Like what?" asked Elizabeth.

"Left and right wings of the party, north and south of the country – countless debts to be cleared with those people who can claim they played a role in getting him into No. 10." Simon yawned.

"Are you saying he could leave you out?"

"Oh yes. But I'll be livid if he does, and I'd certainly want to know who had been given my job – and why."

"And what could you do about it?"

"Nothing. There is absolutely nothing one can do and every back-bencher knows it. The Prime Minister's power of patronage is absolute."

"It won't matter, if you continue driving on the centre line," she said. "Are you sure you wouldn't like me to take a turn at the wheel?"

Louise let Andrew lie in on the Friday morning. She knew he had been expecting to return to a higher ministerial office and had been shattered by the election result.

By the time Andrew woke it was nearly eleven. He sat in silence in his dressing-gown, unshaven, and tapped a hard-boiled egg that refused to crack. An unopened *Times* lay by his side.

"Thank you for all your hard work," he said once the second cup of coffee had taken effect. She smiled.

An hour later, dressed in sports jacket and grey flannels, he toured the constituency in a loudspeaker van, thanking his supporters for returning him to Westminster. Louise was by his side, often able to jog his memory on names he couldn't recall.

After they had shaken the last hand they spent a quiet weekend with Sir Duncan in Stirling – who found it extremely hard to remove the smirk from his face.

Raymond was astonished by the election result. He couldn't believe that the opinion polls had been so wrong. He didn't confide in Joyce that he had hoped a Labour victory would bring him back into office after languishing on the back benches for what seemed an interminable time.

"There's nothing for it," he told her, "but to rebuild a career at the bar. We may be out of office for years."

"But surely that won't be enough to keep you fully occupied?"

"I have to be realistic about the future," he said slowly. "Although I don't intend to let Heath drag us into Europe without putting up one hell of a fight."

"Perhaps they'll ask you to Shadow someone?"

"No, there are always far fewer jobs available in Opposition, and in any case they always give the orators like Fraser the dispatch box when all you can do is to sit and make noises while we wait for another election."

Raymond wondered how he would broach what was really on his mind and tried to sound casual when he said, "Perhaps it's time we considered having our own home in the constituency."

"That seems an unnecessary expense," said Joyce, "especially as there's nothing wrong with your parents' home. And, in any case, wouldn't they be offended?"

"My first interest should be my duty to the constituents and this would be a chance to prove a long-term commitment to them. Naturally my parents will understand."

"But we can't afford the cost of two houses," said Joyce uncertainly.

"I realise that, but it's you who have always wanted to live in Leeds, and this will give you the chance to stop commuting from London every week. After I've done the rounds why don't you stay up, contact a few local estate agents and see what's on the market?"

"All right, if that's what you really want," said Joyce. "I'll start next week."

Charles and Fiona spent a quiet weekend at their cottage in Sussex. Charles tried to do some gardening while he kept one ear open for the telephone. Fiona began to realise how anxious he was when she looked through the French windows and saw her finest delphinium being taken for a weed.

Charles eventually gave the weeds a reprieve and came in and turned on the television to catch Maudling, Macleod, Thatcher and Carrington enter No. 10 Downing Street looking pensive, only to leave smiling. The senior appointments had been made: the Cabinet was taking shape. The new Prime Minister came out and waved to the crowds before being whisked away in his official car.

Would he remember who had organised the young vote for him before he was even the party leader?

"When do you want to go back to Eaton Square?" Fiona enquired from the kitchen.

"Depends," said Charles.

"On what?"

"On whether the phone rings."

Simon sat staring at the television. All those hours of work on Housing and Local Government, and the PM had offered the portfolio to someone else. He had left the set on all day but didn't learn who it was, only that the rest of the Housing and Local Government team had remained intact.

"Why do I bother?" he said out loud. "The whole thing's a farce."

"What were you saying, darling?" asked Elizabeth as she came into the room.

The phone rang again. It was the newly appointed Home Secretary, Reginald Maudling.

"Simon?"

"Reggie, many congratulations on your appointment – not that it came as a great surprise."

"That's what I'm calling about, Simon. Would you like to join me at the Home Office as Under-Secretary?"

"Like to? I'd be delighted."

"Thank heavens for that," said Maudling. "It took me a dickens of a time to convince Ted Heath that you should be released from the Housing and Local Government team."

When Andrew and Louise arrived back at Cheyne Walk after

the weekend a red box was waiting for him in the drawing-room. 'Under-Secretary of State for Scotland' was printed in gold on the side.

"They'll be round to collect that later today," he told Louise. He turned the key to find the box was empty: and then he saw the small envelope in one corner. It was addressed to 'Andrew Fraser Esquire, MP'. He tore it open. It contained a short handwritten note from the Permanent Secretary, the senior civil servant at the Scottish Office.

"In keeping with a long tradition, ministers are presented with the last red box from which they worked. *Au revoir.* No doubt we will meet again."

"I suppose it could be used as a lunch box," said Louise, standing by the door.

"Or perhaps an overnight case," offered Andrew.

"Or a very small cot," added his wife, trying to make her words casual.

Andrew looked up to see Louise looking radiant.

"I let your parents know last night, but I wasn't going to tell you until dinner this evening."

Andrew threw his arms around her.

"By the way," Louise added, "we've already decided on her name."

When Raymond arrived back at Lincoln's Inn he let his clerk know that he wanted to be flooded with work. Over lunch with Sir Nigel Hartwell, the head of chambers, he explained that he thought it unlikely that the Labour party would be in Government again for some considerable time.

"Age is on your side, Raymond. Another full Parliament and you'll be barely forty, so you can still look forward to many years in the Cabinet."

"I wonder," said Raymond, uncharacteristically hesitant.

"Well, you needn't worry about briefs. Solicitors have been calling constantly since it was known you were back on a more permanent basis."

Raymond began to relax.

Joyce phoned him after lunch with the news that she hadn't found anything suitable, but the estate agent had assured her that they were expecting a lot more on the market in the autumn.

"Well, keep looking," said Raymond.

"Don't worry, I will," said Joyce, sounding as if she was enjoying the whole exercise. "If we find something perhaps we can think of starting a family," she added tentatively.

"Perhaps," said Raymond brusquely.

Charles eventually received a call on the Monday night, not from No. 10 Downing Street but from No. 12, the office of the Chief Whip. Because the Chief Whip's is not an official post, .he is paid as the Parliamentary Secretary to the Treasury and he works from No. 12. The Prime Minister and the Chancellor of the Exchequer, being the first and second Lords of the Treasury, live at Nos. 10 and 11 Downing Street respectively.

The Chief Whip had phoned to say he hoped that Charles would be willing to soldier on as a junior Whip. When he heard the disappointment in Charles's voice he added, "For the time being."

"For the time being," repeated Charles and put the phone down.

"At least you're a member of the Government. You haven't been left out in the cold," said Fiona gamely.

"True," he replied.

"People are sure to come and go during the next five years."

Charles had to agree with his wife but it didn't lessen his disappointment. Returning to the Commons as a member of the Government, however, turned out to be far more rewarding than he had expected. This time it was his party that were making the decisions.

The Queen travelled early that July morning to the House of Lords in the Irish State Coach. An escort of the Household Cavalry accompanied her, preceded by a procession of lesser state carriages in which the Imperial State Crown and other royal trappings were transported. Charles could remember watching the ceremony from the streets when he was a boy. Now he was taking part in it. When the Queen arrived at the

Upper House she was accompanied by the Lord Chancellor
through the Sovereign's entrance to the robing room, where
her ladies-in-waiting began to prepare her for the ceremony.

Charles always considered the State opening of Parliament a special occasion for members of both Houses. As a
Whip he watched the members take their seats in the Commons and await the arrival of Black Rod. Once the Queen
was seated on the throne the Lord Great Chamberlain
commanded the Gentleman Usher of Black Rod to inform
the Commons that: "It is Her Majesty's pleasure they attend
her immediately in this House." Black Rod, wearing his
black topcoat, black waistcoat, black knee-breeches, black
stockings and black shoes, resembled the devil's advocate
rather than the Queen's messenger. He marched alone
across the great tiled floor joining the two Chambers until he
reached the doors of the House of Commons which were
slammed in his face when he was just two paces away from
them.

He struck the door three times with the silver tip of his long
thin black rod. In response a little window in the door was
flicked back to check on who it was – not unlike a sleazy
nightclub, Charles's father had once observed. Black Rod
was then allowed admittance to the Lower House. He advanced towards the table and made three obeisances to the
chair before saying, "Mr Speaker, the Queen commands this
Honourable House to attend Her Majesty immediately in
the House of Peers."

With that, the Serjeant-at-Arms, bearing the mace, led Mr
Speaker, in full court dress, a gold embroidered gown of
black satin damask, back towards the Lords. They were
followed by the Clerk of the House and the Speaker's chaplain, behind whom came the Prime Minister, accompanied
by the leader of the Opposition, then Government ministers
with their opposite numbers, and finally as many back-
benchers as could squeeze into the rear of the Lords' Chamber.

The Lords themselves were waiting in the Upper House,
dressed in red capes with ermine collars, looking somewhat like benevolent Draculas, accompanied by peeresses

glittering in diamond tiaras and wearing long evening dresses. The Queen was seated on the throne, in her full Monarchical robes, the Imperial State Crown on her head originally made for George IV. She waited until the procession had filled the Chamber and all was still.

The Lord Chancellor shuffled forward and, bending down on one knee, presented her with a printed document. It was the speech, written by the Government of the day, and although she had read over a copy of the script earlier that morning she had made no personal contribution to its contents, as her role on this occasion was only ceremonial. She looked up at her subjects and began to read.

Charles stood at the back of the cramped gathering, but with his height he had no trouble in following the entire proceedings. Their lordships were all in their places for the Queen's speech, with the law lords seated in their privileged position in the centre of the Chamber, an honour bestowed upon them by an Act of 1539. The Lord Chancellor stood to one side of the Woolsack, which was stuffed with wool from the days when it was the staple commodity of England. When the Lords are in session he acts much as the Speaker does for the Commons.

Charles could spot his elderly father, the Earl of Bridgwater, nodding off during the Queen's speech, which promised that Britain would make a determined effort to become a full member of the EEC. "My Government also intends to bring in a bill to enact trade union reform," she declared. Charles, along with everyone else from the Commons, was counting the likely number of bills that would be presented during the coming months and soon worked out that the Whips' office were going to be in for a busy session.

As the Queen finished her speech Charles took one more look at his father, now sound asleep. How Charles dreaded the moment when he would be standing there watching his brother Rupert in ermine. The only compensation would be if he could produce a son who would one day inherit the title, as it was now obvious Rupert would never marry.

It was not as if he and Fiona had not tried. He was

beginning to wonder if the time had not come to suggest that she visit a specialist. He dreaded finding out she was unable to bear a child.

The speech delivered, the Sovereign left the Upper House followed by Prince Philip and Prince Charles to a fanfare of trumpets. At the other end of the Chamber the procession of MPs, led again by the Speaker, made their way back in pairs from the red benches of the Lords to the green of the Commons.

The leader of the Opposition, having formed his own team, invited Andrew to cover the Home Office brief as number two. Andrew was delighted by the challenge of this new responsibility, especially when he discovered Simon Kerslake was to be his opposite number in Government.

Louise once again became very large in a short period, but Andrew tried to keep his mind off the pregnancy, as he dreaded her going through that amount of pain and sorrow for a third time. He telephoned Elizabeth Kerslake and they agreed to meet privately.

"That's a hard question to answer without ifs and buts," she told Andrew over coffee in her room the following day.

"But what would your advice be if Louise were to lose the third child?"

Elizabeth took a long time considering her reply. "If that happened I cannot believe it would be wise to put her through the same ordeal again," she said flatly. "The psychological repercussions alone might affect her for the rest of her life."

Andrew sat staring in front of him.

"Enough of this morbid talk," Elizabeth added. "I checked Louise last week and I can see no reason why this shouldn't turn out to be a routine birth."

As the first weeks of the new Tory administration took shape, Simon and Andrew became locked in battle over several issues and were soon known as 'the mongoose and the rattlesnake'. When either of the names 'Kerslake' or 'Fraser' was cranked up on the old-fashioned wall machines indicating one of them had risen to speak, members drifted back into the Chamber. Andrew found himself a constant visitor to the table office, a tiny room in the corridor behind the Speaker's chair where members tabled their questions, usually scribbled on yellow sheets, but still acceptable to the omniscient clerks had they been written on postage stamps.

The clerks often helped Andrew reword a question so that it would be acceptable to the chair, a function they carried out for any member, even Tom Carson, who had once accused them of political bias when they suggested one of his questions was out of order. When Carson was finally referred to the Speaker, he was called for and reprimanded, and his question deposited in one of the mock-Gothic waste-paper baskets in the Order office.

Once behind the Speaker's chair, Simon and Andrew would good-humouredly discuss the issues on which they were crossing swords. The opportunity to be out of sight of the Press Gallery above them was often taken by the two opposing members, but once they had both returned to the dispatch box they would tear into each other, looking for any weakness in the other's argument.

On one subject they found themselves in total accord. Ever since August 1969, when the troops had first been sent in, Parliament had been having another of its periodic bouts of trouble with Northern Ireland. In October 1970 the House devoted a full day's business to listen to members' opinions in the never-ending effort to find a solution to the growing clash between the Protestant extremists and the IRA. The motion before the House was to allow emergency powers to be renewed in the province.

Andrew rose from his seat on the front bench to deliver the opening speech for the Opposition. He said he took no side in this unhappy affair, but he felt sure the House was united in condemning violence. Yet however hard he searched for the answer he found neither faction willing to give an inch. 'Goodwill' and 'trust' were words that might as well have been left out of any dictionary printed in Ulster. It was not long before Andrew came to the conclusion that Gladstone was right when he had said, "Every time I find the solution to the Irish question, they change the question."

When Andrew had finished he surprised members by leaving the Chamber and not returning for several minutes.

Simon had been selected to wind up for the Government and had prepared his speech with meticulous care. Although both sides appeared in agreement on the main issue, the mood as always could change in a moment if an unfortunate view was expressed by a Government minister.

During the debate, much to everyone's surprise, Andrew Fraser kept leaving the Chamber. Simon left only twice between three-thirty and the ten o'clock division, once to take a call from his wife, and then again at seven-thirty for a quick supper.

When Simon came back Andrew was still absent from the Chamber, and he had not returned by the time the Shadow Home Secretary began to sum up. Andrew did eventually take his seat on the front bench but Simon had already begun his speech.

As Andrew entered the Chamber and took his place on the front bench, an elderly Conservative rose from his seat.

"On a point of order, Mr Speaker."

Simon sat down immediately and turned his head to listen to the point his colleague wanted to make.

"Is it not a tradition of this House, sir," began the elder statesman rather ponderously, "for a front-bench spokesman to have the courtesy to remain in his seat during the debate in order that he may ascertain views other than his own?"

"That is not a point of order," replied the Speaker above the cries of "Hear, hear" from the Conservative benches. Andrew scribbled a quick note and hurriedly passed it over to Simon. On it was written a single sentence.

"I accept the point my Right Honourable friend makes," Simon began, "and would have complained myself had I not known that the Honourable Gentleman, the member for Edinburgh Carlton, has spent most of the afternoon in hospital." Simon paused to let the effect sink in. "Where his wife was in labour. I am not given to accepting as necessarily accurate all the Opposition tells me," he continued, "but I am able to confirm this statement because it was my wife who delivered the baby." The House began to laugh. "I can assure my Honourable friend that my wife has spent her entire afternoon indoctrinating the infant in the value of Conservative policies as understood by his grandfather, which is why the Honourable Gentleman has found it necessary to be absent himself from so much of the debate." Simon waited for the laughter to subside. "For those members of the House who thrive on statistics, it's a boy and he weighs four pounds three ounces."

There are times in the House when affection is displayed on both sides, thought Andrew, who considered it was ironic that during an Irish debate an Englishman had demonstrated such affection for a Scotsman.

There was no challenge when the Speaker 'collected the voices' at ten o'clock so the matter was decided 'on the nod' and Simon joined Andrew behind the Speaker's chair.

"Just over four pounds doesn't sound very big to me. I thought I'd take a second opinion from the Minister of Health."

"I agree," said Andrew, "the little blighter is stuck in an incubator, but your wife is doing everything she can to fatten him up. I'm off to watch him now."

"Good luck," said Simon.

Andrew sat by the incubator all night, hating the drip, drip, drip of the little plastic tube that passed up the child's nose and down into his stomach. He feared that when he woke his son would be dead and continually went to the wash basin and put a damp, cold cloth over his eyes to ensure he remained awake. He finally lost the battle and dozed off in a 'dad's bed' in the corner.

When his father woke, Robert Bruce Fraser was very much alive. The crumpled father rose from his bed to admire his crumpled offspring, who was receiving milk down the plastic tube from a night nurse.

Andrew stared down at the crinkly face. The boy had inherited his square jaw, but he had his mother's nose and hair colouring. Andrew chuckled at the time Louise had wasted over girls' names. Robert it would be.

Robert Bruce Fraser travelled to Cheyne Walk with his

mother and father three weeks later, having topped the scales earlier that morning at five pounds ten ounces.

Elizabeth Kerslake had told them to be thankful: the post-natal examination had shown that it would not be possible for Louise to bear another child.

CHAPTER
TWELVE

The Chief Whip looked round at his colleagues, wondering which of them would volunteer for such a thankless task.

A hand went up, and he was pleasantly surprised.

"Thank you, Charles."

Charles had already warned Fiona that he was going to volunteer to be the Whip responsible for the issue that had most dominated the last election: Britain's entry into the EEC. Everyone in that room realised that it would be the most demanding marathon of the entire Parliament, and there was an audible sigh of relief when Charles volunteered.

"Not a job for anyone with a rocky marriage," he heard one Whip whisper. At least that's something I don't have to worry about, thought Charles, but he made a note to take home some flowers that night.

"Why was it the bill everyone wanted to avoid?" asked Fiona as she arranged the daffodils.

"Because many of our side don't necessarily back Edward Heath in his lifelong ambition to take Britain into Europe, while quite a few of the Opposition do," said Charles, accepting a large brandy. "Added to that, we have the problem of presenting a bill to curb the trade unions at the same time which may well influence many members of the Labour party from voting with us on Europe. Because of this problem, the Prime Minister requires a regular 'state of play' assessment on Europe even though legislation may not be presented on the floor of the Commons for at least another year. He'll want to know periodically how many of our side are still against entry, and how many from the Opposition we can rely on to break ranks when the crucial vote is taken."

"Perhaps I should become Member of Parliament and then at least I could spend a little more time with you."

"Especially on the European issue if you were a 'don't know'."

The 'Great Debate' was discussed by the media to the point of boredom. Members were nevertheless conscious that they were playing a part in history. And, because of the unusual spectacle of the Whips not being in absolute control of the voting procedure, the Commons sprang to life, and excitement began to build up over the weeks and months of debate.

Charles retained his normal task of watching over fifty members on all normal Government bills, but because of the priority given to the issue of entry into Europe he had been released from all other duties. He knew that this was his chance to atone for his disastrous winding-up speech on the economy which he sensed his colleagues had still not completely forgotten.

"I'm gambling everything on this one," he told Fiona. "And if we lose the final vote I will be sentenced to the back benches for life."

"And if we win?"

"It will be hard to keep me off the front bench," replied Charles.

Robert Fraser was one of those noisy children who after only a few weeks sounded as if he was on the front bench.

"Perhaps he's going to be a politician after all," concluded Louise, staring down at her son.

"What has changed your mind?" asked Andrew.

"He never stops shouting at everyone, he's totally pre-occupied with himself and he falls asleep as soon as someone else offers an opinion," she replied.

"At last I think I've found it." After Raymond heard the news he took the train up to Leeds the following Friday. Joyce had selected four houses for him to consider, but he had to agree with her that the one in Chapel Allerton was exactly what they were looking for. It was also by far the most expensive.

"Can we afford it?" asked Joyce anxiously.

"Probably not, but one of the problems of seeing four houses is that you end up only wanting the best one."

"I could go on looking."

"No, you've found the right house; now I'll have to work out how we can pay for it, and I think I may have come up with an idea."

Joyce said nothing, waiting for him to continue.

"We could sell our place in Lansdowne Road."

"But where would we live when you're in London?"

"I could rent a small flat somewhere between the law courts and the Commons while you set up our real home in Leeds."

"But wouldn't you get lonely?"

"Of course I will," said Raymond, trying to sound convincing. "But almost every member north of Birmingham is parted from his wife during the week. In any case, you've always wanted to settle in Yorkshire, and this might be our best chance. If my practice continues to grow we can buy a second house in London at a later date."

Joyce looked apprehensive.

"One added bonus," said Raymond, "your being in Leeds will ensure I never lose the seat."

She smiled, as she always felt reassured whenever Raymond showed the slightest sign of needing her.

On Monday morning Raymond put in a bid for the house in Chapel Allerton before returning to London. After a little bargaining over the phone during the week, he and the owner settled on a price. By Thursday Raymond had put his Lansdowne Road house on the market and was surprised by the amount the estate agent thought it would fetch.

All Raymond had to do now was find himself a flat.

Simon sent a note to Ronnie expressing his thanks for keeping him so well informed about what was happening at Nethercote and Company. It had been eight months since he had resigned from the board because of his appointment as a minister, but Ronnie saw that the minutes of each meeting were posted to him to study in his own time. 'His own time': Simon had to laugh at the thought.

His overdraft at the bank now stood at a little over £72,000, but as Ronnie intended the shares should be offered at five pounds each when they went public Simon felt sure there was still a fair leeway, as his personal holding should realise £300,000. Elizabeth warned him not to spend a penny of the profit until the money was safely in the bank. He was thankful she didn't know the full extent of his borrowing.

Over one of their occasional lunches at the Ritz, Ronnie spelt out to Simon his plans for the future of the company.

"Now that the Tories are in I think I'll go public in eighteen months' time. This year's profits are up again and next year's look even better. So 1973 looks a perfect bet."

Simon looked apprehensive and Ronnie responded quickly. "If you're having any problem, Simon, I'll be happy to take the shares off your hands at their market value. At least that way you'd show a small profit."

"No, no," said Simon. "I'll hang in there now that I've waited this long."

"Suit yourself," said Ronnie. "Now tell me – how are you enjoying the Home Office?"

Simon put down his knife and fork. "Of the three great offices of state, it's the one most involved with people, so there's a new challenge at a personal level every day, although it can be depressing too. Locking people up in prisons, banning immigrants and deporting harmless aliens isn't my idea of fun. The Home Office never seems to want anyone to enjoy too much freedom."

"And what about Ireland?"

"What about Ireland?" said Simon, shrugging his shoulders.

"I'd give the north back to Eire," said Ronnie, "or let them go independent and give them a large cash incentive to do so. At the moment the whole exercise is money down the drain."

"We're discussing people," said Simon, "not money."

"Ninety per cent of the voters would back me," said Ronnie, lighting a cigar.

"Everyone imagines ninety per cent of the people support their views, until they stand for election," said Simon. "The issue of Ireland is far too important to be glib about. I repeat, we're discussing people, eight million people, all of whom have the same right to justice as you and I. And as long as I work in the Home Office I intend to see that they get it."

Ronnie remained silent.

"I'm sorry, Ronnie," continued Simon. "Too many people have an easy solution to Ireland. If there *was* an easy solution the problem wouldn't have lasted over two hundred years."

"Don't be sorry," said Ronnie. "I'm so stupid, I've only just worked out for the first time why you're in public office."

"You're a typical self-made Fascist," said Simon, teasing his companion once again.

"You may be right, but you won't change my mind on hanging. Your lot should bring back the rope; the streets aren't safe any longer."

"For property developers like you, hoping for a quick killing?"

Both men laughed.

"Andrew, do you want lunch?"

"In a moment, in a moment."

"That's what you said half an hour ago."

"I know, but he's nearly got it. Just give me a few more minutes." Louise waited and watched, but Robert collapsed in a heap again.

"No doubt you're expecting him to play soccer for England by the time he's two."

"No, certainly not," said Andrew, carrying his son back into the house. "Rugby for Scotland."

Louise was touched by the amount of time Andrew spent with Robert. She told her disbelieving friends that he regularly fed and bathed the baby and even changed his nappy.

"Don't you think he's good-looking?" asked Andrew, strapping his son carefully into his chair.

"Yes," said Louise, laughing.

"That's because he looks like me," said Andrew, putting his arms round his wife.

"He most certainly does not," said Louise firmly.

Crash. A bowlful of porridge had been deposited on the floor, leaving just a lump left in the spoon, which Robert was now smearing across his face and hair.

"He looks as if he has just stepped out of a concrete mixer," said Andrew.

Louise stared at her son. "Perhaps you're right. There *are* times when he looks like you."

"How do you feel about rape?" asked Raymond.

"I can't see that it's relevant," Stephanie Arnold replied.

"I think they'll go for me on it," said Raymond.

"But why?"

"They'll be able to pin me in a corner, damage my character."

"But where does it get them? They can't prove lack of consent."

"Maybe, but they will offer it as background to prove the rest of the case."

"Because you raped someone doesn't prove you murdered them."

Raymond and Stephanie Arnold, who was new to chambers, continued discussing their first case together on the way to the Old Bailey, and she left Raymond in no doubt that she was delighted to be led by him. They were to appear together to defend a labourer accused of the rape and murder of his step-daughter.

"Open and shut case unfortunately," said Raymond, "but we're going to make the Crown prove their argument beyond anyone's doubt."

When the case stretched into a second week Raymond began to believe that the jury were so gullible they might even get their client off. Stephanie was sure they would.

The day before the judge's summing up Raymond invited Stephanie to dinner at the House of Commons. That'll make them turn their heads, he thought to himself. They won't have seen anything in a white shirt and black stockings that looks like that for some time, certainly not Mr Speaker.

Stephanie seemed flattered by the invitation and sat through the stodgy meal served in the Strangers' Dining-room, obviously impressed as former Cabinet ministers flitted in and out, all of them acknowledging him.

"How's the new flat?" asked Stephanie.

"Worked out well," replied Raymond. "The Barbican is so convenient for Parliament and the law courts."

"Does your wife like it?" she asked, lighting a cigarette but not looking at him directly.

"She's not in town that much nowadays. She spends most of her time in Leeds – doesn't care much for London."

The awkward pause that followed was interrupted by a sudden clanging of bells.

"Are we on fire?" said Stephanie, quickly stubbing out her cigarette.

"No," said Raymond laughing. "Just the ten o'clock division. I have to leave you and vote. I'll be back in about fifteen minutes."

"Shall I order coffee?"

"No, don't bother," said Raymond. "It's foul. Perhaps . . . perhaps you'd like to come back to the Barbican? Then you can give a verdict on my flat."

"Maybe it's an open and shut case," she smiled.

Raymond returned the smile before joining his colleagues as they flooded out of the dining-room down the corridor towards the Commons Chamber. He didn't have time to explain to Stephanie that he had only six minutes to get into the right lobby. As Raymond had no idea what they were voting on that night he followed the surge of Labour members into the Noes lobby. The bells stopped and the doors were bolted.

Whenever the vote is called for at the end of the debate the Speaker puts the question and the moment he reaches the words, "I think the Ayes have it," the roar of "No" from those opposed to the motion ensures a vote at ten o'clock. Bells peal out over the Palace of Westminster, and in some nearby restaurants and members' homes in the division-bell area.

Members then scurry into the Ayes or Noes division lobby before the cry of "Lock the doors" is heard. Once the doors have been secured each member then files past two clerks seated at a high desk at the far end of the corridor who tick off his name. As Raymond stepped past the clerks he came towards the exit doors which were angled so as to make a funnel through which only one member at a time could pass. The Whip acting as teller shouted out the mounting vote. "Seventy-three," he called as Raymond passed him. The only particular rule relating to voting was that members could not wear a hat or overcoat while in the lobby. A clerk had once told Raymond that this dated from the days when lazy members sent their driver off in the hansom cab, hats over ears, coat buttoned up to the nose, to march through the corridors and give their masters' names. Some of them would have been a damn sight better MPs then their employers, Raymond had often thought.

While in the corridor he discovered that they were voting on a clause of the Trade Union Bill concerning the validity of closed shops. He was in no doubt that he supported his party on that subject.

When he returned to the Strangers' Dining-room after the vote he found Stephanie checking her face in a compact mirror, a small round face with green eyes and brunette hair. She was replacing the trace of lipstick. He suddenly felt conscious of being a little overweight for a man not yet forty.

"Shall we go?" he suggested, after he had signed the bill.

Once they had reached the flat Raymond put on a Charles Aznavour record and retired to the small kitchen to prepare coffee. He was totally oblivious to the fact that women were beginning to find him attractive. A little extra weight and a few grey hairs had not harmed his appearance, if anything giving him an air of authority.

"There's no doubting this is a bachelor flat," Stephanie remarked as she took in the one comfortable leather chair, the pipe stand, and the Spy cartoons of turn-of-the-century judges and politicians.

"I suppose that's because that's what it is," he mused,

setting down a tray laden with coffee and two brandy balloons generously filled with cognac.

"Don't you get lonely?" she asked.

"From time to time," he said, pouring the coffee.

"And between times?"

"Black?" he asked, not looking at her.

"Black," she said.

"Sugar?"

"For a man who has served as a minister of the Crown and who, it's rumoured, is about to become the youngest QC in the country, you're still very unsure of yourself with women."

Raymond blushed, but raised his head and stared into her eyes.

In the silence he caught Aznavour's words, "You've let yourself go . . ."

"Would my Honourable friend care to dance?" she said quietly.

Raymond could still remember the last occasion he had danced. This time he was determined it would be different. He held Stephanie so that their bodies touched and they swayed rather than danced to the music of Marcel Stellman. She didn't notice Raymond slipping off his glasses and putting them into his jacket pocket. He bent over and kissed her neck. She gave a long sigh, and when they parted, she said, "Let's hope this is between times."

Charles studied his chart of 330 Conservatives. He felt confident of 217, not sure about fifty-four and had almost given up on fifty-nine. On the Labour side the best information he could glean was that fifty Socialists were expected to defy the Whip and join the Government's ranks when the great vote took place.

"The main fly in the ointment," Charles reported to the Chief Whip, "is still the Trade Union Reform Bill. The left are trying to convince those Socialists who still support the bill that there is no cause so important for which they should enter the same lobby as those Tory trade union bashers." He went on to explain his fear that unless the Government were willing to modify the Trade Union Bill they might lose

Europe on the back of it. "Alec Pimkin doesn't help matters by trying to gather the waverers in our party round him."

"There's no chance of the Prime Minister modifying one sentence of the Trade Union Bill," said the Chief Whip, draining his gin and tonic. "He promised it in his speech at the party conference, and he intends to deliver by the time he goes to Blackpool at the end of this year. I can also tell you he isn't going to like your conclusions on Pimkin, Charles. He cares almost as passionately about trade union reform as he does about Europe." Charles was about to protest. "I'm not complaining, you've done damn well so far. Just keep working on the fifty waverers. Threaten, cajole, bully, bribe. Try anything, but get them in the right lobby come the night, Pimkin included."

"How about sex?" asked Charles.

"You've been seeing too many American films," said the Chief Whip, laughing. "In any case I don't think we've got anyone other than Miss Norse to offer them."

Charles returned to his office and went over the list once again. His forefinger stopped at the letter 'P'. Charles strolled out into the corridor and looked around; his quarry wasn't there. He checked the Chamber: no sign of him. He passed the library. No need to look in there, he thought, and moved on to the smoking room where he found his man, about to order another gin.

"Alec," said Charles expansively.

The rotund figure of Pimkin looked round.

May as well try bribery first, thought Charles. "Let me get you a drink."

"That's good of you, old fellow," said Pimkin, nervously fingering his bow tie.

"Now, Alec, what's this about your voting against the European Bill?"

Simon was horrified when he read the initial document. Its implications were all too evident.

The report of the new Boundary Commission had been left in the red box for him to study over the weekend. He had agreed at a meeting of Home Office officials that he would steer it through the House as quickly as possible so that it would make the basis for the seats to be contested at the next election. As the Secretary of State reminded him: there must be no hold-ups.

Simon had read the document carefully. In essence the changes made sense and, because of the movement of families from urban to rural areas, it would undoubtedly create more winnable seats for the Conservatives overall. No wonder the party wanted no hold-ups. But what could he do about the decision the Commission had come to on his own constituency, Coventry Central? His hands were tied. If he suggested any change from the Boundary Commission's recommendations he would rightly be accused of jerrymandering.

Because of the city's dwindling population the Commission had recommended that the four constituencies of Coventry become three. Coventry Central was to be the one to disappear, its voters distributed among Coventry West, Coventry East and Coventry North. Simon realised this would leave one safe seat for his sitting colleague and two safe Labour seats. It had never been far from his mind how marginal a constituency he represented. Now he was on the verge of being without one at all. He would have to traipse around the country all over again looking for a new seat to fight at the next election, while at the same time taking care of his constituents in the moribund one; and at the stroke of a pen – *his* pen – they would pass on their loyalties to someone else. If only he had remained in Housing and Local Government he could have put up a case for keeping all four seats.

Elizabeth was sympathetic when he explained the problem but told him not to concern himself too much until he had spoken to the vice-chairman of the party, who advised candidates which constituencies were likely to become available.

"It may even work out to your advantage," she added.

"What do you mean?" said Simon.

"You could get a safer seat nearer London."

"With my luck I'll end up with a marginal in Newcastle."

Elizabeth prepared his favourite meal and spent the evening trying to keep up his spirits. After three portions of shepherd's pie Simon fell asleep almost as soon as he put his head on the pillow. But she stayed awake long into the night.

The casual conversation with the head of Gynaecology at St Mary's kept running through her mind. Although she hadn't confided in Simon, she could recall her supervisor's every word.

"I notice from the roster that you've had far more days off than you are entitled to, Dr Kerslake. You must make up your mind if you want to be a doctor or the wife of an MP."

Elizabeth stirred restlessly as she considered the problem, but came to no conclusion except not to bother Simon while he had so much on his mind.

"Do these boundary changes affect you?" Louise asked, looking up from her copy of *The Times*.

Andrew was bouncing a small rubber ball on Robert's head.

"You'll give him brain damage," said Louise.

"I know, but think of the goals he'll score – and it won't be long before I can start him on rugby."

Robert started to cry when his father stopped to answer his mother's question. "No, Edinburgh isn't affected. There's such a small movement in the population that the seven city seats will remain intact. The only real changes in Scotland will be in Glasgow and the Highlands."

"That's a relief," said Louise. "I should hate to have to look for another constituency."

"Poor old Simon Kerslake is losing his seat altogether and he daren't do anything about it."

"Why not?" asked Louise.

"Because he's the minister in charge of the bill, and if he tried anything clever we would crucify him."

"So what will he do?"

"Have to shop around for a new seat, or convince an older colleague to stand down in his favour."

"But surely ministers find it easy to pick up a plum seat?"

"Not necessarily," said Andrew. "Many constituencies don't like to have someone foisted on them and want to choose their own man. And some actually prefer a local man who will never be a minister, because they feel he can devote more time to them."

"Andrew, can you revert to being some use in Opposition?"

"What are you suggesting?" asked Andrew.

"Just keep throwing that ball at your stupid son's head or he'll be crying all day."

"Take no notice of her, Robert. She'll feel differently when you score your first goal against England."

CHAPTER THIRTEEN

At exactly the time Raymond was ready to stop the affair Stephanie began leaving a set of court clothes in the flat. Although the two had gone their separate ways at the conclusion of the case they continued to see one another a couple of evenings a week. Raymond had had a spare key made so that Stephanie didn't have to spend her life checking when he had a three-line whip.

At first he began simply to avoid her, but she would then seek him out. When he did manage to give her the slip he would often find her back in his flat when he returned from the Commons. When he suggested they should be a little more discreet she began to make threats, subtle at first, but after a time more direct.

During the period of their affair Raymond conducted three major cases for the Crown, all of which had successful conclusions and which added to his reputation. On each occasion his clerk made certain Stephanie was not assigned to be with him. Now that his residency problem had been sorted out Raymond's only worry was how to end their relationship. He quickly discovered that getting rid of Stephanie Arnold was going to prove considerably more difficult than picking her up.

Simon was on time for his appointment at Central Office. He explained his dilemma to Sir Edward Mountjoy – vice-chairman of the party responsible for candidates – in graphic detail.

"What bloody bad luck," said Sir Edward. "But perhaps I

may be able to help," he added, opening the green folder on the desk in front of him. Simon could see that he was studying a list of names. It made him feel once again like an undergraduate who needed someone to die.

"There seem to be about a dozen safe seats that will fall vacant at the next election, caused either by retirement or redistribution."

"Anywhere in particular you could recommend?"

"I fancy Littlehampton."

"Where's that?" said Simon.

"It will be a new seat, safe as houses. It's in Sussex, on the borders of Hampshire." He studied an attached map. "Runs proud to Charles Seymour's constituency which remains unchanged. Can't think you would have many rivals there," said Sir Edward. "But why don't you have a word with Charles? He's bound to know everyone involved in taking the decision."

"Anything else that looks promising?" asked Simon, only too aware that Seymour might not prove altogether co-operative.

"Let me see. Can't afford to put all your eggs in one basket, can we? Ah, yes – Redcorn, in Northumberland." Again the vice-chairman studied the map. "Three hundred and twenty miles from London and no airport within eighty miles, and their nearest main line station is forty miles. I think that one's only worth trying for if you get desperate. My advice would be to speak to Charles Seymour about Littlehampton. He must know the lay of the land in that neck of the woods."

Two clichés in one sentence, thought Simon. Thank heavens Sir Edward would never have to make a speech from the dispatch box.

"I'm sure you're right, Sir Edward," he said.

"Selection committees are being formed already," continued Sir Edward, "so you shouldn't have to wait too long."

"I appreciate your help," said Simon. "Perhaps you could let me know if anything else comes up in the meantime."

"Of course, delighted. The problem is that if one of our side were to die during the sessions you couldn't desert your present seat because that would cause two by-elections. We certainly don't want a by-election in Coventry Central with you being accused of being a carpetbagger somewhere else."

"Don't remind me," said Simon.

Charles had whittled down the fifty-nine anti-Common Market members to fifty-one, but he was now dealing with the hard kernel who seemed quite immune to future advancement or bullying. When he made his next report to the Chief Whip Charles assured him that the Conservatives who would vote against entry into Europe were outnumbered by the Socialists who had declared they would support the Government. The Chief Whip seemed pleased, but asked if Charles had made any progress with Pimkin's disciples.

"Those twelve mad right-wingers?" said Charles sharply. "They seem to be willing to follow Pimkin even into the valley of death. I've tried everything but they're still determined to vote against Europe whatever the cost."

"The maddening thing is that that bloody nuisance Pimkin has nothing to lose," said the Chief Whip. "His seat disappears at the end of this Parliament in the redistribution. I can't imagine anyone with his extreme views would find a constituency to select him, but by then he'll have done the damage." The Chief Whip paused. "If his twelve would even abstain I would feel confident of advising the PM of victory."

"The problem is to find a way of turning Pimkin into Judas and then urging him to lead the chosen twelve into our camp," said Charles.

"You achieve that, and we'd certainly win."

Charles returned to the Whips' office to find Simon Kerslake waiting by his desk.

"I dropped by on the off-chance, hoping you might be able to spare me a few moments," said Simon.

"Of course," said Charles, trying to sound welcoming. "Take a pew."

Simon sat down opposite him. "You may have heard that I lose my constituency as a result of the Boundary Commission report and Edward Mountjoy suggested I have a word with you about Littlehampton, the new seat that borders your constituency."

"It does indeed," said Charles, masking his surprise. He had not considered the problem as his own seat remained intact. He recovered quickly. "And how wise of Edward to send you to me. I'll do everything I can to help."

"Littlehampton would be ideal," said Simon. "Especially while my wife is still working in Paddington."

Charles raised his eyebrows.

"I don't think you've met Elizabeth. She's a doctor at St Mary's," Simon explained.

"Yes, I can see how convenient Littlehampton would be. Why don't I start by having a word with Alexander Dalglish, the constituency chairman, and see what I can come up with?"

"That would be extremely helpful."

"Not at all. I'll call him at home this evening and find out what stage they've reached over selection, and then I'll put you in the picture."

"I'd appreciate that."

"While I've got you, let me give you the whip for next week," said Charles, passing over a sheet of paper. Simon folded it up and put it in his pocket. "I'll call you the moment I have some news."

Simon left feeling happier and a little guilty about his past prejudice concerning Charles, whom he watched disappear into the Chamber to carry out his bench duty.

The European issue had been given six days for debate by back-benchers, the longest period of time allocated to one motion in living memory.

Charles strolled down the aisle leading to the front bench and took a seat on the end to check on another set of speeches. Usually he listened intently to see if he could spot a member wavering in his position; but on this occasion his thoughts were in Littlehampton. Andrew Fraser was on his feet, and Charles was delighted to be able to confirm the tick alongside his name before he drifted into deep thought.

"I for one shall vote for entry into Europe," Andrew was telling the House. "When my party was in power I was a pro-European, and now we are in Opposition I can see no good reason to do a volte-face. The principles that held true two years ago hold true today. Not all of us . . ."

Tom Carson leaped up and asked if his Honourable friend would give way. Andrew resumed his seat immediately.

"Would my Honourable friend really support the peasant farmers of France before the sheep farmers in New Zealand?" asked Carson.

Andrew rose and explained to his colleague that he would certainly expect safeguards for New Zealand, but the initial vote on the floor of the House was on the principle of entry. The details could and should be dealt with in committee. He went on to express the view that had his Honourable friend talked of wogs or Jews in such a context the House would have been in uproar. "Why is it therefore acceptable to the anti-marketeers to describe French farmers as peasants?"

"Perhaps it's you who is the peasant," Carson shouted back, in seven words thus ruining his case for the lamb farmers of New Zealand.

Andrew ignored the jibe and went on to tell the House that he believed in a united Europe as a further insurance against a third world war. He concluded with the words:

"Britain has for a thousand years written history, even the history of the world. Let us decide with our votes whether our children will read that history, or continue to write it." Andrew sat down to acclamation from both sides.

By the time Andrew had resumed his seat Charles had formed a plan and left the Chamber when one of his own colleagues started what promised to be a long, boring and predictable speech.

Instead of returning to the Whips' office which afforded no privacy, Charles disappeared into one of the telephone booths near the cloisters above the Members' Cloakroom. He checked the number and dialled it.

"Alexander, it's Charles. Charles Seymour."

"Good to hear from you, Charles, it's been a long time. How are you?"

"Well. And you?"

"Can't complain. What can I do for a busy man like you?"

"Wanted to chew over the new Sussex constituency with

you, Littlehampton. How's your selection of a candidate going?"

"They've left me to draw up a short list of six for final selection by the full committee in about ten days' time."

"Have you thought of standing yourself, Alexander?"

"Many times," came back the reply. "But the old lady wouldn't allow it, neither would the bank balance. Do you have any ideas?"

"Might be able to help. Why don't you come and have a quiet dinner at my place early next week?"

"That's kind of you, Charles."

"Not at all, it will be good to see you again. It's been far too long. Next Monday suit you?"

"Absolutely."

"Good, let's say eight o'clock, 27 Eaton Square."

Charles put the phone down, returned to the Whips' Office and pencilled a note in his diary.

Raymond had just finished making his contribution to the European debate when Charles returned to take a seat on a half-empty Treasury bench. Raymond had made a coherent economic case for remaining free of the other six European countries and for building stronger links with the Commonwealth and America. He doubted that Britain could take the financial burden of entering a club that had been in existence for so long. If the country had joined at its inception it might have been different, he argued, but he would have to vote against this risky, unproven venture that he suspected could only lead to higher unemployment. When Raymond sat down he did not receive the acclamation that Andrew had and, worse, what praise he did elicit came from the left wing of the party who had spent so much time in the past criticising *Full Employment at any Cost?* Charles put a cross by the name Gould.

A note was being passed along the row to Raymond from one of the House Badge messengers, dressed in white tie and black tails. It read, 'Please ring head of chambers as soon as convenient.'

Raymond left the floor of the House and went to the

nearest telephone in the corner of the Members' Lobby. He was immediately put through to Sir Nigel Hartwell.

"You wanted me to phone?"

"Yes," said Sir Nigel. "Are you free at the moment?"

"I am," said Raymond. "Why? Is it something urgent?"

"I'd rather not talk about it over the phone," said Sir Nigel ominously.

Raymond took a tube from Westminster to Temple and was in chambers fifteen minutes later. He went straight to Sir Nigel's office, sat down in the comfortable chair in the corner of the spacious club-like room, crossed his legs and watched Sir Nigel pace about in front of him. He was clearly determined to get something off his chest.

"Raymond, I have been asked by those in authority about you taking silk. I've said I think you'd make a damn good QC." A smile came over Raymond's face, but it was soon wiped off. "But I need an undertaking from you."

"An undertaking?"

"Yes," said Sir Nigel. "You must stop having this damn silly er . . . relationship with another member of chambers." He rounded on Raymond and faced him.

Raymond turned scarlet but before he could speak the head of chambers continued.

"Now I want your word on it," said Sir Nigel, "that it will end, and end immediately."

"You have my word," said Raymond quietly.

"I'm not a prig," said Sir Nigel, pulling down on his waistcoat, "but if you are going to have an affair for God's sake make it as far away from the office as possible and, if I may advise you, that should include the House of Commons and Leeds. There's still a lot of the world left over and it's full of women."

Raymond nodded his agreement: he could not fault the head of chambers' logic.

Sir Nigel continued, obviously embarrassed. "There's a nasty fraud case starting in Manchester next Monday. Our client has been accused of setting up a series of companies that specialise in life insurance but avoid paying out on the claims: I expect you remember all the publicity. Miss Arnold has been put on the case as a reserve junior. They tell me it could last several weeks."

"She'll try and get out of it," said Raymond glumly.

"She already has, but I made it quite clear that if she felt unable to take the case on she would have to find other chambers."

Raymond breathed a sigh of relief. "Thank you," he said.

"Sorry about this. I know you've earned your silk, old boy, but I can't have members of chambers going around with egg on their faces. Thank you for your co-operation: I can't pretend I enjoyed that."

"Got time for a quiet word?" asked Charles.

"You're wasting your time, dear thing, if you imagine the disciples will change their minds at this late stage," said Alec Pimkin. "All twelve of them will vote against the Government on Europe. That's final."

"I don't want to discuss Europe this time, Alec. It's far more serious, and on a personal level. Let's go and have a drink on the terrace."

Charles ordered the drinks, and the two men strolled out on to the quiet end of the terrace towards the Speaker's house. Charles stopped as soon as he was certain there was no longer anyone within earshot.

"If it's not Europe, what is it?" asked Pimkin, staring out at the Thames.

"What's this I hear about you losing your seat?"

Pimkin turned pale and touched his bow tie nervously. "It's this bloody boundary business. My constituency is swallowed up, and no one seems willing to interview me for a new one."

"What's it worth if I secure you a safe seat for the rest of your life?"

Pimkin looked suspiciously up at Charles. "Almost anything up to a pound of flesh," he added with a false laugh.

"No, I won't need to cut that deep."

The colour returned to Pimkin's cheeks. "Whatever it is, you can rely on me, old fellow."

"Can you deliver the disciples?" said Charles.

Pimkin turned pale again.

"Not on the small votes in committee," said Charles, before Pimkin could reply. "Not on the clauses even, just on the second reading, the principle itself. Standing by the party in their hour of need, no desire to cause an unnecessary general election, all that stuff – you fill in the details for the disciples. I know you can convince them, Alec."

Pimkin still didn't speak.

"I deliver a copper-bottomed seat, you deliver twelve votes. I think we can call that a fair exchange."

"What if I get them to abstain?" said Pimkin.

Charles waited, as if giving the idea considerable thought. "It's a deal," he said, never having hoped for anything more.

Alexander Dalglish arrived at Eaton Square a little after eight. Fiona met him at the door and explained that Charles had not yet returned from the Commons.

"But I expect him any moment," she added. "May I offer you a drink?"

Another thirty minutes passed before Charles hurried in.

"Sorry I'm late, Alexander," he said, grasping his guest by the hand. "Hoped I might make it just before you." He kissed his wife on the forehead.

"Not at all," said Alexander. "I couldn't have asked for more pleasant company."

"What will you have, darling?" asked Fiona.

"A strong whisky, please, and can we go straight into dinner? I've got to be back at the talkshop by ten."

Charles guided his guest towards the dining-room and seated him at the side of the table before taking his place below the Holbein portrait of the first Earl of Bridgwater, an heirloom his grandfather had left him. Fiona took a seat opposite her husband. During the meal of Beef Wellington, Charles spent a great deal of time catching up on what Alexander had been doing since they had last met. Although they had spent three years together in the Guards as brother officers they rarely saw each other outside of regimental reunions since Charles had entered the House. He made no mention of the real purpose behind the meeting until Fiona provided the opportunity when she served coffee.

"I know you two have a lot to talk about, so I'll leave you to get on with it."

"Thank you," said Alexander. He looked up at Fiona and smiled. "For a lovely dinner."

She smiled back and left them alone.

"Now, Charles," said Alexander, picking up the file he had left on the floor by his side. "I need to pick your brains."

"Go ahead, old fellow," said Charles, "only too delighted to be of assistance."

"Sir Edward Mountjoy has sent me a pretty long list for us to consider, among them a Home Office minister and one or two other Members of Parliament who'll be losing their present seats. What do you think of . . .?"

Dalglish opened the file in front of him as Charles poured him a generous glass of port and offered him a cigar from a gold case that he picked up from the sideboard.

"What a magnificent object," said Alexander, staring in awe at the crested box and the engraved C.G.S. along its top.

"A family heirloom," said Charles. "Should have been left to my brother Rupert, but I was lucky enough to have the same initials as my grandfather."

Alexander handed it back to his host before returning to his notes.

"Here's the man who impresses me," he said at last. "Kerslake, Simon Kerslake."

Charles remained silent.

"You don't have an opinion, Charles?"

"Yes."

"So what do you think of Kerslake?"

"Strictly off the record?"

Dalglish nodded, but said nothing.

Charles sipped his port. "Very good," he said.

"Kerslake?"

"No, the port. Taylor's '35. I'm afraid Kerslake is not the same vintage. Need I say more?"

"Well, no, I follow your drift but it's most disappointing. He looks so good on paper."

"On paper is one thing," said Charles, "but having him as your member for twenty years is quite another. You want a man you can rely on. And his wife – never seen in the constituency, you know." He frowned. "I'm afraid I've gone too far."

"No, no," said Alexander. "I've got the picture. Next one is Norman Lamont."

"First class but he's already been selected for Kingston, I'm afraid," said Charles.

Dalglish looked down at his file once again. "Well, what about Pimkin?"

"We were at Eton together. His looks are against him, as my grandmother used to say, but he's a sound man, and very good in the constituency, so they tell me."

"You would recommend him then?"

"I should snap him up before another constituency adopts him."

"That popular, is he?" said Alexander. "Thanks for the tip. Pity about Kerslake."

"That was strictly off the record," said Charles.

"Of course. Not a word. You can rely on me."

"Cigar to your liking?"

"Excellent," said Alexander, "but your judgement has always been so good. You only have to look at Fiona to realise that."

Charles smiled.

Most of the other names Dalglish produced were either unknown, unsuitable or easy to dismiss. When Alexander left shortly before ten Fiona asked him if the chat had been worthwhile.

"Yes, I think we've found the right man."

Raymond had the locks on his flat changed that afternoon. It turned out to be more expensive than he had bargained for, and the carpenter had insisted on cash in advance.

The carpenter grinned as he pocketed the money. "I make a fortune doing this job, Guv'nor, I can tell you. At least one gentleman a day, always cash, no receipt. Means the wife and I can spend a month in Ibiza every year, tax free."

Raymond smiled at the thought. He checked his watch; he could just catch the Thursday seven-ten from King's Cross and be in Leeds by ten o'clock for a long weekend.

Alexander Dalglish phoned Charles a week later to tell him Pimkin had made the short list, and that they hadn't considered Kerslake.

"Pimkin didn't go over very well with the committee at the first interview."

"No, he wouldn't," said Charles. "I warned you his looks were agin' him and he may come over a bit right wing at times but he's as sound as a bell and will never let you down, take my word."

"I'll have to, Charles. Because by getting rid of Kerslake we've removed his only real challenger."

Charles put the phone down and dialled the Home Office.

"Simon Kerslake, please."

"Who's calling?"

"Seymour, Whips' office." He was put straight through.

"Simon, it's Charles. I thought I ought to give you an update on Littlehampton."

"That's thoughtful of you," said Simon.

"Not good news, I'm afraid. It turns out the chairman wants the seat for himself. He's making sure the committee only interviews idiots."

"How can you be so certain?"

"I've seen the short list and Pimkin's the only sitting member they're considering."

"I can't believe it."

"No, I was pretty shocked myself. I pressed the case for you, but it fell on deaf ears. Didn't care for your views on hanging or some such words. Still, I can't believe you'll find it hard to pick up a seat."

"I hope you're right, Charles, but in any case thanks for trying."

"Any time. Let me know of any other seats you put your name in for. I have a lot of friends up and down the country."

"Thank you, Charles. Can you pair me for next Thursday?"

Two days later Alec Pimkin was invited by the Little-hampton Conservatives to attend a short-list interview for the selection of a Tory candidate for the new constitu-ency.

"How do I begin to thank you?" he asked Charles when they met up in the bar.

"Keep your word – and I want it in writing," replied Charles.

"What do you mean?"

"A letter to the Chief Whip saying you've changed your mind on the main European vote, and you and the disciples will be abstaining on Thursday."

Pimkin looked cocky. "And if I don't play ball, dear thing?"

"You haven't got the seat yet, Alec, and I might find it necessary to phone Alexander Dalglish and tell him about that awfully nice little boy you made such a fool of yourself over when you were up at Oxford."

Three days later the Chief Whip received the letter from Pimkin. He immediately summoned his junior Whip.

"*Well done*, Charles. How did you manage to succeed where we've all failed – and the disciples as well?"

"Matter of loyalty," said Charles. "Pimkin saw that in the end."

On the final day of the Great Debate on 'the principle of entry' into Europe the Prime Minister delivered the winding-up speech. He rose at nine-thirty to cheers from both sides. At ten o'clock the House divided and voted in favour of 'the principle' by a majority of 112. Sixty-nine Labour MPs, led by Roy Jenkins, had helped to swell the Government's majority.

Raymond Gould voted against the motion in accordance with his long-held beliefs. Andrew Fraser joined Simon Kerslake and Charles Seymour in the Ayes lobby. Alec Pimkin and the twelve disciples remained in their places on the Commons benches while the vote took place.

When Charles heard the Speaker read out the final result he felt a moment of triumph, although he realised that he still had the committee stage to go through. Hundreds of clauses, any of which could go wrong and turn the bill into a farce. Nevertheless the first round belonged to him.

Ten days later Alec Pimkin defeated a keen young Conservative just down from Cambridge and a local woman councillor to be selected as prospective candidate for Littlehampton.

CHAPTER
FOURTEEN

Andrew studied the case once again and decided to make his own enquiries. Too many constituents had in the past demonstrated that they were willing to lie to him in surgery as happily as they would in the witness box to any judge.

Robert was trying to climb up on to his lap. Andrew hoisted him the remainder of the way in one tug and attempted to return to his papers. "Whose side are you on?" Andrew demanded as his son dribbled all over his freshly written notes. He stopped to pat his bottom. "Ugh," he said, putting the case file by his side on the floor. A few minutes later Robert had been changed and left with his mother.

"I'm afraid your son is not over-anxious to help me in my desire to secure the release of an innocent man," Andrew shouted over his shoulder.

He settled down to go over the papers once more, something about the case didn't ring true . . . Andrew dialled the Procurator Fiscal's number. There was one man who could cut his work in half with a sentence.

"Good morning, Mr Fraser. What can I do for you, sir?"

Andrew had to smile. Angus Sinclair was a contemporary of his father and had known Andrew all his life, but once he was in his office he treated everyone as a stranger, making no exception.

"He even calls his wife 'Mrs Sinclair' when she rings the office," Sir Duncan once told him. Andrew was willing to join in the game.

"Good morning, Mr Sinclair. I need your advice as Procurator Fiscal."

"Always happy to be of service, sir."

"I want to talk to you off the record about the Paddy O'Halloran case. Do you remember it?"

"Of course, everyone in this office remembers that case."

"Good," said Andrew. "Then you'll know what a help you can be to me in cutting through the thicket."

"Thank you, sir," the slight burr came back down the telephone.

"A group of my constituents, whom I wouldn't trust further than I could toss a caber, claim O'Halloran was framed for the Princes Street bank robbery last year. They don't deny he has criminal tendencies" – Andrew would have chuckled if he hadn't been speaking to Angus Sinclair – "but they say he never left a pub called the Sir Walter Scott the entire time the robbery was taking place. All you have to tell me, Mr Sinclair, is that you have no doubt that O'Halloran was guilty and I'll drop my enquiries. If you say nothing, I shall dig deeper."

Andrew waited, but he received no reply.

"Thank you, Mr Sinclair." Although he knew it would elicit no response, he couldn't resist adding: "No doubt I'll see you at the golf club some time over the weekend." The silence continued.

"Goodbye, Mr Sinclair."

"Good day, Mr Fraser."

Andrew settled back: it was going to be a lengthy exercise. He started by checking with all the people who had confirmed O'Halloran's alibi that night but after interviewing the first eight he came to the reluctant conclusion that none of them could be trusted as a witness. Whenever he came across another of O'Halloran's friends the expression 'anyone's for a pint' kept crossing his mind. The time had come to talk with the landlord of the Sir Walter Scott.

"I couldn't be sure, Mr Fraser, but I think he was here that evening. Trouble is, O'Halloran came almost every night. It's hard to recall."

"Do you know anyone who might remember? Someone you could trust with your cash register?"

"That'd be pushing your luck in this pub, Mr Fraser."

The landlord thought for a moment. "However, there's old Mrs Bloxham," he said at last, slapping the drying-up cloth over his shoulder. "She sits in that corner every night." He pointed to a small round table that would have been crowded had it seated more than two people. "If she says he was here, he was."

Andrew asked the landlord where Mrs Bloxham lived and then, hoping she was in, made his way to 43 Mafeking Road, neatly sidestepping a gang of young children playing football in the middle of the street. He climbed some steps that badly needed repairing and knocked on the door of number forty-three.

"Is it another general election already, Mr Fraser?" asked a disbelieving old lady as she peered through the letter-box.

"No, it's nothing to do with politics, Mrs Bloxham," said Andrew, bending down. "I came round to seek your advice on a personal matter."

"A personal matter? Better come on in out of the cold then," she said, opening the door to him. "There's a terrible draught rushes through this corridor."

Andrew followed the old lady as she shuffled down the dingy corridor in her carpet slippers to a room that he would have said was colder than it had been outside on the street. There were no ornaments in the room save a crucifix that stood on a narrow mantelpiece below a pastel print of the Virgin Mary. Mrs Bloxham beckoned Andrew to a wooden seat by a table yet unlaid. She eased her plump frame into an ancient stuffed armchair. It groaned under her weight and a strand of horsehair fell to the floor. Andrew looked more carefully at the old lady. She was wearing a black shawl over a dress she must have worn a thousand times. Once settled in her chair, she kicked off her slippers.

"Feet still giving you trouble, then?" he enquired.

"Doctor doesn't seem to be able to explain the swellings," she said, without bitterness.

Andrew leaned on the table and noticed what a fine piece of furniture it was, and how incongruous it looked in its present surroundings. He was struck by the craftsmanship of the carved Georgian legs. She noticed he was admiring it.

"My great-grandfather gave that to my great-grandmother the day they were married, Mr Fraser."

"It's magnificent," said Andrew.

She didn't seem to hear because all she said was, "What can I do for you, sir?" The second time that day he had been addressed by an elder in that way.

Andrew went over the O'Halloran story again. Mrs Bloxham listened intently, leaning forward slightly and cupping her hand round her ear to be sure she could hear every word.

"That O'Halloran's an evil one," she said, "not to be trusted. Our Blessed Lady will have to be very forgiving to allow the likes of him to enter the kingdom of heaven." Andrew smiled. "Not that I'm expecting to meet all that many politicians when I get there either," she added, giving Andrew a toothless grin.

"Could O'Halloran possibly have been there that Friday night as all his friends claim?" Andrew asked.

"He was there all right," said Mrs Bloxham. "No doubt about that – saw him with my own eyes."

"How can you be so sure?"

"Spilled his beer over my best dress, and I knew something bad would happen on the thirteenth, especially with it being a Friday. I won't forgive him for that. I still haven't been able to get the stain out despite what those washing-powder ads tell you on the telly."

"Why didn't you inform the police immediately?"

"Didn't ask," she said simply. "They've been after him for a long time for a lot of things they couldn't pin on him, but for once he was in the clear."

Andrew finished writing his notes and then rose to leave. Mrs Bloxham heaved herself out of the chair, dispensing yet more horsehair on to the floor. They walked to the door together. "I'm sorry I couldn't offer you a cup of tea but I'm right out at the moment," she said. "If you had come tomorrow it would have been all right."

Andrew paused on the doorstep.

"I get the pension tomorrow, you see," she replied to his unasked question.

It took Elizabeth some time to find a locum to cover for her so that she could travel to Redcorn for the interview. Once again the children had to be left with a baby-sitter. The local and national press had made him the hot favourite for the new seat. Elizabeth put on what she called her best Conservative outfit, a pale blue suit with a dark blue collar that hid everything on top and reached well below her knees.

The journey from King's Cross to Newcastle took three hours and twenty minutes, on what was described in the timetable as 'the express'. At least Simon was able to catch up with a great deal of the paper work that had been stuffed into his red box. Civil servants, he reflected, rarely allowed politicians time to involve themselves in politics. They wouldn't have been pleased to learn that he spent an hour of the journey reading the last four weekly copies of the *Redcorn News*.

At Newcastle they were met by the wife of the Association treasurer, who had volunteered to escort the minister and Mrs Kerslake to the constituency to be sure they were in time for the interview. "That's very thoughtful of you," said Elizabeth, as she stared at the mode of transport that had been chosen to take them the next forty miles.

The ancient Austin Mini took a further hour and a half through the winding B-roads before they reached their destination, and the treasurer's wife never drew breath once throughout the entire journey. When Simon and Elizabeth piled out of the car at the market town of Redcorn they were physically and mentally exhausted.

The treasurer's wife took them through to the constituency headquarters and introduced them both to the agent.

"Good of you to come," he said. "Hell of a journey, isn't it?"

Elizabeth felt unable to disagree with his judgement. But on this occasion she made no comment, feeling that if this was to be Simon's best chance of returning to Parliament she had already decided to give him every support possible. Nevertheless she dreaded the thought of her husband making the journey to Redcorn twice a month as she feared they would see even less of each other than they did at present, let alone the children.

"Now the form is," began the agent, "that we are interviewing six potential candidates and they'll be seeing you last." He winked knowingly.

Simon and Elizabeth smiled uncertainly.

"I'm afraid they won't be ready for you for at least another hour, so you have time for a stroll round the town."

Simon was glad of the chance to stretch his legs and take a closer look at Redcorn. He and Elizabeth walked slowly round the pretty market town, admiring the Elizabethan architecture that had somehow survived irresponsible or greedy town planners. They even climbed the hill to take a look inside the magnificent perpendicular church which dominated the surrounding area.

As he walked back past the shops in the high street Simon nodded to those locals who appeared to recognise him.

"A lot of people seem to know who you are," said Elizabeth, and then they saw the paper rack outside the local newsagent. They sat on the bench in the market square and read the lead story under a large picture of Simon.

'Redcorn's next MP?' ran the headline.

The story volunteered the fact that although Simon Kerslake had to be considered the favourite, Bill Travers, a local farmer who had been chairman of the county council the previous year, was still thought to have an outside chance.

Simon began to feel a little sick in the stomach. It reminded him of the day he had been interviewed at Coventry Central nearly eight years before. Now that he was a minister of the Crown he wasn't any less nervous.

When he and Elizabeth returned to constituency headquarters they were informed that only two more candidates had been seen and the third was still being interviewed. They walked around the town once again, even more slowly this time, watching the shopkeepers put up their coloured shutters and turn 'Open' signs to 'Closed'.

"What a pleasant market town," said Simon, trying to find out how his wife was feeling.

"And the people seem so polite after London," she added.

Simon smiled as they headed back to the party headquarters. As they passed Simon and Elizabeth they bid the strangers "Good evening," courteous people whom Simon felt he would have been proud to represent. But although they walked slowly Elizabeth and he could not make their journey last more than thirty minutes.

When they returned a third time to constituency headquarters the fourth candidate was leaving the interview room. She looked very despondent. "It shouldn't be long now," said the agent, but it was another forty minutes before they heard a ripple of applause, and a man dressed in a Harris tweed jacket and brown trousers left the room. He didn't seem happy either.

The agent ushered Simon and Elizabeth through, and as they entered everyone in the room stood. Ministers of the Crown did not visit Redcorn often.

Simon waited for Elizabeth to be seated before he took the chair in the centre of the room facing the committee. He estimated that there were about fifty people present and they were all staring at him, showing no aggression, merely curiosity. He looked around at the weather-beaten faces. Most of them, male and female, were dressed in tweed. In his dark striped London suit Simon felt out of place.

"And now," said the chairman, "we welcome the Right Honourable Simon Kerslake, MP."

Simon had to smile at the mistake so many people made in thinking that all ministers were automatically members of the Privy Council, and therefore entitled to the prefix 'Right Honourable' instead of the plain 'Honourable' accorded to all MPs – and then only when they were present in the House.

"Mr Kerslake will address us for twenty minutes, and he has kindly agreed to answer questions after that," added the chairman.

Simon felt confident he had spoken well, but even his few carefully chosen quips received no more than a smile, and his more serious comments elicited little response. This was not a group of people given to showing their emotions. When he had finished he sat down to respectful clapping and murmurs.

"Now the minister will take questions," said the chairman.

"Where do you stand on hanging?" said a scowling middle-aged woman in a grey suit seated in the front row.

Simon explained his reasons for being a convinced abolitionist. The scowl did not move from the questioner's face and Simon thought to himself how much happier she would be with Ronnie Nethercote as her member.

A man in a hacking jacket asked: "How do you feel, Mr Kerslake, about this year's farm subsidy?"

"Good on eggs, tough on beef, and disastrous for pig farmers. Or at least that's what I read on the front page of *Farmers Weekly* yesterday." Some of them laughed for the first time. "It hasn't proved necessary for me to have a great knowledge of farming in Coventry Central, but if I am lucky enough to be selected for Redcorn I shall try to learn quickly, and with your help I shall hope to master the farmers' problems." Several heads nodded their approval.

"Miss Pentecost, chairman of the Women's Advisory," announced a tall, thin spinsterish woman who had stood up to catch the chairman's eye. "May I be permitted to ask Mrs Kerslake a question? If your husband were offered this seat, would you be willing to come and live in Northumberland?"

Elizabeth had dreaded the question because she knew that if Simon was offered the constituency she would be expected to resign her post at the hospital. Simon turned and looked towards his wife.

"No," she replied directly. "I am a doctor at St Mary's Hospital, Paddington, where I practise gynaecology. I support my husband in his career but, like Margaret Thatcher, I believe a woman has the right to a good education and then the chance to use her qualifications to their best advantage."

A ripple of applause went round the room and Simon smiled at his wife.

The next question was on Europe, and Simon gave an unequivocal statement as to his reasons for backing the

Prime Minister in his desire to see Britain as part of the Common Market.

Simon continued to answer questions on subjects ranging from trade union reform to violence on television before the chairman asked, "Are there any more questions?"

There was a long silence and just as he was about to thank Simon the scowling lady in the front row, without being recognised by the chair, asked what Mr Kerslake's views were on abortion.

"Morally, I'm against it," said Simon. "At the time of the Abortion Act many of us believed it would stem the tide of divorce. We have been proved wrong: the rate of divorce has quadrupled. Nevertheless, in the cases of rape or fear of physical or mental injury arising from birth I would have to support the medical advice given at the time. Elizabeth and I have two children and my wife's job is to see that babies are safely delivered," he added.

The lips moved from a scowl to a straight line.

"Thank you," said the chairman. "It was good of you to give us so much of your time. Perhaps you and Mrs Kerslake would be kind enough to wait outside."

Simon and Elizabeth joined the other hopeful candidates, their wives and the agent in a small dingy room at the back of the building. When they saw the half-empty trestle table in front of them they both remembered they hadn't had any lunch and devoured what was left of the curling cucumber sandwiches and the cold sausage rolls.

"What happens next?" Simon asked the agent between mouthfuls.

"Nothing out of the ordinary. They'll have a discussion, allowing everyone to express their views, and then vote. It should all be over in twenty minutes."

Elizabeth checked her watch: it was seven o'clock and the last train was at nine-fifteen.

"Ought to make the train comfortably," said Simon.

An hour later when no smoke had emerged from the chimney the agent suggested to all the candidates who had a long journey ahead of them that they might like to check into the Bell Inn just over the road.

When Simon looked around the room it was clear that everyone else had done so in advance.

"You had better stay put in case you're called again," Elizabeth said. "I'll go off and book a room and at the same time call and see how the children are getting on."

"Probably eaten the poor baby-sitter by now," said Simon.

Elizabeth smiled before slipping out and making her way to the small hotel.

Simon opened his red box and tried to complete some work. The man who looked like a farmer came over and introduced himself.

"I'm Bill Travers, the chairman of the new constituency," he began. "I only wanted to say that you'll have my full support as chairman if the committee select you."

"Thank you," said Simon.

"I had hoped to represent this area, as my grandfather did. But I shall understand if Redcorn prefers to choose a man destined for the Cabinet rather than someone who would be happy to spend his life on the back benches."

Simon was touched by his opponent's goodwill, and would have liked to respond in kind but Travers quickly added, "Forgive me, I'll not waste any more of your time. I can see" – he looked down at the red box – "that you have a lot of work to catch up on."

Simon felt guilty as he watched the man walk away. A few minutes later Elizabeth returned and tried to smile. "The only room left is smaller than Peter's and it faces the main road, so it's just about as noisy."

"At least no children to say 'I'm hungry'," he said, touching her hand.

It was a little after nine when a weary chairman came out and asked all the candidates if he could have their attention. Husbands and wives all faced him. "My committee want to thank you for going through this grim procedure. It has been hard for us to decide something that we hope not to have to discuss again for twenty years." He paused. "The committee are going to invite Mr Bill Travers to fight the Redcorn seat at the next election."

In a sentence it was all over. Simon's throat went dry.

He and Elizabeth didn't get much sleep in their tiny room at the Bell Inn, and it hadn't helped that the agent told them the final vote had been twenty-five — twenty-three.

"I don't think Miss Pentecost liked me," said Elizabeth, feeling guilty. "If I had told her that I would have been willing to live in the constituency I think you'd have been offered the seat."

"I doubt it," said Simon. "In any case it's no use agreeing to their terms at the interview and then imposing your own when you have been offered the constituency. My guess is you'll find Redcorn has chosen the right man."

Elizabeth smiled at her husband, grateful for his support.

"There will be other seats," said Simon, only too aware that time was now running out. "You'll see."

Elizabeth prayed that he would prove right, and that next time the choice of a constituency would not make her have to face the dilemma she had so far managed to avoid.

When Raymond took silk, the second Tuesday after the Easter holiday, and became a Queen's Counsel, Joyce made one of her periodic trips to London. The occasion she decided warranted another visit to Harvey Nichols. She recalled her first trip to the store so many years before when she had accompanied her husband to meet the Prime Minister. Raymond had come so far since then although their relationship seemed to have progressed so little. She had given up hope of being a mother, but still wanted him to believe she was a good wife. She couldn't help thinking how much better-looking Raymond had become in middle age, and feared the same could not be said of her.

She enjoyed watching the legal ceremony as her husband was presented in court before the judges. Latin words spoken but not understood. Suddenly her husband was Raymond Gould, QC, MP.

She and Raymond arrived late in chambers for the celebration party. Everyone seemed to have turned out in her husband's honour. Raymond felt full of *bonhomie* and was chatting to the chief clerk when Sir Nigel handed him a glass of champagne. Then he saw a familiar figure by the mantel-piece and remembered that the trial in Manchester was over. He managed to circle the room speaking to everyone but Stephanie Arnold. To his horror he turned to see her introducing herself to his wife. Every time he glanced towards them they seemed deeper in conversation.

"Ladies and gentlemen," said Sir Nigel, banging a table. He waited for silence. "We are always proud in chambers when one of our members takes silk. It is a comment not only on the man but also on his chambers. And when it is the youngest silk – still under forty – it adds to that pride. All of you, of course, know that Raymond also serves in another place in which we expect him to rise to even greater glory. May I add finally how pleasant it is to have his wife Joyce among us tonight. Ladies and gentlemen," he concluded. "The toast is Raymond Gould, QC."

"Raymond Gould, QC," said everyone in chorus. Then, "Speech, speech."

"I would like to thank all those people who made this great honour possible," began Raymond. "My producer, my director, the other stars and not forgetting the criminals, without whom I would have no profession to profess. And finally," he said, "to those of you who want to see the back of me, I direct you all to work tirelessly to ensure the return of a Labour Government at the next election. Thank you."

The applause was sustained and genuine and many of his colleagues were impressed by how relaxed Raymond had become of late. As they came up to congratulate him Raymond couldn't help noticing that Stephanie and Joyce had resumed their conversation. Raymond was handed another glass of champagne just as an earnest young pupil called Patrick Montague who had recently joined them from chambers in Bristol engaged him in conversation. Although Montague had been with them for some weeks Raymond had never spoken to him at length before. He seemed to have very clear views on criminal law and the changes that were necessary. For the first time in his life Raymond felt he was no longer a young man.

Suddenly both women were at his side.

"Hello, Raymond."

"Hello, Stephanie," he said awkwardly and looked anxiously towards his wife. "Do you know Patrick Montague?" he asked, absent-mindedly.

The three of them burst out laughing.

"What's so funny?" asked Raymond.

"You do embarrass me sometimes, Raymond," said Joyce. "Surely you realise Stephanie and Patrick are engaged?"

CHAPTER
FIFTEEN

"With or without civil servants?" asked Simon as Andrew entered the minister's office.

"Without, please."

"Fine," said Simon and pressed a switch on the intercom by his desk.

"I don't want to be disturbed while I'm with Mr Fraser," he said and ushered his colleague towards a comfortable seat in the corner.

"Elizabeth was asking me this morning to find out how Robert was getting on."

"It's his second birthday next month and he's overweight for a scrum-half," replied Andrew. "And how's your search for a seat working out?"

"Not too good. The last three constituencies to come up haven't even asked to see me. I can't put a finger on why, except they all seem to have selected local men."

"It's still a long time to the next election. You're sure to find a seat before then."

"It might not be so long if the Prime Minister decides to go to the country and test his strength against the unions."

"That would be a foolish thing to do," said Andrew. "He might defeat us but he still wouldn't defeat the unions."

A young woman came into the room with two cups of coffee, put them on the low Formica table and left the two men alone.

"Have you had time to look at the file?" Andrew continued.

"Yes, I went over it last night between checking over Peter's prep and helping Michael to build a model galleon."

"And how do you feel?" Andrew asked.

"Not very good. I can't get to grips with this new maths they're now teaching, and my mast was the only one that fell off when Elizabeth launched the galleon in the bath."

Andrew laughed.

"I think you've got a case," said Simon, sounding serious.

"Good," said Andrew. "Now the reason I wanted to see you privately is because I feel there are no party political points to be made out of this case for either of us. I've no plans to try to embarrass your department, and I consider it's in the best interest of my constituents to co-operate as closely as I can with you."

"Thank you," said Simon. "So where do you want to go from here?"

"I'd like to table a planted question for your department in the hope that you would consider opening an enquiry. If the enquiry comes to the same conclusion as I have, I would expect you to order a re-trial."

Simon hesitated. "And if the enquiry goes against you will you agree to no reprisals for the Home Office?"

"You have my word on it."

"Shall I ask the civil servants to come in now?"

"Yes, please do."

Simon returned to his desk and pressed a button. A moment later three men in almost identical suits, white shirts with stiff collars and discreet ties entered the room. Between them they could have ruined any police identification parade.

"Mr Fraser," began Simon, "is asking the Home Office to consider . . ."

"Can you explain why Simon Kerslake missed a vote yesterday?"

Charles looked across the table at the Chief Whip.

"No, I can't," he said. "I've been distributing the weekly whip to him the same as every member of my group."

"What's behind it then?"

"I think the poor man has been spending a lot of his time

traipsing around the country looking for a seat to fight at the next election."

"That's no excuse," said the Chief Whip. "Duties in the House must come first, every member knows that. He missed a vote on a vital clause during the European Bill last Thursday while everyone else in your group has proved reliable. Despite our majority we seem to be in single figures for almost every clause. Perhaps I should have a word with him?"

"No, no, I'd rather you didn't," said Charles, fearing he sounded a little too insistent. "I consider it my responsibility. I'll speak to him and see that it doesn't happen again."

"All right, Charles, if that's the way you want to play it. Thank God it can't last much longer and the damn thing will soon be law, but we must remain vigilant over every clause. The Labour party know only too well that if they defeat us on certain key clauses they can still scupper the whole bill, and if I lost one of those by a single vote I would cut Kerslake's throat. Or anyone else's who was responsible."

"I'll make sure he gets the message," said Charles.

"How's Fiona reacting to all these late nights?" the Chief Whip asked, finally relaxing.

"Very well, considering. In fact now that you mention it I have never seen her looking better."

"Can't say my wife is enjoying 'the prep school antics', as she describes our continual late-night sittings. I've had to promise to take her to the West Indies this winter to make up for it. Well, I'll leave you to deal with Kerslake then. Be firm, Charles. Just remember, we can't afford to lose a vote at this late stage."

"Norman Edwards?" repeated Raymond in disbelief. "The General Secretary of the Haulage Union?"

"Yes," said Fred Padgett, getting up from behind his desk.

"But he burnt *Full Employment at any Cost?* on a public bonfire with every journalist he could lay his hands on to witness the conflagration."

"I know," said Fred, returning a letter to the filing cabinet.

"I'm only your agent, I'm not here to explain the mysteries of the universe."

"When does he want to see me?" asked Raymond.

"As soon as possible."

"Better ask him if he can come for a drink back at the house round six o'clock."

Raymond had had a heavy Saturday morning surgery and thanks to the still imminent Martians had only found time to grab a sandwich at the pub before going off to pursue his favourite pastime. This week Leeds were playing Liverpool at Elland Road. Sitting in the directors' box every other week in full view of his constituents while he supported his local football team killed 30,000 birds with one stone. Later, when talking to the lads in the dressing-room after the match, he found himself lapsing into a pronounced Yorkshire accent that bore no resemblance to the one he used to address high court judges during the week.

Leeds won three–two and after the match Raymond joined the directors for a drink in the boardroom. He became so impassioned about an off-side decision that could have lost them a point that he nearly forgot about his meeting with Norman Edwards.

Joyce was in the garden showing the union leader her early snowdrops when Raymond returned.

"Sorry I'm late," he shouted, as he hung up his yellow and blue scarf. "I've been to the match."

"Who won?" asked Edwards.

"Leeds, of course, three–two."

"Damn," said Norman, his accent leaving the other in no doubt that he had not spent many nights outside of Liverpool.

"Come on in and have a beer," said Raymond.

"I'd prefer a vodka."

The two men went into the house while Joyce continued with her gardening.

"Well," said Raymond, pouring his guest a Smirnoff. "What brings you all the way from Liverpool if it wasn't to watch the football? Perhaps you want a signed copy of my book for your next union bonfire."

"Don't give me any hassle, Ray. I came all this way because I need your help, simple as that."

"I'm all ears," said Raymond.

"We had a full meeting of the General Purposes Committee yesterday, and one of the brothers has spotted a clause in the European Bill which could put us all out of work."

Norman passed over a copy of the bill to Raymond with the relevant clause marked in red. It gave the minister power to make new haulage and lorry regulations which would come before the House as statutory instruments and thus could not be amended.

"If that gets through the House my boys are in deep trouble."

"Why?" said Raymond.

"Because those bloody Frogs know only too well that there's a Channel between us and them, and if my lads are forced by law to sleep a night each side the only people who'll end up making money on the deal will be the guest-house proprietors."

"What's behind it?" asked Raymond.

"They want us to drop the stuff our end, so they can pick it up on the other side."

"But wouldn't that also be true when they need to deliver goods to us?"

"No. Their journeys are much longer to the coast, and they have to stay overnight anyway, not to mention the fact that there are eight of them to one of us. It's diabolical. nothing less."

Raymond studied the wording in detail while Edwards helped himself to another vodka.

"The clause doesn't stop you from going over the next day."

"And how much do you think that will add to your costs?" asked Raymond.

"I'll tell you, enough to make us uncompetitive, that's how much," replied the trade-union leader.

"Point taken," said Raymond. "So what's wrong with asking your own member to put the case?"

"Don't trust him. He's pro-European at any price."

"And what about your sponsored trade union representative in the House?"

"Tom Carson? You must be joking. He's so far to the left that even his own side are suspicious when he supports a cause. We lost the 'tachograph' clause because he championed it. In any case I only put him in the House to get him off my back." Raymond laughed. "Now, all my General Purposes Committee want to know is: would you be willing to fight this clause in the House for us? Not that we can afford the sort of fees you're used to at the bar," he added.

"There would be no fee involved," said Raymond, "but I'm sure you'll be able to repay me in kind sometime in the future."

"Got the picture," said Edwards, touching the side of his nose with a forefinger. "What do I do next?"

"You go back to Liverpool and hope that I am better on an away pitch than your team."

Norman Edwards put on an old raincoat and started to button it up. He smiled at Raymond. "I may have been appalled by your book, Ray. But it doesn't mean I didn't admire it."

The Speaker looked down at the front bench. "Mr Andrew Fraser."

"Number seventeen, sir," said Andrew.

The Speaker looked down to check over the question, seeking a Home Office answer.

Simon rose to the dispatch box, opened his file and said, "Yes, sir."

"Mr Andrew Fraser," called the Speaker again.

Andrew rose from his place on the Opposition front bench to put his supplementary.

"May I thank the minister for agreeing to an enquiry so quickly, and ask him that, if he discovers an injustice has been done to my constituent Mr Paddy O'Halloran, that the Home Secretary will order a re-trial immediately?"

Simon rose again.

"Yes, sir."

"I am grateful to the Honourable Gentleman," said Andrew, half-rising from his place.

All over in less than a minute, but older members who listened to the brief exchange between Fraser and Kerslake in the House that day had no doubt that considerable preparation had gone into that minute from both sides.

"The damn man missed another three-line whip, Charles. It must be the last time. You've been protecting him for far too long."

"It won't happen again," promised Charles convincingly. "I would like to give him one more chance. Allow him that."

"You're very loyal to him," said the Chief Whip. "But next time I'm going to see Kerslake myself and get to the bottom of it."

"It won't happen again," repeated Charles.

"Hm," said the Chief Whip. "Next problem is, are there any clauses on the European Bill that we should be worried about next week?"

"Yes," replied Charles. "This haulage clause that Raymond Gould is fighting. He made a brilliant case on the floor of the House, and got all his own side and half of ours backing him."

"He's not the sponsored MP for the Haulage Union," said the Chief Whip, surprised.

"No, the unions obviously felt Tom Carson wouldn't help the cause and he's hopping mad at the slight."

"Clever of them to pick Gould. He improves as a speaker every time I hear him, and no one can fault him when it comes to a point of law."

"So we'd better face the fact that we're going to lose the clause?"

"Never. We'll redraft the damn thing so that it's acceptable and *seen* to be compassionate. It's not a bad time to be the defender of the union interests. That way we'll keep Gould from getting all the credit. I'll speak to the PM tonight – and don't forget what I said about Kerslake."

Charles returned to his office and realised that in future he would have to be more careful about telling Simon Kerslake

when he was paired for the European Bill. He suspected he
had carried this ploy as far as he could for now.

Simon had read the final report prepared by his department
on the O'Halloran case while Elizabeth was trying to get to
sleep. He only had to go over the details once to realise that
he would have to order a re-trial and institute a full investigation into the past record of the police officers who had been
involved in the case.

When Andrew heard the news, and that the re-trial would
be held in London, he asked Raymond Gould to represent
O'Halloran.

"Praise indeed," said Raymond, who still considered
Andrew among the Commons' finest orators. He somehow
managed to fit O'Halloran into his busy schedule.

The trial was in its third day when Mr Justice Comyns,
after listening to Mrs Bloxham's evidence, stopped proceedings and instructed the jury to return a verdict of not guilty.

Andrew received praise from all quarters of the House, but
he was quick to acknowledge the support given him by Simon
Kerslake and the Home Office. *The Times* even wrote a leader
the next day on the proper use of influence by a constituency
MP.

Some months later the court awarded O'Halloran £25,000
in compensation. The only drawback Andrew's success
caused was that every convict's mother north of Hadrian's
wall queued to tell him about her innocent son at his
fortnightly surgery. But during the year he took only one
seriously and once again began to check into the details.

During the long hot summer of 1972 clause after clause of the
European Bill was voted on, often through the night. On
some occasions the Government managed majorities of only
five or six but somehow the bill remained intact.

Charles would often arrive home at Eaton Square at three
in the morning to find Fiona asleep, only to leave again before
she had woken. Veterans of the House, both servants and
elected, confirmed they had never experienced anything like
it since the Second World War.

And, just as suddenly, the last vote was taken and the marathon was over. The European Bill was through the Commons and on its way to the Upper House to receive their lordships' approval. Charles wondered what he would do with all the hours that were suddenly left him in the day.

When the bill finally received the Royal Assent in October the Chief Whip held a celebration lunch at the Carlton Club in St James's to thank all his team. "And in particular, Charles Seymour," he said, raising his glass during an impromptu speech. When the lunch broke up the Chief Whip offered Charles a lift back to the Commons in his official car. They travelled along Piccadilly, down Haymarket, through Trafalgar Square and into Whitehall. Just as the Commons came into sight the black Rover turned into Downing Street, as Charles assumed, to drop the Chief Whip at No. 12. But as the car stopped the Chief Whip said, "The Prime Minister is expecting you in five minutes."

"What? Why?" said Charles, as he joined his colleague outside No. 10.

"Timed it rather well, didn't I?" said the Chief Whip – and headed off towards No. 12.

Charles stood alone in front of No. 10. The door was opened by a man in a long black coat. "Good afternoon, Mr Seymour."

The Prime Minister saw Charles in his study and, as ever, wasted no time on small talk.

"Thank you for all the hard work you have put in on the European Bill."

"It was a tremendous challenge," said Charles, searching for words.

"As will be your next job," said Mr Heath. "I want you to take over as one of the Ministers of State at the Department of Trade and Industry."

Charles was speechless.

"With all the problems we are going to encounter with the trade unions during the next few months, that should keep you fully occupied."

"It certainly will," said Charles.

He still hadn't been asked to sit down, but as the Prime

Minister was now rising from behind his desk it was clear that the meeting was over.

"You and Fiona must come and have dinner at No. 10 as soon as you've settled into your new department," said the Prime Minister as they walked towards the door.

"Thank you," Charles said.

As he stepped back on to Downing Street a driver opened the back door of a shiny Austin Westminster. It was several moments before Charles realised the car was his.

"The Commons, sir?"

"No, I'd like to return to Eaton Square for a few minutes," he said, sitting back and enjoying the thought of tackling his new job.

The car drove past the Commons, up Victoria Street and on to Eaton Square. He wanted to tell Fiona that all the hard work had been rewarded. He felt guilty about how little he had seen of her lately, although he could not believe it would be much better now that he was to be involved in trade union legislation. How much he still hoped for a son, perhaps even that would prove possible now. The car came to a halt outside the Georgian house. Charles ran up the steps and into the hall. He could hear his wife's voice from the first floor. He took the wide staircase in bounds of two and three at a time, and threw open the bedroom door.

"I'm the new Minister of State at the Department of Trade and Industry," he announced to Fiona, who was lying in bed.

Alexander Dalglish looked up. He showed no sign of interest in Charles's elevation.

When Andrew rang Angus Sinclair at the Procurator Fiscal's office to find that nothing was known of Ricky Hodge and that Sinclair was able to confirm that he had no criminal record, Andrew felt he had stumbled on a case with international implications.

As Ricky Hodge was in a Turkish jail any enquiries had to be made through the Foreign Office. Andrew did not have the same relationship with the Foreign Secretary as he did with Simon, so he felt the direct approach would be best and put down a question to be answered in the House. He worded it carefully: 'What action does the Foreign Secretary intend to take over the confiscation of a British passport from a constituent of the Honourable member for Edinburgh Carlton, details of which have been supplied to him?''

When the question came in front of the House on the following Wednesday the Foreign Secretary rose to answer the question himself. He stood at the dispatch box and peered over his half-moon spectacles and said:

"Her Majesty's Government are pursuing this matter through the usual diplomatic channels."

Andrew was quickly on his feet. "Does the Right Honourable Gentleman realise that my constituent has been in a Turkish prison for six months and has still not been charged?"

"Yes, sir," replied the Foreign Secretary. "I have asked the Turkish Embassy to supply the Foreign Office with more details of the case."

Andrew leaped up again. "How long will my constituent have to be forgotten in Ankara before the Foreign Secretary does more than ask for the details of his case?"

The Foreign Secretary rose again showing no sign of annoyance. "I will report those findings to the Honourable member as quickly as possible."

"When? Tomorrow, next week, next year?" Andrew shouted angrily.

"When?" joined in a chorus of Labour back-benchers, but the Speaker called for the next question above the uproar.

Within the hour Andrew received a handwritten note from the Foreign Office. It read: "If Mr Fraser would be kind enough to telephone, the Foreign Secretary would be delighted to make an appointment to see him."

Andrew phoned from the Commons and was invited to join the Foreign Secretary in Whitehall immediately.

The Foreign Office, known as 'The Palazzo' by its inmates, has an atmosphere of its own. Although Andrew had worked in a Government department as a minister he was still struck by its grandeur. He was met at the courtyard entrance and guided along yards of marble corridors before climbing a fine double staircase at the top of which he was greeted by the Foreign Secretary's Principal Private Secretary.

"Sir Alec will see you immediately, Mr Fraser," he said, and led Andrew past the magnificent pictures and tapestries which lined the way. He was taken into a beautifully proportioned room. The Foreign Secretary stood in front of an Adam fireplace over which hung a portrait of Lord Palmerston.

"Fraser, how kind of you to come at such short notice. I do hope it has not caused you any inconvenience." Platitudes, thought Andrew. Next the silly man will be mentioning my father. "I don't think we have met before, but of course I have known your father for many years. Won't you sit down?"

"I realise you are a busy man. Can we get down to the point at issue, Foreign Secretary?" Andrew demanded.

"Of course," Sir Alec said courteously. "Forgive me for taking up so much of your time." Without a further word, he handed Andrew a file marked 'Richard M. Hodge – Confidential'. "Although Members of Parliament are not subject to the Official Secrets Act I know you will respect the fact that this file is classified."

Another bluff, thought Andrew. He flicked back the cover. It was true: exactly as he had suspected, Ricky Hodge had never been arrested or charged. He turned the page. "Rome, child prostitution; Marseilles, narcotics; Paris, blackmail." Page after page, ending in Turkey, where Hodge had been found in possession of four pounds of heroin which he had been selling in small packets on the black market. In his twenty-nine years Ricky Hodge had spent eleven of the last fourteen in foreign jails.

Andrew closed the file and could feel the sweat on his forehead. It was some moments before he spoke. "I apologise, Foreign Secretary," he said. "I have made a fool of myself."

"When I was a young man," said Sir Alec, "I made a similar mistake on behalf of a constituent. Ernie Bevin was Foreign Secretary at the time. He could have crucified me in the House with the knowledge he had. Instead he revealed everything over a drink in this room. I sometimes wish the public could see members in their quiet moments as well as in their rowdy ones."

Andrew thanked Sir Alec and walked thoughtfully back to the House. The *Evening Standard* poster outside the Commons caught his eye. 'O'Halloran arrested again.' He bought a copy, stood by the railings and began reading. Paddy O'Halloran had been detained in a Glasgow police station and charged with robbing the Bank of Scotland in Sauchiehall Street. Andrew wondered if his friends would allege it was another 'frame up' by the police until he read the next paragraph. "O'Halloran was arrested leaving the bank in possession of a shotgun and £25,000 in used notes. He said when apprehended by the police, 'I've just been clearing my account.'"

At home, Louise told him that Ricky Hodge had done him a favour.

"How's that possible?" asked Andrew.

"You won't take yourself so seriously in future," she smiled.

When Andrew conducted his next surgery in Edinburgh two weeks later he was surprised to see that Mrs Bloxham had made an appointment.

As he greeted her at the door he was even more surprised. She was wearing a bright crimplene dress and a new pair of squeaky brown leather shoes. She also looked as if 'Our Blessed Lady' might have to wait a few more years to receive her after all. Andrew motioned her to a seat.

"I came to thank you, Mr Fraser," she said, once she was settled.

"What for?" asked Andrew.

"For sending that nice young man round from Christie's. They auctioned great-grandma's table for me. I couldn't believe my luck – it fetched £1,400." Andrew smiled. "So it don't matter about the stain on the dress any more." She paused. "It even made up for having to eat off the floor for three months."

Simon steered the new Boundary Commission recommendations unspectacularly through the House as an order in Council, and suddenly he had lost his own constituency. His colleagues in Coventry were understanding, and nursed those wards that would become theirs at the next election in order that he might spend more time searching for a new seat.

Seven seats became available during the year but Simon was only interviewed for two of them. Both were almost on the Scottish border and both put him in second place. He began to appreciate what it must feel like for an Olympic favourite to be awarded the silver medal.

Ronnie Nethercote's monthly board reports began to paint an increasingly sombre picture, thus reflecting in real life what the politicians were decreeing in Parliament. Ronnie had decided to postpone going public until the climate was more advantageous. Simon couldn't disagree with the judgement, but when he checked his special overdraft facility the interest on his loans had pushed the figure in red to over £90,000.

When unemployment first passed the million mark and Ted Heath ordered a pay and prices freeze strikes broke out all over the country.

The new parliamentary session in the autumn was dominated by the issue of a Prices and Incomes policy. Charles Seymour became involved in putting the case for the Government. While he didn't always win every argument, he was now so well-briefed on his subject that he no longer feared making a fool of himself at the dispatch box. Raymond Gould and Andrew Fraser both made passionate speeches on behalf of the unions, but the Conservative majority beat them again and again.

However, the Prime Minister was moving inexorably towards a head-on clash with the unions and an early general election.

When all three party conferences were over members returned to the Commons aware that it was likely to be their last session before the general election. It was openly being said in the corridors that all the Prime Minister was waiting for was a catalyst. The miners provided it. In the middle of a bleak winter they called an all-out strike for more pay in defiance of the Government's new trade union legislation.

In a television interview the Prime Minister told the nation that with unemployment at an unprecedented 2,294,448 and the country on a three-day week he had to call an election to ensure that the rule of law be maintained. The inner Cabinet advised Heath to plump for 28 February 1974.

'Who runs the country?' became the Tory theme but seemed only to emphasise class differences, rather than uniting the country as Edward Heath had hoped.

Andrew Fraser had his doubts but he faced a different threat in his own constituency, where the Scottish National-ists were using the quarrel between the two major parties to promote their own cause. He returned to Scotland, to be warned by his father that the Scottish Nationalists were no longer a joke and that he would be facing a hard campaign against the robust local candidate, Jock McPherson.

Raymond Gould travelled back to Leeds, confident that the north-east industrial area would not tolerate Heath's high-handedness.

Charles felt sure that the people would back any party which had shown the courage to stand up to the unions, although the left wing, led vociferously by Tom Carson, made a great play of the 'two nations' issue, insisting that the Government were out to crush the Labour movement once and for all.

Charles drove down to Sussex to find his supporters glad of the chance to put those 'lazy trade unionists' in their place.

Simon, with no seat to fight, worked on in the Home Office right up to the day of the election, convinced that his career was facing only a temporary setback.

"I'll fight the first by-election that comes up," he promised Elizabeth.

"Even if it's a mining seat in South Wales?" she replied.

Many months had passed before Charles had found it possi-ble even to sustain a conversation with Fiona for any length of time. Neither wanted a divorce, both citing the ailing Earl of Bridgwater as their reason, although inconvenience and loss of face were nearer the truth. In public it would have been hard to detect the change in their relationship since they had never been given to overt affection.

Charles gradually became aware that it was possible for marriages to have been over for years without outsiders knowing it. Certainly the old earl never found out, because even on his death bed he told Fiona to hurry up and produce an heir.

"Do you think you'll ever forgive me?" Fiona once asked her husband.

"Never," he replied, with a finality that encouraged no further discourse.

During the three-week election campaign in Sussex they both went about their duties with a professionalism that masked their true feelings.

"How is your husband bearing up?" someone would enquire.

"Much enjoying the campaign and looking forward to returning to Government," was Fiona's stock reply.

"And how is dear Lady Fiona?" Charles was continuously asked.

"Never better than when she's helping in the constituency," was his.

On Sundays, at one church after another, he read the lesson with confidence while she sang 'Fight the good fight' in a clear contralto.

The demands of a rural constituency are considerably different from those of a city. Every village, however small, expects the member to visit them and to recall the local chairmen's names. Subtle changes were taking place: Fiona no longer whispered the names in Charles's ear. Charles no longer turned to her for advice.

During the campaign Charles would ring the photographer on the local paper to discover which events his editor had instructed him to cover that day. With the list of places and times in his hand Charles would arrive on each occasion a few minutes before the photographer. The Labour candidate complained officially to the local editor that Mr Seymour's photograph was never out of the paper.

"If you were present at these functions we would be only too happy to publish your photo," said the editor.

"But they never invite me," cried the Labour candidate.

They don't invite Seymour either, the editor wanted to say, but he somehow manages to be there. It was never far from the editor's mind that his proprietor was a Tory peer so he kept his mouth shut.

All the way up to election day Charles and Fiona opened bazaars, attended dinners, drew raffles and only just stopped short of kissing babies.

Once, when Fiona asked him, Charles admitted that he hoped to be moved to the Foreign Office as a Minister of State, and perhaps to be made a Privy Councillor.

On the last day of February they dressed in silence and went off to their local polling station to vote. The photographer was there on the steps to take their picture. They stood closer together than they had for some weeks, looking like a smart register office couple. Charles knew it would be the main photograph on the front page of the *Sussex Gazette* the following day, as surely as he knew the Labour candidate would be relegated to a half-column mention on the inside page not far from the obituaries.

The count in a rural seat is always taken the following morning at a more leisurely pace than is customary for its city cousins. So Charles anticipated that by the time he arrived in the town hall the Conservative majority in the House would already be assured. But it was not to be, and the result still hung in the balance that Friday morning.

Edward Heath did not concede when the newscasters predicted he would fail to be given the overall majority he required. Charles spent the day striding around the town hall with an anxious look on his face. The little piles of votes soon became larger and it was obvious that he would hold the seat with at least his usual 21,000 – or was it 22,000? – majority. He never could remember the exact figure. But as the day progressed it became more and more difficult to assess the national verdict.

The last result came in from Northern Ireland a little after four o'clock that afternoon and a BBC commentator announced –

Labour	301
Conservative	296
Liberal	14
Ulster Unionists	11
Scottish Nationalists	7
Welsh Nationalists	2
Others	4

Ted Heath invited the Liberal leader to join him at Downing Street for talks in the hope that they could form a coalition. The Liberals demanded a firm commitment to electoral reform and, in particular, to proportional representation by the next election. Heath knew he could never get his back-benchers to deliver. On the Monday morning he told the Queen in her drawing-room at Buckingham Palace that he was unable to form a Government. She called for Harold Wilson. He accepted her commission and drove back to Downing Street to enter the front door. Heath left by the back.

By the Tuesday afternoon every member, having watched the drama unfold, had returned to London. Raymond had increased his majority and now hoped that the Prime Minister had long since forgotten his resignation and would offer him a job.

Andrew had had the hard and unpleasant fight with Jock McPherson, just as his father had predicted, and held on to his seat by only 2,229.

Charles, still unsure of the exact majority by which he had won, drove back to London, resigned to Opposition. The one compensation was that he would be reinstated on the board of Seymour's where the knowledge he had gained as a minister of Trade and Industry could only be of value.

Simon left the Home Office on 1 March 1974 with little more than an empty red box to show for nine years as a parliamentarian.

BOOK THREE

1974-1977

MINISTERS OF STATE

CHAPTER SIXTEEN

"His diary looks rather full at the moment, Mr Charles."

"Well, as soon as it's convenient," Charles replied over the phone. He held on as he heard the pages being turned.

"12 March at ten-thirty, Mr Charles?"

"But that's nearly a fortnight away," he said, irritated.

"Mr Spencer has only just returned from the States and —"

"How about a lunch, then — at my club?" Charles interrupted.

"That couldn't be until after 19 March."

"Very well, then," said Charles. "12 March, at ten-thirty."

During the fourteen-day wait Charles had ample time to become frustrated by his seemingly aimless role in Opposition. No car came to pick him up and whisk him away to an office where real work had to be done. Worse, no one sought his opinion any longer on matters that affected the nation. He was going through a sharp bout of what is known as 'ex-ministers' blues'.

He was relieved when the day for the appointment with Derek Spencer at last came round. But although he arrived on time he was kept waiting for ten minutes before the chairman's secretary took him through.

"Good to see you after so long," said Spencer, coming round his desk to greet him. "It must be nearly six years since you've visited the bank."

"Yes, I suppose it is," said Charles. "But looking around the old place it feels like yesterday. You've been fully occupied, no doubt?"

"Like a Cabinet minister, but I hope with better results."

They both laughed.

"Of course I've kept in touch with what's been happening at the bank."

"Have you?" said Spencer.

"Yes, I've read all the reports you've sent out over the past years, not to mention the *Financial Times*'s coverage."

"I hope you feel we've progressed satisfactorily in your absence."

"Oh. Yes," said Charles, still standing. "Very impressive."

"Well, now what can I do for you?" asked the chairman, returning to his seat.

"Simple enough," said Charles, finally taking an unoffered chair. "I wish to be reinstated on the board."

There was a long silence.

"Well, it's not quite that easy, Charles. I've just recently appointed two new directors and . . ."

"Of course it's that easy," said Charles, his tone changing. "You have only to propose my name at the next meeting and it will go through, especially as you haven't a member of the family on the board at the present time."

"We have, as a matter of fact. Your brother the Earl of Bridgwater has become a non-executive director."

"What? Rupert never told me," said Charles. "Neither did you."

"True, but things have changed since –"

"Nothing has changed except my estimation of the value of your word," said Charles, suddenly realising that Spencer had never intended he should return to the board. "You gave me your assurance –"

"I won't be spoken to like this in my own office."

"If you're not careful, the next place I shall do it will be in your boardroom. Now, will you honour your undertaking or not?"

"I don't have to listen to threats from you, Seymour. Get out of my office before I have you removed. I can assure you that you will never sit on the board again as long as I'm chairman."

Charles turned and marched out, slamming the door as he

left. He wasn't sure with whom to discuss the problem and returned immediately to Eaton Square to consider a plan of campaign.

"What brings you home in the middle of the afternoon?" asked Fiona.

Charles hesitated, considered the question and then joined his wife in the kitchen and told her everything that had happened at the bank. Fiona continued to grate some cheese as she listened to her husband.

"Well, one thing is certain," she said, not having spoken for several minutes but delighted that Charles had confided in her. "After that fracas, you can't both be on the board."

"So what do you think I ought to do, old girl?"

Fiona smiled; it was the first time he had called her that for nearly two years. "Every man has his secrets," she said. "I wonder what Mr Spencer's are?"

"He's such a dull middle-class fellow I doubt if –"

"I've just had a letter from Seymour's Bank," interrupted Fiona.

"What about?"

"Only a shareholder's circular. It seems Margaret Trubshaw is retiring after twelve years as the board secretary. Rumour has it she wanted to do five more years, but the chairman has someone else in mind. I think I might have lunch with her."

Charles returned his wife's smile.

Andrew's appointment as Minister of State at the Home Office came as no surprise to anyone except his three-year-old son, who quickly discovered how to empty any red boxes that were left unlocked, refilling them with marbles or sweets, and even managing to fit a football into one. As Robert didn't fully understand 'For Your Eyes Only', it didn't seem to make a lot of difference that Cabinet committee papers were sometimes found glued together with old bubble-gum.

"Can you remove that latest stain in the red box?"

"Good heavens, what caused it?" asked Louise, staring down at a jelly-like blob.

"Frog spawn," said Andrew, grinning.

"He's a brain-washed Russian spy," warned Louise, "with a mental age about the same as most of your colleagues in the House. Yes, I'll remove the stain if you sit down and write that letter."

Andrew nodded his agreement.

Among the many letters of commiseration Simon received when he did not return to the House was one from Andrew Fraser. Simon could imagine him sitting in his old office and implementing the decisions he had been involved in making just a few weeks before.

There was also a letter from Ronnie Nethercote inviting him to return to the board of Nethercote and Company at £5,000 a year, which even Elizabeth acknowledged as a generous gesture.

It was not long before Ronnie Nethercote had made Simon an executive director of the company. Simon enjoyed negotiating with the trade unions at a level he had not experienced before. Ronnie made it clear how he would have dealt with the 'Commie bastards' given half a chance. "Lock them all up until they learn to do a day's work."

"You would have lasted about a week in the House of Commons," Simon told him.

"After a week with those windbags I'd have been only too happy to return to the real world."

Simon smiled. Ronnie, he felt, was like so many others – imagining all Members of Parliament were unemployable except the one they knew.

Raymond waited until the last Government appointment was announced before he finally gave up any hope of a job. Several leading political journalists pointed out that he had been left on the back benches while lesser men had been given Government posts but it was scant comfort. Reluctantly he returned to Lincoln's Inn to continue his practice at the bar.

Harold Wilson, starting his third administration, made it

clear that he would govern as long as possible before calling an election. But as he did not have an overall majority in the House few members believed that he could hold out for more than a matter of months.

Fiona returned home after her lunch with Miss Trubshaw with a large Cheshire Cat grin on her face. It remained firmly in place during the hours she had to wait for Charles to get back from the Commons after the last division.

"You look pleased with yourself," said Charles, shaking out his umbrella before closing the front door. His wife stood in the hallway, her arms crossed.

"How has your day been?" she asked.

"So-so," said Charles, wanting to hear the news. "But what about you?"

"Oh, pleasant enough. I had coffee with your mother this morning. She seems very well. A little cold in the head, otherwise –"

"To hell with my mother. How did your lunch with Miss Trubshaw go?"

"I wondered how long it would take you to get round to that."

She continued to wait just as long as it took for them to walk into the drawing-room and sit down. "After seventeen years as secretary to your father and twelve years as secretary to the board there isn't much Miss Trubshaw doesn't know about Seymour's or its present chairman," Fiona began.

"So what did you discover?"

"Which do you want to hear about first, the name of his mistress or the number of his Swiss bank account?"

Fiona revealed everything she had learned over her two-hour lunch, explaining that Miss Trubshaw usually only drank fortified wine but on this occasion she had downed most of a vintage bottle of Pommard. Charles's smile grew wider and wider as each fact came pouring out. To Fiona he looked like a boy who has been given a box of chocolates and keeps discovering another layer underneath.

"Well done, old girl," he said when she had come to the end of her tale. "But how do I get all the proof I need?"

"I've made a deal with our Miss Trubshaw."

"You've what?"

"A deal. With Miss Trubshaw. You get the proof if she remains as secretary to the board for a further five years, and no loss of benefit to her pension."

"Is that all she wants?" said Charles, guardedly.

"And the price of another lunch at the Savoy Grill when you're invited back on the board."

Unlike many of his Labour colleagues Raymond now enjoyed dressing up in white tie and tails and mixing with London society. An invitation to the annual bankers' banquet at the Guildhall was no exception. The Prime Minister was the guest of honour and Raymond wondered if he would drop a hint as to how long he expected the parliamentary session to last before he felt he had to call an election.

At the pre-dinner drinks Raymond had a quick word with the Lord Mayor before becoming involved in a conversation with a circuit court judge on the problems of the parity of sentencing.

When dinner was announced Raymond found his seat on one of the long fingers stretching away from the top table. He checked his place card. Raymond Gould QC, MP. On his right was the chairman of Chloride, Michael Edwardes, and on his left an American banker who had just taken up an appointment in the City.

Raymond found Michael Edwardes's views on how the Prime Minister should tackle the nationalised industries fascinating, but he devoted far more of his attention to the Euro Bond manager from Chase Manhattan. She must have been thirty, Raymond decided, if only because of her elevated position at the bank and her claim to have been an undergraduate at Wellesley at the time of Kennedy's death. He would have put Kate Garthwaite at far younger and was not surprised to learn she played tennis in the summer and swam every day during the winter – to keep her weight down, she confided. She had a warm, oval face, and her dark hair was cut in what Raymond thought was a Mary Quant style. Her nose turned up slightly at the end and would have cost a lot of money for a plastic surgeon to reproduce. There was no chance of seeing her legs as they were covered by a long dress, but what he could see left Raymond more than interested.

"I see there's an 'MP' behind your name, Mr Gould. May I ask which party you represent?" she asked, in an accent heard more often in Boston.

"I'm a Socialist, Mrs Garthwaite. Where do your sympathies lie on this occasion?"

"I would have voted Labour at the last election if I had been qualified," she declared.

"Should I be surprised?" he teased.

"You certainly should. My ex-husband is a Republican congressman."

He was about to ask his next question when the toastmaster called for silence. For the first time Raymond turned his eyes to the top table and the Prime Minister. Harold Wilson's speech stuck firmly to economic problems and the role of a Labour Government in the City and gave no clue as to the timing of the next election. Nevertheless, Raymond considered it a worthwhile evening. He had made a useful contact with the chairman of a large public company. And he had acquired Kate's telephone number.

The chairman of Seymour's reluctantly agreed to see him a second time, but it was obvious from the moment Charles walked in when no hand was proffered that Derek Spencer intended it to be a short interview.

"I thought I ought to see you personally," said Charles as he settled back in the comfortable leather chair and slowly lit a cigarette, "rather than raise my query at the AGM next month."

The first sign of apprehension began to show on the chairman's face, but he said nothing.

"I'm rather keen to discover why the bank should pay out a monthly cheque of £400 to an employee called Miss Janet Darrow, whom I have never come across, although it appears she has been on the payroll for over five years. The cheques, it seems, have been going to a branch of Lloyds in Kensington."

Derek Spencer's face became flushed.

"What I am at a loss to discover," continued Charles after he had inhaled deeply, "is what services Miss Darrow has been supplying to the bank. They must be quite impressive to have earned her £25,000 over the last five years. I appreciate that this is a small amount when you consider the bank's turnover of 123 million last year, but my grandfather instilled in me at an early age the belief that if one took care of the pennies the pounds would take care of themselves."

Still Derek Spencer said nothing, although beads of sweat had appeared on his forehead. Suddenly Charles's tone changed. "If I find I am not a member of the board by the time of the Annual General Meeting I feel it will be my duty to point out this slight discrepancy in the bank's accounts to the other shareholders present."

"You're a bastard, Seymour," the chairman said quietly.

"Now that is not accurate. I am the second son of the former chairman of this bank and I bear a striking resemblance to my father, although everyone says I have my mother's eyes."

"What's the deal?"

"No deal. You will merely keep to your original agreement and see that I am reinstated on the board before the AGM. You will also cease any further payments to Miss Janet Darrow immediately."

"If I agree, will you swear never to mention this matter to anyone again?"

"I will. And, unlike you, I am in the habit of keeping my word."

Charles rose from his chair, leaned over the desk and stubbed out his cigarette in the chairman's ashtray.

Andrew Fraser was surprised when he heard that Jock McPherson wanted to see him. The two men had never been on good terms since McPherson had failed to be elected to the

Scottish Labour Party Executive Committee and had then left the party to stand against him at Edinburgh Carlton. Since McPherson had switched his allegiance they had barely been on speaking terms. However, Andrew realised it would be foolish not to see him after the SNP's sweeping successes in the election.

Andrew was even more surprised when McPherson asked if all seven SNP Members of Parliament could also attend the meeting, not in Andrew's office but somewhere private. He agreed, even more mystified.

McPherson and his band of renegade Scots arrived together at Cheyne Walk, looking as though they had already held a meeting between themselves. Andrew offered them a variety of seats, including the dining-room chairs, a pouffe and even the kitchen stool, apologising that his London flat had never been intended to accommodate nine men in the drawing-room.

While the men settled themselves Andrew remained standing by the mantelpiece, facing Jock McPherson who had obviously been chosen to act as their spokesman.

"I'll get straight to the point," McPherson began. "We want you to fight under the SNP banner at the next election."

Andrew tried not to show his disbelief, and began, "I don't feel . . ."

"Hear me out," said McPherson, raising his massive palms. "We want you to contest the Edinburgh Carlton seat not just as a Scottish Nationalist candidate but as leader of the party."

Andrew still couldn't believe what he was hearing but remained silent.

"We're convinced you'll lose your seat in any case if you stand as a Socialist," McPherson continued, "but we realise that there are many people in Scotland who, whatever their political views, admire what you have achieved in the nine years you have been in the House. After all, man, you were brought up and educated in Edinburgh. With you as leader, we believe we could capture forty to fifty of the seventy-one seats in Scotland. And I may add that your own party is moving inexorably to the left, a state of affairs that I can't believe you are altogether happy about."

Andrew still made no comment. He listened as each one of the MPs put his own view, which became predictable long before the last one had spoken. Every Scottish tone from a Highland lilt to a Glasgow growl was represented in the voices. It became clear that they had given the matter considerable thought and were obviously sincere. "I am very flattered, gentlemen," he began when the last one had said his piece. "And I assure you I will give your offer my serious consideration."

"Thank you," said McPherson. They all stood up like clan leaders in the presence of a new chief.

"We'll wait to hear from you then," said McPherson. One by one they shook hands with their host before filing out.

As soon as they had left Andrew went straight into the kitchen where Robert was still waiting impatiently to play football before going to bed.

"In a moment, in a moment," he said in response to his son's noisy demands. "I'll join you in the garden."

"And what did that lot want?" enquired Louise, as she continued to peel the potatoes.

Andrew went over the details of their proposition.

"And how did you respond?"

"I didn't. I shall wait a week and then decline as gracefully as possible."

"What made you decide against the offer so quickly?"

"I don't like being told by Jock McPherson, or anyone else for that matter, that I will lose my seat at the next election if I don't fall in with their plans." He headed towards the kitchen door. "I'll be back to the red box as soon as I've scored a couple of goals against MacPele." A moment later he had joined Robert in the garden.

"Now listen, clever boots, I'm going to teach you how to feint a pass so that your opponent goes one way while you go the other."

"Sounds just like politics to me," muttered Louise, watching them out of the kitchen window.

27 Eaton Square,
London, SW1
23 April 1974

Dear Derek,

Thank you for your letter of 18 April and your kind
invitation to rejoin the board of Seymour's. I am delighted
to accept and look forward to working with you again.

Yours sincerely,
Charles Seymour.

Fiona checked the wording and nodded. Short and to the
point. "Shall I post it?"

"Yes, please," said Charles as the phone rang.

He picked it up. "730—9712. Charles Seymour speaking."

"Oh, hello, Charles. It's Simon Kerslake."

"Hello, Simon," said Charles, trying to sound pleased to
hear from his former colleague. "What's it like out there in
the real world?"

"Not much fun, which is exactly why I'm phoning. I've
been short-listed for Pucklebridge, Sir Michael Harbour-
Baker's seat. He's nearly seventy and has decided not to
stand again at the next election. As his constituency touches
the south border of yours, I thought you might be able to put
in a word for me again."

"Delighted," said Charles. "I'll speak to the chairman
tonight. You can rely on me, and good luck. It would be nice
to have you back in the House."

Simon gave him his home number which Charles repeated
slowly, as if he were writing it down.

"I'll be in touch," said Charles.

"I really appreciate your help."

Simon put down the phone.

Elizabeth looked up from her copy of *The Lancet*.

"I don't trust that man," she said.

"A woman's intuition again?" said Simon smiling. "You
were wrong about Ronnie Nethercote."

"That's yet to be proved."

It was several days before Kate Garthwaite agreed to see
Raymond again. And when she eventually joined him for

dinner at the House she was not overwhelmed or flattered and she certainly didn't hang on his every word.

She was lively, fun, intelligent and well informed and they began to see each other regularly. As the months passed Raymond found himself missing her at weekends when he was in Leeds with Joyce. Kate enjoyed her independence and made none of the demands on him that Stephanie had, never once suggesting he spend more time with her or that she might leave clothes behind in the flat.

Raymond sipped his coffee. "That was a memorable meal," he said, falling back into the sofa.

"Only by the standards of the House of Commons," replied Kate.

Raymond put an arm round her shoulder before kissing her gently on the lips.

"What! Rampant sex as well as cheap Beaujolais?" she exclaimed, stretching over and pouring herself some more coffee.

"I wish you wouldn't always make a joke of our relationship," said Raymond, stroking the back of her hair.

"I have to," said Kate quietly.

"Why?" Raymond turned to face her.

"Because I'm frightened of what might happen if I take it seriously."

Raymond leant over and kissed her again. "Don't be frightened. You're the best thing that's happened to me in my whole life."

"That's what I'm worried about," said Kate, turning away.

Charles sat through the Annual General Meeting in silence. The chairman made his report for the year ending March 1974 before welcoming two new directors to the board and the return of Charles Seymour.

There were several questions from the floor which Derek Spencer had no trouble in handling. As Charles had promised, there was not even a hint of Miss Janet Darrow. Miss Trubshaw had let Fiona know that the payment had been stopped and also mentioned that she was still worried that her contract was coming to an end on 1 July.

When the chairman brought the AGM to a close Charles asked courteously if he could spare him a moment.

"Of course," said Spencer, looking relieved that the meeting had gone through without a hitch. "What can I do for you?"

"I think it might be wiser to talk in the privacy of your office."

The chairman glanced at him sharply but led him back to his room.

Charles settled himself comfortably in the leather chair once more and removed some papers from his inside pocket. Peering down at them he asked, "What does BX41207122, Bank Rombert, Zurich, mean to you?"

"You said you would never mention –"

"Miss Darrow," said Charles. "And I shall keep my word. But now, as a director of the bank, I am trying to find out what BX41207122 means to you?"

"You know damn well what it means," said the chairman, banging his clenched fist on the desk.

"I know it's your *private*" – Charles emphasised the last word – "account in Zurich."

"You could never prove anything," said Derek Spencer defiantly.

"I agree with you, but what I am able to prove," said Charles, shuffling through the papers that were resting on his lap, "is that you have been using Seymour's money to do private deals, leaving the profit in your Zurich account without informing the board."

"I've done nothing that will harm the bank, and you know it."

"I know the money has been returned with interest, and I could never prove the bank had suffered any loss. Nevertheless, the board might take a dim view of your activities remembering they pay you £40,000 a year to make profits for the bank, not for yourself."

"When they saw all the figures they would at worst rap me over the knuckles."

"I doubt if the Director of Public Prosecutions would take the same lenient attitude if he saw these documents," said Charles, holding up the papers that had been resting on his lap.

"You'd ruin the bank's name."

"And you would probably spend the next ten years in jail. If, however, you did get away with it you would be finished in the City, and by the time your legal fees had been paid there wouldn't be much left of that nest-egg in Zurich."

"So what do you want this time?" demanded Spencer, sounding exasperated.

"Your job," said Charles.

"My job?" said Spencer in disbelief. "Do you imagine because you've been a junior minister you're capable of running a successful merchant bank?" he added scornfully.

"I didn't say I would run it. I can buy a competent chief executive to do that."

"Then what will you be doing?"

"I shall be the chairman of Seymour's which will convince City institutions that we wish to continue in the traditions of generations of my family."

"You're bluffing," stammered Spencer.

"If you are still in this building in twenty-four hours' time," said Charles, "I shall send these to the DPP."

There was a long silence.

"If I agreed," said Spencer at last, "I would expect two years' salary as compensation."

"One year," said Charles. Spencer hesitated, then nodded slowly. Charles rose to his feet and put the papers resting on his lap back into his inside pocket.

They consisted of nothing more than the morning mail from Sussex Downs.

Simon felt the interview had gone well but Elizabeth was not so sure. They sat huddled in a room with five other candidates and their wives, patiently waiting.

He thought back to his answers, and to the eight men and four women on the committee.

"You must admit it's the most ideal seat I've been considered for," said Simon.

"Yes, but the chairman kept eyeing you suspiciously."

"But Millburn mentioned that he had been at Eton with Charles Seymour."

"That's what worries me," whispered Elizabeth.

"A 15,000 majority at the last election and only forty minutes from London. We could even buy a little cottage . . ."

"If they invite you to represent them."

"At least this time you were able to tell them you would be willing to live in the constituency."

"So would anyone in their right mind," said Elizabeth.

The chairman came out and asked if Mr and Mrs Kerslake would be kind enough to return once more to see the committee.

Oh, God, thought Simon. What else can they want to know?

"It's too near London to be my fault this time," chuckled Elizabeth.

The committee sat and stared at them with long faces.

"Ladies and gentlemen," said the chairman. "After our lengthy deliberations, I formally propose that Mr Simon Kerslake be invited to contest Pucklebridge at the next election. Those in favour . . .?"

All twelve hands went up.

"Those against . . .?"

"Carried unanimously," said the chairman. He then turned to Simon. "Do you wish to address your committee?"

The prospective Conservative Member of Parliament for Pucklebridge rose. They all waited expectantly.

"I don't know what to say, except that I'm very happy and honoured and I can't wait for a general election."

They all laughed and came forward and surrounded them. Elizabeth dried her eyes before anyone reached her.

About an hour later the chairman accompanied Simon and Elizabeth back to their car and bade them goodnight. Simon wound down his window.

"I knew you were the right man," Millburn said, "as soon

as Charles Seymour phoned" – Simon smiled – "and warned me to avoid you like the plague."

"Could you tell Miss Trubshaw to come in?" Charles asked his secretary.

Margaret Trubshaw arrived a few moments later and remained standing in front of his desk. She couldn't help but notice the change of furniture in the room. The modern Conran suite had been replaced by a leather club-like sofa. Only the picture of the eleventh Earl of Bridgwater remained in place.

"Miss Trubshaw," began Charles, "since Mr Spencer has felt it necessary to resign so suddenly I think it important for the bank to keep some continuity now that I'm taking over as chairman."

Miss Trubshaw stood like a Greek statue, her hands hidden in the sleeves of her dress.

"With that in mind, the board has decided to extend your contract with the bank for a further five years. Naturally, there will be no loss in your pension rights."

"Thank you, Mr Charles."

"Thank you, Miss Trubshaw."

Miss Trubshaw almost bowed as she left the room.

"And Miss Trubshaw?"

"Yes, Mr Charles," she said, holding on to the door knob.

"I believe my wife is expecting a call from you. Something about inviting you to lunch at the Savoy Grill."

CHAPTER
SEVENTEEN

"A blue shirt," said Raymond, looking at the Turnbull and Asser label with suspicion. "A *blue* shirt," he repeated.

"A fortieth-birthday present," shouted Kate from the kitchen.

I shall never wear it, he thought, and smiled to himself.

"And what's more, you'll wear it," she said, her Boston accent carrying a slight edge.

"You even know what I'm thinking," he complained as she came in from the kitchen. He always thought how elegant she looked in her tailored office suit.

"It's because you're so predictable, Carrot Top."

"Anyway, how did you know it was my birthday?"

"A massive piece of detective work," said Kate, "with the help of an outside agent and a small payment."

"An outside agent. Who?"

"The local paper shop, my darling. In the *Sunday Times* they tell you the name of every distinguished person celebrating a birthday in the following seven days. In a week during which only the mediocre were born, you made it."

Raymond had to laugh.

"Now listen, Carrot Top."

Raymond pretended to hate his new nickname. "Do you have to call me by that revolting name?"

"Yes. I can't stand Raymond."

He scowled. "In any case, carrot tops are green."

"No comment. Try on your shirt."

"Now?"

"Now."

He took off his black coat and waistcoat, removed his white shirt and eased the stud on his stiff collar, leaving a small circle above his Adam's apple. Curly red hairs stuck up all over his chest. He quickly put on the new gift. The fabric had a pleasant soft feel about it. He started to do up the buttons, but Kate walked over and undid the top two.

"You know what? You've brought a whole new meaning to the word 'uptight'."

Raymond scowled again.

"But in the right clothes you could even pass for good looking. Now. Where shall we go to celebrate your birthday?"

"The House of Commons?" suggested Raymond.

"Good God," said Kate. "I said celebrate, not hold a wake. What about Annabel's?"

"I can't afford to be seen in Annabel's."

"With me, you mean?"

"No, no, you silly woman, because I'm a Socialist."

"If members of the Labour party are not allowed to indulge in a good meal then perhaps it's time for you to change parties. In my country one only sees the Democrats in the best restaurants."

"Oh, do be serious, Kate."

"I intend to be. Now what have you been up to in the House lately?"

"Not a lot," said Raymond sheepishly. "I've been snowed under in court and . . ."

"Precisely. It's time you did something positive before your colleagues in Parliament forget you exist."

"Have you anything particular in mind?" asked Raymond, folding his arms across his chest.

"As a matter of fact, I have," said Kate. "I read in the same Sunday paper as the one in which I discovered your best-kept secret that it is proving difficult for the Labour party to repeal the Tories' trade union legislation. It appears there are long-term legal implications which the front bench are still trying to find a way round. Why don't you set that so-called 'first class' mind of yours to working out the legal niceties?"

"Not such a stupid idea." Raymond had become used to Kate's political sense, and when he had remarked on it she had only said, "Just another bad habit I picked up from my ex-husband."

"Now, where do we celebrate?" she asked.

"Compromise," said Raymond.

"I'm all ears."

"The Dorchester."

"If you insist," said Kate, not sounding over-enthusiastic.

Raymond started to change his shirt.

"No, no, no, Carrot Top, people have been known to wear blue shirts at the Dorchester."

"But I haven't got a tie to match," said Raymond triumphantly.

Kate thrust her hand into the Turnbull and Asser bag and drew out a dark blue silk tie.

"But it's got a pattern on it," said Raymond in disgust. "What will you expect next?"

"Contact lenses," said Kate.

Raymond stared at her, and blinked.

On the way out of the door Raymond's gaze fell upon the brightly wrapped package that Joyce had posted from Leeds earlier in the week. He had completely forgotten to open it.

"Damn," said Charles, putting down *The Times* and draining his coffee.

"What's the problem?" asked Fiona as she poured out another cup.

"Kerslake's been selected for Pucklebridge, which means he's back in the House for life. Obviously my chat to Archie Millburn had no effect."

"Why have you got it in for Kerslake?" asked Fiona.

Charles folded the paper and considered the question. "It's quite simple really, old girl. I think he's the only one of my contemporaries who could stop me leading the party."

"Why him in particular?"

"I first came across him when he was President of the Union at Oxford. He was damn good then, and now he's better. He had rivals, but he brushed them aside like flies.

No, despite his background, Kerslake's the one man left who frightens me."

"It's a long race yet, my darling, and he could still stumble."

"So could I, but what he doesn't realise is that I shall be putting out some of his hurdles."

Andrew worded the letter very carefully. He assured Jock McPherson and his colleagues that he had been flattered by their approach, but explained that he had decided his loyalties were still firmly based in the Labour party.

He accepted the point Jock had made about the left trying to gain control, but felt that every democratic party was bound to have a maverick element within its ranks, which was not necessarily unhealthy. He added that he considered the offer to have been confidential on both sides.

"Why add that postscript?" asked Louise when she had read the letter through.

"It's only fair to Jock," said Andrew. "If it gets around I turned him down it will have the opposite effect to the one they were trying to create."

"I'm not so sure they will act in the same magnanimous way when the next election comes round."

"Ah, Jock will make a lot of noise, but he's all right underneath . . ."

"That isn't what your father says about him," said Louise. "He's sure they'll want revenge."

"Father always sees grubs under even the greenest leaf."

"So if we're not about to celebrate your leadership of the Scottish Nationalists we'll have to be satisfied with celebrating your fortieth birthday."

"But that's not for at least —"

"— another month, a week before Robert's fourth birthday."

"How would you like to commemorate the occasion, darling?"

"I thought we might have a week in the Algarve on our own."

"Why don't we have two weeks? Then we can celebrate your fortieth birthday as well?"

"Andrew Fraser, you just lost yourself one vote in Edinburgh Carlton."

Simon listened intently to Ronnie's report at the monthly board meeting. Two tenants had not paid their quarterly rent, and another quarter date was fast approaching. Ronnie's solicitors had sent firm reminders, followed a month later by writs but this action had also failed to elicit any money.

"It only proves what I feared most," said Ronnie.

"What's that?" asked Simon.

"They just haven't got the cash."

"So we will have to replace them with new tenants."

"Simon, when you next travel from Beaufort Street to Whitechapel start counting the 'To Let' signs on office blocks along the way. When you've passed a hundred you'll find you still haven't reached the City."

"So what do you think we should do about it?"

"Try and sell one of our larger properties to secure cash flow. We can at least be thankful that even at these prices they are still worth a lot more than our borrowings. It's the companies who are the other way around that have to call in the receiver."

Simon thought about his overdraft, now approaching £100,000, and was beginning to wish he had accepted Ronnie's generous offer to buy back his shares. He accepted reluctantly that the opportunity had now passed.

When the board meeting was over he drove to St Mary's to pick up Elizabeth. It was to be one of their three-times-a-week journeys to Pucklebridge as Simon tried to get round all the villages before Wilson called an election.

Archie Millburn was turning out to be a conscientious chairman who had accompanied them on nearly every trip.

"He's been very kind to us," said Elizabeth, on their way down.

"He certainly has," said Simon. "Remember he also has to

run Millburn Electronics. But, as he reminds us so often, once he's introduced us to every village chairman we'll be on our own."

"Have you ever discovered why he and Charles Seymour didn't see eye to eye?"

"No, he hasn't mentioned his name since that night. All I know for certain is that they were at school together."

"So what do you intend to do about Seymour?"

"Not a lot I can do," said Simon. "Except keep my eyes very wide open."

"The man who has deserted Edinburgh once too often" – Andrew read the Scottish Nationalist leaflet that had been sent to him that morning by his father. It was full of half-truths and innuendoes.

"Andrew Fraser, the man who has forgotten Edinburgh, should no longer be allowed to represent a Scottish seat." It went on to declare: "He now lives far away from the problems of his constituents in a smart apartment building in fashionable Chelsea among his Tory friends. He visits the City of Edinburgh only a few times a year to make well-publicised appearances . . . Has being a minister gone to his head?"

"How dare they?" cried Louise in a rage. Andrew had never seen his wife so angry. "How dare they come to my home, offer you the leadership of their dreadful little party and then write such a pack of lies? And did you read this?" she added, pointing to the last paragraph, "'His wife Louise, née Forsyth',", she read out aloud, "'comes from one of the wealthiest families in Scotland. She is a close relation of the owners of Forsyth's in Princes Street.' I'm a second cousin once removed, and they don't even give me a discount in the main store."

Andrew started to laugh.

"What's so funny?"

He took her in his arms. "I always suffered under the illusion that you would inherit the Forsyth empire and I would never have to work again," he mocked. "Now we shall have to live off Robert's earnings as a star football player."

"Don't joke, Andrew. It won't seem funny when the election comes round."

"I'm far more concerned about the extreme left trying to infiltrate my General Management Committee," he said, his voice changing, "than I am by Jock McPherson's band of mad little islanders. But at this moment of time my red box is too full to worry about either of them."

Raymond made such a penetrating speech during the second reading of the new Trade Union Bill that the Whips put him on the standing committee, the perfect medium for him to display his skills as the committee debated each clause, point by point. He was able to show his colleagues where the legal pitfalls were and how to find a way round them. The rest of the committee soon learnt from Raymond the meaning of 'mastering a brief', and it was not long before trade union leaders were calling him at the House and even at his flat to learn his views on how their members should react to a host of different legal problems. Raymond showed patience with each of them and, more important, gave them excellent professional advice for the price of a phone call. He found it ironic how quickly they chose to forget that he was the author of *Full Employment at any Cost?* Snippets began to appear in the national press, ranging from laudatory comments from those involved with the bill to a pointed suggestion in the *Guardian* that, whatever had happened in the past, it would be insupportable if Raymond Gould were not made a member of the Government in the near future.

"If they were to offer you a job, would it make any difference to our relationship?" Kate asked.

"Certainly," said Raymond. "I shall have found the perfect excuse not to wear your blue shirts."

Harold Wilson held the crumbling edifice together for a further six months before finally having to call a general election. He chose 10 October 1974.

Raymond immediately returned to his constituency to fight his fifth campaign. When he met Joyce at Leeds City station he couldn't help remembering that his dumpy wife was only four years older than Kate. He kissed her on the cheek as one might a distant relative, then she drove him back to their Chapel Allerton home.

Joyce chatted away on the journey home and it became clear that the constituency was under control and that this time Fred Padgett was well prepared for a general election. "He hasn't really stopped since the last one," she said. As for Joyce, she was undoubtedly better organised than the agent and the secretary put together. What was more, Raymond thought, she enjoyed it. He glanced over at her and couldn't help thinking she even looked prettier at election time.

Unlike his colleagues in rural seats, Raymond did not have to make speech after speech in little village halls. His votes were to be found in the high street where he addressed the midday shoppers through a megaphone, and walked around supermarkets, pubs and clubs, grasping hands before repeating the whole process a few streets away.

Joyce set her husband a schedule that allowed few people in the Leeds community to escape him. Some saw him a dozen times during the three-week campaign – most of them at the football match on the Saturday afternoon before the election.

Once the game was over Raymond was back trooping round the working men's clubs, drinking pint after pint of John Smith's bitter. He accepted it was inevitable that he would put on half a stone during any election campaign. He dreaded what Kate's comments would be when she saw him. Somehow he always found a few minutes in each day to steal away and phone her. She seemed so busy and full of news it only made Raymond feel downcast; she couldn't possibly be missing him.

The local trade unionists backed Raymond to the hilt. They may have found him stuck up and distant in the past, but they knew 'where his heart was', as they confided to anyone who would listen. They banged on doors, delivered leaflets, drove cars to polling booths. They rose before he did in the morning and could still be found preaching to the converted after the pubs had thrown them out at night.

Raymond and Joyce cast their votes in the local secondary

school on the Thursday of election day, looking forward to a large Labour victory. The Labour party duly gained a working majority in the House of forty-three over the Conservatives, but only three over all the parties combined. Nevertheless Harold Wilson looked set for another five years when the Queen invited him to form his fourth administration. The count in Leeds that night gave Raymond his biggest majority ever: 12,207 votes.

He spent the whole of Friday and Saturday thanking his constituents, then set out for London on the Sunday evening.

"He must invite you to join the Government this time," said Joyce, as she walked down the platform of Leeds City station with her husband.

"I wonder," said Raymond, kissing his wife on the other cheek. He waved at her as the train pulled out of the station. She waved back enthusiastically.

"I do like your new blue shirt, it really suits you," were the last words he heard her say.

During the election campaign Charles had had to spend a lot of time at the bank because of a run on the pound. Fiona seemed to be everywhere in the constituency at once, assuring voters that her husband was just a few yards behind.

After the little slips were counted the swing against Charles to the Labour candidate didn't amount to more than one per cent in his 22,000 majority. When he heard the overall result he returned to London resigned to a long spell in Opposition. As he began to catch up with his colleagues in the House, he found many of them already saying openly that Heath had to go after two election defeats in a row.

Charles knew then that he would have to make up his mind once again on where he stood over the election of a new party leader, and that once again he must pick the right man.

Andrew Fraser returned to London after a gruelling and unhappy campaign. The Scottish Nationalists had concentrated their attack on him, Jock McPherson sailing close to libel and slander. Sir Duncan advised his son against any

legal action. "Only plays into their hands," he warned.
"Small parties always benefit from the publicity."

Louise wanted him to inform the press that he had been
offered the leadership of the SNP but Andrew felt it would
serve no purpose, and might even rebound against him: and
he also reminded her that he had given his word. In the last
week of the campaign he spent most of his time trying – and
failing – to stop Frank Boyle, a Communist, who had recently moved from Glasgow, from being elected to his General
Management Committee. On polling day he scraped home
by 1,656, Jock McPherson taking second place. At least he
looked secure for another five years; but it didn't help that the
Scottish Nationalists had increased their overall seats in the
House to eleven.

Andrew, Louise and Robert took the plane to London on
the Sunday night to find the red box awaiting them and a
message that the Prime Minister wanted Andrew to continue
as Minister of State at the Home Office.

Simon had a glorious campaign. He and Elizabeth had
started moving into their new cottage the day the election
was announced, thankful that, now she had to commute, her
salary at the hospital had made it possible for them to employ
a nanny. A double bed and a couple of chairs sufficed as
Elizabeth cooked on an old Aga from provisions still packed
in tea chests. They seemed to use the same two forks for
everything. During the campaign Simon covered the 200-
square-mile constituency for a second time and assured his
wife that she need only take the final week off from from her
duties at St Mary's.

The voters of Pucklebridge sent Simon Kerslake back to
Parliament with a majority of 18,419, the largest in the
constituency's history. The local people had quickly come to
the conclusion that they now had a member who was destined to have a Cabinet career.

Kate kept her remarks very gentle as it became obvious by
the Monday night that the Prime Minister was not going to
offer Raymond a job in the new administration. She cooked

his favourite meal of roast beef – overdone – and Yorkshire pudding in the flat that night, but he didn't comment on it and hardly spoke.

CHAPTER
EIGHTEEN

After Simon had been back at the Commons for a week he felt a sense of *déjà vu*, a feeling that most members returning to the House for a second or even third time often experience. The sense was heightened by finding everything unchanged, even the policeman who greeted him at the Members' Entrance. When Edward Heath announced his Shadow team Simon was not surprised that he wasn't included, as he never had been a known supporter of the Tory leader. He was, however, mystified but not displeased to discover Charles Seymour was not among the names to be found in the Shadow Cabinet.

"Do you regret turning him down now the full team has been published?" asked Fiona, looking up from her copy of the *Daily Mail*.

"It wasn't an easy decision but I think it'll prove right in the long run," replied Charles, buttering another piece of toast.

"What did he offer in the end?"

"Shadow Minister of Industry."

"That sounds rather interesting," said Fiona.

"Everything about it was interesting except the salary, which would have been nothing. Don't forget the bank pays me £40,000 a year while I'm chairman."

Fiona folded her paper. "But you've just appointed a full-time chief executive, so your responsibilities at the bank should be only part-time compared with when you took the chair over. So what's your real reason?"

Charles accepted that he could rarely fool Fiona. "The

truth is that I'm far from certain Ted will be leading the party at the next election."

"Then who will if he doesn't?" asked Fiona.

"Whoever's got the guts to oppose him."

"I'm not sure I understand," said Fiona, beginning to clear away the plates.

"Everyone accepts that he has to allow his name to go forward for re-election now that he's lost twice in a row."

"That's fair enough," agreed Fiona.

"But as he has appointed all possible contenders to the Cabinet or Shadow Cabinet over the last ten years, someone he has selected in the past will have to oppose him. No one of lesser stature would stand a chance."

"Is there a member of the Shadow Cabinet willing to stand?" asked Fiona, returning to her seat at the end of the table.

"One or two are considering it, but the problem is that if they lose it could easily end their political career," said Charles, folding his napkin.

"But if they win?"

"They will undoubtedly be the next Prime Minister."

"Interesting dilemma. And what are you going to do about it?"

"I'm not supporting anyone at the moment, but I've got my eyes wide open," said Charles, folding his copy of *The Times* and rising from the table.

"Is there a front runner?" asked Fiona, looking up at her husband.

"No, not really. Although Kerslake is trying to rally support for Margaret Thatcher, but that idea is doomed from the start."

"A woman leading the Tory party? Your lot haven't got the imagination to risk it," said Elizabeth, tasting the sauce. "The day that happens I shall eat my one and only Tory hat in full view of all the delegates at the party conference."

"Don't be so cynical, Elizabeth. She's the best bet we've got at the moment."

"But what are the chances of Ted Heath standing down? I

always thought the leader of the party stayed on until he was hit by the mythical bus. I don't know Heath very well, but I can never imagine him resigning."

"I agree," said Simon. "So the 1922 Committee will have to change the rules."

"You mean the back-benchers will put pressure on him to go?"

"No, but a lot of the committee in their present mood would be willing to volunteer as driver for that bus."

"If that's true, he must realise that his chances of holding on are slim?"

"I wonder if any leader ever knows that," said Simon.

"You ought to be in Blackpool next week," said Kate, resting her elbow on the pillow.

"Why Blackpool?" Raymond asked, staring up at the ceiling.

"Because, Carrot Top, that's where they are holding this year's Labour party conference."

"What do you imagine I could hope to accomplish there?"

"You'd be seen to be alive. At present you're just a rumour in trade union circles."

"But if you're not a minister or a trade union leader all you do at a party conference is spend four days eating foul food, sleeping in seedy guest houses, and applauding second-rate speeches."

"I've no interest in where you put your weary head at night but I do want you to revive your contacts with the unions during the day."

"Why?" said Raymond. "That lot can't influence my career."

"Not at the moment," said Kate. "But I predict that, like my fellow Americans at their conventions, the Labour party will one day select their leader at the party conference."

"Never," said Raymond. "That is and will always remain the prerogative of elected members of the House of Commons."

"That's the sort of crass, short-sighted, pompous statement I would expect a Republican to make," she said, before plonking a pillow over his head. Raymond feigned death, so she lifted up a corner and whispered in his ear, "Have you read any of the resolutions to be debated at this year's conference?"

"A few," came back Raymond's muffled reply.

"Then it might serve you well to note Mr Anthony Wedgwood Benn's contribution," she said, removing the pillow.

"What's he up to this year?"

"He's calling on 'conference', as he insists on describing your gathering of the brothers, to demand that the next leader be chosen by a full vote of the delegates, making up an electoral college from all the constituencies, the trade union movement and Parliament – I suspect in that order."

"Madness. But what do you expect? He's married to an American."

"Today's extremist is tomorrow's moderate," said Kate blithely.

"A typical American generalisation."

"Benjamin Disraeli, actually."

Raymond placed the pillow back over his head.

Andrew always attended the party conference, although he would never have voted for Tony Benn's resolution on the method of selecting a leader. He feared that if the trade unions were given that sort of power a leader who was totally unacceptable to his colleagues in the House of Commons could be selected. He was relieved when the motion was defeated but he noted that the majority against was far from overwhelming.

Despite being a minister Andrew could only get a small room at Blackpool in a guest house masquerading as a hotel, and that some two miles from the conference centre. Such were the problems created by 4,000 self-important people converging on a seaside resort for a week that many had to forgo the Presidential Suite.

Andrew still had to carry on his job as Minister of State, with red boxes being delivered and taken every morning and afternoon, while making his presence felt at the conference. He spent half his time on a phone in the hotel lobby putting through transfer-charge calls to the Home Office. No one in the Soviet Union would have believed it, especially if they had realised that the Minister of State for Defence, who had the room next to Andrew's, was pacing up and down the corridor waiting for the phone to be free.

Andrew had never addressed the 3,000 delegates at a party conference. Even Cabinet ministers are only allowed a maximum of ten minutes at the rostrum unless they are members of the National Executive. Over half the Labour Cabinet had failed to be elected to this body, which consisted mainly of the leaders of the larger trade unions.

As he left the morning session Andrew was surprised to find Raymond Gould roaming around looking lost. They fell on each other like sane men locked in an asylum and decided to lunch together at the River House, Andrew's favourite restaurant a few miles outside of Blackpool.

Although they had both been in the House for nearly ten years it was the first time they discovered how much they had in common. Andrew had never considered himself a close friend of Raymond's but he had always admired his stand on devaluation.

"You must have been disappointed when the PM didn't ask you to rejoin the Government," Andrew began.

Raymond stared down at the menu. "Very," he finally admitted, as a girl joined them in the bar to take their order.

"Nevertheless, you were wise to come to Blackpool. This is where your strength lies."

"You think so?"

"Come on. Everybody knows you're the trade unions' pin-up boy, and they still have a lot of influence as to who sits in the Cabinet."

"I haven't noticed," said Raymond mournfully.

"You will when they eventually choose the leader."

"That's funny, that's exactly what . . . Joyce said last week."

"Sensible girl, Joyce. I fear it will happen in our time as members."

Bill Scott, the proprietor, told them their table was ready and they went through to the small dining-room.

"Why fear?" asked Raymond, as he took his seat.

"Middle-of-the-road democrats like myself will end up as so many leaves on a bonfire."

"But I'm middle-of-the-road myself, practically right wing on some issues."

"Perhaps. But every party needs a man like you, and at this moment union leaders wouldn't mind if you were a card-carrying Fascist; they'd still back you."

"Then what makes you attend the conference?"

"Thank God it still gives one a chance to keep in touch with the grass roots, and I live in hope that the extreme left will never be much more than an unruly child that the grown-ups have to learn to live with."

"Let's hope you're right," said Raymond, "because they're never going to grow up." Andrew laughed as Raymond continued in a different mood. "I still envy you your job at the Home Office. I didn't go into politics to spend my life on the back benches."

"There may well come a day when I sit and envy you from those same back benches," said Andrew.

As he spoke, the chairman of the Boilermakers' Union shouted across as he passed their table, "Good to see you, Ray." He showed no recognition of Andrew. Raymond turned and smiled at the man and waved back as Caesar might have done to Cassius.

When they had both rejected the choice of date and walnut pudding or Pavlova, Andrew suggested a brandy.

Raymond hesitated.

"You'll see more double brandies drunk here than you will at the Conservative party conference next week. Ask any waitress."

"Have you decided how you're going to vote in the leadership battle?" asked Fiona over breakfast.

"Yes," said Charles, "and at this point in my career I can't afford to make the wrong choice."

"So who have you decided on?" asked Fiona.

"While there isn't a serious contender to oppose Ted Heath it remains in my best interest to continue backing him."

"Isn't there one Shadow Cabinet minister who has the guts to stand against him?"

"The rumour grows that Margaret Thatcher will act as whipping girl. If she gets close enough to force a second ballot the serious contenders will then join in."

"What if she won the first round?"

"Don't be silly, Fiona," said Charles, taking more interest in his scrambled egg. "The Tory party would never elect a woman to lead them. We're far too traditional. That's the sort of immature mistake the Labour party would make to prove how much they believe in equality."

Simon was still pushing Margaret Thatcher to throw her hat in the ring.

"She certainly has enough of them," said Elizabeth.

It amused Andrew and Raymond to watch the Tory party leadership struggle while they got on with their respective jobs. Raymond would have dismissed Thatcher's chances if Kate hadn't reminded him that the Tories had been the first party to choose a Jewish leader, and also the first to select a bachelor.

"So why shouldn't they be the first to elect a woman?" she demanded. He would have continued to argue with her but the damn woman had proved to be right so often in the past. "Let's wait and see," was all he said.

The 1922 Committee announced that the election for leader would take place on 4 February 1975.

At a press conference in early January at the House of Commons Margaret Thatcher announced she would allow her name to go forward to contest the leadership. Simon immediately spent his time exhorting his colleagues to support 'The Lady' and joined a small committee under Airey Neave that was formed for the purpose. Charles Seymour warned his friends that the party could never hope to win a general election with a woman leading them. As the days passed, nothing became clearer than the uncertainty of the outcome.

At four o'clock on a particularly wet and windy day the chairman of the 1922 Committee announced the figures:

> Margaret Thatcher   130
> Edward Heath   119
> Hugh Fraser   16

According to the 1922 Committee rules, the winner needed a fifteen per cent majority and so a second round was necessary. "It will be held in seven days' time," the Chief Whip announced. Three former Cabinet ministers immediately declared they were candidates, while Ted Heath, having been warned that he would get fewer votes a second time round, withdrew from the ballot.

They were the longest days in Simon's life. He did everything in his power to hold Thatcher's supporters together. Charles meanwhile decided to play the second round very low-key. When the time came to vote he put his cross on the ballot paper next to the former Secretary of State he had served under at Trade and Industry. "A man we can all trust," he told Fiona.

When the votes had been counted and confirmed the chairman of the 1922 Committee announced that Margaret Thatcher was the outright winner with a vote of 146 to 79 from her nearest challenger.

Simon was delighted while Elizabeth hoped he had forgotten about the promise to eat her hat. Charles was dumbfounded. They both wrote to their new leader immediately.

11 February 1975

Dear Margaret,

Many congratulations on your victory as the first woman leader of our party. I was proud to have played a small part in your triumph and will continue to work for your success at the next election.

                              Yours,
                              Simon.

27 Eaton Square,
London, SW1
11 February 1975

Dear Margaret,

I made no secret of backing Ted Heath in the first round of the leadership contest having had the privilege of serving in his administration. I was delighted to have supported you on the second ballot. It illustrates how progressive our party is that we have chosen a woman who will undoubtedly be Britain's next Prime Minister.

Be assured of my loyalty.

Yours,

Charles.

Margaret Thatcher answered all her colleagues' letters within the week. Simon received a handwritten letter inviting him to join the new Shadow team as number two in the Education Department. Charles received a typed note thanking him for his letter of support.

CHAPTER
NINETEEN

Seymour's Bank had weathered the Great War, the thirties'
crash, and then the Second World War. Charles had no
intention of being the chairman who presided over its demise
in the seventies. Soon after taking over from Derek Spencer –
at the board's unanimous insistence – he had discovered that
being chairman wasn't quite the relaxed job he expected, and
while he remained confident that the bank could ride the
storm he still wasn't taking any risks. The business sections
of the newspapers were full of stories of the Bank of England
acting as a 'lifeboat' and having to step in to assist ailing
financial institutions, along with daily reports of the collapse
of yet another property company. The time when property
values and rents automatically increased each year had
become a thing of the past.

When he had accepted the board's offer, Charles insisted
that a chief executive be appointed to carry out the day to day
business while he remained the man with whom other City
chairmen dealt. He interviewed several people for the position but he did not find anyone suitable. Head-hunting
seemed to be the next move, the expense of which was saved
when he overheard a conversation at the next table at
White's that the newly appointed chief executive of the 1st
Bank of America was sick of having to report to the board in
Chicago every time he wanted to use a first-class stamp.

Charles immediately invited the chief executive to lunch at
the House of Commons. Clive Reynolds had come from a
similar background to Derek Spencer: London School of
Economics, followed by the Harvard Business School and a
series of successful appointments which had culminated in

his becoming chief executive of the 1st Bank of America. This similarity did not worry Charles, as he made it clear to Mr Reynolds that the appointee would be the chairman's man.

When Reynolds was offered the appointment he drove a hard bargain and Charles looked forward to his doing the same on behalf of Seymour's. Reynolds ended up with £50,000 a year and enough of a profit incentive to ensure that he didn't deal for himself or encourage any other headhunters to invite him to join their particular jungle.

"He's not the sort of fellow we could invite to dinner," Charles told Fiona, "but his appointment will enable me to sleep at night knowing the bank is in safe hands."

Charles's choice was rubber-stamped by the board at their next meeting, and as the months passed it became obvious that the 1st Bank of America had lost one of its prime assets well below the market value.

Clive Reynolds was a conservative by nature, but when he did take what Charles described as a risk – and Reynolds called a 'hunch' – over fifty per cent of them paid off. While Seymour's kept its reputation for caution and good husbandry, they managed a few quite spectacular coups thanks to their new chief executive.

Reynolds had enough sense to treat his new chairman with respect without ever showing deference while their relationship remained at all times strictly professional.

One of Reynolds's first innovations had been to suggest they check on every customer account over £250,000 and Charles had approved.

"When you've handled the account of a company for many years," Reynolds pointed out, "it sometimes is not apparent when one of your traditional customers is heading for trouble as it would be to a newcomer. If there are any 'lame ducks' let's discover them before they hit the ground" – a simile that Charles repeated at several weekend parties.

Charles enjoyed his morning meetings with Clive Reynolds as he picked up a great deal about a profession to which he had previously only brought gut feeling and common sense. In a very short time he learned enough from his new tutor to make him sound like David Rockefeller when he rose to speak in a finance debate on the floor of the House, an unexpected bonus.

Charles knew little of Reynolds's private life except what was on file. He was forty-one, unmarried and lived in Esher, wherever that was. All Charles cared about was that Reynolds arrived each morning at least an hour before him, and left after him every night, even when the House was in recess.

Charles had studied fourteen of the confidential reports on customers with loans over £250,000. Clive Reynolds had already picked out two companies with whom he felt the bank should revise their current position.

Charles still had three more reports to consider before he presented a full assessment to the board.

The quiet knock on the door, however, meant that it was ten o'clock and Reynolds had arrived to make his daily report. Rumours were circulating in the City that the bank rate would go up on Thursday, so Reynolds wanted to go short on dollars and long on gold. Charles nodded. As soon as the announcement had been made about the bank rate, Reynolds continued: "It will be wiser to return to dollars as the new round of pay negotiations with the unions is about to take place. This in turn will undoubtedly start a fresh run on the pound." Charles nodded again.

"I think the dollar is far too weak at two-ten," Reynolds added. "With the unions settling at around twelve per cent the dollar must strengthen, say, to nearer one-ninety." He added that he was not happy about the bank's large holding in Slater Walker and wanted to liquidate half the stock over the next month. He proposed to do so in small amounts over irregular periods. "We also have three other major accounts to consider before we make known our findings to the board. I'm concerned about the spending policy of one of the companies, but the other two appear stable. I think we should go over them together when you have time to consider my reports. Perhaps tomorrow morning, if you could manage that. The companies concerned are Speyward Laboratories, Blackies Limited and Nethercote and Company. It's Speyward I'm worried about."

"I'll take the files home tonight," said Charles, "and give you an opinion in the morning."

"Thank you, Chairman."

Charles had never suggested that Reynolds should call him by his first name.

Archie Millburn held a small dinner party to celebrate Simon's first anniversary as the member for Pucklebridge. Although these occasions had originally been to introduce the party hierarchy to their new member, Simon now knew more about the constituency and its flock than he did, as Archie was the first to admit.

Elizabeth, Peter and Michael had settled comfortably into their small cottage, while Simon, as a member of the Shadow Education team, had visited schools – nursery, primary, public and secondary: universities – red brick, plate glass and Oxbridge; technical colleges, art institutes and even borstals. He had read Butler, Robbins, and Plowden and listened to children and to professors of psychology alike. He felt that after a year he was beginning to understand the subject, and only longed for a general election so that he could once again turn rehearsal into performance.

"Opposition must be frustrating," observed Archie when the ladies had retired after dinner.

"Yes, but it's an excellent way to prepare yourself for Government and do some basic thinking about the subject. I never found time for such luxury as a minister."

"But it must be very different from holding office?" said Archie, clipping a cigar.

"True. In Government," said Simon, "you're surrounded by civil servants who don't allow you to lift a finger or give you a moment to ponder, while in Opposition you can think policy through even if you do often end up having to type your own letters."

Archie pushed the port down to Simon's end of the table. "I'm glad the girls are out," said Archie conspiratorially, "because I wanted you to know I've decided to give up being chairman at the end of the year."

"Why?" said Simon, taken aback.

"I've seen you elected and settled in. It's time for a younger man to have a go."

"But you're only my age."

"I can't deny that, but the truth is that I'm not giving enough time to my electronics company, and the board are continually reminding me of it. No one has to tell you that these are not easy times."

"It's sad," said Simon. "Just as you get to know someone in politics you or they always seem to move on."

"Fear not," said Archie. "I don't intend to leave the area, and I feel confident that you will be my member for at least another twenty years, by which time I will be happy to accept an invitation to dine with you in Downing Street."

"You may find that it's Charles Seymour who is residing at No. 10," said Simon, striking a match to light his cigar.

"Then I won't be getting an invitation," said Archie with a smile.

Charles couldn't sleep that night after his discovery, and his tossing and turning kept Fiona awake. He had opened the Nethercote file when he was waiting for dinner to be served. His first act with any company was to glance down the names of the directors to see if he knew anyone on the board. He recognised no one until his eye stopped at 'S. J. Kerslake, MP'. The cook felt sure that Mr Seymour had not enjoyed his dinner, because he hardly touched the main course.

On his arrival at Seymour's, only moments after Clive Reynolds, he called for his chief executive. He appeared a few minutes later without his usual armful of files, surprised to see the chairman so early. Once Reynolds was seated Charles opened the file in front of him. "What do you know about Nethercote and Company?"

"Private company. Net asset value approaching £10,000,000, running a current overdraft of £7,000,000 of which we service half. Efficiently managed with a good board of directors, will ride out the current problems in my view, and should be well oversubscribed when they eventually go public."

"How much of the company do we own?"

"Seven and a half per cent. As you know, the bank never take eight per cent of any company because then we would have to declare an interest under section twenty-three of the Finance Act. It has always been a policy of this bank to invest in a major client without becoming too involved with the running of the company."

"Who are their principal bankers?"

"The Midland."

"What would happen if we put our seven and a half per cent up for sale and did not renew the overdraft facility at the end of the quarter, but called it in instead?"

"They would have to seek finance elsewhere."

"And if they couldn't?"

"They would have to start selling their assets, which under that sort of forced-sale position would be very damaging for any company, if not impossible, in the present climate."

"And then?"

"I would have to check my file and . . ."

Charles passed over the file and Reynolds studied it carefully, frowning. "They already have a cash-flow problem because of bad debts. With a sudden increased demand they might go under. I would strongly advise against such a move, Chairman. Nethercote have proved a reliable risk over the years, and I think we stand to make a handsome profit when they are quoted on the Stock Exchange."

"For reasons I cannot disclose to you," said Charles, looking up from his chair, "I fear that remaining involved with this company may turn out to be a financial embarrassment for Seymour's." Reynolds looked at him, puzzled. "You will inform the Midland Bank that we will not be renewing this loan at the next quarter."

"Then they would have to look for support from another bank. The Midland would never agree to shoulder the entire amount on their own."

"And try to dispose of our seven and a half per cent immediately."

"But that could lead to a crisis of confidence in the company."

"So be it," said Charles, as he closed the file.

"But I do feel —"

"That will be all, Mr Reynolds."

"Yes, Chairman," said the mystified chief executive, who had never thought of his boss as an irrational man. He turned to leave. Had he looked back he would have been even more mystified by the smile that was spread across Charles Seymour's face.

"They've pulled the rug out from under our feet," said Ronnie Nethercote angrily.

"Who?" said Simon, who had just come into the room.

"The Midland Bank."

"Why would they do that?"

"An outside shareholder put all his stock on the market without warning, and the Midland got worried about their position. They wouldn't be prepared to continue such a large overdraft position on their own."

"Have you been to see the manager?" asked Simon, unable to disguise his anxiety.

"Yes, but he can't do anything. His hands are tied by a main board directive," said Ronnie, slumping deeper into his seat.

"How bad is it?"

"They've given me a month to find another bank. Otherwise I'll have to start selling some of our assets."

"What will happen if we don't manage to come up with another bank?" asked Simon desperately.

"The company could be bankrupt within weeks. Do you know any bankers who are looking for a good investment?"

"Only one, and I can assure you he wouldn't help."

Charles put the phone down satisfied. He wondered if there was anything that could still be regarded as secret. It had taken him less than an hour to find out the size of Kerslake's overdraft. "Banker to banker confidentiality," he had assured them. He was still smiling when Reynolds knocked on the door.

"The Midland weren't pleased," he immediately briefed Charles.

"They'll get over it," his chairman replied. "What's the latest on Nethercote?"

"Only a rumour, but everyone now knows they're in trouble and the chairman is searching around for a new backer," said Reynolds impassively. "His biggest problem is that no one is touching property companies at the moment."

"Once they've collapsed, what's to stop us picking up the pieces and making a killing?"

"A clause that was slipped through in the Finance Act which your Government passed three years ago. The penalties range from a heavy fine to having your banking licence taken away."

"Oh, yes, I remember," said Charles. "Pity. So how long do you expect them to last?"

"Once the month is up," said Reynolds stroking a clean-shaven chin, "if they fail to find a backer the creditors will swarm in like locusts."

"Aren't the shares worth anything?" asked Charles innocently.

"Not the paper they are written on at the moment," said Reynolds, watching his chairman carefully.

This time the chief executive couldn't miss the chairman's smile as Charles thought of Simon Kerslake and his overdraft of £108,000 now backed by worthless shares. Pucklebridge would soon be looking for a new member.

At the end of a month during which no bank came to his rescue Ronnie Nethercote caved in and agreed to call in the receiver and file a bankruptcy notice. He still hoped that he could pay off all his creditors even if the shares he and his fellow directors held remained worthless. He felt as worried for Simon and his career as he did for himself, but he knew there was nothing the receiver would allow him to do to help one individual.

When Simon told Elizabeth she didn't complain. She had always feared this could be the eventual outcome of her husband joining the board of Nethercotes.

"Can't Ronnie help?" she asked. "After all, you've supported him enough in the past."

"No, he can't," replied Simon, avoiding telling her where the real responsibility for his downfall lay.

"But do bankrupts automatically have to leave Parliament?" was Elizabeth's next question.

"No, but I shall because I could never be considered for further promotion – I'd always be rightly tainted with 'lack of judgement'."

"It seems so unfair when you weren't personally to blame."

"There are different rules for those who wish to live in the spotlight," Simon said simply.

"But in time, surely –" began Elizabeth.

"I'm not willing to remain on the back benches for another twenty years only to hear whispered in the corner of the smoking room – Would have made the Cabinet if it hadn't been for . . ."

"Does that mean the children will have to be taken away from school?"

"I'm afraid so," said Simon, his hands shaking. "As a bankrupt I can hardly expect the receiver to view the fees for my sons' education as a dire necessity even if I could find the money."

"So we'll have to get rid of the nanny, too?"

"Not necessarily, but we may both have to make sacrifices in order that she can be part-time."

"But my work at the hospital . . ." began Elizabeth but didn't complete the sentence. "What happens next?"

"I'll have to tell Archie Millburn tonight. I've already written my letter of resignation to hand to him. I shall make an appointment to see the Chief Whip on Monday to explain why I am going to apply for the Chiltern Hundreds."

"What does that mean?"

"It's one of the only ways of leaving the House in mid-session – other than dying. Officially it's a nominal office under the Crown which therefore debars you from membership of the House."

"It all sounds rather formal to me."

"I'm afraid it will cause an embarrassing by-election in Pucklebridge," Simon admitted.

"Can nobody help?"

"There aren't a lot of people around who have a spare £108,000 for a worthless bunch of shares."

"Would you like me to come with you when you go to see Archie?" Elizabeth asked, rising from her seat.

"No, darling. It's kind of you to ask, but I'm the one who made such a fool of myself."

Elizabeth leaned over and pushed back the hair that had fallen over his forehead. She couldn't help noticing some grey strands that must have appeared in the last few weeks. "We'll just have to live off my salary while you look for a job."

Simon drove slowly down to Pucklebridge to keep his impromptu appointment with the chairman. Archie Millburn, standing hands on hips in his garden, listened to the tale with a sad face. "It's been happening to a lot of good people in the City lately, but what I can't understand is: if the company owns such prime properties, why has no one made a takeover bid? Sounds as if it's an asset-stripper's dream."

"It appears to be a matter of confidence," said Simon.

"A sacred word in the City," agreed Archie, while he continued to prune his Roosevelts and Red Mistresses.

Simon handed him the prepared letter of resignation, which Millburn read over and reluctantly accepted.

"I won't mention this to anyone until you've seen the Chief Whip on Monday. I'll call a special meeting of the full committee on Tuesday evening and inform them of your decision then. You had better be prepared for an unfriendly barrage from the press on Tuesday night."

The two men shook hands. "Your misfortune is our misfortune," said Archie. "In a very short time you've gained the respect and the affection of the local people. You'll be missed."

Simon drove back to London and, although the car radio was on low, he did not take in the news flash that they kept repeating every thirty minutes.

CHAPTER
TWENTY

Raymond was among the first to hear the announcement, and was stunned by it. Harold Wilson was going to resign less than half-way through the five-year Parliament, and for no apparent reason other than that he had just passed his sixtieth birthday. He proposed to remain Prime Minister only so long as the Labour party took to select its new leader. Raymond and Kate sat glued to the television, picking up every scrap of information they could. They discussed the implications far into the night.

"Well, Carrot Top, could this mean rehabilitation for our forgotten hero?"

"Who can say?"

"Well, if you can't, who can?"

"The next leader," said Raymond.

The fight for the leadership was a straight battle between the left and right wings of the party, James Callaghan on the right and Michael Foot on the left. Andrew and Raymond both wanted the same man and it was with some relief that they saw Callaghan, despite losing the first ballot, come through to be elected leader. The Queen duly called for Callaghan and asked him to form a new administration.

As tradition demands Andrew sent his resignation to Downing Street, as did every other member of the Government, to allow the new Prime Minister to select his own team.

Raymond was in court listening to the judge's summing up when his junior passed him a note: "Please call 10 Downing Street as soon as possible." The judge took a further thirty minutes, meticulously explaining to the jury the legal definition of manslaughter, before Raymond could escape. He ran down the corridor and stopped at one of the clerks' private boxes to make the call. The plastic dial rotating back into place after each number seemed to take forever.

After he had been passed through three people a voice said, "Good afternoon, Ray": the unmistakable gravelly tones of the new Prime Minister. "I think it's time you rejoined the Government" – Raymond held his breath – "as Minister of State at the Department of Trade." Minister of State: only one place away from the Cabinet.

"You still there, Ray?"

"Yes, Prime Minister, and I'd be delighted to accept."

He put the phone down, immediately picked it up again and dialled the City office of the Chase Manhattan Bank. They put him through to the Euro Bond manager.

Andrew had left his desk at the Home Office and returned to Cheyne Walk. He stayed away from the House of Commons where the lobby correspondents were hanging about like hyenas, scampering off to phone their papers with even the rumour of a rumour. The new Cabinet had been selected, and now it was the turn of the Ministers of State. All Andrew knew for certain was that his old job at the Home Office had been given to someone else.

"Why don't you go and play football with Robert?" Louise suggested. "And stop moping around under my feet?"

"Yes, Dad, yes, Dad, yes, Dad," demanded his son, running upstairs to reappear a few minutes later dressed in the Liverpool kit that he had bought himself from eleven weeks' hard-saved pocket money.

"Go on, Andrew. I can always call you if the phone goes."

Andrew smiled, took off his jacket and put on the pair of old gym shoes Robert was holding out for him. He followed his five-year-old son into the garden to find him already dribbling up and down the thin strip between the flower beds. The little goal he had bought for Robert – or was it for himself? – at Christmas was already set up at the far end of the grass and they took turns defending it. Andrew always had to start in goal. He rubbed his hands together to keep warm as Robert dribbled towards him. He came out of the goal ready to stifle a shot, but Robert kicked the ball to the right and ran to the left, leaving his father spreadeagled on the ground before he pushed the ball gently into the goal. "That's called a feint," he shouted triumphantly, as he ran back past his prostrate father.

Andrew picked himself up. "I know what it's called," he said, laughing. "You seem to have forgotten who taught you the feint in the first place. Let's see if you can do it twice running," he added, returning to defend the goal.

Robert dribbled away from his father until he reached the end of the garden, then turned to face him again. He had begun advancing towards the goal for a second time when there was the sound of the phone ringing. Andrew looked towards the house just as Robert kicked the ball, which rising sharply, struck him in the face. He and the ball fell back into the goal mouth.

Louise opened the kitchen window and shouted, "It's only my mother."

"Wake up, Dad," demanded Robert simultaneously.

Andrew's face was still stinging from the blow. "I'm going to get you for that," he said. "Your turn to defend the goal."

Robert rushed forward to take his place between the posts, jumping up and down trying to touch the crossbar with the tips of his fingers. Andrew took his time as he moved towards his son. When he was about a yard in front of Robert he feinted to the right and ran to the left but Robert had seen the move coming and leaped on the ball shouting, "No goal."

Once again Andrew returned to the end of the garden, thinking over what move he could try next. He suddenly ran straight at Robert and kicked the ball firmly towards the right-hand corner of the goal mouth. But again Robert anticipated the move and caught the ball above his head before pulling it to his chest and shouting, "No goal, Dad, no goal!" He tossed the ball confidently back along the ground to his father's feet.

"Right, the fooling around is over," said Andrew, not quite convinced. He kicked the ball from one foot to the other, trying to look skilful.

"Come on, Dad," Robert complained.

This time Andrew advanced with a look of determination on his face. He tried a change of pace to make his son leave the goal mouth too early. Robert duly came out of the goal; Andrew kicked the ball a little harder and higher than his previous attempt. As he did so he heard the phone ring again and turned his head towards the house. He didn't see his shot cannon against the left-hand corner of the goal post and bounce away.

"It's the Prime Minister," shouted Louise from the window. Andrew turned to walk quickly back towards the house. Out of the corner of his eye he saw the ball bounce on to the path, on its way towards the gate and into the road.

Robert was already running towards the open gate. "I'll save it, Dad, I'll save it."

"No," screamed Andrew at the top of his voice and turned back to run as fast as he could after his son.

Louise froze as she stared out of the window, still holding on to the phone with her rubber gloves. She watched as Andrew turned his back and tore towards the pavement until he was only a yard behind his son. The ball bounced on into the road and Robert dived for it a split second before his father threw himself on his son.

Louise was the only one who saw the driver of the massive Shell tanker slam on its brakes and swerve – too late – to avoid them. Andrew and Robert collided with the corner of the wide metal mudguard and were thrown back together before rolling over and over several times, ending up in the gutter.

"Are you there, Andrew?" asked the Prime Minister.

Louise dropped the phone and ran out of the kitchen towards the open gate. Her husband lay motionless beside the kerb with their son in his arms, the ball still clutched against his chest. She tried to hold on to both of them as Andrew's blood poured down over Robert's red shirt and on to her rubber gloves.

She fell on to her knees by the kerb side. "Let them live, let them live," was all she said.

Robert was crying softly as he held firmly on to the ball and stared at his unconscious father. She had to lean over to hear him repeating, "No goal, Dad, no goal."

When the complete list of ministers was published in *The Times* two days later the only unfilled post left was that of Minister of State for Defence. *The Times*'s political editor, David Wood, surmised that the position was being held open for Mr Andrew Fraser, who was expected to be out of hospital by the end of the week. Wood's final paragraph read:

> Politicians from all parties joined forces in praising Mr Fraser's remarkable courage in diving in front of a moving lorry to rescue his only son, Robert, who was chasing a football. Both father and son were rushed to St Thomas's Hospital with internal injuries, where surgeons operated through the night to save Mr Fraser's life.
>
> As was reported in the final edition of yesterday's paper, his five-year-old son Robert died during the night before Mr Fraser regained consciousness.

"My God," exclaimed Elizabeth, "how dreadful."

"What's dreadful?" asked Simon, as he took his seat at the breakfast table. She passed the paper to her husband and pointed to the picture of Robert.

"Poor kid," said Simon before he had finished the article.

"Certainly puts our own problems into perspective. If Peter or Michael were killed we really would have something to worry about."

Neither of them spoke for several minutes. Then Elizabeth asked, "Are you dreading it?"

"Yes, I am," said Simon. "I feel like a condemned man eating his last breakfast, and the worst part of it is that I have to drive myself to the gallows."

"I wonder if we will ever laugh about today?"

"No doubt – when I collect my parliamentary pension."

"Can we live off that?"

"Hardly. I don't get the first payment until I'm sixty-five, so we have a twenty-five-year wait to find out." He got up. "Can I give you a lift to the hospital?"

"No thanks. I intend to savour the joys of being a two-car family for at least another week. Just let's hope the new Marina holds its price as well as Sir Michael Edwardes claimed it would."

Simon laughed, kissed his wife and left for his appointment with the Chief Whip at the House of Commons. As he started the car Elizabeth rushed out. "I forgot to tell you, Ronnie phoned while you were in the bath."

"I'll call him as soon as I reach the House."

Simon made his way to the Commons. He felt sick as he passed Cheyne Walk and thought of Andrew Fraser and all he must be going through. He made a mental note to write to him immediately. At the Commons the policeman on the gate saluted as he drove in. "Good morning, sir," he said.

"Good morning," said Simon. He parked his car on the second level of the new underground car park and took the escalator up to the Members' Entrance. He couldn't help reflecting that ten years ago he would have taken the stairs. He continued through the Members' Cloakroom, up the marble staircase to the Members' Lobby. Habit made him turn left into the little post office to check whether he had any mail.

"Mr Kerslake," the man behind the counter called into an intercom, and a few seconds later a parcel and a packet of letters held together by a thick elastic band thudded into an office basket. Simon left the parcel marked 'London School of Economics' and the letters on the desk in his room and checked his watch: over forty minutes before his appointment with the Chief Whip. He went to the nearest phone and dialled Nethercote and Company. Ronnie answered the phone himself.

"Sacked the telephone operator last Friday," he explained. "Only me and my secretary left."

"You called, Ronnie," a millimetre of hope in Simon's voice.

"Yes, I wanted to express how I felt. I tried to write you a letter over the weekend but I'm not very good with words." He paused. "Nor it seems with figures. I just wanted to say how desperately sorry I am. Elizabeth told me you were going to see the Chief Whip this morning. I'll be thinking of you."

"That's kind, Ronnie, but I went into it with my eyes wide open. As an advocate of free enterprise, I can hardly complain when I turn out to be one of its victims."

"A very philosophical attitude for this time of the morning."

"How are things your end?"

"The receiver's checking the books. I still believe we can get out with all our creditors fully paid. At least that way I'll avoid the stigma of bankruptcy." There was a longer pause. "Oh Christ, that was tactless."

"Don't worry about it, Ronnie, the overdraft was my decision."

Simon already wished he had been as frank with his wife.

"Let's have lunch one day next week."

"It will have to be somewhere that takes luncheon vouchers," said Simon wryly.

"Good luck, mate," said Ronnie.

Simon decided to fill up the remaining thirty minutes at the House by going to the library and glancing over the rest of the morning press. He settled himself in a corner of the 'B' Room, next to the fireplace over which hung a notice reminding members not to have overloud or prolonged conversations. He leafed through the papers, which all carried photographs of Andrew Fraser and his wife and son. The same portrait of five-year-old Robert appeared on almost every front page. Elizabeth was right: in so many respects they were lucky.

The story of the probable break-up of Nethercote and Company was detailed on the financial pages. They quoted approvingly Ronnie's view that all creditors ought to be paid in full. Not one of the articles mentioned Simon's name, but he could already anticipate the headlines in tomorrow's paper with another picture of a young MP and his happy family. 'The Rise and Fall of Simon Kerslake.' Over ten years' work quickly forgotten: he would be old news within a week.

The library clock inched towards the hour that he could no

longer put off. Simon heaved himself out of the deep leather chair like an old man and walked slowly towards the Chief Whip's office.

Miss Norse, the Chief's ancient secretary, smiled benignly as he came in.

"Good morning, Mr Kerslake," she said brightly. "I'm afraid the Chief is still with Mrs Thatcher but I did remind him of your appointment so I don't expect him to be long. Would you care to have a seat?"

"Thank you," he said.

Alec Pimkin always claimed that Miss Norse had a set patter for every occasion. His imitation of her saying, "I hope I find you in rude health, Mr Pimkin," had brought chuckles to the Members' Dining-room on many occasions. He must have exaggerated, thought Simon.

"I hope I find you in rude health, Mr Kerslake," said Miss Norse, not looking up from her typing. Simon choked back a laugh.

"Very rude, thank you," he said, wondering how many tragic stories or tales of lost opportunities Miss Norse had had to listen to over the years. She stopped suddenly and looked at her note pad.

"I should have mentioned it to you before, Mr Kerslake, a Mr Nethercote rang."

"Thank you, I've spoken to him already."

Simon was leafing through an out-of-date copy of *Punch* when the Chief Whip strode in.

"I can spare you one minute, Simon, one and a half if you are going to resign," he said, laughing, and marched off towards his office. As Simon followed him down the corridor the phone by Miss Norse's side rang. "It's for you, Mr Kerslake," she shouted to their retreating backs.

Simon turned and said, "Can you take the number?"

"He says it's urgent."

Simon stopped, hesitating. "With you in a moment," he said to the Chief Whip, who disappeared into his office. Simon walked back and took the phone from Miss Norse's outstretched hand.

"Simon Kerslake here. Who is it?"

"It's Ronnie."

"Ronnie," said Simon flatly.

"I've just had a call from Morgan Grenfell. One of their clients has made an offer of one pound twenty-five a share for the company and they're willing to take over the current liabilities."

Simon was trying to do the sums in his head.

"Don't bother working it out," Ronnie said. "At one pound twenty-five your shares would be worth £75,000."

"It won't be enough," said Simon, as he recalled his overdraft of £108,712, a figure etched in his memory.

"Don't panic. I've told them I won't settle for anything less than one pound fifty a share and it has to be within seven days, which will give them ample time to check the books. That would bring you in £90,000 but you would still be £18,000 down the Swanee, which you'll have to learn to live with. If you sell the wife as well as the second car you should just about survive."

Simon could tell by the way his friend was speaking that Ronnie already had a cigar between his lips.

"You're a genius."

"Not me – Morgan Grenfell. And I bet they'll make a handsome profit in the long run for their unnamed client who seemed to have all the inside information. If you're still on for lunch next Tuesday, don't bring your luncheon vouchers. It's on me."

Simon put the phone down and kissed Miss Norse on the forehead. She was completely taken aback by a situation for which she had no set reply. She remained silent as the Chief Whip put his head round the door. "An orgy in the Chief Whip's office? You'll be on page three of the *Sun* next, Miss Norse." Simon laughed. "I've got a crisis on over tonight's vote. The Government are reneging on our agreement for pairing, and I have to get a delegation back from Brussels in time for the ten o'clock division. Whatever it is, can it wait, Simon?"

"Yes, of course."

"Can you come to my office, Miss Norse – if I can drag you away from James Double-O-Seven Kerslake?"

Simon left and almost bounced to the nearest phone. First he called Elizabeth and then Archie Millburn at his office. Archie didn't sound all that surprised.

"Don't you think it might be wise for us to stop seeing each other?"

"Why?" said Raymond. "Palmerston had a mistress when he was seventy, and he still beat Disraeli come the election."

"Yes, but that was before the days of a dozen national newspapers *and* investigative journalism. Frankly it wouldn't take a Woodward or Bernstein more than a few hours to discover our little secret."

"We'll be all right. I've destroyed all the tapes."

"Do be serious."

"You're always telling me I'm far too serious."

"Well, I want you to be now. Very."

Raymond turned to face Kate. "I love you, Kate, and I know I always will. Why don't we stop this charade and get married?"

She sighed. "We've been over this a hundred times. I'll want to return to America eventually, and in any case I wouldn't make a very good Prime Minister's wife."

"Three American women have in the past," said Raymond sulkily.

"To hell with your historical precedents – and what's more, I hate Leeds."

"You've never been there."

"I don't need to if it's colder than London."

"Then you'll have to be satisfied with being my mistress." Raymond took Kate in his arms. "You know, I used to think being Prime Minister was worth every sacrifice, but now I'm not so sure."

"It's still worth the sacrifice," said Kate, "as you'll discover when you live at No. 10. Come on, or my dinner will be burnt to a cinder."

"You haven't noticed these," said Raymond smugly, pointing down at his feet.

Kate stared at the fashionable new slip-ons.

"I never thought the day would come," she said. "Pity you're starting to go bald."

When Simon returned home his first words were "We'll survive."

"Thank God for that," Elizabeth said. "But what have you done about your resignation letter?"

"Archie said he would return it the day I became Prime Minister."

"If that's ever to be true I want you to promise me just one thing."

"Anything," said Simon.

"You'll never speak to Ronnie Nethercote again."

For a moment Simon hesitated before saying, "That's not completely fair, Elizabeth, because I haven't been totally straight with you from the beginning." He then sat his wife down on the sofa and told her the whole truth.

It was Elizabeth's turn to remain silent.

"Oh, hell," she said, looking up at Simon. "I do hope Ronnie can forgive me."

"What are you talking about?"

"I phoned him back soon after you had left for the Commons and I spent at least ten minutes telling him why he was the biggest two-faced bastard I'd ever come across, and I didn't want to hear from him again in my life."

It was Simon's turn to collapse on to the sofa. "How did he respond?" he asked anxiously. Elizabeth faced her husband. "That's the strange thing, he didn't even protest. He just apologised."

"Do you think she will ever speak again?"

"God knows, I hope so," said his father, staring at the picture of his grandchild on the mantelpiece. "She's still young enough to have another child."

Andrew shook his head. "No, that's out of the question. The doctor warned me a long time ago that could be dangerous."

He had returned home from hospital ten days after the accident. The first thing he and Louise did was to attend

Robert's funeral. With Andrew on crutches, Sir Duncan had to support Louise during the short service. As soon as the burial was over Andrew took his wife back to Cheyne Walk and put her to bed, before returning downstairs to join his parents.

Andrew's mother bowed her head. "Whatever happens, you must move from this place as soon as possible. Every time Louise looks out of that kitchen window she'll relive the tragedy."

"I hadn't thought of that," said Andrew. "I'll start looking for a new house immediately."

"And what do you plan to do about the Prime Minister's offer?" enquired Sir Duncan.

"I haven't finally made up my mind," he said sharply. "He's given me until Monday to come to a decision."

"You must take it, Andrew. If you don't your political career will be finished. You can't sit at home and mourn Robert's death for the rest of your life."

Andrew looked up at his father. "No goal, Dad, no goal," he murmured and left them to go and sit with Louise in the bedroom. Her eyes were open but there was no expression on her face. Little white hairs had appeared at either side of her head that he had not noticed the week before. "Feeling any better, my darling?" he asked.

There was still no reply.

He undressed and climbed into bed beside her, holding her close, but she did not respond. She felt detached and distant. He watched his tears fall on her shoulder and run down on to the pillow. He fell asleep and woke again at three in the morning. No one had closed the curtains and the moon shone in through the windows, lighting the room. He looked at his wife. She had not moved.

Charles paced up and down the room angrily.

"Give me the figures again."

"Nethercote has accepted a bid of £7,500,000, which works out at one pound fifty a share," said Clive Reynolds.

Charles stopped at his desk and scribbled the figures down on a piece of paper. £90,000, leaving a shortfall of only

£18,000. It wouldn't be enough. "Damn," he said.

"I agree," said Reynolds, "I always thought we were premature to lose our position in the company in the first place."

"An opinion you will not voice outside this room," said Charles.

Clive Reynolds did not reply.

"What's happened to Nethercote himself?" asked Charles, searching for any scrap of information he could find about Simon Kerslake.

"I'm told he's starting up again in a smaller way. Morgan Grenfell were delighted by the deal and the manner in which he handled the company during the takeover. I must say we let it fall into their laps."

"Can we get any stock in the new company?" asked Charles, ignoring his comment.

"I doubt it. It's only capitalised at one million although Morgan Grenfell are giving Nethercote a large overdraft facility as part of the deal."

"Then all that remains necessary is to see the matter is never referred to again."

Andrew spent the weekend reading over the letters of condolence sent to him and Louise. There were over a thousand, many from people he didn't even know. He selected a few to take into the bedroom and read to Louise; not that he was sure she could even hear him. The doctor had told him not to disturb her unless it was really necessary. After such a severe shock she was now suffering from acute depression and must be nursed slowly back to health. Louise had walked a few paces the previous day but needed to rest today, the doctor explained to him.

He sat by the side of their bed, and quietly read the letters from the Prime Minister, from a contrite Jock McPherson, from Simon Kerslake, from Raymond Gould and from Mrs Bloxham. There was no sign that Louise had taken in anything he had said.

"What shall I do about the PM's offer?" he asked. "Shall I accept it?"

She made no response of any kind.

"He's asked me to be the Minister of State for Defence, but I need to know how you would feel." After sitting with her for a few minutes and eliciting no response he left her to rest.

Each night he slept with her and tried to infuse her with his love, but he only felt more alone.

On the Monday morning he called his father and told him he had decided to turn down the Prime Minister's offer. He couldn't leave Louise alone for long periods while she was still in this state.

Andrew returned to the bedroom and sat by her side.

He said in a whisper, as if to himself, "Should I have taken the job?"

Louise gave such a slight nod that Andrew nearly missed it but her fingers were moving. He placed his hand between her fingers and palm and she squeezed gently and repeated the nod, then fell asleep.

Andrew phoned the Prime Minister.

Raymond dug deeper into the red box.

"You enjoying yourself, Carrot Top?"

"It's fascinating," said Raymond. "Do you know –"

"No, I don't. You haven't spoken to me in the last three hours, and when you do it's to tell me how you spend the day with your new mistress."

"My new mistress?"

"The Secretary of State for Trade."

"Oh, him."

"Yes, him."

"What sort of day did you have at the bank?" asked Raymond, not looking up from his papers.

"I had a most fascinating day," replied Kate.

"Why, what happened?"

"One of our customers required a loan," said Kate.

"A loan," repeated Raymond, still concentrating on the file in front of him. "How much?"

"'How much do you want?' I said. 'How much have you got?' they asked. 'Four hundred and seventeen billion at the last count,' I told them. 'That will do fine to start with,' they said. 'Sign here,' I said. But I couldn't close the deal because the lady concerned was only in possession of a £50 banking card."

Raymond burst out laughing and slammed down the lid of the red box. "Do you know why I love you?"

"My taste in men's clothes?" suggested Kate.

"No, no. Just your taste in men."

"I always thought that mistresses were supposed to get fur coats, trips to the Bahamas, the odd solitaire diamond, yet all I ever get is to share you with your red box."

Raymond opened the box once more, took out a small package and handed it to Kate.

"What's this?"

"Why don't you open it and find out?"

Kate slipped off the purple Asprey paper and found inside an exquisitely made miniature, a solid gold replica of a red box on a gold chain. The neat lettering on the side of the lid read, 'For Your Eyes Only'.

"Although they don't announce the birthdays of ministers' mistresses in the *Sunday Times*, I can still remember the day we met."

Andrew made a bid for the house in Pelham Crescent the day he was shown over it, and Louise's mother came down to London immediately to organise the move.

"Let's hope this does the trick," she said.

Andrew prayed for nothing more. The move from Cheyne Walk took about a fortnight, and Louise could still walk only a few paces before she had to sit down. Louise's mother rarely left the house and Andrew began to feel guilty about how much he was enjoying his new job at the Ministry of Defence. Each night and then again in the morning he would try a few words to Louise. She nodded occasionally, touched him once in a while and even began writing notes to him, but never spoke and never cried. The doctor became even more pessimistic. "The crucial time has passed," he explained.

Andrew would sit with her for hours while he worked through the red boxes. Harrier Jump jets for the RAF,

Polaris missiles for the Royal Navy, Chieftain tanks for the Army, what should Labour's attitude be to Trident when Polaris was phased out? Should we allow Cruise to be based on British soil? There was so much to learn before he could face the civil servants on their own ground or the members from the dispatch box. As the months passed Andrew was always asking questions; a year had gone by and he was beginning to know some of the answers.

He looked up at his wife once again. She was gazing at the portrait of Robert on the mantelpiece.

On the anniversary of his son's sixth birthday Andrew stayed at Pelham Crescent all day with Louise. For the first time a tear lodged in her eye. As he held her, he kept remembering the lorry. He could see it so clearly now as if in slow motion. If only the phone hadn't gone, if only the gate had been closed, if only he had turned earlier, if only he had run a little faster. 'No goal, Dad, no goal.'

If only he had scored that goal.

CHAPTER
TWENTY ONE

Raymond entered a Washington ablaze with red, white and blue as the Americans prepared for their bicentennial. He was among the three ministers chosen to represent the United Kingdom when they presented a copy of Magna Carta to the United States Congress. He was making his first trip to America on Concorde only a few weeks after its inaugural flight. Tom Carson had complained to the House about the expense of the trip but his words had fallen upon a silent Chamber.

As the plane taxied to a halt at Dulles airport three limousines drew up. The three ministers were given a car each and motorcycle outriders rushed them to the grounds of the British Embassy on Massachusetts Avenue in less than thirty minutes.

Raymond had an immediate love affair with America, perhaps because it reminded him so much of Kate with its bubbling enthusiasm, its spirit and sense of perpetual innovation. During the ten-day visit he managed to forge several useful contacts in the Senate and House, and over the weekend became an unrepentant sightseer of the beautiful Virginia countryside. He concentrated on getting to know those contemporaries whom he felt would be on the American political stage for the next twenty years, while his more senior colleagues dealt with President Ford and his immediate entourage.

Raymond enjoyed starting each day with the *Washington Post* and the *New York Times*. He quickly learned how to reject those sections that seemed full of endless advertisements for non-essentials he couldn't believe anyone really bought.

Once he had finished reading both papers he found he had to wash his hands as they were always black with newsprint. The one occasion he kept the Outlook section of the *Washington Post* was when it did profiles on the three ministers from London. He tucked the paper away as he wanted to show Kate the paragraph that read: "The two Secretaries of State are interesting men at the end of their careers, but it is Raymond Gould we should keep our eyes on because he has the look of a future Prime Minister."

As Raymond flew out of Washington on his way back to London he presumed, like any lover, that the affair with America could be continued whenever he chose to return.

Simon was in Manchester as a guest of the Business School when he received Elizabeth's message to call her. It was most unusual for Elizabeth to phone in the middle of the day and Simon assumed the worst: something must have happened to the children. The Principal of the Business School accompanied him to his private office, then left him alone.

Dr Kerslake was not at the hospital, he was told, which made him even more anxious. He dialled the Beaufort Street number.

Elizabeth picked up the receiver so quickly that she must have been sitting by the phone waiting for him to call.

"I've been sacked," she said.

"What?" said Simon, unable to comprehend.

"I've been made redundant – isn't that the modern term meant to lessen the blow? The hospital governors have been instructed by the Department of Health and Social Security to make cutbacks and three of us in gynaecology have lost our jobs. I go at the end of the month."

"Darling, I'm sorry," he said, knowing how inadequate his words must have sounded.

"I didn't meant to bother you, but I just wanted someone to talk to," she said. "Everyone else is allowed to complain to their MP, so I thought it was my turn."

"Normally what I do in these circumstances is to put the blame on the Labour party." Simon was relieved to hear Elizabeth laugh.

"Thanks for ringing me back so quickly, darling. See you tomorrow," she said and put the phone down.

Simon returned to his group and explained that he had to leave for London immediately. He took a taxi to the airport and caught the next shuttle to Heathrow. He was back at Beaufort Street within three hours.

"I didn't mean you to come home," Elizabeth said contritely when she saw him on the doorstep.

"I've come back to celebrate," Simon said. "Let's open the bottle of champagne that Ronnie gave us when he closed the deal with Morgan Grenfell."

"Why?"

"Because Ronnie taught me one thing. You should always celebrate disasters, not successes."

Simon hung up his coat and went off in search of the champagne. When he returned with the bottle and two glasses Elizabeth asked, "What's your overdraft looking like nowadays?"

"Down to £16,000, give or take a pound."

"Well, that's another problem then, I won't be giving any pounds in the future, only taking."

"Don't be silly. Someone will snap you up," he said, embracing her.

"It won't be quite that easy," said Elizabeth.

"Why not?" asked Simon, trying to sound cheerful.

"Because I had already been warned about whether I wanted to be a politician's wife or a doctor."

Simon was stunned. "I had no idea," he said. "I'm so sorry."

"It was my choice, darling, but I will have to make one or two decisions if I want to remain in medicine, especially if you're going to become a minister."

Simon remained silent: he had always wanted Elizabeth to make this decision herself and he was determined not to try to influence her.

"If only we weren't so short of money."

"Don't worry about the money," said Simon.

"I do worry, but it may just be an excuse because I worry more about becoming bored when the children have grown

up. I just wasn't cut out to be a politician's wife," she added.
"You should have married someone like Fiona Seymour and
you'd be Prime Minister by now."

"If that's the only way I can be sure of getting the job I'll
stick with you," said Simon, taking Elizabeth in his arms.
Simon couldn't help thinking of all the support his wife
had given him during their marriage and even more so
since his financial crisis. He knew exactly what his wife
must do.

"You mustn't be allowed to give up being a doctor," he
said. "It's every bit as important as wanting to be a minister.
Shall I have a word with Gerry Vaughan? As Shadow
spokesman for Health he might –"

"Certainly not, Simon. If I am to get another job, it'll be
without anyone doing you or me a favour."

Louise was now coping on her own, and had almost returned
to a normal life except she still couldn't speak. She seemed to
be self-sufficient within her own world and the doctor agreed
that she no longer needed a full-time nurse.

The day the nurse left Andrew decided to take Louise off
for a week's holiday abroad. He wanted to return to the
South of France and the Colombe d'Or, but the specialist
had advised against it, explaining that any past association
might trigger off a memory that in itself could cause a further
relapse.

"Witch doctors' mumbo jumbo," Andrew complained but
nevertheless took her to Venice, not Colombe d'Or. Once
there, he was delighted by the interest Louise showed in the
beautiful and ancient city. Her eyes lit up at the sight of
Torcello and she appeared to revel in the trip on a gondola
down the twisting waterways past irreplaceable Italian
architecture. Again and again she squeezed his hand. As they
sat on a piazza for an evening drink, she inclined her head
and listened to a quintet playing on St Mark's Square.
Andrew was confident that she could now hear everything he
told her. The night before they flew back to England he woke
to find her reading James Morris's *Venice* which he had left by
his side of the bed. It was the first time she had opened a book

since the accident. When he smiled at her she grinned back. He laughed, wanting to hear her laugh.

Andrew returned to the Ministry of Defence on Monday. On his desk there was a general directive from the Chancellor of the Exchequer, requiring the budget estimates for all the big-spending Departments of State. Andrew fought hard to keep the Polaris missile after being convinced by the Joint Chiefs of its strategic importance to the nation's defence. He was, however, continually reminded by his colleagues in the House that it was party policy to rid themselves of 'the warmongers' toy'.

When the Secretary of State returned from Cabinet he told Andrew, "We've had our way: the Cabinet were impressed by the case. But I can promise you one thing – you won't be the golden boy at this year's party conference."

"It will make a change for them even to notice me," replied Andrew.

He breathed a sigh of relief while the Joint Chiefs were delighted, but a week later he lost – by default – the same argument with his own General Purposes Committee in Edinburgh. In his absence, they passed a resolution deploring the retention of the Polaris missile and demanded that all the ministers involved should reconsider their decision. They stopped short of naming Andrew, but everyone knew whose scalp they were after. His case was not helped by Tom Carson making yet another inflammatory speech in the House, claiming that Andrew had been browbeaten by the Joint Chiefs and was nothing more than a Polaris puppet.

Andrew's trips to Edinburgh had become less frequent over the past year because of his commitments to Louise and the Defence Department. During the year three members of his General Management Committee had been replaced with a new group calling themselves 'Militant Tendency' led by Frank Boyle. It wasn't just Edinburgh Carlton that was facing the problem of a left-wing insurgence – as Andrew learned from colleague after colleague who was beginning to work out why the left were pushing a resolution at the party conference proposing that members should be re-selected for each election. Some of his more right-wing colleagues had already been replaced, and it didn't take a Wrangler to work out that once a majority of the Trotskyites had secured places on his Management Committee Andrew could be removed at their whim, whatever his past experience or record.

Whenever Andrew was in Edinburgh the local people continually assured him of their support and their confidence in him, but he could not forget, despite their avowals, that it would still take only a handful of votes to remove him. Andrew feared what the outcome would be if many other members were facing the same problem as he faced in Edinburgh.

"Dad, can I have a new cricket bat, please?"

"What's wrong with the old one?" asked Simon, as they came out of the house.

"It's too small," he said, waving it around as if it was an extension to his arm.

"It will have to do, I'm afraid."

"But Martin Henderson's dad has given him a new bat to start the season."

"I'm sorry, Peter, the truth is that Martin's father is far better off than I am."

"I'll tell you one thing," said Peter with feeling. "I'm sure not going to be an MP when I grow up." Simon smiled as his son removed an old cricket ball from his trouser pocket and tossed it over to his father. "Anyway, I bet you can't get me out even though I've only got a small bat."

"Don't forget we still have the junior size stumps left over from last year," said Simon, "so it will be just as hard to hit them."

"Stop making excuses, Dad. Just admit you're past it."

Simon burst out laughing. "We'll see," he said, with more bravado than conviction. Simon always enjoyed a few overs in the garden against his elder son although at the age of thirteen Peter was already able to play his best deliveries with a confidence that was beginning to look ominous.

It was several overs before Simon removed Peter's middle stump and took his turn at the crease.

Michael ran out of the house to join them in the field and

Simon couldn't help noticing that he was wearing a pair of jeans that were far too short and had once belonged to Peter.

"Get behind the wicket, nipper," shouted Peter at his eleven-year-old brother. "Because that's where most of the balls will be going." Michael happily obeyed without comment.

A colleague in the House had recently warned Simon that by fourteen they began to beat you and by sixteen they hoped not to show they weren't trying their hardest any longer.

Simon gritted his teeth as he watched his elder son's fastest ball safely on to the middle of the bat. The way he was going Peter wouldn't have to wait much longer before he could clean bowl him.

He managed to keep his wicket intact for a further five minutes before he was rescued by Elizabeth who came out to tell them that supper was ready.

"What, hamburgers and chips again?" said Michael as his mother put a plate in front of him.

"You're lucky to get anything," Elizabeth snapped back.

Simon cursed again at the damage his own selfish greed had brought upon his family, and marvelled at how little they all complained. He said nothing, only too aware that the previous day Elizabeth had completed her last week at the hospital and was already missing St Mary's.

"How did you all get on?" she asked cheerily.

"I'll survive," said Simon, still thinking about his overdraft.

Once the Chancellor had presented his mini budget, in November 1976, the long process of the Finance Bill, confirming all the new measures proposed, fully occupied the House. Charles, although not a member of the front-bench finance team, regularly took the lead among back-benchers on clauses on which he had specialist knowledge.

He and Clive Reynolds studied the new Finance Bill meticulously and between them picked out the seven clauses that would have an adverse effect on banking.

Reynolds guided Charles through each clause, suggesting changes, rewording, and on some occasions presenting an argument for deleting whole sections of the bill. Charles learned quickly and was soon adding his own ideas; one or two even made Clive Reynolds reconsider. After Charles had put forward amendments to the House on three of the clauses both front benches became respectfully attentive whenever he rose to present a case. One morning, after the Government's defeat on a clause relating to banking loans, he received a note of congratulation from Margaret Thatcher.

The clause Charles most wanted to see removed from the bill concerned a client's right to privacy when dealing with a merchant bank. The Shadow Chancellor was aware of Charles's specialised knowledge on this subject and invited him to oppose clause 110 from the front bench. Charles realised that if he could defeat the Government on this clause he might be invited to join the Shadow finance team in the run-up to the general election.

Judging by the chairman of Ways and Means' selection of amendments the Whips estimated that clause 110 on banking privacy would be reached some time on Thursday afternoon.

On Thursday morning Charles rehearsed his arguments thoroughly with Clive Reynolds, who only had one or two minor amendments to add before Charles set off for the House. When he arrived at the Commons there was a note on the message board asking him to phone the Shadow Chancellor urgently.

"The Government are going to accept a Liberal amendment tabled late last night," the Shadow Chancellor told him.

"Why?" said Charles.

"Minimum change is what they're really after, but it gets them off the hook and at the same time keeps the Liberal vote intact. In essence nothing of substance has changed, but you'll need to study the wording carefully. Can I leave you to handle the problem?"

"Certainly," said Charles, pleased with the responsibility with which they were now entrusting him.

He walked down the long corridor to the vote office and picked up the sheet with clause 110 on it and the proposed

Liberal amendment. He read them both through half a dozen
times before he started to make notes. Parliamentary counsel, with their usual expertise, had produced an ingenious
amendment. Charles ducked into a nearby phone booth and
rang Clive Reynolds at the bank. Charles dictated the
amendment over the phone to him and then remained silent
while Reynolds considered its implications.

"Clever bunch of sharpies. It's a cosmetic job, but it won't
change the power it invests in the Government one iota.
Were you thinking of returning to the bank? That would give
me time to work on it."

"No," said Charles. "Are you free for lunch?"

Clive Reynolds checked his diary: a Belgian banker would
be lunching in the boardroom but his colleagues could
handle that. "Yes, I'm free."

"Good," said Charles. "Why don't you join me at White's
around one o'clock?"

"Thank you," said Reynolds. "By then I should have
had enough time to come up with some credible alternatives."

Charles spent the rest of the morning rewriting his speech
which he hoped would counter the Liberal argument and
make them reconsider their position. If it met with
Reynolds's imprimatur the day could still be his. He read
through the clause once more, convinced he had found a way
through the loophole the civil servants couldn't block. He
placed his speech and the amended clause in his inside
pocket and went down to the Members' Entrance and
jumped into a waiting taxi.

As the cab drove up St James's Charles thought he saw his
wife coming down the opposite side of the road. He pushed
down the window to be sure but she had disappeared into
Prunier's. He wondered with which of her girl friends she was
lunching.

The cab travelled on up St James's and came to a halt
outside White's. Charles found he was a few minutes early so
he decided to walk down to Prunier's and ask Fiona if she
would like to come to the House after lunch and hear him
oppose the clause. Reaching the restaurant he glanced

through the pane-glass window. He froze on the spot. Fiona was chatting at the bar with a man whose back was to Charles but he thought he recognised his profile although he couldn't be certain. He noticed that his wife was wearing a dress he had never seen before. He didn't move as he watched a waiter bow, then guide the pair towards a corner table where they were conveniently out of sight. Charles's first instinct was to march straight in and confront them; but he remained outside. For what seemed an interminable time he stood alone, uncertain what to do next. Finally he crossed back over St James's Street and stood in the doorway of the Economist building going over several plans. In the end he decided to do nothing but wait. He stood there so cold and so incensed that he did not consider returning for his lunch appointment with Clive Reynolds a few hundred yards up the road.

An hour and twenty minutes later the man came out of Prunier's alone and headed up St James's. Charles felt a sense of relief until he saw him turn into St James's Place. He checked his watch: Reynolds would have left by now but he would still be well in time for clause number 110. A few minutes later Fiona stepped out of the restaurant and followed in the man's footsteps. Charles crossed the road, causing a cab to swerve while another motorist slammed on her brakes. He didn't notice. He shadowed his wife, careful to keep a safe distance. When she reached the far end of the passage he watched Fiona enter the Stafford Hotel. Once she was through the swing doors Fiona stepped into an empty lift.

Charles came up to the swing doors and stared at the little numbers above the lift, watching them light up in succession until they stopped at four.

Charles marched through the swing doors and up to the reception desk.

"Can I help you, sir?" the hall porter asked.

"Er – is the dining-room in this hotel on the fourth floor?" asked Charles.

"No, sir," replied the hall porter, surprised. "The dining-room is on the ground floor to your left" – he indicated the way with a sweep of his hand — "there are only bedrooms on the fourth floor."

"Thank you," said Charles and marched back outside.

He returned slowly to the Economist building, incensed, where he waited for nearly two hours pacing up and down St James's before the man emerged from the Stafford Hotel; Alexander Dalglish hailed a taxi and disappeared in the direction of Piccadilly.

Fiona left the hotel about twenty minutes later, and took the path through to the park before setting off towards Eaton Square. On three occasions Charles had to fall back to be certain Fiona didn't spot him; once he was so close he thought he saw a smile of satisfaction come over her face.

He had followed his wife most of the way across St James's Park when he suddenly remembered. He checked his watch, then dashed back to the roadside, hailed a taxi and shouted, "The House of Commons, as fast as you can." The cabby took seven minutes and Charles passed him two pound notes before running up the steps into the Members' Lobby and through to the Chamber out of breath. He stopped by the Serjeant-at-Arms's chair.

From the table where he sat during Committee of the whole House, the Mace lowered on its supports in front of the table, the chairman of Ways and Means faced a packed House. He read from the division list.

"The Ayes to the right 294.
The Noes to the left 293.
The Ayes have it, the Ayes have it."

The Government benches cheered and the Conservatives looked distinctly glum. "What clause were they debating?" a still out of breath Charles asked the Serjeant-at-Arms.

"Clause 110, Mr Seymour."

BOOK FOUR
1977–1989
THE CABINET

CHAPTER TWENTY TWO

Raymond's second trip to the States was at the behest of the Secretary of State for Trade: he was asked to present the country's export and import assessment to the International Monetary Fund, following up a loan granted to Britain the previous November. His civil servants went over the prepared speech with him again and again, emphasising to their minister the responsibility that had been placed on his shoulders. Even the Governor of the Bank of England's private office had been consulted.

"A chance to impress a few people beyond the boundaries of Leeds," Kate assured him.

Raymond's speech was scheduled for the Wednesday morning. He flew into Washington on the Sunday and spent Monday and Tuesday listening to the problems of other nations' trade ministers while trying to get used to the dreadful earphones and the female interpreter.

The conference was attended by most of the leading industrial nations and the British Ambassador, Sir Peter Ramsbotham, told Raymond over dinner at the Embassy that this was a real chance to convince the hard-headed international bankers that Britain cared about economic realities and was still worth their financial backing.

Raymond soon realised that convincing such a gathering required a very different technique from shouting from a soap box on a street corner in Leeds or even addressing the House from the dispatch box. He was glad he had not been scheduled to present his case on the opening day. Over leisurely lunches he re-established his existing contacts in Congress and made some new ones.

The night before he was to deliver his speech Raymond hardly slept. He continued to rehearse each crucial phrase and repeated the salient points that needed to be emphasised until he almost knew them by heart. At three o'clock in the morning he dropped his speech on the floor beside his bed and phoned Kate to have a chat before she went to work.

"I'd enjoy hearing your speech at the conference," she told him. "Although I don't suppose it would be much different from the thirty times I've listened to it in the bedroom."

Once he had said goodbye to Kate he fell into a deep sleep. He woke early that morning and went over the speech one last time before leaving for the conference centre.

All the homework and preparation proved worthwhile. By the time he turned the last page Raymond couldn't be certain how convincing his case had been, but he knew it was the best speech he had ever delivered. When he looked up the smiles all around the oval table assured him that his contribution had been well received. As the ambassador pointed out to him as he rose to leave, any signs of emotion at these gatherings were almost unknown. He felt confident that the IMF loan would be renewed.

There followed two further speeches before they broke for lunch. At the end of the afternoon session Raymond walked out into the clear Washington air and decided to make his way back to the Embassy on foot. He was exhilarated by the experience of dominating an international conference and picked up an evening paper: an article covering the conference suggested that Raymond would be Britain's next Labor Chancellor. He smiled at the spelling. Just the closing day to go, followed by the official banquet and he would be back home by the weekend.

When he reached the Embassy the guard had to double-check: they weren't used to ministers arriving on foot and without a bodyguard. Raymond was allowed to proceed down the tree-lined drive towards the massive Lutyens building. He looked up to see the British flag was flying at half mast and wondered which distinguished American had died.

"Who has died?" he asked the tail-coated butler who opened the door for him..

"The Foreign Secretary, sir."

"Anthony Crosland? I knew he had gone into hospital, but . . ." said Raymond almost to himself. He hurried into the Embassy to find it abuzz with telexes and coded messages. Raymond sat alone in his private sitting-room for several hours and later, to the horror of the security staff, slipped out for a quiet dinner at the Mayflower Hotel with Senator Hart.

Raymond returned to the conference table at nine o'clock the next morning to listen to the French Minister of Commerce put his case for renewed funds. He was savouring the thought of the official banquet at the White House to be held that evening when he was tapped on the shoulder by Sir Peter Ramsbotham, who indicated by touching his lips with his forefinger and pointing that they must have a word in private.

"The Prime Minister wants you to return on the midmorning Concorde," said Sir Peter. "It leaves in an hour. On arrival in Britain you're to go straight to Downing Street."

"What's this all about?"

"I have no idea, that was the only instruction I received from No. 10," confided the ambassador.

Raymond returned to the conference table and made his apologies to the chairman, left the room and was driven immediately to the waiting plane. "Your bags will follow, sir," he was assured.

He was back on English soil three hours and forty-one minutes later, a little after seven-thirty. The purser ensured that he was the first to disembark. A car waiting by the side of the plane whisked him to Downing Street. He arrived just as the Prime Minister was going to dinner, accompanied by an elderly African statesman who was waving his trademark fan back and forth.

"Welcome home, Ray," said the Prime Minister, leaving the African leader. "I'd ask you to join us, but as you can see I'm entertaining the President of Malawi. Let's have a word in my study."

Once Raymond had settled into a chair Mr Callaghan wasted no time.

"Because of Tony's tragic death I have had to make a few changes which will include moving the Secretary of State for Trade. I was hoping you would be willing to take over from him."

Raymond sat up straighter. "I should be honoured, Prime Minister."

"Good. You've earned your promotion, Raymond. I also hear you did us proud in America, very proud."

"Thank you."

"You'll be appointed to the Privy Council immediately and your first Cabinet meeting will be at ten o'clock tomorrow. Now, if you'll excuse me, I must catch up with Dr Banda."

Raymond was left standing in the hall.

He asked his driver to take him back to the flat. All he wanted to do was to tell Kate the news. When he arrived the flat was empty: then he remembered she wasn't expecting him back until the next day. He phoned her home but after twenty continuous rings he resigned himself to the fact that she was out. "Damn," he said out loud, and after pacing around phoned Joyce to let her know the news. Once again there was no reply.

He went into the kitchen and checked to see what was in the fridge: a piece of curled-up bacon, some half-eaten Brie, three eggs. He couldn't help thinking about the banquet he was missing at the White House.

The Right Honourable Raymond Gould QC, MP, Her Britannic Majesty's Principal Secretary of State for Trade, sat on the kitchen stool, opened a tin of baked beans and devoured them with a fork.

Charles closed the file. It had taken him a month to gather all the proof he needed. Albert Cruddick, the private investigator Charles had selected from the Yellow Pages, had been expensive but discreet. Dates, times, places were all fully chronicled. The only name was that of Alexander Dalglish, the same rendezvous, lunch at Prunier's followed by the

Stafford Hotel. They hadn't stretched Mr Cruddick's imagination but at least the detective had spared Charles the necessity of standing in the entrance of the Economist building once, sometimes twice a week for hours on end.

Somehow he had managed to get through that month without giving himself away. He had also made his own notes of the dates and times Fiona claimed she was going to be in the constituency. He had then called his agent in Sussex Downs and, after veiled questioning, elicited answers that corroborated Mr Cruddick's findings.

Charles saw as little of Fiona as possible during this time, explaining that the Finance Bill was occupying his every moment. His lie had at least a semblance of credibility for he had worked tirelessly on the remaining clauses left for debate, and by the time the watered-down bill had become law he had just about recovered from the disaster of the Government's successful retention of clause 110.

Charles placed the file on the table by the side of his chair and waited patiently for the call. He knew exactly where she was at that moment and just the thought of it made him sick to his stomach. The phone rang.

"The subject left five minutes ago," said a voice.

"Thank you," said Charles and replaced the receiver. He knew it would take her about twenty minutes to reach home.

"Why do you think she walks home instead of taking a taxi?" he had once asked Mr Cruddick.

"Gets rid of any smells," Mr Cruddick had replied quite matter-of-factly.

Charles shuddered. "And what about him? What does he do?" He never could refer to him as Alexander, or even Dalglish; or as anything but 'him'.

"He goes to the Lansdowne Club, swims ten lengths or plays a game of squash before returning home. Swimming and squash both solve the problem," Mr Cruddick explained cheerily.

The key turned in the lock. Charles braced himself and picked up the file. Fiona came straight into the drawing-room and was visibly shaken to discover her husband sitting in an armchair with a small suitcase by his side.

She recovered quickly, walked over and kissed him on the cheek. "What brings you home so early, darling? The Socialists taken the day off?" She laughed nervously at her joke.

"This," he said, standing up and holding the file out to her.

She took off her coat and dropped it over the sofa. Then she opened the buff folder and started to read. He watched her carefully. First the colour drained from her cheeks, then her legs gave way and she collapsed on to the sofa. Finally she started to sob.

"It's not true, none of it," she protested.

"You know very well that every detail is accurate."

"Charles, it's you I love, I don't care about him, you must believe that."

"I believe nothing of the sort," said Charles. "You're no longer someone I could live with."

"Live with? I've been living on my own since the day you entered Parliament."

"Perhaps I might have come home more often if you had showed some interest in starting a family."

"And do you imagine I am to blame for that inadequacy," she said.

Charles ignored the innuendo and continued. "In a few moments I am going to my club where I shall spend the night. I expect you to be out of this house within seven days. When I return I want there to be no sign of you or any of your goods or chattels, to quote the original agreement."

"Where will I go?" she cried.

"You could try your lover first, but no doubt his wife might object. Failing that, you can camp down at your father's place."

"What if I refuse to go?" said Fiona, turning to defiance.

"Then I shall throw you out, as one should a whore, and cite Alexander Dalglish in a very messy divorce case."

"Give me another chance. I'll never look at him again," begged Fiona, starting to cry once more.

"I seem to remember your telling me that once before, and indeed I did give you another chance. The results have been all too plain to see." He pointed to the file where it had fallen to the floor.

Fiona stopped weeping when she realised that Charles remained unmoved.

"I shall not see you again. We shall be separated for at least two years, when we will carry through as quiet a divorce as possible in the circumstances. If you cause me a moment of embarrassment I shall drag you both through the mire. Believe me."

"You'll regret your decision, Charles. I promise you. I'll not be pushed aside quite that easily."

"They've done *what*?" said Joyce.

"Two Communists have put their names forward for election to the General Purposes Committee," repeated Fred Padgett.

"Over my dead body." Joyce's voice was unusually sharp.

"I thought that would be your attitude," said Fred.

Joyce searched for the pencil and paper that were normally on the table by the phone.

"When's the meeting?" she asked.

"Next Thursday."

"Have we got reliable people to stand against them?"

"Of course," said Fred. "Councillor Reg Illingworth and Jenny Simpkins from the Co-op."

"They're both sensible enough but between them they couldn't knock the skin off a rice pudding."

"Shall I phone Raymond at the House and get him to come up for the meeting?"

"No," said Joyce. "He's got enough to worry about now that he's in the Cabinet without piling up trouble for him in Leeds. Leave it to me."

She replaced the receiver and sat down to compose her thoughts. A few minutes later she went over to her desk and rummaged about for the full list of the G.P. Committee. She checked the sixteen names carefully, realising that if two Communists were to get themselves elected this time within five years they could control the committee – and then even remove Raymond. She knew how these people worked. With any luck, if they got bloody noses now they might slink off to another constituency.

She checked the sixteen names once more before putting on a pair of sensible walking shoes. During the next four days she visited several homes in the area. "I was just passing," she explained to nine of the wives who had husbands on the committee. The four men who never listened to a word their wives said were visited by Joyce after work. The three who had never cared for Raymond were left well alone.

By Thursday afternoon thirteen people knew only too well what was expected of them. Joyce sat alone hoping he would call that evening. She cooked herself a Lancashire hotpot but only picked at it, then later fell asleep in front of the television when she tried to watch the final episode of *Roots*. The phone woke her at five past eleven.

"Raymond?"

"Hope I didn't wake you," said Fred.

"No, no," said Joyce, now impatient to learn the outcome of the meeting. "What happened?"

"Reg and Jenny walked it. Those two Communist bastards only managed three votes between them."

"Well done," said Joyce.

"I did nothing," said Fred, "except count the votes. Shall I tell Raymond what's been happening?"

"No," said Joyce. "No need to let him think we've had any trouble."

Joyce fell back into the chair by the phone, kicked off her walking shoes, and went back to sleep.

She knew she had to plan the whole operation so that her husband would never find out. She sat alone in the house considering the several alternative ways in which she could deceive him. After hours of unproductive thought the idea finally came in a flash. She went over the problems and repercussions again and again until she was convinced that nothing could go wrong. She leafed through the Yellow Pages and made an appointment for the following morning.

The sales lady helped her to try on several wigs, but only one was bearable.

"I think it makes Modom look most elegant, I must say."

She knew that it didn't – it made Modom look awful – but she hoped it would serve its purpose.

She then applied the eye make-up and lipstick she had acquired at Harrods, and pulled out from the back of her cupboard a floral dress she had never liked. She stood in front of the mirror and checked herself. Surely no one would recognise her in Sussex and she prayed that if he found out he would be forgiving.

She left and drove slowly towards the outskirts of London. How would she explain herself if she was caught? Would he remain understanding when he discovered the truth? When she reached the constituency she parked the car in a side road and walked up and down the high street. No one showed any sign of recognition which gave her the confidence to go through with it. And then she saw him.

She had hoped he'd be in the City that morning. She held her breath as he walked towards her. As he passed she said, "Good morning." He turned and smiled, replying with a casual "Good morning," as he might to any constituent. Her heartbeat returned to normal and she went back to find her car.

She drove off completely reassured she could now get away with it. She went over once again what she was going to say, then all too suddenly she had arrived. She parked the car outside the house opposite, got out and bravely walked up the path.

As Raymond stood outside the Cabinet room several of his colleagues came over to congratulate him. At exactly ten o'clock the Prime Minister walked in, bade everyone "Good morning," and took his place at the centre of the oblong table, while the other twenty-one members of the Cabinet filed in behind him and took their places. The Leader of the House, Michael Foot, sat on his left, while the Foreign Secretary and Chancellor were placed opposite him. Raymond was directed to a seat at the end of the table between the Secretary of State for Wales and the Secretary of State for Education.

"I would like to start the meeting," said the Prime Minister, "by welcoming David Owen as Foreign Secretary and Raymond Gould as Secretary of State for Trade." The other nineteen Cabinet members murmured, "Hear, hear" in a discreetly conservative way. David Owen smiled slightly while Raymond could feel himself going red.

"The first item we must discuss in detail is the proposed pact with the Liberals . . ."

Raymond sat back and decided that today he would only listen.

Andrew sat in the small office and listened carefully to the specialist's opinion. Louise was restored to almost perfect health in every way except for her speech. She was reading regularly and had even begun to write short messages in reply to Andrew's questions. The specialist now felt that she needed some other outside interest to take her mind off Robert. Over a year had passed and she could still spend hours simply staring at his photograph.

"I managed to reach Dr Kerslake at home," the specialist said, "and I must concur with her opinion that it would be unwise for your wife to contemplate another pregnancy. But Dr Kerslake does accept my judgement that you should both consider adoption."

"I've already given the idea a lot of thought, even discussed it with my father," Andrew replied. "But both of us felt that Louise would never agree to it."

"It's a calculated risk in the circumstances," said the specialist. "We mustn't forget it's been a whole year. We know to our cost that Mrs Fraser loves children, and if she is set against such a course she is now well capable of letting you know."

"If Louise shows any response I'd be only too willing to give it a try. But in the end it will all depend on her."

"Good. Find out how she feels," said the specialist, "and if you both decide to go ahead I'll arrange a meeting with the local authority." He rose from behind his desk. "I'm sure it won't be hard to find you a suitable child."

"If it were possible for him to come from a Scottish orphans' home, I would appreciate it."

The specialist nodded. "I'll be in touch with you as soon as I have any news."

When Charles returned home he knew at once Fiona had left. He felt an immediate relief. After a week at his club, he was glad the charade was over, a clean, irrevocable break. He strolled into the drawing-room and stopped: something was wrong. It took him a few moments before he realised what she had done.

Fiona had removed every one of the family paintings.

No Wellington above the fireplace, no Victoria behind the sofa. Where the two Landseers and the Constable had hung there was nothing more than thin dusty outlines indicating the size of each picture she had removed. He walked to the library: the Van Dyck, the Murillo and the two small Rembrandts were also missing. Charles ran down the hall. It couldn't be possible, he thought, as he threw open the dining-room door. It was. He stared at the blank wall where only the previous week the Holbein portrait of the first Earl of Bridgwater had hung.

Charles scrabbled in the back of his pocket diary for the number and dialled it frantically. Mr Cruddick listened to the story in silence.

"Remembering how sensitive you are about publicity, Mr Seymour, there are two avenues of approach," he began in his normal level tone and sounding unperturbed. "You can grin and bear it, or the alternative is one I have used often in the past."

Because of the demands of his new job Raymond saw less of Kate and almost nothing of Joyce apart from his fortnightly visits to Leeds. He worked from eight in the morning until he fell asleep at night.

"And you love every minute of it," Kate reminded him whenever he complained. Raymond had also become aware of the subtle changes that had taken place in his life since he had become a member of the Cabinet, the way he was treated by other people, how quickly his slightest whim was granted, how flattery fell from almost every tongue. He began to enjoy the change in status although Kate reminded him that only the Queen could afford to get used to it.

At the Labour party conference that year he allowed his name to be put forward for a place on the National Executive. Although he failed to be elected he managed to finish ahead of several other Cabinet ministers and polled only a few votes less than Neil Kinnock, the darling of the constituency section.

Andrew Fraser, who now looked upon Raymond as someone he could confide in, joined Raymond for what was becoming their traditional conference lunch together on the third day. Andrew told him of his distress at the party's continued drift to the left.

"If some of those resolutions on defence are passed my life will be made impossible," he said, trying to cut into a very tough steak.

"The hotheads always put up resolutions that are never allowed more than a token discussion."

"Token discussion be damned. Some of their mad ideas are beginning to gain credence which, translated, could become party policy."

"Any particular resolution worrying you?" asked Raymond.

"Yes, Tony Benn's latest proposal that members must be re-selected before every election. His idea of democracy and accountability."

"Why should you fear that?"

"If your management committee is taken over by half a dozen Trots they can reverse a decision 50,000 voters have previously agreed on."

"You're over-reacting, Andrew."

"Raymond, if we lose the next election I can see a split in the party that will be so great we may never recover."

"They've been saying that in the Labour party since the day it was founded."

"I hope you're right, but I fear times have changed," said Andrew. "Not so long ago it was you who envied me."

"That can change again." Raymond abandoned the steak, waved his hand and asked the waitress to bring two large brandies.

Charles picked up the phone and dialled a number he had not needed to look up. The new young Portuguese maid answered.

"Is Lady Fiona at home?"

"Lady no home, sir."

"Do you know where she is?" asked Charles, speaking slowly and clearly.

"Go down to country, expect back six o'clock. Take message please?"

"No, thank you," said Charles. "I'll call this evening." He replaced the receiver.

As always the reliable Mr Cruddick was proved right about his wife's movements. Charles called him immediately. They agreed to meet as planned in twenty minutes.

He drove into the Boltons, parked on the far side of the road a few yards from his father-in-law's house and settled down to wait.

A few minutes later a large anonymous pantechnicon van came round the corner and stopped outside No. 24. Mr Cruddick jumped out from the driver's seat. He was dressed in long brown overalls and a flat cap. He was joined by a young assistant who unlocked the back of the van. Mr Cruddick nodded to Charles before proceeding up the steps to the front door.

The Portuguese maid answered when he pressed the bell.

"We have come to collect the goods for Lady Seymour."

"No understand," said the maid.

Mr Cruddick removed from an inside pocket a long type-written letter on Lady Seymour's personal stationery. The Portuguese maid was unable to read the words of a letter her mistress had addressed to Hurlingham Croquet Club agreeing to be their Ladies' President, but she immediately recognised the letter-head and the signature. She nodded and opened the door wider. All Mr Cruddick's carefully laid plans were falling into place.

Mr Cruddick tipped his hat, the sign for Mr Seymour to join them. Charles got out of the car cautiously, checking both ways before he crossed the road. He felt uncomfortable in brown overalls and hated the cap with which Mr Cruddick had supplied him. It was a little small and Charles was acutely conscious how strange he must look but the Portuguese maid apparently didn't notice the incongruity between his aristocratic mien and the working overalls. It did not take long to discover the whereabouts of most of the pictures. Many were just stacked up in the hall, and only one or two had already been hung.

Forty minutes later the three men had located and loaded into the van all but one of them. The Holbein of the first Earl of Bridgwater was nowhere to be found.

"We ought to be on our way," suggested Mr Cruddick a little nervously, but Charles refused to give up the search. For another thirty-five minutes Mr Cruddick sat tapping the wheel of the van before Charles finally conceded that the painting must have been taken elsewhere. Mr Cruddick tipped his hat to the maid while his partner locked up the back of the van.

"A valuable picture, Mr Seymour?" he enquired.

"A family heirloom that would fetch two million at auction," said Charles matter-of-factly before returning to his car.

"Silly question, Albert Cruddick," said Mr Cruddick to himself as he pulled out from the curb and drove towards Eaton Square. When they arrived the locksmith had replaced all three locks on the front door and was waiting on the top step impatiently.

"Strictly cash, guv'nor. No receipt. Makes it possible for the missus and me to go to Ibiza each year, tax free."

By the time Fiona had returned to the Boltons from her trip to Sussex every picture was back in its place at Eaton Square with the exception of Holbein's first Earl of Bridgwater. Mr Cruddick was left clutching a large cheque and uttering the unpalatable view that Mr Seymour would probably have to grin and bear it.

"I'm delighted," said Simon, when he heard the news. "And at Pucklebridge General Hospital?"

"Yes, I answered an advertisement in *The Lancet* for the post of general consultant in the maternity section."

"But your name must have helped there?"

"Certainly not," said Elizabeth vehemently.

"How come?"

"I didn't apply as Dr Kerslake. I filled out the application form in my maiden name of Drummond."

Simon was momentarily silenced. "But they would have recognised you," he protested.

"I had the full frontal treatment from Estée Lauder to ensure they didn't. The final effect fooled even you."

"Don't exaggerate," said Simon.

"I walked straight past you in Pucklebridge High Street, and said 'Good morning,' and you returned the greeting."

Simon stared at her in disbelief. "But what will happen when they find out?"

"They already have," replied Elizabeth sheepishly. "As soon as they offered me the post I went down to see the senior consultant and told him the truth. He hasn't stopped telling everyone since."

"He wasn't cross?"

"Far from it. In fact he said I nearly failed to be offered the post because he felt I wouldn't be safe let loose on the unmarried doctors."

Andrew held Louise's hand as they approached the door of Grunechan Children's Home on the outskirts of Edinburgh. The matron was waiting on the freshly scrubbed doorstep to greet them.

"Good morning, Minister," she said. "We are honoured that you have chosen our little home."

Andrew and Louise smiled.

"Will you be kind enough to follow me?" She led them down a dimly lit corridor to her room, her starched blue uniform crackling as she walked.

"All the children are in the playground at the moment but you will be able to see them from my window." Andrew had already gone over all the orphans' histories and photographs; he couldn't help noticing how one of them bore a striking resemblance to Robert.

They both looked out of the window for several minutes but Louise showed no interest in any of the children. When the boy who resembled Robert ran towards the window, she turned away and took a seat in the corner.

Andrew shook his head. The matron's lips turned down at the corners.

Coffee and biscuits arrived and while they were eating them Andrew tried once more. "Did you want Matron to bring anyone in to meet you, darling?" Louise shook her head. Andrew cursed himself as he feared the experience might only have done her more harm.

"Have we seen everyone?" he asked, looking for an excuse to leave quickly.

"Yes, sir," said the matron, putting down her cup of coffee. "Well," she hesitated, "there was one girl we didn't bother you with."

"Why not?" asked Andrew out of curiosity.

"Well, you see, she's black."

Andrew stiffened.

"And what's more," continued the matron, "we have absolutely no idea who her parents were. She was left on the doorstep. Not at all the sort of girl to be brought up in a minister's home."

Andrew was so incensed that he quite forgot about consulting Louise who was still resting silently in the corner.

"I should like to see her," he said.

"If you insist," said the matron, a little taken aback. "I'm afraid she hasn't got her best clothes on," she added before she left the room.

Andrew paced up and down, conscious that if Louise hadn't been there he might well have lost his temper with the woman. The matron returned a few moments later with a little girl aged four, perhaps five, and so thin that her dress hung on her like a coathanger. Andrew couldn't see her face because she kept her head bowed.

"Look up, child," commanded the matron. The girl raised

her head slowly. She had the most perfect oval face and olive skin, piercing black eyes and a smile that immediately captivated Andrew.

"What's your name?" he asked quietly.

"Clarissa," she said, and dropped her head again. He wanted to help her so much, and it made him feel guilty that he had put the poor child through such a pointless ordeal.

The matron still looked affronted and with a sniff she said, "You can leave us now, child." Clarissa turned and walked towards the door. Looking at Louise the matron added, "I am sure you agree with me, Mrs Fraser, the girl's not at all suitable."

They both turned to Louise. Her face was alight, her eyes shining in a way Andrew had not seen since Robert's death. She stood up, walked quickly towards the child before she could reach the door, and stared into her black eyes.

"I think you're beautiful," Louise said, "and I do hope you will want to come and live with us."

CHAPTER
TWENTY THREE

'Order, order' had meant nothing to the British electorate until 1978 when the House passed a resolution allowing the proceedings in the Commons to be broadcast on radio. Simon had supported the motion on broadcasting, putting forward the argument that radio was a further extension of democracy as it showed the House at work and allowed the voters to know exactly what their elected representatives were up to. Simon listened carefully to a number of his supplementaries, and realised for the first time that he spoke a little too quickly when he had a minister on the run.

Raymond, on the other hand, did not support the motion as he feared that the cries of "Hear, hear" or "Shame" and the heckling of the Prime Minister would sound to listeners like schoolchildren in a playground squabble. Overhearing the words with only one's imagination to set the scene would, he believed, create a false impression about the many aspects of a member's daily duties. When one evening Raymond heard a parliamentary debate in which he had taken part he was delighted to discover his arguments carried so much conviction.

When Andrew heard his own voice on Radio Four one morning answering questions on defence issues he was suddenly aware that what he had always considered was a faint trace of a Scottish accent was in fact – when he was angry or excited – quite pronounced.

Charles found the morning programme an excellent way of catching up with any proceedings he had missed the previous day. As he now woke each morning alone, 'Yesterday in Parliament' became his constant companion. He hadn't been aware of how upper class he sounded until the occasion on which he followed Tom Carson. He had no intention of changing his voice for the radio.

When the Queen opened the new underground extension to Heathrow airport on 16 December 1977 Raymond was the minister commanded to be present. Joyce made one of her rare trips down to London as they were invited to join the Queen for lunch after the ceremony. When Joyce selected her new dress from Harvey Nichols, she stood in the little cubicle behind a drawn curtain to make sure it was possible for her to curtsey properly. "Good morning, Your Majesty," she practised with a slight wobble, to the bemusement of the shop assistant waiting patiently outside.

By the time she had returned to the flat Joyce was confident that she could carry out her part in the proceedings as well as any courtier. As she prepared for Raymond's return from the morning Cabinet meeting she hoped he would be pleased with her efforts. She had long given up hope of being a mother, but still liked to believe she could be a good wife. Raymond had forewarned her that he would have to change as soon as he arrived at the flat to be sure of being at Green Park before the Queen arrived. After they had accompanied an entourage to Heathrow on the new extension, a journey that would take thirty minutes, they were to return to Buckingham Palace for lunch. Raymond had already come in contact with his monarch on several occasions in his official capacity as a Cabinet minister, but for Joyce it was to be the first time she had been presented.

Once she had had her bath and dressed – she knew Raymond would never forgive her if she were the reason he was late – she began to lay out his clothes. Tail coat, grey pin-striped trousers, white shirt, stiff collar and a silver-grey tie, all hired that morning from Moss Bros. All that he still needed was a clean white handkerchief for his top pocket, just showing in a straight line, as the Duke of Edinburgh always wore his.

Joyce rummaged around in Raymond's chest of drawers, admiring the new shirts as she searched for a handkerchief.

When she first saw the scribbled note peaking out underneath the collar of a pink shirt lying near the bottom of the pile, she assumed it must be an old laundry bill. Then she spotted the word 'Darling'. She felt suddenly sick as she looked more closely.

> Darling Carrot Top,
>   If you ever wear this one I might even agree to marry you.
>
> Kate.

Joyce sank on the end of the bed as the tears trickled down her face. Her perfect day was shattered. She knew at once what course of action she must take. She replaced the unworn shirt and closed the drawer, after first removing the note, and then sat alone in the drawing-room waiting for Raymond to return.

He arrived back at the flat with only a few minutes to spare and was delighted to find his wife changed and ready.

"I'm running it a bit close," he said, going straight into the bedroom.

Joyce followed and watched him don his morning dress suit. When he had straightened his tie in the mirror, she faced him.

"What do you think?" he asked, not noticing the slight paleness in her cheeks.

She hesitated. "You look fantastic, Raymond. Now come along or we'll be late, and that would never do."

When Ronnie Nethercote invited him to lunch at the Ritz, Simon knew things must be looking up again. After a drink in the lounge they were ushered to a corner table overlooking the park in the most palatial dining-room in London. Scattered around the other tables were men who were household names in Ronnie's world as well as in Simon's.

When the head waiter offered them menus Ronnie waved his hand and said, "Order the country vegetable soup, followed by beef off the trolley, take my word for it."

"Sounds like a safe bet," said Simon.

"Unlike our last little venture," Ronnie grunted. "How much are you still in hock because of the collapse of Nethercote and Company?"

"Fourteen thousand three hundred pounds when I last looked but I'm making inroads slowly. It's paying the interest before you can cut down on the capital that really hurts."

"How do you imagine I felt when we were overdrawn seven mill and then the bank decided to pull the rug from under my feet without any warning?"

"As two of the buttons on your waistcoat can no longer reach the holes they were originally tailored for, Ronnie, I must assume those problems are now a thing of the past."

"You're right." He laughed. "Which is why I invited you to lunch. The only person who ended up losing money on that deal was you. If you'd stayed on as the other directors did, at five grand a year, the company would still owe you £11,100 of earned income."

Simon groaned.

The carver wheeled the trolley of beef up to their table.

"Wait a moment, my boy, I haven't even begun. Morgan Grenfell want me to change the structure of the new company and will be injecting a large amount of cash. At the moment Whitechapel Properties – I hope you approve of the name – is still a one-hundred-pound off-the-shelf company. I own sixty per cent and the bank's got forty. Now before the new agreement is signed, I'm going to offer you –"

"Would you like it well done, as usual, Mr Nethercote?"

"Yes, Sam," said Ronnie, slipping the carver a pound note.

"I am going to offer you –"

"And your guest, sir?" the carver said, glancing at Simon.

"Medium, please."

"Yes, sir."

"I am going to offer you one per cent of the new company, in other words one share."

Simon didn't comment, feeling confident Ronnie still hadn't finished.

"Aren't you going to ask?" said Ronnie.

"Ask what?" said Simon.

"You politicians get dumber by the minute. If I am going to offer you a one-pound share, how much do you think I am going to demand in return?"

"Well, I can't believe it's going to be one pound," said Simon grinning.

"Wrong," said Ronnie. "One per cent of the company is yours for one pound."

"Will that be sufficient, sir?" said the carver, putting a plate of beef in front of Simon.

"Hold it, Sam," said Ronnie before Simon could reply. "I repeat I'm offering you one per cent of the company for one pound; now ask your question again, Sam."

"Will that be sufficient, sir?" repeated the carver.

"It's most generous," said Simon.

"Did you hear that, Sam?"

"I certainly did, sir."

"Right, Simon, you owe me a pound."

Simon laughed, removed his wallet from his inside pocket, took out a pound note and handed it over.

"Now the purpose of that little exercise," said Ronnie, turning back to the carver and pocketing the note, "was to prove that Sam here isn't the only person who could make a quid for himself this afternoon." Sam smiled, having no idea what Mr Nethercote was talking about, and placed a large plate of well-done beef in front of him.

Ronnie took out an envelope from his inside pocket and passed it to Simon.

"Do I open it now?" asked Simon.

"Yes – I want to see your reaction."

Simon opened the envelope and studied its contents. A certificate for one share in the new company with a true value of over £10,000.

"Well, well, what do you say?" said Ronnie.

"I'm speechless," said Simon.

"First politician I've known who's ever suffered from that problem."

Simon laughed. "Thank you, Ronnie. It's an incredibly generous gesture."

"No it's not. You were loyal to the old company, so why shouldn't you prosper with the new one?"

"That reminds me, does the name 'Archie Millburn' mean anything to you?" asked Simon.

Ronnie hesitated. "No, no, should it?"

"Only that I thought he might be the man who convinced Morgan Grenfell that you were worth bailing out."

"No, that name doesn't ring any bells. Mind you, Morgan Grenfell have never admitted where they obtained their information from but they knew every last detail about the old company. But if I come across the name Millburn I'll let you know. Enough of business. Fill me in on what's happening in your world. How's your lady wife?"

"Deceiving me."

"Deceiving you?"

"Yes, she's been putting on wigs and dressing up in strange clothes."

Clarissa wet her bed every night for the first month at Pelham Crescent but Louise never complained. Day by day Andrew watched as mother and daughter grew in mutual confidence. Clarissa assumed from her first meeting with Louise that she could talk as normally as any grown-up and chatted away to her night and day. Half the time Louise didn't reply, only because she couldn't get a word in.

Just when Andrew felt everything was getting back on a normal footing at home trouble erupted in Edinburgh. His General Management Committee, which now included five members of Militant Tendency, tabled a motion of no confidence in their member. Their leader, Frank Boyle, had been building up a power base with the sole intention, Andrew suspected, of ousting the member and taking over himself. He didn't discuss the problem with Louise, as the specialist had advised him to avoid any undue stress while Clarissa was settling in.

The five men who wanted Andrew removed had chosen the following Thursday to hold the meeting because they knew the annual Defence Review was due for a full debate in the House that day. If Andrew was unable to attend their meeting Frank Boyle knew they would have a better chance of winning their motion. If he did turn up to defend himself they were also aware that an embarrassing explanation would have to be made for his absence during the debate. When the Prime Minister was informed of the dilemma by the Chief Whip he had no hesitation in telling Andrew to forget the defence debate and go to Edinburgh.

Andrew took the shuttle up on Thursday afternoon and was met at the airport by his chairman, Hamish Ramsey.

"I apologise about you being put through this ordeal, Andrew," he said at once. "I can assure you it's none of my doing, but I must also warn you it's not the same Labour party that I joined over twenty years ago."

"How do you think the vote will go tonight?" asked Andrew.

"You'll win this time. The votes have been decided before the meeting takes place. There's only one waverer and he's so gutless that your very presence will stop him siding with the Trotskies."

When Andrew arrived at his Edinburgh headquarters he was left alone outside the committee room in a cold corridor for over an hour. He knew his opponents were holding things up in the hope he would become frustrated before he eventually had to face them. At last they invited him to join them and he immediately sensed what the Spanish Inquisition must have felt like: question after question from sour-faced men who had never helped him win the seat in the first place and were now alleging that he had shown scant interest in the constituency. Andrew stood his ground and became angry only when Frank Boyle referred to him as 'that son of a Tory'.

"When did you last see your father?" flashed through his mind.

"My father has done more for this city than you could ever hope to do in your lifetime," he told Boyle.

"Then why don't you join his party?" came back Boyle's retort.

Andrew was about to answer when Hamish Ramsey banged the table with his gavel and said, "Enough, enough. It's time to stop this squabbling and vote."

Andrew felt a stab of anxiety as the little slips were passed up to the chairman to be counted. The outcome was five-all and Hamish Ramsey immediately cast his vote in favour of Andrew.

"At least you'll be safe for the coming election, laddie," said Hamish as they drove to the Airport Hotel. "But I wouldn't like to account for much beyond that."

When Andrew arrived back in Pelham Crescent the next morning Louise greeted him at the door.

"Everything all right in Edinburgh?" she asked.

"Fine," said Andrew, taking her in his arms.

"Do you want to hear the good news?"

"Yes," said Andrew, smiling.

"Clarissa didn't wet her bed last night. Perhaps you should stay away more often."

Finally Charles knew he had to discuss what could be done about the stolen Holbein with his solicitor, Sir David Napley. Sir David instructed leading counsel and six weeks later Charles was told that if he sued the Holbein might eventually be returned but not before the story had been on the front page of every national paper. Charles had Albert Cruddick's opinion confirmed: "Grin and bear it."

Fiona had been out of touch for well over a year when the letter came. Charles immediately recognised her handwriting and ripped open the envelope. Only one glance at the writing was enough to make him tear up the missive and deposit the little pieces in the waste-paper basket by his desk. He left for the Commons in a rage.

All through the day he thought of the one word he had taken in from the scrawled hand. Holbein. When he returned from the Commons after the ten o'clock division Charles searched for the remains of the letter, which the daily had conscientiously deposited in the dustbin. After rummaging among potato peelings, eggshells and empty tins Charles spent over an hour Sellotaping the little pieces of paper together. Then he read the letter carefully.

24 The Boltons,
London, S W 10
11 October 1978

Dear Charles,

Enough time has now passed for us to try and treat each
other in a civilised way. Alexander and I wish to marry
and Veronica Dalglish has agreed to an immediate divorce and has not insisted we wait the necessary two years
to establish separation.

"You'll have to wait every day of the two years, you bitch,"
he said out loud. Then he came to the one sentence for which
he was searching.

I realise this might not immediately appeal to you but if
you felt able to fall in with our plans I would be happy to
return the Holbein immediately.
                    Yours ever,
                    Fiona.

He crumpled up the paper in the ball of his hand before
dropping it on the fire.

Charles remained awake into the early hours considering
his reply.

At a Thursday morning Cabinet meeting James Callaghan
informed his colleagues that the Liberal leader, David Steel,
was not willing to continue the Lib/Lab pact after the end of
the current session.

"That can only mean one thing," the Prime Minister
continued. "We must all be prepared for a general election at
any time from now on. I am confident we can hold out until
Christmas, but not for much longer after that."

Raymond was saddened by the news. He felt after two
years in the Cabinet that he was just beginning to be of some
use to the Department of Trade: the changes he was implementing were starting to take effect. But he knew he
needed considerably more time if he hoped to leave a permanent impression on his ministry.

Kate's enthusiasm spurred him on to work even longer

hours and to push through as many of his innovations before the next election as possible.

"I'm trying my damnedest," he told her. "But do remember that the speed of the bureaucratic machine makes British Rail look like Concorde."

The Labour Government struggled on through a session dubbed by the press as 'the winter of discontent': trying to push bills through the House, losing a clause here and a clause there, Raymond was only too delighted to have reached the recess in one piece.

Raymond spent a cold Christmas in Leeds with Joyce. He returned to London early in the New Year aware it could not be long before the Conservatives felt assured enough to put down a motion of no confidence. When it eventually was tabled no one in Parliament was surprised.

The debate caused a day of intense excitement, not least because a strike had caused the Commons bars to run dry and thirsty members were huddled together in the lobbies, the tea room, the smoking room and the dining-rooms. Harassed Whips rushed hither and thither checking lists, ringing up hospitals, board rooms and even great-aunts in their efforts to track down the last few elusive members.

When Mrs Thatcher rose on 6 April to address a packed House the tension was so electric that the Speaker had considerable difficulty keeping control of the over-charged conductors. She addressed the House in firm, strident tones which brought her own side to their feet when she resumed her place. The atmosphere was no different when it was the turn of the Prime Minister to reply. Both leaders made a gallant effort to rise above the petulance of their adversaries but it was the Speaker who had the last word:

> "The Ayes to the right 311,
> The Noes to the left 310.
> The Ayes have it, the Ayes have it."

Pandemonium broke out. Opposition members waved their order papers in triumph, knowing the Prime Minister would now have to call a general election. James Callaghan immediately announced the dissolution of Parliament and after an audience with the Queen election day was set for 3 May 1979.

At the end of that momentous week those few members left at Westminster were stunned by an explosion in the Members' Car Park. Airey Neave, the Shadow spokesman on Northern Ireland, had been blown up by Irish terrorists as he was driving up the exit ramp to leave the Commons. He died on his way to hospital.

Members hurried back to their constituencies. Both Raymond and Andrew found it hard to escape from their departments at such short notice, but Charles and Simon were out in their respective high streets shaking hands with the voters by the morning following the Queen's proclamation.

For three weeks the arguments about who was competent to govern went back and forth, but on 3 May the British people elected their first woman Prime Minister and gave her party a majority of forty-three in the Commons.

Andrew's sixth election turned out to be his most unpleasant to date and he was only glad that he had left Louise and Clarissa in London. Jock McPherson, still the SNP candidate, called him every name under the sun and added one or two new ones in the evening, while the Trotskyites who had voted against him on the committee proved no help when it came to gathering in the votes on election day. But the citizens of Edinburgh, knowing nothing of the committee's opinions, sent Andrew back to Parliament with a majority of 3,738. The Scottish Nationalist vote crumbled, leaving only two members in the House – and Jock McPherson back in Scotland.

Raymond's vote in Leeds was slightly reduced, while Joyce won the office pool for predicting most accurately what her husband's majority would be. He was beginning to accept that she knew more about the constituency than he ever would.

A few days later when Raymond returned to London Kate

had never seen him so depressed and decided to hold off telling him her own news when he said, "God knows how many years it will be before I can be of some use again."

"You can spend your time in Opposition making sure the Government doesn't dismantle all your achievements."

"With a majority of forty-three they could dismantle me if they wanted to," he told her. He placed the red leather box marked 'Secretary of State for Trade' in the corner, next to the ones marked 'Minister of State at the Department of Trade' and 'Parliamentary Under-Secretary at the Department of Employment'.

"They're only your first three," Kate tried to reassure him.

Simon increased his majority at Pucklebridge to 19,461, notching up another record after which he and Elizabeth spent the weekend in their cottage with the boys waiting for Mrs Thatcher to select her team.

Simon was surprised when the Prime Minister phoned personally and asked if he could come up to see her in Downing Street: that was an honour usually afforded only to Cabinet ministers. He tried not to anticipate what she might have in mind.

He duly travelled up from the country and spent thirty minutes alone with the new Prime Minister. When he heard what Mrs Thatcher wanted him to do he was touched that she had taken the trouble to see him in person. She knew that no member ever found it easy to accede to such a request but Simon accepted without hesitation. Mrs Thatcher added that no announcement would be made until he had had time to talk his decision over with Elizabeth.

Simon thanked her and travelled back to his cottage in Pucklebridge. Elizabeth sat in silence as she listened to Simon's account of his conversation with the Prime Minister.

"Oh, my God," she said, when he had finished. "She's offered you the chance to be a Minister of State, but in return we have no certainty of peace for the rest of our lives."

"I can still say no," Simon assured her.

"That would be the act of a coward," said Elizabeth, "and you've never been that."

"Then I'll phone the Prime Minister and tell her I accept."

"I ought to congratulate you," she said. "But it never crossed my mind for one moment . . ."

Charles's was one of the few Tory seats in which the majority went down. A missing wife is hard to explain especially when it is common knowledge that she is living with the former chairman of the adjoining constituency. Charles had faced a certain degree of embarrassment with his local committee and he made sure that the one woman who couldn't keep her mouth shut was told his version of the story 'in strictest confidence'. Any talk of removing him had died when it was rumoured that Charles would stand as an independent candidate if replaced. When the vote was counted Sussex Downs still returned Charles to Westminster with a majority of 20,176. He sat alone in Eaton Square over the weekend, but no one contacted him. He read in the Monday *Telegraph* – how he missed *The Times* – the full composition of the new Tory team.

The only surprise was Simon Kerslake's appointment as Minister of State for Northern Ireland.

CHAPTER
TWENTY FOUR

"Well, say something."

"Very flattering, Kate. What reason did you give for turning the offer down?" asked Raymond, who had been surprised to find her waiting for him at the flat.

"I didn't need a reason."

"How did they feel about that?"

"You don't seem to understand. I accepted their offer."

Raymond removed his glasses and tried to take in what Kate was saying. He steadied himself by holding on to the mantelpiece.

Kate continued. "I had to, darling."

"Because the offer was too tempting?"

"No, you silly man. It had nothing to do with the offer as such, but it gives me the chance to stop letting my life drift. Can't you see it was *because* of you?"

"Because of me you're going to leave London and go back to New York."

"To work in New York and start getting my life in perspective. Raymond, don't you realise it's been five years?"

"I know how long it is and how many times I've asked you to marry me."

"We both know that isn't the answer; Joyce can't be brushed aside that easily. And it could even end up being the single reason you fail in your career."

"We can overcome that problem, given time," Raymond reasoned.

"That sounds fine now, until the party wins the next

election and lesser men than you are offered the chance to shape future policy."

"Can't I do anything to make you change your mind?"

"Nothing, my darling. I've handed Chase my resignation and begin my new job with Chemical Bank in a month."

"Only four weeks," said Raymond.

"Yes, four weeks. I had to hold off telling you until I had severed all the bonds, had resigned and could be sure of not letting you talk me out of it."

"Do you know how much I love you?"

"I hope enough to let me go, before it's too late."

Charles would not have normally accepted the invitation. Lately he had found cocktail parties to consist of nothing but silly little bits of food, never being able to get the right drink and rarely enjoying the trivial conversation. But when he glanced on his mantelpiece and saw an 'At Home' from Lady Carrington he felt it might be an amusing break from the routine he had fallen into since Fiona had left. He was also keen to discover more about the rumoured squabbles in Cabinet over expenditure cuts. He checked his tie in the mirror, removed an umbrella from the hat stand and left Eaton Square for Ovington Square.

He and Fiona had been apart for nearly two years. Charles had heard from several sources that his wife had now moved in with Dalglish on a permanent basis despite his unwillingness to co-operate over a divorce. He had remained discreetly silent on his wife's new life except for one or two selected titbits dropped selectively in the ears of well-chosen gossips. That way he had elicited for himself sympathy from every quarter while remaining the magnanimous loyal husband.

Charles had spent most of his spare time in the Commons, and his most recent budget speech had been well received both by the House and the national press. During the committee stage of the Finance Bill he had allowed himself to be burdened with a lot of the donkey work. Clive Reynolds had been able to point out discrepancies in some clauses of the bill, which Charles passed on to a grateful Chancellor.

Thus Charles received praise for saving the Government from any unnecessary embarrassment. At the same time he disassociated himself from the 'wets' as the Prime Minister referred to those of her colleagues who did not unreservedly support her monetarist policies. If he could keep up his work output he was confident he would be preferred in the first reshuffle.

By spending his mornings at the bank and afternoons and evenings in the Commons Charles managed to combine both worlds with the minimum of interruption from his almost non-existent private life.

He arrived at Lord Carrington's front door a little after six-forty-five. A maid answered his knock, and he walked straight through to a drawing-room that could have held fifty guests and very nearly did.

He even managed to be served with the right blend of whisky before joining his colleagues from both the Upper and Lower Houses. He saw her first over the top of Alec Pimkin's balding head.

"Who is she?" asked Charles, not expecting Pimkin to know.

"Amanda Wallace," said Pimkin, glancing over his shoulder. "I could tell you a thing or two . . ." but Charles had already left his colleague in mid-sentence. The sexual aura of the woman was attested to by the fact that she spent the entire evening surrounded by attentive men, like moths around a candle. If Charles had not been one of the tallest men in the room he might never have seen the flame. It took him another ten minutes to reach her side of the room where Julian Ridsdale, a colleague of Charles's in the Commons, introduced them only to find himself dragged away moments later by his wife.

Charles was left staring at a woman who would have looked beautiful in anything from a ballgown to a towel. Her slim body was encased in a white silk dress, and her fair hair touched her bare shoulders. But what struck Charles most was the translucent texture of her skin. It had been years since he had found it so hard to make conversation.

"I expect you already have a dinner engagement?"

Charles asked her in the brief intervals before the vultures closed in again.

"No," she replied and smiled encouragingly. She agreed to meet him at Walton's in an hour's time. Charles dutifully began to circulate round the room but it was not long before he found his eyes drawn back to her. Every time she smiled he found himself responding but Amanda didn't notice because she was always being flattered by someone else. When he left an hour later he smiled directly at her, and this time did win a knowing grin.

Charles sat alone at a corner table in Walton's for another hour. He was just about to admit defeat and return home when she was ushered to the table. The anger that had developed from being kept waiting was forgotten the moment she smiled and said, "Hello, Charlie."

He was not surprised to learn that his tall, elegant companion earned her living as a model. As far as Charles could see she could have modelled anything from tooth paste to stockings.

"Shall we have coffee at my place?" Charles asked after an unhurried dinner. She nodded her assent and he called for the bill, not checking the addition for the first time in many years.

He was delighted, if somewhat surprised, when she rested her head on his shoulder in the cab on the way back to Eaton Square. By the time they had been dropped off at Eaton Square most of Amanda's lipstick had been removed. The cabbie thanked Charles for his excessive tip and couldn't resist adding, "Good luck, sir."

Charles never did get round to making the coffee. When he woke in the morning, to his surprise he found her even more captivating, and for the first time in weeks quite forgot 'Yesterday in Parliament'.

Elizabeth listened carefully as the man from Special Branch explained how the safety devices worked. She tried to make Peter and Michael concentrate on not pressing the red buttons that were in every room and would bring the police at a moment's notice. The electricians had already wired the rooms in Beaufort Street and now they had nearly finished at the cottage.

At Beaufort Street a uniformed policeman stood watch by the front door night and day. In Pucklebridge, because the cottage was so isolated, they had to be surrounded by arc lamps that could be switched on at a moment's notice.

"It must be damned inconvenient," suggested Archie Millburn during dinner. After his arrival at the cottage he had been checked by security patrols with dogs before he was able to shake hands with his host.

"Inconvenient is putting it mildly," said Elizabeth. "Last week Peter broke a window with a cricket ball and we were immediately lit up like a Christmas tree."

"Do you get any privacy?" asked Archie.

"Only when we're in bed. Even then you can wake up to find you're being licked; you sigh and it turns out to be an Alsatian."

Archie laughed. "Lucky Alsatian."

Every morning when Simon was driven to work he was accompanied by two detectives, a car in front and another to the rear. He had always thought there were only two ways from Beaufort Street to Westminster. For the first twenty-one days as minister he never travelled the same route twice.

Whenever he was due to fly to Belfast he was not informed of either his departure time or from which airport he would be leaving. While the inconvenience drove Elizabeth mad the tension had the opposite effect on Simon. Despite everything, it was the first time in his life he didn't feel it was necessary to explain to anyone why he had chosen to be a politician.

Inch by inch he worked to try to bring the Catholics and Protestants together. Often after a month of inches he would lose a yard in one day, but he never displayed any anger or prejudice except perhaps, as he told Elizabeth, "a prejudice for common sense". Given time, Simon believed, a break-through would be possible – if only he could find on both sides a handful of men of goodwill.

During the all-party meetings both factions began to treat him with respect and – privately – with affection. Even the

Opposition spokesman at Westminster openly acknowledged that Simon Kerslake was turning out to be an excellent choice for the 'dangerous and thankless ministry'.

Andrew also knew he would require a handful of men of goodwill when Hamish Ramsey resigned as chairman of Edinburgh Carlton.

"I don't need the hassle any longer," Hamish told him. "I'm not in politics for the same reason as that bunch of trouble-makers." Andrew reluctantly let him go and had to work hard to convince Hamish's deputy, David Connaught, that he should stand in his place. When David finally agreed to allow his name to go forward he was immediately opposed by Frank Boyle, who had already made his opinion of the sitting member abundantly clear. Andrew canvassed every person on the committee during the run up to election for the new chairman. He estimated the voting was going to be seven-all, which would still allow Hamish to give his casting vote in favour of Connaught.

Andrew phoned Hamish at home an hour before the meeting was due to begin. "I'll call and leave a message for you at the House when it's all over," Ramsey told him. "Don't worry, you're safe this time. At least I'll leave you with the right chairman."

Andrew left Pelham Crescent after he had tucked Clarissa up in bed and read her another chapter of *Jacob Two Two*. He told Louise he would return from Westminster straight after the ten o'clock vote. He sat in the Chamber and listened to Charles Seymour deliver a well-argued discourse on monetarist policy. Andrew didn't always agree with the logic of Seymour's case and he had never cared much for the man himself: but he had to admit that such talent was wasted on the back benches.

During the speech a note was passed to Andrew by an attendant. He unfolded the little white slip. Stuart Gray, the lobby correspondent for *The Scotsman*, needed to speak to him urgently. Andrew slipped from his place on the front bench, stepping over the feet of Shadow ministers still intent on

Seymour's speech. He felt like a small boy leaving a cinema in the middle of a film in pursuit of an ice lolly. He found Gray waiting for him in the Members' Lobby.

Andrew had known Stuart since he had first entered the House, when the journalist had told him, "You and I are each other's bread and butter, so we'd better make a sandwich." Andrew had laughed, and they had had few differences of opinion in the fifteen years since. Stuart suggested that they go down to Annie's Bar for a drink. They strolled along the corridor and took the stairway near the tea room to the basement bar, named after a former barlady.

Andrew settled down on a couch at the side of a pillar while Stuart went up to the bar to order two whiskies.

"Cheers," said the journalist, putting Andrew's glass down on the table in front of him.

Andrew took a long gulp. "Now, what can I do for you?" he asked. "Is my father being tiresome again?"

"I'd call him a supporter compared with your new chairman."

"What do you mean? I've always found David Connaught to be a sound fellow myself," said Andrew, a little pompously.

"I'm not interested in your views of David Connaught," said Stuart. "I want an opinion on your new chairman, Frank Boyle." The journalist sounded very much on the record.

"What?"

"He won the vote tonight seven to six."

"But . . ." Andrew fell silent.

"Come on, Andrew. We both know the bloody man's a Commie trouble-maker, and my editor is screaming for a quote."

"I can't say anything, Stuart, not until I know all the facts."

"I've just told you all the facts: now, are you going to give me a quote?"

"Yes." Andrew paused. "I am sure Mr Boyle will continue to serve in the best traditions of the Labour party, and I look forward to working in close co-operation with him."

"Balls," said Stuart. "They will only print that in Pseuds Corner in *Private Eye*."

"It's the only quote you're going to get out of me tonight," said Andrew.

Stuart looked at his friend and could see lines on his face that he had never noticed before. "I'm sorry," he said. "I went too far. Please get in touch when the time's right. With that bastard Boyle in charge you might be in need of my help."

Andrew thanked him absent-mindedly, downed his whisky in one gulp, then walked out of Annie's Bar and along the terrace corridor to the phone booths at the foot of the stairs. He dialled Ramsey's home number.

"What in heaven's name happened?" was all he could ask.

"One of our voters didn't show," said Hamish Ramsey. "Claimed he was held up in Glasgow and couldn't get back in time. I was just about to ring you."

"Bloody irresponsible of him," said Andrew. "Why didn't you postpone the vote?"

"I tried to, but Frank Boyle produced the rule book. 'Any motion proposed fourteen days before a meeting cannot be postponed without the agreement of the proposer and seconder.' I'm sorry, Andrew: my hands were tied."

"It's not your fault, Hamish. I couldn't have had a better chairman than you. I'm only sorry you didn't leave in a blaze of glory."

Hamish chuckled. "Don't you ever forget, Andrew, the voters have the last word in a democracy. In Edinburgh you're the man who has served them for more than fifteen years and they won't forget that quickly."

"You can get dressed now, Miss Wallace," said the gynaecologist returning to her desk.

Amanda started to slip back into her latest Dior outfit – a light blue denim suit bought the previous day in Conduit Street in an attempt to cheer herself up.

"It's the third time in five years," said Elizabeth Kerslake, leafing through the confidential file and trying not to sound accusing.

"I may as well book into the same clinic as before," said Amanda, matter-of-factly.

Elizabeth was determined to make her reconsider the consequences. "Is there any chance that the father would want you to have this child?"

"I can't be certain who the father is," said Amanda, looking shame-faced for the first time. "You see, it was the end of one relationship and the beginning of another."

Elizabeth made no comment other than to say, "I estimate that you are at least eight weeks pregnant, but it could be as much as twelve." She looked back down at the file. "Have you considered giving birth to the child and then bringing it up yourself?"

"Good heavens, no," said Amanda. "I make my living as a model, not as a mother."

"So be it," Elizabeth sighed, closing the file. "I'll make all the" – she avoided saying usual – "necessary arrangements. You must see your GP immediately and ask him to sign the required clearance forms. Then phone me in about a week, rather than make the trip down to Pucklebridge again."

Amanda nodded her agreement. "Could you let me know what the clinic is going to charge this time? I'm sure they are suffering from inflation like the rest of us."

"Yes, I will look into that, Miss Wallace," said Elizabeth, just managing to keep her temper as she showed Amanda to the door. Once her patient had left Elizabeth picked up the confidential file from her desk, walked over to the cabinet and flicked through S, T, U, until she found the right slot. Perhaps she should have been sterner with her but she was convinced that it would have made little difference. She paused, wondering if having the child might change the woman's cavalier attitude to life.

Charles returned home after the debate feeling pleased with himself. He had received praise for his latest speech from every wing of the party, and the Chief Whip had made it quite clear that his efforts on the Finance Bill had not gone unnoticed.

As he drove back to Eaton Square he wound down the car

window and let the fresh air rush in and the cigarette smoke out. His smile widened at the thought of Amanda sitting at home waiting for him. It had been a glorious couple of months. At forty-eight he was experiencing realities he had never even dreamed of in fantasy. As each day passed he expected the infatuation to wear off, but instead it only grew more intense. Even the memory the day after was better than anything he had experienced in the past.

Once the Holbein had been restored to his dining-room wall Charles planned to talk to Amanda about their future; if she said "Yes" he would even be willing to grant Fiona a divorce. He parked the car and took out his latch key, but she was already there opening the front door to throw her arms around him.

"Why don't we go straight to bed?" she greeted him.

Charles would have been shocked had Fiona uttered such feelings even once in their fifteen years of married life, but Amanda made it appear quite natural. She was already lying naked on the bed before Charles could get his waistcoat off. After they had made love and she was settled in his arms Amanda told him she would have to go away for a few days.

"Why?" said Charles, puzzled.

"I'm pregnant," she said matter-of-factly. "I've already booked myself into a clinic. Don't worry. I'll be as right as rain in no time."

"But why don't we have the baby?" said a delighted Charles, looking down into her grey eyes. "I've always wanted a son."

"Don't be silly, Charlie. There's years ahead of me for that."

"But if we were married?"

"You're already married. Besides, I'm only twenty-six."

"I can get a divorce in a moment and life wouldn't be so bad with me, would it?"

"Of course not, Charlie. You're the first man I've ever really cared for."

Charles smiled hopefully. "So you'll think about the idea?"

Amanda looked into Charles's eyes anxiously. "If I *were* to have a child I do hope he'd have blue eyes like yours."

"Will you marry me?" he asked.

"I'll think about it. In any case, you may have changed your mind by morning."

Raymond drove Kate to Heathrow. He was wearing the pink shirt she had chosen for him; she was wearing the little red box. He had so much to tell her on the way to the airport that she hardly spoke at all. The last four weeks had gone by in a flash. It was the first time he had been grateful for being in Opposition.

"It's all right, Carrot Top. Don't fuss. We'll see each other whenever you come to New York."

"I've only been to America twice in my life," he said. She tried to smile.

Once she had checked her eleven bags in at the counter, a process that seemed to take forever, she was allocated a seat.

"Flight BA 107, gate number fourteen, boarding in ten minutes," she was informed.

"Thank you," she said and rejoined Raymond, who was sitting on the end of an already crowded tubular settee. He had bought two plastic cups of coffee while Kate had been checking in. They were both already cold. They sat and held hands like children who had met on a summer holiday and had now to return to separate schools.

"Promise me you won't start wearing contact lenses the moment I've gone."

"Yes, I can promise you that," said Raymond, touching the bridge of his glasses.

"I've so much I still want to tell you," she said.

He turned towards her. "Vice-presidents of banks shouldn't cry," he said, brushing a tear from her cheek. "The customers will realise you're a soft touch."

"Neither should Cabinet ministers," she replied. "All I wanted to say, is that if you really feel . . ." she began.

"Hello, Mr Gould."

They both looked up to see a broad smile spread across the face of someone whose tan proved that he had just arrived from a sunnier climate.

"I'm Bert Cox," he said, thrusting out his hand, "I don't suppose you remember me." Raymond let go of Kate's hand and shook Mr Cox's.

"We were at the same primary school in Leeds, Ray. Mind you, that was a million light years ago. You've come a long way since then."

How can I get rid of him? wondered Raymond desperately.

"This is the missus," Bert Cox continued obliviously, gesturing at the silent woman in a flowery dress by his side. She smiled but didn't speak. "She sits on some committee with Joyce, don't you, love?" he said, not waiting for her reply.

"This is the final call for Flight BA 107, now boarding at gate number fourteen."

"We always vote for you, of course," continued Bert Cox. "The missus" – he pointed to the lady in the flowered dress again – "thinks you'll be Prime Minister. I always say –"

"I must go, Raymond," said Kate, "or I'll miss my flight."

"Can you excuse me for a moment, Mr Cox?" said Raymond.

"Delighted. I'll wait. I don't often get a chance to have a word with my MP."

Raymond walked with Kate towards the barrier. "I am sorry about this. I'm afraid they're all like that in Leeds – hearts of gold, but never stop talking. What were you going to say?"

"Only that I would have been happy to live in Leeds, however cold it is. I never envied anyone in my life, but I do envy Joyce." She kissed him gently on the cheek and walked towards the barrier before he could reply. She didn't look back.

"Are you feeling all right, madam?" asked an airport official as she went through the security barrier.

"I'm fine," said Kate, brushing aside her tears. She walked slowly towards gate fourteen, happy that he had worn the pink shirt for the first time. She wondered if he had found the note she had left underneath the collar. If he had asked her just one more time . . .

Raymond stood alone and then turned to walk aimlessly towards the exit.

"An American lady, I would have guessed," said Mr Cox rejoining him. "I'm good on accents."

"Yes," said Raymond, still alone.

"A friend of yours?" he asked.

"My best friend," said Raymond.

When ten days had passed and Elizabeth had not yet heard from Miss Wallace she decided she had no choice but to contact her direct. She flicked through her personal file and noted the latest number Amanda had given.

Elizabeth picked up the phone and dialled. It was some time before anybody answered.

"730-9712. Charles Seymour speaking." There was a long silence. "Is anyone there?"

Elizabeth couldn't reply. She replaced the receiver and felt her whole body come out in a cold sweat. She closed Amanda Wallace's file and returned it to the cabinet.

CHAPTER
TWENTY FIVE

Simon had spent nearly a year preparing a White Paper entitled 'A Genuine Partnership for Ireland' for consideration by the House. The Government's aim was to bring north and south together for a period of ten years at the end of which a more permanent arrangement could be considered. During those ten years both sides would remain under the direct rule of Westminster and Dublin. Both Protestants and Catholics had contributed to 'the Charter', as the press had dubbed the complex agreement. With considerable skill, patience and fortitude Simon had convinced the political leaders of Northern Ireland to append their names to the final draft when and if it was approved by the House.

He admitted to Elizabeth that the agreement was only a piece of paper, but he felt it was a foundation stone on which the House could base an eventual settlement. On both sides of the Irish Sea politicians and journalists alike were describing the Charter as a genuine breakthrough.

The Secretary of State for Northern Ireland was to present the White Paper to the Commons when Irish business was next scheduled on the parliamentary calendar. Simon, as the architect of the Charter, had been asked to deliver the winding-up speech on behalf of the Government. He knew that if the House backed the concept of the document he might then be allowed to prepare a parliamentary bill and thus overcome a problem so many other politicians had failed to solve before him. If he succeeded Simon felt that all the sacrifices he had made in the past would prove worthwhile.

When Elizabeth sat down to read through the final draft in Simon's study that evening even she admitted for the first time that she was pleased he had accepted the Irish appointment.

"Now, embryonic statesman," she continued, "are you ready for your dinner like every normal human being at this time in the evening?"

"I certainly am." Simon moved his copy of the 129-page Charter from the dining-room table to the sideboard, planning to go over it yet again once he had finished dinner.

"Damn," he heard Elizabeth say from the kitchen.

"What is it?" he asked, not looking up from his toy, like a child studying a jigsaw and wondering where a colourless piece fitted in.

"I'm out of Bisto."

"I'll go and buy some," Simon volunteered. The two policemen on the door were chatting when the minister came out.

"Come on, my wife needs a packet of Bisto, so affairs of state must be held up for the time being."

"I'm very sorry, sir," said the sergeant. "When I was told you would be in for the rest of the evening I allowed the official car to go off duty. But Constable Barker can accompany you."

"That's no problem," said Simon. "We can take my wife's car. I'll just find out where she's parked the damn thing."

He slipped back into the house but returned a moment later. "Been in the force long?" he asked Constable Barker as they walked down the road together.

"Not that long, sir. Started on the beat just over a year ago."

"Are you married, Constable?"

"Fine chance on my salary, sir."

"Then you won't have encountered the problem of being Bisto-less."

"They've never heard of gravy in the police canteen, sir."

"You should try the House of Commons sometime," said Simon. "I don't think you'd find it any better – the food, that is, not to mention the salary."

The two men laughed as they headed off towards the car.

"What does your wife think of the Mini Metro?" the constable asked as Simon put the key in the door.

Like everyone else in Beaufort Street, Elizabeth heard the explosion, but she was the first to realise what it had to be. She ran out of the front door in search of the duty policeman. She saw him running down the road and quickly followed.

The little red Metro was scattered all over the side street, the glass from its windows making the pavement look as though there had been a sudden hailstorm.

When the sergeant saw the severed head he pulled Elizabeth back. Two other bodies lay motionless in the road, one of them an old lady with the contents of her shopping bag spread around her.

Within minutes, six police cars had arrived and Special Branch officers had cordoned off the area with white ribbon. An ambulance rushed the bodies to Westminster Hospital. The job of picking up the remains of the police constable needed a very resolute man.

Elizabeth was taken to the hospital in a police car, where she learned that the old lady had died before arrival while her husband was on the critical list. When she told the surgeon in charge that she was a doctor he was more forthcoming and answered her questions candidly. Simon was suffering from multiple fractures, a dislocated hip and a severe loss of blood. The only question he was not willing to be drawn on was when she asked about his chances.

She sat alone outside the operating theatre waiting for any scrap of news. Hour after hour went by, and Elizabeth kept recalling Simon's words: "Be tolerant. Always remember there are still men of goodwill in Northern Ireland." She found it almost impossible not to scream, to think of the whole lot of them as evil murderers. Her husband had worked tirelessly on their behalf. He wasn't a Catholic or a Protestant, just a man trying to do an impossible task. Although she couldn't help thinking that it was she who had been the intended target.

Another hour passed.

A tired, grey-faced man came out into the corridor through

the flapping rubber doors. "He's still hanging on, Dr Kerslake. Your husband has the constitution of an ox; most people would have let go by now." He smiled. "Can I find you a room so that you can get some sleep?"

"No, thank you," Elizabeth replied. "I'd prefer to be near him."

She rang home to check the children were coping and her mother answered the phone. She had rushed over the moment she had heard the news and was keeping them away from the radio and television.

"How is he?" she asked.

Elizabeth told her mother all she knew, then spoke to the children.

"We're taking care of Grandmother," Peter told her.

Elizabeth couldn't hold back the tears. "Thank you, darling," she said, and quickly replaced the receiver. She returned to the bench outside the operating theatre, kicked off her shoes, curled her legs under her body and tried to snatch some sleep.

She woke with a start in the early morning. Her back hurt and her neck was stiff. She walked slowly up and down the corridor in her bare feet stretching her aching limbs, searching for anyone who could tell her some news. Finally a nurse brought her a cup of tea and assured her that her husband was still alive. But what did 'still alive' mean? She stood and watched the grim faces coming out of the operating theatre and tried not to recognise the tell-tale signs of despair. The surgeon told her she ought to go home and rest: they would have nothing to tell her for several hours. A policeman kept all journalists – who were arriving by the minute – in an ante-room off the main corridor.

Elizabeth didn't move from the corridor for another day and another night, and she didn't return home until the surgeon told her it was all over.

When she heard the news she fell on her knees and wept.

"God must want the Irish problem solved as well," he added. "Your husband will live, Dr Kerslake, but it's a miracle."

"Got time for a quick one?" asked Alexander Dalglish.

"If you press me," said Pimkin.

"Fiona," shouted Alexander. "It's Alec Pimkin, he's dropped in for a drink."

She came through to join them. She was dressed in a bright yellow frock and had allowed her hair to grow down past her shoulders.

"It suits you," said Pimkin, tapping his bald head.

"Thank you," said Fiona. "Why don't we all go through to the drawing-room?"

Pimkin happily obeyed and had soon settled himself into Alexander's favourite chair.

"What will you have?" asked Fiona, as she stood by the drinks cabinet.

"A large gin with just a rumour of tonic."

"Well, how's the constituency faring since my resignation?"

"It ticks along, trying hard to survive the biggest sex scandal since Profumo," chuckled Pimkin.

"I only hope it hasn't harmed your election chances," said Alexander.

"Not a bit of it, old fellow," said Pimkin, accepting the large Beefeaters and tonic Fiona handed him. "On the contrary, it's taken their minds off me for a change."

Alexander laughed.

"In fact," continued Pimkin, "interest in the date of your wedding has only been eclipsed by Charles and Lady Di. Gossips tell me," he continued, clearly enjoying himself, "that my Honourable friend, the member for Sussex Downs, made you wait the full two years before you could place an announcement in *The Times*."

"Yes, that's true," said Fiona. "Charles didn't even answer my letters during that period, but lately when any problem's arisen he's been almost friendly."

"Could that be because he also wants to place an announcement in *The Times*?" said Pimkin, downing his gin quickly in the hope of being offered a second.

"What do you mean?"

"The fact that he has lost his heart to another."

"Another?" said Alexander Dalglish.

"No less –" Pimkin paused as he sipped pointedly at his empty glass "– than Miss Amanda Wallace, only daughter of the late and little lamented Brigadier Boozer Wallace."

"Amanda Wallace?" said Fiona in disbelief. "Surely he's got more sense than that."

"I don't think it has a lot to do with sense," said Pimkin holding out his glass. "More to do with sex."

"But he's old enough to be her father."

"If that is the case," said Pimkin, "Charles can always adopt her."

Alexander laughed.

"But I am informed by a reliable source," continued Pimkin, "that marriage is being proposed."

"You can't be serious," said Fiona flatly.

"The subject has most certainly been broached for she is undoubtedly pregnant and Charles is hoping for a son," said Pimkin in triumph as he accepted his second double gin.

"That's not possible," said Fiona under her breath.

"And I am also informed," continued Pimkin, "that some of the more ungenerous of our brethren are already suggesting the name of several candidates for the role of father."

"Alec, you're incorrigible."

"My dear, it is common knowledge that Amanda has slept with half the Cabinet and a considerable cross section of back-benchers."

"Stop exaggerating," said Fiona.

"And what's more," continued Pimkin as if he hadn't heard her, "she has only stopped short of the Labour front bench because her mother told her they were common and she might catch something from them."

Alexander laughed again. "But surely Charles hasn't fallen for the pregnancy trick?"

"Hook, line and sinker. He's like an Irishman who's been locked into a Guinness brewery over the weekend. Dear Amanda has my Honourable friend uncorking her at every opportunity."

"But she's plain stupid," said Alexander. "The only time I

met her she assured me that Michael Parkinson was turning out to be an excellent chairman of the party."

"Stupid she may well be," said Pimkin, "but plain she is not and together, I'm told, they are updating the *Kama Sutra*."

"Enough, Alec, enough," said Fiona laughing.

"You're right," said Pimkin, aware that his glass was nearly empty once again. "A man of my impeccable reputation cannot afford to be seen associating with people living in sin. I must leave immediately, darlings," he said, rising to his feet. Pimkin put his glass down and Alexander accompanied him to the front door.

As it closed Alexander turned to Fiona. "Never short of useful information, our former member," he said.

"I agree," said Fiona. "So much gleaned for such a small investment in Beefeaters."

As Alexander walked back into the drawing-room he added, "Does it change your plans for the return of the Holbein?"

"Not in any way," said Fiona.

"So you'll still be at Sotheby's next week for their Old Masters sale?"

Fiona smiled. "Certainly. And if the price is right we won't have to worry about what we give Charles for a wedding present."

Three weeks after the bombing Simon left the Westminster Hospital on crutches, Elizabeth by his side. His right leg had been so shattered that he had been told he would never walk properly again. As he stepped out on to Horseferry Road a hundred cameras flashed to meet their editors' demand to capture the instant hero. He smiled as if there were no pain. "Don't let those murderers think they got to you," he was warned by both sides. Elizabeth's smile showed only relief that her husband was still alive.

After three weeks of complete rest Simon returned to his Irish Charter against doctor's orders, knowing the document was still due to be debated in the House in less than a fortnight. The Secretary of State and the other Minister of

State for Northern Ireland visited him at home on several occasions and it was agreed that the Minister of State would take over Simon's responsibilities temporarily and deliver the winding-up speech. During his absence the whole Northern Ireland office grew to realise just how much work Simon had put into the Charter, and no one was at all complacent about taking his place.

The attempt on Simon's life and the build up to the special debate on the Charter became of such national interest that the BBC decided to broadcast the entire proceedings on Radio Four from three-thirty to the vote at ten o'clock.

On the afternoon of the debate Simon sat up in bed listening to every word on the radio as if it were the final episode in his favourite serial and he was desperate to know the outcome. The speeches opened with a clear and concise presentation of the Charter by the Secretary of State for Northern Ireland, which left Simon feeling confident that the whole House would support him. The Opposition spokesman followed with a fair-minded speech, raising one or two queries he had over the controversial Patriots' Clause with its special rights for Protestants in the south and Catholics in the north, and also how it would affect the Catholics unwilling to register in Northern Ireland. Otherwise he reassured the House that the Opposition supported the Charter and would not be calling for a division.

Simon began to relax for the first time as the debate continued, but his mood changed as some back-bench members started to express more and more anxiety over the Patriots' Provision. One or two back-benchers were even insisting that the Charter should not be sanctioned by the House until the need for the Patriots' Provision was fully explained by the Government. Simon realised that a few narrow-minded men were simply playing for time in the hope the Charter would be held up and later forgotten. For generations such men had succeeded in stifling the hopes and aspirations of the Irish people while they allowed bigotry to undermine any real desire for peace.

Elizabeth came in and sat on the end of the bed. "How's it going?" she asked.

"Not well," said Simon, "it will all depend on the Opposition spokesman."

They both sat and listened. But no sooner had the Opposition spokesman risen than Simon realised that he too had misunderstood the real purpose of the Patriots' Provision and that what Simon had agreed to with both sides in Dublin and Belfast was not being accurately explained to the House. There was no malice in the speech and he was clearly following what had been agreed through the usual channels but Simon could sense that his lack of conviction was sowing doubts in the minds of his fellow members. He feared a division might be called after all.

After one or two members had interrupted to voice further doubts about the Patriots' Clause the Shadow minister suggested: "Perhaps we should wait until the Minister of State is fully recovered and able to report to the House himself." A few 'hear, hears' could be heard around the Chamber.

Simon felt sick. He was going to lose the Charter if it didn't get through the House tonight. All the hard work and goodwill would count for nothing. He made a decision.

"I'd love a hot cup of cocoa," he said, trying to sound casual.

"Of course, darling. I'll just go and turn the kettle on. Would you like a biscuit while I'm up?"

Simon nodded. Once the bedroom door was closed, he slipped quietly out of bed and dressed as quickly as possible. He picked up his blackthorn stick, a gift from Dr Fitzgerald, the Irish Prime Minister, which had been among the dozens of presents awaiting his return from hospital. Then he hobbled silently down the stairs and across the hall, hoping Elizabeth would not hear him. He eased the front door open. When the policeman on duty saw him Simon put a finger to his lips and closed the door very slowly behind him. He made his way laboriously up to the police car, lurched into the back and said, "Switch on the radio, please, and drive me to the House as quickly as possible."

Simon continued to listen to the Opposition spokesman as the police car weaved in and out of the traffic on a route he hadn't travelled before. They arrived at the St Stephen's entrance to the Commons at nine-twenty-five.

Visitors stood to one side as they might for royalty but Simon didn't notice. He hobbled on through the Central Lobby, oblivious to the awkwardness of his gait, turning left past the policeman and on towards the entrance of the House. He prayed he would reach the Chamber before the Government spokesman rose to deliver his winding-up speech. Simon passed an astonished chief doorkeeper and arrived at the bar of the House as the new digital clock showed nine-twenty-nine.

The Opposition spokesman was resuming his place on the front bench to muffled cries of "Hear, hear." The Speaker rose but before he had time to call upon the Minister of State to reply Simon stepped slowly forward on to the green carpet of the Commons. For a moment there was a stunned silence; then the cheering began. It had reached a crescendo by the time Simon arrived at the front bench. His blackthorn stick fell to the floor as he clutched the dispatch box. The Speaker called out his name *sotto voce*.

Simon waited for the House to come to complete silence.

"Mr Speaker, I must thank the House for its generous welcome. I return this evening because having listened to every word of the debate on the radio I feel it necessary to explain to Honourable members what was behind my thinking with the Patriots' Provision. This was not some superficial formula for solving an intractable problem, but an act of good faith to which the representatives from all sides felt able to put their names. It may not be perfect, since words can mean different things to different people – as lawyers continually demonstrate to us."

The laughter broke the tension that had been building up in the House.

"But if we allow this opportunity to pass today it will be another victory for those who revel in the mayhem of Northern Ireland whatever their reason, and a defeat for all men of goodwill."

The House was silent as Simon went on to explain in detail the thinking behind the Patriots' Provision and the effect it would have on both Protestants and Catholics in north and south. He also covered the other salient clauses in the Charter, answering the points that had been raised during the debate until, in glancing up at the clock above the Speaker's chair, he realised he had less than a minute left.

"Mr Speaker, we in this great House, who have in the past decided the fate of nations, are now given an opportunity to succeed today where our predecessors have failed. I ask you to support this Charter – not unreservedly, but to show the bombers and the murderers that here in Westminster we can cast a vote for the children of tomorrow's Ireland. Let the twenty-first century be one in which the Irish problem is only a part of history. Mr Speaker, I seek the support of the whole House."

The motion on the Charter was agreed without division.

Simon immediately returned home and on arrival silently crept upstairs. He closed the bedroom door behind him and fumbled for the switch. The light by the side of the bed went on and Elizabeth sat up.

"Your cocoa's gone cold and I've eaten all the biscuits," she said, grinning, "but thank you for leaving the radio on, at least I knew where you were."

CHAPTER TWENTY SIX

Charles and Amanda were married at the most inconspicuous register office in Hammersmith. They then departed for a long weekend in Paris. Charles had told his bride that he preferred her not to let anyone learn of the marriage for at least another week. He didn't want Fiona to find yet a further excuse for not returning the Holbein. Amanda readily agreed, and then remembered – but surely Alec Pimkin didn't count.

Paris turned out to be fun, even though Charles was sensitive about Amanda's obvious pregnancy – never more so than when they arrived on the Friday night at the Plaza Athenée and were escorted to a suite overlooking the courtyard. Later, over dinner, Amanda astonished the waiters with her appetite as well as the cut of her dress.

Over breakfast in bed the next day Charles read in the *Herald Tribune* that Mrs Thatcher was considering a reshuffle that very weekend. He cut the honeymoon short and returned to London on the Saturday, two days earlier than planned. Amanda was not overjoyed. Her husband spent the whole of Sunday at Eaton Square alongside a phone that never rang.

That same Sunday evening the Prime Minister called for Simon Kerslake and told him that he was to be made a Privy Councillor and would be moved from the Northern Ireland Office to Defence as Minister of State.

He had started to protest, but Mrs Thatcher forestalled any discussion. "I don't want any more dead heroes, Simon," she said sharply.

Elizabeth was relieved when she heard the news, although

it took her some time to get used to her husband being
referred to as 'the Right Honourable Simon Kerslake'. For
some weeks the old joke of 'rarely right and never honourable' had to be suffered by both of them from countless
well-meaning constituents who imagined they were the only
people who had thought of the quip.

Mrs Thatcher called Charles Seymour on the Monday
morning while he was waiting in Eaton Square for the return
of the Holbein. Both sides' solicitors had agreed that the first
Earl of Bridgwater should be back at Charles's home by
eleven that morning. Only the Queen or Mrs Thatcher could
have kept Charles from being there to receive it.

The Prime Minister's call came long after he thought the
reshuffle was over, but then Mrs Thatcher had been informed that Charles was in Paris on his honeymoon and
wouldn't be back until the Monday morning.

Charles took a taxi to Downing Street and was quickly
ushered into the Prime Minister's study. Mrs Thatcher
began by complimenting him on the work he had carried out
on successive Finance Bills in Opposition and in Government. She then invited him to join the front-bench team as
the Financial Secretary to the Treasury.

Charles accepted gracefully, and after a short policy discussion with the Prime Minister drove back to Eaton Square
to celebrate both his triumphs. Amanda met him at the door
to tell him the Holbein had been returned. Fiona had kept
her part of the bargain: the painting had been delivered at
eleven o'clock sharp.

Charles strode confidently into his drawing-room and was
delighted to find the bulky package awaiting him. He was by
no means so pleased to be followed by Amanda, a cigarette in
one hand and a glass of gin in the other; but this was not a day
for quarrels, he decided. He told her of his appointment, but
she didn't seem to take in its significance until her husband
opened a bottle of champagne.

Charles poured out two glasses and handed one to his
bride.

"A double celebration. What fun," she said, first draining
the gin.

Charles took a quick sip of the champagne before he began to untie the knots and tear away the smart red wrapping paper that covered his masterpiece. Once the paper had been removed he pulled back the final cardboard covers. Charles stared with delight at the portrait.

The first Earl of Bridgwater was back home. Charles picked up the gold frame he knew so well to return it to its place in his study but he noticed that the picture had come a little loose. "Damn," he said.

"What's the matter?" asked Amanda still leaning against the door.

"Nothing important, only I shall have to get the frame fixed. I'll drop it into Oliver Swann on the way to the bank. I've waited nearly three years; another couple of days won't make any difference."

Now that Charles had accepted the post of Financial Secretary to the Treasury he knew there was one little arrangement he had to clear up before the appointment became public knowledge. With that in mind, he left Eaton Square and dropped the Holbein off at the framer. He then went on to the bank and summoned Clive Reynolds to his office. It was clear from Reynolds's manner that the news of Charles's ministerial appointment had not yet leaked out.

"Clive," Charles called him for the first time. "I have a proposition to put to you."

Clive Reynolds remained silent.

"The Prime Minister has offered me a post in the Government."

"Congratulations," said Reynolds, "and well deserved, if I may say so."

"Thank you," said Charles. "Now: I'm considering offering you the chance to stand in for me as chairman during my absence."

Clive Reynolds looked surprised.

"On the clear understanding that if the Conservatives were to return to Opposition or I were to lose my appointment in Government I would be reinstated as chairman immediately."

"Naturally," said Reynolds. "I should be delighted to fill the appointment for the interim period."

"Good man," said Charles. "It can't have escaped your notice what happened to the last chairman in the same situation."

"I shall make certain that will not happen again."

"Thank you," said Charles. "I shall not forget your loyalty when I return."

"And I shall also endeavour to carry on the traditions of the bank in your absence," said Reynolds, his head slightly bowed.

"I feel sure you will," said Charles.

The board accepted the recommendation that Clive Reynolds be appointed as temporary chairman and Charles vacated his office happily to take up his new post at the Treasury.

Charles considered it had been the most successful week of his life and on the Friday evening on the way back to Eaton Square he dropped into Oliver Swann's gallery to pick up the Holbein.

"I'm afraid the picture didn't quite fit the frame," said Mr Swann.

"Oh, I expect it's worked loose over the years," Charles said non-committally.

"No, Mr Seymour, this frame was put on the portrait quite recently," said Swann.

"That's not possible," said Charles. "I remember the frame as well as I remember the picture. The portrait of the first Earl of Bridgwater has been in my family for over 400 years."

"Not this picture," said Swann.

"What do you mean?" said Charles, beginning to sound anxious.

"This picture came up for sale at Sotheby's about three weeks ago."

Charles went cold as Swann continued.

"It's the school of Holbein, of course," he said, "probably painted by one of his pupils around the time of his death. I should think there are a dozen or so in existence."

"A dozen or so," repeated Charles, the blood drained from his face.

"Yes, perhaps even more. At least it's solved one mystery for me," said Swann, chuckling.

"What's that?" asked Charles, choking out the words.

"I couldn't work out why Lady Fiona was bidding for the picture, and then I remembered that your family name is Bridgwater."

"At least *this* wedding has some style," Pimkin assured Fiona between mouthfuls of sandwich at the reception after her marriage to Alexander Dalglish. Pimkin always accepted wedding invitations as it allowed him to devour mounds of smoked salmon sandwiches and consume unlimited quantities of champagne. "I particularly enjoyed that *short* service of blessing in the Guards' Chapel; and Claridges can always be relied on to understand my little proclivities." He peered round the vast room and only stopped to stare at his reflection in a chandelier.

Fiona laughed. "Did you go to Charles's wedding?"

"My darling, the only Etonians who have ever been seen in Hammersmith pass through it as quickly as possible on a boat, representing either Oxford or Cambridge."

"So you weren't invited," said Fiona.

"I'm told that only Amanda was invited, and even she nearly found she had another engagement. With her doctor, I believe."

"Well, Charles certainly can't afford another divorce."

"No, not in his present position as Her Majesty's Financial Secretary. One divorce might go unnoticed but two would be considered habit-forming, and all diligent readers of Nigel Dempster have been able to observe that consummation has taken place."

"But how long will Charles be able to tolerate her behaviour?"

"As long as he still believes she has given him a son who will inherit the family title. Not that a marriage ceremony will necessarily prove legitimacy," added Pimkin.

"Perhaps Amanda won't produce a son."

"Perhaps whatever she produces it will be obvious that it's not Charles's offspring," said Pimkin, falling into a chair that had been momentarily left by a large buxom lady.

"Even if it was I can't see Amanda as a housewife."

"No, but it suits Amanda's current circumstances to be thought of as the loving spouse."

"Time may change that too," said Fiona.

"I doubt it," said Pimkin. "Amanda is stupid, that has been proved beyond reasonable doubt, but she has a survival instinct second only to a mongoose. So while Charles is spending all the hours of the day advancing his glittering career she would be foolish to search publicly for greener pastures. Especially when she can always lie in them privately."

"You're a wicked old gossip," said Fiona.

"I cannot deny it," said Pimkin, "for it is an art at which women have never been as accomplished as men."

"Thank you for such a sensible wedding present," said Alexander, joining his wife of two hours. "You selected my favourite claret."

"Giving a dozen bottles of the finest claret serves two purposes," said Pimkin, his hands resting lightly on his stomach. "First, you can always be assured of a decent wine when you invite yourself to dine."

"And second?" asked Alexander.

"When the happy couple split up you can feel relieved that they will no longer have your present to quarrel over."

"Did you give Charles and Amanda a present?" asked Fiona.

"No," said Pimkin, deftly removing another glass of champagne from a passing waiter. "I felt your return of the bogus Earl of Bridgwater was quite enough for both of us."

"I wonder where he is now?" said Alexander.

"He no longer resides in Eaton Square," said Pimkin with the air of one who has divulged a piece of information which can only guarantee further rapt attention.

"Who would want the phoney earl?"

"We are not aware of the provenance of the buyer, as he

emanates from one of Her Majesty's former colonies, but the seller . . ."

"Stop teasing, Alec. Who?"

"None other than Mrs Amanda Seymour."

"Amanda?"

"Yes. Amanda, no less. The dear, silly creature retrieved the false earl from the cellar where Charles had buried him with full military honours."

"But she must have realised it was a fake."

"My dear Amanda wouldn't know the difference between a Holbein and an Andy Warhol but she still happily accepted £10,000 for the impersonation. I am assured that the dealer who purchased this fabricated masterpiece made what I think vulgar people in the City describe as 'a quick turn'."

"Good God," said Alexander. "I only paid £8,000 for it myself."

"Perhaps you should get Amanda to advise you on these matters in future," said Pimkin. "In exchange for my invaluable piece of information I'm bound to enquire if the real Earl of Bridgwater is to remain in hiding."

"Certainly not, Alec. He is merely awaiting the right moment to make a public appearance," said Fiona, unable to hide a smile.

"And where is Amanda now?" asked Alexander, obviously wanting to change the subject.

"In Switzerland producing a baby, which we can but hope will bear sufficient resemblance to a white Caucasian to convince one of Charles's limited imagination that he is the father."

"Where *do* you get all your information from?" asked Alexander.

Pimkin sighed dramatically. "Women have a habit of pouring their hearts out to me, Amanda included."

"Why should she do that?" asked Alexander.

"She lives safe in the knowledge that I am the one man she knows who has no interest in her body." Pimkin drew breath, but only to devour another smoked salmon sandwich.

Charles phoned Amanda every day while she was in Geneva. She kept assuring him all was well, and that the baby was expected on time. He had considered it prudent for Amanda not to remain in England advertising her pregnancy, a less than recent occurrence to even the most casual observer. She for her part did not complain. With £10,000 safely tucked away in a private Swiss account there were few little necessities she could not have brought to her, even in Geneva.

It had taken a few weeks for Charles to become accustomed to Government after such a long break. He enjoyed the challenge of the Treasury and quickly fell in with its strange traditions. He was constantly reminded that his was the department on which the Prime Minister kept the closest eye, making the challenge even greater. The civil servants, when asked their opinion of the new Financial Secretary, would reply variously: able, competent, efficient, hard-working — but without any hint of affection in their voices. When someone asked his driver, whose name Charles could never remember, the same question he proffered the view, "He's the sort of minister who always sits in the back of a car. But I'd still put a week's wages on Mr Seymour becoming Prime Minister."

Amanda produced her child in the middle of the ninth month. After a week's recuperation she was allowed to return to England. She discovered travelling with her offspring was a nuisance and by the time she arrived at Heathrow she was more than happy to turn the child over to the nanny Charles had selected.

Charles had sent a car to pick her up from the airport. He had an unavoidable conference with a delegation of Japanese businessmen, he explained, all of them busy complaining about the new Government tariffs on imports. At the first opportunity to be rid of his oriental guests he bolted back to Eaton Square.

Amanda was there to meet him at the door. Charles had almost forgotten how beautiful his wife was, and how long she had been away.

"Where's my child?" he asked, after he had given her a long kiss.

"In a nursery that's more expensively furnished than our bedroom," she replied a little sharply.

Charles ran up the wide staircase and along the passage. Amanda followed. He entered the nursery and stopped in his tracks as he stared at the future Earl of Bridgwater. The little black curls and deep brown eyes came as something of a shock.

"Good heavens," said Charles, stepping forward for a closer examination. Amanda remained by the door, her hand clutching its handle.

She had a hundred answers ready for his question.

"He's the spitting image of my great-grandfather. You skipped a couple of generations, Harry," said Charles, lifting the boy high into the air, "but there's no doubt you're a real Seymour."

Amanda sighed with inaudible relief. The hundred answers she could now keep to herself.

"It's more than a couple of generations the little bastard has skipped," said Pimkin. "It's an entire continent." He took another sip of christening champagne before continuing. "This poor creature, on the other hand," he said, staring at Fiona's firstborn, "bears a striking resemblance to Alexander. Dear little girl should have been given a kinder legacy with which to start her life."

"She's beautiful," said Fiona, picking Lucy up from the cradle to check her nappy.

"Now we know why you needed to be married so quickly," added Pimkin between gulps. "At least this child made wedlock, even if it was a close-run thing."

Fiona continued as if she had not heard his remark. "Have you actually seen Charles's son?"

"I think we should refer to young Harry as Amanda's child," said Pimkin. "We don't want to be had up under the Trade Descriptions Act."

"Come on, Alec, have you seen Harry?" she asked, refusing to fill his empty glass.

"Yes, I have. And I am afraid he also bears too striking a resemblance to his father for it to go unnoticed in later life."

"Anyone we know?" asked Fiona, probing.

"I am not a scandalmonger," said Pimkin, removing a crumb from his waistcoat. "As you well know. But a certain Brazilian *fazendeiro* who frequents Cowdray Park and Ascot during the summer months has obviously maintained his interest in English fillies."

Pimkin confidently held out his glass.

CHAPTER
TWENTY SEVEN

James Callaghan's resignation as Labour party leader in October 1980 took none of the political analysts by surprise. Unlike his predecessor he was over sixty-five, the age at which his party had recommended retirement.

Those same analysts were surprised, however, when Michael Foot, the veteran left-winger, defeated Denis Healey by 139 votes to 129 to become the new leader of the Labour party. The analysts immediately predicted a long spell of opposition for the socialists.

The Conservatives took much pleasure in watching a leadership struggle from the sidelines for a change. When Charles Seymour heard the result it amused him that the Labour party had ended up replacing a sixty-year-old with a sixty-four-year-old, who in turn was being replaced by a sixty-seven-year-old. Lord Shinwell, who at the age of ninety-six was the oldest living former Labour Cabinet minister, declared that he would be a candidate for party leadership when Foot retired.

When the election for the Shadow Cabinet came a week later Andrew decided not to submit his name. Like many of his colleagues he liked the new leader personally but had rarely been able to agree with him on domestic issues and was totally opposed to his defence and European policies. Instead he took on the chairmanship of the Select Committee on Scottish Affairs. Raymond for his part considered that Foot was destined to be no more than an interim leader and was therefore quite happy to serve under him. When the election to the Shadow Cabinet was announced Raymond

came eighth. Michael Foot invited him to continue shadowing the Trade portfolio.

When Andrew entered the Commons Chamber the day
after the election he walked up the gangway and took a seat
on the back benches for the first time in fourteen years. He
looked down at Raymond lounging on the front bench and
recalled his own words: "There may well come a day when I
sit and envy you from the same back benches."

Andrew was not surprised when he heard from his local
committee in Edinburgh that he would once again have to
submit himself to re-selection as their candidate some time
during 1981. When the Labour conference the previous
October had approved the mandatory re-selection of Labour
MPs he had realised his biggest battle would be internal.
Frank Boyle had even managed to replace another of
Andrew's supporters with one of his own henchmen.

Roy Jenkins, the former deputy leader of the Labour party,
was returning from Brussels as soon as his term as President
of the European Commission came to an end. After delivering the Dimbleby lecture on television Jenkins made no
secret of the fact that he was considering founding a new
party that would take in those moderate radicals who felt the
Labour party had swung too far to the left. The party
conference had removed the power of selection of the leaders
from Members of Parliament; for many this was the final
straw, and several Labour MPs told Jenkins they were ready
to defect. Andrew would have preferred to remain loyal to the
party and try to change it from the inside, but he was fast
coming to the conclusion that that hour had passed.

In his morning mail was a curt note from the constituency
secretary informing him that Frank Boyle was going to
oppose him for the nomination. Andrew flew up to Edinburgh on the day of the meeting, fearing the worst. No one
met him at the airport, and at party headquarters David
Connaught greeted him with a glum face.

Andrew stood in front of the committee in a cold, cheerless
room and answered the same questions that had been put to
him only three years before. He gave exactly the same

answers: where he stood on nuclear disarmament, why he was in favour of a close association with the United States, his attitude to a wealth tax – on and on, predictable question after predictable question, but he never once allowed them to exasperate him.

He ended with the words: "I have been proud to serve the people of Edinburgh Carlton for almost twenty years as the Labour member and hope to do so for at least another twenty. If you now feel unable to re-select me I would have to consider standing as an independent candidate." For the first time, one or two members of the committee looked anxious.

"We are not intimidated by your threats, Mr Fraser," said Frank Boyle. "The Labour party has always been bigger than any individual. Now we know where Mr Fraser's real interests lie I suggest we move to a vote."

Twelve little slips of paper were passed out. 'Fraser' or 'Boyle' were scribbled on them before they were sent back to the chairman.

Frank Boyle slowly gathered up the slips, clearly relishing Andrew's discomfort. He unfolded the first slip of paper. "Boyle," he said, glancing at the others round the table.

He opened a second – "Fraser" – then a third, "Boyle", followed by "Fraser, Fraser, Fraser."

Andrew kept count in his head: four-two in his favour.

"Fraser," followed by "Boyle, Boyle, Fraser."

Six-four in Andrew's favour, with two still unopened: he only needed one more vote. "Boyle." Six-five. The chairman took some considerable time opening the last slip.

"Boyle," he announced in triumph.

He paused for effect. "Six votes all," he declared. "Under standing order forty-two of the Party Constitution," he said, as if he had learnt the words off by heart before the meeting, "in the result of a tie the chairman shall have the casting vote." He paused once again.

"Boyle," he said, lingering for a moment. "I therefore declare that Frank Boyle is selected as the official Labour party candidate for the constituency of Edinburgh Carlton at the next general election." He turned to Andrew and said,

"We shall no longer be requiring your services, Mr Fraser."

"I would like to thank those of you who supported me," Andrew said quietly and left without another word.

The next day the *Scotsman* came out with a lengthy article on the dangers of a small group of wilful people having the power to remove a member who had served his constituents honourably over a long period of time. Andrew phoned Stuart Gray to thank him. "I only wish the article had come out the day before," he said.

"It was set up for yesterday," Stuart told him, "but the announcement from Buckingham Palace of Prince Charles's engagement to Lady Diana Spencer moved everything else out – even the Rangers–Celtic report. By the way, doesn't Boyle's nomination have to be confirmed by his General Management Committee?"

"Yes, but they are putty in his hands. That would be like trying to explain to your mother-in-law about your wife's nagging."

"Then why don't you appeal to the National Executive and ask for the decision to be put to a full meeting of the constituency party?"

"Because it would take weeks to get the decision over-turned and more importantly I'm no longer certain that I want to fight the seat as a Labour candidate."

Andrew listened to the reporter's question and said, "Yes, you may quote me."

As the date for an election drew nearer Charles decided it might be wise to introduce Amanda to the constituency. He had explained to those who inquired that his wife had had rather a bad time of it after the birth, and had been told by her doctors not to participate in anything that might raise her blood pressure – though one or two constituents considered that the Sussex Downs' Conservatives would find it hard to raise the blood pressure of a ninety-year-old with a pace-maker. Charles had also decided to leave Harry at home, explaining that it was he who had chosen a public life, not his son.

The annual Garden Party held in the grounds of Lord

Cuckfield's country home seemed to Charles to be the ideal opportunity to show off Amanda and he asked her to be certain to wear something appropriate.

He was aware that designer jeans had come into fashion, and that his clothes-conscious wife never seemed to dress in the same thing twice. He also knew that liberated women didn't wear bras. But he was nevertheless shocked when he saw Amanda in a near see-through blouse and jeans so tight it looked as if she had been poured into them. Charles was genuinely horrified.

"Can't you find something a little more . . . conservative?" he suggested.

"Like the things that old frump Fiona used to wear?"

Charles couldn't think of a suitable reply. "The Garden Party will be frightfully dull," said Charles desperately. "Perhaps I should go on my own."

Amanda turned and looked him in the eye. "Are you ashamed of me, Charlie?"

He drove his wife silently down to the constituency and every time he glanced over at her he wanted to make an excuse to turn back. When they arrived at Lord Cuckfield's home his worst fears were confirmed. Neither the men nor the women could take their eyes off Amanda as she strolled around the lawns devouring strawberries. Many of them would have used the word 'hussy' if she hadn't been the member's wife.

Charles might have escaped lightly had it only been the one *risqué* joke Amanda told – to the bishop's wife – or even her curt refusals to judge the baby contest or to draw the raffle; but he was not to be so lucky. The chairman of the Women's Advisory Committee had met her match when she was introduced to the member's wife.

"Darling," said Charles. "I don't think you've met Mrs Blenkinsop."

"No, I haven't," said Amanda, ignoring Mrs Blenkinsop's outstretched hand.

"Mrs Blenkinsop," continued Charles, "was awarded the OBE for her services to the constituency."

"OBE?" Amanda asked innocently.

Mrs Blenkinsop drew herself up to her full height.

"Order of the British Empire," she said.

"I've always wondered," said Amanda, smiling. "My dad used to tell me it stood for 'other buggers' efforts'."

"Seen the Persil anywhere?" asked Louise.

"No, I stopped washing my own pants some time ago," replied Andrew.

"Ha, ha," said Louise. "But if you haven't taken them who has – two giant packets are missing?"

"The phantom Persil thief strikes again. Whatever next?" said Andrew. "The Bovril perhaps?"

"Stop making a fool of yourself and go and fish Clarissa out of the bath."

Andrew pulled himself out of the armchair, dropped *The Economist* on the carpet and ran upstairs. "Time to get out, young lady," he said even before he reached the bathroom door. First he heard the sobbing then when he opened the door he found Clarissa covered from head to toe in soap flakes. Her thick black curly hair was matted with them. Andrew burst out laughing but he stopped when he saw Clarissa's knees and shins were bleeding. She held a large scrubbing brush in one hand which was covered in a mixture of soap powder and blood.

"What's the matter, darling?" asked Andrew, kneeling on the bath mat.

"It isn't true," said Clarissa, not looking at him.

"What isn't true?" asked Andrew gently.

"Look on the box," she said pointing at the two empty packets which were standing on the end of the bath. Andrew glanced at the familiar picture on the box of a little fair-haired girl in a white party dress.

"What isn't true?" he repeated, still uncertain what Clarissa meant.

"It isn't true that Persil washes whiter and can remove even the blackest spots. Two large packets and I'm still black," she said.

Andrew had to smile which only made Clarissa cry even more. After he had washed off all the suds and gently dried her he put antiseptic ointment on the cuts and bruises.

"Why am I so black?" she asked.

"Because your mother and father were black," replied Andrew, guiding his daughter through to her bedroom.

"Why can't you be my father? Then I'd be white."

"I am your father now so you don't need to be."

"Yes, I do."

"Why?"

"Because the children at school laugh at me," Clarissa said, clutching firmly on to Andrew's hand.

"When I was at school they used to laugh at me because I was small," said Andrew. "They called me puny."

"What did you do about it?" asked Clarissa.

"I trained hard and ended up as captain of the school rugby team and that made them stop laughing."

"But by then you were big. I can't train to be white."

"No, I was still small, and you won't need to train."

"Why?" asked Clarissa, still not letting go of his hand.

"Because you're going to be beautiful, and then all those ugly white girls will be oh so jealous."

Clarissa was silent for some time before she spoke again.

"Promise, Daddy?"

"I promise," he said, remaining on the edge of the bed.

"Like Frank Boyle is jealous of you?"

Andrew was startled. "What do you know about him?"

"Only what I heard Mummy say, that he's going to be the Labour man for Edinburgh, but you'll still beat him."

Andrew was speechless.

"Is he going to be the Labour man, Daddy?" she asked.

"Yes, he is."

"And will you beat him?"

"I'll try."

"Can I help?" Clarissa asked, a tiny smile appearing on her face.

"Of course. Now off you go to sleep," said Andrew, getting up and drawing the curtains.

"Is he black?"

"Who?" asked Andrew.

"The nasty Frank Boyle."

"No," said Andrew laughing, "he's white."

"Then he ought to be made to have my skin then I could have his."

Andrew turned off the light, relieved Clarissa could no longer see his face.

Harry's second birthday party was attended by all those two-year-olds in the vicinity of Eaton Square whom his nanny considered acceptable. Charles managed to escape from a departmental meeting accompanied by a large paint board and a red tricycle. As he parked his car in Eaton Square he spotted Fiona's old Volvo driving away towards Sloane Square. He dismissed the coincidence although he still had plans for regaining the priceless Holbein. Harry naturally wanted to ride the tricycle round and round the dining-room table. Charles sat watching his son and couldn't help noticing that he was smaller than most of his friends. Then he remembered that great-grandfather had only been five feet eight inches tall.

It was the moment after the candles had been blown out, and nanny switched the light back on, that Charles was first aware that something was missing. It was like the game children play with objects on a tray: everyone shuts his eyes, nanny takes one away and then you all have to guess which piece it was.

It took Charles some time to realise that the missing object was his gold cigar box. He walked over to the sideboard and studied the empty space. He continued to stare at the spot where the small gold box left to him by his great-grandfather had been the previous night. Now all that was left in its place was the matching lighter.

He immediately asked Amanda if she knew where the heirloom was, but his wife seemed totally absorbed in lining up the children for a game of musical chairs. After checking carefully in the other rooms Charles went into his study and phoned the Chelsea police.

An inspector from the Crime Squad came round immediately and took down all the details. Charles was able to supply the police officer with a photograph of the box which carried the initials C.G.S. He stopped just short of mentioning Fiona by name. The inspector assured Charles that he would deal with the investigation personally. Charles returned to the party to find nannies arriving to gather their wards.

When the Edinburgh Carlton Labour party issued a press statement after their AGM announcing that Frank Boyle had been selected to fight the seat as their candidate, Andrew was surprised and touched by the flood of letters and calls of goodwill he received, many from people he didn't even know. Most of the messages begged him to stand at the next general election as an Independent.

Twenty Labour MPs and one Conservative had joined the newly formed Social Democratic Party and many others were expected to follow. Andrew knew he would have to make an announcement soon if he didn't want his supporters to drift away. He spent agonising hours discussing with Louise the problem of severing the final bonds with the party.

"What shall I do?" he asked, yet again.

"I can't tell you that; I just hope you make up your mind fairly quickly."

"Why quickly?"

"Because I'm going to vote for the Social Democrats at the next election, so you had better be my local candidate."

A few days later Roy Jenkins, Andrew's old chief at the Home Office, phoned to say he was fighting a by-election in Glasgow as the SDP candidate.

"I do hope you will feel able to join us," said Jenkins.

Andrew had always admired Jenkins's firm stand against the left and felt he was the one man who might break the two-party system.

"I need a little more time," he replied.

A week later Andrew made up his mind and informed the Chief Whip that he was leaving the party and would be joining the SDP. Then he packed a bag and travelled to Glasgow.

Roy Jenkins won the seat at Glasgow Hillhead with a large enough swing to worry both main parties. By Easter, a total of twenty-nine Members of Parliament had broken away to join him, while the alliance of SDP and Liberal MPs together could muster more than forty votes on the floor of the House.

With opinion polls putting them in second place, it began to look possible that the Social Democrats might hold the balance of power after the next election. The Conservatives were now running a poor third in all the national opinion polls.

Charles heard nothing for three weeks about the missing gold box and was beginning to despair when the inspector phoned to say that the family heirloom had been found.

"Excellent news," said Charles. "Are you able to bring the box round to Eaton Square?"

"It's not quite as simple as that, sir," said the policeman.

"What do you mean?"

"I would prefer not to discuss the matter over the phone. May I come and see you, sir?"

"By all means," said Charles, slightly mystified.

He waited impatiently for the inspector to arrive, although the policeman was at the front door barely ten minutes later. His first question took Charles by surprise.

"Are we alone, sir?"

"Yes," said Charles. "My wife and son are away visiting my mother-in-law in Wales. You say you've found the gold box," he continued, impatient to hear the inspector's news.

"Yes, sir."

"Well done, Inspector. I shall speak to the Commissioner personally," he added, guiding the officer towards the drawing-room.

"I'm afraid there's a complication, sir."

"How can there be when you've found the box?"

"We cannot be sure there was anything illegal about its disappearance in the first place."

"What do you mean, Inspector?"

"The gold case was offered to a dealer in Grafton Street for £2,500."

"And who was doing the selling?" asked Charles impatiently.

"That's the problem, sir. The cheque was made out to Amanda Seymour and the description fits your wife," said the inspector. Charles was speechless. "And the dealer has a receipt to prove the transaction." The inspector passed over a copy of the receipt. Charles was unable to steady his shaking hand as he recognised Amanda's signature.

"Now, as this matter has already been referred to the Director of Public Prosecutions I thought I ought to have a word with you in private, as I am sure you would not want us to prefer charges."

"Yes, no, of course, thank you for your consideration, Inspector," said Charles flatly.

"Not at all, sir. The dealer has made his position clear: he would be only too happy to return the cigar box for the exact sum he paid for it. I don't think that could be fairer."

Charles made no comment other than to thank the inspector again before showing him out.

He returned to his study, phoned Amanda at her mother's house and told her to return immediately. She started to protest, but he had already hung up.

Charles remained at home until they all arrived back at Eaton Square late that night. The nanny and Harry were immediately sent upstairs.

It took Charles about five minutes to discover that only a few hundred pounds of the money was left. When his wife burst into tears he struck her across the face with such force that she fell to the ground. "If anything else goes missing from this house," he said, "you will go with it and I will also make sure you spend a very long time in jail." Amanda ran out of the room sobbing uncontrollably.

The next day Charles advertised for a full-time governess. He also moved his own bedroom to the top floor so that he could be close to his son. Amanda made no protest.

Once the governess had settled in Amanda quickly became bored with the child and began disappearing for long periods. Charles couldn't be sure where she was most of the time, and didn't care.

After Pimkin had recounted the latest state of affairs to Alexander Dalglish in well-embroidered detail Fiona remarked to her husband, "I never thought the day would come when I would feel sorry for Charles."

On a sleepy Thursday in April 1982 Argentina attacked and occupied two small islands whose 1,800 British citizens were forced to lower the Union Jack for the first time in over a hundred years. Few members returned to their constituency that Friday and the House met unusually on a Saturday morning to debate the crisis while the nation followed every word on the radio.

The same day Mrs Thatcher immediately despatched a task force halfway around the globe to recapture the islands. Her fellow countrymen followed every scrap of news so intently that the London theatres found themselves empty at the height of the season.

Simon felt exhilarated to be a member of the Defence team at such an historic moment, and Elizabeth didn't begrudge him those days when he left before she had woken and arrived home after she had fallen asleep.

Under less public scrutiny but almost equal pressure, Charles beavered away at the Treasury addressing the economic problems that had been presented. He spent day after day in the House helping to put the Government's case. Like Simon he found he could only snatch moments to be at home but, unlike Elizabeth, his wife remained in bed until midday. When Charles did manage to slip away from the department he spent all his spare time with Harry, whose progress he followed with delighted concern.

At the time when the Union Jack was raised once again in the Falklands, the budget became an Act.

CHAPTER
TWENTY EIGHT

'PM to go in Nov' and 'Will Maggie wait till June?' were two of the headlines Andrew read on the first day of the new Parliamentary session.

Anyone who is defending a marginal seat is always on edge as the statutory five years draws to a close, and the new SDP members all treated their seats as marginal. Andrew was no exception.

He had worked hard to prove he was worth his place in the group the leader of the Social Democrats was beginning to form in the Commons. When Roy Jenkins had announced the make-up of his Shadow team Andrew was appointed Defence spokesman and enjoyed the challenge of pitting himself against the two main parties in the Commons in the run-up to the election. But once the Falklands crisis was over he knew his real problems were not going to be in Westminster but in Edinburgh, where he spent an increasing amount of his time. Hamish Ramsey phoned to ask him if there was anything he could do to help.

"Be my chairman for the election campaign," said Andrew simply.

Ramsey agreed without hesitation and within a fortnight four members of Andrew's old Labour party committee had defected to join him. Support for Andrew came from the most surprising quarters, including Jock McPherson, who pledged that the Scottish Nationalists would not be contesting the Edinburgh Carlton seat as they had no desire to see Frank Boyle in Parliament. Sir Duncan Fraser kept very quiet about what the Conservatives were up to until they

announced that Jamie Lomax would be their standard-
bearer.

"Lomax. Lomax," repeated Andrew. "He and I were at
school together," he told his father. "He was known as Loopy
Lomax. You've selected the biggest idiot of his generation."

"That's a disgraceful slur on an able man," said Sir
Duncan, trying to keep a straight face. "I can assure you it
took a lot of convincing the committee to make certain
Lomax was selected."

"How did you fix it?"

"I must admit it wasn't easy. We had some very good
applicants, but I managed to undermine every one of them
and point out how blemish-free Lomax's political past was,"
said Sir Duncan, winking.

"Non-existent careers make for the best blemish-free
pasts," said Andrew, and burst out laughing.

"Yes, I'm afraid one or two of the committee noticed that.
But you must admit Lomax is a fine figure of a man," added
his father.

"What's that got to do with it?" asked Andrew. "You
weren't looking for a male model as candidate."

"I know, but it did help me to swing the ladies on the
Women's Advisory Committee round to my way of thinking."

"You're a rogue, Father."

"No, I'm not. There isn't a Conservative in Scotland who
would rather see Frank Boyle in the House than you, and as
we have no chance of winning the seat, why let *him* in?"

Louise and Clarissa spent the Christmas recess in Edinburgh. Sir Duncan warned Louise that if Andrew lost this
election he could never hope to return to the House of
Commons again.

During 1983 Margaret Thatcher stuck firm to her monetarist
policies and brought inflation below four per cent, while in
parts of Scotland unemployment rose to fifteen per cent. She
had gradually stifled any opposition from the 'wets' and by
the end of her first administration they were totally outman-
oeuvred. But it was the outcome of the Falklands crisis that

had kept her ahead in the opinion polls for over a year. The press speculated on the date of the general election all through the month of April, and after the Conservatives' success in the local elections on 5 May the Prime Minister sought an audience with the Queen. Shortly afterwards Margaret Thatcher told the nation that she needed another five years to continue her policies and prove that they worked. The election date was set for 9 June.

Once the election campaign had begun in earnest Stuart Gray interviewed all three candidates on behalf of the *Scotsman* and told Andrew he had a plan to help him.

"You can't," said Andrew. "You're bound to remain neutral and give all three candidates equal column inches during the campaign."

"Agreed," said Stuart. "But on the one hand we know Frank Boyle is sharp and has the looks of an escaped convict, while Jamie Lomax looks like a film star but makes crass statements every time he opens his mouth."

"So?" said Andrew.

"So I'm going to cover the political pages with the worst shots I can find of Boyle and fill up inch after inch with the sayings of Lomax. They'll both get equal coverage while at the same time they'll lose votes."

"They'll suss it out and complain to the editor."

"I doubt it," said Stuart. "I have yet to meet a politician who complained about having his photo in the paper, or one who was angered by seeing his mad views aired to a larger audience than he could have hoped to influence in the past."

"And what do you propose to do about me?"

"That's a problem," admitted Stuart, laughing. "Perhaps I'll leave the columns blank. That's one way you can't lose votes."

Whenever Andrew carried out a door-to-door canvass he found a clear division between those who still backed him and those who thought he had been disloyal to the Labour party. As the canvass returns came in and the colours were put out on the trestle tables in the new party headquarters it became clear from even a cursory glance that it was going to be his toughest election yet.

Andrew had experienced some dirty campaigns over the years, especially when he had been up against the Scottish Nationalists, but after only a few days he had sweet memories of Jock McPherson who was Little Red Riding Hood compared with Boyle. Andrew could just about tolerate hearing that he had been thrown out of the Labour party because he was such a lazy member, even that he had left them in the lurch because he had been told he could never hope to be a minister again, but when it was repeated to him that the Boyle camp were spreading a rumour that Louise had lost her voice because, when she had her baby, it turned out to be black he was furious.

If Andrew had seen Boyle that day he would undoubtedly have hit him. Sir Duncan counselled restraint, pointing out that any other action could only harm Louise and Clarissa. Andrew took a deep breath and said nothing.

With a week to go a local opinion poll in the *Scotsman* showed Boyle leading by thirty-five per cent to Andrew's thirty-two. The Conservatives had nineteen per cent but fourteen per cent remained undecided. Jock McPherson had kept his word: no Scottish Nationalist candidate had entered the lists.

On the Friday before the election McPherson went one better by issuing a statement advising his supporters to back Andrew Fraser.

When Andrew phoned to thank him, he said, "I'm returning a favour."

"I don't remember ever doing you a favour," said Andrew.

"You certainly did, remembering you're an Edinburgh man. One mention to the press of my offer of the leadership of the Scottish Nationalists and I'd have been sunk down the nearest pothole."

With five days to go Alliance supporters from the two Edinburgh constituencies which were not fielding an SDP candidate swarmed in to help Andrew, and he began to believe the canvass returns that were now showing he could win. With two days to go the *Scotsman* proclaimed it was thirty-nine per cent to thirty-eight per cent in Boyle's favour, but also went on to point out that the Labour party would have a better-oiled machine to depend on when it came to polling day.

In his eve-of-poll message Andrew issued a clear statement on why his views differed from those of his opponent in the Labour party, and how he saw the future of Britain if the Alliance gained enough seats to hold the balance of power. He reminded voters that without exception the national opinion polls showed the SDP now running neck and neck with Labour.

Frank Boyle also put out an eve-of-poll message, delivered to every house in the constituency, showing a picture of Andrew holding Clarissa in his arms under the caption 'Does your member tell you the whole truth?' There was no mention of Louise or Clarissa in the text but the innuendo could not have been clearer. Andrew didn't see the sheet until the morning of polling day by which time he knew there was nothing effective he could do to refute Boyle's implied slur. Issuing a writ that could not be dealt with until weeks after the election was over could only prove impotent. He either won the day or he lost it.

To that end, he and Louise never stopped working from seven that morning until ten at night. Helpers arrived from the most unexpected places, as if to prove the *Scotsman* wrong about the Labour party machine, but Andrew couldn't help noticing that there were red rosettes everywhere he went.

Towards the end of the day even Sir Duncan joined him and began chauffeuring SDP voters to the polls in his Rolls Royce.

"We've faced the fact that our candidate has lost so now I've come to help you," he told Andrew bluntly.

As the city hall clock struck ten Andrew sat down on the steps of the last polling station. He knew there was nothing he could do now. He had done everything possible, only avoiding members of the House of Lords and lunatics – neither of which group was entitled to vote.

An old lady was coming out of the polling station with a smile on her face.

"Hello, Mrs Bloxham," said Andrew. "How are you?"

"I'm fine, Andrew," she smiled. "I nearly forgot to vote and that would never have done."

He raised his tired head.

"Now don't fret yourself, laddie," she continued, "I never failed to vote for the winner in fifty-two years and that's longer than you've lived." She chuckled and left him sitting on the steps.

Andrew somehow picked himself up and made his way through the dark cobbled streets to his election head-quarters. They cheered him as he entered the room, and the chairman offered him a 'wee dram of whisky'.

"To hell with a wee dram," said Andrew. "Just keep pouring."

He tried to get round the room to thank everyone before Hamish Ramsey told him it was time to go over to the city hall for the count. A small band of supporters accompanied the Frasers to the city hall to witness the proceedings. As he entered the hall the first person he saw was Boyle, who had a big smile on his face. Andrew was not discouraged by the smile as he watched the little slips of paper pour out of the boxes. Boyle had yet to learn that the first boxes to be counted were always from the inner wards, where most of the committed Socialists lived.

As both men walked round the tables, the little piles began to be checked – first in tens, then hundreds, until they were finally placed in thousands and handed over to the Sheriff. As the night drew on Boyle's smile turned to a grin, from a grin to a poker face, and finally to a look of anxiety as the piles grew closer and closer in size.

For over three hours the process of emptying the boxes continued and the scrutineers checked each little white slip before handing in their own records. At one twenty-two in the morning the Sheriff added up the list of numbers in front of him and asked the three candidates to join him.

He told them the result.

Frank Boyle smiled once again. Andrew showed no emo-tion, but called for a recount.

For over an hour, he paced nervously around the room as

the scrutineers checked and double-checked each pile: a change here, a mistake there, a lost vote discovered and, on one occasion, the name on the top of a pile of one hundred votes was not the same as the ninety-nine beneath it. At last the scrutineers handed back their figures. Once again the Sheriff added up the columns of numbers and asked the candidates to join him.

This time Andrew smiled while Boyle looked surprised and demanded another recount. The Sheriff acquiesced, but said it must be the last time. Both candidates agreed in the absence of their Conservative rival, who was sleeping soundly in a corner, secure in the knowledge that no amount of recounting would alter his position in the contest.

Once again the piles were checked and double-checked and five mistakes were discovered in the 42,588 votes cast. At three-twenty a.m., with counters and checkers falling asleep at their tables, the Sheriff once more asked the two candidates to join him. They were both stunned when they heard the result and the Sheriff informed them that there would be a further recount in the morning after his staff had managed to get some sleep.

All the voting papers were then placed carefully back in the black boxes, locked and left in the safe-keeping of the local constabulary while the candidates crept away to their beds.

Andrew slept in fits and starts through the remainder of the night. Louise, pale with exhaustion but still grinning, brought him a cup of tea at eight in the morning. He took a cold shower, shaved slowly and was back at the city hall a few minutes before the count was due to recommence. As he walked up the steps he was greeted by a battery of television cameras and journalists who had heard rumours as to why the count had been held up overnight and knew they couldn't afford to be absent as the final drama unfolded.

The counters looked eager and ready when the Sheriff checked his watch and nodded. The boxes were unlocked and placed in front of the staff for the fourth time. Once again the little piles grew from tens into hundreds and then into thousands. Andrew paced around the tables, more to burn up his nervous energy than out of a desire to keep checking. He had thirty witnesses registered as his counting agents to make sure he didn't lose by sleight of hand or genuine mistake.

Once the counters and scrutineers had finished they sat in front of their piles and waited for the slips to be collected and taken to the Sheriff. When the Sheriff had added up his little columns of figures for the final time he found that no votes had changed hands.

He explained to Andrew and Frank Boyle the procedure he intended to adopt in view of the outcome. He told both candidates that he had spoken to Lord Wylie at nine that morning and the Lord Advocate had read out the relevant statute in election law that was to be followed in such circumstances. Both candidates agreed on which of the two choices they preferred.

The Sheriff walked up on to the stage with Andrew Fraser and Frank Boyle in his wake, both looking anxious.

Everyone in the room stood to be sure of a better view of the proceedings. When the pushing back of chairs, the coughing and the nervous chattering had stopped, the Sheriff began. First he tapped the microphone that stood in front of him to be sure it was working. The metallic scratch was audible throughout the silent room. Satisfied, he began to speak.

"I, the returning officer for the district of Edinburgh Carlton, hereby declare the total number of votes cast for each candidate to be as follows:

Frank Boyle	18,437
Jamie Lomax	5,714
Andrew Fraser	18,437."

The supporters of both the leading candidates erupted into a noisy frenzy. It was several minutes before the Sheriff's voice could be heard above the babble of Scottish burrs.

"In accordance with section sixteen of the Representation of the People Act 1949 and rule fifty of the Parliamentary Election Rules in the second schedule to that Act, I am

obliged to decide between tied candidates by lot," he announced. "I have spoken with the Lord Advocate of Scotland, and have confirmed that the drawing of straws or the toss of a coin may constitute decision by lot for this purpose. Both candidates have agreed to the latter course of action."

Pandemonium broke out again as Andrew and Boyle stood motionless on each side of the Sheriff waiting for their fate to be determined.

"I have borrowed from the Royal Bank of Scotland," continued the Sheriff, aware that twenty million people were watching him on television for the first and probably the last time in his life, "a golden sovereign. On one side is the head of King George III, on the other Britannia. I shall invite the sitting member, Mr Fraser, to call his preference." Boyle curtly nodded his agreement. Both men inspected the coin.

The Sheriff rested the golden sovereign on his thumb, Andrew and Boyle still standing on either side of him. He turned to Andrew and said, "You will call, Mr Fraser, while the coin is in the air."

The silence was such that they might have been the only three people in the room. Andrew could feel his heart thumping in his chest as the Sheriff spun the coin high above him.

"Tails," he said clearly when the coin was at its zenith. The sovereign hit the floor and bounced, turning over several times before settling at the feet of the Sheriff.

Andrew stared down at the lady and sighed audibly. The Sheriff cleared his throat before declaring, "Following the decision by lot, I declare the aforementioned Mr Andrew Fraser to be the duly elected Member of Parliament for Edinburgh Carlton."

Andrew's supporters charged forward and on to the stage and carried him on their shoulders out of the city hall and through the streets of Edinburgh. Andrew searched for Louise and Clarissa, but they were lost in the crush.

The Royal Bank of Scotland presented the golden sovereign to the member the next day, and the editor of the

Scotsman rang to ask if there had been any particular reason why he had selected tails.

"Naturally," Andrew replied. "George III lost America for us. I wasn't going to let him lose Edinburgh for me."

CHAPTER
TWENTY NINE

Raymond read the *Daily Mail* caption again and smiled: 'On the toss of a coin'.

It saddened Raymond that Andrew had felt it necessary to leave the Labour party, although he was delighted that he had been returned to the Commons. Raymond was only thankful that there had been no Frank Boyles in his constituency. He often wondered if it was because Joyce kept such a watchful eye on all the committees.

Margaret Thatcher's second victory had come as a bitter blow to him although he couldn't have pretended it was a surprise. Her overall majority of 144 was even larger than had been predicted, while the SDP managed only six seats – although the Alliance were only two percentage points behind Labour in actual votes cast. Raymond was enough of a realist to know that now nothing was going to stop the Tories from governing for another five-year term.

Once again Raymond returned to his practice at the bar and a new round of time-consuming briefs. When the Lord Chancellor, Lord Hailsham, offered him the chance to become a High Court judge, with a place in the House of Lords, Raymond gave the matter considerable thought before finally asking Joyce for her opinion.

"You'd be bored to tears in a week," she told him.

"No more bored than I am now."

"Your turn will come."

"Joyce, I'm nearly fifty, and all I have to show for it is the chairmanship of the Select Committee on Trade and Industry. If the party fails to win next time I may never hold office again. Don't forget that the last occasion we lost this badly we were in Opposition for thirteen years."

"Once Michael Foot has been replaced the party will take on a new look, and I bet you'll be offered one of the senior Shadow jobs."

"That'll depend on who's our next leader," said Raymond. "And I can't see a great deal of difference between Neil Kinnock who looks unbeatable, and Michael Foot – except that Kinnock's ten years younger than I am."

"Then why not stand yourself?" asked Joyce.

"It's too early for me," said Raymond.

"Then why don't you at least wait until we know who's going to be the leader of the party," said Joyce. "You can be a judge at any time – they die off just as quickly as Cabinet ministers."

When Raymond returned to his chambers the following Monday he followed Joyce's advice and let Lord Hailsham know that he was not interested in being a judge in the foreseeable future, and settled down to keep a watchful eye on Cecil Parkinson, the new Secretary of State for Trade and Industry.

Only a few days later Michael Foot announced that he would not be standing for leader when the party's annual conference took place. When he informed the Shadow Cabinet several faces lit up at the thought of the forthcoming battle at Brighton in October. Neil Kinnock and Roy Hattersley became the front runners, while during the weeks leading up to the conference several trade unionists and MPs approached Raymond and asked him to stand; but he told them all "next time".

The vote for the new leader took place on the Sunday before the conference began: as Raymond predicted Kinnock won easily and Hattersley, his closest rival, was elected as his deputy.

After the conference Raymond returned to Leeds for the weekend, still confident that he would be offered a major post in the Shadow Cabinet despite the fact he hadn't supported the winner. Having completed his morning surgery he hung around the house waiting for the new leader to call him, even missing the match against Chelsea. He didn't like being in the second division.

When Neil Kinnock eventually phoned late that evening Raymond was shocked by his offer and replied without hesitation that he was not interested. It was a short conversation.

Joyce came into the drawing-room as he sank back into his favourite armchair.

"Well, what did he offer you?" she asked, facing him.

"Transport. Virtually a demotion."

"What did you say?"

"I turned him down, of course."

"Who has he given the main jobs to?"

"I didn't ask and he didn't volunteer, but I suspect we'll only have to wait for the morning papers to find out. Not that I'm that interested," he continued, staring at the floor, "as I intend to take the first place that comes free on the bench. I've wasted too many years already."

"So have I," said Joyce quietly.

"What do you mean?" asked Raymond, looking up at his wife for the first time since she had come into the room.

"If you're going to make a complete break, I think it's time for me to do so as well."

"I don't understand," said Raymond.

"We haven't been close for a long time, Ray," said Joyce, looking straight into her husband's eyes. "If you're thinking of giving up the constituency and spending even more time in London I think we should part." She turned away.

"Is there someone else?" asked Raymond, his voice cracking.

"No one special."

"But someone?"

"There is a man who wants to marry me," said Joyce, "if that's what you mean. We were at school in Bradford together. He's an accountant now and has never married."

"But do you love him?"

Joyce considered the question. "No, I can't pretend I do. But we're good friends, he's very kind and understanding and, more important, he's there."

Raymond couldn't move.

"And the break would at least give you the chance to ask Kate Garthwaite to give up her job in New York and return to London." Raymond gasped. "Think about it and let me know what you decide." She left the room quickly so that he could not see her tears.

Raymond sat alone in the room and thought back over his years with Joyce – and Kate – and knew exactly what he wanted to do now that the whole affair was out in the open.

He caught the last train to London the same evening because he had to be in court by ten o'clock the next morning to attend a judge's summing up. In the flat that night he slept intermittently as he thought about how he would spend the rest of his new life. Before he went into court the next morning he ordered a dozen red roses via Interflora. He phoned the Attorney General. If he was going to change his life he must change it in every way.

When the summing up was over and the judge had passed sentence Raymond checked the plane schedules. Nowadays you could be there in such a short time. He booked his flight and took a taxi to Heathrow. He sat on the plane praying it wasn't too late and that too much time hadn't passed. The flight seemed endless and he took another taxi from the airport.

When he arrived at her front door she was astonished. "What are you doing here on a Monday afternoon?"

"I've come to try and win you back," said Raymond. "Christ, that sounds corny," he added.

"It's the nicest thing you've said in years," she said as he held her in his arms; over Joyce's shoulder Raymond could see the roses brightening up the drawing-room.

"Let's go and have a quiet dinner."

Over dinner Raymond told Joyce of his plans to accept the Attorney General's offer to join the bench, but only if she would agree to live in London. After a second bottle of champagne which Joyce had been reluctant to open they finally returned home.

When they arrived back a little after one the phone was

ringing. Raymond opened the door and stumbled towards it while Joyce groped for the light switch.

"Ray, I've been trying to get you all night," a lilting Welsh voice said.

"Have you now?" Raymond said thickly, trying to keep his eyes open.

"You sound as if you've been to a good party."

"I've been celebrating with my wife."

"Celebrating before you've heard the news?"

"What news?" said Raymond, collapsing into the armchair.

"I've been juggling the new team around all day and I was hoping you would agree to join the Shadow Cabinet as . . ."

Raymond sobered up very quickly and listened carefully to the new leader. "Can you hold the line?"

"Of course," said the surprised voice the other end.

"Joyce," said Raymond, as she came out of the kitchen clutching two mugs of very black coffee. "Would you agree to live with me in London if I don't become a judge?"

A broad smile spread across Joyce's face with the realisation that he was seeking her approval.

She nodded several times.

"I'd be delighted to accept," he said.

"Thank you, Raymond. Perhaps we could meet at my room in the Commons tomorrow and talk over policy in your new field."

"Yes, of course," said Raymond. "See you tomorrow." He dropped the phone on the floor and fell asleep in the chair.

Joyce replaced the phone and didn't discover until the following morning that her husband was the new Shadow Secretary of State for Social Services.

Raymond sold his flat in the Barbican, and he and Joyce moved into a small Georgian house in Cowley Street, only a few hundred yards from the House of Commons.

Raymond watched Joyce decorate his study first, then she set about the rest of the house with the energy and enthusiasm of a newly-wed. Once she had completed the guest bedroom Raymond's parents came down to spend the weekend. He burst out laughing when he greeted his father at the door clutching on to a bag, marked 'Gould, the family butcher'.

"They do have meat in London, you know," said Raymond.

"Not like mine, son," his father replied.

Over the finest beef Raymond could remember he watched Joyce and his mother chatting away. "Thank God I woke up in time," he said out loud.

"What did you say?" asked Joyce.

"Nothing, my dear, nothing."

Although Raymond spent most of his time on the overall strategy for a future Labour Government, like all politicians he had pet anomalies that particularly upset him. His had always been war widows' pensions, a preoccupation which dated back to his living with his grandmother in Leeds. He remembered the shock when he first realised shortly after leaving university that his grandmother had eked out an existence for thirty years on a weekly widow's pension that wouldn't have covered the cost of a decent meal in a London restaurant.

From the back benches, he had always pressed for the redeeming of war bonds and higher pensions for war widows. His weekly mail showed unequivocally just how major a problem war widows' pensions had become. During his years in Opposition he had worked doggedly to achieve ever-increasing, smaller rises, but he vowed that were he to become Secretary of State he would enact something more radical.

Joyce left a cutting from the *Standard* for him to read when he returned from the Commons that night. She had scribbled across it: "This could end up on the front page of every national paper."

Raymond agreed with her, and the following day he tried to press his view on to a reluctant Shadow Cabinet who seemed more concerned with the planned series of picketing by the Yorkshire miners' union than the case of Mrs Dora Benson.

Raymond researched the story carefully and discovered that the case didn't differ greatly from the many others he had looked into over the years, except for the added ingredient of a Victoria Cross. By any standards, Mrs Dora Benson highlighted Raymond's cause. She was one of the handful of surviving widows of the First World War and her husband, Private Albert Benson, had been killed at the Somme leading an attack on a German trench. Nine Germans had been killed before Albert Benson died, which was why he had been awarded the VC. His widow had continued working as a cleaner in the King's Head at Barking for over fifty years. Her only possessions of any value were her war bonds, but with no redemption date they were still passing hands at twenty-five pounds each. Mrs Benson's case might have gone unnoticed if in desperation she had not asked Sotheby's to auction her husband's medal.

Once Raymond had armed himself with all the facts he put down a question to the minister concerned asking if he would at last honour the Government's long-promised pledges in such cases. A sleepy but packed House heard Simon Kerslake, as Minister of State for Defence, reply that his department was once again considering the problem and he would make known their findings in the near future. Simon settled back on to the green benches satisfied that would pacify Gould. But Raymond's supplementary stunned him and woke up the House.

"Does the Right Honourable Gentleman realise that this eighty-four-year-old widow, whose husband was killed in action and won the Victoria Cross, has a lower income than a sixteen-year-old cadet on his first day in the armed forces?"

Simon rose once more, determined to put a stop to the issue until he had had more time to study the details of this particular case.

"I was not aware of this fact, Mr Speaker, and I can assure the Right Honourable Gentleman that I shall take into consideration all the points he has mentioned."

Simon felt confident the Speaker would now move on to the next question. But Raymond rose again, the Opposition benches spurring him on.

"Is the Right Honourable Gentleman also aware that an admiral, on an index-linked income, can hope to end his career with a pension of over £500 a week while Mrs Dora Benson's weekly income remains fixed at £47.32?"

There was a gasp even from the Conservative benches as Raymond sat down.

Simon rose again, painfully aware that he was unprepared for Gould's attack and that he had to stifle it as quickly as he could. "I was not aware of that particular comparison either, but once again I can assure the Right Honourable Gentleman I will give the case my immediate consideration."

To Simon's horror Raymond rose from the benches for yet a third time. He could see that Labour members opposite were enjoying the rare spectacle of watching him up against the ropes. "Is the Right Honourable Gentleman also aware that the annuity for a Victoria Cross is £100 with no extra pension benefits? We pay our fourth-division footballers more, while keeping Mrs Benson in the bottom league of the national income bracket."

Simon looked distinctly harassed when he in turn rose for a fourth time and made an uncharacteristic remark that he regretted the moment he said it.

"I take the Right Honourable Gentleman's point," he began, his words coming out a little too quickly. "And I am fascinated by his sudden interest in Mrs Benson. Would it be cynical of me to suggest that it has been prompted by the wide publicity this case has enjoyed in the national press?"

Raymond made no attempt to answer but sat motionless with his arms folded and his feet up on the table in front of him while his own back-benchers screamed their abuse at Simon.

The national papers the next day were covered with pictures of the arthritic Dora Benson with her bucket and mop alongside photos of her handsome young husband in private's uniform. Many of the papers went on to describe how Albert Benson had won his VC, and some of the tabloids used considerable licence. But all of them picked up Raymond's point that Mrs Benson was in the bottom one per cent of the income bracket and that the annuity for a Victoria Cross was a pathetic £100.

It was an enterprising and unusually thorough journalist from the *Guardian* who led her story on a different angle which the rest of the national press had to turn to in their second edition. It transpired that Raymond Gould had put down forty-seven questions concerning war widows' pension rights during his time in the House and spoken on the subject in three budgets and five social service debates from the back benches. He had also made the subject the thrust of his maiden speech over twenty years before. But when the journalist revealed that Raymond gave £500 a year to the Erskine Hospital for wounded soldiers every member knew that Simon Kerslake would have to retract his attack and make an apology to the House.

At three-thirty the Speaker rose from his chair and told a packed house that the Minister of State for Defence wished to make a personal statement.

Simon Kerslake rose warily from the front bench and stood nervously at the dispatch box.

"Mr Speaker," he began. "With your permission and that of the House I would like to make a personal statement. During a question put to me yesterday I impugned the integrity of the Right Honourable Gentleman, the member for Leeds North. It has since been brought to my attention that I did him a gross injustice and I offer the House my sincere apologies, and the Right Honourable Gentleman the assurances that I will not question his integrity a third time."

While younger members were puzzled by the reference, Raymond smiled to himself.

Aware of how rare personal statements were in anyone's parliamentary career, members looked on eagerly to see how he would respond.

He moved slowly to the dispatch box.

"Mr Speaker, I accept the gracious manner in which the Right Honourable Gentleman has apologised and hope that he will not lose sight of the greater issue, namely that of war widows' benefits, and in particular the plight of Mrs Dora Benson."

Simon looked relieved and nodded courteously.

Many Opposition members told Raymond he should have gone for Simon when he had him on the run, while Tom Carson continued shouting at Simon long after the House had proceeded to the next business. *The Times* leader writer proved them wrong when he wrote the next morning: "In an age of militant demands from the left, Parliament and the Labour party have found a new Clement Attlee on their front bench. Britain need have no fear for human dignity or the rights of man should Raymond Gould ever accede to the high office which that gentleman held."

When Raymond returned home from the Commons that night he found Joyce had cut out all the press comments for him to study and had also somehow managed to make inroads into his overflowing correspondence.

Joyce turned out to have a better feel for gut politics than the entire Shadow Cabinet put together.

Alec Pimkin threw a party for all his Tory colleagues who had entered the House in 1964, "To celebrate the first twenty years in the Commons," as he described the occasion in an impromptu after-dinner speech.

Over brandy and cigars the corpulent, balding figure sat back and surveyed his fellow members. Many had fallen by the wayside over the years, but of those that were left, he believed only two men now dominated the intake.

Pimkin's eyes first settled on his old friend Charles Seymour. Despite studying him closely he was still unable to spot a grey hair on the Treasury minister's head. From time to time Pimkin still saw Amanda, who had returned to being a full-time model and was rarely to be found in England nowadays. Charles, he suspected, saw more of her on the covers of magazines than he ever did in his home at Eaton Square. Pimkin had been surprised by how much time Charles was willing to put aside for little Harry. Charles was the last man he would have suspected of ending up a doting father. Certainly there was no sign of his ambitions diminishing, and Pimkin suspected that only one man remained a worthy rival for the party leadership.

His eyes moved on to someone for whom in 1984 Orwell's big brother seemed to hold no fears. Simon Kerslake was deep in animated conversation about his work on the proposed disarmament talks between Thatcher, Gorbachov and Reagan. Pimkin studied the Defence minister intently. He considered that had *he* been graced with such looks he would not have had to fear for his dwindling majority. Rumours of some financial crisis had long since died away, and Kerslake now seemed well set for a formidable future.

The party began to break up, as one by one his contemporaries came over to thank him for such a 'splendid', 'memorable', 'worthwhile' evening. When the last one had departed and Pimkin found himself alone he drained the drop of brandy that remained in his balloon and stubbed out the dying cigar. He sighed as he speculated on the fact that he could now never hope to be made a minister. He therefore determined to become a kingmaker, for in another twenty years there would be nothing left on which to speculate.

Raymond celebrated his twenty years in the House by taking Joyce to the Guinea Restaurant off Berkeley Square for dinner. He admired the long burgundy dress his wife had chosen for the occasion and even noticed that one or two women gave it more than a casual glance throughout their meal.

He too reflected on his twenty years in the Commons, and he told Joyce over a brandy that he hoped he would spend more of the next twenty years in Government. 1984 had not turned out to be a good year for the Conservatives, and Raymond was already forming plans to make 1985 as uncomfortable for the Government as possible.

A few weeks later Tony Benn, who had lost his seat at the general election, returned to the House of Commons as the member for Chesterfield. The Conservatives came a poor third and went on to lose two more by-elections early in 1985. Even the press began to acknowledge that the Labour party was once again looking like a serious alternative Government.

The winter of 1985 brought a further rise in the unemployment figures which only increased the Labour party's lead in the polls. And then after the resignation of two cabinet ministers over a small helicopter company in the West Country and the loss of two further by-elections, the Conservatives fell into third place for the first time in five years.

A drop in the price of oil from $22 to $10 a barrel in the space of six weeks did not help the Chancellor's budget judgement. After a long, hot summer Mrs Thatcher decided on a further cabinet reshuffle bringing in those who would be formulating policy in the run-up to the general election. The average age of the cabinet fell by seven years and the press dubbed it, 'Mrs Thatcher's new lamps for old reshuffle'.

CHAPTER THIRTY

Andrew was on his way to the House of Commons when he heard the first reports on his car radio. There had been no mention of the news in the morning papers so it must have happened overnight. It began with a news flash: just the bare details. HMS *Broadsword*, one of the Navy's destroyers, had been passing through the Gulf of Surt between Tunis and Benghazi when she was boarded by a group of mercenaries, posing as coastguard officials, who took over the ship in the name of Colonel Gaddafi. The newscaster went on to say that there would be a more detailed report in their ten o'clock bulletin.

Andrew had reached his room in the House of Commons by nine-thirty, and he immediately phoned the SDP leader David Owen to discuss the political implications of the news. Once a course of action had been agreed on Andrew took a handwritten letter round to the Speaker's office before the noon deadline, requesting an emergency debate following question time that afternoon. He also sent a copy of the letter by messenger to the Foreign Secretary and the Secretary of State for Defence.

By staying near a radio most of the morning Andrew was able to learn that HMS *Broadsword* was now in the hands of over a hundred guerillas. They were demanding the freedom of all Libyan prisoners in British jails in exchange for the 217-strong crew of the *Broadsword*, who were being held hostage in the engine room.

By twelve o'clock the ticker-tape machine in the Members' Corridor was hovered over by craning necks, and the dining-rooms were so full that many members had to go without lunch.

Question time that day had been allocated to Welsh Affairs, so the Chamber itself did not start filling up until nearly three-fifteen although the Palace of Westminster was already packed and buzzing with each new snippet of information. Political correspondents waited hawk-like in the Members' Lobby seeking opinions on the crisis from any senior politicians as they passed to and from the Chamber. Few were rash enough to say anything that might be re-interpreted the next day.

When Andrew came into the Chamber he took his seat next to David Owen on the Opposition front bench below the gangway. Since Andrew had the overall responsibility for the Alliance Defence portfolio he was expected to represent the other twenty-two Alliance members. At three-twenty-seven the Prime Minister, followed by the Foreign Secretary and the Secretary of State for Defence, filed into the House and took their places on the Treasury bench. All three looked suitably sombre. The last two questions on Welsh Affairs had the largest audience of members since the Aberfan disaster of 1966.

At three-thirty Mr Speaker Weatherill rose and called for order.

"Statements to the House," he announced in his crisp, military style. "There will be two statements on HMS *Broadsword* before the House debates Welsh Affairs." The Speaker then called the Secretary of State for Defence.

Simon Kerslake rose from the front bench and placed a prepared statement on the dispatch box in front of him.

"Mr Speaker, with your permission and that of the House, I would like to make a statement concerning Her Majesty's frigate *Broadsword*. At seven-forty GMT this morning HMS *Broadsword* was passing through the Gulf of Surt between Tunis and Benghazi when a group of guerillas, posing as official coastguards, boarded the ship and seized the officer in command, Captain Lawrence Packard, and placed the crew under arrest. The captain and his company did everything possible to resist but were outnumbered three to one. The guerillas, claiming to represent the People's Liberation Army, have since placed Captain Packard and the crew in the engine room of the ship. As far as it is possible to ascertain from our Embassy in Tripoli no lives have been lost, although Captain Packard sustained severe injuries during the battle, and we cannot be certain of his fate. There is no suggestion that *Broadsword* was doing anything other than going about her lawful business. This barbaric act must be looked upon as piracy under the 1958 Geneva Convention on the High Seas. The guerillas are demanding the release of all Libyan prisoners in British prisons in exchange for the return of HMS *Broadsword* and her crew. My Right Honourable friend, the Home Secretary, informs me there are only nine known Libyans in British jails at the present time, two of whom have been sentenced to three months for persistent shoplifting, two who were convicted on more serious drug charges, and the five who tried to hijack a British Airways 747 last year. Her Majesty's Government cannot and will not interfere with the due process of law and has no intention of releasing any of these men."

Loud "Hear, hears," came from all sections of the House.

"My Right Honourable friend, the Foreign Secretary, has made Her Majesty's Government's position clear to the Libyan Ambassador, in particular that Her Majesty's Government cannot be expected to tolerate this sort of treatment of British subjects or of British property. We have demanded and expect immediate action from the Libyan Government."

Simon sat down to loud and prolonged cheers before the leader of the Opposition rose from his place to say that he would wish it to be known that the Opposition gave the Government their full backing. He asked if any plans had been formulated at this early stage for the recovery of *Broadsword*.

Simon rose again. "We are, Mr Speaker, at present seeking a diplomatic solution, but I have already chaired a meeting of the Joint Chiefs and I anticipate making a further statement to the House tomorrow."

"Mr Andrew Fraser," said the Speaker.

Andrew rose from his place. "May I inform the Right

Honourable Gentleman that we in the Alliance also concur with his views that this is an act of piracy. But can he tell the House how long he will allow negotiations to continue when it is well known throughout the diplomatic world that Gaddafi is a master of procrastination, especially if we were to rely on the United Nations to adjudicate on this issue?" From the noise that greeted Andrew's question it seemed that his views were shared by the majority of the House.

Simon rose to answer the question. "I accept the point the Honourable Gentleman is making but he will know, having been a Minister of State for Defence himself, that I am not in a position to divulge any information which might imperil the safety of *Broadsword*."

Question after question came at Simon. He handled them with such confidence that visitors to the Strangers' Gallery would have found it hard to believe that he had been invited to join the Cabinet only five weeks before.

At four-fifteen, after Simon had answered the last question the Speaker was going to allow, he sank back on the front bench to listen to the statement from the Foreign Office. The House fell silent once again as the Foreign Secretary rose from his place and checked the large double-spaced sheets in front of him. All eyes were now on the tall, elegant man who was making his first official statement since his appointment.

"Mr Speaker, with your permission and that of the House, I too would like to make a statement concerning HMS *Broadsword*. Once news had reached the Foreign Office this morning of the plight of Her Majesty's ship *Broadsword* my office immediately issued a strongly worded statement to the Government of Libya. The Libyan Ambassador has been called to the Foreign Office and I shall be seeing him again immediately this statement and the questions arising from it has been completed."

Raymond looked up at the Strangers' Gallery from his place on the Opposition front bench. It was one of the ironies of modern diplomacy that the Libyan Ambassador was sitting in the gallery making notes while the Foreign Secretary delivered his statement. He couldn't imagine Colonel Gaddafi inviting the British Ambassador to take notes while he sat in his tent addressing his followers. Raymond was pleased to see an attendant ask the ambassador to stop writing; the prohibition dated from the time when the House had jealously guarded its privacy. Raymond's eyes dropped back to the front bench, and he continued to listen to Charles Seymour.

"Our ambassador to the United Nations has tabled a resolution to be debated by the General Assembly this afternoon, asking representatives to back Britain against this flagrant violation of the 1958 Geneva Convention on the High Seas. I confidently expect the support of the free world over this act of piracy against Her Majesty's ship *Broadsword*. Her Majesty's Government will do everything in its power to ensure a diplomatic solution bearing in mind that the lives of 217 British servicemen are still at risk."

The leader of the Opposition rose for a second time and asked at what point the Foreign Secretary would consider once again breaking off diplomatic relations with Libya.

"I naturally hope it will not come to that, Mr Speaker, and I expect the Libyan Government to deal quickly with their own mercenaries."

Charles continued to answer questions from all sections of the House but could only repeat that there was little new intelligence to offer the House at the present time. Raymond watched his two contemporaries as they displayed over twenty years of parliamentary skill in presenting their case. He wondered if this episode would make one of them Mrs Thatcher's obvious successor.

At four-thirty, the Speaker, realising nothing original had been said for some time, announced that he would allow one further question from each side before returning to the business of the day. He shrewdly called Alec Pimkin who sounded to Raymond like 'the very model of a modern major-general' and then Tom Carson who suggested that Colonel Gaddafi was often grossly misrepresented by the British press. Once Carson had sat down, Mr Speaker found it easy to move on to other business.

The Speaker rose again and thanked the Honourable Gentleman, the member for Edinburgh Carlton, for his courtesy in informing him that he would be making an application under standing order number ten for an emergency debate. The Speaker said he had given the matter careful thought but he reminded the House that, under the terms of the standing order, he did not need to divulge the reasons for his decision, merely decide whether the matter should have precedence over the orders of the day. He ruled that the matter was not proper for discussion within the terms of standing order number ten.

Andrew rose to protest but as the Speaker remained standing he had to resume his seat.

"This does not mean, however," continued Mr Speaker, "that I would not reconsider such a request at a later date."

Andrew realised that Charles Seymour and Simon Kerslake must have pleaded for more time, but he was only going to allow them twenty-four hours. The clerk at the table rose and bellowed above the noise of members leaving the Chamber, "Adjournment." The Speaker called the Secretary of State for Wales to move the adjournment motion on the problems facing the Welsh mining industry. The Chamber emptied of all but the thirty-eight Welsh MPs who had been waiting weeks for a full debate on the Principality's affairs.

Andrew went straight to his office and tried to piece together the latest information from news bulletins before preparing himself for a full debate the following day. Simon made his way back to the Ministry of Defence to continue discussions with the Joint Chiefs of Staff, while Charles was driven quickly to the Foreign Office.

When Charles reached his room, he was told by the Permanent Under-Secretary that the Libyan Ambassador awaited him.

"Does he have anything new to tell us?" asked Charles.

"Frankly, nothing; it seems that we're not the only people who are unable to make any contact with Colonel Gaddafi."

"Send him in then."

Charles stubbed out his cigarette and stood by the mantelpiece below a portrait of Palmerston. Charles had never met the ambassador before, largely because he had taken over at the Foreign Office only five weeks previously.

When Mr Kadir, the five-foot-one, dark-haired, immaculately dressed Ambassador for Libya entered the room, the office resembled nothing so much as a study in which a headmaster was about to tick off an unruly boy from the lower fifth.

Charles was momentarily taken aback when he noticed the ambassador's old Etonian tie. He recovered quickly.

"Foreign Secretary?" began Mr Kadir.

"Her Majesty's Government wishes to make it abundantly clear to your Government," began Charles, not allowing the ambassador to complete his sentiments, "that we consider the act of boarding and holding Her Majesty's ship *Broadsword* against her will as one of piracy on the high seas."

"May I say –?" began Mr Kadir.

"No, you may not," said Charles, "and until our ship has been released, we shall do everything in our power to bring pressure, both diplomatic and economic, on your Government."

"But may I just say –?" Mr Kadir tried again.

"My Prime Minister also wants you to know that she wishes to speak to your Head of State at the soonest possible opportunity, so I shall expect to hear back from you within the hour."

"Yes, Foreign Secretary, but may I –"

"And you may further report that we will reserve our right to take any action we deem appropriate if you fail to secure the release into safe custody of HMS *Broadsword* and her crew by twelve noon tomorrow, GMT. Do I make myself clear?"

"Yes, Foreign Secretary, but I would like to ask –"

"Good day, Mr Kadir."

After the Libyan Ambassador was shown out Charles couldn't help wondering what it was he had wanted to know.

"What do we do now?" he asked when the Permanent Under-Secretary returned, having deposited Mr Kadir in the lift.

"We act out the oldest diplomatic game in the world."

"What do you mean?" said Charles.

"Our sit-and-wait policy. We're awfully good at it," said

the Permanent Under-Secretary, "but then we've been at it for nearly a thousand years."

"Well, while we sit let's at least make some phone calls. I'll start with Secretary of State Kirkpatrick in Washington and then I'd like to speak to Gromyko in Moscow."

When Simon arrived back at the Ministry of Defence from the Commons he was told that the Joint Chiefs were assembled in his office waiting for him to chair the next strategy meeting. As he entered the room to take his place at the head of the table the Joint Chiefs rose.

"Good afternoon, gentlemen," Simon said. "Please be seated. Can you bring me up to date on the latest situation, Sir John?"

Admiral Sir John Fieldhouse, Chief of the Defence Staff, pushed up the half-moon glasses from the end of his nose and checked the notes in front of him.

"Very little has changed in the last hour, sir," he began. "The Prime Minister's office has still had no success in contacting Colonel Gaddafi. I fear we must now treat the capture of *Broadsword* as a blatant act of terrorism, rather similar to the occupation seven years ago of the American Embassy in Iran by students who backed the late Ayatollah Khomeini. In such circumstances we can either 'jaw-jaw or war-war', to quote Churchill. With that in mind, this committee will have formed a detailed plan by the early evening for the recapture of HMS *Broadsword*, as we assume the Foreign Office are better qualified to prepare for jaw-jaw." Sir John replaced his glasses and looked towards his minister.

"Are you in a position to give me a provisional plan which I could place in front of the Cabinet for their consideration?"

"Certainly, Minister," said Sir John, removing his glasses again before opening a large blue file in front of him.

Simon listened intently as Sir John went over his provisional strategy. Around the table sat eight of the senior-ranking staff officers of the Army, Navy and Air Force, and even the first draft plan bore the stamp of their 300 years of military experience. He couldn't help remembering that his call-up status was still that of a Second Lieutenant. For an hour he asked the Joint Chiefs questions that ranged from the elementary to ones that demonstrated a clear insight into their problems. By the time Simon left the room to attend the Cabinet meeting at No. 10 the Joint Chiefs were already up-dating their plan.

Simon walked slowly across Whitehall from the Department of Defence to Downing Street, his private detective by his side. Downing Street was thronged with people curious to see the comings and goings of ministers involved in the crisis. Simon was touched that the crowd applauded him all the way to the front door of No. 10, where the journalists and TV crews awaited each arrival. The great television arc lights were switched on as he reached the door and a microphone was thrust in front of him, but he made no comment. Simon was surprised by how many of the normally cynical journalists called out, "Good luck" and "Bring our boys home."

The front door opened and he went straight through to the corridor outside the Cabinet room, where twenty-two of his colleagues were already waiting. A moment later the Prime Minister walked into the Cabinet room and took her seat in the centre of the table with Charles and Simon opposite her.

Mrs Thatcher began by telling her colleagues that she had been unable to make any contact with Colonel Gaddafi and that they must therefore decide on a course of action that did not involve his acquiescence. She invited the Foreign Secretary to brief the Cabinet first.

Charles went over the actions in which the Foreign Office was involved at the diplomatic level. He reported his meeting with Ambassador Kadir, and the resolution which had been tabled at the UN and was already being debated at an emergency session of the General Assembly. The purpose of asking the United Nations to back Britain on Resolution 12/40, he said, was to gain the diplomatic initiative and virtually guarantee international sympathy. Charles went on to tell the Cabinet that he expected a vote to take place in the General Assembly in New York that evening which would demonstrate overwhelming support for the United Kingdom's resolution, and which would be regarded as a moral victory by the whole world. He was delighted to be able to report to the Cabinet that the Foreign Ministers of both the United States and Russia had agreed to back the UK in her diplomatic endeavours as long as she launched no retaliatory action. Charles ended by reminding his colleagues of the importance of treating the whole affair as an act of piracy, rather than an injury at the hands of the Libyan Government itself.

A legal nicety, thought Simon as he watched the faces of his colleagues round the table. They were obviously impressed that Charles had brought the two super powers together in support of Britain. The Prime Minister's face remained inscrutable. She called upon Simon to air his views.

He was able to report that *Broadsword* had, since the last meeting of the Cabinet, been towed into the Bay of Surt and moored; there was no hope of boarding her except by sea. Captain Packard and his crew of 216 remained under close arrest in the engine room on the lower deck of the ship. From confirmed reports Simon had received in the last hour it appeared that the ship's company were bound, gagged and that the ventilation systems had been turned off. "Captain Packard," he informed the House, "had refused to co-operate with the guerillas in any way, and we remain unsure of his fate." He paused. "I therefore suggest," Simon continued, "that we have no choice but to mount a rescue operation in order to avoid a protracted negotiation that can only end in grave loss of morale for the entire armed forces. The longer we put off such a decision the harder our task will become. The Joint Chiefs are putting the final touches to a plan code-named 'Shoplifter' which they feel must be carried out in the next forty-eight hours, if the men and the ship are to be saved." Simon added that he hoped diplomatic channels would be kept open while the operation was being worked out, in order that the rescue team could be assured of the greatest element of surprise.

"But what if your plan fails?" interrupted Charles. "We would risk losing not only *Broadsword* and her crew but also the goodwill of the free world."

"There is no serving officer in the British Navy who will

thank us for leaving *Broadsword* in Libyan waters while we negotiate a settlement in which, at best, our ship will be returned when it suits the guerillas – to say nothing of the humiliation of our Navy. Gaddafi can laugh at the United Nations while he has captured not only one of our most modern frigates but also the headlines of the world's press. As Ayatollah Khomeini did, he will want to keep them both for as long as he can. These headlines can only demoralise our countrymen and invite the sort of election defeat Carter suffered at the hands of the American people after the Iranian Embassy débâcle."

"We would be foolish to take such an unnecessary risk while we have world opinion on our side," protested Charles. "Let us at least wait a few more days."

"I fear that if we wait," said Simon, "the crew will be transferred from the ship to a military prison, which would only result in our having two targets to concentrate on, and then Gaddafi can sit around in the desert taking whatever amount of time suits him."

Simon and Charles weighed argument against counter-argument while the Prime Minister listened, taking note of the views of her other colleagues round the table to see if she had a majority for one course or the other. Three hours later, when everyone had given his opinion, she had 'fourteen-nine' written on the pad in front of her.

"I think we have exhausted the arguments, gentlemen," she said, "and having listened to the collective views around this table I feel we must on balance allow the Secretary of State for Defence to proceed with Operation Shoplifter. I therefore propose that the Foreign Secretary, the Defence Secretary, the Attorney General and myself make up a sub-committee, backed up by a professional staff, to consider the Joint Chiefs' plan. The utmost secrecy will be required from us at all times, so the subject will not be raised again until the plan is ready for presentation to a full meeting of the Cabinet. Therefore, with the exception of the sub-committee, all ministers will return to their departments and carry on with their normal duties. We must not lose sight of the fact that the country still has to be governed. Thank you, gentlemen." The Prime Minister asked Charles and Simon to join her in the study.

As soon as the door was closed she said to Charles, "Please let me know the moment you hear the result of the vote in the General Assembly. Now that the Cabinet has favoured a military initiative, it is important that you are seen to be pressing for a diplomatic solution."

"Yes, Prime Minister," said Charles without emotion.

Mrs Thatcher then turned to Simon. "When can I have a run-down on the details of the Joint Chiefs' plan?"

"We anticipate working on the strategy through the night, Prime Minister, and I should be able to make a full presentation to you by ten tomorrow."

"No later, Simon," said the Prime Minister. "Now our next problem is tomorrow's proposed emergency debate. Andrew Fraser will undoubtedly put in a second request for a full debate under standing order number ten and the Speaker gave a clear hint today he will allow it. Anyway, we can't avoid making a policy statement without an outcry from the Opposition benches – and I suspect our own – so I've decided that we will grasp the nettle and no doubt get stung."

The two men looked at each other, exasperated at the thought of having to waste precious hours in the Commons.

"Charles, you must be prepared to open the debate for the Government, and Simon, you will wind up. At least the debate will be on Thursday afternoon; that way some of our colleagues may have gone home for the weekend, though frankly I doubt it. But with any luck we will have secured a moral victory at the United Nations, and we can keep the Opposition minds concentrating on that. When you sum up, Simon, just answer the questions put during the debate without offering any new initiative."

She then added, "Report any news you hear direct to me. I shan't be sleeping tonight."

Charles walked back to the Foreign Office, at least thankful that Amanda was somewhere in South America.

Simon returned to the Joint Chiefs to find a large map of Libyan territorial waters pinned to a blackboard. Generals, admirals and air marshals were studying the contours and ocean depths like children preparing for a geography test.

They all stood again when Simon entered the room. They looked at him in anticipation, men of action who were suspicious of talk. When Simon told them the Cabinet's decision was to back the Ministry of Defence the suggestion of a smile came over the face of Sir John. "Perhaps that battle will turn out to be our hardest," he said, just loud enough for everyone to hear.

"Take me through the plan again," said Simon, ignoring Sir John's comment. "I have to present it to the Prime Minister by ten o'clock tomorrow."

Sir John placed the tip of a long wooden pointer on a model of HMS *Broadsword* in the middle of a stretch of water in a well-protected bay.

When Charles reached his office the international telegrams and telexes of support for a diplomatic solution were piled high on his desk. The Permanent Under-Secretary reported that the debate in the United Nations had been so one-sided that he anticipated an overwhelming majority when they came to vote. Charles feared his hands were tied; he had to be seen to go through the motions, even by his own staff, although he had not yet given up hopes of undermining Simon's plan. He intended the whole episode to end up as a triumph for the Foreign Office and not for 'those war-mongers' at the Ministry of Defence. After consulting the Permanent Under-Secretary Charles appointed a small Libyan task force consisting of some older Foreign Office mandarins with experience of Gaddafi and four of the department's most promising high fliers.

Mr Oliver Miles, the former Ambassador to Libya, had his leave cancelled and was deposited in a tiny room in the upper reaches of the Foreign Office so that Charles could call on his local knowledge at any time, day or night, throughout the crisis.

Charles asked the Permanent Under-Secretary to link him up with Britain's ambassador at the United Nations.

"And keep trying to raise Gaddafi."

Simon listened to Sir John go over the latest version of Operation Shoplifter. Thirty-seven men from the crack Special Boat Service, the Marine equivalent of the SAS regiment which had been involved in the St James's Square siege in April 1984, were now in Rosyth on the Scottish coast, preparing to board HMS *Brilliant*, the sister ship to *Broadsword*.

The men were to be dropped from a submarine a mile outside Rosyth harbour and to swim the last mile and a half under water until they reached the ship. They would then board *Brilliant* and expect to recapture her from a mock Libyan crew in an estimated twelve minutes. *Brilliant* would then be sailed to a distance of one nautical mile off the Scottish coast. The operation was to be completed in sixty-five minutes. The SBS planned to rehearse the procedure on *Brilliant* three times before first light the following morning, when they hoped to have the entire exercise down to one hour.

Simon had already confirmed the order to send two submarines from the Mediterranean full steam in the direction of the Libyan coast. The rest of the fleet was to be seen to be conspicuously going about its normal business while the Foreign Office appeared to be searching for a diplomatic solution.

Simon's request to the Joint Chiefs came as no surprise and was granted immediately. He phoned Elizabeth to explain why he wouldn't be home that night. An hour later the Secretary of State for Defence was strapped into a helicopter and on his way to Rosyth.

Charles followed the proceedings at the United Nations live in his office on a satellite link-up. At the end of a brief debate a vote was called for. The Secretary General announced 147-3 in Great Britain's favour, with twenty-two abstentions. Charles wondered if such an overwhelming vote would be enough to get the Prime Minister to change her mind over Kerslake's plan. He checked over the voting list carefully. The Russians, along with the Warsaw Pact countries and the Americans, had kept their word and voted with the UK.

Only Libya, South Yemen and Djibouti had voted against. Charles was put through to Downing Street and passed on the news. The Prime Minister, although delighted with the diplomatic triumph, refused to change course until she had heard from Gaddafi. Charles put the phone down and asked his Permanent Under-Secretary to call Ambassador Kadir to the Foreign Office once more.

"But it's two o'clock in the morning, Foreign Secretary."

"I am quite aware what time it is but I can see no reason why, when we are all awake, he should be having a peaceful night's sleep."

When Mr Kadir was shown into his room it annoyed Charles to see the little man still looking fresh and dapper. It was obvious that he had just shaved and put on a clean shirt.

"You called for me, Foreign Secretary?" asked Mr Kadir politely, as if he had been invited to afternoon tea.

"Yes," said Charles. "We wished to be certain that you are aware of the vote taken at the United Nations an hour ago supporting the United Kingdom's Resolution 12/40."

"Yes, Foreign Secretary."

"In which your Government was condemned by the leaders of ninety per cent of the people on the globe" – a fact the Permanent Under-Secretary had fed to Charles a few minutes before Mr Kadir had arrived.

"Yes, Foreign Secretary."

"My Prime Minister is still waiting to hear from your Head of State."

"Yes, Foreign Secretary."

"Have you yet made contact with Colonel Gaddafi?"

"No, Foreign Secretary."

"But you have a direct telephone link to his head-quarters."

"Then you will be only too aware, Foreign Secretary, that I have been unable to speak to him," said Mr Kadir with a wry smile.

Charles saw the Permanent Under-Secretary lower his eyes. "I shall speak to you on the hour every hour, Mr Kadir, but do not press my country's hospitality too far."

"No, Foreign Secretary."

"Good night, Ambassador," said Charles.

"Good night, Foreign Secretary."

Kadir turned and left the Foreign Office to be driven back to his Embassy. He cursed the Right Honourable Charles Seymour. Didn't the man realise that he hadn't been back to Libya, except to visit his mother, since the age of four? Colonel Gaddafi was ignoring his ambassador every bit as much as he was the British Prime Minister. He checked his watch: it was two forty-four.

Simon's helicopter landed in Scotland at two forty-five. He and Sir John were immediately driven to the dockside, then ferried out to HMS *Brilliant* through the misty night.

"The first Secretary of State not to be piped on board in living memory," said Sir John as Simon made his way with difficulty, his blackthorn stick tapping up the gangplank. The captain of the *Brilliant* couldn't disguise his surprise when he saw his uninvited guests and took them quickly to the bridge. Sir John whispered something in the captain's ear which Simon missed.

"When is the next raid due?" asked Simon, staring out from the bridge but unable to see more than a few yards in front of him.

"They leave the sub at 0300, sir," said the captain, "and should reach *Brilliant* at approximately three-twenty. They hope to have taken command of the ship in eleven minutes and be a mile beyond territorial waters in under the hour."

Simon checked his watch: it was five to three. He thought of the SBS preparing for their task, unaware that the Secretary of State and the Chief of the Defence Staff were on board *Brilliant* waiting for them. He pulled his coat collar up.

Suddenly he was thrown to the deck, a black and oily hand clamped over his mouth before he could protest. He felt his arms whipped up and tied behind his back as his eyes were blindfolded and he was gagged. He tried to retaliate and received a sharp elbow in the ribs. Then he was dragged down a narrow staircase and dumped on to a wooden floor. He lay trussed up like a chicken for what he thought was about ten minutes before he heard the ship's engines revving up and felt the movement of the ship below him. The Secretary of State could not move for another fifteen minutes.

"Release them," Simon heard a voice say in distinctly Oxford English. The rope around his arms was untied and the blindfold and gag removed. Standing over the Secretary of State was an SBS frogman, black from head to toe, his white teeth gleaming. Simon was still slightly stunned as he turned to see the Services Chief also being untied.

"I must apologise, Minister," said Sir John, as soon as his gag was removed, "but I told the captain not to inform the submarine commander we were on board. If I am going to risk 217 of my men's lives I wanted to be sure this rabble from the SBS knew what they were up to." Simon backed away from the six-foot-two giant who towered over him, still grinning.

"Good thing we didn't bring the Prime Minister along for the ride," said Sir John.

"I agree," said Simon, looking up at the SBS commando. "She would have broken his neck." Everyone laughed except the frogman who pursed his lips.

"What's wrong with him?" said Simon.

"If he utters the slightest sound during the first sixty minutes he has no hope of being selected for the final team."

"The Conservative party could do with some back-bench Members of Parliament like that," said Simon, "especially when I have to address the House tomorrow and explain why I'm doing nothing."

By three-forty-nine *Brilliant* was a mile beyond territorial waters. The newspaper headlines that morning ranged from 'Diplomatic Victory' in *The Times* to 'Gaddafi the Pirate' in the *Mirror*.

At a meeting of the inner Cabinet held at ten in the morning Simon reported his first-hand experience of Shoplifter to the Prime Minister. Charles was quick to follow him. "But after the overwhelming vote in our favour at the UN it must be sensible for us to postpone anything that might be construed as an outright act of aggression."

"If the SBS don't go tomorrow morning we will have to

wait another month, Prime Minister," said Simon, inter-rupting him. All eyes at the meeting of the inner Cabinet turned to Kerslake.

"Why?" asked Mrs Thatcher.

"Because Ramadan, when Moslems fast and cannot take drink during daylight hours, will be coming to an end tomorrow. Traditionally the heaviest eating and drinking takes place the following day, which means tomorrow night will be our best chance to catch the guerillas off guard. I have been over the entire operation in Rosyth and by now the SBS are well on their way to the submarines and preparing for the assault. It's all so finely tuned, Prime Minister, that obviously we can't throw away such a strategic advantage."

"That's good reasoning," she concurred. "With the weekend ahead of us we must pray that this mess will be all over by Monday morning. Let's put on our negotiating faces for the Commons this afternoon. I expect a very convincing performance from you, Charles."

When Andrew rose at three-thirty that Thursday afternoon to ask for a second time for an emergency debate under standing order number ten the Speaker granted his request, directing that the urgency of the matter warranted a debate to commence at seven o'clock that evening.

The Chamber emptied quickly as the members scuttled off to prepare their speeches, although they all knew that less than two per cent of them could hope to be called. The Speaker departed the Chamber and did not return until five to seven when he took over the chair from his deputy.

By seven o'clock, when Charles and Simon had entered the House, all thirty-seven SBS men were aboard Her Majesty's submarine *Conqueror*, lying on the ocean bed about sixty nautical miles off the Libyan coast. A second submarine, *Courageous*, was ten miles to her rear. Neither had broken radio silence for the past twelve hours.

The Prime Minister had still not heard from Colonel Gaddafi and they were now only eight hours away from Operation Shoplifter. Simon looked around him. The atmosphere resembled Budget Day and an eerie silence fell as the Speaker called Andrew Fraser to address the House.

He began by explaining, under standing order number ten, why the matter he had raised was specific, important and needed urgent consideration. He quickly moved on to demand that the Foreign Secretary confirm that if negotiations with Gaddáfi failed or dragged on the Secretary of State for Defence would not hesitate to take the necessary action to recover HMS *Broadsword*. Simon sat on the front bench looking glum and shaking his head.

"Gaddafi's nothing more than a pirate," said Andrew. "Why talk of diplomatic solutions?"

The House cheered as each well-rehearsed phrase rolled off Andrew's tongue. When he sat down the cheers came from all parts of the Chamber and it was several minutes before the Speaker could bring the House back to order. Mr Kadir sat in the distinguished Strangers' Gallery staring impassively down, trying to memorise the salient points that had been made and the House's reaction to them, so that – if he were ever given the chance – he could pass them on to Colonel Gaddafi.

"The Foreign Secretary," called the Speaker and Charles rose from his place on the Treasury bench. He placed his speech on the dispatch box in front of him and waited. Once again the House fell silent.

Charles opened his case by emphasising the significance of the United Nations' vote as the foundation for a genuine negotiated settlement. He went on to say that his first priority was to secure the lives of the 217 men on board HMS *Broadsword* and that he intended to work tirelessly to that end. The Secretary General was hoping to contact Gaddafi personally and brief him on the strong feelings of his colleagues in the General Assembly. Charles stressed that taking any other course at the present time could only lose the support and goodwill of the free world. When Charles sat down he realised that the rowdy House was not convinced.

The contribution from the back benches confirmed the Prime Minister's and Simon's beliefs that they had gauged the feelings of the nation correctly, but neither of them allowed the slightest show of emotion to cross their faces and give hope to those who were demanding military action.

By the time Simon rose to wind up for the Government at nine-thirty that night he had spent two and a half hours in the Chamber listening to men and women tell him to get on with exactly what he was already doing. Blandly, he backed the Foreign Secretary in his pursuit of a diplomatic solution. The House became restive, and when the clock reached ten Simon sat down to cries of "Resign" from some of his own colleagues and the more right-wing of the Labour benches.

Andrew watched carefully as Kerslake and Seymour left the Chamber. He wondered what was really going on in his old department.

He arrived home after the debate. Louise congratulated him on his speech and added, "But it didn't evoke much of a response from Simon Kerslake."

"He's up to something," said Andrew. "I only wish I was sitting in his office tonight and could find out what it is."

When Simon arrived in that office he phoned Elizabeth and explained that he would be spending another night at the ministry.

"Some women do lose their men to the strangest mistresses," said Elizabeth. "By the way, your younger son wants to know if you will have time to watch him play hockey in his cuppers' match at Oxford on Saturday."

"What's today?"

"It's still Thursday," she said, "and you're the one in charge of the nation's defences."

Simon knew the rescue attempt would be all over one way or the other by lunchtime the next day. Why shouldn't he watch his son play hockey?

"Tell him I'll be there," he said.

Although nothing could be achieved between midnight and six o'clock now the submarines were in place, none of the Joint Chiefs left the operations room. Radio silence was not broken once through the night as Simon tried to occupy himself with the bulging red boxes containing other pressing matters which still demanded his attention. He took advantage of the presence of the Joint Chiefs and had a hundred queries answered in minutes that would normally have taken him a month.

At midnight the first editions of the morning papers were brought to him. Simon pinned up the *Telegraph*'s headline on the operations board. 'Kerslake's in his Hammock till the great Armada comes.' The article demanded to know how the hero of Northern Ireland could be so indecisive while our sailors lay bound and gagged in foreign waters, and ended with the words 'Captain, art thou sleeping there below?' "Not a wink," muttered Simon. 'Resign' was the single-word headline in the *Daily Express*. Sir John looked over the minister's shoulder and read the opening paragraph.

"I shall never understand why anyone wants to be a politician," he said before reporting: "We have just heard from reconnaissance in the area that both submarines *Conqueror* and *Courageous* have moved up into place."

Simon picked up his stick from the side of his desk and left the Joint Chiefs to go to Downing Street. He took the private lift to the basement and then walked through the tunnel which runs under Whitehall direct to the Cabinet room, thus avoiding the press and any curious onlookers.

He found the Prime Minister sitting alone in the Cabinet room.

Simon went over the final plan with her in great detail, explaining that everything was ready and would be over by the time most people were having their breakfasts.

"Let me know the moment you hear anything, however trivial," she concluded, before returning to the latest gloomy study of the economy from the Wynne Godley team, who were suggesting the pound and the dollar would be on an equal parity by 1988. "One day you may have all these problems on *your* shoulders," she said.

Simon smiled and left her to walk back through the private tunnel to his office on the other side of Whitehall.

He took the lift back up to his room on the sixth floor and joined the Joint Chiefs. Although it was past midnight none of them looked tired despite their all having shared the lonely vigil with their comrades 2,000 miles away. They told stories

of Suez and the Falklands, and there was frequently laughter. But it was never long before their eyes returned to the clock.

As Big Ben struck two chimes, Simon thought: four o'clock in Libya. He could visualise the men falling backwards over the side of the boat and deep into the water before starting the long, slow swim towards *Broadsword*.

When the phone rang, breaking the eerie silence like a fire alarm, Simon picked it up to hear Charles Seymour's voice.

"Simon," he began, "I've finally got through to Gaddafi and he wants to negotiate." Simon looked at his watch; the SBS men could only be a few hundred yards from *Broadsword*.

"It's too late," he said. "I can't stop them now."

"Don't be such a bloody fool – order them to turn back. Don't you understand we've won a diplomatic coup?"

"Gaddafi could negotiate for months and still end up humiliating us. No, I won't turn back."

"We shall see how the Prime Minister reacts to your arrogance," said Charles and slammed down the receiver.

Simon sat at his desk and waited for the telephone to ring. He wondered if he could get away with taking the damn thing off the hook – the modern equivalent of Nelson placing the telescope to his blind eye, he considered. He needed a few minutes, but the phone rang again only seconds later. He picked it up and heard Margaret Thatcher's unmistakable voice.

"Can you stop them if I order you to, Simon?"

He considered lying. "Yes, Prime Minister," he said.

"But you would still like to carry it through, wouldn't you?"

"I only need a few minutes, Prime Minister."

"Do you understand the consequences if you fail, with Charles already claiming a diplomatic victory?"

"You would have my resignation within the hour."

"I suspect mine would have to go with it," she said. "In which case Charles would undoubtedly be Prime Minister by this time tomorrow." There was a moment's pause before she continued. "Gaddafi is on the other line and I am going to tell him that I *am* willing to negotiate." Simon felt defeated.

"Perhaps that will give you enough time, and let's hope it's Gaddafi who has to worry about resignations at breakfast."

Simon nearly cheered.

"Do you know the hardest thing I have had to do in this entire operation?"

"No, Prime Minister."

"When Gaddafi rang in the middle of the night, I had to pretend to be asleep so that he didn't know I was sitting by the phone."

He laughed.

"Good luck, Simon. I'll phone and explain my decision to Charles."

The clock read three-thirty.

On his return the bevy of admirals were variously clenching their fists, tapping the table or walking around it, and Simon began to sense what the Israelis must have felt like as they waited for news from Entebbe.

The phone rang again. He knew it couldn't be the Prime Minister this time as she was the one woman in England who never changed her mind. It was Charles Seymour.

"I want it clearly understood, Simon, that I gave you the news concerning Gaddafi's desire to negotiate at three-twenty. That is on the record, so there will be only one minister handing in his resignation later this morning."

"I know exactly where you stand, Charles, and I feel confident that whatever happens you'll come through your own mound of manure smelling of roses." He slammed down the phone just as four o'clock struck. For no fathomable reason everyone in the room stood up, but as the minutes passed again one by one they sat back down.

At seven minutes past four radio silence was broken with the five words, "Shoplifter apprehended, repeat Shoplifter apprehended."

Simon watched the Joint Chiefs cheer like schoolchildren reacting to the winning goal at a football match. *Broadsword* was on the high seas in neutral waters. He sat down at his desk and asked to be put through to No. 10. The Prime Minister came on the line. "Shoplifter apprehended," he told her.

"Congratulations, continue as agreed," was all she said.

The next move was to be sure that all the Libyan prisoners who had been taken aboard *Broadsword* would be discharged at Malta and sent home unharmed. Simon waited impatiently for radio silence to be broken again, as agreed, at five o'clock.

Captain Lawrence Packard came on the line as Big Ben struck five. He gave Simon a full report on the operation: one Libyan guerilla had been killed and eleven injured. There had been no, repeat no, British deaths and only a few minor injuries sustained. The thirty-seven SBS men were back on board the submarines *Conqueror* and *Courageous*. HMS *Broadsword* had two engines out of action and currently resembled an Arab bazaar, but was sailing the high seas on her way home. God Save the Queen.

"Congratulations, Captain," said Simon. He returned to Downing Street, no longer bothering to use the secret tunnel. As he limped up the road journalists with no idea of the news that was about to be announced were already gathering outside No. 10. Once again he answered none of their shouted questions. When he was shown into the Cabinet room he found Charles already there with the Prime Minister. He told them both the latest news.

"Well done, Simon," said Mrs Thatcher.

Charles made no comment.

It was agreed that the Prime Minister would make a statement to the House at three-thirty that afternoon.

"I must admit that my opinion of Charles Seymour has gone up," said Elizabeth in the car on the way to Oxford to watch Peter play in his hockey match.

"What do you mean?" asked Simon.

"He's just been interviewed on television. He said he had backed your judgement all along while having to pretend to carry out pointless negotiations. He had a very good line to the effect that it was the first time in his life that he had felt honourable about lying."

"Smelling like roses," Simon said sharply. Elizabeth didn't understand her husband's response.

He went on to tell his wife everything that had gone on between them during the last few hours.

"Why didn't you say something?"

"And admit that the Foreign Secretary and I were quarrelling throughout the entire operation? It would only show up the Government in a bad light and give the Opposition something to latch on to."

"I'll never understand politics," said Elizabeth resignedly.

It amused Simon to watch his son massacred in the mud while he stood on the touchline in the rain only hours after he had feared Gaddafi might have done the same to him. "It's a walkover," he told the Principal when Peter's college were four goals down by half-time.

"Perhaps he'll be like you and surprise us all in the second half," came back the reply.

At eight o'clock on the following Saturday morning Simon sat in his office and heard the news that *Broadsword* had all engines on full speed and was expected to reach Portsmouth by three o'clock, exactly one week after his son had lost his college match eight–nil: they hadn't had a good second half. Simon had tried to console his downcast son but it didn't help that he had been the goalkeeper.

He was smiling when his secretary interrupted his thoughts to remind him that he was due in Portsmouth in an hour. As Simon reached the door the phone rang. "Explain to whoever it is I'm already late," he said.

His secretary replied, "I don't think I can, sir."

Simon turned round, puzzled. "Who is it?" he asked.

"Her Majesty the Queen."

Simon returned to his desk, picked up the receiver and listened to the sovereign. When she had finished Simon thanked her and said he would pass on her message to Captain Packard as soon as he reached Portsmouth. During the flight down Simon looked out of the helicopter and stared at a traffic jam that stretched from the coast to London with people who were going to welcome *Broadsword* home. The helicopter landed an hour later.

The Secretary of State for Defence stood on the pier and was able to pick out the destroyer through a pair of binoculars. She was about an hour away but was already so surrounded by a flotilla of small craft that it was hard to identify her.

Sir John told him that Captain Packard had signalled to ask if the Secretary of State wished to join him on the bridge as they sailed into port. "No, thank you," said Simon. "It's his day, not mine."

"Good thing the Foreign Secretary isn't with us," said Sir John. A squad of Tornadoes flew over, drowning Simon's reply. As *Broadsword* sailed into port, the ship's company were all on deck standing to attention in full dress uniform. The ship itself shone like a Rolls-Royce that had just come off the production line.

By the time the captain descended the gangplank a crowd of some 500,000 were cheering so loudly that Simon could not hear himself speak. Captain Packard saluted as the Secretary of State leaned forward and whispered the Queen's message in his ear:

"Welcome home, Rear-Admiral Sir Lawrence Packard."

CHAPTER
THIRTY ONE

The *Broadsword* factor remained in the memories of the electorate for a far shorter time than had the Falklands victory and the Conservative cause was not helped by the breakdown in Geneva of the disarmament talks between Reagan, Gorbachov and Thatcher.

The Russians put the blame for the breakdown on Mrs Thatcher's 'aggressive stance' over *Broadsword* after they had backed her for a diplomatic solution at the UN. Within six months the Conservative lead in the opinion polls had dropped to three per cent.

"The truth is," noted Raymond at a Shadow Cabinet meeting, "Mrs Thatcher has had nearly eight years at No. 10 and no Prime Minister has served two full terms in succession – let alone three – since Lord Liverpool in 1812."

At that time of the year when referees leave the field to be replaced by umpires Raymond watched his predictions become history. Once the Christmas recess had ended he felt sure the Prime Minister would go to the country in late May or some time in June rather than face another winter. When the Conservatives held on to the marginal seat in Birmingham and fared better than expected at the local elections in May no one believed the Prime Minister would delay the announcement much longer.

Margaret Thatcher seemed to care nothing for Lord Liverpool or historical precedent, because she called an election for late June, believing that the month that had been a winner for her in the past would prove to be good for her again.

"It's time to let the nation choose who is to govern for the next five years," she declared on *Panorama*.

"Of course, it's got nothing to do with the fact she's regained a slight lead in the opinion polls," said Joyce tartly.

"A lead that could well disappear during the next few weeks," Raymond added.

He returned to Yorkshire for only three days of the campaign. As one of the party's leading spokesmen he had to travel around the country addressing meeting after meeting in marginal seats. Many journalists went as far as to suggest that were Raymond leading the party they would be in a far stronger position to win the election. On the few occasions he was back in Leeds he enjoyed the electioneering and felt completely relaxed with his constituents for the first time in his life. He also felt his age when he discovered that the new Tory candidate for Leeds North had been born in 1964, the year he had first entered Parliament. When they met the only insult Raymond suffered at his young rival's hands was being called 'sir'.

"Please call me by my Christian name," said Raymond.

"Raymond –" began the young man.

"No, Ray will do just fine."

Charles and Simon also saw little of their constituencies as they too toured the marginal seats, adding more and more to their schedules as the polling day became closer. Half-way through the campaign the Conservatives mounted a massive attack on the Alliance, as opinion polls were continuing to show that they were making considerable inroads into the Conservative vote, while traditional Labour supporters were returning to their old allegiance.

Andrew had to remain in Edinburgh for the entire campaign, to face Frank Boyle once again. But this time, as Stuart Gray informed the constituents of Edinburgh Carlton through his columns in the *Scotsman*, it was a Frank Boyle without teeth. Andrew felt what was left of those teeth a few times during the final three weeks but at least the Royal Bank of Scotland did not find it necessary to part with a second golden sovereign in their 300-year history. Andrew retained his seat by over 2,000 votes, to be returned to Parliament for the eighth time. Louise claimed that her husband's majority were the 2,000 people who had fallen in love with the thirteen-year-old coltish Clarissa, who was already fulfilling her father's prophecy as gauche fifteen-year-old Scots blushed in her presence.

The final result of the election did not become clear until four o'clock on the Friday afternoon as several recounts took place up and down the country.

"It will be a hung Parliament," David Dimbleby told the viewers tuned into the BBC 'Election Special' programme that afternoon. He repeated the detailed figures for those people still returning from work:

Conservative	313
Labour	285
Liberal/SDP Alliance	31
Irish/Ulster Unionist	17
Speaker and others	4

Dimbleby went on to point out that there was no necessity for Mrs Thatcher to resign as she was still the leader of the largest party in the Commons. But one thing was apparent, the SDP might well hold the balance at the next election.

The Prime Minister made very few changes to her front-bench team as she clearly wished to leave an impression of unity despite her small majority. The press dubbed it 'The cosmetic Cabinet'. Charles moved to the Home Office while Simon became Foreign Secretary.

Everyone at Westminster was thankful when a few weeks later Parliament broke up for the summer recess and politicians returned home for a rest.

That rest was to last a complete week before Tony Benn rolled a thundercloud across the clear blue summer sky by announcing he would contest the leadership of the Labour party at the October conference.

Benn claimed that Kinnock's naivety and gauche approach as leader had been the single reason that the Labour party had not been returned to power. There were many Socialists who agreed with this judgement, but they also felt they would have fared considerably worse under Benn.

What his announcement did, however, was to make respectable the claim of any other candidates who wished their names to be put forward. Roy Hattersley and John Smith joined Benn and Kinnock for the first ballot. Many Members of Parliament, trade-union leaders and constituency activists pressed Raymond to stand for the leadership.

"If you don't stand now," Joyce told him, "you'll have no chance in the future."

"It's the future I'm thinking about," replied Raymond.

"What do you mean?" she asked.

"I want to stand for deputy leader against Michael Meacher and John Cunningham, and that will secure me a power base in the party which would afford me a better chance next time."

Raymond waited another week before he launched his candidacy. On the following Monday, at a packed press conference, he announced he would be standing for deputy leader.

With four candidates in the field for the leadership no clear favourite emerged although most prophets accepted Benn would lead after the first ballot. Hattersley came to an agreement with Smith that whichever one of them captured the most votes in the first round the other would drop out and support the leader of the right in the final ballot.

When the vote had been counted Benn, as predicted, topped the first ballot, with Kinnock in third place. To everyone's surprise when Kinnock dropped out he advised his supporters not to back Benn as he felt it could only spell a further prolonged period of Opposition for the Labour party.

A few hours later the party chairman announced that Tony Benn had been soundly beaten. The Labour party had a new moderate leader.

The vote then took place for the deputy leadership and although the new leader made clear his preference for Raymond everyone still expected it to be close. Joyce spent the last hour running from delegate to delegate while

Raymond tried to appear calm. At eleven o'clock that Sunday night the chairman of the Labour party's National Executive announced that by a mere three per cent Raymond Gould was the newly elected deputy leader of the Labour party.

The new leader immediately appointed Raymond Shadow Chancellor of the Exchequer.

Among the many letters and telegrams Raymond received was one from Kate, which read: Congratulations. But have you read standing order no. 5(4) of the party constitution? Raymond replied: Hadn't. Have now. Let's hope it's an omen.

In their first twelve months the new Labour team looked fresh and innovative as Mrs Thatcher began to look tired and out of touch. She was not helped in her cause by the election of Gary Hart to the White House in November 1988. President Hart's avowed intention to lower unemployment and spend more of the nation's wealth to help 'genuine Democrats' left Britain with a handful of new problems. The pound strengthened against the dollar overnight, and large export orders sat gathering dust in dockside warehouses.

But what threw her economic forecasts into total disarray was the decision of the recently elected Governments of Brazil and Argentina to refuse to repay any of the loans negotiated by their former military rulers leaving the Bank of England with what could only be described as an overdraft.

During the long cold winter of 1988 the Conservatives lost several votes on the floor of the House and many more upstairs in committee. The Prime Minister seemed somewhat relieved to find herself spending Christmas at Chequers.

The relief did not last long as two elderly Conservative members died before the House convened in January. The press dubbed the Government the 'lame drake' administration.

Both of the pending by-elections were held in May: the Conservatives fared far better than might have been expected, holding on to one and just losing the other. For a third time Mrs Thatcher plumped for a June election.

After a decade of the lady from Grantham Raymond sensed the mood was for change. The monthly unemployment, inflation and import/export figures announced at regular intervals during the campaign all augured badly for the Conservatives.

The Prime Minister's reiterated plea that a Government shouldn't be judged on one month's figures now sounded unconvincing, and by the final week the only point of contention was whether the Labour party would end up with a decent working majority.

Raymond woke up on the Friday morning after the election to be told by Joyce that the computer predictions indicated an overall majority of four seats. Together they toured the constituency that morning before joining Raymond's parents for a late lunch. When they left the little butcher's shop that afternoon there was a crowd of well-wishers awaiting them on the pavement who cheered them all the way to their car. Raymond and Joyce travelled down to London and were back in Cowley Street in time to watch the first Labour Prime Minister since 1979 emerge from Buckingham Palace with the television cameras following him all the way back until he took up residence at 10 Downing Street.

This time Raymond did not have long to wait for a telephone call because the first appointment the new Prime Minister confirmed was his Chancellor. Raymond and Joyce travelled to No. 11 later that afternoon, instructing estate agents to lease their Cowley Street house on a six-month let that might or might not be renewable. Joyce spent hours checking over her new home and replacing some of the objects she had inherited from Diana Brittan while Raymond called his team over from Transport House to prepare the Labour party's first budget, and replace even more of what Leon Brittan had left behind.

After Raymond's advisers returned to Transport House that night he started to go over the hundreds of letters and telegrams of congratulations that had been flooding in throughout the day. One from America made him particularly happy, and he returned his own best wishes to Mrs Kate Wilberhoff.

Andrew had defeated Frank Boyle for a third time and the
left-winger announced that he would not be standing again.

Andrew had also spent a weekend thanking all his helpers.
When he returned to the Commons on the Monday morning
he found a note awaiting him on the Members' Letter-board.

Over lunch in the Members' Dining-room David Owen
informed him privately that he would not be seeking re-
election as leader of the SDP: seven years had been quite
enough. Although the party had slightly improved their
position in the House he accepted that they now faced a
five-year Parliament, and he wanted Andrew to take over.

As soon as Owen had issued an official press statement
Geoffrey Parkhouse of the *Glasgow Herald* was the first to
phone and ask Andrew, "When will you be announcing your
bid for the SDP leadership?"

Leaving the Home Office came as a great blow to Charles.
His period of time there had been so short that he felt he had
achieved very little. The civil servants had procrastinated
over all major decisions as they waited for another general
election and a clear mandate. He informed Amanda over
breakfast on the Monday after the election that he would be
returning to Seymour's Bank and that his salary would once
again be sufficient for her allowance to remain constant – so
long as she kept to her part of the bargain. Amanda nodded
and left the breakfast table without comment just as Harry
came in.

It was an important morning for Harry as he was to be
taken to his first day of prep school at Hill House to begin the
academic course mapped out for him by his father. Charles
tried to convince him that it would be the start of a wonderful
future, but Harry looked apprehensive. Once he had deposited a tearful eight-year-old with his first headmaster
Charles continued on to the City, cheerful at the prospect of
returning to the world of banking.

When he arrived at Seymour's, he was met by Clive
Reynolds's secretary who immediately took him through to
the boardroom and asked him if he would like a coffee.

"Thank you," said Charles, taking off his gloves, placing

his umbrella in the stand and settling himself in the chairman's seat at the head of the table. "And would you tell Mr Reynolds I'm in?"

"Certainly," said the secretary.

Clive Reynolds joined him a few moments later.

"Good morning, Mr Seymour. How nice to see you again after such a long time," he said, shaking Charles by the hand.

"Good morning, Clive. It's nice to see you too. First I must congratulate you on the manner in which you have conducted the bank's affairs in my absence."

"It's kind of you to say so, Mr Seymour."

"I was particularly impressed by the Distillers takeover; that certainly took the City by surprise."

"Yes, quite a coup, wasn't it?" said Reynolds, smiling. "And there's another one in the pipeline."

"I shall look forward to hearing the details."

"Well, I'm afraid it remains confidential at the moment," said Clive, taking the seat beside him.

"Of course, but now I have returned I had better be briefed fairly soon."

"I'm afraid shareholders cannot be briefed until we are certain the deals have been concluded. We can't afford any rumours harming our chances, can we?"

"But I'm not an ordinary shareholder," said Charles sharply. "I am returning as chairman of the bank."

"No, Mr Seymour," said Reynolds quietly. "I am chairman of this bank."

"Do you realise whom you are addressing?" said Charles.

"Yes, I think so. A former Foreign Secretary, a former Home Secretary, a former chairman of the bank and a two per cent shareholder."

"But you are fully aware that the board agreed to have me back as chairman when the Conservatives went into Opposition," Charles reminded him.

"The composition of the board has changed considerably since those days," said Reynolds. "Perhaps you've been too busy running the rest of the world to notice minor comings and goings in Cheapside."

"I shall call a board meeting."

"You don't have the authority."

"Then I shall demand an Extraordinary General Meeting," said Charles.

"And tell the shareholders what? That you had a standing order to return as Chairman when you felt like it? That won't sound like a former Foreign Secretary."

"I'll have you out of this office in twenty-four hours," Charles continued, his voice suddenly rising.

"I don't think so, Mr Seymour. Miss Trubshaw has completed her five years and left us on a full pension, and it won't take you long to discover that I don't possess a Swiss bank account or a well-compensated mistress."

Charles went red in the face. "I'll get you removed. You don't begin to understand how far my influence stretches."

"I hope I'm not removed, for your sake," said Reynolds calmly.

"Are you threatening me?"

"Certainly not, Mr Seymour, but I would hate to have to explain how Seymour's lost over £500,000 on the Nethercote account because of your personal wish to ruin Simon Kerslake's career. It may interest you to know that the only thing the bank gained from that fiasco was goodwill, and we only managed that because I recommended that Morgan Grenfell pick up the pieces."

Charles couldn't resist a smile. "When I make that public it will finish you," he said triumphantly.

"Perhaps," said Reynolds calmly, "but it would also stop you from becoming Prime Minister."

Charles turned, picked up his umbrella, put on his gloves and walked away. As he reached the door, a secretary walked in holding two cups of coffee. Charles passed her without a word and slammed the door.

"I'll only be needing one, Miss Bristow."

During the first week after the Queen's Speech Andrew was pleased to discover that a majority of his colleagues wrote to say that they would support him if he put his name forward for the leadership of the SDP.

At their weekly parliamentary meeting the party Whip asked that names for the post of party leader be submitted to his office within seven days. Each candidate had to be proposed and seconded by Members of Parliament.

For the next week the popular press tried to suggest, conjure up or even invent a rival for Andrew. Louise, who believed almost everything she read in the papers, took to perusing the *Morning Star*, the only paper which showed no interest in the outcome. But by five o'clock on the seventh day it had become obvious that Andrew was to be the sole nomination.

At the next parliamentary meeting of the SDP he was not so much elected as anointed. On the following Saturday, having been made a Privy Councillor the day before, Andrew addressed the party faithful at a packed Albert Hall. After a well-received speech, the press unanimously predicted – yet again – an SDP-Liberal revival. One or two journalists were quick to point out that if the balance of power did ever rest in his hands the Right Honourable Andrew Fraser might not know which way to jump: with on the one hand a father who was a distinguished Tory, while on the other having been a member of the Labour party himself for twenty years, which party would he consider the lesser of the two evils? Andrew always told the press that he would worry about that when the problem arose, because the SDP might not even be able to come to an agreement with the Liberals.

Numerous articles on the new SDP leader appeared in newspapers and magazines across the country. They all reported the stories of his attempt to save his son's life, the gradual recovery of his wife after Robert's death, the successful adoption of Clarissa and his re-election to Parliament on the toss of a golden sovereign.

All the publicity made Clarissa feel like a film star, she told her father. She was the most popular girl in school, she added, so he had better become Prime Minister. He laughed but proceeded to lead his party with a determination and energy that caused him to be talked of in the same breath as the leaders of the two main parties.

No sooner had the publicity over Andrew's election died

down than the press started speculating as to whether Mrs Thatcher would now make way for a younger man.

"Don't you know any other restaurant?"

"Yes, but they don't know me," replied Ronnie Nethercote, as the two men strolled into the Ritz for the first time in a couple of years. Heads turned as people leaned forward and whispered Simon's name to their guests.

"What are you up to nowadays? I can't believe Opposition fully occupies you," Ronnie said as they took their seats.

"Not really. I might also be described as one of the four million unemployed," replied Simon.

"That's what we're here to talk about," said Ronnie, "but first I recommend the country vegetable soup and the . . ."

"Beef off the trolley," interjected Simon.

"You remembered."

"It's the one thing you've always been right about."

Ronnie laughed more loudly than people normally did in the Ritz before saying, "Now you no longer have the entire armed forces at your disposal or ambassadors to call you Your Eminence or whatever they call you now, why don't you join the board of my new company?"

"It's kind of you to ask, Ronnie, but the answer has to be no."

They both broke off their conversation to allow the head waiter to take their orders.

"There's a salary of £20,000 a year that goes with it."

"I can't deny that Elizabeth and I could do with the money. With Peter staying up at Oxford to do a D.Phil. and Michael bent on being an actor I wonder if my bank account will ever be in credit."

"Then why not come in with us?" asked Ronnie.

"Because I'm a committed politician," said Simon, "and I no longer want to involve myself in any commercial activities."

"That might stop you becoming Prime Minister?"

Simon hesitated at the bluntness of Ronnie's question then said, "Frankly, yes. I've got a better than outside chance and

I'd be foolish to lengthen the odds by becoming involved in anything else right now."

"But everyone knows that as soon as Margaret announces she's going to pack up you'll be the next leader. It's as simple as that."

"No, Ronnie, it's never as simple as that."

"Then tell me, who could beat you?"

"Charles Seymour, for one."

"Seymour? He's a toffee-nosed git," said Ronnie.

"He has a lot of friends in the party, and his patrician background still counts for something with the Tories. Sir Alec remains the best loved of our most recent Prime Ministers."

"Yes, but he was given the leadership by the magic circle," said Ronnie. "You'd kill Seymour with every elected member of the party having a vote."

"Time will tell," said Simon, bored with a conversation he had had with so many people lately. "But what have you been up to?" he asked, deliberately changing the subject.

"I've been working my backside off in preparation for going public in about a year's time, which is why I wanted you on the board."

"You never give up."

"No, and I hope you haven't given up your one per cent of the company."

"Elizabeth has it locked away somewhere."

"Then you had better find the key."

"Why?" asked Simon.

"Because when I put out ten million shares on the market at three quid a time, your one original share will be exchanged for 100,000 shares of common stock. I know you weren't ever Chancellor but that's £300,000 of anyone's money."

Simon was speechless.

"Well, say something," said Ronnie.

"Frankly I'd forgotten the share existed," Simon finally managed.

"Well, I think I can safely say," said Ronnie, parodying

one of Mrs Thatcher's favourite phrases, "that's not a bad investment for a pound, and one you will never regret."

As the budget debate drew nearer Raymond found twenty-four hours each day were not enough, even without sleep. He discussed the changes he required with the Treasury mandarins, but it became more obvious as each week passed that he would have to make sacrifices. He was sick of being told that there would always be next year, feeling he had waited far too long already. He often went over to Transport House to discuss with his party researchers those promises in the manifesto which they considered the top priorities. Raymond had been pleased by the party's decision to leave Walworth Road and return to Transport House as the party headquarters soon after their victory at the polls.

As the weeks passed, compromises were reached and cut-backs agreed but Raymond managed to cling to the changes about which he felt most passionate. By the Friday morning before the budget the mandarins had handed him his speech. It ran to 143 pages and they estimated it would keep him at the dispatch box for two and a half hours.

On the Tuesday morning of Budget Day he spelt out his tax changes to the Cabinet, who traditionally did not hear the full details until a few hours before the budget was presented to the House.

Budget Day in the House of Commons is a traditional affair. Ambassadors, diplomats, bankers and members of the House of Lords rub shoulders with the general public in the tiny Strangers' Gallery. The queue for seats often stretches for a quarter of a mile from St Stephen's to Westminster Bridge, but only half a dozen people at the front of the line actually hear the Chancellor's speech, because every other place has been allocated even before the queue has begun to form. The Chamber itself is usually packed by two-thirty although the Chancellor does not rise until an hour later. The Press Gallery is equally overcrowded with correspondents ready to run to the nearest phone as soon as any change in taxation is announced. Back-benchers, who because of the size of the Chamber cannot be guaranteed their normal places, are mostly seated by two-twenty-five. Conservatives can reserve their seats by filling in a small prayer card during the morning and leaving it on the place they wish to occupy. Socialists, who consider the system undemocratic, refuse to use the prayer cards and make a mad rush for places at two-thirty. The atheists on both sides wait for the chaplain to finish prayers before they charge in, hoping to find their usual places free.

Budget Day is also traditionally one for eccentric dress. A few top hats can be observed on the Conservative benches and the odd miner's helmet rests on a Labour head. Tom Carson arrived in a boiler suit with a Liverpool scarf around his neck, while Alec Pimkin satisfied himself with a red silk waistcoat and a white carnation in the buttonhole of his morning coat.

The green leather of the two front benches begins to disappear long before three o'clock, and by then any straggling back-bencher will be relegated to the floor or to the upstairs galleries, known as the 'Members' Side Galleries', which lack the atmosphere of the House and from which members traditionally do not rise to interrupt or make a speech.

At ten past three Raymond stepped out of No. 11 and held the famous battered budget box, first used by Gladstone, high above his head, so that the press photographers could take the traditional picture before he was driven off to the Commons.

By three-fifteen, when the Prime Minister rose to answer questions, the Chamber had taken on the look of an opening night in the West End, for what members were about to experience was pure theatre.

At three-twenty-five Raymond entered the Chamber to be greeted by cheers from his own side. Every place in the Commons except his had been filled. He looked up to see Joyce in the Strangers' Gallery, and smiled. At three-thirty, when the Prime Minister had finished answering questions, the chairman of Ways and Means – who traditionally takes the Speaker's place for a budget debate as the Speaker, being 'the King's man', does not preside over money matters – rose from his chair and called:

"Budget statement, Mr Chancellor of the Exchequer."

Raymond rose and placed his speech in front of him. He began with a review of the world economic position and went on to inform the House of the philosophy behind his first budget, namely to bring down unemployment without driving up inflation. He spoke for the first hour and a half without divulging to the House any of the fiscal changes that he would be making, so abiding by the tradition that no irreversible decisions could be considered until the Stock Exchange had closed, but also giving him the opportunity to tease the House with the odd hint or suggestion.

Raymond took a sip from the glass of water by his side when he had turned page seventy-eight. He had finished with the theory and was now ready to start on the practice.

"Old-age pensions will be raised to a record level," he declared, "as will allowances for single-parent families and disablement grants." Raymond paused and taking a faded sheet from his inside pocket read from the first speech he had ever delivered in public. "No woman whose husband has sacrificed his life for his country shall be allowed to suffer because of an ungrateful nation. War widows' pensions will go up by fifty per cent and war bonds will be honoured at their full face value." The cheering after this statement lasted for some considerable time. Once the House had settled again he continued. "The tax on beer, cigarettes, petrol and perfume will go up by five per cent. Taxes on salaries of more than £30,000 a year will be raised to eighty-five per cent and capital gains tax to fifty per cent." Several Conservatives looked glum. The Chancellor went on to announce an expansion programme in the regions to stimulate employment. He detailed his plan region by region, to cheers from different sections of the House.

He ended his speech by saying, "My purpose as the first Labour Chancellor for ten years is not to rob the rich and give to the poor, but rather to make those who live in comparative ease pay taxes that will alleviate the plight of those in genuine need. Let me tell those Honourable members who sit on the benches opposite that this is only a fifth of what I intend to achieve in the lifetime of this Parliament, and by then Britain can hope to be a more equal and just society. We intend to create a generation in which class is as outdated as the debtors' prison, in which talent, hard work and honesty are their own reward, a Socialist society that is the envy of the East as well as the West. This budget, Mr Speaker, is nothing more than the architect's plan for that dream. I look forward to being given enough time to build the reality."

When Raymond resumed his seat after two hours and twenty minutes, the length of time it takes to run a world-class marathon, he was greeted by cheers and the waving of order papers from the benches behind him.

The leader of the Opposition was faced with the almost impossible task of an immediate response, and couldn't hope to do more than pick up one or two weaknesses in the Chancellor's philosophy. The House did not hang on her every word.

BOOK FIVE
1989-1991
PARTY LEADERS

CHAPTER
THIRTY TWO

After the success of Raymond's first budget the leader of the Opposition made changes to her Shadow Cabinet as quickly as was diplomatic. She moved the former Chancellor to cover the Foreign Office, Simon to tackle Home Affairs and Charles to counter the formidable problems now raised by Raymond Gould at the Treasury.

Raymond soon discovered his task of pushing legislation through became that much harder when Charles had added the enthusiasm of his new young team to his own considerable experience of financial matters.

Raymond's success continued, however, even if it was at a slower pace than that for which he would have hoped. Labour won the first two by-elections occasioned by members' deaths, which in itself was remarkable in Government. The by-election results only started a fresh round of rumours that Denis Thatcher was pressing his wife to retire.

Charles Seymour knew that when such moves were finally made they could happen so suddenly that everyone seemed unprepared and uncertain what to do next. By the time Mrs Thatcher announced her resignation he had been building up a loyal team around him for several months.

The former Prime Minister sent a letter to Sir Cranley Onslow, the new chairman of the 1922 Committee, letting him know that she would not be putting her name forward for re-election. She explained that she would be over sixty-five at the next election and had already led the party for fourteen years, the longest period for any Conservative since Churchill, and that she now felt she was ready to pass the leadership on to new blood.

The moment everyone in the party had said the usual phrases about the retiring leader being the greatest Prime Minister since Churchill, they proceeded to look for the new Churchill.

Within hours of Mrs Thatcher's resignation both Charles Seymour and Simon Kerslake had received calls and messages from about fifty or sixty supporters, and been contacted by all the leading political journalists. Charles went about his campaign in the thorough manner in which he approached everything, appointing lieutenants to cover each intake of new members since 1964. Simon had invited Bill Travers to organise his back-up team. Travers, like any farmer, rose early each morning to gather in his harvest.

Both Simon and Charles were nominated within twenty-four hours of the necessary seven days, and by the weekend none of the rumoured third candidates had appeared in the lists which convinced the press it would be a two-horse race.

The *Financial Times* went one better than its rivals. Its political editor, Peter Riddell, spent the whole week trying to contact the 289 Tory members. He succeeded in reaching 228 of them and was able to report to his readers that 101 had said they would vote for Simon Kerslake, ninety-eight for Charles Seymour, while twenty-nine had refused to give any opinion. The article's headline read 'Narrow lead for Kerslake', and went on to point out that although the two men were polite about each other in public no one pretended they were friends.

'King Kerslake' ran the banner headline in the Monday editions of the *Sun*, and its political editor predicted Simon would win by 116 to 112: Simon suspected that they had done little more than divide the *Financial Times*'s don't-knows down the middle. With eight days to go he was being quoted at two–one on with Charles eleven–eight against by the veteran ex-Labour MP Lord Mikardo, who had run a book on the last fourteen leadership contests irrespective of party. When Elizabeth told him the odds Simon remained sceptical, as he knew from bitter experience that it never paid to underestimate the Right Honourable member for Sussex

Downs. Elizabeth agreed and then pointed to a small paragraph in the paper which he had overlooked. Ronnie's new company was going public, and the shares looked certain to be well over-subscribed.

"That's one prediction that's turned out to be accurate," said Simon, smiling.

With twelve hours to go to the close of nominations a new candidate appeared in the lists, which came as a shock to everyone because until that moment the general public were entirely unaware of Alec Pimkin. Some of his colleagues even expressed surprise that he had been able to find a proposer and a seconder. As it had been assumed that Pimkin's supporters were all men who would have backed Charles it was considered a blow to his cause, although most political pundits doubted if Pimkin could scrape together more than seven or eight out of the 289 votes to be cast.

Charles pleaded with Pimkin to withdraw but he stubbornly refused, admitting to Fiona that he was thoroughly enjoying his brief moment of glory. He held a press conference in the Commons, gave endless interviews to television, radio and the national press, and found he was receiving considerable political attention for the first time in his life since the Common Market debate. He even enjoyed the cartoon that appeared in the *Daily Telegraph* of the three candidates in the 100 metres which had Charles portrayed as a string bean, Simon as a jumping bean and Alec as a has-bean waddling in a long way behind the other two. But Alexander Dalglish remained puzzled as to what had made Pimkin place his name in the lists in the first place.

"My majority in Littlehampton had plummeted from over 12,000 to 3,200 since I was first elected, and frankly the Social Democrats have been getting a little too close for comfort. That tiresome fellow Andrew Fraser is in Sussex once a month making speeches on behalf of his candidate and there are still over four years to go until the election."

"But how many votes can you hope to pick up?" asked Fiona.

"Many more than those drunken scribblers realise. I have

nine votes already pledged, not including my own, and I could well end up with as many as fifteen."

"Why so many?" asked Fiona, immediately realising how tactless the question must have sounded.

"Dear, simple creature," Pimkin replied. "There are some members of our party who do not care to be led either by a middle-class pushy minor public schoolboy or an aristocratic, arrogant snob. By voting for me they can lodge their protest very clearly."

"But isn't that irresponsible of you?" asked Fiona, annoyed by the 'simple' quip.

"Irresponsible it may be, but you can't begin to imagine the invitations I have been receiving during the last few days. They should continue for at least a year after the election is over."

Bombshells occur in the House of Commons only on rare occasions, mainly because the elements of bad luck and timing have to come together. Something that will create a headline one week may be hardly worthy of a mention the next. On the Thursday before the leadership election the House was packed for questions to the Chancellor. Raymond and Charles were having their usual verbal battles across the dispatch box, Charles coming out slightly on top. As the Treasury wasn't his portfolio, all Simon could do was sit with his legs up on the table and listen while his rival scored points.

Tom Carson seemed extremely anxious to get in a supplementary on almost any question that was down on the order paper. Between two-thirty and five past three he had leaped up from his place no less than a dozen times. The digital clock above the Speaker's chair had reached three-twelve when, out of exasperation, the Speaker called him on a seemingly innocuous question on windfall profits.

With Prime Minister's questions just about to begin Carson faced a packed House and a full press gallery. He paused for a moment before putting his question.

"What would be my Right Honourable friend's attitude to a man who invests one pound in a company and, five years

later, receives a cheque for £300,000 despite not being on the
board or appearing to be involved in any way with that
company?"

Raymond was puzzled as he had no idea what Carson was
talking about. He did not notice that Simon Kerslake had
turned white.

Raymond rose to the dispatch box. "I would remind my
Honourable friend that I put capital gains tax up to fifty per
cent which might dampen his ardour a little," he said. It was
about the only attempt at humour Raymond had made at the
dispatch box that year, which may have been the reason so
few members laughed. As Carson rose a second time Simon
slipped a note across to Raymond which he hurriedly skim-
med.

"But does the Chancellor consider that such a person
would be fit to be Prime Minister or even leader of the
Opposition?"

Members started talking amongst themselves, trying to
work out at whom the question was directed while the
Speaker stirred restlessly in his seat, anxious to bring a halt to
such disorderly supplementaries. Raymond returned to the
dispatch box and told Carson that the question was not
worthy of an answer. There the matter might have rested had
Charles not risen to the dispatch box.

"Mr Speaker, is the Chancellor aware that this personal
attack is aimed at my Right Honourable friend, the member
for Pucklebridge, and is a disgraceful slur on his character
and reputation? The Honourable member for Liverpool
Dockside should withdraw his allegation immediately."

The Conservatives cheered their colleague's magnanimity
while Simon remained silent, knowing that Charles had
successfully put the story on the front page of every national
paper.

Simon read the papers over breakfast on the Friday morning,
and was not surprised by the coverage of Charles's bogus
supplementary. The details of his transaction with Ronnie
Nethercote were chronicled in the fullest extent, and it did
not read well that he had received £300,000 from a 'property

speculator' for a one pound investment. Some of the papers felt 'bound to ask' what Nethercote hoped to gain out of the transaction. No one seemed to realise that Simon had been on the previous company's board for five years, had invested £60,000 of his own money in that company and had only recently finished paying off the overdraft.

By the Sunday Simon had made a full press statement to put the record straight, and most of the papers had given him a fair hearing. However, Sir Peter McKay, the editor of the *Sunday Express*, didn't help matters with a comment in his widely-read PM column on the centre page.

> I would not suggest for one moment that Simon Kerslake has done anything that might be described as dishonest, but with the spotlight turned so fiercely on him there may be some Members of Parliament who feel they cannot risk going into a general election with an accident-prone leader. Mr Seymour, on the other hand, has made his position abundantly clear. He did not seek to return to his family bank in Opposition while he was still hoping to hold public office.

The Monday papers were reassessing the outcome of the ballot to take place the next day and were predicting that Seymour now had the edge. Some journalists went so far as to suggest that Alec Pimkin might profit from the incident as members waited to see if there would be a second chance to give their final verdict.

Simon had received several letters of sympathy during the week, including one from Raymond Gould. Raymond assured Simon that he had not been prepared for the Carson supplementary and apologised for any embarrassment his first answer might have caused.

"It never crossed my mind that he had," said Simon, as he passed Raymond's letter over to Elizabeth.

"The Times was right," she said a few moments later. "He is a very fair man."

A moment later Simon passed his wife another letter.

Seymour's Bank,   15 May 1989
202 Cheapside,
London, EC1

Dear Mr Kerslake,

   I write to correct one fact to which the press have
continually referred. Mr Charles Seymour, the former
chairman of this bank, did seek to return to Seymour's
after the Conservatives went into Opposition. He hoped
to continue as chairman on a salary of £40,000 a year.

   The board of Seymour's did not fall in with his wishes.

                                   Yours sincerely,
                                   Clive Reynolds.

"Will you use it?" asked Elizabeth, when she had finished
reading the letter through.

"No. It will only draw more attention to the issue."

Elizabeth looked at her husband as he continued to read
the letters, and remembered the file that she still possessed on
Amanda Wallace. She would never reveal its contents to
Simon; but perhaps the time had come to make Charles
Seymour sweat a little.

On the Monday evening Simon sat on the front bench
listening to the Financial Secretary moving those clauses of
the short Finance Bill which were being taken in committee
on the floor of the House. Charles never let any of Raymond
Gould's team get away with a phrase or even a comma if he
could see a weakness in their case, and the Opposition were
enjoying every moment. Simon sat and watched the votes
slipping away, knowing he could do nothing to stop the
process.

Of the three candidates only Pimkin slept well the night
before the election.

Voting began promptly at nine o'clock the next day in the
Grand Committee room of the House of Commons, the party
Whips acting as tellers. By three-ten all but one of those
entitled to vote had done so. John Cope, the Chief Whip,
stood guard over the large black tin box until Big Ben struck
four, when it became apparent that Mrs Thatcher had
decided to remain neutral.

At four o'clock the box was removed to the Chief Whip's

office and the little slips were tipped out and checked twice in less than fifteen minutes. As John Cope left his room he was followed, Pied Piper-like, by lobby correspondents hoping to learn the result, but he had no intention of divulging anything before he reached the 1922 Committee who were keenly awaiting him.

Committee room fourteen was filled to overflowing, with some 280 of the 289 Conservative Members of Parliament present. Their chairman, Sir Cranley Onslow, welcomed the Chief Whip and asked him to join him on the small raised platform. He did so and passed over a folded piece of paper. The chairman of the 1922 Committee rose, faced the committee, unfolded the piece of paper and pushed up his glasses. He hesitated as he took in the figures.

"The result of the ballot carried out to select the leader of the parliamentary party is as follows:

> Charles Seymour   138
> Simon Kerslake   135
> Alec Pimkin   15"

There was a gasp followed by prolonged chatter, which lasted until members noticed that the chairman remained standing as he waited for some semblance of order to return among his colleagues.

"There being no outright winner," Sir Cranley continued, "a second ballot will take place next Tuesday without Mr Pimkin."

The national press surrounded Pimkin as he left the Commons that afternoon, wanting to know whom he would advise his supporters to vote for in the second ballot. Pimkin, obviously relishing every moment, declared a little pompously that he intended to interview both candidates in the near future and ask them one or two apposite questions. He was at once dubbed 'Kingmaker' by the press, and the phones at his home and office never stopped ringing. Whatever their private thoughts, both Simon and Charles agreed to see Pimkin before he told his supporters how he intended to cast his vote.

Elizabeth sat alone at her desk willing herself to go through with it. She glanced down at the faded file that she had not looked at for so many years. She sipped the brandy from the tumbler by her side, both of which she had discovered in the medicine cabinet a few minutes before. All her years of training and commitment to the Hippocratic oath went against what she felt she must now do. While Simon had slept soundly she had lain awake considering the consequences, then made the final decision. Simon's career came first. She picked up the receiver, dialled the number and waited. She nearly replaced it at once when she heard his voice.

"730–9712. Charles Seymour speaking."

"It's Elizabeth Kerslake," she said, trying to sound confident. There was a long silence in which neither of them spoke.

Once Elizabeth had taken another sip of brandy she added, "Don't hang up, Mr Seymour, because I feel confident you'll be interested in what I have to say."

Charles still didn't speak.

"Having watched you from a distance over the years I am sure that your reaction to Carson's question in the Commons last week was not spontaneous."

Charles cleared his throat but still didn't speak.

"And if anything else happens this week that could cause my husband to lose the election, be assured I shall not sit by and watch."

There was still no reply.

"I have a file in front of me marked 'Miss Amanda Wallace', and if you wish all its contents to remain confidential I would advise you to avoid any repercussion of your antics. It's packed with names *Private Eye* would wallow in for months."

Charles said nothing.

Elizabeth's confidence was growing. "You needn't bother to inform me that such an action would get me struck off the medical register. That would be a small penalty for watching you have to suffer the way my husband has this week." She paused. "Good day, Mr Seymour."

Charles still didn't speak.

Elizabeth put the phone down and swallowed the remainder of the brandy. She prayed that she had sounded convincing because she knew she could never carry out such a threat.

Charles took Pimkin to dinner at White's – where Alec had always wanted to be a member – and was escorted to a private room on the first floor.

Charles didn't wait long to ask, "Why are you going through with this charade? Don't you realise I would have won it in the first round, if you hadn't stood?"

Pimkin bridled. "No doubt, but I haven't had so much fun in years."

"Who the hell got you your seat in the first place?"

"I well remember," said Pimkin. "And I also remember the price you exacted for it. But now it's my turn to call the tune, and this time I require something quite different."

"What are you hoping for? Chancellor of the Exchequer in my first administration?" said Charles, barely able to keep the sarcasm from his voice.

"No, no," said Pimkin, "I know my worth; I am not a complete fool."

"So what do you want? Membership of White's? Perhaps I could fix that."

"Nothing as mundane. In return for putting you into Downing Street I expect to be translated to the House of Lords."

Charles hesitated. He could always give Pimkin his word; and who other than Pimkin would notice if in three years' time he didn't carry it through?

"If you and your fifteen men vote for me next Tuesday I'll put you in the Lords," said Charles. "You have my word on it."

"Good," said Pimkin. "But one small thing, old chum," he added as he closely folded his napkin.

"Christ – what do you want now?" asked Charles, exasperated.

"Like you, I want the agreement in writing."

Charles hesitated again, but this time he knew he was beaten. "I agree," he said.

"Good, then it's a deal," said Pimkin. Looking round for a waiter he added, "I rather think champagne is called for."

When Pimkin put the same proposition two days later Simon Kerslake took some time before he answered. Then he said, "That's a question I would have to consider on its merits at the time, if and when I became Prime Minister."

"So bourgeois," said Pimkin as he left Simon's room. "I offer him the keys to No. 10 and he treats me like a locksmith."

Charles left the Commons that night having spent his time going round a large cross-section of his supporters, and he was reassured to discover they were standing firm. Wherever he went in the long Gothic corridors members singly or in groups came up to pledge their support. It was true that Kerslake's windfall of £300,000 was fast becoming yesterday's news, but Charles still felt enough blood had been let from that wound to ensure his final victory, even though he still cursed Pimkin for holding up the result. One anonymous note, with all the necessary details, sent to the right Labour member, had certainly proved most effective. Charles cursed as he realised Elizabeth Kerslake had successfully stopped any further covert attacks on his rival.

When he arrived home he was appalled to find Amanda waiting for him in the drawing-room.

"I thought I told you to stay away until the middle of next week?"

"I changed my mind, Charlie," said Amanda.

"Why?" he asked suspiciously.

"I think I've earned a little reward for being such a good girl."

"What do you have in mind?" he asked as he stood by the mantelpiece.

"Fair exchange."

"For what?"

"For the world rights to my life story."

"Your *what*?" said Charles in disbelief. "Who is going to be the slightest bit interested in you?"

"It's not me they're interested in, Charlie, it's you. The *News of the World* have offered me £100,000 for the unexpurgated story of life with Charles Seymour." She added dramatically, "Or what it's like to live with the second son of an earl who will go to any lengths to become Prime Minister."

"You can't be serious," said Charles.

"Deadly serious. I've made quite a few notes over the years. How you got rid of Derek Spencer but failed to pull the same trick on Clive Reynolds. The extremes you went to trying to keep Simon Kerslake out of the House. How your first wife swapped the famous Holbein picture of the first Earl of Bridgwater. But the story which will cause the most interest is the one in which the real father of young Harry Seymour is revealed because his dad's life story was serialised in the *People* a couple of years ago, and that seems to be one episode they missed out."

"You bitch. You know Harry is my son," said Charles, advancing towards her. But Amanda stood her ground.

"And perhaps I should include a chapter on how you assault your wife behind the closed doors of your peaceful Eaton Square mansion."

Charles came to a halt. "What's the deal?"

"I keep quiet for the rest of my life and you present me with £50,000 now and a further £50,000 when you become leader."

"You've gone mad."

"Not me, Charlie, I've always been sane. You see, I don't have a paranoia to work out on dear harmless brother Rupert. The *News of the World* will love that part now that he's the fifteenth Earl. I can just see the picture of him wearing his coronet and decked out in his ermine robes."

"They wouldn't print it."

"They would when they learn that he's as queer as a two-pound note, and therefore our only son will collect the earldom when he's not entitled to it."

"No one would believe it, and by the time they print the story it will be too late," said Charles.

"Not a bit," said Amanda. "I am assured by my agent that the true reason behind the resignation of the leader of the

Conservative party would be an even bigger scoop than that of a one-time contestant."

Charles sank down in the nearest armchair.

"Twenty-five thousand," he said.

"Fifty thousand," replied his wife. "It's only fair. After all, it's a double deal: no story to the press and you become leader of the Conservative party."

"All right," whispered Charles, rising to leave the room.

"Wait a minute, Charlie. Don't forget I've dealt with you in the past."

"What else are you hoping for?" said Charles, swinging round.

"Just the autograph of the next Tory leader," she replied producing a cheque.

"Where the hell did you get hold of that?" asked Charles, pointing to the slip of paper.

"From your cheque book," said Amanda innocently.

"Don't play games with me."

"From the top drawer of your desk."

Charles snatched it from her and nearly changed his mind. Then he thought of his brother in the House of Lords, his only son not inheriting the title and having to give up the leadership. He took out his pen and scribbled his name on the cheque before leaving his wife in the drawing-room holding £50,000. She was checking the date and the signature carefully.

Simon and Elizabeth spent a quiet weekend in their country cottage while the photographers pitched camp in Eaton Square. They had received a leak from an 'authoritative' source that Pimkin would come out in support of his old school chum.

"A brilliant move," said Elizabeth over breakfast on the Sunday morning admiring the picture on the front page of the *Observer*.

"Another photo of Seymour telling us what he will do when he's Prime Minister?" said Simon, not looking up from the *Sunday Times*.

"No," said Elizabeth, and passed her paper across the

table. Simon stared at the Holbein portrait of the first Earl of Bridgwater under the headline 'A gift to the nation'.

"Good God," said Simon. Are there no depths he will not sink to, to win this election?"

"My dear, by any standards you have delivered the *coup de grâce*," said Pimkin to Fiona over lunch that Sunday.

"I thought you would appreciate it," said Fiona, pouring him another glass of his own wine.

"I certainly did and I particularly enjoyed the director of the National Gallery's comments – 'that Charles's gesture of presenting the priceless painting to the nation was the act of a selfless man'."

"Of course, once the story had been leaked to the press Charles was left with no choice," said Alexander Dalglish.

"I realise that," said Pimkin, leaning back, "and I would have given a dozen bottles of my finest claret to have seen Charles's face the moment he realised the first Earl of Bridgwater had escaped his clutches for ever. If he had denied giving the earl to the nation the publicity that would have followed would have certainly ensured defeat in the election on Tuesday."

"Win or lose next week, he daren't then suggest it was all done without his approval," said Alexander.

"I love it, I love it," said Pimkin. "I am told that Princess Diana will be unveiling the portrait on behalf of the nation – and rest assured that when she performs the official ceremony, I shall be there to bear witness."

"Ah, but will Charles?" asked Fiona.

On Monday morning Charles's brother phoned from Somerset to ask why he had not been consulted about donating the Holbein to the nation.

"It was my picture to dispose of as I pleased," Charles reminded him and slammed down the phone.

By nine o'clock on Tuesday morning, when the voting took place for the last time, the two contestants had spoken to nearly every member twice. Charles joined his colleagues in the Members' Dining-room for lunch while Simon took Elizabeth to Locketts in Marsham Street. She showed him some coloured brochures of a holiday on the Orient Express which would be the most perfect way to see Venice. She hoped that they wouldn't have time to go on the trip. Simon hardly mentioned the vote that was simultaneously taking place in the Commons but it never was far from either of their minds.

The voting ended at three-fifty but once again the Chief Whip did not remove the black box until four o'clock. By four-fifteen he knew the winner but did not reveal his name until the 1922 Committee had assembled at five o'clock. He informed their chairman at one minute to five.

Once again, Sir Cranley Onslow stood on the small raised platform in the committee room fourteen to declare the result. There was no need to ask if the people at the back could hear.

"Ladies and gentlemen," he said, his words echoing round the room, "the result of the second ballot for the leadership of the Tory Party is as follows:

Charles Seymour   130
Simon Kerslake   158."

Just over half the members present rose and cheered while Bill Travers ran all the way to Simon's room to be the first to report the news. When he arrived Simon swung round and faced the open door.

"You look and sound as though you'd run a marathon."

"Like Pheidippides, I bring great news of victory."

"I hope that doesn't mean you're going to drop down dead," said Simon, grinning.

The new leader of the Conservative party said nothing more for a few moments. It was obvious that Pimkin had come out in favour of him. Later that night, one or two other members also admitted that they had changed their minds during the second week because they hadn't liked the blatant opportunism of Charles presenting a priceless portrait to the nation only a few days before the final vote.

The following morning Fiona phoned Pimkin to ask him

why he had acted as he did. "My dear Fiona," he replied, "like Sidney Carton I considered it would be good to go to my grave knowing I had done one honourable thing in my life."

It took only a week for Simon's little house in Beaufort Street to be transformed. He could not as much as turn his head without facing a camera. Everywhere he went he was followed by a platoon of press men. He was surprised how quickly the experience became part of his daily routine, although Elizabeth never found it an edifying experience. She was, however, as booked up as Simon and once again they seemed only to meet in the evenings. He spent his first two weeks selecting the Shadow Cabinet he wanted to take into the next general election. He was able to announce the composition of his new team to the press fourteen days after his election as leader of the Conservative party. He made one sentimental appointment: that of Bill Travers as Shadow Minister of Agriculture.

When asked at a press conference why his defeated rival would not be serving in the team Simon explained that he had offered Charles Seymour the deputy leadership and any portfolio of his choice, but Charles had turned the offer down, saying he preferred to return to the back benches for the present time.

Charles had left for Scotland the same morning for a few days' rest by the river Spey, taking his son with him. Although he spent much of their short holiday feeling depressed about the final outcome of the leadership struggle, Harry's original efforts at fishing helped deaden some of the pain. Harry even ended up with the biggest fish.

Amanda, on the other hand, realising how slim her chances were of coaxing any more cash out of her husband, re-opened negotiations over her life story with the *News of the World*.

When Nick Lloyd, the editor, read through Amanda's notes he decided on two things. She would require a ghost writer and the paper would have to halve their original offer.

"Why?" demanded Amanda.

"Because we daren't print the better half of your story."

"Why not?"

"No one would believe it."

"But every word is true," she insisted.

"I'm not doubting the veracity of the facts," said Lloyd, "only readers' ability to swallow them."

"They accepted that a man climbed the walls of Buckingham Palace and found his way into the Queen's bedroom."

"Agreed," replied Lloyd, "but only after the Queen had confirmed the story. I'm not so sure that Charles Seymour will be quite as co-operative."

Amanda remained silent long enough for her agent to close the deal.

The watered-down version of 'My Life with Charles Seymour' appeared a few months later to coincide with Charles's much-publicised divorce, but it made no more than a faint ripple in political circles. Now that Charles had no prospect of leading his party it was very much yesterday's news.

Amanda came out of the divorce settlement with another £50,000 but lost custody of Harry, which was all Charles really cared about. He prayed her irresponsible remarks reported in the papers concerning the boy's claim to the title had been quickly forgotten.

Then Rupert phoned from Somerset and asked to see him privately.

A week later they sat facing each other in Charles's drawing-room at Eaton Square.

"I am sorry to broach such an embarrassing subject," said Rupert, "but I feel it is my duty to do so."

"Duty, poppycock," said Charles, stubbing out his cigarette. "I tell you Harry is my son, and as such will inherit the title. He's the spitting image of great-grandfather and that ought to be enough proof for anyone."

"In normal circumstances I would agree with you, but the recent publicity in the *News of the World* has been brought to my notice and I feel . . ."

"That sensationalist tabloid," said Charles sarcastically, his voice rising. "Surely you don't take their word before mine?"

"Certainly not," said Rupert, "but if Amanda is to be believed Harry is not your son."

"How am I meant to prove he is?" asked Charles, trying to control his temper. "I didn't keep a diary of the dates when I slept with my wife."

"But it seems Amanda did so I have had to take legal advice on the matter," continued Rupert, "and am informed that a blood test is all that will prove necessary to verify Harry's claim to the title. We both share a rare blood group as did our father and grandfather, and if Harry is of that group I shall never mention the subject again. If not, then the title will eventually be inherited by our second cousin in Australia."

"And if I don't agree to put my son through this ridiculous test?"

"Then the matter must be placed in the hands of our family solicitors," said Rupert, sounding unusually in control. "And they must take whatever course they consider fit."

CHAPTER
THIRTY THREE

Simon's first year as leader was one of unbounded energy and
ideas which bore fruit as the Conservatives picked up three
seats at by-elections and whittled away the Government's
majority. The press were already predicting that the Socialists wouldn't be able to complete their full five-year term,
which moved Simon to goad Central Office into a perpetual
state of readiness for an election.

Raymond continued to gain respect at the Treasury as his
policies began to show results. He had to cut back on some of
the more ambitious projects as his gloomy predictions about
American interest rates and the drop in the production of
North Sea oil proved daily more accurate. After his second
budget the financial press felt he had done all that was
possible, given the world situation. When unemployment fell
below two million and strikes to their lowest level since the
Second World War some members hailed Raymond as the
unions' Messiah, while others noted that he had been shrewd
enough to steal some of the Opposition's co-inflation clothes
in the absence of Charles Seymour.

As Raymond entered his third year as Chancellor the
opinion polls showed the two main parties neck and neck
again, with a surprising proportion of people saying that they
would vote for the Alliance for the first time.

The Liberals still held sixteen seats in the Commons but,
as in the past three elections, they had decided to fight under
the collective banner as the Social Democrats during the
general election campaign.

As the time for election drew near both small parties knew they would have to declare their choice for overall leader if a combination of Liberals and Social Democrats ever held the balance of power in Parliament. When the pollsters dug a little deeper it transpired that Andrew Fraser had become the most popular political leader in the country despite the fact he only led forty-two members in the Commons.

Andrew spent a lot of his time addressing meetings all over the country trying to convince the voters that at the next election the political balance would change. He said it so often he began to believe it himself, and two good by-election victories early in 1990 helped his supporters feel it was possible too. The press began to take such claims seriously when at the local election in May the Alliance captured 102 council seats at the expense of both the major parties.

"Daddy, Daddy, open my school report."

Charles left the morning mail unopened as he held Harry in his arms. He knew nothing could ever part them now but he dreaded Harry finding out that he might not be his real father.

"Please open it," pleaded Harry, wriggling free.

The school doctor had been asked to take a sample of Harry's blood along with six other boys from his form so that he would not consider the request unusual. Even the doctor hadn't been told the full significance of the action.

Harry extracted the envelope from the pile by Charles's side – the one with the school crest in the top left-hand corner – and held it out for his father to open. He looked excited and seemed hardly able to contain himself. Charles had promised he would phone his brother as soon as the result of the blood test was confirmed. He had wanted to phone the doctor a hundred times during the past week but had always stopped himself, knowing it would only add to the man's curiosity.

"Come on, Dad, read the report and you'll see it's true."

Charles tore open the letter and removed the little book which would reveal the result of all Harry's efforts during the term. He flicked through the pages – Latin, English, History, Geography, Art, Divinity, Games, Form master, Headmaster. He reached the last page, a small yellow sheet headed: 'Term medical report'. It started: Harry Seymour, age eleven, height four feet nine inches – he's suddenly sprung up, thought Charles – weight five stone four pounds. He glanced up at Harry who looked as if he was about to burst.

"It is true, Dad, isn't it?"

Charles read on without answering the boy's question. At the foot of the page was a typewritten note signed by the school doctor. Charles read it twice before he understood its full significance and then a third time. "As requested I took a sample of Harry's blood and analysed it. The result shows that Harry shares a rare blood group . . ."

"Is it true, Dad?" asked Harry yet again.

"Yes, my son, it's true."

"I told you, Dad – I knew I'd be top in the class. That means I'll be captain of the school next term. Just like you."

"Just like me," said his father, as he picked up the phone by his side and began to dial his brother's number in Somerset.

When the Prime Minister went into hospital for a minor operation the press immediately started to speculate on his resignation. Ten days later when he walked out looking better than ever the rumours ceased immediately. In the Prime Minister's absence as deputy leader Raymond chaired Cabinet meetings and stood in for him during questions in the Commons. This gave the lobby correspondents a chance to proclaim, like Caesarian soothsayers plucking at entrails, that Raymond was *primus inter pares*.

Raymond enjoyed presiding over the Cabinet, but was surprised that the civil servants expected him to spend his entire Tuesday and Thursday mornings preparing for Prime Minister's questions.

Both Simon Kerslake and Andrew Fraser had gained formidable reputations during Prime Minister's questions, and Raymond found the fifteen-minute encounter more demanding than a full winding-up speech in a major debate;

in retrospect, he was relieved that he had prepared so thoroughly. The lobby correspondents seemed to be in agreement that Raymond had held his own on both occasions and that, if anything, Simon Kerslake had underestimated him.

The Prime Minister returned to Downing Street the following week and assured Raymond that the operation had been a success and the likelihood of any recurrence of the trouble was, in the surgeon's opinion, minimal. He admitted to Raymond that he hoped to lead the party to a second victory at the polls, by which time he would be within a few years of his seventieth birthday and ready to bow out quietly. He told Raymond bluntly that he hoped he would be his successor. But Raymond couldn't help remembering that Neil Kinnock was eight years younger than he was.

Raymond returned to the Treasury to prepare for what looked like his final budget before the general election. His stewardship had made it possible to loosen the reins slightly with an election in mind. He described the loosening to the Cabinet as no more than a percentage point or two; he had no intention, he assured them, of letting three years' hard work be sacrificed at the altar of vote-catching. Some of his colleagues round the Cabinet table wished he were not quite so unbending at times.

Whenever Raymond spoke around the country more and more people approached him about standing for the leadership. He always thanked them courteously but maintained his loyalty to the Prime Minister, which loyalty, he added, would remain constant until he chose to resign.

Simon and Andrew also spent every weekend in planes, cars or trains fulfilling speaking engagements right up until the party conferences in October.

Andrew, in his summing-up speech to the SDP conference at Weston-super-Mare, told the delegates that they should expect to hold the balance of power between the two major parties after the next election. For the first time, he told them, they would have the chance to participate in a national Government. He sent the delegates home warning them to prepare for an election within the coming twelve months, by which time they would be able to welcome SDP Members of

Parliament who would already be playing a major role in the running of the nation. Andrew's supporters left the West Country keyed up for battle.

The Labour party conference followed a week later at Brighton and Raymond delivered a keynote speech on the state of the nation's finances. He pressed the unions to continue supporting their Government by keeping the twin evils of inflation and unemployment at acceptable levels. "Let us not pass on three years of achievement to be squandered by a Conservative Government," he told the cheering delegates. "Brothers, I look forward to presenting five more Labour budgets that will make it impossible for the Tories to imagine a future victory at the polls."

Raymond received one of the rare standing ovations to be given to any Cabinet minister at a Labour party conference. The delegates had never doubted his ability, but over the years they had grown to respect his sincerity as well as his judgement.

Seven more days passed before Simon addressed the Tory faithful at the Conservative party conference in Blackpool. By tradition, the leader always receives a four-to-six-minute standing ovation after he completes his speech on the final day. "He'd still get four minutes," said Pimkin to a colleague, "if he read them *Das Kapital*."

Simon had spent six weeks preparing for the occasion since, like Andrew, he was convinced this would be the last conference before the election. He was pleasantly surprised to find Charles Seymour coming forward with new ideas on tax reform which he hoped might be considered for inclusion in the leader's speech to the conference.

Charles had recently been making useful contributions in the House during finance debates, and Simon hoped that it would not be long before he would be willing to return to the front bench. His main preoccupation in the House had been as a member of the Chairmen's Panel from which committee chairmen were recruited for each bill. Charles had mellowed considerably during his time on the back benches and many of his friends feared he had lost his ambition for high office and might not even stand at the next election. Simon hoped this wasn't the case as he desperately needed someone of Charles's ability to counter Raymond Gould at the Treasury. Simon included Charles's suggestions in the final draft of his speech and dropped him a handwritten note of thanks.

On that Friday morning in Blackpool, in front of 2,000 delegates and millions more watching on television, Simon presented a complete and detailed plan of what he hoped to achieve when the Conservatives were returned to Government.

"*Power* is what we want and *power* is what we seek," he told a mesmerised audience. "For without *power* we cannot serve."

After the peroration the delegates duly rose for a genuine six-minute ovation. When the noise had died down Pimkin was heard to remark, "I think I made the right decision."

The conference season over, members made their way back from the three seasides to Westminster. Sadness overcame the House in their first week back when the ageing Mr Speaker Weatherill suffered a minor heart attack and retired to the Lords. The Government's overall majority was only two at the time and the Labour party Chief Whip feared that if they supplied the new Speaker from their own ranks and the Conservatives were to retain the old Speaker's safe seat the Government majority would cease to exist.

Simon reluctantly agreed that the Speaker should come from his own benches and asked his Chief Whip to suggest a suitable candidate.

When Charles Seymour asked to be granted a private interview with the leader Simon agreed immediately.

Charles arrived at the Opposition leader's office the following morning. It was the first time they had talked alone since the leadership battle. A head of white hair had grown from the roots of Charles's once Odyssean locks, and the deeper lines in Charles's face gave him a more gentle look. Simon couldn't help noticing a slight stoop had replaced his ramrod bearing. Looking at them now no one would have suggested they were contemporaries. Charles's request came as a shock to Simon for he had never once considered his great rival as a candidate for that particular job.

"But I want you to return to the front bench and be my Chancellor," said Simon. "You must know I would be delighted to have you back in the team."

"That's considerate of you," said Charles. "But I would prefer the more restful life of being an arbitrator rather than an antagonist. I've lost that desire always to be on the attack. For over twenty years you've had the advantage of Elizabeth and two sons to keep your feet on the ground. It's only quite recently that Harry has done the same for me."

All men are thought to have one great moment in their careers in the House, and for Alec Pimkin it was to be that day. The election of a Speaker in the Commons is a quaint affair. By ancient tradition no one must appear to want the honour, and it is rare for more than one person to be proposed for the post. During Henry VI's reign three Speakers were beheaded within a year, although in modern times it has been more the heavy burden of duties that has often led to an early grave. This tradition of reluctance has carried on through the ages, and for that reason a future Speaker frequently does not know who has sponsored him. Dressed in a smart blue suit, sporting a red carnation and his favourite pink-spotted bow tie, Alec Pimkin rose from his seat on the back benches to move that 'the Right Honourable Charles Seymour does take the chair of this House as Speaker'. His speech was serious yet witty, informed but personal. Pimkin held the House in his grasp for nine minutes and never once let it go. "He's done his old friend proud," one member muttered to another across the gangway when Pimkin sat down, and indeed the look on Charles's face left no doubt that he felt the same way, whatever had taken place in the past.

After Charles had been seconded the tradition of dragging the Speaker-elect to the chair was observed. This normally humorous affair, usually greeted with hoots of laughter and cheering, became even more of a farce with the sight of the small, portly Pimkin and his Labour seconder dragging the six-foot-four former Guards' officer from the third row of the back benches all the way to the chair.

Charles surveyed the Commons from his new vantage point. He began by expressing his grateful thanks for the high honour the House had bestowed on him. From the moment he rose and stood his full height, every member knew they had selected the right man to guide them through the parliamentary calendar. The sharpness of his tongue may have gone but there remained a firm delivery and natural authority that left none of his colleagues in any doubt that Mr Speaker Seymour intended to keep 'order' for many years to come.

The Conservatives held the Croydon North-East seat comfortably at the by-election, and captured a marginal six weeks later. The press pointed out that it only needed the Tories and the SDP/Liberal Alliance to join together for the Government and Opposition to be in equal numbers, leaving the seventeen Irish members to decide the fate of the Parliament. Raymond was determined that the Government should hold on for another few weeks so that he could deliver his third budget, which he was convinced would act as a launching pad on which to fight the election.

Andrew had realised that Raymond's next budget might help Labour's chances at the polls, and he sought an official meeting with the leader of the Opposition to discuss the possibility of a 'no confidence' motion.

Simon agreed with Andrew's suggestion and thought that they should time the debate for the end of March. If they won that would ensure an election before the budget.

Raymond had accepted an invitation to address a large Labour rally in Cardiff the weekend before the vote of 'no confidence'. He boarded the train at Paddington, settled into his compartment and began to check over his speech. As the train pulled into Swindon a railway official stepped on board and, having discovered where the Chancellor of the Exchequer was seated, asked if he could speak to him privately for a few minutes. Raymond listened carefully to what the man had to say, replaced the speech in his brief case, got off the train, crossed the platform and returned by the first available train to London.

On the journey back he tried to work out all the consequences of the news he had just been told. As soon as he arrived at Paddington he made his way through the waiting photographers and journalists, answering no questions. A car took him straight to Westminster Hospital. Raymond was shown into a private room, to find the Prime Minister sitting upright in bed.

"Now don't panic," he said before Raymond could speak. "I'm in fine shape considering I'm over sixty and with all the pressure we've been under this last year."

"What's wrong with you?" asked Raymond, taking a chair next to the bed.

"Recurrence of the old trouble, only this time they say it will take major surgery. I'll be out of this place in a month, six weeks at the most, and then I'll live as long as Harold Macmillan, they tell me. Now, to more important matters. I want you to take over for me again, which will mean you will have to speak in my place during the 'no confidence' debate on Wednesday. If we lose the vote, I shall resign as leader."

Raymond tried to protest as he had already worked out the implications the moment he had heard his leader was ill again. The Prime Minister held up his hand and continued talking. "No party can fight an election with its leader laid up in bed for six weeks, however well he might be when they release him. If there is to be an election, the voters have the right to know who is going to lead the party in Parliament, and of course in such an emergency under standing order number five (four) of the Labour party's constitution," continued the Prime Minister, "the National Executive would meet and automatically select you to take over as party leader."

Raymond raised his head. "Yes. The importance of that particular standing order has already been pointed out to me."

The Prime Minister smiled. "Joyce, no doubt."

"Her name was Kate, actually."

The Prime Minister looked puzzled and then continued. "I think you must get used to the idea, Raymond, that you may well be running for Prime Minister in three weeks' time. Because if we lose the 'no confidence' vote on Wednesday I am given no choice but to advise the Queen to call an immediate general election."

Raymond remained silent.

"I can assure you," continued the Prime Minister, "the National Executive will not want an internal blood bath three weeks before a general election. Nothing could be more certain to guarantee a Tory victory. If, however, we do win the 'no confidence' vote then it's a different matter altogether because I'll be back and running the ship long before the Easter recess is over. That will give us enough time to call the election after you've delivered your third budget. So make sure you win on Wednesday."

"I am unable to express how much we will all miss your leadership," said Raymond, without guile.

"As every member of the House except the Irish will know which lobby they'll be voting in long before the debate begins, my leadership may turn out to be less important than any single vote. And don't forget it will be the first occasion at which they've allowed television on the floor of the Commons, so make sure Joyce picks out one of those smart shirts you sometimes wear."

Raymond spent the final few days before the 'no confidence' vote preparing his speech. He cancelled all the engagements in his diary except for the Speaker's dinner to celebrate the Queen's sixty-fifth birthday, at which he would be standing in for the Prime Minister.

The Government and Opposition Whips spent Monday and Tuesday checking that every member would be present in the House by ten o'clock on Wednesday night. The political journalists pointed out that, if the vote were a tie, Mr Speaker Seymour had already made it clear that he would abide by the ancient tradition of giving his casting vote to the Government of the day. Charles was armed with precedents from Speaker Addington in the eighteenth century to Speaker Denison in the nineteenth. Charles pointed out that, in line with the principle, he must vote in such a manner as not to make the decision of the chair final.

Simon was to open the debate for the Opposition while Andrew was being allowed to wind up, the only concession Simon had granted the SDP/Liberal Alliance for ensuring their support in the lobbies. Neil Kinnock was to open for the Government with Raymond winding up.

When Raymond read his speech out to Joyce on the Tuesday night the entire rehearsal took only twenty-four minutes, but he explained to her that with the noise and interruptions that would occur in the Chamber he would be on his feet the full thirty minutes. In fact he might have to cut short some lines on the night.

The following day members began arriving hours before the debate was due to begin. The Strangers' Gallery had been booked days in advance, with many senior ambassadors and even some Privy Councillors unable to be guaranteed a seat. The Press Gallery was filled and editors were sitting at the feet of their political journalists' desks. The Commons itself was like a stand at a cup final where twice as many tickets had been sold as there were seats. The only difference from a Budget Day was that the House was taken up with lighting equipment that had been tested a dozen times that morning.

Between two-thirty and three-thirty Mr Speaker Seymour had been unable to stop members chattering during questions to Mr Meacher, the Secretary of State for Education, but at three-thirty he duly shouted for "Order" and did not have to wait long for silence before calling: "The leader of the Opposition."

Simon rose from his place on the front bench to be greeted with cheers from his own side. He was momentarily surprised by the brightness of the arc lights which he had been assured he would hardly notice, but soon he was into his stride. Without a note in front of him he addressed the House for fifty minutes, tearing into the Government one moment, then switching to the policies he would implement the next. He ended his peroration by describing the Labour party as "the party of wasted opportunity" then added – jabbing his finger at Raymond – "but you will be replaced by a party of ideas and ideals."

He sat down to the cheers of his back-benchers who thought they had already won the vote – if not the next election as well. The noise continued for some time before Charles could bring the House back to order and call the next speaker.

Neil Kinnock had always revelled in his Welsh ancestry and had often been compared by older members to Aneurin Bevan. The *bête noire* of the Tories set in to the Opposition leader with a vengeance, expounding his beliefs and rousing his own side to cheers when he said that the Tories would be routed and would regret this no confidence 'trick' for a decade. "The Right Honourable Gentleman," he said, pointing at Simon, "has the nerve to call us the party of wasted opportunities. For the past two years it is he who has led the party of opportunists, and who will be the leader of the Opposition until it is time for him to be replaced." When Kinnock sat down the television producers couldn't be blamed for thinking that they were covering a lions *v* Christians slaughter. Again it took the Speaker several minutes to bring the House back to order.

The back-benchers also rose to the occasion with speeches from past ministers quoting precedent and from young turks demanding change, which helped confirm old and established new reputations. The House remained packed that night right up until nine o'clock when the Speaker called Andrew Fraser to wind up for the Opposition.

Andrew delivered a 'plague on both your houses' speech and shouted above the protests from the two main parties. "When the time comes you will both need to call on an honest broker." At nine-thirty when he resumed his seat Andrew was cheered as loudly as forty-two members in unison could manage.

When it came to Raymond's turn to wind up, members wondered how he would make himself heard above the noise that greeted him. He rose to the dispatch box and, looking grave, with head bowed, almost whispered his first words, "Mr Speaker, I know the whole House would wish me to open my speech by saying how sad we all are that the Prime Minister is unable to be present tonight. I am sure all Honourable members will want to join me in sending him, his wife and family our best wishes as he prepares for his operation."

Suddenly the House was silent and, having caught its mood Raymond raised his head and delivered for the eleventh time the speech he had prepared so assiduously. When he had seen Simon give his apparently impromptu speech Raymond had torn up his notes. He spelt out the achievements of the Government during the past two and a half years and assured the House that he was only half-way through his time as Chancellor. "I have not been able to achieve equality in three years, but of one thing I am certain: I look forward to delivering my next budget whatever the outcome of the vote tonight. We shall not see the opportunist Government of the Conservatives or the Alliance's so-called 'honest broker'. Indeed, looking at the Alliance I can say there is no one less honest and no one more broke. We, Mr Speaker, will see the return of a Labour Government for another full Parliament." Raymond sat down as the clock reached ten. He found, like the speakers before him, that he was drenched in sweat from the heat sent out by the powerful arc lights.

The Speaker rose and his first words were lost as he put the question:

"This House has no confidence in Her Majesty's Government. As many as are of that opinion say Aye, to the contrary, No. I think the Ayes have it."

"No," hollered back the voices from the Government benches.

"Clear the lobbies," called the Speaker above the cheers for Raymond Gould. Members departed to the lobbies to cast their votes. The Irish members surprised no one by dividing among themselves. Fourteen minutes later the tellers returned to a noisy Chamber to give the result of the division to the clerk at the table who then entered the figures on a division paper. The four tellers lined up and advanced towards the table from the bar of the House. They came to a halt and bowed for a third time. One of the Opposition Whips read out: "Ayes to the right 323, Noes to the left 322" and passed the piece of paper to the Speaker who tried to repeat it above the bedlam. Few members heard him say:

"The Ayes have it, the Ayes have it."

Raymond sat on the front bench and watched the delighted Tories bobbing up and down like children on a carousel. He reflected that if the Prime Minister had been present to register his vote the Government would have saved the day.

Her Majesty the Queen visited her Prime Minister in hospital twenty-four hours after his successful operation. He advised the monarch to dissolve Parliament immediately and asked that the general election be set for 9 May. He explained to the Queen that he intended to resign as leader of his party that morning and would relinquish the office of Prime Minister as soon as the outcome of the election was clear.

Before she left the Westminster Hospital the Queen spent some time discussing a private constitutional issue with the Prime Minister. He suggested that when the Labour party had confirmed their new leader he must be the man to offer her advice on such a personal matter.

The National Executive of the Labour party met behind the closed doors of Transport House in Smith Square at ten o'clock the following morning to select their new leader.

Three hours and twenty minutes later the committee issued a one-line press statement: "Mr Raymond Gould has been invited to lead the party at the forthcoming general election."

Although no one was in any doubt about the fierce arguments that must have taken place during the meeting the press were met by a unified voice once the committee finally broke up.

As Lord Broadstairs, the former Prime Minister, wrote in the centre page of the *Sunday Express* that weekend, "The Labour party in selecting their leader resembled nothing less than the old-fashioned magic circle of Lord Rosebery in their

determination to prove unity." The only leak he had managed to gather from the meeting was that Raymond Gould's acceptance speech had impressed every one present.

But Lord Broadstairs went on to point out that if the Labour party should lose the general election Raymond Gould could be the shortest serving leader in the Labour party's history, as under standing order five (four) of the constitution his appointment had to be confirmed by the delegates at the next party conference in October.

It had been two hours before Raymond was able to leave Transport House and escape the press. When he eventually got away he went straight to Westminster Hospital to visit the Prime Minister. The operation had visibly aged him. He was in good spirits, but admitted that he was glad not to be facing a gruelling election campaign. After he had congratulated Raymond on his new post he went on to say: "You're dining with the Queen tonight?"

"Yes, to celebrate her sixty-fifth birthday," said Raymond.

"There's more to it than that," said the Prime Minister gravely and he then revealed the private conversation that he had had with the monarch the previous day.

"And will her decision depend on the four people in that room?"

"I suspect it will."

"And what's your attitude?"

"That's no longer relevant because I shall resign as Prime Minister the day after the election, so it's more important the new Prime Minister considers what is best for the country."

For the first time Raymond felt like the leader of the party.

CHAPTER
THIRTY FOUR

Elizabeth straightened Simon's white tie and took a pace back to look at him.

"Well, at least you *look* like a Prime Minister," she said, smiling.

Her husband checked his watch. Still a few minutes to spare before he needed to be at the Speaker's private apartments – not that he was willing to risk being late for this particular birthday celebration. Elizabeth helped him on with his overcoat and after a search realised he had lost another pair of gloves.

"I do hope you can take care of the nation's belongings a little better than you do your own," she sighed.

"I'm sure I'll find it hard to lose a whole country," said Simon.

"Do remember that Raymond Gould will be trying to help you," said Elizabeth.

"Yes, that's true. I only wish I was fighting Kinnock."

"Why?" she asked.

"Because Gould was born into the wrong party," said Simon as he kissed his wife and walked towards the front door, "and a lot of the electorate have already reached the same conclusion."

The policeman on the gates of New Palace Yard saluted as Simon was driven into the courtyard and dropped at the Members' Entrance. He glanced at his watch again: ten minutes to spare. He never could resist checking how many people were in the Chamber or what the latest news was on the ticker-tape machine.

He put his head round the door of the smoking room. A few
members were scattered around, mainly from safe seats they
felt did not need nursing. Pimkin, surrounded by his usual
cronies, hailed him. His face lit up when he saw Simon
formally dressed. "I say, waiter, mine's a double gin and
tonic." His companions duly laughed. Simon responded by
asking the barman to give Mr Pimkin a large gin and tonic
and to charge it to his account.

He spent a few minutes moving from group to group
chatting to members about how the election might go in their
constituencies. Pimkin assured Simon that the Tories would
return in triumph. "I wish everyone was as confident as you
are," Simon told him before leaving for the Speaker's private
apartments as Pimkin ordered another gin.

He strolled along the library corridor, lined from floor to
ceiling with venerable old journals of the House, until he
reached the Speaker's office, which is the route members take
to the Speaker's private rooms. When Simon reached the
Grand Stairway dominated by Speaker Addington's portrait
he was met by the Speaker's train-bearer clad in white tie and
black tails.

"Good evening, Mr Kerslake," he said and led Simon
down the corridor into the antechamber where a relaxed
Charles Seymour stood ready to receive his guests. Charles
shook Simon's hand warmly. Simon thought how well his
colleague looked compared with their meeting of a few
months before.

Andrew Fraser had already arrived and soon the three
men were deep into a discussion about the course the election
would take when another guest walked in.

"The Right Honourable Raymond Gould," announced
the train-bearer. Charles went over to greet his guest.

"Many congratulations on your election as leader," were
his first words. "You've had one hell of a week; you must be
exhausted."

"Exhilarated, to be honest," replied Raymond.

He moved towards Simon, who in turn offered his congratulations. The two men shook hands and for a moment
resembled medieval knights who had lowered their visors

before the final joust. The unnatural silence that followed was broken by Andrew.

"Well, I hope it's going to be a clean fight," he said. Both men laughed.

The train-bearer came to the Speaker's side to inform him that Her Majesty had left Buckingham Palace a few moments earlier.

Charles excused himself while the three leaders continued their conversation.

"Has either of you been told the real reason why we are bidden here this evening?" asked Raymond.

"Isn't the Queen's sixty-fifth birthday enough?" said Simon.

"No, that's just an excuse for us to meet without suspicion. I think it might be helpful for you both to know that Her Majesty has a highly sensitive question to put to us."

Simon and Andrew listened as Raymond revealed the substance of his discussion with the Prime Minister.

Charles waited in the entrance of the courtyard of the Speaker's House to welcome the Queen.

It was only a few minutes before he spotted two police outriders entering the gates of New Palace Yard followed by the familiar maroon Rolls Royce, which displayed no numberplate. A tiny white light on the centre of the roof blinked in the evening dusk. As soon as the car had come to a halt a footman leaped down and opened the back door.

The Queen stepped out, to be greeted by the commoner history had judged to be the monarch's man. She was dressed in a simple cocktail dress. The only jewellery she wore was a string of pearls and a small diamond brooch. Charles bowed before shaking hands and taking his guest up the carpeted staircase to his private apartments. Her three party leaders stood in line waiting to greet her. She shook hands first with the new leader of the Labour party and congratulated him on his election that afternoon before enquiring how the Prime Minister was faring. Then she shook hands with her leader of the Opposition and asked how his wife was coping at Pucklebridge General Hospital after the new National

Health cutbacks. Simon was always amazed by how much the Queen could recall from her past conversations, few of which could ever last more than a few moments. She then moved on to Andrew whom she teased about his father's recent speech in Edinburgh on the Social Democrats' greatest weakness being their lack of leadership.

"He's very old, ma'am," insisted Andrew.

"Not as old as Gladstone when he formed his last administration," she replied.

She removed the gin and tonic offered to her on a silver tray and looked around the magnificent room. "My husband and I are great admirers of the Gothic revival in architecture, though being infrequent visitors to Westminster we are, however, usually forced to view the better examples from the outside of railway stations or from the inside of cathedrals."

The four men smiled and a few minutes later Charles suggested they adjourn to the State dining-room where five places were set out round an oval table covered with silver which glittered in the candlelight. The four men waited until the Queen was seated at the head of the table.

Charles had placed Raymond on the Queen's right and Simon on her left while he and Andrew filled the other two places.

When the champagne was served Charles and his colleagues rose and toasted the Queen's health. She reminded them that her birthday was not for another two weeks and remarked that she had twenty-four official birthday engagements during the month, which didn't include the family's private celebrations. "I would happily weaken but the Queen Mother attended more functions for her ninetieth birthday last year than I have planned for my sixty-fifth. I can't imagine where she gets the energy."

"Perhaps she would like to take my place in the election campaign," said Raymond.

"Don't suggest it," the Queen replied. "She would leap at the opportunity without a second thought."

The chef had prepared a simple dinner of smoked salmon followed by lamb in red wine and aspic. His only flamboyant gesture was a birthday cake in the shape of a crown resting on a portcullis of sponge. No candles were evident.

After the meal had been cleared away and the cognac served the servants left them alone. The four men remained in a light mood until the Queen without warning put to them a delicate question that surprised only Charles. She waited for an answer.

No one spoke.

"Perhaps I should ask you first," said the Queen, turning to Raymond, "as you are standing in for the Prime Minister."

Raymond didn't hesitate. "I am in favour, ma'am," he said quietly.

She next turned to Simon.

"I would also support such a decision, Your Majesty," he replied.

"Thank you," said the Queen, and turned to Andrew.

"At heart I am a traditionalist, Your Majesty, but I confess to having given the subject a great deal of thought over the last few years and I have come round to supporting what I think is described as the 'modern approach'."

"Thank you," she repeated, her eyes finally resting on Charles Seymour.

"Against, ma'am," he said without hesitation, "but then I have never been a modern man."

"That is no bad thing in Mr Speaker," she said, and paused before adding: "Some years ago I asked a former Lord Chancellor to draw up the necessary papers. He assured me then that if none of my parliamentary leaders was against the principle the legislation could be carried through while both Houses were still in session."

"That is correct, ma'am," said Charles. "It would require two or three days at most if all the preparations have already been completed. It's only a matter of proclamation to both Houses of Parliament: your decision requires no vote."

"Excellent, Mr Speaker. Then the matter is settled."

BOOK SIX

1991

PRIME MINISTER

CHAPTER THIRTY FIVE

Her Majesty's proclamation passed through the Lords and Commons without a division.

Once the initial shock had been absorbed by the nation the election campaign took over. The first polls gave the Tories a two-point lead. The press attributed this to the public's unfamiliarity with the new Labour leader, but by the end of the first week the Tories had slipped a point while the press had decided that Raymond Gould had begun his stewardship well.

"A week is a long time in politics," he quoted.

"And there are still two to go," Joyce reminded him.

The pundits put forward the theory that Raymond had increased his popularity during the first week because of the extra coverage he had received as the new leader of the Labour party. He warned the press department at Transport House that it might well be the shortest honeymoon on record, and they certainly couldn't expect him to be treated like a bridegroom for the entire three weeks. The first signs of a broken marriage came when the Department of Employment announced that inflation had taken an upturn for the first time in nine months.

"And who has been Chancellor for the last three years?" demanded Simon in that night's speech in Manchester.

Raymond tried to dismiss the figures as a one-off monthly hiccup but the next day Simon was insistent that there was more bad news just around the corner.

When the Department of Trade announced the worst deficit in the balance of payments for fourteen months Simon took on the mantle of a prophet and the Tories edged back into a healthy lead, but with the Social Democrats stealing a point from both of them.

"Honeymoon, broken marriage and divorce, all in a period of fourteen days," said Raymond wryly. "What can happen in the last seven?"

"Reconciliation, perhaps?" suggested Joyce.

During the campaign all three leaders managed to visit most of the one hundred marginal seats in which the outcome of any general election is decided. None of them could afford to spend too much time worrying about those 550 of the 650 seats that could not change hands without a swing of at least eight per cent.

Andrew was willing to make one exception to the eight per cent rule in the case of Alec Pimkin's seat in Littlehampton, which he had considered vulnerable for some time. The Social Democrats had selected an able young candidate who had nursed the constituency assiduously over the past three years and couldn't wait to take on Pimkin.

Alec Pimkin eventually made an appearance in Littlehampton – only after the local chairman had tracked him down to his London flat to say they were becoming desperate. The Alliance yellow lines were almost as abundant on the canvass returns as the Conservative blue ones, he warned.

"Don't you realise that I have had grave responsibilities in the Commons?" Pimkin declared. "No one could have anticipated that members would have been called back for a special declaration by the monarch."

"Everyone knows about that," said the chairman. "But the bill commanded by the Queen went through all its three readings last week without a division."

Pimkin inwardly cursed the day they allowed television into the House. "Don't fuss," he soothed. "Come the hour, cometh the man and the voters will remember that I have had a long and distinguished parliamentary career. Damn it, old thing, have you forgotten that I was a candidate for the leadership of the Tory party?"

No, and how many votes did you receive on that occasion, the chairman wanted to say, but he took a deep breath and

repeated his urgent request that the member visit the constituency as soon as possible.

Pimkin arrived seven days before the election and, as in
past campaigns, settled himself in the private bar of the Swan
Arms – the only decent pub in the constituency, he assured
those people who took the trouble to come over and seek his
opinion.

"But the Alliance candidate has visited every pub in the
division," wailed the chairman.

"More fool he. We can say that he's looking for any excuse
for a pub crawl," said Pimkin, roaring with laughter.

From time to time Pimkin did stroll over to his local
committee headquarters to find a few loyal workers, licking
envelopes and folding election messages. On the one occasion on which he ventured into the high street he was
appalled to discover Andrew Fraser standing on an upturned
box extolling the virtues of the Alliance candidate to a large
crowd. Pimkin wandered over to listen to what Andrew had
to say and was not pleased to find that hardly anyone in the
crowd recognised him.

"Humbug," said Pimkin at the top of his voice. Andrew
waved back. "Littlehampton needs a member who lives in
the constituency," declared Andrew genially, and went on
with his speech. Pimkin turned to retreat to the warmth of the
fireside at the Swan Arms. After all, as the landlord had
assured him, put up a donkey with a blue ribbon as the
Conservative candidate in Littlehampton and they would
elect it. Pimkin had not been overwhelmed by the analogy.

With six days to go Andrew held a meeting with the
Liberals to discuss tactics. The Alliance began to record over
twenty-two per cent in some polls while the Labour and
Conservative vote remained neck and neck with thirty-eight
per cent each. Andrew's continual claim that he would hold
the balance of power in the next Parliament was analysed
seriously by the *Observer* and *Sunday Times* over the last
weekend of the campaign, and few political pundits were now
disagreeing with him. Both the BBC and ITV were already
trying to book him for the first interview after the election.
Andrew made no commitment.

He travelled up from Liverpool to Glasgow on the Monday before the election and then trekked across Scotland, pursued by a pack of journalists, until he reached Edinburgh on the Wednesday night.

The same evening Simon returned to Pucklebridge to deliver his last speech of the campaign in the local village hall. Four hundred and eighteen sat inside to hear his speech. Four thousand more stood outside in the cold listening to his words being relayed by loudspeaker. Simon's final message to his supporters all over the country was, "Be sure you go to the polls tomorrow. Every vote will be vital."

The statement turned out to be the most accurate any of the three leaders had made during the entire three-week campaign.

Raymond had returned to Leeds on the evening and was met on the platform of Leeds City station by the Lord Mayor and over half the Corporation. He was driven to the town hall to deliver his last appeal to the electorate before an audience of 2,000 people. Somehow he raised himself to give one more speech, and the cheers that greeted his arrival at the town hall made him forget he hadn't had more than four hours' sleep a night during the last month. Introducing the Labour leader the Mayor said, "Ray has come home."

Raymond stood up and delivered his speech as vigorously as if it were the opening day of the campaign. When he sat down forty minutes later he felt his legs give way. As soon as the hall was cleared Joyce and Fred Padgett took the exhausted candidate home. He fell asleep in the car on the way back so the two of them helped him upstairs, undressed him and let him sleep on until six the next morning.

All three leaders were up by six preparing for interviews on both breakfast television channels followed by the obligatory photo of each arriving at a polling station accompanied by his wife to cast their votes.

Andrew enjoyed being back in Edinburgh where for a few hours he was allowed to recall the days of recounts and catch up with the many old friends who had made it possible for him to remain in Parliament. Once again he ended up on the steps of the final polling station as the city hall clock struck ten. No Mrs Bloxham was there to remind him that she only voted for winners; she had died the previous year. Andrew, Louise and Clarissa walked back to the local SDP head-quarters arm in arm to join their supporters and watch the results as they came in on television.

Raymond and Joyce remained in Leeds overnight while Simon and Elizabeth returned to London to follow the outcome at Central Office in Smith Square. Raymond couldn't remember when he had last watched television for three hours without a break. The first result came from Guildford at eleven-twenty-one, and showed a two per cent swing to the Conservatives.

"Not enough," said Simon from the party chairman's room at Central Office.

"It may not be enough," said Raymond when the next two seats delivered their verdict, and the swing remained the same. The first shock came a few minutes after midnight when the Social Democrats captured the Labour seat of Rugby, and less than thirty minutes later followed it by taking Billericay from the Conservatives. When the first hundred seats had been declared the pundits were certain of only one thing: they were uncertain what the final outcome would be. Opinions, expert and amateur, were still fluid at one o'clock that morning, by which time 200 results were in, and remained so at two o'clock when over 300 constituencies had selected their member.

Raymond went to bed with a lead of 236–191 over Simon, knowing it would be offset by the county shires the next day. Andrew had gained four seats and lost one, to give the Alliance thirty-two seats overnight.

The next morning pundits were back on radio and televi-sion by six o'clock, all agreeing with the *Daily Mail*'s headline 'Stalemate'. Raymond and Joyce returned to London on the early morning train while the rural seats were proving their traditional loyalty to the Conservatives. Simon travelled down to Pucklebridge to acknowledge a record majority. He wished he could have sacrificed a couple of thousand for the marginals that weren't going his way. By twelve-thirty-three when Raymond had reached No. 11 Downing Street, the

Labour lead had fallen to 287–276 while the Alliance had captured forty-four seats.

At twelve o'clock that Friday morning, the cameras from all four channels swung over to Edinburgh where the Sheriff was declaring that Andrew Fraser had been returned to the House with a majority of over 7,000. The cameras moved on to show the victor, hands high above his head. The number on the SDP chart flicked up to forty-five. By one o'clock the Social Democrats had notched up their forty-sixth victory by a mere seventy-two votes, a result which saddened Simon.

"The House won't be quite the same without Alec Pimkin," he told Elizabeth.

At two-twenty-three that Friday afternoon both the major parties had 292 seats with only two safe Tory-held seats still to be declared. Simon retained the first but Andrew picked up the last after three re-counts.

At four o'clock Lord Day of Langham announced from the BBC studios the final result of the 1991 election:

Conservative	293
Labour	292
SDP/Liberal	47
Irish	17
Speaker	1

Lord Day went on to point out that the popular vote made the outcome even more finely balanced with Labour taking 12,246,341 (35.2 per cent), Conservatives 12,211,907 (35.1 per cent) and the Alliance 8,649,881 (25.4 per cent). He told viewers that he had never experienced a result like it in his thirty-six years as a political journalist. He apologised for his failure to get an interview with Andrew Fraser who now held the key as to who would form the next Government.

Andrew phoned Simon first, then Raymond. He listened intently to both men and what they were willing to offer before telling them that he intended to hold a meeting of his members in London on Sunday and relay their comments. He would report back with their decision in the hope that a Government could be formed by Monday.

Andrew and Louise flew down from Edinburgh on the

Saturday morning together with a planeload of journalists but by the time Andrew disappeared outside Terminal One into a waiting car the press had nothing new to report.

Sir Duncan had already told the *Scotsman* that his son would naturally back the Conservatives, while the former Prime Minister announced from his bedside that Andrew had always been a good Socialist at heart and would have nothing to do with the capitalist cause.

On the Saturday Andrew held several informal meetings in Pelham Crescent with senior members of the Alliance to ascertain the views of his colleagues, old and new. By the time he went to bed he still had no clear mandate and when a newscaster said no one was sure how the SDP/Liberal Alliance would vote the following day in their private meeting Andrew added out loud, "Me included." Even so he had decided after much deliberation on the qualities of the two men and what they stood for and that helped him make up his mind which party he thought should form the next Government.

At the Commons the next morning he and every other SDP and Liberal member had to run the gauntlet of journalists and photographers on the way to a closely guarded committee room on the third floor. The Whip had deliberately selected one of the less accessible rooms and had asked the Serjeant-at-Arms to be certain the recording machines were disconnected.

Andrew opened the meeting by congratulating his colleagues on their election to the House of Commons. "But it is important to remember," he continued, "that the nation will never forgive us if we are irresponsible with our new power. We cannot afford to say we will support one party, then change our minds after only a few weeks, causing another general election. We must be seen to be responsible. Or you can be sure that when the next election comes every one of us will forfeit our seats."

He went on to describe in detail how both the major party leaders had accepted the general direction in which he felt the new Government should be moving. He reported that they had both accepted that two members of the Alliance should have seats in the Cabinet. Both had also agreed to back a motion in the Commons for a referendum on proportional representation. For three hours the SDP/Liberal members gave their views, but by the end of that time Andrew was still unable to steer them to a consensus and had to call for a ballot. Andrew did not vote himself and left the SDP Liberal and Chief Whips to count the votes and announce the result.

Twenty-three votes each was the decision of his members.

The Chief Whip informed the parliamentary party that they would have to allow their elected leader to make the final decision. He, after all, was the biggest single reason they had been returned to the House in such relatively large numbers. After twenty-seven years in the Commons he must have the clearest view of which man and which party was most capable of governing the country.

When the Chief Whip sat down, the word "Agreed" came over clearly from the lips of the members sitting round the long table, and the meeting broke up.

Andrew returned to Pelham Crescent and told Louise which man he had decided to support. She seemed surprised. Later that night he left for a quiet dinner at the Atheneum with the sovereign's private secretary. The equerry returned to Buckingham Palace a little after eleven o'clock and briefed the monarch on the salient points of their discussion.

"Mr Fraser," the private secretary said, "is not in favour of another quick election and has made it quite clear which party the Social Democrats are willing to support in the Commons."

The monarch nodded thoughtfully, thanked his private secretary and retired to bed.

CHAPTER
THIRTY SIX

King Charles III made the final decision.

As Big Ben struck ten o'clock on that Saturday morning, a private secretary to the Royal household phoned the Right Honourable Simon Kerslake and asked if he would be kind enough to attend His Majesty at the palace.

Simon stepped out of the Conservative party headquarters on the corner of Smith Square and into the clear morning sunlight to be greeted by crowds of wellwishers, television cameras and journalists. He only smiled and waved as this was not the occasion to make a statement. He slipped quickly through the police cordon and into the back of his black Rover. Motor cycle outriders guided the chauffeur-driven car through the dense crowds slowly past Transport House. Simon wondered what would be going through Raymond Gould's mind at that moment as he considered the decision Andrew Fraser must have made.

The chauffeur drove on to Millbank past the House of Commons, round Parliament Square and left into Birdcage Walk before reaching the Mall.

Scotland Yard had been briefed as to which party leader had been called to see the King and the car never stopped once on its journey to the palace.

The chauffeur then swung into the Mall and Buckingham Palace loomed in front of Simon's eyes. At every junction a policeman held up the traffic and then saluted. Suddenly it was all worthwhile: Simon went back over the years and then considered the future. His first thoughts were of Elizabeth and the children. How he wished they could be with him now. He recalled his selection at Coventry, the loss of his seat and the continual rejections before Pucklebridge. The financial crisis, the resignation letter that Archie Millburn had promised to return the day he became Prime Minister. The Irish Charter, *Broadsword*, and his final battle with Charles Seymour.

The Rover reached the end of the Mall and circled the statue of Queen Victoria before arriving at the vast wrought-iron gates outside Buckingham Palace. A sentry in the scarlet uniform of the Grenadier Guards presented arms. The huge crowds that had been waiting round the gates from the early hours craned their necks in an effort to see who had been chosen to lead them. Simon smiled and waved. In response some of them waved back and cheered more loudly while others looked sulky and downcast.

The Rover continued on its way past the sentry and across the courtyard through the archway and into the quadrangle before coming to a halt on the gravel by a side entrance. Simon stepped out of the car to be met by the King's private secretary. The silent equerry led Simon up a semicircular staircase, past the Alan Ramsey portrait of George III and down a long corridor before entering the audience chamber. He bowed and left Simon alone with his new sovereign.

Simon could feel his pulse quicken as he took three paces forward, bowed and waited for the King to speak.

The forty-three-year-old monarch showed no sign of nervousness in carrying out his first official duty, despite its unusual delicacy.

"Mr Kerslake," he began, "I wanted to see you first as I thought it would be courteous to explain to you in detail why I shall be inviting Mr Raymond Gould to be my first Prime Minister."

The End

THE ELEVENTH COMMANDMENT

To Neil and Monique

CONTENTS

ACKNOWLEDGEMENTS

I would like to thank the following for their help in researching this book:

The Hon. William Webster, former Director of the CIA and the FBI
The Hon. Richard Thornburgh, former United States Attorney-General
The Hon. Samuel Berger, United States National Security Advisor
Patrick Sullivan, United States Secret Service, Washington Field Office
Special Agent J. Patrick Durkin, United States Diplomatic Secret Service
Melanne Verveer, Chief of Staff to Hillary Rodham Clinton
John Kent Cooke Jr, owner, Washington Redskins
Robert Petersen, Superintendent, United States Senate Press Gallery
Jerry Gallegos, Superintendent, House Press Gallery
King Davis, Chief of Police, Sierra Madre, California

Mikhail Piotrovsky, Director, Hermitage Museum and the Winter
    Palace, St Petersburg
Dr Galina Andreeva, Keeper of the Department of Eighteenth and
    Nineteenth Century Painting, State Tretyakov Gallery, Moscow
Aleksandr Novoselov, Assistant to the Ambassador, Embassy of the
    Russian Federation, Washington DC
Andrei Titov
Three members of the St Petersburg Mafya who refused to allow their
    names to appear

Malcolm Van de Riet and Timothy Rohrbaug, Nicole Radner, Robert
Van Hoek, Phil Hochberg, David Gries, Judy Lowe and Philip
Verveer, Nancy Henrietta, Lewis K. Loss, Darrell Green, Joan
Komlos, Natasha Maximova, John Wood and Chris Ellis.
    And, in particular, Janet Brown, Commission on Presidential
Debates; and Michael Brewer of the Brewer Consulting Group.

BOOK ONE

The Team Player

CHAPTER ONE

AS HE OPENED THE DOOR the alarm went off.

The sort of mistake you would expect an amateur to make, which was surprising, as Connor Fitzgerald was considered by his peers to be the professional's professional.

Fitzgerald had anticipated that it would be several minutes before the local *policia* responded to a burglary in the San Victorina district.

There were still a couple of hours to go before the kick-off of the annual match against Brazil, but half the television sets in Colombia would already be switched on. If Fitzgerald had broken into the pawn shop after the game had started, the *policia* probably wouldn't have followed it up until the referee had blown the final whistle. It was well known that the local criminals looked upon the match as a ninety-minute parole period. But his plans for that ninety minutes would have the *policia* chasing their shadows for days. And it would be weeks, probably months, before anyone worked out the real significance of the break-in that Saturday afternoon.

The alarm was still sounding as Fitzgerald closed the back door and made his way quickly through the small store room towards the front of the shop. He ignored the rows of watches on their little stands, emeralds in their cellophane bags and gold objects of every size and shape displayed behind a fine-mesh grille. All were care-fully marked with a name and date, so their impoverished owners could return within six months and reclaim their family heirlooms. Few ever did.

Fitzgerald swept aside the bead curtain that divided the store room from the shop, and paused behind the counter. His eyes rested on a battered leather case on a stand in the centre of the window. Printed on the lid in faded gold letters were the initials 'D.V.R.' He remained absolutely still until he was certain that no one was look-ing in.

When Fitzgerald had sold the hand-crafted master-piece to the shopkeeper earlier that day, he had explained that as he had no intention of returning to Bogotá, it could go on sale immediately. Fitzgerald was not surprised that the piece had already been placed in the window. There wouldn't be another one like it in Colombia.

He was about to climb over the counter when a young man strolled past the window. Fitzgerald froze, but the man's attention was wholly occupied by a small radio he was pressing to his left ear. He took about as much notice of Fitzgerald as he would of a tailor's dummy. Once he was out of sight, Fitzgerald straddled the counter and walked to the window. He glanced up and down the road to check for any casual observers, but there were none. With one movement he removed the leather case from its stand and walked quickly back. He leapt over the counter and turned to look out of the window again to reassure himself that no inquisitive eyes had witnessed the burglary.

Fitzgerald swung round, pulled aside the bead curtain and strode on towards the closed door. He checked his watch. The alarm had been blaring away for ninety-eight seconds. He stepped into the alley and listened. Had he heard the whine of a police siren, he would have turned left and disappeared into the maze of streets that ran behind the pawnbroker's shop. But apart from the alarm, everything remained silent. He turned right and walked casually in the direction of Carrera Septima.

When Connor Fitzgerald reached the pavement he glanced left and then right, weaved through the light traffic and, without looking back, crossed to the far side of the street. He disappeared into a crowded restaurant, where a group of noisy fans were seated around a large-screen television.

Nobody gave him a glance. Their only interest was in watching endless replays of the three goals Colombia had scored the previous year. He took a seat at a corner table. Although he couldn't see the television screen clearly, he had a perfect view across the street. A battered sign with the words '*J. Escobar. Monte de Piedad, establecido 1946*' flapped in the afternoon breeze above the pawn shop.

Several minutes passed before a police car screeched to a halt outside the shop. Once Fitzgerald had seen the two uniformed officers enter the building, he left his table and walked nonchalantly out of the back door onto another quiet Saturday afternoon street. He hailed the first empty taxi and said in a broad South African accent, 'El Belvedere on the Plaza de Bolívar, *por favor*.' The driver nodded curtly, as if to make it clear that he had no wish to become involved in a prolonged conversation. As Fitzgerald slumped into the back of the battered yellow cab, he turned up the radio.

Fitzgerald checked his watch again. Seventeen minutes past one. He was running a couple of minutes behind schedule. The speech would have already begun, but as they always lasted for well over forty minutes, he still had more than enough time to carry out his real reason for being in Bogotá. He moved a few inches to his right, so as to be sure the driver could see him clearly in the rear-view mirror.

Once the *policia* began their enquiries, Fitzgerald needed everyone who had seen him that day to give roughly the same description: male, Caucasian, fiftyish, a shade over six foot, around 210 pounds, unshaven, dark unruly hair, dressed like a foreigner, with a foreign accent, but not American. He hoped that at least one of them would be able to identify the South African nasal twang. Fitzgerald had always been good at accents. In high school he had regularly been in trouble for mimicking his teachers.

The taxi's radio continued to pump out the views of expert after expert on the likely outcome of the annual fixture. Fitzgerald mentally switched off from a language he had little interest in mastering, although he had recently added '*falta*', '*fuera*' and '*gol*' to his limited vocabulary.

When the little Fiat drew up outside the El Belvedere seventeen minutes later, Fitzgerald handed over a ten-thousand-peso note, and had slipped out of the cab before the driver had a chance to thank him for such a generous tip. Not that the taxi drivers of Bogotá are well known for their overuse of the words '*muchas gracias*'.

Fitzgerald ran up the hotel steps, past the liveried door-man and through the revolving doors. In the foyer, he headed straight for the bank of elevators opposite the check-in desk. He had to wait only a few moments before one of the four lifts returned to the ground floor. When the doors slid open he stepped inside and pressed the button marked '8', and the 'Close' button immediately afterwards, giving no one a chance to join him. When the doors opened on the eighth floor, Fitzgerald walked down the thinly carpeted corridor to room 807. He pushed a plastic card into the slot and waited for the green light to glow before he turned the handle. As soon as the door opened, he placed the '*Favor de no Molestar*' sign on the outside knob, closed the door and bolted it.

He checked his watch yet again: twenty-four minutes to two. By now he calculated that the police would have left the pawn shop, having concluded that it was a false alarm. They would phone Mr Escobar at his home in the country to inform him that everything appeared to be in order, and would suggest that when he returned to the city on Monday, he should let them know if anything was missing. But long before then, Fitzgerald would have replaced the battered leather case in the window. On Monday morning the only items that Escobar would report stolen would be the several small packets of uncut emeralds that had been removed by the *policia* on their way out. How long would it be before he discovered the only other thing that was missing? A day? A week? A month? Fitzgerald had already decided he would have to leave the odd clue to help speed up the process.

Fitzgerald took off his jacket, hung it over the nearest chair and picked up the remote control from a table by the side of the bed. He pressed the 'On' button and sat down on the sofa in front of the television. The face of Ricardo Guzman filled the screen.

Fitzgerald knew that Guzman would be fifty next April, but at six foot one, with a full head of black hair and no weight problem, he could have told the adoring crowd that he had not yet turned forty, and they would have believed him. After all, few Colombians expected their politicians to tell the truth about anything, especially their age.

Ricardo Guzman, the favourite in the upcoming presidential election, was the boss of the Cali cartel, which controlled 80 per cent of the New York cocaine trade, and made over a billion dollars a year. Fitzgerald had not come across this information in any of Colombia's three national newspapers, perhaps because the supply of most of the country's newsprint was controlled by Guzman.

'The first action I shall take as your President will be to nationalise any company in which Americans are the majority shareholders.'

The small crowd that surrounded the steps of the

Congress building on the Plaza de Bolívar screamed their approval. Ricardo Guzman's advisors had told him again and again that it would be a waste of time making a speech on the day of the match, but he had ignored them, calculating that millions of television viewers would be flicking through the channels in search of the soccer, and would come across him on their screens, if only for a moment. The same people would then be surprised, only an hour later, to see him striding into the packed stadium. Football bored Guzman, but he knew that his entrance moments before the home team were due to take the field would divert the crowd's attention away from Antonio Herrera, the Colombian Vice-President and his main rival in the election. Herrera would be seated in the VIP box, but Guzman would be in the midst of the crowd behind one of the goals. The image he wished to portray was of a man of the people.

Fitzgerald estimated that there was about six minutes of the speech left. He had already heard Guzman's words at least a dozen times: in crowded halls, in half-empty bars, on street corners, even in a coach station while the candidate had addressed the local citizens from the back of a bus. He pulled the leather case off the bed and onto his lap.

'. . . Antonio Herrera is not the Liberal candidate,' hissed Guzman, 'but the American candidate. He is nothing more than a ventriloquist's dummy, whose every word is chosen for him by the man who sits in the Oval Office.' The crowd cheered again.

Five minutes, Fitzgerald calculated. He opened the case and stared down at the Remington 700 that had been out of his sight for only a few hours.

'How dare the Americans assume that we will always fall in line with whatever is convenient for them?' Guzman barked. 'And simply because of the power of the God-almighty dollar. To hell with the God-almighty dollar!' The crowd cheered even more loudly as the candidate took a dollar bill from his wallet and tore George Washington into shreds.

'I can assure you of one thing,' continued Guzman, scattering the tiny pieces of green paper over the crowd like confetti.

'God isn't an American . . .' mouthed Fitzgerald.

'God isn't an American!' shouted Guzman.

Fitzgerald gently removed the McMillan fibreglass stock from the leather case.

'In two weeks' time, the citizens of Colombia will be given the opportunity to let their views be heard right across the world,' Guzman shouted.

'Four minutes,' murmured Fitzgerald, as he glanced up at the screen and mimicked the smile of the candidate. He took the Hart stainless steel barrel from its resting place and screwed it firmly into the stock. It fitted like a glove.

'Whenever summits are held around the world, Colombia will once again be sitting at the conference table, not reading about it in the press the following day. Within a year I will have the Americans treating us not as a Third World country, but as their equals.'

The crowd roared as Fitzgerald lifted the Leupold 10 Power sniper scope from its place and slid it into the two little grooves on the top of the barrel.

'Within a hundred days you will see changes in our country that Herrera wouldn't have believed possible in a hundred years. Because when I am your President . . .'

Fitzgerald slowly nestled the stock of the Remington 700 into his shoulder. It felt like an old friend. But then, it should have done: every part had been hand-crafted to his exact specifications.

He raised the telescopic sight to the image on the television screen, and lined up the little row of mil dots until they were centred an inch above the heart of the candidate.

'. . . conquer inflation . . .'

Three minutes.

'. . . conquer unemployment . . .'

Fitzgerald breathed out.

'. . . and thereby conquer poverty.'

Fitzgerald counted three . . . two . . . one, then gently squeezed the trigger. He could barely hear the click above the noise of the crowd.

Fitzgerald lowered the rifle, rose from the sofa and put the empty leather case down. It would be another ninety seconds before Guzman reached his ritual condemnation of President Lawrence.

He removed one of the hollow-point bullets from its little leather slot inside the lid of the case. He broke the stock and slipped the bullet into its chamber, then snapped the barrel shut with a firm upward movement.

'This will be a last chance for the citizens of Colombia to reverse the disastrous failures of the past,' cried Guzman, his voice rising with every word. 'So we must be sure of one thing . . .'

'One minute,' murmured Fitzgerald. He could repeat word for word the final sixty seconds of a Guzman speech. He turned his attention from the television and walked slowly across the room towards the french windows.

'. . . that we do not waste this golden opportunity . . .'

Fitzgerald pulled back the lace curtain that obscured the view of the outside world, and stared across the Plaza de Bolívar to the north side of the square, where the Presidential candidate was standing on the top step of the Congress building, looking down on the crowd. He was about to deliver his *coup de grâce*.

Fitzgerald waited patiently. Never leave yourself in the open for longer than is necessary.

'*Viva la Colombia!*' Guzman cried. '*Viva la Colombia!*' the mob screamed back in a frenzy, although many of them were no more than paid flunkies strategically placed among the crowd.

'I love my country,' declared the candidate. Thirty seconds of the speech left. Fitzgerald pushed open the french windows, to be greeted by the full volume of the masses repeating Guzman's every word.

The candidate dropped his voice almost to a whisper: 'And let me make one thing clear – my love of my country is my only reason for wishing to serve as your President.'

For a second time, Fitzgerald pulled the stock of the Remington 700 slowly up into his shoulder. Every eye was looking at the candidate as he boomed out the words, '*Dios guarde a la Colombia!*' The noise became deafening as he raised both arms high in the air to acknowledge the roars of his supporters shouting back '*Dios guarde a la Colombia!*' Guzman's hands remained triumphantly in the air for several seconds, as they did at the end of every speech. And, as always, for a few moments he remained absolutely still.

Fitzgerald lined up the tiny mil dots until they were an inch above the candidate's heart, and breathed out as he tightened the fingers of his left hand around the stock. 'Three . . . two . . . one,' he murmured under his breath, before gently squeezing the trigger.

Guzman was still smiling as the boat-tailed bullet tore into his chest. A second later he slumped to the ground like a stringless puppet, fragments of bone, muscle and tissue flying in every direction. Blood spurted over those who were standing nearest to him. The last Fitzgerald saw of the candidate was his outstretched arms, as if he were surrendering to an unknown enemy.

Fitzgerald lowered the rifle, broke the stock and quickly closed the french windows. His assignment was completed.

His only problem now was to make sure he didn't break the Eleventh Commandment.

CHAPTER TWO

'SHOULD I SEND a message of condolence to his wife and family?' asked Tom Lawrence.

'No, Mr President,' replied the Secretary of State. 'I think you should leave that to an Assistant Secretary for Inter-American Affairs. It now looks certain that Antonio Herrera will be the next President of Colombia, so he'll be the person you'll have to do business with.'

'Will you represent me at the funeral? Or should I send the Vice-President?'

'Neither of us, would be my advice,' replied the Secretary of State. 'Our Ambassador in Bogotá can represent you quite adequately. As the funeral will take place this weekend, we couldn't be expected to be available at such short notice.'

The President nodded. He had become accustomed to Larry Harrington's matter-of-fact approach to everything, including death. He could only wonder what line Larry would adopt were he himself to be assassinated.

'If you have a moment, Mr President, I think I should brief you in greater detail on our present policy in Colombia. The press may want to question you on the possible involvement of . . .'

The President was about to interrupt him when there was a knock on the door, and Andy Lloyd entered the room.

It must be eleven o'clock, thought Lawrence. He

hadn't needed a watch since he had appointed Lloyd as his Chief of Staff.

'Later, Larry,' said the President. 'I'm about to give a press conference on the Nuclear, Biological, Chemical and Conventional Arms Reduction Bill, and I can't imagine many journalists will be interested in the death of a presidential candidate in a country that, let's face it, most Americans couldn't even place on a map.'

Harrington said nothing. He didn't feel it was his responsibility to point out to the President that most Americans still couldn't place Vietnam on a map either. But once Andy Lloyd had entered the room, Harrington knew that only the declaration of a world war would have given him priority. He gave Lloyd a curt nod and left the Oval Office.

'Why did I ever appoint that man in the first place?' Lawrence asked, his eyes fixed on the closed door.

'Larry was able to deliver Texas, Mr President, at a moment when our internal polls showed that the majority of southerners considered you a northern wimp who would quite happily appoint a homosexual as Chairman of the Joint Chiefs of Staff.'

'I probably would,' said Lawrence, 'if I thought he was the right man for the job.'

One of the reasons Tom Lawrence had offered his old college friend the post of White House Chief of Staff was that after thirty years, they had no secrets from each other. Andy told it as he saw it, without any suggestion of guile or malice. This endearing quality ensured that he could never hope to be elected to anything himself, and would therefore never be a rival.

The President flicked open the blue file marked 'IMMEDIATE' that Andy had left for him earlier that morning. He suspected that his Chief of Staff had been up most of the night preparing it. He began to go over the questions Andy considered were the most likely to be asked at the midday press conference:

How much taxpayers' money do you anticipate saving by this measure?

'I suppose Barbara Evans will be asking the first question, as usual,' said Lawrence, looking up. 'Do we have any idea what it might be?'

'No, sir,' Lloyd replied. 'But as she's been pressing for an Arms Reduction Bill ever since the day you beat Gore in New Hampshire, she's hardly in a position to complain now that you're ready to deliver it.'

'True. But that won't necessarily stop her asking an unhelpful question.'

Andy nodded his agreement as the President glanced at the next question.

How many Americans will lose their jobs as a result of this?

Lawrence looked up. 'Is there anyone in particular you want me to avoid?'

'The rest of the bastards,' said Lloyd with a grin. 'But when you wrap it up, go to Phil Ansanch.'

'Why Ansanch?'

'He backed the Bill at every stage, and he's among your dinner guests tonight.'

The President smiled and nodded as he continued to run his finger down the list of anticipated questions. He stopped at number seven.

Isn't this another example of America losing its way?

He looked up at his Chief of Staff. 'Sometimes I think we're still living in the Wild West, the way certain members of Congress have reacted to this Bill.'

'I agree, sir. But as you know, 40 per cent of Americans still consider the Russians our greatest threat, and nearly 30 per cent expect us to go to war with Russia in their lifetime.'

Lawrence cursed, and ran a hand through his thick, prematurely grey hair before returning to the list of questions, stopping again when he reached nineteen.

'How much longer am I going to be asked questions about burning my draft card?'

'As long as you're the Commander-in-Chief, would be my guess,' replied Andy.

The President mumbled something under his breath and moved on to the next question. He looked up again. 'Surely there's no chance of Victor Zerimski becoming the next President of Russia?'

'Probably not,' said Andy, 'but he's moved up to third place in the latest opinion poll, and although he's still well behind Prime Minister Chernopov and General Borodin, his stand against organised crime is beginning to make a dent in their leads. Probably because most Russians believe Chernopov is financed by the Russian Mafia.'

'What about the General?'

'He's been losing ground, since most of the Russian army haven't been paid for months. The press have been reporting that soldiers are selling their uniforms to tourists on the streets.'

'Thank God the election's still a couple of years away. If it looked as if that fascist Zerimski had the slightest chance of becoming the next President of Russia, an Arms Reduction Bill wouldn't get past first base in either House.'

Lloyd nodded as Lawrence turned the page. His finger continued to run down the questions. He stopped at twenty-nine.

'How many members of Congress have weapons manufacturing and base facilities in their districts?' he asked, looking back up at Lloyd.

'Seventy-two Senators and 211 House members,' said Lloyd, without having to refer to his unopened file. 'You'll need to convince at least 60 per cent of them to support you to guarantee a majority in both Houses. And that's assuming we can count on Senator Bedell's vote.'

'Frank Bedell was demanding a comprehensive Arms Reduction Bill when I was still in high school in Wisconsin,' said the President. 'He has no choice but to support us.'

'He may still be in favour of the Bill, but he feels you haven't gone far enough. He's just demanded that you reduce our defence expenditure by over 50 per cent.'

'And how does he expect me to pull that off?'

'By withdrawing from NATO and allowing the Europeans to be responsible for their own defence.'

'But that's totally unrealistic,' said Lawrence. 'Even the Americans for Democratic Action would come out against that.'

'You know that, I know that, and I suspect that even the good Senator knows that. But it doesn't stop him appearing on every television station from Boston to Los Angeles, claiming that a 50 per cent reduction in defence expenditure would solve America's health-care and pension problems overnight.'

'I wish Bedell spent as much time worrying about the defence of our people as he does about their health care,' said Lawrence. 'How do I respond?'

'Lavish praise on him for his tireless and distinguished record of defending the interests of the elderly. But then go on to point out that, as long as you are Commander-in-Chief, the United States will never lower its defences. Your first priority will always be to ensure that America remains the most powerful nation on earth, *et cetera, et cetera.* That way we should keep Bedell's vote, and perhaps even sway one or two of the hawks as well.'

The President glanced at his watch before turning to the third page. He gave out a deep sigh when he came to question thirty-one.

How can you hope to get this Bill enacted, when the Democrats don't have a majority in either House?

'OK, Andy. What's the answer to that one?'

'You explain that concerned Americans are making it clear to their elected representatives right across the country that this Bill is long overdue, and no more than common sense.'

'I used that line last time, Andy. For the Drugs Enforcement Bill, remember?'

'Yes, I do remember, Mr President. And the American people backed you all the way.'

Lawrence let out another deep sigh before saying, 'Oh, to govern a nation that doesn't have elections every two years and isn't hounded by a press corps convinced it could do a better job than the democratically elected government.'

'Even the Russians are having to come to terms with the phenomenon of the press corps,' said Lloyd.

'Who would have believed we'd live to see that?' said Lawrence, as he scanned the final question. 'My hunch is that if Chernopov promised the Russian voters that he intended to be the first President to spend more on health care than on defence, he'd romp home.'

'You may be right,' said Lloyd. 'But you can also be certain that if Zerimski were elected, he'd start rebuilding Russia's nuclear arsenal long before he considered building new hospitals.'

'That's for sure,' said the President. 'But as there's no chance of that maniac being elected . . .'

Andy Lloyd remained silent.

CHAPTER THREE

FITZGERALD KNEW that the next twenty minutes would decide his fate.

He walked quickly across the room and glanced at the television. The crowd were fleeing from the square in every direction. Noisy elation had turned to blind panic. Two of Ricardo Guzman's advisers were bending over what remained of his body.

Fitzgerald retrieved the spent cartridge and replaced it in its slot inside the leather case. Would the owner of the pawn shop notice that one of the bullets had been used?

From the other side of the square, the unmistakable whine of a police siren rose above the noise of the screaming crowd. This time the response had been a lot quicker.

Fitzgerald unclipped the viewfinder and placed it in its sculpted slot. He then unscrewed the barrel, slipped it into position, and finally replaced the stock.

He glanced at the television screen for the last time and watched the local *policia* pouring into the square. He grabbed the leather case, pocketed a book of matches from an ashtray on top of the television, then crossed the room and opened the door.

He looked up and down the empty corridor, then walked quickly in the direction of the freight elevator.

He jabbed the little white button on the wall several times. He had unlocked the window that led to the fire escape only moments before he left for the pawn shop, but he knew that if he had to fall back on his contingency plan, a posse of uniformed police would probably be waiting for him at the bottom of the rickety metal staircase. There would be no Rambo-type helicopter, blades whirring, offering him an escape to glory as bullets flew past his ears, hitting everything except him. This was the real world.

When the heavy lift doors slid slowly open, Fitzgerald came face to face with a young waiter in a red jacket carrying an overloaded lunch tray. He had obviously drawn the short straw, and not been given the afternoon off to watch the match.

The waiter was unable to hide his surprise at the sight of a guest standing outside the freight elevator. '*No, señor, perdone, no puede entrar,*' he tried to explain as Fitzgerald brushed past him. But the guest had jabbed the button marked '*Planta Baja*' and the doors had closed long before the young man could tell him that particular lift ended up in the kitchen.

When he reached the ground floor, Fitzgerald moved deftly between the stainless steel tables covered with row upon row of *hors d'oeuvres* waiting to be ordered, and bottles of champagne that would only be uncorked if the home side won. He had reached the far end of the kitchen, pushed his way through the swing doors and disappeared out of sight long before any of the white-clad staff could think of protesting. He ran down a poorly-lit corridor – he had removed most of the lightbulbs from their sockets the previous night – to a heavy door that led to the hotel's underground car park.

He removed a large key from his jacket pocket, closed the door behind him and locked it. He headed straight for a small black Volkswagen parked in the darkest corner. He took a second, smaller key from his trouser pocket, unlocked the car's door, slipped behind the wheel, placed the leather case under the passenger seat and turned on the ignition. The engine immediately sprang into life, even though it had not been used for the past three days. He revved the accelerator for a few seconds before easing the gear lever into first.

Fitzgerald manoeuvred the vehicle unhurriedly between the rows of parked cars and drove up the steep ramp out onto the street. He paused at the top of the slope. The *policia* were breaking into a parked car, and didn't even glance in his direction. He turned left and headed slowly away from the Plaza de Bolívar.

And then he heard the whining sound behind him. He glanced at the rear-view mirror to see two *policia* outriders bearing down on him, their flashing lights full on. Fitzgerald pulled over to the side of the road as the outriders and the ambulance carrying Guzman's lifeless body sped past him.

He took the next left down a side street and began a long, circuitous route to the pawn shop, often doubling back on himself. Twenty-four minutes later he drove into an alley and parked behind a truck. He retrieved the battered leather case from under the passenger seat and left the car unlocked. He planned to be back behind the wheel in less than two minutes.

He quickly checked up and down the alley. There was no one in sight.

Once again as Fitzgerald entered the building, the alarm went off. But this time he was not worried about the speedy arrival of a passing patrol – most of the *policia* would be fully occupied, either at the stadium, where the game was due to kick off in half an hour, or arresting anyone who was still within a mile of the Plaza de Bolívar.

Fitzgerald closed the back door of the pawn shop behind him. For the second time that day he moved quickly through the rear office and, sweeping back the bead curtains, stopped behind the counter. He checked for passers-by before returning the battered leather case to its original place in the window.

When Escobar returned to the shop on Monday morning, how long would it be before he discovered that one of the six boat-tailed magnum bullets had been fired, and only the casing remained in place? And even then, would he bother to pass on the information to the police?

Fitzgerald was back behind the wheel of the Volkswagen in less than ninety seconds. He could still hear the clanging alarm as he drove onto the main street and began to follow the signs for Aeropuerto El Dorada. No one showed the slightest interest in him. After all, the game was just about to kick off. In any case, what possible connection could there be between an alarm going off in a pawn shop in the San Victorina district and the assassination of a presidential candidate in the Plaza de Bolívar?

Once Fitzgerald had reached the highway, he stuck to the centre lane, never once exceeding the speed limit. Several police cars shot past him, on their way into the city. Even if anyone had stopped him to check his papers, they would have found that everything was in order. The packed suitcase on the back seat would reveal nothing unusual for a businessman who was visiting Colombia to sell mining equipment.

Fitzgerald slipped off the highway when he reached the exit for the airport. After a quarter of a mile he suddenly swung right and drove into the parking lot of the San Sebastian hotel. He opened the glove compartment and removed a much-stamped passport. With the book of matches he had taken from the El Belvedere, he set Dirk van Rensberg alight. When his fingers were about to be burnt, he opened the car door, dropped the remains of the passport on the ground and stamped out the flames, making sure the South African crest was still recognisable. He put the matches on the passenger seat, grabbed his suitcase from the back and slammed the door closed, leaving the keys in the ignition. He walked towards the front door of the hotel and deposited the remains of Dirk van Rensberg's passport and a large, heavy key in the litter bin at the bottom of the steps.

Fitzgerald pushed through the revolving doors behind a group of Japanese businessmen, and remained in their slipstream as they were ushered towards an open elevator. He was the only passenger to step out on the third floor. He headed straight for room 347, where he extracted another plastic card that unlocked another room, booked in another name. He tossed the suitcase onto the bed and checked his watch. One hour and seventeen minutes until take-off.

He removed his jacket and threw it over the only chair, then opened the suitcase and took out a washbag before disappearing into the bathroom. It was some time before the water was warm enough for him to place the plug in the basin. While he waited he cut his nails, then he scrubbed his hands as thoroughly as a surgeon preparing for an operation.

It took Fitzgerald twenty minutes to remove every trace of his week-old beard, and several handfuls of shampoo needed to be rubbed in firmly under the warm shower before his hair returned to its natural wavy state and sandy colour.

Fitzgerald dried himself as best he could with the single thin towel the hotel had provided, then returned to the bedroom and put on a clean pair of jockey shorts. He walked over to the chest of drawers on the far side of the room, pulled open the third drawer and felt about until he found the packet taped to the drawer above. Although he hadn't occupied the room for several days, he was confident that no one would have come across his hiding place.

Fitzgerald ripped open the brown envelope and quickly checked its contents. Another passport in yet another name. Five hundred dollars in used notes and a first-class ticket to Cape Town. Escaping assassins don't travel first class. Five minutes later he left room 347, his old clothes strewn all over the floor and a '*Favor de no Molestar*' sign on the door.

Fitzgerald took the guest elevator to the ground floor, confident that no one would give a fifty-one-year-old man in a blue denim shirt, striped tie, sports jacket and grey flannels a second look. He stepped out of the elevator and strolled across the lobby, making no attempt to check out. When he'd arrived eight days earlier, he had paid cash in advance for the room. He had left the mini-bar locked, and never once rung room service, made an outside call or watched a pay film. There would be no extra charges on this guest's account.

He only had to wait for a few minutes before the shuttle bus swept up to the entrance. He checked his watch. Forty-three minutes to take-off. He wasn't at all anxious about missing Aeroperu's Flight 63 to Lima. He felt sure nothing was going to run on time that day.

Once the bus had dropped him at the airport he made his way slowly in the direction of the check-in counter, where he was not surprised to be told that the flight to Lima had been held up by over an hour. Several *policia* in the overcrowded, chaotic departures hall were suspiciously eyeing every passenger, and although he was stopped and questioned several times, and his case searched twice, he was eventually allowed to proceed to Gate 47.

He slowed his pace when he saw a couple of backpackers being dragged off by airport security staff. He idly wondered just how many innocent unshaven male Caucasians would spend the night being questioned in cells because of his actions earlier that afternoon.

When Fitzgerald joined the queue that led to Passport Control, he repeated his new name under his breath. It was his third that day. The blue-uniformed official in the little cubicle flicked open the New Zealand passport and carefully studied the photograph inside, which bore an undeniable resemblance to the smartly dressed man standing in front of him. He handed back the passport and allowed Alistair Douglas, a civil engineer from Christchurch, to stroll through to the departure lounge. After a further delay, the flight was finally called. A stewardess guided Mr Douglas to his seat in the first-class section.

'Would you care for a glass of champagne, sir?'

Fitzgerald shook his head. 'No, thank you. A glass of still water will be just fine,' he replied, trying out his New Zealand accent.

He fastened his seatbelt, sat back and pretended to read the in-flight magazine as the aircraft began its slow progress down the bumpy runway. Because of the extended line of planes waiting to take off in front of them, there was enough time for Fitzgerald to choose the dishes he would eat and the movie he would watch long before the 727 began its acceleration for take-off. When the wheels finally left the ground, Fitzgerald started to relax for the first time that day.

Once the aircraft had reached its cruising altitude, he disposed of the in-flight magazine, closed his eyes, and began to think about what needed to be done once he landed in Cape Town.

'This is your captain speaking,' said a sombre voice. 'I have an announcement to make which I know will cause some of you considerable distress.' Fitzgerald sat bolt upright. The one eventuality he hadn't planned for was an unscheduled return to Bogotá.

'I'm sorry to have to inform you that a national tragedy has taken place in Colombia today.'

Fitzgerald lightly gripped the armrest of his seat and concentrated on breathing evenly.

The captain hesitated for a moment. 'My friends,' he declared gravely, 'Colombia has suffered a terrible loss.' He paused. 'Our national team has been defeated by Brazil, by two goals to one.'

An audible groan went through the cabin, as if crashing into the nearest mountain would have been a preferable alternative. Fitzgerald allowed the suggestion of a smile to cross his lips.

The stewardess reappeared by his side. 'Can I fix a drink for you now we're on our way, Mr Douglas?'

'Thank you,' Fitzgerald replied. 'I think I'll have that glass of champagne after all.'

CHAPTER FOUR

As Tom Lawrence entered the packed room, the press corps rose to their feet.

'The President of the United States,' declared the Press Secretary, just in case there was a visitor from outer space.

Lawrence climbed the one step up to the podium and placed Andy Lloyd's blue file on the lectern. He waved at the assembled journalists in a now-familiar gesture to let them know they could resume their seats.

'I am delighted to announce,' began the President, sounding relaxed, 'that I will be sending to Congress a Bill which I promised the American people during the election campaign.'

Few of the senior White House correspondents seated in front of him wrote down a word, as most of them knew that if there was going to be a story worth printing, it was much more likely to come during the question-and-answer session than from any prepared statement. In any case, the President's opening remarks would be handed to them in a press kit as they left the room. Old pros only fell back on the prepared text when they had to fill extra column inches.

This did not stop the President from reminding them that the passing of an Arms Reduction Bill would allow him to release more revenue for long-term health care, so that elderly Americans could expect a better standard of living during their retirement.

'This is a Bill that will be welcomed by any decent, caring citizen, and I am proud to be the President who will guide it through Congress.' Lawrence looked up and smiled hopefully, feeling satisfied that his opening statement at least had gone well.

Shouts of 'Mr President!' came from every direction as Lawrence opened his blue file and glanced down at the thirty-one likely questions. He looked up and smiled at a familiar face in the front row. 'Barbara,' he said, pointing to the veteran UPI journalist whose right it was, as the doyenne of the press corps, to ask the first question.

Barbara Evans rose slowly to her feet. 'Thank you, Mr President.' She paused for a moment before asking, 'Are you able to confirm that the CIA had no involvement in the assassination of the Colombian presidential candidate, Ricardo Guzman, in Bogotá on Saturday?'

A buzz of interest rippled around the room. Lawrence stared down at the redundant thirty-one questions and answers, wishing he hadn't dismissed Larry Harrington's offer of a more detailed briefing quite so casually.

'I'm glad you asked that question, Barbara,' he responded, without missing a beat. 'Because I want you to know that while I'm President, such a suggestion doesn't even arise. This administration would never in any circumstances interfere with the democratic process of a sovereign state. In fact, only this morning, I instructed the Secretary of State to call Mr Guzman's widow and pass on my personal condolences.'

Lawrence was relieved that Barbara Evans had mentioned the dead man's name, because otherwise he wouldn't have been able to recall it. 'It may also be of interest to you to know, Barbara, that I have already asked the Vice-President to represent me at the funeral, which I understand will be held in Bogotá this weekend.'

Pete Dowd, the Secret Service agent in charge of the Presidential Protective Division, immediately left the room to warn the Vice-President before the press got to him.

Barbara Evans looked unconvinced, but before she could follow up with a second question the President had turned his attention to a man standing in the back row who, he hoped, would have no interest in the presidential election in Colombia. But once he had asked his question, Lawrence began to wish he had. 'What chance does your Arms Reduction Bill have of becoming law if Victor Zerimski looks likely to be the next Russian President?'

For the next forty minutes Lawrence answered several questions about the Nuclear, Biological, Chemical and Conventional Arms Reduction Bill, but they were interspersed with demands to be told about the CIA's current role in South America, and how he would deal with Victor Zerimski should he become the next Russian President. As it became all too apparent that Lawrence didn't know a great deal more than they did about either subject, the hacks, scenting blood, began to badger him on them to the exclusion of all others, including the Arms Reduction Bill.

When Lawrence at last received a sympathetic question from Phil Ansanch on the subject of the Bill, he gave a long, discursive reply, and then without warning wrapped up the press conference by smiling down at the baying journalists and saying, 'Thank you, ladies and gentlemen. It's been a pleasure, as always.' Without another word he turned his back on them, quickly left the room and headed in the direction of the Oval Office.

The moment Andy Lloyd had caught up with him, the President growled under his breath, 'I need to speak to Larry Harrington immediately. As soon as you've tracked him down, call Langley. I want the Director of the CIA in my office within the hour.'

'I wonder, Mr President, if it might be wiser . . .' began the Chief of Staff.

'Within the hour, Andy,' said the President, not even looking at him. 'If I find out that the CIA had any involvement in that assassination in Colombia, I'll hang Dexter out to dry.'

'I'll ask the Secretary of State to join you immediately, Mr President,' said Lloyd. He disappeared into a side office, picked up the nearest phone and dialled Larry Harrington at the State Department. Even over the phone the Texan was unable to disguise his pleasure at being proved right so quickly.

When Lloyd had put the phone down, he made his way back to his own office, closed the door and sat silently at his desk for a few moments. Once he had thought through exactly what he needed to say, he dialled a number that only one person ever answered.

'The Director,' was all Helen Dexter said.

Connor Fitzgerald handed over his passport to the Australian customs official. It would have been ironic if the document had been challenged, because for the first time in three weeks he was using his real name. The uniformed officer tapped out the details on his keyboard, checked the computer screen, then pressed a few more keys.

Nothing untoward appeared, so he stamped the tourist visa and said, 'Hope you enjoy your visit to Australia, Mr Fitzgerald.'

Connor thanked him and walked through to the baggage hall, where he took a seat opposite the motionless console and waited for his luggage to appear. He never allowed himself to be the first to pass through customs, even when he had nothing to declare.

When he had landed in Cape Town the previous day, Connor had been met off the plane by his old friend and colleague Carl Koeter. Carl had spent the next couple of hours debriefing him before they enjoyed a long lunch discussing Carl's divorce and what Maggie and Tara were up to. It was the second bottle of 1982 Rustenberg Cabernet Sauvignon that nearly caused Connor to miss his flight to Sydney. In the duty-free shop he hurriedly chose presents for his wife and daughter that were clearly stamped 'Made in South Africa'. Even his passport gave no clue that he had arrived in Cape Town via Bogotá, Lima and Buenos Aires.

As he sat in the baggage collection zone waiting for the console to start up, he began to think about the life he had been leading for the past twenty-eight years.

Connor Fitzgerald had been brought up in a family dedicated to the cause of law and order.

His paternal grandfather, Oscar, named after another Irish poet, had emigrated to America from Kilkenny at the turn of the century. Within hours of landing at Ellis Island he had headed straight for Chicago, to join his cousin in the police department.

During Prohibition Oscar Fitzgerald was among the small band of cops who refused to take bribes from the mob. As a result he failed to rise above the rank of sergeant. But Oscar did sire five Godfearing sons, and only gave up when the local priest told him it was the Almighty's will that he and Mary wouldn't be blessed with a daughter. His wife was grateful for Father O'Reilly's words of wisdom – it was difficult enough raising five strapping lads on a sergeant's salary. Mind you, if Oscar had ever given her one cent more than she was entitled to from his weekly pay packet, Mary would have wanted to know in great detail where it came from.

On leaving high school, three of Oscar's boys joined the Chicago PD, where they quickly gained the promotion their father had deserved. Another took holy orders, which pleased Mary, and the youngest, Connor's father, studied criminal justice at De Paul on the GI Bill.

After graduating, he joined the FBI. In 1949 he married Katherine O'Keefe, a girl who lived two doors away on South Lowe Street. They only had one child, a son, whom they christened Connor.

Connor was born in Chicago General Hospital on 8 February 1951, and even before he was old enough to attend the local Catholic school it had become clear that he was going to be a gifted football player. Connor's father was delighted when his son became captain of the Mount Carmel High School team, but his mother still kept him working late into the night, to make sure he always completed his homework. 'You can't play football for the rest of your life,' she continually reminded him.

The combination of a father who stood whenever a woman entered the room and a mother who verged on being a saint had left Connor, despite his physical prowess, shy in the presence of the opposite sex. Several girls at Mount Carmel High had made it only too obvious how they felt about him, but he didn't lose his virginity until he met Nancy in his senior year. Shortly after he had led Mount Carmel to another victory one autumn afternoon, Nancy had taken him behind the bleachers and seduced him. It would have been the first time he'd ever seen a naked woman, if she'd taken off all her clothes.

About a month later, Nancy asked him if he'd like to try two girls at once.

'I haven't even had two girls, let alone at once,' he told her. Nancy didn't seem impressed, and moved on.

When Connor won a scholarship to Notre Dame, he didn't take up any of the numerous offers that came the way of all the members of the football team. His team-mates seemed to take great pride in scratching the names of the girls who had succumbed to their charms on the inside of their locker doors. Brett Coleman, the team's place-kicker, had seventeen names inside his locker by the end of the first semester. The rule, he informed Connor, was that only penetration counted: 'The locker doors just aren't big enough to include oral sex.' At the end of his first year, 'Nancy' was still the only name Connor had scratched up. After practice one evening he checked through the other lockers, and discovered that Nancy's name appeared on almost every one of them, occasionally bracketed with that of another girl. The rest of the team would have given him hell for his low scoring if he hadn't been the best freshman quarterback Notre Dame had seen for a decade.

It was during Connor's first few days as a sophomore that everything changed.

When he turned up for his weekly session at the Irish Dance Club, she was putting on her shoes. He couldn't see her face, but that didn't matter much, because he was unable to take his eyes off those long, slim legs. As a football hero, he had become used to girls staring at him, but now the one girl he wanted to impress didn't seem aware that he even existed. To make matters worse, when she stepped onto the dance floor, she was partnered by Declan O'Casey, who had no rival as a dancer. They both held their backs rigidly straight, and their feet moved with a lightness Connor could never hope to match.

When the number came to an end, Connor still hadn't discovered her name. And, worse, she and Declan had left before he could find some way of being introduced to her. In desperation, he decided to follow them back to the women's dorms, walking fifty yards behind and always remaining in the shadows, just as his father had taught him. He grimaced as they held hands and chatted happily. When they reached Le Mans Hall she kissed Declan on the cheek and disappeared inside. Why, he wondered, hadn't he concentrated more on dancing and less on football?

After Declan had headed off in the direction of the men's dorms, Connor began to stroll casually up and down the sidewalk below the dormitory windows, wondering if there was anything he could do. He finally caught a glimpse of her in a dressing gown as she drew the curtain, and hung around for a few more minutes before reluctantly returning to his room. He sat on the end of his bed and began composing a letter to his mother, telling her that he had seen the girl he was going to marry, although he hadn't actually spoken to her yet – and come to think of it, he didn't even know her name. As Connor licked the envelope, he tried to convince himself that Declan O'Casey was nothing more to her than a dancing partner.

During the week, he tried to find out as much as he could about her, but he picked up very little other than that she was called Maggie Burke, had won a scholarship to St Mary's, and was in her freshman year studying Art History. He cursed the fact that he had never entered an art gallery in his life; in fact the nearest he'd come to painting was whenever his father asked him to touch up the fence surrounding their little back yard on South Lowe Street. Declan, it turned out, had been dating Maggie since her last year at school, and was not only the best dancer in the club, but was also considered the university's brightest mathematician. Other institutions were already offering him fellowships to pursue a post-graduate degree, even before the results of his final exams were known. Connor could only hope that Declan would be offered an irresistible post far away from South Bend as soon as possible.

Connor was the first to turn up at the dance club the following Thursday, and when Maggie appeared from the changing room in her cream cotton blouse and short black skirt, the only question he had to consider was whether to stare up into those green eyes or down at her long legs. Once again she was partnered by Declan all evening, while Connor sat mutely on a bench, trying to pretend he wasn't aware of her presence. After the final number the two of them slipped off. Once again Connor followed them back to Le Mans Hall, but this time he noticed that she wasn't holding Declan's hand.

After a long chat and another kiss on the cheek, Declan disappeared off in the direction of the men's dorms. Connor slumped down on a bench opposite her window and stared up at the balcony of the girls' dormitory. He decided to wait until he had seen her draw the curtains, but by the time she appeared at the window, he'd dozed off.

The next thing he remembered was waking from a deep sleep in which he had been dreaming that Maggie was standing in front of him, dressed in pyjamas and a dressing gown.

He woke with a start, stared at her in disbelief, jumped up and thrust out his hand. 'Hi, I'm Connor Fitzgerald.'

'I know,' she replied as she shook his hand. 'I'm Maggie Burke.'

'I know,' he said.

'Any room on that bench?' she asked.

From that moment, Connor never looked at another woman.

On the following Saturday Maggie went to a football game for the first time in her life, and watched him pull off a series of remarkable plays in front of what was for him a packed stadium of one.

The next Thursday, she and Connor danced together all evening, while Declan sat disconsolately in a corner. He looked even more desolate when the two of them left together, holding hands. When they reached Le Mans Hall, Connor kissed her for the first time, then fell on one knee and proposed. Maggie laughed, turned bright red, and ran inside. On his way back to the men's dorms Connor also laughed, but only when he spotted Declan hiding behind a tree.

From then on Connor and Maggie spent every moment of their spare time together. She learned about touchdowns, end zones and lateral passes, he about Bellini, Bernini and Luini. Every Thursday evening for the next three years he fell on one knee and proposed to her. Whenever his team-mates asked him why he hadn't scratched her name on the inside of his locker, he replied simply, 'Because I'm going to marry her.'

At the end of Connor's final year, Maggie finally agreed to be his wife – but not until she had completed her exams.

'It's taken me 141 proposals to make you see the light,' he said triumphantly.

'Oh, don't be stupid, Connor Fitzgerald,' she told him. 'I knew I was going to spend the rest of my life with you the moment I joined you on that bench.'

They were married two weeks after Maggie had graduated *summa cum laude*. Tara was born ten months later.

CHAPTER FIVE

'DO YOU EXPECT ME TO BELIEVE that the CIA didn't even *know* that an assassination attempt was being considered?'

'That is correct, sir,' said the Director of the CIA calmly. 'The moment we became aware of the assassination, which was within seconds of it taking place, I contacted the National Security Advisor, who, I understand, reported directly to you at Camp David.'

The President began to pace around the Oval Office, which he found not only gave him more time to think, but usually made his guests feel uneasy. Most people who entered the Oval Office were nervous already. His secretary had once told him that four out of five visitors went to the rest room only moments before they were due to meet the President. But he doubted if the woman sitting in front of him even knew where the nearest rest room was. If a bomb had gone off in the Rose Garden, Helen Dexter would probably have done no more than raise a well-groomed eyebrow. Her career had outlasted three Presidents so far, all of whom were rumoured at some point to have demanded her resignation.

'And when Mr Lloyd phoned to tell me that you required more details,' said Dexter, 'I instructed my deputy, Nick Gutenburg, to contact our people on the ground in Bogotá and to make extensive enquiries as to exactly what happened on Saturday afternoon. Gutenburg completed his report yesterday.' She tapped the file on her lap.

Lawrence stopped pacing and came to a halt under a portrait of Abraham Lincoln that hung above the fireplace. He looked down at the nape of Helen Dexter's neck. She continued to face straight ahead.

The Director was dressed in an elegant, well-cut dark suit with a simple cream shirt. She rarely wore jewellery, even on state occasions. Her appointment by President Ford as Deputy Director at the age of thirty-two was meant to have been a stopgap to placate the feminist lobby a few weeks before the 1976 election. As it was, Ford turned out to be the stopgap. After a series of short-term directors who either resigned or retired, Ms Dexter finally ended up with the coveted position. Many rumours circulated in the hothouse atmosphere of Washington about her extreme right-wing views and the methods she had used to gain promotion, but no member of the Senate dared to question her appointment. She had graduated *summa cum laude* from Bryn Mawr, followed by the University of Pennsylvania Law School, before joining one of New York's leading law firms. After a series of rows with the board over the length of time it took women to become partners, ending in litigation that was settled out of court, she had accepted an offer to join the CIA.

She began her life with the Agency in the office of the Directorate of Operations, eventually rising to become its Deputy. By the time of her appointment, she had made more enemies than friends, but as the years passed they seemed to disappear, or were fired, or took early retirement. When she was appointed Director she had just turned forty. The *Washington Post* described her as having blasted a hole through the glass ceiling, but that didn't stop the bookies offering odds on how many days she would survive. Soon they altered that to weeks, and then months. Now they were taking bets on whether she would last longer as the head of the CIA than J. Edgar Hoover had at the FBI.

Within days of Tom Lawrence taking up residence in the White House, he had discovered the lengths to which Dexter would go to block him if he tried to encroach on her world. If he asked for reports on sensitive subjects, it was often weeks before they appeared on his desk, and when they eventually did, they inevitably turned out to be long, discursive, boring and already out of date. If he called her into the Oval Office to explain unanswered questions, she could make a deaf mute appear positively forthcoming. If he pushed her, she would play for time, obviously assuming she would still be in her job long after the voters had turned him out of his.

But it was not until he proposed his nomination for a vacancy on the Supreme Court that he saw Helen Dexter at her most lethal. Within days, she had placed files on his desk that went to great lengths to point out why the nominee was unacceptable.

Lawrence had pressed on with the claims of his candidate – one of his oldest friends, who was found hanging in his garage the day before he was due to take up office. He later discovered that the confidential file had been sent to every member of the Senate Selection Committee, but he was never able to prove who had been responsible.

Andy Lloyd had warned him on several occasions that if he ever tried to remove Dexter from her post, he had better have the sort of proof that would convince the public that Mother Teresa had held a secret bank account in Switzerland regularly topped up by organised crime syndicates.

Lawrence had accepted his Chief of Staff's judgement. But he now felt that if he could prove the CIA had been involved in the assassination of Ricardo Guzman without even bothering to inform him, he could have Dexter clearing her desk within days.

He returned to his chair and touched the button

under the rim of his desk which would allow Andy to listen in on the conversation, or pick it up off the tape later that evening. Lawrence realised that Dexter would know exactly what he was up to, and he suspected that the legendary handbag which never left her side lacked the lipstick, perfume and compact usually associated with her sex, and had already recorded every syllable that had passed between them. Nevertheless, he still needed his version of events for the record.

'As you seem to be so well informed,' the President said as he sat down, 'perhaps you could brief me in more detail on what actually happened in Bogotá.'

Helen Dexter ignored his sarcastic tone, and picked up a file from her lap. The white cover bearing a CIA logo had printed across it the words 'FOR THE PRESIDENT'S EYES ONLY'. Lawrence wondered just how many files she had stashed away across the river marked 'FOR THE DIRECTOR'S EYES ONLY'.

She flicked the file open. 'It has been confirmed by several sources that the assassination was carried out by a lone gunman,' she read.

'Name one of these sources,' snapped the President.

'Our Cultural Attaché in Bogotá,' replied the Director.

Lawrence raised an eyebrow. Half the Cultural Attachés in American embassies around the world had been placed there by the CIA simply to report back directly to Helen Dexter at Langley without any consultation with the local Ambassador, let alone the State Department. Most of them would have thought the Nutcracker Suite was a dish to be found on the menu of an exclusive restaurant.

The President sighed. 'And who does *he* think was responsible for the assassination?'

Dexter flicked over a few pages of the file, extracted a photograph and pushed it across the Oval Office desk. The President looked down at a picture of a well-dressed, prosperous-looking middle-aged man.

'And who's this?'

'Carlos Velez. He runs the second-largest drug cartel in Colombia. Guzman, of course, controlled the biggest.'

'And has Velez been charged?'

'Unfortunately he was killed only a few hours after the police had obtained a warrant to arrest him.'

'How convenient.'

The Director didn't blush. Not possible in her case, thought Lawrence: after all, blushing requires blood.

'And did this lone assassin have a name? Or did he also die only moments after a court order was . . .'

'No, sir, he's still very much alive,' the Director replied firmly. 'His name is Dirk van Rensberg.'

'What's known about him?' asked Lawrence.

'He's South African. Until recently he lived in Durban.'

'Until recently?'

'Yes. He went underground immediately after the assassination.'

'That would be quite easy to do, if you were never above ground in the first place,' said the President. He waited for the Director to react, but she remained impassive. Eventually he said, 'Do the Colombian authorities go along with your account of what happened, or is our Cultural Attaché your only source of information?'

'No, Mr President. We picked up the bulk of our intelligence from Bogotá's Chief of Police. In fact, he already has in custody one of van Rensberg's accomplices, who was employed as a waiter at the El Belvedere hotel, the building from which the shot was fired. He was arrested in the corridor only moments after he had helped the assassin to escape in the freight elevator.'

'And do we know anything of van Rensberg's movements following the assassination?'

'He seems to have taken a flight to Lima in the name of Alistair Douglas, and then continued on to Buenos Aires, using the same passport. We lost track of him after that.'

'And I doubt if you'll ever find him again.'

'Oh, I wouldn't be that pessimistic, Mr President,' said Dexter, ignoring Lawrence's tone. 'Hired assassins tend to be loners who often disappear for several months following a job of this importance. Then they reappear once they feel the heat is off.'

'Well,' said the President, 'let me assure you that in this case I intend to keep the heat on. When we next meet, I may well have a report of my own for you to consider.'

'I shall look forward to reading it,' said Dexter, sounding like the school bully who had no fear of the headmaster.

The President pressed a button under his desk. A moment later there was a tap on the door and Andy Lloyd entered the room.

'Mr President, you have a meeting with Senator Bedell in a few minutes,' he said, ignoring Dexter's presence.

'Then I'll leave you, Mr President,' said Dexter, rising from her place. She put the file on the President's desk, picked up her handbag and left the room without another word.

The President didn't speak until the Director of the CIA had closed the door behind her. Then he turned to his Chief of Staff. 'I don't believe a word of it,' he muttered as he dropped the file into the out tray. Lloyd made a mental note to retrieve it as soon as his boss had left the room. 'I guess the best we can hope for is that we've put the fear of God in her, and that she won't consider carrying out another operation like that while I'm in the White House.'

'Remembering the way she treated you when you were a Senator, Mr President, I wouldn't put a lot of money on that.'

'As I can hardly employ an assassin to remove her, what do you suggest I do?'

'In my opinion she has left you with two choices, Mr

President. You can either sack her and face the inevitable Senate inquiry, or accept defeat, go along with her version of what took place in Bogotá, and hope you can get the better of her next time.'

'There could be a third choice,' the President said quietly.

Lloyd listened intently, making no attempt to interrupt his boss. It quickly became clear that the President had given considerable thought to how he might remove Helen Dexter from her post as Director of the CIA.

Connor collected his thoughts as he glanced up at the baggage arrivals screen. The console was beginning to spew out the luggage from his flight, and some passengers were already stepping forward to pick up the first bags.

It still saddened him that he had not been present at his daughter's birth. While he had doubts about the wisdom of the United States's policy in Vietnam, Connor shared his family's patriotism. He volunteered for military service, and completed officers' candidate school while he waited for Maggie to graduate. They ended up only having time for a wedding and a four-day honeymoon before Second Lieutenant Fitzgerald left for Vietnam in July 1972.

Those two years in Vietnam were now a distant memory. Being promoted to first lieutenant, captured by the Vietcong, escaping while saving another man's life – it all seemed so long ago that he was almost able to convince himself that it had never actually happened. Five months after he returned home, the President awarded him the nation's highest military decoration, the Medal of Honor, but after eighteen months as a prisoner of war in Vietnam he was just happy to be alive and reunited with the woman he loved. And the moment he saw Tara, he fell in love for a second time.

Within a week of returning to the States, Connor

began to look for a job. He had already been interviewed for a position at the CIA's Chicago field office when Captain Jackson, his old company commander, turned up unannounced and invited him to be part of a special unit that was being set up in Washington. Connor was warned that should he agree to join Jackson's elite team, there would be aspects of the job he could never discuss with anyone, including his wife. When he learned what was expected of him, he told Jackson that he would need a little time to think about it before he came to a decision. He discussed the problem with Father Graham, the family priest, who simply advised him: 'Never do anything you consider dishonourable, even if it's in the name of your country.'

When Maggie was offered a job at the Admissions Office at Georgetown University, Connor realised just how determined Jackson was to recruit him. He wrote to his old company commander the following day and said he would be delighted to join 'Maryland Insurance' as an executive trainee.

That was when the deception had begun.

A few weeks later Connor, Maggie and Tara moved to Georgetown. They found a small house on Avon Place, the deposit being covered by the Army paycheques Maggie had deposited in Connor's account, refusing to believe he was dead.

Their only sadness during those early days in Washington was that Maggie suffered two miscarriages, and her gynaecologist advised her to accept that she could have only one child. It took a third miscarriage before Maggie finally accepted his advice.

Although they had now been married for thirty years, Maggie was still able to arouse Connor simply by smiling and running her hand down his back. He knew that when he walked out of customs and saw her waiting for him in the arrivals hall, it would be as if it was for the first time. He smiled at the thought that she would have been at the airport for at least an hour before the plane was scheduled to land.

His case appeared in front of him. He grabbed it from the conveyor and headed towards the exit.

Connor passed through the green channel, confident that even if his luggage was searched, the customs officer wouldn't be that interested in a wooden springbok marked clearly on the foot 'Made in South Africa'.

When he stepped out into the arrivals hall, he immediately spotted his wife and daughter standing among the crowd. He quickened his pace and smiled at the woman he adored. Why had she even given him a second look, let alone agreed to be his wife? His smile broadened as he took her in his arms.

'How are you, my darling?' he asked.

'I only come alive again when I know you're safely back from an assignment,' she whispered. He tried to ignore the word 'safely' as he released her and turned to the other woman in his life. A slightly taller version of the original, with the same long red hair and flashing green eyes, but a calmer temperament. Connor's only child gave him a huge kiss on the cheek that made him feel ten years younger.

At Tara's christening, Father Graham had asked the Almighty that the child might be blessed with the looks of Maggie and the brains of – Maggie. As Tara had grown up, her grades in high school, and the turned heads of young men, had proved Father Graham not only to be a priest, but a prophet. Connor had soon given up fighting off the stream of admirers who had knocked on the front door of their little house in Georgetown, or even bothering to answer the phone: it was almost invariably another tongue-tied youth who hoped his daughter might agree to a date.

'How was South Africa?' Maggie asked as she linked arms with her husband.

'It's become even more precarious since Mandela's

death,' Connor replied – he'd had a full briefing from Carl Koeter on the problems facing South Africa over their long lunch in Cape Town, supplemented by a week of local papers that he read during the flight to Sydney. 'The crime rate's so high in most of the major cities that it's no longer against the law to drive through a red light after dark. Mbeki is doing his best, but I'm afraid I'm going to have to recommend that the company cut back its investment in that part of the world – at least until we're confident that the civil war is under control.'

' "*Things fall apart; the centre cannot hold; mere anarchy is loosed upon the world*",' Maggie said.

'I don't think Yeats ever visited South Africa,' said Connor.

How often he had wanted to tell Maggie the whole truth, and explain why he had lived a lie for so many years. But it was not that easy. She may have been his mistress, but they were his masters, and he had always accepted the code of total silence. Over the years, he had tried to convince himself that it was in her best interests not to know the whole truth. But when she unthinkingly used words like 'assignment' and 'safely', he was aware that she knew far more than she ever admitted. Did he talk in his sleep? Soon, though, it would no longer be necessary to continue deceiving her. Maggie didn't know it yet, but Bogotá had been his last mission. During the holiday he would drop a hint about an expected promotion that would mean far less travelling.

'And the deal?' Maggie asked. 'Were you able to settle it?'

'The deal? Oh, yes, it all went pretty much to plan,' said Connor. That was the nearest he would get to telling her the truth.

Connor began to think about spending the next two weeks basking in the sun. As they passed a news-stand, a small headline in a right-hand column of the *Sydney Morning Herald* caught his eye.

45

American Vice-President to Attend Funeral in
Colombia

Maggie let go of her husband's arm as they walked out
of the Arrivals hall into the warm summer air and headed
for the parking lot.

'Where were you when the bomb went off in Cape
Town?' Tara asked.

Koeter hadn't mentioned anything about a bomb in
Cape Town. Would he ever be able to relax?

CHAPTER SIX

HE INSTRUCTED HIS DRIVER to take him to the National Gallery.

As the car pulled away from the White House staff entrance, a Secret Service Uniformed Division officer in the guard booth opened the reinforced metal gate and raised a hand to acknowledge him. The driver turned onto State Place, drove between the South Grounds and the Ellipse, and past the Department of Commerce.

Four minutes later, the car drew up outside the gallery's east entrance. The passenger walked quickly across the cobbled driveway and up the stone steps. When he reached the top step, he glanced back over his shoulder to admire the vast Henry Moore sculpture that dominated the other side of the square, and checked to see if anyone was following him. He couldn't be sure, but then, he wasn't a professional.

He walked into the building and turned left up the great marble staircase that led to the second-floor galleries where he had spent so many hours in his youth. The large rooms were crowded with schoolchildren, which was not unusual on a weekday morning. As he walked into Gallery 71, he looked around at the familiar Homers, Bellows and Hoppers, and began to feel at home – a sensation he never experienced in the White House. He moved on to Gallery 66, to admire once again

August Saint-Gaudens' *Memorial to Shaw and the 54th Massachusetts Regiment.* The first time he'd seen the massive life-size frieze he had stood in front of it, mesmerised, for over an hour. Today he could only spare a few moments.

Because he couldn't stop stopping, it took him another quarter of an hour to reach the rotunda at the centre of the building. He walked quickly past the statue of Mercury and down the stairs, doubled back through the bookstore, ran down another flight of stairs and along the underground concourse before finally emerging in the East Wing. Taking one flight of steps up, he passed below the large Calder mobile hanging from the ceiling, then pushed his way through the revolving doors out of the building onto the cobbled driveway. By now he was confident no one was following him. He jumped into the back of the first taxi in the queue. Glancing out of the window, he saw his car and driver on the far side of the square.

'A.V.'s, on New York Avenue.'

The taxi turned left on Pennsylvania, then headed north up Sixth Street. He tried to marshal his thoughts into some sort of coherent order, grateful that the driver didn't want to spend the journey offering him his opinions on the Administration or, particularly, on the President.

They swung left onto New York Avenue and the taxi immediately began to slow down. He passed a ten-dollar bill to the driver even before they had come to a halt, then stepped out onto the street and shut the back door of the cab without waiting for the change.

He passed under a red, white and green awning which left no doubt of the proprietor's origins, and pushed open the door. It took a few moments for his eyes to grow accustomed to the light, or lack of it. When they did, he was relieved to find that the place was empty except for a solitary figure seated at a small table at the far end of the room, toying with a half-empty glass of tomato juice. His smart, well-cut suit gave no indication that he was unemployed. Although the man still had the build of an athlete, his prematurely balding dome made him look older than the age given in his file. Their eyes met, and the man nodded. He walked over and took the seat opposite him.

'My name is Andy . . .' he began.

'The mystery, Mr Lloyd, is not who you are, but why the President's Chief of Staff should want to see me in the first place,' said Chris Jackson.

'And what *is* your specialist field?' Stuart McKenzie asked.

Maggie glanced at her husband, knowing he wouldn't welcome such an intrusion into his professional life.

Connor realised that Tara couldn't have warned the latest young man to fall under her spell not to discuss her father's work.

Until that moment, he couldn't remember enjoying a lunch more. Fish that must have been caught only hours before they had sat down at the corner table in the little beach café at Cronulla. Fruit that had never seen preservatives or a tin, and a beer he hoped they exported to Washington. Connor took a gulp of coffee before leaning back in his chair and watching the surfers only a hundred yards away – a sport he wished he'd discovered twenty years before. Stuart had been surprised by how fit Tara's father was when he tried out the surfboard for the first time. Connor bluffed by telling him that he still worked out two or three times a week. Two or three times a day would have been nearer the truth.

Although he would never consider anyone good enough for his daughter, Connor had to admit that over the past few days he had come to enjoy the young lawyer's company.

'I'm in the insurance business,' he replied, aware that his daughter would have told Stuart that much.

'Yes, Tara said you were a senior executive, but she didn't go into any details.'

Connor smiled. 'That's because I specialise in kidnap and ransom, and have the same attitude to client confidentiality that you take for granted in your profession.' He wondered if that would stop the young Australian pursuing the subject. It didn't.

'Sounds a lot more interesting than most of the run-of-the-mill cases I'm expected to advise on,' said Stuart, trying to draw him out.

'Ninety per cent of what I do is fairly routine and boring,' Connor said. 'In fact, I suspect I have even more paperwork to deal with than you do.'

'But I don't get trips to South Africa.'

Tara glanced anxiously in her father's direction, knowing that he wouldn't be pleased that this information had been passed on to a relative stranger. But Connor showed no sign of being annoyed.

'Yes, I have to admit my job has one or two compensations.'

'Would it be breaking client confidentiality to take me through a typical case?'

Maggie was about to intervene with a line she had used many times in the past, when Connor volunteered, 'The company I work for represents several corporate clients who have large overseas interests.'

'Why don't those clients use companies from the country involved? Surely they'd have a better feel for the local scene.'

'Con,' interrupted Maggie, 'I think you're burning. Perhaps we ought to get back to the hotel before you begin to look like a lobster.'

Connor was amused by his wife's unconvincing intervention, especially as she had made him wear a hat for the past hour.

'It's never quite that easy,' he said to the young lawyer. 'Take a company like Coca-Cola, for example – whom,

I should point out, we don't represent. They have offices all over the world, employing tens of thousands of staff. In each country they have senior executives, most of whom have families.'

Maggie couldn't believe that Connor had allowed the conversation to go this far. They were fast approaching the question that always stopped any further enquiry dead in its tracks.

'But we have people well qualified to carry out such work in Sydney,' said Stuart, leaning forward to pour Connor some more coffee. 'After all, kidnap and ransom isn't unknown even in Australia.'

'Thank you,' said Connor. He took another gulp while he considered this statement. Stuart's scrutiny didn't falter – like a good prosecuting counsel, he waited patiently in the hope that the witness would at some stage offer an unguarded response.

'The truth is that I'm never called in unless there are complications.'

'Complications?'

'Let's say, for example, that a company has a large presence in a country where crime is rife and kidnap and ransom fairly common. The chairman of that company – although it's more likely to be his wife, because she will have far less day-to-day protection – is kidnapped.'

'That's when you move in?'

'No, not necessarily. After all, the local police may well be experienced at handling such problems, and there aren't many firms that welcome outside interference, especially when it comes from the States. Often I'll do no more than fly in to the capital city and start carrying out my own private enquiries. If I've visited that part of the world before and built up a rapport with the local police, I might make my presence known, but even then I'd still wait for them to ask me for assistance.'

'What if they don't?' asked Tara. Stuart was surprised

that she had apparently never asked her father that question before.

'Then I have to go it alone,' said Connor, 'which makes the process all the more precarious.'

'But if the police aren't making any headway, why wouldn't they want to enlist your help? They must be aware of your particular expertise,' said Stuart.

'Because it's not unknown for the police to be involved at some level themselves.'

'I'm not sure I understand,' said Tara.

'The local police could be receiving part of the ransom,' suggested Stuart, 'so they wouldn't welcome any outside interference. In any case, they might think the foreign company involved could well afford to pay it.'

Connor nodded. It was quickly becoming clear why Stuart had landed a job with one of the most prestigious criminal practices in Sydney.

'So what do you do if you think the local police might be taking a cut?' asked Stuart.

Tara began to wish she had warned Stuart not to push his luck too far, although she was fast coming to the conclusion that Australians had no idea where 'too far' was.

'When that happens you have to consider opening negotiations yourself, because if your client is killed, you can be sure that the ensuing investigation won't exactly be thorough, and it's unlikely that the kidnappers will ever be caught.'

'And once you've agreed to negotiate, what's your opening gambit?'

'Well, let's assume that the kidnapper demands a million dollars – kidnappers always ask for a round figure, usually in US dollars. Like any professional negotiator, my primary responsibility is to get the best possible deal. And the most important element of that is making sure that the company's employee comes to no harm. But I would never allow things to reach the negotiation stage if I felt that my client could be released without the company having to hand over a penny. The more you pay out, the more likely it is that the criminal will repeat the exercise a few months later, sometimes kidnapping exactly the same person.'

'How often do you reach the negotiating stage?'

'About 50 per cent of the time. That's the point when you discover whether or not you're dealing with professionals. The longer you can stretch out the negotiations, the more likely it is that amateurs will become anxious about being caught. And after a few days they often grow to like the person they've kidnapped, which makes it almost impossible for them to carry out their original plan. In the Peruvian Embassy siege, for example, they ended up holding a chess competition, and the terrorists won.'

All three of them laughed, which helped Maggie to relax a little.

'Is it the pros or the amateurs who send ears through the post?' asked Stuart with a wry smile.

'I'm happy to say I didn't represent the company that negotiated on behalf of Mr Getty's grandson. But even when I'm dealing with a pro, some of the best cards will still be in my hand.' Connor hadn't noticed that his wife and daughter had allowed their coffee to go cold.

'Please continue,' said Stuart.

'Well, the majority of kidnaps are one-off affairs, and although they're nearly always carried out by a professional criminal, he may have little or no experience of how to negotiate in a situation like that. Professional criminals are almost always over-confident. They imagine they can handle anything. Not unlike a lawyer who thinks he can open a restaurant simply because he eats three meals a day.'

Stuart smiled. 'So what do they settle for once they realise they're not going to get the mythical million?'

'I can only speak from my own experience,' said

Connor. 'I usually end up handing over around a quarter of the sum demanded – in used, traceable notes. On a few occasions I've parted with as much as half. Only once did I agree to hand over the full amount. But in my defence, counsel, on that particular occasion even the island's Prime Minister was taking a cut.'

'How many of them get away with it?'

'Of the cases I've handled over the past seventeen years, only three, which works out at roughly 8 per cent.'

'Not a bad return. And how many clients have you lost?'

They were now entering territory even Maggie hadn't ventured onto before, and she began to shift uneasily in her chair.

'If you do lose a client, the company backs you to the hilt,' said Connor. He paused. 'But they don't allow anyone to fail twice.'

Maggie rose from her place, turned to Connor and said, 'I'm going for a swim. Anyone care to join me?'

'No, but I'd like another go on the board,' said Tara, eagerly assisting her mother's attempt to end the interrogation.

'How many times did you fall in this morning?' Connor asked, confirming that he also thought it had gone quite far enough.

'A dozen or more,' said Tara. 'That was the worst one.' She pointed proudly to a large bruise on her right thigh.

'Why did you let her go that far, Stuart?' asked Maggie, sitting back down to take a closer look at the bruise.

'Because it gave me the chance to rescue her and look heroic.'

'Be warned, Stuart, she'll have mastered surfing by the end of the week, and she'll end up rescuing you,' said Connor with a laugh.

'I'm well aware of that,' Stuart replied. 'But the moment it happens I plan to introduce her to bungee jumping.'

Maggie turned visibly white, and quickly looked in Connor's direction.

'Don't worry, Mrs Fitzgerald,' Stuart added quickly. 'You'll all be back in America long before then.' None of them wanted to be reminded.

Tara grabbed Stuart by the arm. 'Let's go, Superman. It's time to find another wave you can rescue me from.'

Stuart leapt up. Turning to Connor, he said, 'If you ever discover your daughter's been kidnapped, I won't be demanding a ransom, and I won't be willing to settle – in US dollars or any other currency.'

Tara blushed. 'Come on,' she said, and they ran down the beach towards the breakers.

'And for the first time, I don't think I'd try to negotiate,' Connor said to Maggie, stretching and smiling.

'He's a nice young man,' said Maggie, taking his hand. 'It's just a pity he's not Irish.'

'It could have been worse,' said Connor, rising from his chair. 'He might have been English.'

Maggie smiled as they began walking towards the surf. 'You know, she didn't get home until five this morning.'

'Don't tell me you still lie awake all night whenever your daughter goes out on a date,' said Connor with a grin.

'Keep your voice down, Connor Fitzgerald, and try to remember she's our only child.'

'She's not a child any longer, Maggie,' he said. 'She's a grown woman, and in less than a year she'll be Dr Fitzgerald.'

'And you don't worry about her, of course.'

'You know I do,' said Connor, taking her in his arms. 'But if she's having an affair with Stuart – which is none of my business – she could have done a lot worse.'

'I didn't sleep with you until the day we were married, and even when they told me you were missing in Vietnam, I never looked at another man. And it wasn't because of a lack of offers.'

55

'I know, my darling,' said Connor. 'But by then you'd realised I was irreplaceable.'

Connor released his wife and ran towards the waves, making sure he always remained just one stride ahead of her. When she finally caught up with him, she was out of breath.

'Declan O'Casey proposed to me long before . . .'

'I know, my darling,' he replied, looking down into her green eyes and brushing back a stray wisp of hair. 'And never a day goes by when I'm not thankful that you waited for me. It was the one thing that kept me alive after I'd been captured in 'Nam. That and the thought of seeing Tara.'

Connor's words reminded Maggie of the sadness she had felt at her miscarriages and the knowledge that she couldn't have any more children. She had been brought up in a large family, and longed to have a brood herself. She could never accept her mother's simple philosophy – it's God's will.

While Connor had been away in Vietnam, she had spent many happy hours with Tara. But the moment he returned the young madam had transferred her affections overnight, and although she remained close to her daughter, Maggie knew that she could never have the same relationship with Tara that Connor enjoyed.

When Connor signed up with Maryland Insurance as a management trainee, Maggie had been puzzled by his decision. She had always thought that, like his father, Connor would want to be involved in law enforcement. That was before he explained who he would really be working for. Although he didn't go into great detail, he did tell her who his paymaster was, and the significance of being a non-official cover officer, or NOC. She kept his secret loyally over the years, though not being able to discuss her husband's profession with her friends and colleagues was sometimes a little awkward. But she decided this was a minor inconvenience, compared with what so many other wives were put through by husbands only too happy to discuss their work in endless detail. It was their extracurricular activities they wanted to keep secret.

All she really hoped was that one day her daughter would find someone willing to wait on a park bench all night just to see her draw a curtain.

CHAPTER SEVEN

JACKSON LIT A CIGARETTE, and listened carefully to every word the man from the White House had to say. He made no attempt to interrupt him.

When Lloyd eventually came to the end of his prepared piece, he took a sip of the *acqua minerale* in front of him and waited to hear what the former Deputy Director of the CIA's first question would be.

Jackson stubbed out his cigarette. 'May I ask why you thought I was the right person for this assignment?'

Lloyd was not taken by surprise. He had already decided that if Jackson asked that particular question, he would simply tell the truth. 'We know that you resigned your post with the CIA because of a . . . difference of opinion' – he emphasised the words – 'with Helen Dexter, despite the fact that your record with the Agency had been exemplary, and until then you were considered her natural successor. But since resigning for reasons that on the face of it seem somewhat bizarre, I believe you have not been able to find a job worthy of your qualifications. We suspect that Dexter also has something to do with that.'

'It only takes one phone call,' said Jackson, 'off the record, of course – and suddenly you find you've been removed from any shortlist. I've always been wary of speaking ill of the living, but in the case of Helen Dexter, I'm happy to make an exception.' He lit another cigarette. 'You see, Dexter believes that Tom Lawrence has the second most important job in America,' he continued. '*She* is the true defender of the faith, the nation's last bastion, and to her elected politicians are nothing more than a temporary inconvenience who will, sooner or later, be ejected by the voters.'

'The President has been made aware of that on more than one occasion,' Lloyd said, with some feeling.

'Presidents come and go, Mr Lloyd. My bet is that, like the rest of us, your boss is human, and therefore you can be sure that Dexter will have a file on him which is filled with the reasons why Lawrence isn't qualified for a second term. And by the way, she'll have one almost as thick on you.'

'Then we'll have to start building up our own file, Mr Jackson. I can think of no one better qualified to carry out the task.'

'Where would you like me to begin?'

'By investigating who was behind the assassination of Ricardo Guzman in Bogotá last month,' said Lloyd. 'We have reason to believe that the CIA might have been involved, directly or indirectly.'

'Without the President's knowledge?' said Jackson in disbelief.

Lloyd nodded, removed a file from his briefcase and slid it across the table. Jackson flicked it open.

'Take your time,' said Lloyd, 'because you're going to have to memorise everything.'

Jackson began reading, and started making observations even before he had come to the end of the first page.

'If we assume that it was a lone gunman, trying to get any reliable information will be virtually impossible. That sort of character doesn't leave a forwarding address.' Jackson paused. 'But if it *is* the CIA we're dealing with, then Dexter has a ten-day start on us. She's probably already turned every avenue that might lead to the assassin into a blind alley – unless . . .'

'Unless . . . ?' echoed Lloyd.

'I'm not the only person that woman has crossed over the years. It's just possible that there might be someone else based in Bogotá who –' He paused. 'How long have I got?'

'The new President of Colombia is making an official visit to Washington in three weeks' time. It would help if we had something by then.'

'It's already beginning to feel like the old days,' said Jackson as he stubbed out his cigarette. 'Except this time there's the added pleasure of Dexter being officially on the other side.' He lit another cigarette. 'Who will I be working for?'

'Officially you're freelance, but unofficially you work for me. You'll be paid at the same level as you were when you left the Agency, your account credited on a monthly basis, although for obvious reasons your name won't appear on any books. I'll contact you whenever . . .'

'No you won't, Mr Lloyd,' said Jackson. 'I'll contact *you* whenever I have anything worthwhile to report. Two-way contacts only double the chance of someone stumbling across us. All I'll need is an untraceable phone number.'

Lloyd wrote down seven figures on a cocktail napkin. 'This gets straight through to my desk, bypassing even my secretary. After midnight it's automatically transferred to a phone by the side of my bed. You can call me night or day. You needn't bother about the time difference when you're abroad, because I don't care about being woken up.'

'That's good to know,' said Jackson. 'Because I don't think Helen Dexter ever sleeps.'

Lloyd smiled. 'Have we covered everything?'

'Not quite,' said Jackson. 'When you leave, turn right and then take the next right. Don't look back, and don't hail a taxi until you've walked at least four blocks. From now on you're going to have to think like Dexter, and be warned, she's been at it for thirty years. There's only one person I know who's better than she is.'

'I hope that's you,' said Lloyd.

'I'm afraid not,' said Jackson.

'Don't tell me he already works for Dexter.'

Jackson nodded. 'Even though he's my closest friend, if Dexter ordered him to kill me, there isn't an insurance company in town that would take out a policy on my life. If you expect me to beat both of them, you'd better hope I haven't gone rusty over the past eight months.'

The two men rose. 'Goodbye, Mr Lloyd,' said Jackson as they shook hands. 'I'm sorry that this will be our first and last meeting.'

'But I thought we agreed –' said Lloyd, looking anxiously at his new recruit.

'To work together, Mr Lloyd, not to meet. You see, Dexter wouldn't consider two meetings a coincidence.'

Lloyd nodded. 'I'll wait to hear from you.'

'And Mr Lloyd,' said Jackson, 'don't visit the National Gallery again, unless it's for the sole purpose of seeing the paintings.'

Lloyd frowned. 'Why not?' he asked.

'Because the half-asleep guard in Gallery 71 was planted there on the day of your appointment. It's all in your file. You go there once a week. Is Hopper still your favourite artist?'

Lloyd's mouth went dry. 'Then Dexter already knows about this meeting?'

'No,' said Jackson. 'You got lucky this time. It's the guard's day off.'

Although Connor had seen his daughter cry many times when she was younger, over a cut leg, a bruised ego or simply not getting her own way, this was quite different. While she clung to Stuart he pretended to be absorbed in a rack of bestselling books at the news-stand, and reflected on one of the most enjoyable holidays he could remember. He'd put on a couple of pounds and had managed to almost master the surfboard, although he had rarely experienced more pride before more falls. During the past fortnight he had come first to like, and later to respect Stuart. And Maggie had even stopped reminding him every morning that Tara hadn't returned to her room the previous night. He took that to be his wife's reluctant seal of approval.

Connor picked up the *Sydney Morning Herald* from the news-stand. He flicked over the pages, only taking in the headlines until he came to the section marked 'International News'. He glanced towards Maggie, who was paying for some souvenirs that they would never display or even consider giving as presents, and which would undoubtedly end up in Father Graham's Christmas sale.

Connor lowered his head again. 'Landslide for Herrera in Colombia' was the headline running across three columns at the foot of the page. He read about the new President's one-sided victory over the National Party's last-minute replacement for Ricardo Guzman. Herrera, the article went on to say, planned to visit America in the near future to discuss with President Lawrence the problems Colombia was currently facing. Among the subjects uppermost . . .

'Do you think this would be all right for Joan?'

Connor glanced across at his wife, who was holding up a Ken Done print of Sydney Harbour.

'A bit modern for her, I would have thought.'

'Then we'll have to get her something from duty free once we're on the plane.'

'This is the last call for United Airlines Flight 816 to Los Angeles,' said a voice that echoed around the airport. 'Will all those who have not yet boarded the aircraft please make their way immediately to Gate 27.'

Connor and Maggie began walking in the direction of the large departure sign, trying to stay a few paces in front of their daughter and Stuart, who were locked together as if they were in a three-legged race. Once they had gone through passport control, Connor hung back, while Maggie carried on towards the departure lounge to tell the gate agent that the last two passengers would be following shortly.

When Tara reluctantly appeared round the corner a few moments later, Connor placed an arm gently around her shoulders. 'I know it's not much of a consolation, but your mother and I think he's . . .' Connor hesitated.

'I know,' she said between sobs. 'As soon as I get back to Stanford, I'm going to ask if they'll allow me to complete my thesis at Sydney University.' Connor spotted his wife talking to a stewardess by the gate to the aircraft.

'Is she that afraid of flying?' the stewardess whispered to Maggie when she saw the young woman sobbing.

'No. She just had to leave something behind that they wouldn't let her take through customs.'

Maggie slept almost the entire fourteen-hour flight from Sydney to Los Angeles. Tara always marvelled at how she managed it. She could never do more than doze during a flight, however many pills she took. She held her father's hand firmly. He smiled at her but didn't speak.

Tara returned his smile. For as long as she could remember, he had been the centre of her world. It never worried her that she might not meet a man who could take his place; more that when she did, he wouldn't be able to accept it. Now that it had happened, she was relieved to discover just how supportive he was. If anything, it was her mother who was proving to be the problem.

Tara knew that if her mother had her way, she would still be a virgin, and probably still living at home. It wasn't until the eleventh grade that she stopped believing that if you kissed a boy you'd become pregnant. That was when a classmate passed on to her a much-thumbed copy of *The Joy of Sex*. Each night, curled up under the sheets with a torch, Tara would turn the pages.

But it was only after her graduation from Stone Ridge that she lost her virginity – and if everyone else in her class had been telling the truth, she must have been the last. Tara had joined her parents for a long-promised visit to her great-grandfather's birthplace. She fell in love with Ireland and its people within moments of landing at Dublin. Over dinner in their hotel on the first night, she told her father that she couldn't understand why so many of the Irish were not content to remain in their homeland, but had to emigrate.

The young waiter who was serving them looked down at her and recited:

> 'Ireland never was contented.'
> 'Say you so? You are demented.
> Ireland was contented when
> All could use the sword and pen.'

'Walter Savage Landor,' Maggie said. 'But do you know the next line?'

The waiter bowed.

> 'And when Tara rose so high . . .'

Tara blushed, and Connor burst out laughing. The waiter looked puzzled.

'It's my name,' Tara explained.

He bowed again before clearing away the plates. While her father was settling the bill and her mother was collecting her coat, the waiter asked Tara if she would like to join him for a drink at Gallagher's when he came off duty. Tara happily agreed.

She spent the next couple of hours watching an old movie in her room, before creeping downstairs just after midnight. The pub Liam had suggested was only a few hundred yards down the road, and when Tara walked in she found him waiting at the bar. Liam wasted no time in introducing her to the joys of Guinness. She wasn't surprised to discover that he had taken the job as a waiter during the holidays before he completed his final year at Trinity College, studying the Irish poets. Liam was surprised, however, to find how well she could quote Yeats, Joyce, Wilde and Synge.

When he took her back to her room a couple of hours later, he kissed her gently on the lips and asked, 'How long are you staying in Dublin?'

'Two more days,' she replied.

'Then don't let's waste a moment of it.'

After three nights during which she hardly slept, Tara departed for Oscar's birthplace in Kilkenny, feeling qualified to add a footnote or two to *The Joy of Sex.*

As Liam carried their bags down to the hire car, Connor gave him a large tip and whispered 'Thank you.' Tara blushed.

At Stanford in her sophomore year, Tara had what might have been described as an affair with a medical student. But it wasn't until he proposed that she realised she didn't want to spend the rest of her life with him. It hadn't taken her a year to reach a very different conclusion about Stuart.

They had first met when they bumped into each other. It was her fault – she wasn't looking when she crossed his path as he swooped down the face of a large wave. Both of them went flying. When he lifted her out of the water, Tara waited for a richly deserved tirade of abuse.

Instead he just smiled and said, 'In future, try and keep out of the fast lane.' She performed the same trick later that afternoon, but this time on purpose, and he knew it.

He laughed and said, 'You've left me with two choices. Either I start giving you lessons, or we can have a coffee. Otherwise our next meeting might well be in the local hospital. Which would you prefer?'

'Let's start with the coffee.'

Tara had wanted to sleep with Stuart that night, and

by the time she was due to leave ten days later, she wished she hadn't made him wait three days. By the end of the week . . .

'This is your captain speaking. We're now beginning our descent into Los Angeles.'

Maggie woke with a start, rubbed her eyes and smiled at her daughter. 'Did I fall asleep?' she asked.

'Not until the plane took off,' Tara replied.

After they'd collected their luggage, Tara said goodbye to her parents and went off to join her connecting flight to San Francisco. As she disappeared into the crowd of arriving and departing passengers, Connor whispered to Maggie, 'It wouldn't surprise me if she turned round and took the next plane back to Sydney.' Maggie nodded.

They headed off in the direction of the domestic terminal, and climbed aboard the 'red-eye'. This time Maggie was asleep even before the video describing the safety drill had been completed. As they flew across the States, Connor tried to dismiss Tara and Stuart from his thoughts, and to concentrate on what needed to be done once he was back in Washington. In three months' time he was due to be taken off the active list, and he still had no idea which department they planned to transfer him to. He dreaded the thought of being offered a nine-to-five job at headquarters, which he knew would consist of giving lectures to young NOCs on his experiences in the field. He had already warned Joan that he would resign if they didn't have anything more interesting to offer him. He wasn't cut out to be a teacher.

During the past year there had been hints about one or two front-line posts for which he was being considered, but that was before his boss had resigned without explanation. Despite twenty-eight years of service and several commendations, Connor was aware that now Chris Jackson was no longer with the Company, his future might not be quite as secure as he'd imagined.

CHAPTER EIGHT

'ARE YOU CERTAIN Jackson can be trusted?'

'No, Mr President, I'm not. But I am certain of one thing: Jackson loathes – I repeat, loathes – Helen Dexter as much as you do.'

'Well, that's as good as a personal recommendation,' said the President. 'What else made you pick him? Because if loathing Dexter was the primary qualification for the job, there must have been a fairly large number of candidates.'

'He also has the other attributes I was looking for. There's his record, as an officer in Vietnam and as head of counter-intelligence, not to mention his reputation as Deputy Director of the CIA.'

'Then why did he suddenly resign when he still had such a promising career ahead of him?'

'I suspect that Dexter felt it was a bit too promising, and he was beginning to look like a serious contender for her post.'

'If he can prove that she gave the order to assassinate Ricardo Guzman, he still might be. It looks as if you've chosen the best man for the job, Andy.'

'Jackson told me there was one better.'

'Then let's recruit him as well,' said the President.

'I had the same idea. But it turns out that he's already working for Dexter.'

'Well, at least he won't know Jackson's working for us. What else did he have to say?'

Lloyd opened the file and began to take the President through the conversation he had had with the former Deputy Director of the CIA.

When he'd finished, Lawrence's only comment was, 'Are you telling me I'm expected to just sit around twiddling my thumbs while we wait for Jackson to come up with something?'

'Those were his conditions, Mr President, if we wanted him to take on the assignment. But I have a feeling that Mr Jackson isn't the sort of person who sits around twiddling *his* thumbs.'

'He'd better not be, because every day Dexter's at Langley is a day too many for me. Let's hope Jackson can supply us with enough rope to hang her publicly. And while we're at it, let's hold the execution in the Rose Garden.'

The Chief of Staff laughed. 'That might have the double advantage of getting a few more Republicans to vote with us on the Safe Streets and Crime Reduction Bill.'

The President smiled. 'Who's next?' he asked.

Lloyd glanced at his watch. 'Senator Bedell has been waiting in the lobby for some time.'

'What does he want now?'

'He was hoping to talk you through his latest set of proposed amendments to the Arms Reduction Bill.'

The President frowned. 'Did you notice how many points Zerimski has picked up in the latest opinion poll?'

Maggie began dialling the 650 number moments after she had turned the key in the lock of their little house in Georgetown. Connor started to unpack, listening to one end of the conversation between his wife and his daughter.

'Just phoned to let you know that we've arrived back safely,' Maggie tried as an opener.

Connor smiled at the unconvincing ploy. Tara was far too acute to fall for it, but he knew that she would play along.

'Thanks for calling, Mom. It's good to hear you.'

'Everything all right at your end?' asked Maggie.

'Yes, fine,' Tara said, before spending the next few minutes trying obliquely to assure her mother that she wasn't about to do something impetuous. When she was convinced that Maggie was convinced, she asked, 'Is Dad around?'

'He's right here.' She handed the phone across the bed to Connor.

'Can you do me a favour, Dad?'

'You bet.'

'Please explain to Mom that I'm not about to do anything silly. Stuart's already rung twice since I got back, and as he's planning to' – she hesitated – 'to come over to the States for Christmas, I'm pretty sure I can hang on until then. By the way, Dad, I thought I'd better warn you that I already know what I'd like for Christmas.'

'And what's that, my darling?'

'That you'll pay for my overseas calls for the next eight months. I have a feeling that might end up being more expensive than buying that used car you promised me if I get my PhD.'

Connor laughed.

'So you'd better get that promotion you mentioned when we were in Australia. Bye, Dad.'

'Bye, darling.'

Connor hung up, and gave Maggie a reassuring smile. He was about to tell her for the tenth time to stop worrying, when the phone rang again. He picked up the receiver, assuming it would be Tara again. It wasn't.

'Sorry to call the moment you arrive back,' said Joan, 'but I've just heard from the boss, and it sounds like an emergency. How quickly can you come in?'

Connor checked his watch. 'I'll be with you in twenty minutes,' he said, and put the phone down.

'Who was that?' asked Maggie, as she continued unpacking.

'Joan. She just needs me to sign a couple of outstanding contracts. Shouldn't take too long.'

'Damn,' said Maggie. 'I forgot to get her a present on the plane.'

'I'll find her something on the way to the office.'

Connor quickly left the room, and ran down the stairs and out of the house before Maggie could ask any more questions. He climbed into the old family Toyota, but it was some time before he could get the engine to splutter into life. He eventually eased the 'old tank', as Tara described it, out onto Twenty-Ninth Street. Fifteen minutes later he turned left on M Street, before taking another left and disappearing down a ramp into an unmarked underground carpark.

As Connor entered the building, the security guard touched the rim of his peaked hat and said, 'Welcome back, Mr Fitzgerald. I wasn't expecting to see you until Monday.'

'That makes two of us,' said Connor, returning the mock-salute and heading towards the bank of elevators. He took one to the seventh floor. When he stepped out into the corridor, he was greeted by a smile of recognition from the receptionist who sat at a desk below the boldly printed caption 'Maryland Insurance Company'. The directory on the ground floor stated that the distinguished firm occupied the seventh, eighth, ninth and tenth floors.

'How nice to see you, Mr Fitzgerald,' said the receptionist. 'You have a visitor.'

Connor smiled and nodded before continuing down the corridor. As he turned the corner, he spotted Joan standing by the door of his office. From the expression on her face, he suspected she had been waiting there for some time. Then he remembered Maggie's words just before he left home – not that Joan looked as if a present was uppermost in her thoughts.

'The boss arrived a few minutes ago,' Joan said, holding the door open for him.

Connor strode into his office. Sitting on the other side of his desk was someone he'd never known to take a holiday.

'I'm sorry to have kept you waiting, Director,' he said. 'I only . . .'

'We have a problem,' was all Helen Dexter said, pushing a file across the desk.

'Just give me one decent lead, and I'll do all the groundwork,' said Jackson.

'I only wish I could, Chris,' replied Bogotá's Chief of Police. 'But it has already been made clear to me by one or two of your former colleagues that you are now *persona non grata*.'

'I've never thought of you as someone who gave a damn about such niceties,' said Jackson as he poured the Police Chief another whisky.

'Chris, you have to understand that when you were a representative of your government, it was all above board.'

'Including your kickbacks, if I remember correctly.'

'But of course,' said the policeman nonchalantly. 'You'll be the first to appreciate that expenses still have to be met.' He took a gulp from his crystal glass. 'And as you know only too well, Chris, inflation in Colombia remains extremely high. My salary doesn't cover even my day-to-day expenses.'

'From that little homily,' said Jackson, 'am I to understand that the rate remains the same, even if one is *persona non grata*?'

The Chief of Police downed his last drop of whisky, wiped his moustache and said, 'Chris, Presidents come and go in both our countries – but not old friends.'

Jackson gave him a thin smile before removing an envelope from an inside pocket and sliding it under the table. The Chief of Police glanced inside it, unbuttoned a tunic pocket and slipped the envelope out of sight.

'I see that your new masters have not, alas, allowed you the same degree of latitude when it comes to – expenses.'

'One decent lead, that's all I ask,' repeated Jackson.

The Chief of Police held up his empty glass and waited until the barman had filled it to the brim. He took another long gulp. 'I have always believed, Chris, that if you're looking for a bargain, there's no better place to start than a pawn shop.' He smiled, drained his glass and rose from the table. 'And remembering the dilemma you are currently facing, my old friend, I would begin in the San Victorina district, and I wouldn't bother to do much more than window-shop.'

Once Connor had finished reading the details of the confidential memorandum, he passed the file back to the Director.

Her first question took him by surprise. 'How long is it before you're due to retire from the service?'

'I come off the active list on the first of January next year, but naturally I hope to remain with the Company.'

'It may not be quite that easy to accommodate your particular talents at the present time,' Dexter said matter-of-factly. 'However, I do have a vacancy I would feel able to recommend you for.' She paused. 'As director of our Cleveland office.'

'Cleveland?'

'Yes.'

'After twenty-eight years' service with the Company,' said Connor, 'I was rather hoping you might be able to find me something in Washington. I'm sure you know that my wife is the Dean of Admissions at Georgetown.

It would be almost impossible for her to find an equivalent post in . . . Ohio.'

A long silence followed.

'I'd like to help,' Dexter said in the same flat tone, 'but there's nothing suitable for you at Langley at the present time. If you did feel able to take up the appointment in Cleveland, it might be possible to bring you back in a couple of years.'

Connor stared across the table at the woman he had served for the past twenty-six years, painfully aware that she was now using the same lethal blade on him as she had on so many of his colleagues in the past. But why, when he had always carried out her orders to the letter? He glanced at the file. Had the President demanded that someone should be sacrificed after he had been questioned so closely about the CIA's activities in Colombia? Was Cleveland to be his reward for all his years of service?

'Is there any alternative?' he asked.

The Director didn't hesitate. 'You could always opt for early retirement.' She sounded as if she was suggesting the replacement of a sixty-year-old janitor in her apartment building.

Connor sat in silence, unable to believe what he was hearing. He'd given his whole life to the Company, and like so many of its officers, he'd put that life on the line several times.

Helen Dexter rose from her place. 'Perhaps you'd let me know when you've reached a decision.' She left the room without another word.

Connor sat alone at his desk for some time, trying to take in the full implications of the Director's words. He recalled that Chris Jackson had told him of an almost identical conversation he had had with her eight months before. In his case, the position he'd been offered was in Milwaukee. 'It could never happen to me,' he remembered telling Chris at the time. 'After all, I'm a team player, and no one would suspect me of wanting her job.' But Connor had committed an even graver sin. By carrying out Dexter's orders, he had unwittingly become the cause of her possible downfall. If he were no longer around to embarrass her, she might survive yet again. How many other good officers had been sacrificed over the years, he wondered, on the altar of her ego?

Connor's thoughts were interrupted when Joan entered the room. She didn't need to be told that the meeting had gone badly.

'Anything I can do?' she asked quietly.

'No, not a thing, thanks, Joan.' After a short silence he added, 'You know I'm due to come off the active list soon.'

'On the first of January,' she said. 'But with your record, the Company's certain to offer you a large desk, civilised hours for a change, and perhaps a long-legged secretary thrown in.'

'It seems not,' said Connor. 'The only job the Director had in mind for me was to head up the office in Cleveland, and there certainly wasn't any mention of a long-legged secretary.'

'Cleveland?' repeated Joan incredulously.

Connor nodded.

'The bitch.'

Connor glanced up at his long-serving secretary, unable to hide a look of surprise. This was the strongest language he had heard her use about anyone in nineteen years, let alone the Director.

Joan looked him in the eye and said, 'What will you tell Maggie?'

'I don't know. But as I've been deceiving her for the past twenty-eight years, I'm sure I'll be able to come up with something.'

As Chris Jackson opened the front door, a bell rang to warn the shopkeeper that someone had entered the premises.

There are more than a hundred pawn shops in Bogotá, most of them in the San Victorina district. Jackson hadn't done so much footwork since he had been a junior agent. He even began to wonder if his old friend the Chief of Police had sent him off on a wild goose chase. But he kept going, because he knew that this particular policeman always made sure there would be another envelope stuffed full of notes at some time in the future.

Escobar looked up from behind his evening paper. The old man reckoned that he could always tell, even before a customer had reached the counter, if he was a buyer or a seller. The look in their eyes, the cut of their clothes, even the way they walked towards him. It took only a glance at this particular gentleman to make him feel pleased that he hadn't closed early.

'Good evening, sir,' Escobar said, rising from his stool. He always added 'sir' when he thought it was a buyer. 'How may I assist you?'

'The gun in the window . . .'

'Ah, yes. I see that you are most discerning. It is indeed a collector's item.' Escobar lifted the counter lid and walked across to the window. He removed the case, placed it on the counter, and allowed his customer to have a closer look at its contents.

Jackson only needed a cursory glance at the hand-crafted rifle to know its provenance. He wasn't surprised to find that one of the cartridges had been fired.

'How much are you asking for it?'

'Ten thousand dollars,' replied Escobar, having identified the American accent. 'I cannot let it go for any less. I have already received so many enquiries.'

After three days of traipsing round the hot and humid city, Jackson was in no mood to bargain. But he didn't have that amount of cash on him, and he couldn't just write out a cheque or present a credit card.

'Can I leave a down-payment,' he asked, 'and pick it up first thing in the morning?'

'Certainly, sir,' said Escobar. 'Although for this particular item, I would require a 10 per cent deposit.'

Jackson nodded, and removed a wallet from his inside pocket. He extracted some used notes and passed them across the counter.

The shopkeeper counted the ten hundred-dollar bills slowly, then placed them in the cash register and wrote out a receipt.

Jackson looked down at the open case, smiled, removed the spent cartridge and put it in his pocket.

The old man was puzzled, not by Jackson's action, but because he could have sworn that all twelve bullets had been in place when he had bought the rifle.

'I'd pack up everything and join you tomorrow,' she said, 'if it weren't for my parents.'

'I'm sure they'd understand,' said Stuart.

'Maybe,' said Tara. 'But it wouldn't stop me feeling guilty about all the sacrifices my father's made over the years so I could finish my PhD. Not to mention my mother. She'd probably have a heart attack.'

'But you said you'd find out if your Faculty Advisor would allow you to finish off your doctorate in Sydney.'

'My Faculty Advisor isn't the problem,' said Tara. 'It's the Dean.'

'The Dean?'

'Yes. When my Faculty Advisor discussed the idea with him yesterday, he told her it was out of the question.' There was a long silence before Tara said, 'Are you still there, Stuart?'

'Sure am,' he said, followed by a sigh that would have done credit to a Shakespearean lover.

'It's only another eight months,' Tara reminded him. 'In fact, I can even tell you how many days. And don't forget, you'll be over here for Christmas.'

'I'm looking forward to that,' said Stuart. 'I only hope

76

your parents don't feel I'm imposing on them. After all, they won't have seen you for some time.'

'Don't be silly. They were delighted when I told them you'd be joining us. Mom adores you, as you well know, and you're the first man Dad has ever had a good word for.'

'He's a remarkable man.'

'What do you mean?'

'I suspect you know exactly what I mean.'

'I'd better hang up, or Dad will need a raise just to cover my phone bills. By the way, it's your turn next time.'

Stuart pretended he hadn't noticed how suddenly Tara had changed the subject.

'It always seems strange to me,' she continued, 'that you're still at work while I'm fast asleep.'

'Well, I can think of one way of changing that,' said Stuart.

When he opened the door, the alarm went off. A carriage clock in the outer office struck twice as he swept aside the bead curtain and stepped into the shop. He stared across at the stand in the window. The rifle was no longer in its place.

It took him several minutes to find it, hidden under the counter.

He checked each item, and noted that one cartridge was missing, placed the case under his arm and left as quickly as he had entered. Not that he had any anxiety about being caught: the Chief of Police had assured him that the break-in would not be reported for at least thirty minutes. He glanced at the carriage clock before closing the door behind him. It was twelve minutes past two.

The Chief of Police could hardly be blamed if his old friend didn't have enough cash on him to buy the rifle. And in any case, he did so like being paid twice for the same piece of information. Especially when the currency was dollars.

She poured him a second cup of coffee.

'Maggie, I'm considering resigning from the company and looking for a job that means I don't have to travel so much.' He glanced across the kitchen table and waited to see how his wife would react.

Maggie replaced the coffee pot on the warmer and took a sip from her own cup before she spoke. 'Why now?' she asked simply.

'The Chairman has told me I'm to be taken off kidnap and ransom and replaced by a younger man. It's company policy at my age.'

'But there must be plenty of other jobs in the company for someone with your experience.'

'The Chairman did come up with a suggestion,' said Connor. 'She offered me the chance to head up our field office in Cleveland.'

'Cleveland?' said Maggie in disbelief. She remained silent for some time, then said quietly, 'Why is the Chairman suddenly so keen to see the back of you?'

'Oh, it's not that bad. After all, if I turn the offer down, I'm still eligible for a full retirement package,' said Connor, making no attempt to answer her question. 'In any case, Joan assures me there are several large insurance companies in Washington who would be only too happy to employ someone with my experience.'

'But not the one you're currently working for,' said Maggie, still looking directly at her husband. Connor met her eyes, but couldn't think of a convincing reply. There followed an even longer silence.

'Don't you think the time has come to tell me the whole truth,' said Maggie. 'Or am I simply expected to go on believing every word you say, like a dutiful wife?'

Connor lowered his head and remained silent.

'You've never hidden the fact that "Maryland Insurance" is nothing more than a front for the CIA. And I've never pressed you on the subject. But lately even your well-disguised trips have left a little mud on your shoes.'

'I'm not sure I understand,' Connor said lamely.

'When I picked up your suit from the dry cleaners, they told me they'd found this in the pocket.' Maggie placed a tiny coin on the table. 'I'm told it has no value outside Colombia.'

Connor stared at a ten-peso piece, that would cover a local call in Bogotá.

'Many wives would immediately jump to one conclusion, Connor Fitzgerald,' Maggie continued. 'But don't forget, I've known you for over thirty years, and I'm well aware you're not capable of that particular deception.'

'I promise you, Maggie . . .'

'I know, Connor. I've always accepted that there had to be a good reason why you haven't been completely candid with me over the years.' She leaned across, took her husband's hand and said, 'But if you're now to be dumped on the scrapheap for no apparent reason, don't you feel I have a right to be told exactly what you've been up to for the past twenty-eight years?'

Jackson asked the taxi driver to pull up outside the pawn shop and wait. He would only be a few minutes, he said, and then he wanted to be taken on to the airport.

As soon as he entered the shop, Escobar came scurrying through from the outer office. He looked agitated. When he saw who the customer was, he bowed his head and without a word pressed a key on the cash register and pulled open the drawer. He slowly extracted ten hundred-dollar bills and handed them across the counter.

'I must apologise, sir,' he said, looking up at the tall

American, 'but I fear the rifle was stolen at some time during the night.'

Jackson didn't comment.

'The funny thing about it,' continued Escobar, 'is that whoever stole it dïdn't take any cash.'

Jackson still said nothing. Escobar couldn't help thinking, after his customer had left the shop, that he hadn't seemed all that surprised.

As the taxi headed towards the airport, Jackson placed a hand in his jacket pocket and removed the spent cartridge. He might not be able to prove who had pulled the trigger, but he was now in no doubt who had given the order to assassinate Ricardo Guzman.

CHAPTER NINE

THE HELICOPTER LANDED SOFTLY on a patch of grass by the Reflecting Pool between the Washington and Lincoln Memorials. As the rotor blades slowed, a short flight of steps unfolded. The door of *Nighthawk* swung open and President Herrera appeared, sporting a full-dress uniform that made him look like a minor character in a B-movie. He stood to attention and returned the salute of the waiting Marines, then walked the short distance to his armoured Cadillac limousine. As the motorcade proceeded up Seventeenth Street, every flagstaff was flying the Colombian, American and District of Columbia flags.

Tom Lawrence, Larry Harrington and Andy Lloyd were waiting for him at the south portico of the White House. 'The better-tailored the outfit, the more colourful the sash, the more numerous the medals, the less significant the country,' Lawrence thought as he stepped forward to greet his visitor.

'Antonio, my dear old friend,' said Lawrence as Herrera embraced him, though they had only met once before. When Herrera eventually released his host, Lawrence turned to introduce him to Harrington and Lloyd. Cameras flashed and videotapes whirred as the presidential party made its way into the White House. Several more 'grip and grin' pictures were taken in the long corridor below a full-length portrait of George Washington.

After the requisite three-minute photo-op the President ushered his guest into the Oval Office. While Colombian coffee was being served and yet more photographs taken, they discussed nothing of significance. When they were eventually left alone, the Secretary of State began to guide the conversation on to the current relationship between the two countries. Lawrence was grateful for the briefing he had received from Larry earlier that morning. He felt able to speak authoritatively about extradition agreements, this year's coffee crop, the drug problem, even the new metro being constructed in Bogotá by an American company as part of an overseas aid package.

As the Secretary of State broadened the discussion to take in the repayment of extended dollar loans and the disparity of exports and imports between the two countries, Lawrence found his mind wandering to the problems he would have to face later that day.

The Arms Reduction Bill was getting bogged down in committee, and Andy had already warned him that the votes just weren't stacking up. He would probably need to see several Congressmen individually if he was to have any chance of pushing it through. He was aware that these ritual visits to the White House were usually nothing more than ego-massaging, so that the elected representatives could return to their districts and inform the voters – if they were Democrats – how close their relationship was with the President, or – if they were Republicans – how the President was dependent on their support to get any legislation through. With the mid-term elections less than a year away, Lawrence realised that there would have to be quite a few unscheduled meetings during the coming weeks.

He was brought back to the present with a jolt when Herrera said, '. . . and for that I must thank you particularly, Mr President.' A large smile appeared on the face of Colombia's leader as the three most powerful men in America stared at him in disbelief.

'Would you care to repeat that, Antonio?' said the President, not quite sure that he had heard his visitor correctly.

'As we are in the privacy of the Oval Office, Tom, I just wanted to say how much I appreciated the personal role you played in my election.'

'How long have you been working for Maryland Life, Mr Fitzgerald?' asked the Chairman of the Board. It was his first question in an interview that had already lasted for over an hour.

'Twenty-eight years in May, Mr Thompson,' replied Connor, looking directly at the man who sat at the centre of the large table facing him.

'Your record is most impressive,' said the woman sitting on the Chairman's right. 'And your references are impeccable. I'm bound to ask why you want to leave your present job. And, perhaps more important, why Maryland Life seems willing to let you go.'

Connor had discussed how he should answer this question with Maggie over dinner the previous evening. 'Just tell them the truth,' she had said. 'And don't bother with any guile; you've never been any good at it.' He hadn't expected any different advice.

'My only immediate chance of promotion would have meant moving to Cleveland,' he answered, 'and I felt I couldn't ask my wife to give up her job at Georgetown University. It would be hard for her to find an equivalent post in Ohio.'

The third member of the interviewing board nodded. Maggie had briefed him that one member of the panel had a son who was in his senior year at Georgetown.

'I don't think that we need to detain you any longer,' said the Chairman. 'I'd just like to thank you, Mr Fitzgerald, for coming to see us this afternoon.'

'My pleasure,' said Connor, standing to leave.

To his surprise the Chairman rose from behind the long table and came round to join him. 'Would you and your wife care to have dinner with us one evening next week?' he asked as he escorted Connor to the door.

'We'd be delighted, sir,' Connor replied.

'Ben,' said the Chairman. 'Nobody at Washington Provident calls me sir, and certainly not my senior executives.' He smiled and shook Connor warmly by the hand. 'I'll ask my secretary to phone your office tomorrow morning and fix a date. I look forward to meeting your wife – Maggie, isn't it?'

'Yes, sir,' Connor replied. He paused. 'And I look forward to meeting Mrs Thompson, Ben.'

The White House Chief of Staff picked up the red phone, but didn't immediately recognise the voice.

'I have some information you might find useful. I'm sorry it's taken so long.'

Lloyd quickly grabbed a blank yellow pad and flicked the top off a felt-tip pen. He didn't need to press any buttons – every conversation that took place on that particular phone was automatically recorded.

'I've just returned from ten days in Bogotá, and someone down there was making sure that doors were not only slammed in my face, but locked and bolted.'

'So Dexter must have found out what you were up to,' said Lloyd.

'Within minutes of my speaking to the local Chief of Police, would be my bet.'

'Does that mean she also knows who you're working for?'

'No, I covered myself on that front, which is why I've taken so long getting back to you. And I can promise you that after the wild goose chase I led one of her junior officers on, she'll never be able to fathom who I'm reporting back to. Our Cultural Attaché in Bogotá is now following up every known drug baron, every junior official in the narcotics department, and half the local police force. His report will fill so many pages it will take them a month just to read it, let alone figure out what the hell I was doing down there.'

'Did you come up with anything we could pin on Dexter?' Lloyd asked.

'Nothing she wouldn't be able to explain away with the usual smoke and mirrors. But all the evidence suggests that the CIA was behind the assassination.'

'We already know that,' said Lloyd. 'The President's problem is that, although our informant's credentials are impeccable, he could never appear on the stand, because he's the person who directly benefited from the assassination. Do you have anything that could stand up in court?'

'Only Bogotá's Chief of Police, and his credentials certainly aren't impeccable. If he were to stand up in court, you could never be certain which side he'd end up supporting.'

'Then how can you be so sure the CIA was involved?'

'I saw the rifle that I'm confident was used to kill Guzman. I even got hold of the spent cartridge of the bullet that hit him. What's more, I'm fairly sure I know the man who made the gun. He's the best in the business, and he's contracted to work for a small number of NOCs.'

'NOCs?'

'Non-official cover officers, unattached to any government agency. That way the CIA can deny all knowledge of their activities if anything goes wrong.'

'So the assassin is a serving officer of the CIA,' said Lloyd.

'It looks that way. Unless it turns out to be the one Dexter pensioned off a few days ago.'

'Well there's one person we ought to have on our payroll.'

There was a long silence before Jackson finally said,

'That may be the way you do things at the White House, Mr Lloyd, but this man wouldn't betray a former employer, however large a bribe you offered him. Threatening him won't work either: he wouldn't give you the time of day if you put a gun to his head.'

'How can you be so sure?'

'He served under me in 'Nam, and even the Vietcong couldn't get anything out of him. If you really want to know, he's about the only reason I'm still alive. In any case, Dexter will already have convinced him that her orders came direct from the White House.'

'We could tell him she was lying,' said Lloyd.

'That would only put his own life in danger. No, I have to be able to prove Dexter's involvement without him finding out what we're up to. And that won't be easy.'

'So how do you intend to do it?'

'By going to his retirement party.'

'Are you serious?'

'Yes, because there'll be one person there who loves him even more than she loves her country. And she might just be willing to talk. I'll be in touch.'

The phone went dead.

When Nick Gutenburg, the Deputy Director of the CIA, entered the drawing room of the Fitzgeralds' home, the first person he saw was his predecessor Chris Jackson, deep in conversation with Joan Bennett. Was he telling her who he'd been working for in Bogotá? Gutenburg would have liked to overhear what they were talking about, but first he had to say hello to his host and hostess.

'I'll do another nine months with the company,' Joan was saying. 'By then I'll be eligible for my full pension. After that, I'm hoping to join Connor in his new job.'

'I've only just heard about that,' said Jackson. 'It sounds ideal. From what Maggie was telling me, he won't have to spend quite so much time travelling.'

'That's right, but his appointment isn't official yet,'

said Joan. 'And you know how Connor feels about things being cut and dried. But as the Chairman of Washington Provident has invited him and Maggie to dinner tomorrow night, I think we can assume he's landed the job. Unless, of course, Mr Thompson simply wants to make up a bridge four.'

'Good of you to come, Nick,' said Connor warmly, passing the Deputy Director a glass of Perrier. He didn't need to be reminded that Gutenburg never allowed alcohol to pass his lips.

'Wouldn't have missed it for the world, Connor,' replied Gutenburg.

Turning to his wife, Connor said, 'Maggie, this is Nick Gutenburg, a colleague of mine. He works in . . .'

'Loss adjustment,' Gutenburg interjected quickly. 'We're all going to miss your husband at Maryland Life, Mrs Fitzgerald,' he said.

'Well, I'm sure your paths will cross again,' said Maggie, 'now that Connor's taking up another job in the same line of business.'

'It hasn't been confirmed yet,' said Connor. 'But as soon as it is, Nick, you'll be the first to hear about it.'

Gutenburg's eyes returned to Jackson, and when he moved away from Joan Bennett, Gutenburg slipped across the room to join her.

'I was delighted to hear that you'll be staying with the company, Joan,' were his opening words. 'I thought you might be leaving us to join Connor in his new job.'

'No, I'll be remaining with the firm,' said Joan, uncertain how much the Deputy Director knew.

'I just thought that as Connor's continuing in the same line of business . . .'

You're on a fishing trip, thought Joan. 'I wouldn't know,' she said firmly.

'Who's Chris Jackson talking to?' Gutenburg asked.

Joan looked across the room. She would like to have been able to say she had no idea, but she knew she wouldn't get away with it. 'That's Father Graham, the Fitzgeralds' local parish priest from Chicago, and Tara, Connor's daughter.'

'And what does she do?' asked Gutenburg.

'She's completing a PhD at Stanford.'

Gutenburg realised that he was wasting his time trying to get any real information out of Connor's secretary. After all, she had worked for Fitzgerald for nearly twenty years, so there wasn't much doubt where her loyalties lay – though there was nothing in her file to suggest that their relationship was anything but professional. And, looking at Miss Bennett, he suspected she might be the last forty-five-year-old virgin left in Washington. When Connor's daughter went over to the drinks table to refill her glass, Gutenburg left Joan without another word.

'My name's Nick Gutenburg,' he told her, thrusting out his hand. 'I'm a colleague of your father's.'

'I'm Tara,' she said. 'Do you work at the downtown office?'

'No, I'm based in the suburbs,' said Gutenburg. 'Are you still on the West Coast doing graduate work?'

'That's right,' Tara replied, looking a little surprised. 'And what about you? Which branch of the company do you work for?'

'Loss adjustment. It's rather boring compared with what your father does, but someone has to stay at home and do the paperwork,' he said, letting out a little laugh. 'By the way, I was delighted to hear about your dad's new appointment.'

'Yes, Mom was pleased that such a prestigious firm snapped him up so quickly. Although it's still not official.'

'Will he be working out of Washington?' Gutenburg asked, sipping his Perrier.

'Yes, the company's based just a couple of blocks from his old office . . .' Tara stopped talking when she heard a sharp noise. She turned to see Chris Jackson banging the table to bring the guests to order.

'Excuse me,' she whispered. 'That's my cue to resume my official duties for the evening.' She walked quickly away, and Gutenburg turned to listen to his predecessor at Langley.

'Ladies and gentlemen,' Chris began. He waited until everyone was silent before he continued. 'It's my privilege to propose a toast to two of my oldest friends, Connor and Maggie. Over the years, Connor has consistently proved to be the one man most likely to get me into a scrape.'

The guests laughed. One called out, 'Only too true,' and another added, 'I know the problem.'

'But once you're in a scrape, I don't know anyone better to get you out of it.' This was greeted by warm applause. 'We first met . . .'

Gutenburg felt his pager buzz, and quickly pulled it off his belt. 'TROY ASAP', it read. He flicked it off, and slipped out of the room into the hall. He picked up the nearest phone as if he was in his own home and dialled a number that wasn't in any directory. It hadn't even rung before a voice said, 'The Director.'

'I got your message, but I'm on a non-secure line.' He didn't need to announce who he was.

'What I have to tell you, everyone in the world will know about in a few hours.'

Gutenburg didn't speak. It wasted time.

'Yeltsin died of a heart attack seventeen minutes ago,' said Helen Dexter. 'Report to my office immediately, and cancel everything you're doing for the next forty-eight hours.' The line went dead. No call from a non-secure line to Dexter's office ever lasted more than forty-five seconds. She kept a stop-watch on her desk.

Gutenburg replaced the phone and slipped out of the front door without bothering to say goodbye to his hostess. He was being driven down the Parkway on his way back to Langley by the time Chris raised his glass and said, 'To Connor and Maggie, and whatever the future holds for them.'

All the guests raised their glasses. 'To Connor and Maggie.'

CHAPTER TEN

'I'LL TELL YOU EXACTLY where my information came from,' said Tom Lawrence. 'From the President of Colombia himself. He thanked me personally for "the role I played in his election".'

'That's hardly proof,' Helen Dexter said, showing no sign of emotion.

'Are you doubting my word?' The President made no attempt to hide his anger.

'Certainly not, Mr President,' said Dexter calmly. 'But if you're accusing the Agency of carrying out covert operations without your knowledge, I hope it's not going to be simply on the word of a South American politician.'

The President leaned forward. 'I suggest that you listen carefully to a recording of a conversation that took place in this office quite recently,' he said. 'Because what you're about to hear struck me as having a ring of truth about it – something I suspect you haven't had much exposure to in recent years.'

The Director remained impassive, although Nick Gutenburg, seated on her right, shifted uneasily in his seat. The President nodded in the direction of Andy Lloyd, who reached over and pressed a button on a tape recorder that had been placed on the corner of the President's desk.

'*Would you care to go into greater detail?*'

'*Of course, although I'm sure I can't tell you anything you don't already know. My only real rival, Ricardo Guzman, was conveniently removed from the contest just two weeks before the election.*'

'Surely you're not suggesting . . .' It was Lawrence's voice.

'*Well, if it wasn't your people, it certainly wasn't mine,*' Herrera cut in before the President could finish his sentence.

There followed such a long silence that Gutenburg began to wonder if the conversation had come to an end, but as Lawrence and Lloyd didn't move, he assumed there was more to follow.

'*Do you have any actual evidence to link the assassination with the CIA?*' asked Lloyd eventually.

'*The bullet that killed him was traced to a rifle that had been sold to a pawn shop before the assassin fled the country. The rifle was later removed from the shop by one of your operatives and shipped back to America via the diplomatic pouch.*'

'*How can you be so sure of that?*'

'*My Chief of Police is obviously a lot more forthcoming with me than the CIA are with you.*'

Andy Lloyd flicked off the tape recorder. Helen Dexter looked up to find the President's eyes boring into hers.

'Well?' Lawrence asked. 'What simple explanation do you have this time?'

'From that conversation there is absolutely no proof of any CIA involvement in Guzman's assassination,' she said evenly. 'All it suggests to me is that Herrera is trying to shield the person who carried out his orders.'

'I assume you're referring to the "lone assassin" who has since conveniently disappeared somewhere in South Africa,' said the President sarcastically.

'The moment he surfaces, Mr President, we'll find him, and then I'll be able to supply the proof you've asked for.'

'An innocent man shot in a back street in Johannesburg will not be enough proof for me,' said Lawrence.

'Nor me,' said Dexter. 'When I produce the man who was responsible for the assassination, there won't be any doubt about who he was working for.' There was a slight edge to her voice.

'If you fail to do so,' said the President, 'I wouldn't be surprised if this tape' – he tapped the recorder – 'ended up in the hands of a certain reporter at the *Washington Post* who isn't exactly known for his love of the CIA. We can leave it to him to decide if Herrera is covering himself, or simply telling the truth. Either way, you're going to have to answer an awful lot of awkward questions.'

'If that were ever to happen, you might have to answer one or two yourself, Mr President,' said Dexter, not flinching.

Lawrence rose angrily from his chair and glared down at her. 'Let me make it clear that I still require positive proof of the existence of your missing South African. And if you fail to produce it within twenty-eight days, I'll expect both of your resignations on my desk. Now get out of my office.'

The Director and her Deputy rose to leave the room without another word. Neither of them spoke until they were seated in the back of Dexter's car. Once they had been driven out of the grounds of the White House, she touched a button on her armrest and a smoked-glass window slid up so that the driver – a senior operative – was unable to hear the conversation taking place behind him.

'Have you found out which company it was that interviewed Fitzgerald?'

'Yes,' replied Gutenburg.

'Then you're going to have to give their Chairman a call.'

'My name is Nick Gutenburg. I'm the Deputy Director of the CIA. You may wish to call me back. The switchboard number at the Agency is 703 482 1100. If you give the operator your name, she will put you straight through to my office.' He put the phone down.

Gutenburg had found over the years that not only were such calls invariably returned, usually in under a minute, but that the little subterfuge nearly always gave him the upper hand.

He sat at his desk, waiting. Two minutes passed, but he wasn't concerned. He knew that this particular gentleman would want to verify the number. Once he had confirmed that it was the CIA's switchboard, Gutenburg would be in an even stronger position.

When the phone eventually rang three minutes later, Gutenburg let it continue for some time before answering it. 'Good morning, Mr Thompson,' he said, not waiting to hear who it was. 'I'm grateful to you for calling back so promptly.'

'My pleasure, Mr Gutenburg,' said the Chairman of Washington Provident.

'I fear it's a delicate matter that I need to speak to you about, Mr Thompson. I wouldn't be making such a call unless I felt it was in your best interests.'

'I appreciate that,' said Thompson. 'How can I help?'

'You have recently been interviewing candidates to head up your kidnap and ransom department. A post that demands the highest standards of integrity.'

'Of course,' said Thompson. 'But I think we've found the ideal person for the position.'

'I have no idea who you've selected for the job, but I should let you know that we are currently investigating one of the applicants, and should the case end up in court, it might not reflect too well on your firm. However, Mr Thompson, if you are confident that you have found the right man, the CIA certainly has no desire to stand in his way.'

'Now wait a moment, Mr Gutenburg. If you're aware of something I should know about, I'll be only too happy to listen.'

Gutenburg paused before saying, 'May I ask, in the strictest confidence, the name of the candidate to whom you are thinking of offering this position?'

'You most certainly can, because I'm in no doubt about his reputation, background or propriety. We are about to sign a contract with a Mr Connor Fitzgerald.' There was a long silence before Thompson said, 'Are you still there, Mr Gutenburg?'

'I am, Mr Thompson. I wonder if you could find the time to visit me at Langley? I think I should brief you more fully on the fraud investigation we are presently undertaking. You might also want to examine some confidential papers that have come into our possession.'

This time it was Thompson's turn to remain silent. 'I'm very sorry to hear that. I don't think a visit will be necessary,' said the Chairman quietly. 'He seemed like such a good man.'

'I'm equally distressed to have had to make this call in the first place, Mr Thompson. But you would have been more angry with me if I hadn't, and the whole sorry affair had ended up on the front page of the *Washington Post.*'

'I can't disagree with that,' said Thompson.

'May I add,' said the Deputy Director, 'though of course it's not pertinent to the case we're investigating, that I've been a policyholder with Washington Provident since the day I began working for the CIA.'

'I'm glad to hear that, Mr Gutenburg. I'd just like to say how much I appreciate the thoroughness with which you people carry out your job.'

'I only hope I've been of some service, Mr Thompson. Goodbye, sir.'

Gutenburg replaced the receiver, and immediately pressed '1' on the phone nearest to him.

'Yes?' said a voice.

'I don't think Washington Provident will be offering Fitzgerald a job after all.'

'Good. Why don't we leave it for three days, then *you* can tell him about his new assignment.'

'Why wait three days?'

'You've obviously never read Freud's paper on maximum vulnerability.'

We are sorry to inform you . . .

Connor was reading the letter for the third time when the phone on his desk rang. He felt numb with disbelief. What could possibly have gone wrong? The dinner at the Thompsons' home couldn't have been more agreeable. When he and Maggie left a few minutes before midnight, Ben had suggested a round of golf at Burning Tree the following weekend, and Elizabeth Thompson had asked Maggie to drop by for coffee while the men were out chasing little white balls. The next day his lawyer had rung to say that the contract Washington Provident had sent for his approval needed no more than a few minor adjustments.

Connor picked up the phone.

'Yes, Joan.'

'I have the Deputy Director on the line.'

'Put him through,' he said wearily.

'Connor?' said a voice he had never trusted. 'Something important has come up, and the Director's asked me to brief you immediately.'

'Of course,' said Connor, not really taking in Gutenburg's words.

'Shall we make it three o'clock, the usual place?'

'Of course,' Connor repeated. He was still holding the phone long after he had heard the click. He read the letter for a fourth time, and decided not to tell Maggie about it until he had been shortlisted for another job.

Connor was the first to arrive in Lafayette Square. He sat down on a bench facing the White House. A few minutes later Nick Gutenburg took a seat on the other end of the bench. Connor took care not to even glance in his direction.

'The President himself requested that you should take on this assignment,' murmured Gutenburg, looking fixedly in the direction of the White House. 'He wanted our best man.'

'But I'm due to leave the Company in ten days' time,' said Connor.

'Yes, the Director told him. But the President insisted that we do everything in our power to convince you to stay until this assignment has been completed.'

Connor remained silent.

'Connor, the outcome of the elections in Russia could affect the future of the free world. If that lunatic Zerimski is elected, it would mean a return to the Cold War overnight. The President could forget his Arms Reduction Bill, and Congress would be demanding an increase in the defence budget that could bankrupt us.'

'But Zerimski's still way behind in the polls,' said Connor. 'Isn't Chernopov expected to win comfortably?'

'That's how it may look right now,' said Gutenburg. 'But there are still three weeks to go, and the President' – he emphasised the word while continuing to stare at the White House – 'feels that with an electorate that volatile, anything could happen. He'd be a lot happier knowing you were out there, just in case your particular expertise is needed.'

Connor didn't respond.

'If it's your new job you're worrying about,' continued Gutenburg, 'I'd be happy to have a word with the Chairman of the company you're joining and explain to him that it's only a short-term assignment.'

'That won't be necessary,' said Connor. 'But I'll need a little time to think about it.'

'Of course,' said Gutenburg. 'When you've made up your mind, please call the Director and let her know your decision.' He rose and walked away in the direction of Farragut Square.

Three minutes later, Connor strolled off in the opposite direction.

Andy Lloyd picked up the red phone. This time he recognised the voice immediately.

'I'm almost certain I know who carried out the assignment in Bogotá,' said Jackson.

'Was he working for the CIA?' Lloyd asked.

'Yes, he was.'

'Do you have enough proof to convince the Congressional Select Committees on Intelligence?'

'No, I don't. Almost all the evidence I have would be thrown out as circumstantial. But when it's all put together, there are far too many coincidences for my liking.'

'For example?'

'The agent who I suspect pulled the trigger was sacked shortly after the President saw Dexter in the Oval Office and demanded to know who was responsible for Guzman's assassination.'

'Not even admissible as evidence.'

'Perhaps not. But the same agent was about to take up a new appointment with Washington Provident as head of their kidnap and ransom department when suddenly, without any explanation, the job offer was withdrawn.'

'A second coincidence.'

'There's a third. Three days later, Gutenburg met the agent in question on a park bench in Lafayette Square.'

'Why would they want to take him back?'

'To carry out a one-off assignment.'

'Do we have any idea what that assignment is?'

'No. But don't be surprised if it takes him a long way from Washington.'

'Have you any way of finding out where?'

'Not at the moment. Even his wife doesn't know.'

'OK, let's look at it from their point of view,' said Lloyd. 'What do you think Dexter will be doing right now to make sure her ass is covered?'

'Before I could begin to answer that I'd need to know the outcome of her last meeting with the President,' said Jackson.

'He gave her and Gutenburg twenty-eight days to prove that the Agency wasn't involved in the assassination of Guzman, and to provide cast-iron proof of who *did* kill him. He also left them in no doubt that if they fail, he'll demand their resignations and release all the evidence in his possession to the *Washington Post*.'

There was a long silence before Jackson said, 'That means the agent in question has less than a month to live.'

'She'd never eliminate one of her own people,' said Lloyd in disbelief.

'Don't forget that he's an NOC. The section of the CIA he works for doesn't even exist officially, Mr Lloyd.'

'This guy's a good friend of yours, isn't he?' said Lloyd.

'Yes,' replied Jackson quietly.

'Then you'd better make sure he stays alive.'

'Good afternoon, Director. It's Connor Fitzgerald.'

'Good afternoon, Connor. How nice to hear from you,' Dexter said in a warmer tone than the one she had adopted at their previous meeting.

'The Deputy Director asked me to call you once I'd come to a decision on the matter he and I discussed on Monday.'

'Yes,' said Dexter, reverting to her normal clipped style.

'I'm willing to take the assignment.'

'I'm glad to hear that.'

'On one condition.'

'And what's that?'

'I will require proof that the operation has been sanctioned by the President.'

There was a long silence before Dexter said, 'I'll inform the President of your request.'

'So how does it work?' asked the Director. She couldn't remember when she had last visited the OTS lab at Langley.

'It's quite simple really,' said Professor Ziegler, the CIA's Director of Technical Services. He turned to a bank of computers and pressed some keys. Tom Lawrence's face appeared on the screen.

After Dexter and Nick Gutenburg had listened to the words of the President for a few moments, she said, 'What's so remarkable about that? We've all heard Lawrence making a speech before.'

'Maybe, but you've never heard him make that particular speech,' said Ziegler.

'What do you mean?' asked Gutenburg.

An almost childlike smile of satisfaction spread across the professor's face. 'I have stored in my computer – codename "Tommy" – over a thousand speeches, television and radio interviews and telephone conversations the President has given or taken part in during the past two years. Every word or phrase he has used in that time is stored in this memory bank. That means I can make him deliver a speech on any subject you choose. I can even decide what his position is on any given issue.'

Dexter began to consider the possibilities. 'If Tommy were to be asked a question, could he give a convincing reply?' she asked.

'Not spontaneously,' admitted Ziegler. 'But if you had some idea of the questions he might be expected to answer, I believe I could fool Lawrence's own mother.'

'So all we have to do,' said Gutenburg, 'is anticipate what the other party is likely to say.'

'Which may not be as difficult as you might think,'

said Ziegler. 'After all, if *you* were to receive a call from the President, you'd be unlikely to ask him about the strength of the dollar, or what he had for breakfast, would you? In most cases you'd know the reason he was calling. I have no idea why you might need Tommy, but if you were to prepare opening and closing remarks, as well as – say – the fifty questions or statements he was most likely to have to respond to, I could almost guarantee he could conduct a plausible conversation.'

'I'm sure we can do that,' said Gutenburg.

The Director nodded her agreement, then asked Ziegler: 'Why did we develop this piece of equipment in the first place?'

'It was set up in case the President died while America was at war, and we needed the enemy to believe he was still alive. But Tommy has many other uses, Director. For example . . .'

'I'm sure he does,' interrupted Dexter.

Ziegler looked disappointed, aware that the Director was coming to the end of her attention span.

'How long would it take you to prepare a specific programme?' Gutenburg asked.

'How long will it take you to work out what the President needs to say?' replied Ziegler, the childlike smile returning to his face.

She kept her finger on the buzzer until Connor finally picked up the phone on his desk.

'What's the problem, Joan? I'm not going deaf.'

'I've got Ruth Preston, the President's personal secretary, on the line.'

The next voice Connor heard was a woman's. 'Is that Connor Fitzgerald?'

'Speaking,' Connor replied. He could feel the sweat in the palm of the hand holding the phone. That never happened when he was waiting to pull the trigger.

'I have the President on the line for you.'

He heard a click. 'Good afternoon,' a familiar voice said.

'Good afternoon, Mr President.'

'I think you know why I'm calling.'

'Yes, sir, I do.'

Professor Ziegler pressed 'Opening Statement'. The Director and Deputy Director held their breath.

'I felt I had to call and let you know just how important I consider this assignment to be.' *Pause.* 'Because I have no doubt that you're the right person to carry it out.' *Pause.* 'So I hope you will agree to take on the responsibility.'

Ziegler pressed the 'Wait' button.

'I appreciate your confidence in me, Mr President,' said Connor, 'and I'm grateful to you for taking the time to phone personally . . .'

'*Number 11*,' said Ziegler, who knew all the replies by heart.

'I felt it was the least I could do in the circumstances.' *Pause.*

'Thank you, Mr President. Although Mr Gutenburg assured me of your involvement, and the Director herself called later that afternoon to confirm it, as you know, I still felt unable to take on the assignment unless I was certain that the order had come directly from you.'

'*Number 7.*'

'I can quite understand your anxiety.' *Pause.*

'*Number 19.*

'Perhaps when this is all over you and your wife would come and visit me at the White House – that is, if the Director will allow it.' *Pause.*

'*Number 3*,' said Ziegler sharply. There was a burst of loud laughter.

Connor moved the phone slightly away from his ear. 'We would be honoured, sir,' he said once the laughter had died away.

'*Closing statement*,' said Ziegler.

'Good. I'll look forward to seeing you as soon as you return.' *Pause.* 'I often think it's sad that America doesn't always appreciate its unsung heroes.' *Pause.* 'It was good talking to you. Goodbye.'

'Goodbye, Mr President.'

Connor was still holding the phone when Joan came into the room. 'So that's another myth exploded,' she said as Connor replaced the receiver. He looked up at her and raised an enquiring eyebrow.

'That the President always calls everyone by their first name.'

CHAPTER ELEVEN

GUTENBURG HANDED HIM a large brown envelope containing four passports, three airline tickets and a bundle of notes in different currencies.

'Don't I have to sign for all this?' asked Connor.

'No. As it's all been a bit rushed, we'll deal with the paperwork when you get back. Once you arrive in Moscow, you're to go to Zerimski's campaign headquarters and show them your credentials as a freelance reporter from South Africa. They'll give you a press pack detailing his schedule for the run-up to the election.'

'Do I have a contact in Moscow?'

'Yes. Ashley Mitchell.' Gutenburg hesitated. 'It's his first big assignment, and he's been briefed strictly on a need-to-know basis. He's also been instructed only to get in touch with you if it's a green light, in which case he'll supply you with the weapon.'

'Make and model?'

'The usual custom-made Remington 700,' said Gutenburg. 'But if Chernopov stays ahead in the polls, I don't expect your services will be needed, in which case you're to return to Washington the day after the election. I'm afraid this mission may turn out to be a bit of a non-event.'

'Let's hope so,' said Connor, and left the Deputy Director without shaking hands.

'I'm afraid my arm was twisted so far up my back that I couldn't say no,' said Connor, putting another blue shirt in his suitcase.

'You could have refused,' said Maggie. 'Starting a new job on the first of the month would have been a convincing enough excuse.' She paused. 'What was Ben Thompson's reaction?'

'He's been very understanding,' said Connor. 'He has no problem with me starting a month later. It seems December is always a quiet time.' Connor pressed his clothes down, wondering how he would fit his spongebag in. He was already wishing he had allowed Maggie to pack for him, but hadn't wanted her to come across several items that didn't tie in with his story. He sat down heavily on the suitcase lid. Maggie snapped the lock shut, and they fell on the bed, laughing. He took her in his arms and held on to her a little too long.

'Is everything all right, Connor?' she asked quietly.

'Everything's just fine, honey,' he said, releasing her.

He picked up the case and carried it downstairs. 'I'm sorry I won't be here for Thanksgiving. Don't forget to tell Tara I'm looking forward to seeing her at Christmas,' he said as Maggie followed him out of the front door. He stopped beside a car she had never seen before.

'And Stuart too,' she reminded him.

'Yes, of course,' he said as he placed the suitcase in the boot. 'It will be good to see him again.' Once more he took his wife in his arms. This time he made sure he didn't hold on too long.

'Heavens, what are we going to give Tara for Christmas?' Maggie suddenly said. 'I haven't even thought about it.'

'If you'd seen her latest phone bill, you wouldn't have to think about it,' said Connor, climbing behind the wheel.

'I don't remember this car,' said Maggie.

'It's one of the company's,' he explained as he turned on the ignition. 'By the way, could you let Father Graham know he'll have to find someone else to make up his bridge four on Saturday? Goodbye, honey.'

Without another word he put the car into drive and eased it out onto the road. He hated saying goodbye to Maggie, and always tried to keep their farewells as short as possible. He checked in the rear-view mirror. She was standing at the end of the drive, waving, as he turned the corner onto Cambridge Place and headed for the airport.

When he reached the end of the Dulles access road, he didn't need to look for the arrow pointing to the long-term parking lot. He drove down the ramp and took a ticket from the machine, then parked in a far corner. He locked the car and headed towards the airport entrance, then took the escalator up one flight to the United Airlines check-in desk.

'Thank you, Mr Perry,' said the uniformed assistant who checked his ticket. 'Flight 918 is almost ready for boarding. Please make your way to Gate C7.'

After clearing security, Connor boarded a mobile lounge to the mid-field terminal. In the waiting area he sat in the far corner, and when the passengers were asked to board he took his usual window seat near the back. Twenty minutes later he was listening to the captain explaining that although they would not be taking off on time, they would somehow miraculously still be arriving on schedule.

Back in the terminal, a young man in a dark blue suit dialled a number on his cellphone.

'Yes?' said a voice.

'Agent Sullivan calling from "Coach House". The bird has flown.'

'Good. Report in again as soon as you've carried out the rest of your assignment.' The line went dead.

The young man switched off his phone and took the

escalator to the ground floor. He walked over to a car in the far corner of the long-term carpark, unlocked it, drove out of the lot, paid the parking ticket, and headed east.

Thirty minutes later he returned the keys to the car pool and signed the daily log. It showed that the vehicle had been checked out in his name and returned in his name.

'Can you be absolutely sure there'll be no trace of his ever having existed?' asked the Director.

'No trace whatsoever,' said Gutenburg. 'Don't forget that as an NOC he was never on the Company's books in the first place.'

'But what about his wife?'

'Why should she suspect anything? His monthly pay-cheque has been paid into their joint account. She won't give it a second thought. As far as she's concerned, he's resigned from his present position and will be joining Washington Provident on the first of January.'

'There's still his former secretary.'

'I've had her transferred to Langley so I can keep an eye on her.'

'What division?'

'Middle East.'

'Why Middle East?'

'Because she'll have to be at the office during their working hours, from six in the evening until three in the morning. And for the next eight months I'm going to work her so hard that she'll be too tired to think about anything other than what she's going to do once she retires.'

'Good. Where's Fitzgerald at this moment?'

Gutenburg checked his watch. 'Halfway across the Atlantic. He'll be landing at London Heathrow in about four hours.'

'And the car?'

'Has already been returned to the pool. It's currently being resprayed and given a new set of plates.'

'What about his office on M Street?'

'It will be stripped overnight, and that floor will be placed in the hands of real estate agents on Monday.'

'You seem to have thought of everything except what happens when he returns to Washington,' said the Director.

'He isn't going to return to Washington,' replied Gutenburg.

Connor joined the long queue waiting to go through passport control. When he eventually reached the front, an official checked his passport and said, 'I hope you have an enjoyable fortnight in Britain, Mr Perry.'

In the little box asking 'How long do you intend to stay in the United Kingdom?' Mr Perry had written 'Fourteen days.' But then, it would be Mr Lilystrand who returned to the airport the following morning.

Two men watched him as he left Terminal Three and boarded the bus for Victoria Coach Station. Forty-two minutes later, the same two men saw him join the queue at a taxi rank. Separately they followed the black cab to the Kensington Park Hotel, where one of them had already left a package for him in reception.

'Any messages for me?' Connor asked as he signed the registration form.

'Yes, Mr Lilystrand,' said the concierge. 'A gentleman left this for you this morning.' He handed Connor an enormous brown envelope. 'Your room number is 211. The porter will bring up your luggage.'

'I can manage it myself, thank you,' he said.

As soon as Connor entered the room, he tore open the envelope. Inside was a ticket to Geneva in the name of Theodore Lilystrand, and a hundred Swiss francs. He slipped off his jacket and lay down on the bed, but despite being exhausted he was unable to sleep. He turned on the television and flicked through endless programmes – what Tara called channel surfing – but it didn't help.

He had always disliked the waiting game. That was the only time doubts ever set in. He kept reminding himself that this would be his last mission. He began to think about Christmas with Maggie and Tara – and, yes, Stuart. He disliked not being allowed to carry photographs with him, always having to visualise them in his mind. Most of all, he hated not being able to just pick up a phone and talk to either of them whenever he felt like it.

Connor didn't stir from his bed until it was dark. Then he emerged from his overnight prison cell to go in search of a meal. He bought an *Evening Standard* from a corner news-vendor and strolled into a small Italian restaurant on High Street, Kensington that was only half full.

The waiter showed him to a quiet table in the corner. The light was barely strong enough for him to read the paper. He ordered a Diet Coke with lots of ice. The British would never understand the meaning of 'lots of ice', and he was not surprised when the waiter returned a few minutes later bearing a long glass with three small ice cubes floating in it, and a tiny piece of lemon.

He ordered cannelloni and a side salad. Funny how he picked Maggie's favourite dishes whenever he was abroad. Anything to remind him of her.

'The one thing you have to do before you start your new job is find a decent tailor,' Tara had said to him when they last spoke. 'And I want to come with you so I can pick your shirts and ties.'

'Your new job.' Once again he thought about that letter. *I am sorry to have to inform you . . .* However many times he went over it, he still couldn't think of a reason for Thompson to have changed his mind. It simply didn't add up.

He began to read the front page of the paper: nine candidates were contesting an election to be the first

Mayor of London. That's odd, thought Connor: haven't they always had a Mayor – what about Dick Whittington? He looked at the photographs of the contenders and their names, but they meant nothing to him. One of them would be running England's capital in a couple of weeks' time. He wondered where he would be then.

He paid the bill in cash and left a tip that would not give the waiter any reason to remember him. When he was back in his hotel room he switched on the television and watched a few minutes of a comedy that didn't make him laugh. After trying a couple of movies, he slept intermittently. But he was comforted by the thought that at least he was better off than the two men stationed outside on the pavement, who wouldn't sleep at all. He had spotted them within moments of landing at Heathrow.

He checked his watch. A few minutes after midnight – a few minutes after seven in Washington. He wondered what Maggie would be doing that evening.

'And how's Stuart?' Maggie asked.

'Still hanging in there,' Tara replied. 'He arrives in LA in fifteen days. I can't wait.'

'Will you both be flying straight here?'

'No, Mom,' said Tara, trying not to sound exasperated. 'As I've told you several times already, we're going to rent a car and drive up the West Coast. Stuart's never been to America, and he wants to see LA and San Francisco. Remember?'

'Do drive carefully, won't you?'

'Mother, I've been driving for nine years without even a ticket, which is more than can be said for you or Dad. Now, will you stop worrying and tell me what you're doing this evening?'

'I'm going to hear Placido Domingo in *La Bohème*. I decided to wait until your father was out of town before I went, because I know he'd fall asleep before the first act was over.'

'Are you going on your own?'

'Yes.'

'Well, be careful, Mother, and make sure you don't sit in the first six rows.'

'Why not?' asked Maggie innocently.

'Because some rich, handsome man might leap out of one of the boxes and ravish you.'

Maggie laughed. 'I consider myself properly chastised.'

'Why don't you ask Joan to go with you? Then you can both talk about Dad all night.'

'I called her at the office, but the number seems to be out of order. I'll try her at home later.'

'Bye, Mom, talk to you tomorrow,' said Tara. She knew her mother would call every day while Connor was away.

Whenever Connor travelled abroad or took an evening off to partner Father Graham at the bridge club, Maggie would catch up with some of her university activities. Anything from GULP, the Georgetown University Litter Patrol, of which she was a founder member, to the Alive Women's Poetry Society and the Irish dance class, where she gave lessons. The sight of the young students dancing, their backs straight, their feet tapping away, brought back memories of Declan O'Casey. He was now a distinguished professor, with a chair at the University of Chicago. He had never married, and still sent her a card every Christmas, and an unsigned one on Valentine's Day. The old typewriter with the crooked 'e' always gave away his identity.

She picked up the phone again and dialled Joan's home number, but there was no reply. She fixed herself a light salad, which she ate alone in the kitchen. After she had put the plate in the dishwasher she rang Joan again. There was still no answer, so she set off for the Kennedy Center. A single ticket was always easy to come by, however celebrated the guest tenor happened to be.

Maggie was transfixed by the first act of *La Bohème*, and only wished she had someone with whom to share the experience. When the curtain came down, she joined the throng heading for the foyer. As she approached the crowded bar, Maggie thought she caught a glimpse of Elizabeth Thompson. She remembered that she had invited her for coffee, but had never followed it up. She had been surprised, because the offer had sounded so genuine at the time.

When Ben Thompson turned and caught her eye, Maggie smiled and walked over to join them.

'How nice to see you, Ben,' she said.

'And you too, Mrs Fitzgerald,' he replied, but not in the warm voice she remembered from dinner a fortnight before. And why hadn't he called her Maggie?

Undaunted, she ploughed on. 'Domingo is magnificent, don't you think?'

'Yes, and we were extremely lucky to lure Leonard Slatkin from St Louis,' said Ben Thompson. Maggie was surprised that he didn't offer to buy her a drink, and when she finally ordered an orange juice, she was even more puzzled when he made no attempt to pay for it.

'Connor is so looking forward to joining you all at Washington Provident,' she said, taking a sip of her juice. Elizabeth Thompson appeared surprised, but didn't comment.

'He's particularly grateful to you, Ben, for allowing him to put it off for a month so he could complete that unfinished contract for his old firm.'

Elizabeth was just about to say something when the three-minute bell sounded.

'Well, we'd better get back to our seats,' said Ben Thompson, although his wife had only half-finished her drink. 'Nice to have seen you again, Mrs Fitzgerald.' He took his wife firmly by the arm and guided her towards the auditorium. 'I hope you enjoy the second act.'

Maggie didn't enjoy the second act. She couldn't concentrate, as the conversation that had just taken place in the foyer kept running through her mind. But however many times she went over it, she couldn't reconcile his attitude with what had taken place at the Thompsons' only a fortnight before. If she had known how to get in touch with Connor, she would have broken the rule of a lifetime and phoned him. So she did the next best thing. The moment she arrived home, she called Joan Bennett again.

The phone rang and rang.

The following morning Connor rose early. He settled his bill in cash, hailed a taxi and was on his way to Heathrow before the duty porter even realised he'd left. At seven forty he boarded Swissair Flight 839 to Geneva. The flight took just under two hours, and he readjusted his watch to ten thirty as the wheels of the aircraft touched the ground.

During the stopover he took advantage of Swissair's offer to take a shower. He entered the 'exclusive facility' – the description in their in-flight magazine – as Theodore Lilystrand, an investment banker from Stockholm, and emerged forty minutes later as Piet de Villiers, a reporter with the *Johannesburg Mercury*.

Even though he still had over an hour to kill, Connor did not browse in any of the duty-free shops, buying only a croissant and a cup of coffee from one of the most expensive restaurants in the world.

Eventually he walked across to Gate 23. There wasn't a long queue for the Aeroflot flight to St Petersburg. When the passengers were called a few minutes later, he made his way to the back of the aircraft. He began to think about what needed to be done the following morning, once the train had pulled in to Moscow's Raveltay station. He went over the Deputy Director's final briefing again, wondering why Gutenburg had repeated the words, 'Don't get caught. But if you are, deny absolutely that you have anything to do with the CIA. Don't worry – the Company will always take care of you.'

Only raw recruits were ever reminded of the Eleventh Commandment.

'The flight to St Petersburg has just taken off, and our package is on board.'

'Good,' said Gutenburg. 'Anything else to report?'

'I don't think so,' replied the young CIA agent. He hesitated. 'Except . . .'

'Except what? Come on, spit it out.'

'It's just that I thought I recognised someone else who boarded the plane.'

'Who was it?' snapped Gutenburg.

'I can't remember his name, and I'm not that certain it was him. I couldn't risk taking my eyes off Fitzgerald for more than a few seconds.'

'If you remember who it was, call me immediately.'

'Yes, sir.' The young man switched off his phone and made his way to Gate 9. In a few hours he would be back behind his desk in Berne, resuming his role as Cultural Attaché at the American Embassy.

'Good morning. This is Helen Dexter.'

'Good morning, Director,' replied the White House Chief of Staff stiffly.

'I thought the President would want to know immediately that the man he asked us to track down in South Africa is on the move again.'

'I'm not sure I follow you,' said Lloyd.

'The head of our Johannesburg office has just informed me that Guzman's killer boarded a South African Airways flight to London two days ago. He was carrying a passport in the name of Martin Perry. He only stayed in London overnight. The following morning he took a Swissair flight to Geneva, using a Swedish passport in the name of Theodore Lilystrand.'

Lloyd didn't interrupt her this time. After all, he could play the tape back if the President wanted to hear exactly what she had said.

'At Geneva he boarded an Aeroflot flight to St Petersburg. This time he was carrying a South African passport in the name of Piet de Villiers. From St Petersburg, he took the overnight train to Moscow.'

'Moscow? Why Moscow?' asked Lloyd.

'If I recall correctly,' said Dexter, 'an election is about to take place in Russia.'

When the plane landed in St Petersburg, Connor's watch claimed that it was five fifty. He yawned, stretched and waited for the aircraft to taxi to a halt before altering the hands to local time. He looked out of the window at an airport that was in semi-darkness because half the lightbulbs were missing. Light snow was falling, but didn't settle. The hundred weary passengers had to wait another twenty minutes before a bus arrived to transport them to the terminal. Some things simply didn't change, whether the KGB or organised criminals were in charge. Americans had come to refer to them as the Mafya, to avoid confusion with the Italian version.

Connor was the last to leave the aircraft, and the last to get off the bus.

A man who had travelled first class on the same flight rushed to the front of the queue to be sure of being the first through immigration and customs. He was grateful that Connor followed the textbook routine. Once the man had stepped off the bus, he never looked back. He knew Connor's eyes would always be moving.

When Connor walked out of the airport onto the pot-holed road thirty minutes later, he hailed the first available taxi and asked to be taken to Protsky station.

The first-class traveller followed Connor into the booking hall, which looked more like an opera house than a railway station. He watched closely to see which train he would be boarding. But there was another man standing in the shadows who even knew the number of the sleeping compartment he would be occupying.

The American Cultural Attaché in St Petersburg had passed up an invitation to the Kirov Ballet that evening so he could inform Gutenburg when Fitzgerald had boarded the overnight train to Moscow. It wouldn't be necessary to accompany him on the journey, as Ashley Mitchell, his colleague in the capital, would be waiting on Platform 4 the following morning to confirm that Fitzgerald had reached his destination. It had been made clear to the Attaché that this was Mitchell's operation.

'One first-class sleeper to Moscow,' said Connor in English to the booking clerk.

The man pushed a ticket across the wooden counter, and was disappointed when the customer handed over a ten-thousand-rouble note. He had been hoping that this passenger would give him an opportunity to make a small turn on the exchange rate – his second that night.

Connor checked his ticket before making his way towards the Moscow express. He walked down the crowded platform, passing several old green carriages that looked as if they predated the 1917 Revolution, stopped at Coach K and presented his ticket to a woman standing by the open door. She clipped it and stood aside to allow him to climb aboard. Connor strolled down the corridor, looking for booth Number 8. Once he had found it, he switched on the light and locked himself in; not because he was afraid of being robbed by bandits, as was so often reported in the American press, but because he needed to change his identity once again.

He had seen the fresh-faced youth standing under the arrivals board at Geneva airport, and had wondered where they were recruiting them from these days. He didn't bother trying to spot the agent in St Petersburg: he knew someone would be there to check on his arrival, and someone else would be waiting on the platform in

Moscow. Gutenburg had already briefed him fully on Agent Mitchell, who he had described as fairly raw, and unaware of Fitzgerald's status as an NOC.

The train left St Petersburg at exactly one minute to midnight, and the gentle, rhythmic sound of the carriage wheels clattering over the tracks soon made Connor feel drowsy. He woke with a start, and checked his watch: four thirty-seven. The most sleep he'd managed in the past three nights.

Then he recalled his dream. He had been sitting on a bench in Lafayette Square, facing the White House and talking with someone who never once looked in his direction. The meeting he'd had with the Deputy Director the previous week was being replayed word for word, but he couldn't recall what it was about the conversation that continued to nag away at him. Just as Gutenburg came to the sentence he wanted to hear repeated, he had woken up.

He was no nearer to solving the problem when the train pulled in to Raveltay station at eight thirty-three that morning.

'Where are you?' asked Andy Lloyd.

'A phone booth in Moscow,' Jackson replied. 'Via London, Geneva and St Petersburg. As soon as he got off the train he led us all on a wild goose chase. He managed to lose our man in Moscow in less than ten minutes. If it hadn't been me who taught him the doubling-back technique in the first place, he would have shaken me off as well.'

'Where did he end up?' asked Lloyd.

'He checked into a small hotel on the north side of the city.'

'Is he still there?'

'No, he left about an hour later, but he was so well disguised that I nearly missed him myself. If it hadn't been for the walk, he might have given me the slip.'

'Where did he go?' asked Lloyd.

'He took another circuitous route, and ended up at the campaign headquarters of Victor Zerimski.'

'Why Zerimski?'

'I don't know yet, but he came out of the building carrying all Zerimski's campaign literature. Then he bought a map from a news-stand and had lunch in a nearby restaurant. In the afternoon, he hired a small car and returned to his hotel. He hasn't left the building since.'

'Oh my God,' said Lloyd suddenly. 'It's going to be Zerimski this time.'

There was a long pause at the other end of the line before Jackson said, 'No, Mr Lloyd, that's not possible.'

'Why not?'

'He'd never agree to carry out such a sensitive assignment unless the order had come directly from the White House. I've known him long enough to be certain of that.'

'Try not to forget that your friend carried out exactly the same assignment in Colombia. No doubt Dexter was able to convince him that that operation had also been sanctioned by the President.'

'There could be an alternative scenario,' said Jackson quietly.

'Namely?'

'That it's not Zerimski they're planning to kill, but Connor.'

Lloyd wrote the name down on his yellow pad.

BOOK TWO

The Loner

CHAPTER TWELVE

'AMERICAN?'

'Yes,' said Jackson, not looking down at the source of the piping voice.

'You need anything?'

'No thanks,' he said, still not taking his eyes off the front door of the hotel.

'You must need something. Americans always need something.'

'I don't need anything. Now go away,' said Jackson firmly.

'Caviar? Russian dolls? General's uniform? Fur hat? Woman?'

Jackson looked down at the boy for the first time. He was draped from head to toe in a sheepskin jacket three sizes too large for him. On his head he wore a cap made out of rabbitskin that Jackson felt he needed more every minute. The boy's smile revealed two missing teeth.

'A woman? At five o'clock in the morning?'

'Good time for woman. But perhaps you prefer man?'

'How much do you charge for your services?'

'What type of services?' asked the boy, looking suspicious.

'As a runner.'

'Runner?'

'Helper, then.'

'Helper?'

'Assistant.'

'Ah, you mean partner, like in American movies.'

'OK, so now we've agreed on your job description, wiseguy, how much do you charge?'

'Per day? Per week? Per month?'

'Per hour.'

'How much you offer?'

'Quite the little entrepreneur, aren't we?'

'We learn from Americans,' said the boy, with a grin that stretched from ear to ear.

'One dollar,' said Jackson.

The boy began laughing. 'I may be wiseguy, but you are comedian. Ten dollars.'

'That's nothing less than extortion.'

The boy looked puzzled for the first time.

'I'll give you two.'

'Six.'

'Four.'

'Five.'

'Agreed,' said Jackson.

The boy raised the palm of his right hand high in the air, something else he'd seen in American movies. Jackson slapped it. The deal was struck. The boy immediately checked the time on his Rolex watch.

'So, what's your name?' Jackson asked.

'Sergei,' replied the boy. 'And yours?'

'Jackson. How old are you, Sergei?'

'How old you want me to be?'

'Cut the crap and tell me your age.'

'Fourteen.'

'You're not a day over nine.'

'Thirteen.'

'Ten.'

'Eleven.'

'OK,' said Jackson. 'I'll settle for eleven.'

'And how old are you?' demanded the boy.

'Fifty-four.'

'I'll settle for fifty-four,' said Sergei.

Jackson laughed for the first time in days. 'How come your English is so good?' he asked, still keeping an eye on the hotel door.

'My mother live with American for long time. He return to States last year, but not take us.'

This time Jackson believed he was telling the truth.

'So what's the job, partner?' asked Sergei.

'We're keeping an eye on someone who's staying at that hotel.'

'Is a friend or enemy?'

'Friend.'

'Mafya?'

'No, he works for the good guys.'

'Don't treat me like child,' said Sergei, with an edge to his voice. 'We're partners, remember.'

'OK, Sergei. He's a friend,' said Jackson, just as Connor appeared in the doorway. 'Don't move.' He placed a hand firmly on the boy's shoulder.

'Is that him?' asked Sergei.

'Yes, that's him.'

'He has kind face. Maybe better I work for him.'

Victor Zerimski's day hadn't begun well, and it was still only a few minutes past eight a.m. He was chairing a meeting of the Central Council of the Communist Party which was being briefed by Dmitri Titov, his Chief of Staff.

'An international body of observers has arrived in Moscow to monitor the electoral process,' Titov was telling them. 'They are looking principally for any suggestion of ballot-rigging, but their chairman has already admitted that with an electorate so vast and so widespread, there is no way they can spot every irregularity.' Titov ended his report by saying that now that Comrade Zerimski had climbed to second place in the polls, the Mafya were pouring even more money into Chernopov's campaign.

Zerimski stroked his thick moustache as he looked in turn at each of the men seated round the table. 'When I am President,' he said, rising from his place at the head of the table. 'I'll throw those Mafya bastards in jail one by one. Then the only thing they'll count for the rest of their lives will be rocks.' The members of the Central Council had heard their leader lambast the Mafya many times before, though he never mentioned them by name in public.

The short, muscle-bound man thumped the table. 'Russia needs to return to the old-fashioned values the rest of the world used to respect us for.' The twenty-one men facing him nodded, despite having heard these words repeatedly over the past few months.

'For ten years we have done nothing but import the worst America has to offer.'

They continued to nod, and kept their eyes firmly fixed on him.

Zerimski ran a hand through his thick black hair, sighed, and slumped back into his chair. He looked across at his Chief of Staff. 'What am I doing this morning?'

'You're paying a visit to the Pushkin Museum,' said Titov. 'They're expecting you at ten o'clock.'

'Cancel it. A complete waste of time when there are only eight days until the election.' He banged the table again. 'I should be out on the streets where the people can see me.'

'But the director of the museum has applied for a grant from the government to restore the works of leading Russian artists,' said Titov.

'A waste of the people's money,' said Zerimski.

'And Chernopov has been criticised for cutting the arts subsidy,' continued the Chief of Staff.

'All right. I'll give them fifteen minutes.'

'Twenty thousand Russians visit the Pushkin every

week,' Titov added, looking down at the typewritten notes in front of him.

'Make it thirty minutes.'

'And Chernopov accused you on television last week of being an uneducated thug.'

'He did *what?*' bellowed Zerimski. 'I was studying law at Moscow University when Chernopov was still a farm labourer.'

'That is of course true, Chairman,' said Titov, 'but our internal polls show that it is not the public perception, and that Chernopov is getting his message across.'

'Internal polls? Something else we have to thank the Americans for.'

'They put Tom Lawrence in office.'

'Once I'm elected, I won't need polls to keep me in office.'

Connor's love of art had begun when Maggie had dragged him around galleries while they were still at college. At first he had gone along just so he could spend more time in her company, but within weeks he became a convert. Whenever they travelled out of town together he would happily accompany her to any gallery she chose, and as soon as they moved to Washington they had become Friends of the Corcoran and Members of the Phillips. While Zerimski was being guided around the Pushkin by its director, Connor had to be careful not to become distracted by the many masterpieces, and to concentrate on observing the Communist leader.

When Connor had first been sent to Russia back in the 1980s, the nearest any senior politician got to the people was to stare down at them from the Praesidium during May Day parades. But now that the masses could make a choice on a ballot paper, it had suddenly become necessary for those who hoped to be elected to move among them, even to listen to their views.

The gallery was as crowded as Cooke Stadium for a

Redskins game, and wherever Zerimski appeared, the crowds parted as if he were Moses approaching the Red Sea. The candidate moved slowly among the Muscovites, ignoring the paintings and sculptures in favour of their outstretched hands.

Zerimski was shorter than he looked in his photographs, and had surrounded himself with an entourage of even smaller aides so as not to emphasise the fact. Connor recalled President Truman's comment about size: 'When it comes down to inches, my boy, you should only consider the forehead,' he once told a Missouri student. 'Better to have a spare inch between the top of your nose and the hairline than between the ankle and the kneecap.' Connor noticed that Zerimski's vanity hadn't affected his dress-sense. His suit was badly cut, and his shirt was frayed at the collar and cuffs. Connor wondered if it was wise for the director of the Pushkin to be wearing a hand-tailored suit that obviously hadn't been made in Moscow.

Although Connor was aware that Victor Zerimski was a shrewd and educated man, it soon became clear that his visits to art galleries over the years must have been infrequent. As he bustled through the crowd he occasionally jabbed a finger in the direction of a canvas and informed the onlookers of the name of the artist in a loud voice. He managed to get it wrong on several occasions, but the crowd still nodded their agreement. He ignored a magnificent Rubens, showing more interest in a mother standing in the crowd clinging to her child than in the genius with which the same scene was depicted behind her. When he picked up the child and posed for a picture with the mother, Titov suggested he should take a pace to the right. That way they would get the Virgin Mary into the photograph as well. No front page would be able to resist it.

Once he had walked through half a dozen galleries, and was sure that everyone visiting the Pushkin was aware of his presence, Zerimski became bored and switched his attention to the journalists following closely behind him. On the first-floor landing he began to hold an impromptu press conference.

'Go on, ask me anything you like,' he said, glowering at the pack.

'What is your reaction to the latest opinion polls, Mr Zerimski?' asked the Moscow correspondent of *The Times*.

'Heading in the right direction.'

'You now appear to be in second place, and therefore Mr Chernopov's only real rival,' shouted another journalist.

'By election day *he* will be *my* only real rival,' said Zerimski. His entourage laughed dutifully.

'Do you think Russia should return to being a Communist state, Mr Zerimski?' came the inevitable question, delivered with an American accent.

The wily politician was far too alert to fall into that trap. 'If by that you mean a return to higher employment, lower inflation, and a better standard of living, the answer must be yes.' He sounded not unlike a Republican candidate during an American primary.

'But that's exactly what Chernopov claims is the government's present policy.'

'The government's present policy,' said Zerimski, 'is to make sure that the Prime Minister keeps his Swiss bank account overflowing with dollars. That money belongs to the Russian people, which is why he is not fit to be our next President. I'm told that when *Fortune* magazine next publishes its list of the ten richest people in the world, Chernopov will be in seventh place. Elect him as President and within five years he'll knock Bill Gates off the top spot. No, my friend,' he added. 'You are about to learn that the Russian people will vote resoundingly for a return to those days when we were the most respected nation on earth.'

'And the most feared?' suggested another journalist.

'I'd rather that than continue the present situation, where we are simply ignored by the rest of the world,' said Zerimski. Now the journalists were writing down his every word.

'Why is your friend so interested in Victor Zerimski?' whispered Sergei at the other end of the gallery.

'You ask too many questions,' said Jackson.

'Zerimski bad man.'

'Why?' asked Jackson, his eyes fixed on Connor.

'If elected, he put people like me in jail and we all go back to "the good old days", while he's in Kremlin eating caviar and drinking vodka.'

Zerimski began striding towards the gallery's exit, with the director and his entourage trying to keep up with him. The candidate stopped on the bottom step to be photographed in front of Goya's vast *Christ Descending from the Cross*. Connor was so moved by the painting that he was almost knocked over by the pursuing crowd.

'You like Goya, Jackson?' whispered Sergei.

'I haven't seen that many,' admitted the American. 'But yes,' he said, 'it's quite magnificent.'

'They have several more in the basement,' said Sergei. 'I could always arrange for one . . .' he rubbed his thumb against his fingers.

Jackson would have cuffed the boy if it wouldn't have drawn attention to them.

'Your man's on the move again,' said Sergei suddenly. Jackson looked up to see Connor disappearing out of a side entrance of the gallery with Ashley Mitchell in pursuit.

Connor sat alone in a Greek restaurant on the Prechinstenka and considered what he had seen that morning. Although Zerimski was always surrounded by a bunch of thugs, their eyes staring in every direction, he was still not as well protected as most Western leaders. Several of his strong-arm men might be brave and resourceful, but only three of them appeared to have any previous experience of protecting a world statesman. And they couldn't be on duty all the time.

He tried to digest a rather bad moussaka as he went over the rest of Zerimski's itinerary, right through to election day. The candidate would be seen in public on twenty-seven different occasions during the next eight days. By the time a waiter had placed a black coffee in front of him, Connor had shortlisted the only three locations worth considering if Zerimski's name needed to be removed from the ballot paper.

He checked his watch. That evening the candidate would address a Party gathering in Moscow. The following morning he would travel by train to Yaroslavl, where he would open a factory before returning to the capital to attend a performance by the Bolshoi Ballet. From there he would take the midnight train to St Petersburg. Connor had already decided to shadow Zerimski in Yaroslavl. He had also booked tickets for the ballet and the train to St Petersburg.

As he sipped his coffee he thought about Ashley Mitchell at the Pushkin, slipping behind the nearest pillar whenever Connor had glanced in his direction, and tried not to laugh. He had decided that he would allow Mitchell to follow him during the day – he might prove useful at some point – but he wouldn't let him find out where he slept at night. He glanced out of the window to see the Cultural Attaché seated on a bench, reading a copy of *Pravda*. He smiled. A professional should always be able to watch his prey without being seen.

Jackson removed a wallet from inside his jacket, extracted a hundred-rouble note and passed it to the boy.

'Get us both something to eat, but don't go anywhere near that restaurant,' he said, nodding across the road.

'I've never been inside a restaurant. What would you like?'

'I'll have the same as you.'

'You catching on fast, Jackson,' said Sergei as he scurried away.

Jackson checked up and down the road. The man seated on the bench reading a copy of *Pravda* wasn't wearing an overcoat. He had obviously assumed that surveillance was only carried out in warm, comfortable surroundings, but having lost Fitzgerald the previous day, there was clearly no way he could risk moving. His ears were bright red, his face flushed with the cold, and he had no one to fetch him something to eat. Jackson doubted if they would be seeing him tomorrow.

Sergei returned a few minutes later, carrying two paper bags. He passed one up to Jackson. 'A big Mac with French fries and ketchup.'

'Why do I have a feeling that if Zerimski becomes President, he'll close down McDonald's?' said Jackson. He took a bite of the hamburger.

'And I thought you might need this,' said Sergei, handing him an officer's hat made of rabbit's fur.

'Did a hundred roubles cover all this?' asked Jackson.

'No, I stole the hat,' said Sergei matter-of-factly. 'I thought your need was greater than his.'

'You could get us both arrested.'

'Not likely,' said Sergei. 'There are over two million soldiers in Russia. Half of them haven't been paid for months, and most would sell you their sister for a hundred roubles.'

Jackson tried on the hat – it fitted perfectly. Neither of them spoke while they devoured their lunch, their eyes pinned on the restaurant.

'See that man sitting on the bench reading *Pravda*, Jackson?'

'Yes,' said Jackson between bites.

'He was at the gallery this morning.'

'You also catch on fast,' said Jackson.

'Don't forget that I have a Russian mother,' replied Sergei. 'By the way, which side is the bench man on?'

'I know who's paying him,' said Jackson, 'but I don't know which side he's on.'

CHAPTER THIRTEEN

CONNOR WAS AMONG THE LAST to arrive at the Lenin Memorial Hall. He took a seat at the back of the room in the section reserved for the press and tried to make himself as inconspicuous as possible. He couldn't help remembering the last time he'd attended a political meeting in Russia. On that occasion he had also come to listen to the Communist candidate, but that was in the days when there was only one name on the ballot paper. Which was possibly why the turnout on election day had been only 17 per cent.

Connor glanced around the hall. Although there was another fifteen minutes to go before the candidate was due to arrive, every seat had already been taken, and the gangways were almost full. At the front of the hall, a few officials were milling around on the stage, making sure everything would be as the leader expected it. An old man was placing a grandiose chair towards the back of the stage.

The gathering of Party faithful couldn't have been in greater contrast to an American political convention. The delegates, if that was what they were, were dressed in drab clothes. They looked undernourished, and sat in silence as they waited for Zerimski to appear.

Connor lowered his head and began scribbling some notes on his pad; he had no desire to get involved in a conversation with the journalist on his left. She had already told the correspondent on the other side of her that she represented the *Istanbul News*, the sole English-language paper in Turkey, and that her editor thought it would be a disaster if Zerimski were ever to become President. She went on to say she had recently reported that the Communist candidate might just pull it off. If she had asked Connor's opinion, he would have had to agree. The odds on his being required to carry out his assignment were shortening by the hour.

A few moments later, the Turkish journalist began sketching a portrait of Zerimski. Her paper obviously couldn't afford the luxury of a photographer, and was probably relying on wire services and whatever she came up with. He had to admit that the drawing was a good likeness.

Connor checked the room again. Would it be possible to assassinate someone in a room as crowded as this? Not if you hoped to escape. Getting at Zerimski while he was in his car was another option, although it was certain to be well protected. No professional would consider a bomb, which often ended up killing innocent people while failing to eliminate the target. If he was to have any chance of escaping, he would have to rely on a high-powered rifle in an open space. Nick Gutenburg had assured him that a customised Remington 700 would be safely in the US Embassy long before he arrived in Moscow – another misuse of the diplomatic pouch. If Lawrence gave the order, they would leave him to decide the time and place.

Now that he'd studied Zerimski's itinerary in detail, Connor had decided that his first choice would be Severodvinsk, where the Communist leader was addressing a rally in a shipyard two days before the election. Connor had already begun to study the various cranes which operated at Russian docks, and the possibility of remaining hidden inside one for a long period of time.

Heads were beginning to turn towards the back of the room, and Connor looked around. A group of men in badly cut suits with bulges under their arms were filling the back of the hall, scanning the room before their leader made his entrance.

Connor could see that their methods were primitive and ineffective, but like all security forces they probably hoped that their presence and sheer weight of numbers would make anyone think twice before trying anything. He checked the faces – all three of the professionals were back on duty.

Suddenly loud applause burst from the rear of the hall, followed by cheering. As Zerimski entered, the Party members rose as one to acclaim their leader. Even the journalists were forced to stand to catch a glimpse of him. Zerimski's progress toward the stage was continually held up as he stopped to clasp outstretched hands. When he finally reached the platform, the noise became almost deafening.

The elderly chairman who had been waiting patiently at the front of the hall led Zerimski up the steps and onto the stage, guiding him towards the large chair. Once Zerimski had sat down, he walked slowly forward to the microphone. The audience resumed their places and fell silent.

He didn't do a good job of introducing 'the next President of Russia', and the longer he spoke, the more restless the audience became. Zerimski's entourage, who were standing behind him, began to fidget and look annoyed. The old man's final flourish was to describe the speaker as 'the natural successor to Comrade Vladimir Ilyich Lenin'. He stood aside to make way for his leader, who didn't look at all certain that Lenin was the most fortunate comparison that could have been chosen.

As Zerimski rose from his place at the back of the stage and walked slowly forward, the crowd began to come alive again. He threw his arms high in the air, and they cheered more loudly than ever.

Connor's eyes never left Zerimski. He carefully noted his every movement, the stances he took, the poses he struck. Like all energetic men, he hardly remained still for a moment.

After Zerimski felt the cheering had gone on for long enough, he waved his audience back down into their seats. Connor noted that the whole process from start to finish had taken a little over three minutes.

Zerimski didn't begin to speak until everyone had resumed their places and he had complete silence.

'Comrades,' he began in a firm voice, 'it is a great honour for me to stand before you as your candidate. As each day passes, I become more and more aware that the Russian people are demanding a fresh start. Although few of our citizens wish to return to the old totalitarian regime of the past, the majority want to see a fairer distribution of the wealth that has been created by their skills and hard work.'

The audience began clapping again.

'Let us never forget,' Zerimski continued, 'that Russia can once again become the most respected nation on earth. If other countries entertain any doubt about that, under my presidency they will do so at their peril.'

The journalists scribbled away furiously, and the audience cheered even more loudly. Nearly twenty seconds passed before Zerimski was able to speak again.

'Look at the streets of Moscow, comrades. Yes, you will see Mercedes, BMWs and Jaguars, but who is driving them? Just a privileged few. And it is those few who are hoping that Chernopov will be elected so they can continue to enjoy a lifestyle no one in this room can ever hope to emulate. The time has come, my friends, for this wealth – *your* wealth – to be shared among the many, not the few. I look forward to the day when Russia no longer has more limousines than family cars, more yachts than fishing boats, and more secret Swiss bank accounts than hospitals.'

Once again the audience greeted his words with prolonged applause.

When the noise eventually died down, Zerimski
dropped his voice, but every word still carried to the back
of the hall. 'When I become your President, I shall not
be opening bank accounts in Switzerland, but factories
all over Russia. I shall not be spending my time relaxing
in a luxurious dacha, but working night and day in my
office. I shall be dedicating myself to your service, and
be more than satisfied with the salary of a President,
rather than taking bribes from dishonest businessmen
whose only interest is in pillaging the nation's assets.'

This time the applause was so enthusiastic that it was
over a minute before Zerimski was able to continue.

'At the back of the room,' he said, pointing a stubby
finger at the assembled journalists, 'are the representatives of the world's press.' He paused, curled his lip and
added, 'And may I say how welcome they are.'

No applause followed this particular remark.

'However, let me remind them that when I am President, they'll need to be in Moscow not only during the
run-up to an election, but permanently. Because then
Russia will not be hoping for handouts whenever the
Group of Seven meet, but will once again be a major
participant in world affairs. If Chernopov were elected,
the Americans would be more concerned about the views
of Mexico than those of Russia. In future, President Lawrence will have to listen to what *you* are saying, and not
just soft-talk the world's press by telling them how much
he liked Boris.'

Laughter spread around the hall.

'He may call everyone else by their first name, but
he'll call me "Mr President".'

Connor knew that the American media would report
that remark from coast to coast, and that every word of
the speech would be raked over in the Oval Office.

'There are only eight days to go, my friends, before

the people decide,' Zerimski said. 'Let us spend every moment of that time making sure we have an overwhelming victory on election day. A victory that will send out a message to the whole world that Russia is back as a power to be reckoned with on the global stage.' His voice was beginning to rise with every word. 'But don't do it for me. Don't even do it for the Communist Party. Do it for the next generation of Russians, who will then be able to play their part as citizens of the greatest nation on earth. Then, when you have cast your vote, you will have done so knowing that we can once again let the people be the power behind the nation.' He paused, and looked around the audience. 'I ask for only one thing – the privilege of being allowed to lead those people.' Dropping his voice almost to a whisper, he ended with the words, 'I offer myself as your servant.'

Zerimski took a pace backwards and threw his arms in the air. The audience rose as one. The final peroration had taken forty-seven seconds, and not for a moment had he remained still. He had moved first to his right and then to his left, each time raising the corresponding arm, but never for more than a few seconds at a time. Then he bowed low, and after remaining motionless for twelve seconds he suddenly stood bolt upright and joined in the clapping.

He remained in the centre of the stage for another eleven minutes, repeating several of the same gestures again and again. When he felt he had milked every ounce of applause he could drag out of the audience, he descended the steps from the stage, followed by his entourage. As he walked down the centre aisle, the noise rose higher than ever, and even more arms were thrust out. Zerimski grabbed as many as he could during his slow progress to the back of the hall. Never once did Connor's eyes leave him. Even after Zerimski had left the hall, the cheering continued. It didn't die down until the audience began to leave.

Connor had noted several characteristic movements of the head and hands, small mannerisms that were often repeated. He could see already that certain gestures regularly accompanied certain phrases, and he knew that soon he would be able to anticipate them.

'Your friend just left,' said Sergei. 'I follow him?'

'That won't be necessary,' said Jackson. 'We know where he's spending the night. Mind you, that poor bastard a few paces behind him is going to be led a merry dance for the next hour or so.'

'What do we do next?' asked Sergei.

'You grab some sleep. I have a feeling tomorrow's going to be a long day.'

'You haven't paid me for today yet,' said Sergei, thrusting out his hand. 'Nine hours at $6 an hour is – $56.'

'I think you'll find it's eight hours at $5 an hour,' said Jackson. 'But nice try.' He passed $40 over to Sergei.

'And tomorrow?' his young partner asked after he had counted and pocketed the notes. 'What time you want me?'

'Meet me outside his hotel at five o'clock, and don't be late. My guess is we'll be following Zerimski on his travels to Yaroslavl, and then returning to Moscow before going on to St Petersburg.'

'You're lucky, Jackson. I was born in St Petersburg, and there's nothing I don't know about the place. But remember, I charge double outside Moscow.'

'You know, Sergei, if you go on like this, it won't be long before you price yourself out of the market.'

CHAPTER FOURTEEN

MAGGIE DROVE OUT of the university parking lot at one minute past one. She swung left onto Prospect Street, braking only briefly at the first stop sign before accelerating away. She only ever took an hour for lunch, and if she failed to find a parking spot near the restaurant it would cut down their time together. And today she needed every minute of that hour.

Not that any of her staff in the Admissions Office would have complained if she had taken the afternoon off. After twenty-eight years working for the university – the last six as Dean of Admissions – if she had put in a backdated claim for overtime, Georgetown University would have had to launch a special appeal.

At least today the gods were on her side. A woman was pulling out of a spot a few yards from the restaurant where they had arranged to meet. Maggie put four quarters in the meter to cover an hour.

When she entered the Café Milano, Maggie gave the maître d' her name. 'Yes, of course, Mrs Fitzgerald,' he said, and guided her to a table by the window to join someone who had never been known to be late for anything.

Maggie kissed the woman who had been Connor's secretary for the past nineteen years, and took the place opposite her. Joan probably loved Connor as much as she had any man, and for that love she had never been rewarded with more than the occasional peck on the cheek and a gift at Christmas, which Maggie inevitably ended up buying. Though Joan was not yet fifty, her sensible tweeds, flat shoes and cropped brown hair revealed that she had long ago given up trying to attract the opposite sex.

'I've already decided,' Joan said.

'I know what I'm going to have too,' said Maggie.

'How's Tara?' asked Joan, closing her menu.

'Hanging in there, to use her own words. I only hope she'll finish her thesis. Although Connor would never say anything to her, he'll be very disappointed if she doesn't.'

'He speaks warmly of Stuart,' Joan said as a waiter appeared by her side.

'Yes,' said Maggie, a little sadly. 'It looks as if I'm going to have to get used to the idea of my only child living thirteen thousand miles away.' She looked up at the waiter. 'Cannelloni and a side salad for me.'

'And I'll have the angel-hair pasta,' said Joan.

'Anything to drink, ladies?' the waiter asked hopefully.

'No, thank you,' said Maggie firmly. 'Just a glass of water.' Joan nodded her agreement.

'Yes, Connor and Stuart got on well,' said Maggie once the waiter had left. 'Stuart will be joining us for Christmas, so you'll have a chance to meet him then.'

'I look forward to that,' said Joan.

Maggie sensed that she wanted to add something, but after so many years she had learned that there was no point in pressing her. If it was important, Joan would let her know when she was good and ready.

'I've tried to call you several times in the past few days. I hoped you might be able to join me at the opera or come for dinner one evening, but I seem to keep missing you.'

'Now that Connor's left the company, they've closed

the office on M Street and moved me back to head-quarters,' said Joan.

Maggie admired the way Joan had chosen her words so carefully. No hint of where she was working, no suggestion of for whom, not a clue about what her new responsibilities were now that she was no longer with Connor.

'It's no secret that he hopes you'll eventually join him at Washington Provident,' said Maggie.

'I'd love to. But there's no point in making any plans until we know what's happening.'

'What do you mean, "happening"?' asked Maggie. 'Connor's already accepted Ben Thompson's offer. He has to be back before Christmas, so he can start his new job at the beginning of January.'

A long silence followed before Maggie said quietly, 'So he didn't get the job with Washington Provident after all.'

The waiter arrived with their meals. 'A little parmesan cheese, madam?' he asked as he placed them on the table.

'Thank you,' said Joan, staring intently at her pasta.

'So that's why Ben Thompson cold-shouldered me at the opera last Thursday. He didn't even offer to buy me a drink.'

'I'm sorry,' said Joan, as the waiter left them. 'I just assumed you knew.'

'Don't worry. Connor would have let me know the moment he'd got another interview, and then told me it was a far better job than the one he'd been offered at Washington Provident.'

'How well you know him,' said Joan.

'Sometimes I wonder if I know him at all,' said Maggie. 'Right now I have no idea where he is or what he's up to.'

'I don't know much more than you do,' said Joan. 'For the first time in nineteen years, he didn't brief me before he left.'

'It's different this time, isn't it, Joan?' said Maggie, looking straight at her.

'What makes you say that?'

'He told me he was going abroad, but left without his passport. My guess is that he's still in America. But why . . .'

'Not taking his passport doesn't prove he isn't abroad,' said Joan.

'Possibly not,' said Maggie. 'But this is the first time he's hidden it where he knew I would find it.'

A few minutes later, the waiter reappeared and whisked away their plates.

'Would either of you care for dessert?' he asked.

'Not for me,' said Joan. 'Just coffee.'

'Me too,' said Maggie. 'Black, no sugar.' She checked her watch. She only had sixteen minutes left. She bit her lip. 'Joan, I've never asked you to break a confidence before, but there's something I have to know.'

Joan looked out of the window and glanced at the good-looking young man who had been leaning against the wall on the far side of the street for the past forty minutes. She thought she had seen him somewhere before.

When Maggie left the restaurant at seven minutes to two, she didn't notice the same young man take out a mobile phone and dial an unlisted number.

'Yes?' said Nick Gutenburg.

'Mrs Fitzgerald has just finished lunch with Joan Bennett at Café Milano on Prospect. They were together for forty-seven minutes. I've recorded every word of their conversation.'

'Good. Bring the tape in to my office immediately.'

As Maggie ran up the steps to the Admissions Office, the clock in the university courtyard was showing one minute to two.

It was one minute to ten in Moscow. Connor was enjoying the finale of *Giselle*, performed by the Bolshoi Ballet. But unlike most of the audience, he didn't keep his opera glasses trained on the prima ballerina's virtuoso performance. From time to time he would glance down to the right and check that Zerimski was still in his box. Connor knew how much Maggie would have enjoyed the Dance of the Wilis, the spirits of thirty-six young brides dressed in their wedding gowns, pirouetting in the moonlight. He tried not to be mesmerised by their *pliés* and arabesques, and to concentrate on what was going on in Zerimski's box. Maggie often went to the ballet when he was out of town, and she would have been amused to know that the Russian Communist leader had achieved in a single evening what she had failed to do in thirty years.

Connor studied the men in the box. On Zerimski's right was Dmitri Titov, his Chief of Staff. On his left sat the elderly man who had introduced him before he gave his speech the previous evening. Behind him in the shadows stood three guards. Connor assumed that there would be at least another dozen in the corridor outside.

The vast theatre, with its beautiful tiered balconies and its stalls filled with gilt chairs covered in red velvet plush, was always sold out for weeks in advance. But the Maggie theory had also applied in Moscow – you can always pick up a single ticket, even at the last minute.

Moments before the conductor was due to arrive in the orchestra pit, a section of the crowd began to applaud. Connor had looked up from his programme to see one or two people pointing towards a box on the second tier. Zerimski had timed his entrance to perfection. He stood at the front of the box, waving and smiling. A little under half the audience rose and cheered loudly, while the rest remained seated, some clapping politely, others continuing their conversations as if he wasn't there. This seemed to confirm the accuracy of the opinion polls – that Chernopov was now leading his rival by only a few percentage points.

Once the curtain had risen, Connor quickly discovered that Zerimski showed about as much interest in ballet as he did in art. It had been another long day for the candidate, and Connor was not surprised to see him stifling the occasional yawn. His train had left for Yaroslavl early that morning, and he had immediately begun his programme with a visit to a clothes factory on the outskirts of the town. When he left the union officials an hour later, he had grabbed a sandwich before dropping in to a fruit market, then a school, a police station and a hospital, followed by an unscheduled walkabout in the town square. Finally he had been driven back to the station at speed and jumped onto a train that had been held up for him.

The dogma Zerimski proclaimed to anyone who cared to listen hadn't changed a great deal from the previous day, except that 'Moscow' had been replaced with 'Yaroslavl'. The thugs who surrounded him as he toured the factory looked even more amateurish than those who had been with him when he delivered his speech at the Lenin Memorial Hall. It was clear that the locals were not going to allow any Muscovites onto their territory. Connor concluded that an attempt on Zerimski's life would have a far better chance of succeeding outside the capital. It would need to be in a city that was large enough to disappear in, and proud enough not to allow the three professionals from Moscow to call the tune.

Zerimski's visit to the shipyard in Severodvinsk in a few days' time still looked his best bet.

Even on the train back to Moscow, Zerimski didn't rest. He called the foreign journalists into his carriage for another press conference. But before anyone could ask a question, he said, 'Have you seen the latest opinion polls, which show me running well ahead of General Borodin and now trailing Chernopov by only one point?'

'But you've always told us in the past to ignore the

polls,' said one of the journalists bravely. Zerimski scowled.

Connor stood at the back of the mêlée and continued to study the would-be President. He knew he had to anticipate Zerimski's every expression, movement and mannerism, as well as be able to deliver his speech verbatim.

When the train pulled into Protsky station four hours later, Connor had a sense that someone on board was watching him, other than Mitchell. After twenty-eight years, he was rarely wrong about these things. He was beginning to wonder if Mitchell wasn't just a little too obvious, and if there might be someone more professional out there. If there was, what did they want? Earlier in the day, he'd had a feeling that someone or something had flitted across his path that he'd noticed before. He disapproved of paranoia, but like all professionals, he didn't believe in coincidences.

He left the station and doubled back to his hotel, confident that no one had followed him. But then, they wouldn't need to if they knew where he was staying. He tried to dismiss these thoughts from his mind as he packed his bag. Tonight he would lose whoever was trailing him – unless, of course, they already knew exactly where he was going. After all, if they knew why he was in Russia, they had only to follow Zerimski's itinerary. He checked out of the hotel a few minutes later, paying his bill in cash.

He had changed taxis five times before allowing the last one to drop him outside the theatre. He checked his bag in with an old woman seated behind a counter in the basement, and rented a pair of opera glasses. Leaving the bag gave the management confidence that the glasses would be returned.

When the curtain was finally lowered at the end of the performance, Zerimski rose and waved to the audience once again. The response was not quite so enthusiastic as before, but Connor thought he must have left feeling that his visit to the Bolshoi had been worthwhile. As he strode down the steps of the theatre he loudly informed the departing audience how much he had enjoyed the magnificent performance of Ekaterina Maximova. A line of cars awaited him and his entourage, and he slipped into the back of the third. The motorcade and its police escort whisked him off to another train waiting at another station. Connor noted that the number of motorcycle outriders had been increased from two to four.

Other people were obviously beginning to think he might be the next President.

Connor arrived at the station a few minutes after Zerimski. He showed a security guard his press pass before purchasing a ticket for the eleven fifty-nine to St Petersburg.

Once he was inside his sleeping compartment he locked the door, switched on the light over his bunk and began to study the itinerary for Zerimski's visit to St Petersburg.

In a carriage at the other end of the train, the candidate was also going over the itinerary, with his Chief of Staff.

'Another first-thing-in-the-morning-to-last-thing-at-night sort of day,' he was grumbling. And that was before Titov had added a visit to the Hermitage.

'Why should I bother to go to the Hermitage when I'm only in St Petersburg for a few hours?'

'Because you went to the Pushkin, and not to go to Russia's most famous museum would be an insult to the citizens of St Petersburg.'

'Let's be thankful that we leave before the curtain goes up at the Kirov.'

Zerimski knew that by far the most important meeting of the day would be with General Borodin and the military high command at Kelskow Barracks. If he could persuade the General to withdraw from the presidential race and back him, then the military – almost two and a half million of them – would surely swing behind him, and the prize would be his. He had planned to offer Borodin the position of Defence Secretary until he discovered that Chernopov had already promised him the same post. He knew that Chernopov had been to see the General the previous Monday, and had left empty-handed. Zerimski took this as a good sign. He intended to offer Borodin something he would find irresistible.

Connor also realised that tomorrow's meeting with the military leader might decide Zerimski's fate. He switched off the light above his bunk a few minutes after two a.m., and fell asleep.

Mitchell had turned off his light the moment the train had pulled out of the station, but he didn't sleep.

Sergei had been unable to hide his excitement at the thought of travelling on the Protsky express. He had followed his partner to their compartment like a contented puppy. When Jackson pulled open the door, Sergei announced, 'It's bigger than my flat.' He leapt onto one of the bunks, kicked off his shoes and pulled the blankets over him without bothering to take off any clothes. 'Saves washing and changing,' he explained as Jackson hung his jacket and trousers on the flimsiest wire hanger he'd ever seen.

As the American prepared for bed, Sergei rubbed the steamed-up window with an elbow, making a circle he could peer through. He didn't say another word until the train began to move slowly out of the station.

Jackson climbed into his bunk and switched his light off.

'How many kilometres to St Petersburg, Jackson?'

'Six hundred and thirty.'

'And how long will it take us to get there?'

'Eight and a half hours. We've got another long day ahead of us, so try to get some sleep.'

Sergei switched off his light, but Jackson remained awake. He was now certain that he knew why his friend had been despatched to Russia. Helen Dexter obviously wanted Connor out of the way, but Jackson still didn't know how far she would go to save her own skin.

He had attempted to ring Andy Lloyd earlier that afternoon on his cellphone, but hadn't been able to get through. He didn't want to risk calling from the hotel, so he decided to try again after Zerimski had delivered his speech in Freedom Square the following day, by which time Washington would have woken up. Once Lloyd knew what was going on, Jackson was sure he would be given the authority to abort the whole operation before it was too late. He closed his eyes.

'Are you married, Jackson?'

'No, divorced,' he replied.

'There are now more divorces each year in Russia than in the States. Did you know that, Jackson?'

'No. But I've come to realise over the past couple of days that that's just the sort of useless information you carry around in that head of yours.'

'What about children? You have any?'

'None,' said Jackson. 'I lost . . .'

'Why don't you adopt me? Then I go back to America with you.'

'I don't think Ted Turner could afford to adopt *you*. Now go to sleep, Sergei.'

There was another long silence.

'One more question, Jackson?'

'Tell me how I'm going to stop you.'

'Why is this man so important to you?'

Jackson waited some time before answering. 'Twenty-nine years ago he saved my life in Vietnam, so I guess you could say I owe him for those years. Does that make any sense?'

Sergei would have replied, but he'd fallen fast asleep.

CHAPTER FIFTEEN

VLADIMIR BOLCHENKOV, St Petersburg's Chief of Police, had enough on his mind without having to worry about four mysterious phone calls. Chernopov had visited the city on Monday, and had brought the traffic to a standstill by demanding that his motorcade should be the same size as the late President's.

Borodin was refusing to allow his men to leave their barracks until they were paid, and now that it looked as if he was out of the race for President, rumours of a military coup were beginning to surface once again. 'It's not hard to work out which city Borodin will want to take over first,' Bolchenkov had warned the Mayor. He had set up a whole department to deal with the threat of terrorism during the election campaign. If any of the candidates were going to be assassinated, it wouldn't be on his territory. That week alone, the department had received twenty-seven threats on Zerimski's life. The Chief had dismissed them as the usual assortment of weirdoes and lunatics -- until a young lieutenant had rushed into his office earlier that morning, white-faced and talking far too quickly.

The Chief sat and listened to the recording the Lieutenant had made moments before. The first call had come through at nine twenty-four, fifty-one minutes after Zerimski had arrived in the city.

'There will be an attempt on Zerimski's life this afternoon,' said a male voice with an accent that Bolchenkov couldn't quite place. Mid-European, perhaps; certainly not Russian.

'While Zerimski is addressing the rally in Freedom Square, a lone gunman hired by the Mafya will make the attempt. I will call back with more details in a few minutes' time, but I will speak only to Bolchenkov.' The line went dead. The brevity of the call meant there was no possibility of tracing it. Bolchenkov knew immediately that they were dealing with a professional.

Eleven minutes later the second call came through. The Lieutenant bluffed for as long as he could, claiming they were trying to find the Chief, but all the caller said was, 'I will phone again in a few minutes' time. Just be sure Bolchenkov is standing by the phone. It's your time that's being wasted, not mine.'

That was when the Lieutenant had burst into the Chief's office. Bolchenkov had been explaining to one of Zerimski's sidekicks why his motorcade couldn't be allocated the same number of police outriders as Chernopov's. He immediately stubbed out his cigarette and went to join his team in the terrorism unit. It was another nine minutes before the caller phoned again.

'Is Bolchenkov there?'

'This is Bolchenkov speaking.'

'The man you are looking for will be posing as a foreign journalist, representing a South African newspaper that doesn't exist. He arrived in St Petersburg on the express from Moscow this morning. He is working alone. I will call you again in three minutes.'

Three minutes later the whole department was assembled to listen to him.

'I'm sure that by now the entire anti-terrorism division of the St Petersburg Police are hanging on my every word,' was the caller's opening salvo. 'So allow me to give you a helping hand. The assassin is six foot one, has blue eyes and thick sandy hair. But he'll probably be disguised. I don't know what he will be wearing, but then, you must do something to earn your wages.' The line went dead.

The whole unit listened to the tapes again and again over the next half-hour. Suddenly the Chief stubbed out another cigarette and said, 'Play the third tape again.' The young Lieutenant pressed a button, wondering what his boss had picked up that the rest of them had missed. They all listened intently.

'Stop,' said the Chief after only a few seconds. 'I thought so. Go back and start counting.'

Count what? the Lieutenant wanted to ask as he pressed the playback button. This time he heard the faint chime of a carriage clock in the background.

He rewound the tape and they listened once again. 'Two chimes,' said the Lieutenant. 'If it was two in the afternoon, our informant was calling from the Far East.'

The Chief smiled. 'I don't think so,' he said. 'It's more likely that the call was made at two in the morning, from the east coast of America.'

Maggie picked up the phone by her bed and dialled a 650 number. It only rang a couple of times before it was picked up.

'Tara Fitzgerald,' said a brisk voice. No 'Hello, good evening,' or confirmation that the caller had dialled the correct number. Just the bold announcement of her name, so no one needed to waste any time. How like her father, Maggie thought.

'It's Mom, honey.'

'Hi, Mom. Has the car broken down again, or is it something serious?'

'Nothing, honey, I'm just missing your father,' she replied, laughing. 'I hoped you'd have time for a chat.'

'Well, at least you're only missing *one* man,' said Tara, trying to lighten the tone. 'I'm missing two.'

'Maybe, but at least you know where Stuart is, and can give him a call whenever you want to. My problem is that I haven't a clue where your father is.'

'There's nothing new about that, Mom. We all know the rules when Dad's away. The womenfolk are expected to sit at home dutifully waiting for their master to return. Typically Irish . . .'

'Yes, I know. But I have an uneasy feeling about this particular trip,' said Maggie.

'I'm sure there's no need to be anxious, Mother. After all, he's only been away for a week. Remember how many times in the past he's turned up when you least expected it. I've always assumed it was a dastardly plot to make sure you don't have a lover on the side.'

Maggie laughed unconvincingly.

'Something else is worrying you, isn't it, Mom?' said Tara quietly. 'Do you want to tell me about it?'

'I discovered an envelope addressed to me hidden in one of his drawers.'

'The old romantic,' said Tara. 'What did he have to say?'

'I've no idea. I haven't opened it.'

'Why not, for heaven's sake?'

'Because he's written clearly on the outside, "Not to be opened before 17 December".'

'Mom, it's probably just a Christmas card,' said Tara lightly.

'I doubt it,' said Maggie. 'I don't know many husbands who give their wives Christmas cards, and certainly not in a brown envelope hidden in a drawer.'

'If you're that anxious about it, Mom, I'm sure Dad would want you to open it. Then you might find out you've been worrying about nothing.'

'Not until 17 December,' said Maggie quietly. 'If Connor arrived home before then and discovered I'd opened it, he'd . . .'

'When did you find it?'

'This morning. It was among his sports clothes, in a drawer I hardly ever open.'

'I'd have opened it straight away if it had been addressed to me,' said Tara.

'I know you would,' said Maggie, 'but I still think I'd better leave it for a few more days before I do anything. I'll put it back in the drawer in case he suddenly turns up. Then he'll never know I'd even come across it.'

'Perhaps I should fly back to Washington.'

'Why?' asked Maggie.

'To help you open it.'

'Stop being silly, Tara.'

'No sillier than you just sitting there on your own fretting about what might be inside.'

'Perhaps you're right.'

'If you're so uncertain, Mother, why don't you give Joan a call and ask her advice?'

'I already have.'

'And what did she say?'

'Open it.'

Bolchenkov sat on the desk at the front of the operations room and looked down at the twenty hand-picked men. He struck a match and lit his seventh cigarette of the morning.

'How many people are we expecting in the square this afternoon?' he asked.

'It's only a guess, Chief,' said the most senior uniformed officer present, 'but it could be as many as a hundred thousand.'

A murmur of whispered conversations broke out.

'Quiet,' said the Chief sharply. 'Why so many, Captain? Chernopov only managed seventy thousand.'

'Zerimski's a far more charismatic figure, and now that the polls are moving in his direction, I predict he'll prove a much bigger draw.'

'How many officers can you spare me on the ground?'

'Every available man will be in the square, Chief, and I've cancelled all leave. I've already issued the man's description, in the hope that we can pick him up before he even reaches the square. But not many of them have any experience of something this big.'

'If there are really going to be a hundred thousand people in the square,' said Bolchenkov, 'it will be a first for me as well. Have all your officers been issued with the description?'

'Yes, but he may be in disguise. In any case, there are a lot of tall foreigners with blue eyes and sandy hair out there. And don't forget, they haven't been told why he's wanted for questioning. We don't need a panic on our hands.'

'Agreed. But I don't want to frighten him off now, just to give him a second chance later. Has anyone picked up any more information?'

'Yes, Chief,' replied a younger man leaning against the back wall. The Chief stubbed out his cigarette and nodded.

'There are three South African journalists officially covering the election. From the description given to us by our informant, I'm fairly confident it's the one who calls himself Piet de Villiers.'

'Anything on the computer about him?'

'No,' said the young officer. 'But the police in Johannesburg were extremely cooperative. They have three men on their files answering to that name, with crimes ranging from petty theft to bigamy, but none of them fitted the description, and in any case two of them are currently locked up. They've no idea of the whereabouts of the third. They also mentioned a Colombian connection.'

'What Colombian connection?'

'A few weeks ago the CIA circulated a confidential memo giving details about the murder of a presidential candidate in Bogotá. It seems they traced the assassin to

South Africa, then lost him. I called my contact at the
CIA, but all he could tell me was that they knew the man
was on the move again, and that he was last seen boarding
a plane for Geneva.'

'That's all I need,' said the Chief. 'I don't suppose
there was any sign of de Villiers when Zerimski visited
the Hermitage this morning?'

'No, Chief,' said another voice, 'not if he was with the
press corps. There were twenty-three journalists there,
and only two of them vaguely fitted the description.
One was Clifford Symonds, an anchor with CNN, and
the other I've known for years. I play chess with him.'
Everyone in the room laughed, helping to break the
tension.

'Rooftops and buildings?' said the Chief.

'I have a dozen men detailed to cover the rooftops
around the square,' said the head of the small-arms unit.
'Most of the buildings are public offices, so I'll station
plain-clothes officers at every entrance and exit. If anyone fitting the description tries to enter the square, or
any of the buildings overlooking it, he'll be arrested on
the spot.'

'Be careful you don't arrest some foreign dignitary and
get us into even worse trouble. Any questions?'

'Yes, Chief. Have you considered calling off the rally?'
asked a voice from the back.

'I have, and I decided against it. If I were to cancel a
meeting every time I received a threat to a public figure,
our telephone lines would be blocked with calls from
every half-baked radical with nothing better to do than
cause mayhem. In any case, it could still be a false alarm.
And even if de Villiers is roaming around the city, when
he sees our presence on the ground he might have
second thoughts. Any more questions?'

No one stirred.

'If any of you picks up anything, and I mean anything,
I want to know immediately. Heaven help the man who

tells me afterwards, "I didn't mention it, Chief, because I didn't think it was important at the time."'

Connor kept the television on while he shaved. Hillary Bowker was bringing viewers up to date with what was happening in the States. The Arms Reduction Bill had passed the House, squeaking home by a mere three votes. Tom Lawrence was nevertheless claiming the result as a triumph for common sense. The pundits, on the other hand, were already warning that the Bill would face a far tougher passage once it reached the floor of the Senate.

'Not at all,' the President had assured the assembled journalists at his morning press briefing. Connor smiled. 'The House was simply carrying out the will of the people, and I'm confident that the Senate will want to do exactly the same.'

The President was replaced by a pretty girl with bright red hair who reminded Connor of Maggie. In my line of work I should have married a newscaster, he had once told her.

'And now, to find out more about the upcoming elections in Russia, we go over to Clifford Symonds, our correspondent in St Petersburg.'

Connor stopped shaving and stared at the screen.

'The opinion polls show that the two leading candidates, Prime Minister Grigory Chernopov and Communist Party leader Victor Zerimski, are now running neck and neck. The Communist candidate will be addressing a rally in Freedom Square this afternoon that the police are predicting could be attended by as many as a hundred thousand people. This morning Mr Zerimski will have a private meeting with General Borodin, who is expected shortly to announce his withdrawal from the race following his poor showing in the latest opinion polls. Uncertainty remains as to which of the two front-runners he will support, and on that decision could hang the result of the election. This is Clifford Symonds, CNN International, St Petersburg.'

Hillary Bowker's face reappeared on the screen. 'And now for the weather,' she said with a broad smile.

Connor flicked off the television, as he had no interest in being told the temperature in Florida. He rubbed some more lather into his stubble and continued shaving. He had already decided that he wasn't going to attend Zerimski's morning press conference, which would be nothing more than a panegyric from his press secretary about what his boss had achieved even before breakfast, or go to the Hermitage and spend most of his time avoiding Mitchell. He would concentrate on Zerimski's main public appearance that day. He had already found a convenient restaurant on the west side of the square. It wasn't known for its cuisine, but it did have the advantage of being on the second floor, and overlooking Freedom Square. More important, it had a rear door, so he wouldn't have to enter the square before it was necessary.

Once he had left his hotel, he called the restaurant from the nearest public phonebox and booked a corner table by the window for twelve o'clock. He then went in search of a rented car, which was even harder to find in St Petersburg than it had been in Moscow. Forty minutes later he drove into the centre of the city and left the vehicle in an underground carpark only a couple of hundred yards from Freedom Square. He had decided to drive back to Moscow after the speech. That way he would soon find out if anyone was following him. He walked up into the street, strolled into the nearest hotel and slipped the head porter a twenty-dollar bill, explaining that he needed a room for about an hour so that he could take a shower and change his clothes.

When he came back down in the lift a few minutes before twelve, the head porter didn't recognise him. Connor left a duffle bag with him and said he would be back to pick it up around four. When the porter placed the bag under the counter he noticed the briefcase for the first time. As each bore a label with the same name, he put them together.

Connor walked slowly up the side street next to Freedom Square. He passed two policemen who were questioning a tall, sandy-haired foreigner. They didn't give him a second glance as he slipped inside and took the lift to the second-floor restaurant. He gave the head waiter his name, and was immediately directed to a corner table. He sat so that he was shielded from most of the other diners, but still had a bird's-eye view of the square below.

He was thinking about Tom Lawrence, and wondering how late he would leave it before he made up his mind, when a waiter appeared by his side and handed him the menu. Connor glanced out of the window, and was surprised to find that the square was already filling up, although there were still two hours to go before Zerimski was due to deliver his speech. Among the crowd he spotted several plain-clothes policemen. One or two of the younger ones were already clinging to statues and checking carefully around the square. But what were they looking for? Was the Chief of Police being over-cautious, or did he fear there might be some form of demonstration during Zerimski's speech?

The head waiter returned. 'Could I please take your order, sir? The police have instructed us to close the restaurant before two o'clock.'

'Then I'd better have the minute steak,' said Connor.

CHAPTER SIXTEEN

'WHERE DO YOU THINK HE IS RIGHT NOW?' asked Sergei.

'He'll be out there somewhere, but if I know him he'll be damn near impossible to find in this crowd,' said Jackson. 'It will be like looking for a needle in a haystack.'

'Who ever lost a needle in a haystack?'

'Stop making smart-assed remarks and do what you're being paid for,' said Jackson. 'I'll give you a ten-dollar bonus if you can spot him. Remember, he's likely to be well disguised.'

Sergei suddenly took a far greater interest in the crowd milling around in the square. 'See that man on the top step in the north corner?' he said. 'Talking to a policeman.'

'Yes,' replied Jackson.

'That's Vladimir Bolchenkov, the Chief of Police. A fair man, even though he's the second most powerful person in St Petersburg.'

'Who's the first?' asked Jackson. 'The Mayor?'

'No, his brother Joseph. He's the city's Mafya boss.'

'Doesn't that cause a slight conflict of interest?'

'No. You only get arrested in St Petersburg if you're not Mafya.'

'Where do you get all your information?' asked Jackson.

'My mother. She's slept with both of them.'

Jackson laughed as they continued to watch the Chief talking to the uniformed officer. He would have liked to overhear their conversation. If it had been taking place in Washington, the CIA would have been able to play back every word that passed between them.

'You see the young men draped around the statues?' said the senior police officer standing next to Bolchenkov.

'What about them?' said the Chief.

'Just in case you were wondering why I haven't arrested them, they're all members of my team, and have a better view of the crowd than anyone. Look behind you, Chief: the hotdog salesman, the two men on the flower barrows and the four news-vendors are also mine. And I've got twelve busloads of uniformed police less than a block away, who can be pulled in at a moment's notice. There will also be another hundred plain-clothes men drifting in and out of the square during the next hour. Every exit is covered, and anyone who has a view of the square will have one of my men within a few feet of him.'

'If he's as good as I think he is,' said the Chief, 'he'll have found somewhere you haven't thought of.'

Connor ordered a cup of coffee and continued to watch the activity taking place in the square below. Although there were still thirty minutes to go before the candidate was due to arrive, the square was already packed with everyone from Zerimski-worshippers to the simply curious. He was amused by how hard the hotdog vendor was trying to disguise the fact that he was a policeman. The poor man had just received another voluble complaint – probably forgotten the ketchup. Connor turned his attention to the far side of the square. The little stand erected for the press was now the only area that remained unoccupied. He wondered why so many plain-clothes detectives were milling around, far more than was necessary to keep a casual passer-by from straying into a reserved area. Something didn't add up. He was distracted by a hot coffee being placed in front of him. He checked his watch. Zerimski should have finished his meeting with General Borodin by now. The outcome would lead the news on all the networks that evening. Connor wondered if he would be able to tell from Zerimski's manner if a deal had been struck.

He called for the bill, and while he waited he concentrated on the scene below him for the last time. No professional would ever have considered Freedom Square a suitable target area. Besides all the problems he had already identified, the Chief of Police's thoroughness was evident for anyone to see. Despite this, Connor felt that the sheer size of the crowd would give him his best opportunity yet to study Zerimski at close quarters, which was why he had decided not to sit among the press on this occasion.

He paid his bill in cash, walked slowly over to the girl seated in the little booth and passed her a ticket. She handed him his hat and coat, and he gave her a five-rouble note. Old people always leave small tips, he'd read somewhere.

He joined a large group of workers streaming out of offices on the first floor, who had obviously been given time off to attend the rally. Any managers within a mile of the square had probably accepted that not much work was going to be done that afternoon. Two plain-clothes policemen standing a few yards from the door were scrutinising the group of workers, but because of the freezing air they were revealing as little of themselves as possible. Connor found himself being borne along by the crowd as it flowed out onto the pavement.

Freedom Square was already packed as Connor tried to squeeze between the bodies and make his way towards the podium. The crowd must be well over seventy thousand strong. He knew that the Chief of Police would have been praying for a thunderstorm, but it was a typical winter's day in St Petersburg – cold, sharp and clear. He looked towards the roped-off press enclosure, which still seemed to have a considerable amount of activity going on around it. He smiled when he spotted Mitchell in his usual place, about ten feet from where he himself would normally have been seated. Not today, my friend. At least this time Mitchell was wearing a warm overcoat and the appropriate headgear.

'Good day for pickpockets,' said Sergei, scanning the crowd.

'Would they risk it with this sort of police presence?' asked Jackson.

'You can always find a cop when you don't need one,' said Sergei. 'I've already seen some old lags leaving with wallets. But the police don't seem interested.'

'Perhaps they've got enough problems on their hands, what with a crowd of nearly a hundred thousand and Zerimski expected to arrive at any moment.'

Sergei's eyes settled on the Chief of Police. 'Where is he?' Bolchenkov was asking a sergeant with a walkie-talkie.

'He left the meeting with Borodin eighteen minutes ago, and is being driven down Preyti Street. He should be with us in about seven minutes.'

'Then in seven minutes our problems begin,' said the Chief, checking his watch.

'Don't you think it's possible our man might just try taking a shot at Zerimski while he's in the car?'

'Not a chance,' said the Chief. 'We're dealing with a pro. He wouldn't consider a moving target, especially one in a bulletproof car. In any case, he couldn't be certain which vehicle Zerimski was in. No, our man's out there in that crowd somewhere, I feel it in my bones. Don't forget, the last time he tried something like this, it was a standing target in the open. That way it's almost impossible to hit the wrong person; and with a big crowd you have a better chance of escaping.'

Connor was still edging his way slowly towards the platform. He cast an eye round the crowd, and identified several more plain-clothes policemen. Zerimski wouldn't mind, as they would only add to the numbers. All he would care about was having a larger turnout than Chernopov.

Connor checked the roofs. A dozen or so marksmen were scanning the crowd with binoculars. They couldn't have been more obvious if they'd been wearing yellow tracksuits. There were also at least a couple of hundred uniformed police standing around the perimeter of the square. The Chief obviously believed in the value of deterrence.

The windows of the buildings around the square were crammed with office-workers trying to get the best possible view of what was going on below them. Once again Connor glanced towards the roped-off press enclosure, which was now beginning to fill up. The police were checking everyone's credentials carefully – nothing unusual about that, except that some of the journalists were being asked to remove their headgear. Connor watched for a few moments. Everyone being challenged had two things in common: they were male, and they were tall. It caused him to stop in his tracks. Then, out of the corner of his eye, he caught sight of Mitchell a few paces away from him in the crowd. He frowned. How had the young agent recognised him?

Suddenly, without warning, a loud roar came from behind him, as if a rock star had arrived on stage. He turned and watched Zerimski's motorcade make its slow progress around three sides of the square, coming to a halt in the north-west corner. The crowd was applauding enthusiastically, although they couldn't possibly see the candidate, as the windows of all the cars were black. The doors of the Zil limousines were opened, but there was no way of knowing if Zerimski was among those who had stepped out, as he was surrounded by so many burly bodyguards.

When the candidate finally mounted the steps a few moments later, the crowd began cheering even louder, reaching a climax as he walked to the front of the stage. He stopped and waved first in one direction and then another. By now Connor could have told you how many paces he would take before he turned and waved again.

People were leaping up and down to get a better view, but Connor ignored the bedlam all around him. He kept his eye on the police, most of whom were looking away from the stage. They were searching for something, or someone, in particular. A thought flashed across his mind, but he dismissed it at once. No, it wasn't possible. Paranoia setting in. He'd once been told by a veteran agent that it was always at its worst on your last assignment.

But if you were in any doubt, the rule was always the same: get yourself out of the danger area. He looked around the square, quickly weighing up which exit he should take. The crowd was beginning to calm down as they waited for Zerimski to speak. Connor decided he would start moving towards the north end of the square the moment there was a burst of prolonged applause. That way it was less likely that he'd be noticed slipping through the crowd. He glanced, almost as a reflex action, to see where Mitchell was. He was still standing a few yards to his right, if anything a little closer than when he had first spotted him.

Zerimski approached the microphone with his hands raised, to let the crowd know that he was about to begin his speech.

'I've seen the needle,' said Sergei.

'Where?' demanded Jackson.

'There, about twenty paces from stage. He has differ-

ent-coloured hair and walks like an old man. You owe
me ten dollars.'

'How did you pick him out from this distance?' asked
Jackson.

'He is the only one trying to leave the square.'

Jackson passed over a ten-dollar bill as Zerimski
stopped in front of the microphone. The old man who
had introduced him in Moscow sat alone at the back of
the stage. Zerimski didn't allow that kind of mistake to
happen a second time.

'Comrades,' he began resonantly, 'it is a great honour
for me to stand before you as your candidate. As each
day passes, I become more and more aware . . .'

As Connor scanned the crowd, he once again caught
sight of Mitchell. He'd taken another step towards him.

'Although few of our citizens wish to return to the old
totalitarian days of the past, the vast majority . . .'

Just the odd word change here and there, thought
Connor. He noticed that Mitchell had taken another
step towards him.

'. . . want to see a fairer distribution of the wealth that
has been created by their skills and hard work.' As the
crowd began to cheer, Connor quickly moved a few paces
to his right. When the applause died down, he froze, not
moving a muscle.

'Why is the man on the bench following your friend?'
asked Sergei.

'Because he's an amateur,' said Jackson.

'Or a professional who knows exactly what he's doing?'
suggested Sergei.

'My God, don't tell me I'm losing my touch,' said
Jackson.

'So far he's done everything but kiss him,' said Sergei.

'Look at the streets of St Petersburg, comrades,' continued Zerimski. 'Yes, you will see Mercedes, BMWs and
Jaguars, but who is driving them? Only the privileged
few . . .'

When the crowd burst into applause again, Connor took a few more steps towards the north end of the square.

'I look forward to the day when this is not the only country on earth where limousines outnumber family cars . . .'

Connor glanced back to find that Mitchell had taken two or three more steps in his direction. What was he playing at?

'. . . and where there are more Swiss bank accounts than hospitals.'

He would have to lose him during the next burst of applause. He concentrated on Zerimski's words, to anticipate exactly when he would make his move.

'I think I've spotted him,' said a plain-clothes policeman who was sweeping the crowd through a pair of binoculars.

'Where, where?' demanded Bolchenkov, grabbing the glasses.

'Twelve o'clock, fifty yards back, not moving a muscle. He's in front of a woman wearing a red scarf. He doesn't look like his photograph, but whenever there's a burst of applause he moves too quickly for a man of that age.'

Bolchenkov began focusing the glasses. 'Got him,' he said. After a few seconds he added, 'Yes, it might just be him. Brief those two at one o'clock to move in and arrest him, and tell the pair twenty yards in front of him to cover them. Let's get it over with as quickly as possible.' The young officer looked anxious. 'If we've made a mistake,' said the Chief, 'I'll take the responsibility.'

'Let us never forget,' continued Zerimski, 'that Russia can once again be the greatest nation on earth . . .'

Mitchell was now only a pace away from Connor, who was studiously ignoring him. In just a few more seconds there would be an extended ovation when Zerimski told the crowd what he intended to do when he became President. No bank accounts supplied by the bribes of dishonest businessmen – that always got the loudest cheer of all. Then he'd be clean away, and would make sure that Mitchell was transferred to a desk job in some mosquito-infested backwater.

'. . . I shall be dedicating myself to your service, and be more than satisfied with the salary of a President, rather than taking bribes from dishonest businessmen whose only interest is in pillaging the nation's assets.'

The crowd erupted into cheers. Connor turned suddenly and began moving to his right. He had taken almost three strides when the first policeman grabbed his left arm. A second later another came at him from the right. He was thrown to the ground, but made no attempt to resist. Rule one: when you've nothing to hide, don't resist arrest. His hands were wrenched behind his back and a pair of handcuffs snapped around his wrists. The crowd began to form a little circle around the three men on the ground. They were now far more interested in the sideshow than in Zerimski's words. Mitchell hung back slightly, and waited for the inevitable 'Who is he?'

'Mafya hitman,' he whispered into the ears of those nearest him. He moved back towards the press enclosure, muttering the words 'Mafya hitman' periodically.

'Let me leave you good citizens in no doubt that if I were to be elected President, you can be sure of one thing . . .'

'You're under arrest,' said a third man whom Connor couldn't see because his nose was being pressed firmly against the ground.

'Take him away,' said the same authoritative voice, and Connor was bundled off towards the north end of the square.

Zerimski had spotted the disturbance in the crowd, but like an old pro he ignored it. 'If Chernopov were to be elected, the Americans would be more concerned about the views of Mexico than those of Russia,' he continued unfalteringly.

Jackson never took his eyes off Connor as the crowd quickly divided, making a path to allow the police through.

'My friends, there are only six days to go before the people decide . . .'

Mitchell walked quickly away from the commotion and headed towards the press stand.

'Don't do it for me. Don't even do it for the Communist Party. Do it for the next generation of Russians . . .'

The police car, surrounded by four motorcycles, began to make its way out of the square.

'. . . who will then be able to play their part as citizens of the greatest nation on earth. I ask for only one thing – the privilege of being allowed to lead those people.' This time he was silent until he was sure he had the attention of everyone in the square, before ending softly with the words, 'Comrades, I offer myself as your servant.'

He stood back, and suddenly the noise of the police sirens was obliterated by the roar of a hundred thousand voices.

Jackson looked towards the press enclosure. He could see that the journalists were far more interested in the disappearing police car than in Zerimski's frequently repeated words.

'Mafya hitman,' the Turkish journalist was informing a colleague – a 'fact' that she had picked up from someone in the crowd, whom she would later quote as 'an authoritative source'.

Mitchell was looking up at a row of television cameramen who were following the progress of the police car as it disappeared out of sight, its blue lamp flashing. His eyes settled on the one person he needed to speak to. He waited patiently for Clifford Symonds to look in his direction, and when he eventually did, Mitchell waved his arms to indicate that he needed to speak to him urgently. The CNN reporter quickly joined the American Cultural Attaché among the cheering throng.

Zerimski remained in the centre of the platform, soaking up the adulation of the crowd. He had no intention of leaving while they were still howling their approval.

Symonds listened carefully to what Mitchell had to tell him. He was due on air in twelve minutes. The smile on his face became broader by the second.

'Are you absolutely certain?' he asked, when Mitchell had finished speaking.

'Have I ever let you down in the past?' Mitchell asked, trying to sound offended.

'No,' said Symonds apologetically. 'You never have.'

'But you must keep this piece of information a million miles away from the Embassy.'

'Of course. But who shall I say is my source?'

'A resourceful and diligent police force. That's the last thing the Chief of Police is going to deny.'

Symonds laughed. 'I'd better get back to my producer if I'm going to lead on this for the morning newscast.'

'OK,' said Mitchell. 'Just remember – make sure it can't be traced back to me.'

'Have I ever let *you* down in the past?' retorted Symonds. He turned and dashed back towards the press enclosure.

Mitchell slipped away in the opposite direction. There was still one more receptive ear in which he needed to plant the story, and it would have to be done before Zerimski left the stage.

A protective line of bodyguards was barring any over-enthusiastic supporters from getting near the candidate. Mitchell could see his press secretary only a few yards away, basking in the cheers his leader was receiving.

Mitchell told one of the guards in perfect Russian who he needed to speak to. The thug turned around and shouted at the press secretary. If Zerimski was elected, thought Mitchell, it wasn't exactly going to be a subtle administration. The press secretary made an immediate sign to let the American through, and he entered the cordoned-off area and joined another of his chess partners. He briefed him quickly, telling him that de Villiers had been disguised as an old man, and which hotel he'd been seen leaving just before he'd entered the restaurant.

By the end of the day, it would have dawned on Fitzgerald and Jackson that they had both been dealing with a real professional.

CHAPTER SEVENTEEN

THE PRESIDENT and his Chief of Staff sat alone in the
Oval Office, watching the early-morning news. Neither
of them spoke as Clifford Symonds presented his report.

'An international terrorist was arrested in Freedom
Square this afternoon during a speech given by the Communist leader Victor Zerimski. The as-yet unnamed man
is being held in the notorious Crucifix Prison in the
centre of St Petersburg. The local police are not ruling
out the possibility that this may be the same man who
was recently linked with the assassination of Ricardo Guzman, a presidential candidate in Colombia. The man
who police have arrested is thought to have been following Zerimski for several days while he was campaigning
around the country. Only last week he was described in
Time magazine as the most expensive hired gun in the
west. He is thought to have been offered a million dollars
by the Russian Mafya to remove Zerimski from the presidential race. When the police tried to arrest him, it took
four of them just to hold him down.'

Some footage followed of a man being arrested in
the crowd and hustled away, but the best shot they had
managed was the back of a head covered in a fur hat.
Symonds' face reappeared on the screen.

'The Communist candidate continued to deliver his
speech, although the arrest took place only a few yards

in front of the platform. Zerimski later praised the St Petersburg police for their diligence and professionalism, and vowed that however many attempts were made on his life, nothing would deter him from his fight against organised crime. Zerimski is currently running neck and neck with Prime Minister Chernopov in the opinion polls, but many observers feel that today's incident will give a boost to his popularity in the final run-up to the election.

'A few hours before Zerimski addressed the rally, he held a private meeting with General Borodin at his headquarters on the north side of the city. No one knows the outcome of those talks, but the General's spokesmen are not denying that he will soon be making a statement about whether he intends to continue his campaign for President, and perhaps more importantly, which of the two remaining candidates he would pledge to support were he to withdraw. The election has suddenly been thrown wide open. This is Clifford Symonds, CNN International, in Freedom Square, St Petersburg.'

'On Monday the Senate will continue to debate the Nuclear, Biological, Chemical and Conventional Arms Reduction . . .'

The President pressed a button on his remote control, and the screen went blank.

'And you're telling me that the man they've arrested has no connection with the Russian Mafya, but is a CIA agent?'

'Yes. I'm waiting for Jackson to call in and confirm that it's the same man who killed Guzman.'

'What do I say to the press if they question me about this?'

'You'll have to bluff, because we don't need anyone to know that the man they're holding is one of ours.'

'But it would finish off Dexter and her little shit of a Deputy once and for all.'

'Not if you claimed you knew nothing about it, because

then half the population would dismiss you as a CIA dupe. But if you admit you did know, the other half would want you impeached. So for now, I suggest you confine yourself to saying that you are awaiting the result of the Russian elections with interest.'

'You bet I am,' said Lawrence. 'The last thing I need is for that evil little fascist Zerimski to become President. We'd be back to Star Wars overnight.'

'I expect that's exactly why the Senate is holding out on your Arms Reduction Bill. They won't want to make a final decision until they know the outcome of the election.'

Lawrence nodded. 'If it's one of ours they've got holed up in that goddamn jail, we've got to do something about it, and quickly. Because if Zerimski does become President, then God help him. I certainly wouldn't be able to.'

Connor didn't speak. He was wedged between two officers in the back of the police car. He knew these young men had neither the rank nor the authority to question him. That would come later, and from someone with a lot more braid on his lapel.

As they drove through the vast wooden gates of the Crucifix prison and into a cobbled yard, the first thing Connor saw was the reception party. Three massive men in prisoners' garb stepped forward, almost pulled the car's back door off its hinges and dragged him out. The young policemen who had been sitting on either side of him looked terrified.

The three thugs quickly bundled the new prisoner across the yard and into a long, bleak corridor. That was when the kicking and punching began. Connor would have protested, but their vocabulary seemed to consist only of grunts. When they reached the far end of the corridor, one of them pulled open a heavy steel door and the other two threw him into a tiny cell. He made no effort to struggle when they removed first his shoes, then his watch, wedding ring and wallet – from which they would learn nothing. They left, slamming the cell door closed behind them.

Connor rose slowly to his feet and warily stretched his limbs, trying to discover if any bones had been broken. There didn't seem to be any permanent damage, he decided, although the bruises were already beginning to appear. He looked around the room, which wasn't much larger than the sleeping compartment he'd travelled in from Moscow. The green brick walls looked as if they hadn't seen a splash of paint since the turn of the century.

Connor had spent eighteen months in a far more restricted space in Vietnam. Then his orders had been clear: when questioned by the enemy, give only your name, rank and serial number. The same rules did not apply to those who lived by the Eleventh Commandment:

> *Thou shalt not get caught. But if you are, deny absolutely that you have anything to do with the CIA. Don't worry – the Company will always take care of you.*

Connor realised that in his case he could forget 'the usual diplomatic channels', despite Gutenburg's reassurances. Lying on the bunk in his tiny cell, it now all fell so neatly into place.

He hadn't been asked to sign for the cash, or for the car. And he now remembered the sentence he'd been trying to recall from the recesses of his mind. He went over it word by word:

'If it's your new job you're worrying about, I'd be happy to have a word with the Chairman of the company you're joining and explain to him that it's only a short-term assignment.'

How did Gutenburg know he'd been interviewed for a new job, and that he was dealing directly with the Chairman of the company? He knew because he'd already spoken to Ben Thompson. That was the reason they had withdrawn their offer. '*I'm sorry to inform you . . .*'

As for Mitchell, he should have seen through that angelic choirboy façade. But he was still puzzled by the phone call from the President. Why had Lawrence never once referred to him by name? And the sentences had been a little disjointed, the laugh a little too loud.

Even now he found it hard to believe the lengths to which Helen Dexter was willing to go to save her own skin. He stared up at the ceiling. If the President had never made the phone call in the first place, he realised he had no hope of being released from the Crucifix. Dexter had successfully removed the one person who might expose her, and Lawrence could do nothing about it.

Connor's unquestioning acceptance of the CIA operative's code had made him a willing pawn in her survival plan. No Ambassador would be making diplomatic protests on his behalf. There would be no food parcels. He would have to take care of himself, just as he had in Vietnam. And he had already been told by one of the young officers who'd arrested him of another problem he would face this time: no one had escaped from the Crucifix in eighty-four years.

The cell door suddenly swung open, and a man dressed in a light blue uniform covered in gold braid walked in. He took his time lighting a cigarette. His fifteenth that day.

Jackson remained in the square until the police car was out of sight. He was furious with himself. He finally turned and marched off, leaving the cheering mob behind him, walking so quickly that Sergei had to run to keep up with him. The young Russian had already decided that this was not a time to be asking questions. The word 'Mafya' was on the lips of everyone they passed in the street. Sergei was relieved when Jackson stopped and hailed a taxi.

Jackson could only admire how well Mitchell – no doubt guided by Dexter and Gutenburg – had carried out the whole operation. It was a classic CIA sting, but with a difference: this time it was one of their own they had ruthlessly left languishing in a foreign jail.

He tried not to think about what they would be putting Connor through. Instead he concentrated on the report he was about to make to Andy Lloyd. If only he had been able to contact him the previous night, he might have got the go-ahead to pull Connor out. His cellphone still wasn't working, so he was going to have to risk using the phone in his hotel room. After twenty-nine years, he had been given one chance to balance the books. And he had been found wanting.

The taxi stopped outside Jackson's hotel. He paid the fare and ran inside. Not bothering to wait for the elevator, he leapt up the stairs until he reached the first floor and then sprinted down the corridor to Room 132. Sergei had only just caught up with him by the time he had turned the key and opened the door.

The young Russian sat on the floor in the corner of the room and listened to one half of a conversation Jackson had with someone called Lloyd. When he eventually put the phone down, Jackson was white and trembling with rage.

Sergei spoke for the first time since they had left the square: 'Maybe it's time I called one of my mother's customers.'

'Congratulations,' said Dexter the moment Gutenburg entered her office. The Deputy Director smiled as he took the seat opposite his boss and placed a folder on her desk.

'I've just been watching the headlines on ABC and CBS,' she said. 'They've both run with Symonds' version of what took place in Freedom Square. Is there any feel yet as to how big the press are going to play the story tomorrow?'

'They're already losing interest. Not a shot was fired, not even a punch was thrown, and the suspect turned out to be unarmed. And no one's suggesting that the man they've arrested might be an American. By this time tomorrow, the story will only be making the front pages in Russia.'

'How are we responding to any press enquiries?'

'We're saying that it's an internal problem for the Russians, and that in St Petersburg hired gunmen come cheaper than a decent wristwatch. I tell them they only have to read *Time*'s piece on the Russian Godfather last month to appreciate the problems they're facing. If they push me, I point them in the direction of Colombia. If they keep on pushing, I throw in South Africa. That gives them several column inches to feed their hungry editors.'

'Did any of the networks show footage of Fitzgerald after he'd been arrested?'

'Only the back of his head, and even then he was surrounded by police. Otherwise you can be sure they'd have run it over and over.'

'What chance is there of him appearing in public and making a statement that would compromise us, and that the press might follow up?'

'Virtually none. If they ever do hold a trial, the foreign press will certainly be excluded. And if Zerimski's elected, Fitzgerald will never set foot outside the Crucifix again.'

'Have you prepared a report for Lawrence?' asked Dexter. 'Because you can be sure he'll be trying to make two and two equal six.'

Gutenburg leant forward and tapped the file he had placed on the Director's desk.

She flicked it open and began reading, showing no sign of emotion as she turned the pages. When she reached the end, she closed the file and allowed a flicker of a smile to cross her face before passing it back across the table.

'See that it's signed in your name and sent over to the White House immediately,' she said. 'Because whatever doubts the President may have at this moment, if Zerimski becomes President, he will never want to refer to the subject again.'

Gutenburg nodded his agreement.

Helen Dexter looked across the desk at her deputy. 'It's a pity we had to sacrifice Fitzgerald,' she said. 'But if it helps to get Zerimski elected, it will have served a double purpose. Lawrence's Arms Reduction Bill will be rejected by Congress, and the CIA will have far less interference from the White House.'

Connor swung his legs off the bunk, placed his bare feet on the stone floor and faced his visitor. The Chief took a long drag on his cigarette and blew the smoke high into the air. 'Filthy habit,' he said, in flawless English. 'My wife never stops telling me to give it up.'

Connor showed no emotion.

'My name is Vladimir Bolchenkov. I am the Chief of Police of this city, and I thought we might have a little chat before we think about putting anything on the record.'

'My name is Piet de Villiers. I am a South African citizen working for the *Johannesburg Journal*, and I wish to see my Ambassador.'

'Now there's my first problem,' said Bolchenkov, the cigarette dangling from the corner of his mouth. 'You see, I don't believe your name is Piet de Villiers, I'm fairly sure you're not South African, and I know for certain that you don't work for the *Johannesburg Journal*, because there's no such paper. And just so we don't waste too much of each other's time, I have it on the highest authority that you were not hired by the Mafya. Now, I admit that I don't yet know who you are, or even which country you come from. But whoever it is that sent you has, to use a modern colloquialism, dropped you in deep shit. And, if I may say so, from a very great height.'

Connor didn't even blink.

'But I can assure you that they are not going to do the same thing to me. So if you feel unable to assist with my enquiries, there is nothing I can do except leave you here to rot, while I continue to bask in the glory that is currently being undeservedly heaped upon me.'

Connor still didn't react.

'I see that I'm not getting through to you,' said the Chief. 'I feel it's my duty to point out that this isn't Colombia, and that I will not be switching my allegiance according to who I've spoken to most recently, or who offers me the thickest wad of dollars.' He paused and drew on his cigarette again before adding, 'I suspect that's one of the many things we have in common.'

He turned and began walking towards the cell door, then stopped. 'I'll leave you to think it over. But if I were in your shoes, I wouldn't wait too long.'

He banged on the door. 'Let me assure you, whoever you are,' he added as the door was opened, 'there will be no thumbscrews, no rack, or any other, more sophisticated forms of torment while I'm St Petersburg's Chief of Police. I don't believe in torture; it's not my style. But I cannot promise you everything will be quite so friendly if Victor Zerimski is elected as our next President.'

The Chief slammed the cell door closed, and Connor heard a key turn in the lock.

CHAPTER EIGHTEEN

THREE WHITE BMWs drew up outside the hotel. The man seated next to the driver in each car leapt out onto the pavement and checked up and down the road. Once they were satisfied, the back door of the middle car was opened to allow Alexei Romanov to step out. The tall young man was wearing a long black cashmere coat, and didn't look to either side as he walked quickly into the hotel. The other three men followed, forming a semi-circle around him.

From the description he had been given over the phone, Romanov immediately recognised the tall American standing in the middle of the hall, looking as if he was waiting for someone.

'Mr Jackson?' enquired Romanov in a guttural accent.

'Yes,' Jackson replied. He would have shaken hands if Romanov had not simply turned round and headed straight back towards the entrance.

The three cars' engines were running and their doors were still open when Jackson stepped out onto the street. He was ushered towards the back door of the centre vehicle, and sat between the man who hadn't been willing to shake hands with him and another equally silent but more heavily built man.

The three cars slipped into the centre lane, and as if by magic every other vehicle moved out of their path.

Only the traffic lights didn't seem to know who they were.

As the little motorcade swept through the city, Jackson cursed himself again. None of this would have been necessary if he had been able to get through to Lloyd twenty-four hours earlier. But that was hindsight, he thought – a gift only politicians are born with.

'You need to meet Nicolai Romanov,' Sergei had said. He had dialled his mother's number, and when the phone was eventually answered, he behaved in a way Jackson had not witnessed before. He was respectful, listened attentively, and never once interrupted. Twenty minutes later he put the phone down.

'I think she'll make the call,' he said. 'The problem is that you can't become a member of the "Thieves in Law" – or the Mafya, as you call them – until you're fourteen. It was the same even for Alexei, the Czar's only son.'

Sergei went on to explain that he had asked that Jackson should be granted a meeting with the Czar, the leader of the Thieves in Law. The organisation had been founded at the time when Russia was ruled by a real Czar, and had survived to become the most feared and respected criminal organisation in the world.

'My mother is one of the few women the Czar will talk to. She will ask him to grant you an audience,' said Sergei.

The phone rang, and he immediately picked it up. As he listened carefully to what his mother had to say, he turned white and began to tremble. He hesitated for some time, but finally agreed to whatever she was suggesting. His hand was still shaking when he put the receiver down.

'Has he agreed to see me?' asked Jackson.

'Yes,' said Sergei quietly. 'Two men come to pick you up tomorrow morning: Alexei Romanov, the Czar's son, who will succeed him when he dies, and Stefan Ivanitsky, Alexei's cousin, who is third in command.'

'Then what's the problem?'

'As they do not know you, they make one condition.'

'And what's that?'

'If the Czar thinks you waste his time, the two men will come back and break one of my legs, to remind me not to bother them again.'

'Then you'd better make sure you're not around when I get back.'

'If I'm not here they pay a call on my mother and break her leg. And when they catch me, they break both my legs. It is the unwritten code of the Mafya.'

Jackson wondered if he should cancel the meeting. He didn't want to be responsible for Sergei ending up on crutches. But the boy told him it was too late. He had already accepted their terms.

One glance at Stefan Ivanitsky, the Czar's nephew, who was seated on his right, was enough to convince Jackson that breaking a leg would take him only a moment, and would be forgotten even more quickly.

Once the BMWs had passed the city boundaries, the little motorcade quickly accelerated to sixty miles per hour. As they climbed the winding roads up into the hills, they met few other vehicles. They sped past peasants on the side of the road with their heads bowed, and no sign in their faces that they cared about either the past or the future. Jackson began to understand why Zerimski's words might excite any last flicker of hope left in them.

Without warning, the leading car suddenly swung left and stopped outside a massive wrought-iron gate dominated by a crest with a black falcon's outstretched wings. Two men holding Kalashnikovs stepped forward, and the first driver lowered a smoked-glass window to allow them to peer in. It reminded Jackson of arriving outside the CIA's headquarters – except that at Langley the guards had to be satisfied with side-arms that remained in their holsters.

After all three cars had been inspected, one of the guards nodded and the wings of the falcon split open. The motorcade proceeded at a more stately pace along a gravel drive that wound through a thick forest. It was another five minutes before Jackson caught his first glimpse of the house – though house it was not. A century before it had been the palace of an Emperor's first-born. It was now inhabited by a remote descendant who also believed in his hereditary position.

'Don't speak to the Czar unless he speaks first,' Sergei had warned him. 'And always treat him like his imperial ancestors.' Jackson preferred not to tell Sergei that he had no idea how to treat a member of the Russian Royal Family.

The cars crunched to a halt outside the front door. A tall, elegant man in a long black tailcoat, white shirt and bow tie stood waiting on the top step. He bowed to Jackson, who tried to look as if he was used to this sort of treatment. After all, he had once met Richard Nixon.

'Welcome to the Winter Palace, Mr Jackson,' said the butler. 'Mr Romanov awaits you in the Blue Gallery.'

Alexei Romanov and Stefan Ivanitsky accompanied Jackson through the open door. Jackson and the young Romanov followed the butler down a long marble corridor, while Ivanitsky remained standing by the entrance. Jackson would have liked to stop and admire the paintings and statues that would have graced any museum in the world, but the steady pace of the butler did not allow it. The butler stopped when he reached two white doors at the end of the corridor that stretched almost to the ceiling. He knocked, opened one of the doors, and stood aside to allow Jackson to enter.

'Mr Jackson,' he announced, and left the room, closing the door quietly behind him.

Jackson stepped into a vast, lavishly furnished drawing room. The floor was covered by a single carpet a Turk would have traded his life for. From a Louis XIV winged chair of red velvet rose an elderly man in a blue pin-striped suit. His hair was silver, and the pallor of his skin suggested that he had suffered a long illness. His thin body was slightly stooped as he took a step forward to shake hands with his guest.

'It is kind of you to come all this way to see me, Mr Jackson,' he said. 'You must forgive me, but my English is a little rusty. I was forced to leave Oxford in 1939, soon after the war broke out, although I was only in my second year. You see, the British never really trusted the Russians, even though we were later to become allies.' He smiled sweetly. 'I'm sure they show much the same attitude when dealing with the Americans.'

Jackson wasn't sure how to react.

'Do have a seat, Mr Jackson,' said the old man, gesturing towards the twin of the chair he had been sitting in.

'Thank you,' said Jackson. They were the first words he had spoken since leaving the hotel.

'Now, Mr Jackson,' said Romanov, lowering himself slowly into his chair, 'if I ask you a question, be sure to answer it accurately. If you are in any doubt, take your time before replying. Because should you decide to lie to me – how shall I put it? – you will find that it's not only this meeting that will be terminated.'

Jackson would have walked out there and then, but he knew that the old man was probably the one person on earth who could get Connor out of the Crucifix prison alive. He gave a curt nod to show that he understood.

'Good,' said Romanov. 'And now I should like to learn a little more about you, Mr Jackson. I can tell at a glance that you work for a law enforcement agency, and as you are in my country' – he emphasised the word *my* – 'I assume it has to be the CIA rather than the FBI. Am I right?'

'I worked for the CIA for twenty-eight years, until quite recently when I was – replaced.' Jackson chose his words carefully.

'It's against the rules of nature to have a woman as your boss,' commented Romanov, without even the suggestion of a smile. 'The organisation I control would never indulge in such stupidity.'

The old man leant across to a table on his left and picked up a small glass full of a colourless liquid that Jackson hadn't noticed until that moment. He took a sip, and replaced the glass on the table before asking his next question.

'Are you currently working for another law enforcement agency?'

'No,' said Jackson firmly.

'So you have gone freelance?' suggested the old man. Jackson didn't reply.

'I see,' he said. 'From your silence I am bound to deduce that you are not the only person who doesn't trust Helen Dexter.'

Again Jackson said nothing. But he was quickly learning why it wouldn't pay to lie to Romanov.

'Why did you want to see me, Mr Jackson?'

Jackson suspected that the old man knew exactly why, but played along with the charade. 'I came on behalf of a friend of mine who, because of my stupidity, has been arrested and is currently locked up in the Crucifix Prison.'

'An establishment that isn't known for its humanitarian record, especially when it comes to considering appeals or granting parole.'

Jackson nodded his agreement.

'I am aware that it was not your friend who was responsible for informing the press that my organisation had offered him a million dollars to remove Zerimski from the presidential race. Had that been the case, he would have been found hanging in his cell long before now. No, I suspect that the person peddling that particular piece of misinformation,' Romanov continued, 'is one of Helen Dexter's minions. If only you had come to me a little earlier, Mr Jackson, I could have warned you about Mitchell.' He took another sip from his glass and added, 'One of the few of your countrymen I would consider recruiting into my organisation. I see you are surprised by the extent of my knowledge.'

Jackson thought he hadn't moved a muscle.

'Mr Jackson, surely you wouldn't be shocked to learn that I have my own people well placed in the upper echelons of both the CIA and the FBI?' The thin smile returned to his face. 'And if I thought it would prove useful, I would also have someone working for me in the White House. But as President Lawrence will reveal anything he is asked at his weekly news conference, it's hardly necessary. Which leads on to my next question. Your friend works for the CIA?'

Jackson didn't reply.

'Ah, I see. Just as I thought. Well, I think he can be confident that Helen Dexter will not be riding to his rescue on this occasion.'

Jackson still said nothing.

'Good,' said the old man. 'So now I know exactly what you expect of me.' He paused. 'But I am at a loss to understand what you have to offer in return.'

'I have no idea what the going rate is,' said Jackson.

The old man began laughing. 'You can't believe for one moment, Mr Jackson, that I dragged you out here to discuss money, can you? Look around and you will see that however much you have to offer, it wouldn't be enough. *Time* was well short of the mark when it speculated on the extent of my power and wealth. Last year alone my organisation had a turnover of $187 billion, more than the economy of Belgium or Sweden. We now have fully operational branches in 142 countries. A new one opens every month, to paraphrase McDonald's slogan. No, Mr Jackson, I do not have enough days left on earth to waste any of them discussing money with a penniless man.'

'Then why did you agree to see me in the first place?' asked Jackson.

'You don't ask questions, Mr Jackson,' said Romanov sharply. 'You only answer them. I'm surprised that you don't appear to have been properly briefed.'

The old man took a further sip of the colourless liquid before spelling out exactly what he expected in return for assisting Connor to escape. Jackson knew he didn't have the authority to accept Romanov's terms on Connor's behalf, but as he had been instructed not to ask questions, he remained silent.

'You may need a little time to think over my proposition, Mr Jackson,' continued the old man. 'But should your friend agree to my terms and then fail to carry out his side of the bargain, he must be made fully aware of the consequences of his actions.' He paused to draw breath. 'I do hope, Mr Jackson, that he's not the sort of person who, having signed an agreement, then relies on some clever lawyer to identify a loophole that will get him out of honouring it. You see, in this court I am both judge and jury, and I shall be appointing my son Alexei as prosecuting counsel. I have made it his personal responsibility to see that this particular contract is carried out to the letter. I have already given orders that he will accompany you both back to the United States, and he will not return until the agreement has been honoured. I hope I make myself clear, Mr Jackson.'

Zerimski's office could not have been in greater contrast to the Czar's country palace. The Communist leader occupied the third floor of a dilapidated building in a northern suburb of Moscow – although anyone who was invited to stay at his dacha on the Volga quickly became aware that Zerimski was no stranger to luxury.

The last vote had been cast at ten o'clock the previous evening. Now all Zerimski could do was sit and wait for the officials from the Baltic to the Pacific to count the ballot papers. He knew only too well that in some districts people would have voted several times. In others the ballot boxes would simply never reach the town hall. But he was confident that once he had agreed terms with Borodin, and the General had withdrawn from the race, he was in with a real chance of winning. But he was enough of a realist to know that, with the Mafya backing Chernopov, he would need to poll well over half of the votes cast to have the slightest chance of being declared the winner. For that reason he had decided to make an ally in the Czar's camp.

The result of the election would not be known for a couple of days, as they still tallied the votes by hand in most parts of the country. He didn't need to be reminded of Stalin's oft-quoted remark that it doesn't matter how many people vote, only who counts them.

Zerimski's inner circle were working the phones as they tried to keep track of what was happening across the vast nation. But all the state chairmen were willing to say was that it looked too close to call. The Communist leader thumped the table more times that day than he had during the past week, and remained closeted in his room for long periods of time making private calls.

'That's good news, Stefan,' Zerimski was saying. 'As long as you can take care of the problem of your cousin.' He was listening to Ivanitsky's response when there was a knock on the door. He put the phone down the moment he saw his Chief of Staff enter the room. He had no desire for Titov to find out who he had been talking to.

'The press are wondering if you'll speak to them,' said Titov, hoping it might keep his master occupied for a few minutes. The last time Zerimski had seen the vultures, as he referred to them, was the previous morning, when they had all turned out to watch him cast his vote in Koski, the district of Moscow in which he was born. It would have been no different if he had been running for President of the United States.

Zerimski nodded reluctantly, and followed Titov down

the stairs and out onto the street. He had instructed his staff never to allow a member of the press to enter the building, for fear that they would discover just how inefficient and understaffed his organisation was. That was something else which would change once he got his hands on the state coffers. He hadn't told even his Chief of Staff that if he won, this would be the last election the Russian people would vote in while he was alive. And he didn't give a damn how many protests there were in foreign newspapers and magazines. In a very short time they would have a zero circulation east of Germany.

When Zerimski stepped out onto the pavement, he was met by the largest gathering of journalists he'd seen since the campaign had begun.

'How confident are you of victory, Mr Zerimski?' someone shouted, before he even had a chance to say good afternoon.

'If the winner is the man who the most people have voted for, I will be the next President of Russia.'

'But the chairman of the international panel of observers says that this has been the most democratic election in the history of Russia. Do you not accept that judgement?'

'I will if I'm declared victor,' replied Zerimski. The journalists laughed politely at his little pun.

'If elected, how long will it be before you visit President Lawrence in Washington?'

'Soon after he has visited me in Moscow,' came back the immediate reply.

'If you become President, what will happen to the man who was arrested in Freedom Square and accused of plotting to assassinate you?'

'That will be a decision for the courts. But you can be sure he will receive a fair trial.'

Zerimski suddenly became bored. Without warning he turned and disappeared back into the building, ignoring the questions shouted at his retreating back.

'Have you offered Borodin a post in your cabinet?'

'What will you do about Chechnya?'

'Will the Mafya be your first target?'

As he wearily climbed the worn stone stairs to the third floor he decided that, win or lose, that was the last occasion he would ever speak to the press. He didn't envy Lawrence trying to run a country where journalists expected to be treated as equals. When he reached his office he slumped into the only comfortable chair in the room, and slept for the first time in days.

The key turned in the lock, and the cell door swung open. Bolchenkov entered, carrying a large duffel bag and a battered leather briefcase.

'As you see, I have returned,' said St Petersburg's Chief of Police, sitting down opposite Connor. 'From which you can assume that I want another off-the-record chat. Though I am bound to say I hope it will be a little more productive than our last encounter.'

The Chief stared down at the man sitting on the bunk. Connor looked as if he had lost several pounds in the past five days.

'I see that you haven't yet become accustomed to our *nouvelle cuisine*,' said Bolchenkov, lighting a cigarette. 'I must confess that it does take a few days even for the low life of St Petersburg to fully appreciate the Crucifix's menu. But they come round to it once they realise that they're here for the rest of their lives, and that there is no *à la carte* alternative.' He drew deeply on his cigarette and blew the smoke out of his nose.

'In fact,' he continued, 'you may have read in the press quite recently that one of our inmates ate a fellow prisoner. But what with the food shortage and the problem of overcrowding, we didn't think it worth making a fuss about.'

Connor smiled.

'Ah, I see you are alive after all,' said the Chief. 'Now,

I have to tell you that there have been one or two interesting developments since our last meeting, which I have a feeling you will want to know about.'

He placed the duffel bag and the briefcase on the floor. 'These two pieces of luggage were reported as unclaimed by the head porter of the National Hotel.'

Connor raised an eyebrow.

'Just as I thought,' said the Chief. 'And to be fair, when we showed him your photograph, the porter confirmed that although he remembered a man fitting your description leaving the bag, he couldn't recall the briefcase. Nevertheless, I suspect you won't need to have its contents described to you.'

The Chief flicked up the knobs of the case and lifted the lid to reveal a Remington 700. Connor stared straight ahead, feigning indifference.

'Although I'm sure you have handled this type of weapon before, I'm confident that you have never seen this particular rifle, despite the initials P.D.V. being so conveniently printed on the case. Even a raw recruit could work out that you have been set up.'

Bolchenkov drew deeply on his cigarette.

'The CIA must think we have the dumbest police force on earth. Did they imagine for a moment that we don't know what Mitchell's real job is? Cultural Attaché!' he snorted. 'He probably thinks the Hermitage is a department store. Before you say anything, I have another piece of news that might be of interest to you.' He inhaled again, allowing the nicotine to reach down into his lungs. 'Victor Zerimski has won the election, and will be installed as President on Monday.'

Connor smiled weakly.

'And as I can't imagine that he'll be offering you a front-row seat for the inauguration,' said the Chief, 'perhaps the time has come for you to tell us your side of the story, Mr Fitzgerald.'

CHAPTER NINETEEN

PRESIDENT ZERIMSKI swaggered into the room. His colleagues immediately rose from their places around the long oak table and applauded until he had taken his seat below a portrait of Stalin, resurrected from the basement of the Pushkin where it had languished since 1956.

Zerimski was dressed in a dark blue suit, white shirt and red silk tie. He looked quite different from the other men seated round the table, who were still garbed in the ill-fitting clothes they had worn throughout the election campaign. The message was clear – they should all visit a tailor as soon as possible.

Zerimski allowed the applause to continue for some time before waving down his colleagues as if they were just another adoring crowd.

'Although I do not officially take office until next Monday,' he began, 'there are one or two areas where I intend to make some immediate changes.' The President looked around at those supporters who had stood by him through the lean years, and were about to be rewarded for their loyalty. Many of them had waited half a lifetime for this moment.

He turned his attention to a short, squat man who was staring blankly in front of him. Joseph Pleskov had been promoted from Zerimski's bodyguard to a full member of the Politburo the day after he had shot three men who had tried to assassinate his boss while he was on a visit to Odessa. Pleskov had one great virtue, which Zerimski would require of any cabinet minister: as long as he understood his orders, he would carry them out.

'Joseph, my old friend,' Zerimski said. 'You are to be my Minister of the Interior.' Several faces around the table tried not to show surprise or disappointment; most of them knew they were far better qualified to do the job than the former docker from the Ukraine, and some suspected he couldn't even spell 'interior'. The short, thickset man beamed at his leader like a child who had been given an unexpected toy.

'Your first responsibility, Joseph, will be to deal with organised crime. I can think of no better way of setting about that task than by arresting Nicolai Romanov, the so-called Czar. Because there will be no room for Czars, imperial or otherwise, while I am President.'

One or two of the faces that had looked sullen only a moment before suddenly cheered up. Few of them would have been willing to take on Nicolai Romanov, and none of them believed Pleskov was up to it.

'What shall I charge him with?' asked Pleskov innocently.

'Anything you like, from fraud to murder,' said Zerimski. 'Just be sure it sticks.'

Pleskov was already looking a little apprehensive. It would have been easier if the boss had simply ordered him to kill the man.

Zerimski's eye circled the table. 'Lev,' he said, turning to another man who had remained blindly loyal to him. 'I shall give you responsibility for the other half of my law and order programme.'

Lev Shulov looked nervous, unsure if he should be grateful for what he was about to receive.

'You are to be my new Justice Minister.'

Shulov smiled.

'Let me make it clear that there is far too much of a logjam in the courts at present. Appoint a dozen or so new judges. Be sure they are all long-standing Party members. Begin by explaining to them that I have only two policies when it comes to law and order: shorter trials and longer sentences. And I am keen to make an example of someone newsworthy in the first few days of my presidency, to leave no doubt about the fate of those who cross me.'

'Did you have anyone in mind, Mr President?'

'Yes,' replied Zerimski. 'You will remember . . .' There was a quiet knock on the door. Everyone turned to see who dared to interrupt the new President's first cabinet meeting. Dmitri Titov entered noiselessly, gambling that Zerimski would have been even more annoyed not to be interrupted. The President drummed his fingers on the table as Titov walked the length of the room, then bent down and whispered in his ear.

Zerimski immediately burst out laughing. The rest of them wanted to join in, but were unwilling to until they had heard the joke. He looked up at his colleagues. 'The President of the United States is on the line. It seems that he wishes to congratulate me.' Now they all felt able to join in the laughter.

'My next decision as your leader is whether I should put him on hold – for another three years . . .' They all laughed even louder, except for Titov, '. . . or whether I should take the call.'

No one offered an opinion.

'Shall we find out what the man wants?' asked Zerimski. They all nodded. Titov picked up the phone by his side and handed it to his boss.

'Mr President,' said Zerimski.

'No, sir,' came back the immediate reply. 'My name is Andy Lloyd. I am the White House Chief of Staff. May I put you through to President Lawrence?'

'No, you may not,' said Zerimski angrily. 'Tell your

President next time he calls to be on the end of the line himself, because I don't deal with messenger boys.' He slammed the phone down, and they all laughed again.

'Now, what was I saying?'

Shulov volunteered. 'You were about to tell us, Mr President, who should be made an example of in order to demonstrate the new discipline of the Justice Department.'

'Ah, yes,' said Zerimski, the smile returning to his lips just as the phone rang again.

Zerimski pointed at his Chief of Staff, who picked up the receiver.

'Would it be possible,' a voice enquired, 'to speak to President Zerimski?'

'Who's calling him?' asked Titov.

'Tom Lawrence.'

Titov handed the receiver to his boss. 'The President of the United States,' was all he said. Zerimski nodded and took the phone.

'Is that you, Victor?'

'This is President Zerimski. Who am I addressing?'

'Tom Lawrence,' said the President, raising an eyebrow to the Secretary of State and the White House Chief of Staff, who were listening in on their extensions.

'Good morning. What can I do for you?'

'I was just calling to add my congratulations to all the others you must be receiving after your impressive' – Lawrence had wanted say 'unexpected', but the State Department had counselled against it – 'victory. A very close-run thing. But everyone in politics experiences that problem from time to time.'

'It's not a problem I will experience again,' said Zerimski. Lawrence laughed, assuming this was meant to be funny. He wouldn't have done so if he could have seen the stony-faced looks of those seated around the cabinet table in the Kremlin.

Lloyd whispered, 'Keep going.'

'The first thing I'd like to do is get to know you a little better, Victor.'

'Then you will have to start by understanding that only my mother calls me by my first name.'

Lawrence looked down at the notes spread across his desk. His eye settled on Zerimski's full name, Victor Leonidovich. He underlined 'Leonidovich', but Larry Harrington shook his head.

'I'm sorry,' said Lawrence. 'How would you like me to address you?'

'The same way you would expect anyone *you* don't know to address you.'

Though they could hear only one side of it, those seated around the table in Moscow were enjoying the first encounter between the two leaders. Those in the Oval Office were not.

'Try a different tack, Mr President,' suggested the Secretary of State, cupping a hand over his phone.

Tom Lawrence glanced down at Andy Lloyd's prepared questions and skipped a page. 'I was hoping it wouldn't be too long before we could find an opportunity to meet. Come to think of it,' he added, 'it's rather surprising that we haven't bumped into each other before now.'

'It's not all that surprising,' said Zerimski. 'When you last visited Moscow, in June, your Embassy failed to issue me or any of my colleagues with an invitation to the dinner that was held for you.' There were murmurs of support from around the table.

'Well, I'm sure you know only too well that on overseas trips one is very much in the hands of one's local officials . . .'

'I shall be interested to see which of those local officials you feel need replacing after such a fundamental miscalculation.' Zerimski paused. 'Starting with your Ambassador, perhaps.'

There followed another long silence while the three

men in the Oval Office checked through the questions they had assiduously prepared. So far they had not anticipated one of Zerimski's replies.

'I can assure you,' Zerimski added, 'that I will not be allowing any of my officials, local or otherwise, to overrule *my* personal wishes.'

'Lucky man,' said Lawrence, giving up bothering with any of the prepared answers.

'Luck is not a factor I ever take into consideration,' said Zerimski. 'Especially when it comes to dealing with my opponents.'

Larry Harrington was beginning to look desperate, but Andy Lloyd scribbled a question on a pad and pushed it under the President's nose. Lawrence nodded.

'Perhaps we should try to arrange an early meeting so that we can get to know each other a little better?'

The White House trio sat waiting for the offer to be robustly rejected.

'I'll give that my serious consideration,' said Zerimski, to everyone's surprise, at both ends. 'Why don't you tell Mr Lloyd to get in touch with Comrade Titov, who is responsible for organising my meetings with foreign leaders.'

'I certainly will,' said Lawrence, feeling relieved. 'I'll ask Andy Lloyd to call Mr Titov in the next couple of days.' Lloyd scribbled another note, and handed it to him. It read: 'And of course I would be happy to visit Moscow.'

'Goodbye, Mr President,' said Zerimski.

'Goodbye – Mr President,' Lawrence replied.

As Zerimski put the phone down, he stalled the inevitable round of applause by quickly turning to his Chief of Staff and saying, 'When Lloyd rings, he will propose that I visit Washington. Accept the offer.'

His Chief of Staff looked surprised.

'I am determined,' said the President, turning back to his colleagues, 'that Lawrence should realise as soon as possible what sort of man he is dealing with. More importantly, I wish the American public to find out for themselves.' He placed his fingers together. 'I intend to begin by making sure that Lawrence's Arms Reduction Bill is defeated on the floor of the Senate. I can't think of a more appropriate Christmas present to give ... Tom.'

This time he allowed them to applaud him briefly, before silencing them with another wave of his hand.

'But we must return for the moment to our domestic problems, which are far more pressing. You see, I believe it is important that our own citizens are also made aware of the mettle of their new leader. I wish to provide them with an example that will leave no one in any doubt about how I intend to deal with those who consider opposing me.' They all waited to see who Zerimski had selected for this honour.

He turned his gaze to the newly appointed Justice Minister. 'Where is that Mafya hitman who tried to assassinate me?'

'He's locked up in the Crucifix,' said Shulov. 'Where I assume you'll want him to remain for the rest of his life.'

'Certainly not,' said Zerimski. 'Life imprisonment is far too lenient a sentence for such a barbarous criminal. This is the ideal person to put on trial. We will make him our first public example.'

'I'm afraid the police haven't been able to come up with any proof that he ...'

'Then manufacture it,' said Zerimski. 'His trial isn't going to be witnessed by anyone except loyal Party members.'

'I understand, Mr President,' said the new Justice Minister. He hesitated. 'What did you have in mind?'

'A quick trial, with one of our new judges presiding and a jury made up exclusively of Party officials.'

'And the sentence, Mr President?'

'The death penalty, of course. Once the sentence has

been passed, you will inform the press that I shall be attending the execution.'

'And when will that be?' asked the Justice Minister, writing down Zerimski's every word.

The President flicked over the pages of his diary and began searching for a fifteen-minute gap. 'Eight o'clock next Friday morning. Now, something far more important – my plans for the future of the armed forces.' He smiled at General Borodin, who was seated on his right, and who hadn't yet opened his mouth.

'For you, Deputy President, the greatest prize of all . . .'

CHAPTER TWENTY

As a PRISONER in the Nan Dinh camp, Connor had developed a system for counting the days he'd been in captivity.

At five every morning a Vietcong guard would appear carrying a bowl of rice swimming in water – his only meal of the day. Connor would remove a single grain and place it inside one of the seven bamboo poles that made up his mattress. Every week he would transfer one of the seven grains to the beam above his bed, and then eat the other six. Every four weeks he would remove one of the grains from the beam above his bed and put it between the floorboards under his bed. The day he and Chris Jackson escaped from the camp, Connor knew he had been in captivity for one year, five months and two days.

But lying on a bunk in a windowless cell in the Crucifix, even he couldn't come up with a system to record how long he had been there. The Chief of Police had now visited him twice, and left with nothing. Connor began to wonder how much longer it would be before he became impatient with his simply repeating his name and nationality, and demanding to see his Ambassador. He didn't have to wait long to find out. Only moments after Bolchenkov had left the room the second time, the three men who had greeted him on the afternoon of his arrival came charging into his cell.

Two of them dragged him off the bunk and threw him into the chair recently occupied by the Chief. They wrenched his arms behind his back and handcuffed him.

That was when Connor first saw the cut-throat razor. While two of them held him down, the third took just fourteen strokes of the rusty blade to shave every hair off his head, along with a considerable amount of skin. He hadn't wasted any time applying soap and water. The blood continued to run down Connor's face and soak his shirt long after they had left him slumped in the chair.

He recalled the words of the Chief when they had first met: 'I don't believe in torture; it's not my style.' But that was before Zerimski had become President.

He eventually slept, but for how long he could not tell. The next thing he remembered was being pulled up off the floor, hurled back into the chair and held down for a second time.

The third man had replaced his razor with a long, thick needle, and used the same degree of delicacy he had shown as a barber to tattoo the number '12995' on the prisoner's left wrist. They obviously didn't believe in names when you booked in for room and board at the Crucifix.

When they returned a third time, they yanked him up off the floor and pushed him out of the cell into a long, dark corridor. It was at times like this that he wished he lacked any imagination. He tried not to think about what they might have in mind for him. The citation for his Medal of Honor had described how Lieutenant Fitzgerald had been fearless in leading his men, had rescued a brother officer, and had made a remarkable escape from a North Vietnamese prisoner of war camp. But Connor knew he had never come across a man who was fearless. In Nan Dinh he had held out for one year, five months and two days – but then he was only twenty-two, and at twenty-two you believe you're immortal.

When they hurled him out of the corridor and into the morning sun, the first thing Connor saw was a group of prisoners erecting a scaffold. He was fifty-one now. No one needed to tell him he wasn't immortal.

When Joan Bennett checked in for work at Langley that Monday, she knew exactly how many days she had served of her eight-month sentence, because every evening, just before she left home, she would feed the cat and cross off one more date on the calendar hanging on the kitchen wall.

She left her car in the west parking lot, and headed straight for the library. Once she had signed in, she took the metal staircase down to the reference section. For the next nine hours, with only a break for a meal at midnight, she would read through the latest batch of e-mailed newspaper extracts from the Middle East. Her main task was to search for any mention of the United States and, if it was critical, electronically copy it, collate it and e-mail it to her boss on the third floor, who would consider its consequences at a more civilised hour later that morning. It was tedious, mind-deadening work. She had considered resigning on several occasions, but was determined not to give Gutenburg that satisfaction.

It was just before her midnight meal-break that Joan spotted a headline in the *Istanbul News*: 'Mafya Killer to go on Trial'. She could still only think of the Mafia as being Italian, and was surprised to discover that the article concerned a South African terrorist on trial for the attempted murder of the new President of Russia. She would have taken no further interest if she hadn't seen the line drawing of the accused man.

Joan's heart began to thump as she carefully read through the lengthy article by Fatima Kusmann, the *Istanbul News*'s Eastern European correspondent, in which she claimed to have sat next to the professional killer during a rally in Moscow which Zerimski had addressed.

Midnight passed, but Joan remained at her desk.

As Connor stood in the prison courtyard and stared up at the half-constructed scaffold, a police car drew up and one of the thugs shoved him into the back seat. He was surprised to find the Chief of Police waiting for him. Bolchenkov hardly recognised the gaunt, crop-headed man.

Neither of them spoke as the car made its way through the gates and out of the prison. The driver turned right and drove along the banks of the Neva at exactly fifty kilometres an hour. They passed three bridges before swinging left and crossing a fourth that would take them into the centre of the city. As they crossed the river, Connor stared out of the side window at the pale green palace of the Hermitage. It couldn't have been in greater contrast to the prison he had just left. He looked up at the clear blue sky, and back down at the citizens walking up and down the streets. How quickly he had been made aware of how much he valued his freedom. Once they were on the south side of the river the driver swung right, and after a few hundred yards pulled up in front of the Palace of Justice. The car door was opened by a waiting policeman. If Connor had any thoughts of escape, the other fifty officers on the pavement would have caused him to think again. They formed a long reception line as he climbed the steps into the huge stone building.

He was marched to the front desk, where an officer pinned his left arm to the counter, studied his wrist and entered the number '12995' on the charge sheet. He was then taken down a marble corridor towards two massive oak doors. When he was a few paces away the doors suddenly swung open, and he entered a packed courtroom.

He looked around at the sea of faces, and it was obvious they had been waiting for him.

* * *

Joan typed a search string into the computer: *attempt on Zerimski's life*. What press reports there were all seemed to agree on one thing: that the man who had been arrested in Freedom Square was Piet de Villiers, a South African hitman hired by the Russian Mafya to assassinate Zerimski. A rifle discovered among his belongings was identified as identical to that which had been used to assassinate Ricardo Guzman, a presidential candidate in Colombia, two months earlier.

Joan scanned the Turkish newspaper's line drawing of de Villiers into her computer, and enlarged it until it filled the entire screen. She then zoomed in on the eyes, and blew them up to life size. She was now certain of the true identity of the man about to go on trial in St Petersburg.

Joan checked her watch. It was a few minutes past two. She picked up the phone by her side and dialled a number she knew by heart. It rang for some time before a sleepy voice answered, 'Who's this?'

Joan said only, 'It's important that I see you. I'll be at your place in a little over an hour,' and replaced the phone.

A few moments later, someone else was woken by a ringing telephone. He listened carefully before saying, 'We'll just have to advance our original schedule by a few days.'

Connor stood in the dock, and looked around the courtroom. His eyes first settled on the jury. Twelve good men and true? Unlikely. Not one of them even glanced in his direction. He suspected that it hadn't taken long to swear them in, and that there wouldn't have been any requests for alternates.

Everyone in the courtroom rose as a man in a long black gown emerged from a side door. He sat down in the large leather chair in the centre of the raised dais, below a full-length portrait of President Zerimski. The clerk of the court rose from his place and read out the charge, in Russian. Connor was barely able to follow the proceedings, and he certainly wasn't asked how he wished to plead. The clerk resumed his seat, and a tall, sombre-looking middle-aged man rose from the bench directly below the judge and began to address the jury.

Holding the lapels of his jacket, the prosecutor spent the rest of the morning describing the events that had led up to the arrest of the defendant. He told the jury how de Villiers had been seen stalking Zerimski for several days before he was apprehended in Freedom Square. And how the rifle with which the defendant had intended to assassinate their beloved President had been discovered among his personal belongings in a hotel lobby. 'Vanity got the better of the accused,' the prosecutor said. 'The case that contained the weapon had his initials clearly printed on it.' The judge allowed the rifle and the briefcase to be examined by the jury.

'Even more damning, a slip of paper was found secreted in the accused's spongebag,' continued the prosecutor, 'which confirmed the transfer of one million US dollars to a numbered bank account in Geneva.' Again, the jury was given the chance to study this piece of evidence. The prosecutor went on to praise the diligence and resourcefulness of the St Petersburg police force for preventing this heinous act, and its professionalism in catching the criminal who had intended to perpetrate it. He added that the nation owed a considerable debt of gratitude to Vladimir Bolchenkov, the city's Chief of Police. Several members of the jury nodded their agreement.

The prosecutor completed his monologue by informing the jury that whenever the defendant had been asked if he had been hired to carry out the killing on behalf of the Mafya, he had refused to answer. 'You must make what you will of his silence,' he said. 'My own conclusion is that having heard the evidence, there can only be one verdict, and one sentence.' He smiled thinly at the judge and resumed his seat.

Connor looked around the courtroom to see who had been appointed to defend him. He wondered how his counsel would go about the task when they hadn't even met.

The judge nodded towards the other end of the bench, and a young man who looked as if he hadn't long been out of law school rose to address the court. He did not clasp the lapels of his jacket as he looked up towards the bench, or smile at the judge, or even address the jury. He simply said, 'My client offers no defence,' and resumed his seat.

The judge nodded, then turned his attention to the foreman of the jury, a grave-looking man who knew exactly what was expected of him. He rose from his place on cue.

'Having listened to the evidence in this case, Mr Foreman, how do you find the defendant?'

'Guilty,' said the man, delivering his one-word script without needing to be prompted or to consult any other member of the jury.

The judge looked at Connor for the first time. 'As the jury has reached a unanimous verdict, all that is left for me to do is pass sentence. And, by statute, there is only one penalty for your crime.' He paused, stared impassively at Connor and said, 'I sentence you to death by hanging.' The judge turned to the defence counsel. 'Do you wish to appeal against the sentence?' he asked rhetorically.

'No, sir,' came back the immediate response.

'The execution will take place at eight a.m. on Friday.'

Connor was surprised only that they were waiting until Friday to hang him.

Before she left, Joan checked over several of the articles again. The dates exactly matched Connor's absences abroad. First the trip to Colombia, then the visit to St Petersburg. There were, to quote one of Connor's favourite maxims, just too many coincidences.

By three o'clock, Joan felt drained and exhausted. She didn't look forward to telling Maggie the results of her detective work. And if it really was Connor on trial in St Petersburg, there wasn't a moment to waste, because the Turkish papers were already a couple of days old.

Joan shut down her computer, locked her desk and hoped her boss wouldn't notice that his e-mail in-box was almost empty. She walked up the old staircase to the ground floor, inserted her electric pass-key in the exit security control, and passed the trickle of workers arriving for the early-morning shift.

Joan switched on her headlights and drove her brand-new car out of the parking lot and through the gate, turning east onto the George Washington Parkway. The road was still covered with patchy ice from the previous evening's storm, and highway crews were working to clear it before the morning rush-hour. Normally she enjoyed driving through Washington's deserted early-morning streets, past the magnificent monuments that commemorated the nation's history. At school in St Paul she had sat silently at the front of the class while her teacher regaled them with tales of Washington, Jefferson, Lincoln and Roosevelt. It was her admiration for these heroic figures that had fuelled her ambition to work in the public service.

After studying government at the University of Minnesota, she had filled in application forms for the FBI and the CIA. Both had asked to interview her, but once she had seen Connor Fitzgerald she had cancelled her appointment with the FBI. Here was a man who had returned from a futile war with a medal he never mentioned, and who continued to serve his country without fanfare or recognition. If she ever expressed these thoughts to Connor, he only laughed and told her she was being sentimental. But Tom Lawrence had been right when he had described Connor as one of the nation's unsung heroes. Joan would suggest to Maggie that she contact the White House immediately, as it was Lawrence who had asked Connor to take on this assignment in the first place.

Joan was trying to put her thoughts into some logical order when a large green sanding truck passed her on the outside and began moving across into her lane moments before it had fully overtaken her. She flashed her lights, but the truck didn't pull away as she expected. She checked her rear-view mirror and eased into the centre lane. The truck immediately began to drift across into her path, forcing her to veer sharply into the left-hand lane.

Joan had to decide in an instant whether to slam on her brakes or to try to accelerate past the thoughtless driver. Once again she checked her rear-view mirror, but this time she was horrified to see a large black Mercedes coming up fast behind her. She slammed her foot down on the accelerator as the highway banked steeply to the left near Spout Run. The little Passat responded immediately, but the sanding truck also accelerated, and she couldn't pick up enough speed to pass it.

Joan had no choice but to move further to her left, almost into the median strip. She looked into her rear-view mirror and saw that the Mercedes had also drifted across, and was now close to her rear bumper. She could feel her heart pounding. Were the truck and the car working together? She tried to slow down, but the Mercedes just moved closer and closer to her rear bumper. Joan slammed her foot down on the accelerator again and her car leapt forward. Sweat was running down her forehead and into her eyes as she drew level with the front of the sanding truck, but even with her foot flat on the floor she just couldn't overtake it. She stared up into the cab and tried to attract the driver's attention, but he ignored her waving hand, and went on implacably easing the truck inch by inch further to his left, forcing her to slow down and fall in behind him. She checked her rear-view mirror: the Mercedes was, if anything, even closer to her bumper.

As she looked forward the truck's tailplate rose, and its load of sand began to pour out onto the road. Instinctively Joan slammed on her brakes, but the little car careered out of control, skidded across the ice-encrusted median strip and hurtled down the grass embankment towards the river. It hit the water like a flat stone, and after floating for a moment, disappeared out of sight. All that was left were the skidmarks on the bank and a few bubbles. The sanding truck moved back into the centre lane and continued its journey in the direction of Washington. A moment later the Mercedes flashed its lights, overtook the truck and accelerated away.

Two cars that were heading towards Dulles Airport came to a halt on the median strip. One of the drivers leapt out and slid down the bank towards the river to see if he could help, but by the time he reached the water there was no sign of the car. All that remained were the skidmarks on the snowy bank and a few bubbles. The other driver scribbled down the sanding truck's licence number. He handed it to the first cop to arrive on the scene, who punched it into his dashboard computer. After a few seconds he frowned. 'Are you sure you wrote down the correct number, sir?' he asked. 'The Washington Highway Department has no record of such a vehicle.'

When Connor was bundled into the back of the car, he found the Chief of Police waiting for him once again. As the driver began the return journey to the Crucifix, Connor couldn't resist asking Bolchenkov a question.

'I'm puzzled to know why they're waiting until Friday to hang me.'

'Bit of luck, really,' said the Chief. 'It seems our beloved President insisted on witnessing the execution.' Bolchenkov inhaled deeply on his cigarette. 'And he doesn't have a spare fifteen minutes in his schedule before Friday morning.'

Connor gave a wry smile.

'I'm glad you've found your tongue at last, Mr Fitzgerald,' continued the Chief. 'Because I think the time has come to let you know that there is an alternative.'

CHAPTER TWENTY-ONE

MARK TWAIN ONCE SAID of a friend, 'If he didn't turn up on time, you would know he was dead.'

Once four o'clock had come and gone, Maggie started checking her watch every few minutes. By four thirty she began to wonder if she had been so sleepy when Joan called that she might have misunderstood what she had said.

At five o'clock, Maggie decided it was time to give Joan a call at home. No answer, just a continual ringing tone. Next she tried her car phone, and this time she did get a message: 'This number is temporarily out of order. Please try again later.'

Maggie began pacing round the kitchen table, feeling sure that Joan must have some news of Connor. It had to be important, otherwise why would she have woken her at two in the morning? Had he been in contact with her? Did she know where he was? Would she be able to tell her when he was coming home? By six, Maggie had decided it was now an emergency. She switched on the television to check the exact time. Charlie Gibson's face appeared on the screen. 'In the next hour we'll talk about Christmas decorations that even the kids can help you with. But first we'll go over to Kevin Newman for this morning's news.'

Maggie began pacing round the kitchen as a reporter

predicted that the President's Nuclear, Biological, Chemical and Conventional Arms Reduction Bill was almost certain to be voted down in the Senate now that Zerimski had been elected as the Russian leader.

She was wondering if she should break a lifetime's rule and try to ring Joan at Langley when a trailer appeared under Kevin Newman's image: '*GW Parkway crash involves sanding truck and Volkswagen – driver of car presumed drowned. Details on Eyewitness News at 6.30.*' The words crawled across the screen and disappeared.

Maggie tried to eat a bowl of cornflakes while the early-morning bulletin continued. Andy Lloyd appeared on the screen, announcing that President Zerimski would be making an official visit to Washington just before Christmas. 'The President welcomed the news,' said a reporter, 'and hoped it would go some way to convincing Senate leaders that the new Russian President wished to remain on friendly terms with America. However, the majority leader of the Senate said he would wait until Zerimski had addressed . . .'

When Maggie heard the little thud on the mat, she went out into the hall, picked up the seven envelopes lying on the floor and checked through them as she walked back into the kitchen. Four were for Connor; she never opened his letters while he was away. One was a Pepco bill; another was postmarked Chicago, and the letter 'e' on 'Maggie' was at an angle, so it could only have been Declan O'Casey's annual Christmas card. The last letter bore the distinctive handwriting of her daughter. She tossed the others to one side and tore it open.

Dear Mother,

Just a note to confirm that Stuart arrives in Los Angeles on Friday. We plan to drive up to San Francisco for a few days before flying to Washington on the fifteenth.

Maggie smiled.

We're both looking forward to spending Christmas with you and Dad. He hasn't phoned me, so I assume he isn't back yet.

Maggie frowned.

I've had a letter from Joan, who doesn't seem to be enjoying her new job. I suspect that, like all of us, she is missing Dad. She tells me she is buying a sexy new Volkswagen...

Maggie read the sentence a second time before her hand began trembling. 'Oh my God, no!' she said out loud. She checked her watch – six twenty. On the television, Lisa McRee was holding up a paperchain of holly and berries. 'Festive Christmas decorations the children can help with,' she declared brightly. 'Now we turn to the topic of Christmas trees.'

Maggie flicked over to Channel 5. Another newscaster was speculating about whether Zerimski's planned visit would influence Senate leaders before they cast their vote on the Arms Reduction Bill.

'Come on, come on,' said Maggie.

Finally the newscaster said, '*And now we have more on that accident on the George Washington Parkway. We go live to our on-the-spot correspondent, Liz Fullerton.*'

'*Thank you, Julie. I'm standing on the median of the George Washington Parkway, where the tragic accident took place at approximately three fifteen this morning. Earlier I interviewed an eye-witness who told Channel 5 what he had seen.*'

The camera focused on a man who clearly hadn't expected to be on television that morning.

'*I was headed into Washington,*' he told the reporter, '*when this sanding truck deposited its load on the highway, causing the car behind to swerve and run out of control. The car skidded right across the road, down the bank and into the*

Potomac.' The camera swung across to show a wide angle of the river, focusing on a group of police divers before returning to the reporter.

'*No one seems to be quite sure exactly what happened,*' she continued. '*It's even possible that the driver of the sanding truck, sitting high up in his cab, continued on his journey unaware that an accident had taken place.*'

'No! No!' screamed Maggie. 'Don't let it be her!'

'*Behind me you can see police divers, who have already located the vehicle, apparently a Volkswagen Passat. They hope to bring it to the surface within the next hour. The identity of the driver is still unknown.*'

'No, no, no,' repeated Maggie. 'Please, God, not Joan.'

'*The police are requesting that the driver of a black Mercedes who may have witnessed the accident should come forward to help with their enquiries. We hope to bring you more news on the hour, so until then . . .*'

Maggie ran into the hall, grabbed her coat and rushed out of the front door. She leapt into her car, and was relieved when the old Toyota spluttered into life almost immediately. She eased it slowly out onto Avon Place, before accelerating down Twenty-Ninth Street and east on M Street in the direction of the Parkway.

If she had checked her rear-view mirror, she would have seen a small blue Ford making a three-point turn before chasing after her. The passenger in the front seat was dialling an unlisted number.

'Mr Jackson, it is so good of you to come and see me again.'

Jackson was amused by Nicolai Romanov's elaborate courtesy, especially as it carried with it the pretence that he might have had some choice in the matter.

The first meeting had been at Jackson's request, and obviously hadn't been considered 'a waste of time', as Sergei was still running around on both legs. Each subsequent meeting had followed a summons from

Romanov to bring Jackson up to date with the latest plans.

The Czar sank back in his winged chair, and Jackson noticed the usual glass of colourless liquid on the table by his side. He remembered the old man's reaction on the one occasion he had asked a question, and waited for him to speak.

'You'll be glad to hear, Mr Jackson, that with the exception of a single problem that still needs to be resolved, everything required to make good your colleague's escape has been arranged. All we need now is for Mr Fitzgerald to agree our terms. Should he find himself unable to do so, I can do nothing to prevent him from being hanged at eight o'clock tomorrow morning.' Romanov spoke without feeling. 'Allow me to take you through what we have planned so far, should he decide to go ahead. I am certain that, as a former Deputy Director of the CIA, your observations will prove useful.'

The old man pressed a button in the armrest of his chair, and the doors at the far end of the drawing room opened immediately. Alexei Romanov entered the room.

'I believe you know my son,' said the Czar.

Jackson glanced in the direction of the man who always accompanied him on his journeys to the Winter Palace, but rarely spoke. He nodded.

The young man pushed aside an exquisite fourteenth-century tapestry depicting the Battle of Flanders. Behind it was concealed a large television set. The flat silver screen looked somewhat incongruous in such magnificent surroundings, but no more so, Jackson thought, than its owner and his acolytes.

The first image to come up on the screen was an exterior shot of the Crucifix prison.

Alexei Romanov pointed to the entrance. 'Zerimski is expected to arrive at the jail at seven fifty. He will be in the third of seven cars, and will enter through a side gate situated here.' His finger moved across the screen. 'He will be met by Vladimir Bolchenkov, who will accompany him into the main courtyard, where the execution will take place. At seven fifty-two . . .'

The young Romanov continued to take Jackson through the plan minute by minute, going into even greater detail when it came to explaining how Connor's escape would be achieved. Jackson noticed that he seemed unconcerned by the one remaining problem, obviously confident that his father would come up with a solution before the following morning. When he had finished, Alexei switched off the television, replaced the tapestry and gave his father a slight bow. He then left the room without another word.

When the door had closed, the old man asked, 'Do you have any observations?'

'One or two,' said Jackson. 'First, let me say that I'm impressed by the plan, and convinced it has every chance of succeeding. It's obvious you've thought of almost every contingency that might arise – that is, assuming Connor agrees to your terms. And on that, I must repeat, I have no authority to speak on his behalf.'

Romanov nodded.

'But you're still facing one problem.'

'And do you have a solution?' asked the old man.

'Yes,' replied Jackson. 'I have.'

Bolchenkov spent nearly an hour spelling out Romanov's plan in great detail, then left Connor to consider his response. He didn't need to be reminded that he was faced with an unalterable time limit: Zerimski was due to arrive at the Crucifix in forty-five minutes.

Connor lay on his bunk. The terms could not have been expressed more explicitly. But even if he did accept those terms, and his escape was successfully engineered, he was not at all confident that he would be able to carry out his side of the bargain. If he failed, they would kill him. It was that simple – except that Bolchenkov had promised that it would not be the quick and easy death of the hangman's noose. He had also spelled out – in case Connor should be in any doubt – that all contracts made with the Russian Mafya and not honoured automatically became the responsibility of the offender's next of kin.

Connor could still see the cynical expression on the Chief's face as he extracted the photographs from an inside pocket and passed them over to him. 'Two fine women,' Bolchenkov had said. 'You must be proud of them. It would be a tragedy to have to shorten their lives for something they knew nothing about.'

Fifteen minutes later the cell door swung open again, and Bolchenkov returned, an unlit cigarette dangling from his mouth. This time he didn't sit down. Connor continued to look up at the ceiling as if he wasn't there.

'I see that our little proposal is still presenting you with a dilemma,' said the Chief, lighting the cigarette. 'Even after our brief acquaintance, that does not surprise me. But perhaps when you hear my latest piece of news, you will change your mind.'

Connor went on gazing at the ceiling.

'It appears that your former secretary, Joan Bennett, has met with an unfortunate car accident. She was on her way from Langley to visit your wife.'

Connor swung his legs off the bed, sat up and stared at Bolchenkov.

'If Joan is dead, how could you possibly know she was on her way to see my wife?'

'The CIA aren't the only people who are tapping your wife's telephone,' replied the Chief. He took a last drag from his cigarette, allowed the stub to fall from his mouth and ground it out on the floor.

'We suspect that your secretary had somehow discovered who it was that we arrested in Freedom Square. And without putting too fine a point on it, if your wife is as proud and headstrong as her profile suggests, I think we can assume that it won't be long before she reaches the same conclusion. If that is the case, I fear Mrs Fitzgerald is destined to suffer the same fate as your late secretary.'

'If I agree to Romanov's terms,' Connor said, 'I wish to insert a clause of my own into the contract.'

Bolchenkov listened with interest.

'Mr Gutenburg?'

'Speaking.'

'This is Maggie Fitzgerald. I'm the wife of Connor Fitzgerald, who I believe is currently abroad on an assignment for you.'

'I don't recall the name,' said Gutenburg.

'You attended his farewell party at our home in Georgetown only a couple of weeks ago.'

'I think you must have mistaken me for someone else,' replied Gutenburg calmly.

'I have not mistaken you for anyone else, Mr Gutenburg. In fact, at eight twenty-seven on the second of November, you made a phone call from my home to your office.'

'I made no such call, Mrs Fitzgerald, and I can assure you that your husband has never worked for me.'

'Then tell me, Mr Gutenburg, did Joan Bennett ever work for the Agency? Or has she also been conveniently erased from your memory?'

'What are you suggesting, Mrs Fitzgerald?'

'Ah, I've caught your attention at last. Allow me to repair your temporary loss of memory. Joan Bennett was my husband's secretary for nearly twenty years, and I have a feeling you would find it hard to deny that you knew she was on her way from Langley to see me when she met her death.'

'I was sorry to read of Miss Bennett's tragic accident, but I'm at a loss to understand what it has to do with me.'

'The press are apparently mystified about what actually took place on the George Washington Parkway yesterday morning, but they might be a step nearer to the solution if they were told that Joan Bennett used to work for a man who has disappeared from the face of the earth while carrying out a special assignment for you. I've always found in the past that journalists consider a story involving a Medal of Honor winner to be of interest to their readers.'

'Mrs Fitzgerald, I can't be expected to remember every one of the seventeen thousand people the CIA employs, and I certainly don't recall ever meeting Miss Bennett, let alone your husband.'

'I see I'll have to jog that failing memory of yours a little further, Mr Gutenburg. As it happens, the party you didn't attend and didn't telephone from was, fortunately or unfortunately, depending on your perspective, videotaped by my daughter. She'd hoped to surprise her father by giving him the tape for Christmas. I've just had another look at it, Mr Gutenburg, and although you play only a minor role, I can assure you that your tête-à-tête with Joan Bennett is there for all to see. This conversation is also being recorded, and I have a feeling that the networks will consider your contribution worth airing on the early evening news.'

This time Gutenburg didn't reply for some time. 'Perhaps it might be a good idea for us to meet, Mrs Fitzgerald,' he said eventually.

'I can see no purpose in that, Mr Gutenburg. I already know exactly what I require from you.'

'And what is that, Mrs Fitzgerald?'

'I want to know where my husband is at this moment, and when I can expect to see him again. In return for those two simple pieces of information, I will hand over the tape.'

'I'll need a little time . . .'

'Of course you will,' said Maggie. 'Shall we say forty-eight hours? And Mr Gutenburg, don't waste your time tearing my home apart searching for the tape, because you won't find it. It's been hidden somewhere that even a mind as devious as yours wouldn't think of.'

'But . . .' began Gutenburg.

'I should also add that if you decide to dispose of me in the same way you did Joan Bennett, I've instructed my lawyers that if I die in suspicious circumstances, they are to immediately release copies of the tape to all three major networks, Fox and CNN. If, on the other hand, I simply disappear, the tape will be released seven days later. Goodbye, Mr Gutenburg.'

Maggie put the phone down and collapsed onto the bed, bathed in sweat.

Gutenburg shot through the connecting door between his office and the Director's.

Helen Dexter glanced up from her desk, unable to hide her surprise that her Deputy had entered the room without bothering to knock.

'We have a problem,' was all he said.

CHAPTER TWENTY-TWO

THE CONDEMNED MAN ate no breakfast.

The kitchen staff always made an effort to remove the lice from the bread for a prisoner's last meal, but this time they had failed. He took one look at the offering and put the tin plate under his bunk.

A few minutes later, a Russian Orthodox priest entered the cell. He explained that although he was not of the same denomination as the prisoner, he would be happy to perform the last rites.

The holy sacrament was the only food he would eat that day. After the priest had performed the little ceremony, they knelt together on the cold stone floor. At the end of a short prayer the priest blessed him and left him to his solitude.

He lay on his bunk staring up at the ceiling, not for one moment regretting his decision. Once he had explained his reasons, Bolchenkov had accepted them without comment, even nodding curtly as he left the cell. It was the nearest the Chief would ever get to admitting that he admired a man's moral courage.

The prisoner had faced the prospect of death once before. It didn't hold the same horror for him a second time. On that occasion he had thought about his wife, and the child he would never see. But now he could only think of his parents, who had died within a few days of each other. He was glad that neither of them had gone to their graves with this as their final memory of him.

For them, his return from Vietnam had been a triumph, and they were delighted when he had told them that he intended to go on serving his country. He might even have become Director if a President in trouble hadn't decided to appoint a woman, in the hope that it would help his flagging campaign. It hadn't.

Although it was Gutenburg who had placed the knife firmly between his shoulderblades, there wasn't any doubt about who had handed him the weapon; she would have enjoyed playing Lady Macbeth. He would go to his grave knowing that few of his fellow countrymen would ever be aware of the sacrifice he had made. For him that only made it all the more worthwhile.

There would be no ceremonial farewell. No coffin draped with the American flag. No friends and relatives standing by the graveside to hear the priest extolling the dedication and public service which had been the hallmark of his career. No Marines raising their rifles proudly in the air. No twenty-one-gun salute. No folded flag given on behalf of the President to his next of kin.

No. He was destined to be just another of Tom Lawrence's unsung heroes.

For him, all that was left was to be hanged by the neck in an unloved and unloving land. A shaven head, a number on his wrist, and an unmarked grave.

Why had he made that decision which had so moved the usually passionless Chief of Police? He didn't have time to explain to him what had taken place in Vietnam, but that was where the die had been irrevocably cast.

Perhaps he should have faced the firing squad all those years ago in another far-off land. But he had survived. This time there was no one to rescue him at the last moment. And it was too late now to change his mind.

* * *

The Russian President woke in a foul mood that morning. The first person he took it out on was his chef. He swept his breakfast onto the floor and shouted, 'Is this the sort of hospitality I can expect when I come to Leningrad?'

He stormed out of the room. In his study, a nervous official placed on his desk documents for signing which would empower the police to arrest citizens without having to charge them with any crime. This did nothing to change Zerimski's black mood. He knew that it was merely a ploy to get a few pickpockets, dope peddlers and petty criminals off the streets. It was the Czar's head he wanted delivered to him on a platter. If the Minister for the Interior continued to fail him, he would have to consider replacing him.

By the time his Chief of Staff arrived, Zerimski had signed away the lives of another hundred men whose only crime had been to support Chernopov during the election campaign. Rumours were already circulating around Moscow that the former Prime Minister planned to emigrate. The day he left the country, Zerimski would sign a thousand such orders, and would imprison everybody who had ever served Chernopov in any capacity.

He threw his pen down on the desk. All this had been achieved in less than a week. The thought of the havoc he was going to cause in a month, a year, made him feel a little more cheerful.

'Your limousine is waiting, Mr President,' said a petrified official whose face he couldn't see. He smiled at the thought of what would undoubtedly be the highlight of his day. He had been looking forward to a morning at the Crucifix as others would anticipate an evening at the Kirov.

He left his study and strode down the long marble corridor of the newly commandeered office block towards the open door, his entourage moving swiftly ahead of him. He paused for a moment on the top step to look down at the gleaming motorcade. He had instructed Party officials that he must always have one more limousine than any previous President.

He climbed into the back of the third car and checked his watch: seven forty-three. The police had cleared the road an hour before so that the motorcade could proceed without encountering a single vehicle travelling in either direction. Holding up the traffic makes the local inhabitants aware that the President is in town, he explained to his Chief of Staff.

The traffic police estimated that the journey, which would normally have taken twenty minutes, should be completed in less than seven. As Zerimski shot through traffic lights of whatever colour and swung across the river, he didn't even glance in the direction of the Hermitage. Once they reached the other side of the Neva, the driver of the leading car pushed the speedometer up to a hundred kilometres an hour to be sure the President would be on time for his first official engagement that morning.

As he lay on his bunk, the prisoner could hear the guards marching down the stone passageway towards him, the noise of their boots becoming a little louder with each step. He wondered how many of them there would be. They stopped outside his cell. A key turned in the lock and the door swung open. When you have only moments to live, you notice every detail.

Bolchenkov led them in. The prisoner was impressed that he had got back so quickly. He lit a cigarette and inhaled once before offering it to the prisoner. He shook his head. The Chief shrugged his shoulders, ground the cigarette out on the stone floor with his foot, and left to greet the President.

The next person to enter the cell was the priest. He was carrying a large open bible and softly chanting some words that meant nothing to the prisoner. Next were three men he recognised immediately. But this time there was no razor, no needle, just a pair of handcuffs. They stared at him, almost willing him to put up a fight, but to their disappointment he calmly placed his hands behind his back and waited. They slapped on the cuffs and pushed him out of the cell into the corridor. At the end of the long grey tunnel he could just make out a pinprick of sunlight.

The President stepped out of his limousine, to be welcomed by the Chief of Police. It amused him that he had awarded Bolchenkov the Order of Lenin on the same day as he had signed an order to arrest his brother.

Bolchenkov led Zerimski into the yard where the execution would take place. No one suggested removing the President's fur-lined coat or hat on such a bitterly cold morning. As they crossed the courtyard, the small crowd huddled up against one wall began to applaud. The Chief saw a frown cross Zerimski's face. The President had expected far more people to turn up to witness the execution of a man who had been sent to kill him.

Bolchenkov had anticipated that this might present a problem, so he leaned over and whispered in the President's ear, 'I was instructed to permit only Party members to attend.' Zerimski nodded. Bolchenkov didn't add how difficult it had been to drag even the few people present into the Crucifix that morning. Too many of them had heard the stories of how once you were in, you never got out.

The Chief came to a halt by a plush eighteenth-century chair that Catherine the Great had bought from the estate of the British Prime Minister Robert Walpole in 1779, and that had been requisitioned from the Hermitage the previous day. The President sank into the comfortable seat directly in front of the newly erected gallows.

After only a few seconds Zerimski began fidgeting

impatiently as he waited for the prisoner to appear. He looked across at the crowd, and his eyes rested on a young boy who was crying. It didn't please him.

At that moment the prisoner emerged from the dark corridor into the stark morning light. The bald head covered in dried blood and the thin grey prison uniform made him look strangely anonymous. He appeared remarkably calm for someone who had only a few more moments to live.

The condemned man stared up into the morning sun and shivered as an officer of the guard marched forward, grabbed his left wrist and checked the number: 12995. The officer then turned to face the President and read out the court order.

While the officer went through the formalities, the prisoner looked around the yard. He saw the shivering crowd, most of them wary of moving a muscle for fear that they might be ordered to join him. His eyes settled on the boy, who was still weeping. If they had allowed him to make a will, he would have left everything to that child. He glanced briefly at the scaffold, then settled his gaze on the President. Their eyes met. Although he was terrified, the prisoner held Zerimski's gaze. He was determined not to let him have the satisfaction of knowing just how frightened he was. If the President had stopped staring back at him and looked down at the ground between his feet, he would have seen for himself.

The officer, having completed his commission, rolled up his scroll and marched away. This was the sign for two of the thugs to come forward, grab one of the prisoner's arms each, and lead him to the scaffold.

He walked calmly past the President and on towards the gallows. When he reached the first of the wooden steps, he glanced up at the clock tower. Three minutes to eight. Few people, he thought, ever know exactly how long they have left to live. He almost willed the clock to strike. He had waited twenty-eight years to repay his debt.

Now, in these final moments, it all came back to him.

It had been a hot, sweaty May morning in Nan Dinh. Someone had to be made an example of, and as the senior officer, he had been singled out. His second-in-command had stepped forward and volunteered to take his place. And, like the coward he was, he had not protested. The Vietcong officer had laughed and accepted the offer, but then decided that both men should face the firing squad the following morning.

In the middle of the night, the same Lieutenant had come to his bedside and said they must try to escape. They would never have another chance. Security at the camp was always lax, because to the north lay a hundred miles of jungle occupied by the Vietcong, and to the south twenty-five miles of impenetrable swamp. Several men had tried their luck with that route before, and their luck had run out.

The Lieutenant said he would rather risk dying in the swamps than face the certainty of death by firing squad. As he stole away into the night, the Captain had reluctantly joined him. When the sun appeared above the horizon a few hours later, the camp was still within sight. Across the stinking, mosquito-infested swamp they could hear the guards laughing as they took turns to fire potshots at them. They had dived below the surface of the swamp, but after only a few seconds they had to come up and struggle on. Eventually, after the longest day of his life, darkness fell. He had begged the Lieutenant to carry on without him, but he had refused.

By the end of the second day, he wished he had been allowed to face the firing squad instead of dying in that godforsaken swamp in that godforsaken country. But on and on the young officer went. For eleven days and twelve nights they didn't eat, surviving only by drinking from the endless torrents of rain. On the twelfth morning they reached dry land and, delirious from illness and exhaustion, he collapsed. He later learned that for four more days the Lieutenant had carried him through the jungle to safety.

The next thing he recalled was waking in an army hospital.

'How long have I been here?' he asked the nurse who was tending him.

'Six days,' she said. 'You're lucky to be alive.'

'And my friend?'

'He's been up for the past couple of days. He's already visited you once this morning.'

He fell asleep again, and when he woke he asked the nurse for a pen and paper. He spent the rest of the day sitting in his hospital bed writing and rewriting the citation. When he had made a fair copy, he asked that it should be sent to the commanding officer.

Six months later, he had stood on the White House lawn between Maggie and her father and had listened to the citation being read out. Lieutenant Connor Fitzgerald stepped forward and the President had awarded him the Medal of Honor.

As he began to mount the steps of the gallows, he thought of the one man who would mourn him when he discovered the truth. He had warned them not to tell him, because if he found out, he would break the contract, give himself up and return to the Crucifix. 'You must understand,' he had explained to them, 'that you are dealing with a totally honourable man. So be sure that the clock has struck eight before he finds out he's been deceived.'

The first chime sent a shiver through his body, and his thoughts were brought back to the moment.

On the second chime, the little boy who had been crying ran up to the foot of the gallows and fell on his knees.

On the third, the Chief placed a restraining arm on a young Corporal who had taken a step forward to drag the child away.

On the fourth, the prisoner smiled down at Sergei as if he were his only son.

On the fifth, the two thugs pushed him forward so that he was standing directly below the dangling rope.

On the sixth, the hangman placed the noose around his neck.

On the seventh, he lowered his eyes and stared directly at the President of the Russian Republic.

On the eighth, the hangman pulled the lever and the trapdoor opened.

As the body of Christopher Andrew Jackson swung above him, Zerimski began to applaud. Some of the crowd half-heartedly joined in.

A minute later the two thugs carried the lifeless body down from the gallows. Sergei rushed forward to help them lower his friend into the crude wooden coffin that lay on the ground beside the scaffold.

The Chief accompanied the President back to his limousine and the motorcade sped out of the prison gates even before the coffin lid had been nailed down. Four prisoners lifted the heavy casket onto their shoulders and headed towards the graveyard. Sergei walked by their side, out of the yard to a patch of rough ground at the back of the prison. Even the dead were not allowed to escape from the Crucifix.

If Sergei had looked back, he would have seen the rest of the crowd running out through the prison gates before they were slammed shut and the vast wooden bolts pushed back in place.

The pallbearers stopped by the side of an unmarked grave that other prisoners had just finished digging. They dropped the casket unceremoniously into the gaping hole and then, without a prayer or even a moment's pause, shovelled the recently dug sods of earth on top of it.

The boy didn't move until they had completed their task. A few minutes later, the guards herded the prisoners back to their cells. Sergei fell on his knees, wondering how long they would allow him to remain by the grave.

A moment later a hand was placed on the boy's shoulder. He looked up and saw the Chief standing above him. A fair man, he'd once told Jackson.

'Did you know him well?' the Chief asked.

'Yes, sir,' said Sergei. 'He was my partner.'

The Chief nodded. 'I knew the man he gave his life for,' he said. 'I only wish I had such a friend.'

CHAPTER TWENTY-THREE

'MRS FITZGERALD is not quite as clever as she thinks she is,' said Gutenburg.

'Amateurs rarely are,' said Helen Dexter. 'Does that mean you've got hold of the video?'

'No, although I have got a pretty good idea where it is,' said Gutenburg. He paused. 'But not *exactly* where.'

'Stop being a smartass,' said Dexter, 'and get to the point. You don't need to prove to me how clever you are.'

Gutenburg knew that this was about as near as he would ever get to receiving a compliment from the Director.

'Mrs Fitzgerald doesn't realise that her home and office have been bugged for the past month, and that we've had agents watching her since the day her husband flew out of Dulles three weeks ago.'

'So what have you found out?'

'Not a lot when the individual bits of information are taken in isolation. But if you piece them together, they start making a picture.' He pushed a file and a tape recorder across the table.

The Director ignored them. 'Talk me through it,' she said, beginning to sound a little irritated.

'During Mrs Fitzgerald's lunch with Joan Bennett at the Café Milano, the conversation was inconsequential until just before she left to return to work. It was then that she asked Bennett a question.'

'And what was that question?'

'Perhaps you'd like to hear for yourself.' The Deputy Director pressed the 'Play' button on the tape recorder and sat back.

'*Me too. Black, no sugar.*' Footsteps could be heard walking away. '*Joan, I've never asked you to break a confidence before, but there's something I have to know.*'

'*I hope I can help, but as I've already explained, if it concerns Connor, I'm probably as much in the dark as you are.*'

'*Then I need the name of someone who isn't in the dark.*'

There followed a long silence before Joan said, '*I suggest you look at the guest-list for Connor's farewell party.*'

'*Chris Jackson?*'

'*No. Unfortunately, he's no longer employed by the Company.*'

There was another long silence.

'*That smooth little man who left without saying goodbye? The one who said he worked in loss adjustment?*'

Gutenburg flicked off the tape.

'Why did you ever go to that party?' snapped Dexter.

'Because you instructed me to find out if Fitzgerald had landed a job that would keep him in Washington. Don't forget that it was his daughter who gave us the lead that made it possible to convince Thompson that it might not be wise to employ him. I'm sure you recall the circumstances.'

The Director frowned. 'What happened after Mrs Fitzgerald left the Café Milano?'

'Nothing significant until she returned home that night, when she made several calls – she never makes personal calls from the office – including one to Chris Jackson's cellphone.'

'Why would she do that, when she knew he'd left the Company?'

'They go back a long way. He and Fitzgerald served in Vietnam together. In fact, it was Jackson who recommended Fitzgerald for the Medal of Honor, and who recruited him as an NOC.'

'Did Jackson tell her about you?' asked Dexter in disbelief.

'No, he didn't have a chance,' replied Gutenburg. 'I gave an order to block his cellphone the moment we discovered he was in Russia.' He smiled. 'We can, however, still identify who's been trying to call him, and who he's been trying to call.'

'Does that mean you've found out who he's reporting back to?'

'Jackson has only dialled one number on that line since he landed in Russia, and I suspect he only risked that because it was an emergency.'

'Who did he call?' asked Dexter impatiently.

'An unlisted number at the White House.'

Dexter didn't even blink. 'Our friend Mr Lloyd, no doubt.'

'No doubt,' replied Gutenburg.

'Is Mrs Fitzgerald aware that Jackson is reporting directly to the White House?'

'I don't think so,' said Gutenburg. 'Otherwise I suspect she would have tried to contact him herself some time ago.'

Dexter nodded. 'Then we must make certain that she *never* finds out.'

Gutenburg showed no emotion. 'Understood. But I can't do anything about that until I've got my hands on the family video.'

'What's the latest status on that?' asked Dexter.

'We wouldn't have progressed an inch if we hadn't picked up a clue in an intercepted phone call. When Joan Bennett rang Mrs Fitzgerald from Langley at two in the morning to say she'd be with her in an hour, one of my people checked what she'd been calling up on the reference library's computer. It soon became clear that she must have stumbled on something that made her suspect it was her old boss who was in prison in St Petersburg. But, as you know, she never kept her appointment with Mrs Fitzgerald.'

'A little too close for comfort.'

'Agreed. But when she failed to turn up, Mrs Fitzgerald drove out to the GW Parkway and waited for the police to dredge up the car.'

'She probably saw a report on TV, or heard about it on the radio,' said Dexter.

'Yes, that's what we assumed – the story led the local news that morning. Once she knew for certain it was Bennett in the car, she immediately phoned her daughter at Stanford. If she sounds a little sleepy, that's because it was only five o'clock in the morning in California.' He leant forward again and touched the 'Play' button on the tape recorder.

'*Hi, Tara. It's Mom.*'

'*Hi, Mom. What time is it?*'

'*I'm sorry to call so early, darling, but I have some very sad news.*'

'*Not Dad?*'

'*No, Joan Bennett – she's been killed in a car crash.*'

'*Joan's dead? I can't believe it. Tell me it's not true.*'

'*I'm afraid it is. And I have a terrible feeling that in some way it's connected to the reason Connor hasn't returned home.*'

'*Come on, Mom, aren't you getting a little paranoid? After all, Dad's only been away for three weeks.*'

'*You may be right, but I've still decided to move that video you made of his farewell party to a safer place.*'

'*Why?*'

'*Because it's the only proof I have that your father ever met a man called Nick Gutenburg, let alone worked for him.*'

The Deputy Director touched the 'Stop' button. 'The conversation continues for some time, but it doesn't add a great deal to our knowledge. When Mrs Fitzgerald left the house a few minutes later carrying a videotape, the officer listening in realised the significance of what he'd just heard, and tailed her to the university. She didn't go straight to the Admissions Office as usual, but dropped in at the library, where she went to the computer section on the first floor. She spent twenty minutes searching for something on one of the computers, and left with a printout of about a dozen pages. Then she took the elevator down to the audio-visual research centre on the ground floor. The officer didn't want to risk joining her in the elevator, so once he knew which floor she'd stopped at, he went to the computer she'd been working on and tried to call up the last file that had been opened.'

'She'd erased everything, of course,' said Dexter.

'Of course,' said Gutenburg.

'But what about the printout?'

'Again, no clue as to what was on it.'

'She can't have lived with Connor Fitzgerald for twenty-eight years and not picked up something about the way we work.'

'The officer left the library and waited in his car. After a few minutes Mrs Fitzgerald came out of the building. She was no longer carrying the tape, but she was . . .'

'She must have deposited it in the audio-visual centre.'

'Exactly my thought,' said Gutenburg.

'How many tapes does the university store in its library?'

'Over twenty-five thousand,' said Gutenburg.

'We don't have enough time to go through them all,' said Dexter.

'We wouldn't have, if Mrs Fitzgerald hadn't made her first mistake.'

Dexter didn't interrupt this time.

'When she left the library she didn't have the video, but she did have the printout. Our agent followed her to the Admissions Office, where I'm happy to say her principles got the better of her.'

Dexter raised an eyebrow.

'Before returning to her office, Mrs Fitzgerald called

in at the recycling centre. She's not the Vice-President of GULP by accident.'

'GULP?'

'Georgetown University Litter Patrol. She dumped the printout in the paper depository.'

'Good. So what did you find on it?'

'A complete list of the videos currently on loan and unlikely to be returned until the beginning of next term.'

'So she must have felt it was safe to leave her video in an empty box, because no one would come across it for weeks.'

'Correct,' said Gutenburg.

'How many videos are there that fall into that category?'

'Four hundred and seventy-two,' replied Gutenburg.

'Presumably you've requisitioned every one.'

'I thought about doing that, but if an inquisitive student or member of staff became aware of a CIA presence on the campus, all hell would break loose.'

'Good thinking,' said Dexter. 'So how do you intend to go about finding that video?'

'I've detailed a dozen hand-picked officers, all recent graduates, to check out every one of the titles on that list until they come across a home-made video in what should be an empty box. The problem is that, despite their being dressed like students, I can't afford to leave any one of them inside the library for longer than twenty minutes, or let them go there more than twice in a day, if they're not going to stick out like sore thumbs, especially as there's hardly anyone around at this time of year. So the exercise is proving rather time-consuming.'

'How long do you think it will be before they find it?'

'We could get lucky and come across it almost immediately, but my bet is that it will probably take a day or two, three at the most.'

'Don't forget you have to be back in touch with Mrs Fitzgerald in less than forty-eight hours.'

'I hadn't forgotten. But if we find the tape before then, that won't be necessary.'

'Unless Mrs Fitzgerald also recorded her phone conversation with you.'

Gutenburg smiled. 'She did, but it was erased within seconds of her replacing the receiver. You should have seen the pleasure it gave Professor Ziegler to demonstrate his latest toy.'

'Excellent,' said Dexter. 'Ring me the moment you get your hands on that video. Then there will be nothing to stop us eliminating the one person who could still . . .' The red phone on her desk began to ring, and she grabbed it without completing her sentence.

'The Director,' she said, pressing a button on her stopwatch. 'When did this happen? . . . Are you absolutely certain? . . . And Jackson? Where is he?' When she had heard the reply, she immediately put the phone down. Gutenburg noticed that the stopwatch had reached forty-three seconds.

'I do hope you find that videotape within the next forty-eight hours,' said the Director, looking across the desk at her Deputy.

'Why?' asked Gutenburg, looking anxious.

'Because Mitchell tells me that Fitzgerald was hanged at eight o'clock this morning St Petersburg time, and that Jackson has just boarded a United Airlines flight out of Frankfurt, bound for Washington.'

BOOK THREE

The Hired Assassin

CHAPTER TWENTY-FOUR

AT SEVEN A.M., the three thugs entered his cell and marched him off to the Chief's office. Once they had left the room Bolchenkov locked the door, and without a word went over to a wardrobe in the corner. Inside was a policeman's uniform, which he indicated Connor should change into. Because of his loss of weight over the past week, the clothes hung on him, and he was grateful for the braces. But with the aid of a wide-brimmed hat and a long blue coat, he managed to look like any of the thousand policemen who would be walking the beat in St Petersburg that morning. He left his prison clothes at the bottom of the wardrobe, wondering how the Chief would dispose of them. Still without saying a word, Bolchenkov ushered him out of his office and into a tiny anteroom, then locked him in.

After a long silence, Connor heard a door opening, then footsteps, followed by another door opening, which could have been the wardrobe in the Chief's office. He didn't move a muscle as he tried to work out what was going on. The first door opened again and two, possibly three, people rushed noisily into the office. They left a few seconds later, dragging something or someone out of the room and slamming the door behind them.

Moments later the door was unlocked, and Bolchenkov indicated that he should come out. They went through the office and back into the corridor. If the Chief turned left, they would be returning to his cell; but he turned right. Connor's legs felt very weak, but he followed as quickly as he could.

The first thing he saw when he stepped into the court-yard was the scaffold, and someone placing a magnificent gilded chair with plush red upholstery a few paces in front of it. He didn't need to be told who would be sitting there. As he and Bolchenkov walked across the yard, Connor noticed a group of policemen dressed in long blue coats like the one he was wearing dragging passers-by off the street, presumably to witness the execution.

The Chief moved quickly across the gravel to a car on the far side of the courtyard. Connor was about to open the passenger door when Bolchenkov shook his head and pointed to the driver's seat. Connor took his place behind the wheel.

'Drive up to the gate and then stop,' said the Chief as he got into the passenger seat.

Connor kept the car in first gear as he drove slowly across the yard, stopping in front of two guards posted by the closed gate. One of them saluted the Chief and immediately began checking under the vehicle, while the other looked through the back window and inspected the boot.

The Chief leaned across and pulled down the sleeve on Connor's left wrist. When the guards had completed their search, they returned to their positions and saluted Bolchenkov once again. Neither of them took the slight-est interest in the driver. The vast wooden bolts were removed and the great gates of the Crucifix Prison were pulled open.

'Get moving,' said the Chief under his breath as a small boy ran into the prison compound, looking as if he knew exactly where he was going.

'Which way?' Connor whispered.

'Right.'

Connor swung the car across the road and began driving alongside the Neva towards the city centre. There wasn't another car in sight.

'Cross the next bridge,' said Bolchenkov, 'then take the first left.'

As they passed the prison on the far side of the river, Connor glanced across at its high walls. The police were still trying to coax people in to add to the small crowd who had already gathered to witness his hanging. How was Bolchenkov going to get away with it?

Connor continued driving for another couple of hundred metres, until Bolchenkov said, 'Pull over here.' He slowed down and brought the car to a halt behind a large white BMW with one of its rear doors open.

'This is where we part company, Mr Fitzgerald,' said Bolchenkov. 'Let's hope we never meet again.'

Connor nodded his agreement. As he stepped out of the car, the Chief added, 'You are privileged to have such a remarkable friend.'

It was to be some time before Connor understood the full significance of his words.

'Your flight leaves from Gate 11, Mr Jackson. It will be boarding in twenty minutes.'

'Thank you,' said Connor, as he picked up his boarding pass. He began walking slowly towards Departures, hoping the official wouldn't check his passport too closely. Although they had replaced Jackson's photograph with his, Chris was three years older than him, two inches shorter, and was bald. If he was asked to remove his hat, he would have to explain why his head was covered in Gorbachev-like marks. In California they would simply have assumed he was a cult member.

He handed his passport over with his right hand – if he had used his left, the sleeve would have risen to reveal the tattooed number on his wrist. Once he was back in

America he would buy himself a wider watchstrap.

The official gave the passport only a cursory glance before allowing him through. His newly acquired suitcase, containing nothing more than a change of clothes and a spongebag, passed through security without hindrance. He picked it up and made his way to Gate 11, where he took a seat in the far corner of the lounge facing away from the exit that led to the plane.

In the twenty-four hours since he had left the Crucifix, Connor hadn't relaxed for one moment.

'*This is the first call for Finnair Flight 821 to Frankfurt,*' said a voice over the intercom.

Connor didn't move. If they had told him the truth, he would never have allowed Chris to take his place. He tried to piece together everything that had happened after he had left Bolchenkov.

He had got out of the police car and walked as quickly as he could to the waiting BMW. The Chief had already begun his return journey to the Crucifix by the time Connor climbed into the back of the car and sat beside a pale, thin young man wearing a long black cashmere coat. Neither he nor the two similarly-dressed men seated in the front of the car spoke, or even acknowledged his presence.

The BMW eased out onto the empty road and moved quickly away from the city. Once they joined the highway, the driver ignored the speed limit. As 8.00 flicked up on the dashboard clock, a road sign told Connor that they were 150 kilometres from the Finnish border.

As the distance on the signs dropped to a hundred kilometres, then fifty, then thirty, then ten, Connor began to wonder how they were going to explain the presence of a Russian policeman to the border guards. But no explanation proved necessary. When the BMW was about three hundred metres from the no man's land that divided the two countries, the driver flashed his lights four times. The barrier at the frontier rose immediately, allowing them to cross the border into Finland without even dropping their speed. Connor was beginning to appreciate the extent of the Russian Mafya's influence.

No one in the car had uttered a word since their journey had begun, and once again the road signs gave Connor the only clue as to where they were heading. He began to think Helsinki must be their destination, but a dozen kilometres before they reached the outskirts of the city, they took a slip road off the highway. The car slowed as the driver manoeuvred over potholes and around blind bends that led deeper and deeper into the countryside. Connor gazed at the barren landscape, covered in a thick layer of snow.

'This is the second call for Finnair Flight 821 to Frankfurt. Would all passengers please board the aircraft.'

Connor still didn't move.

Forty minutes after leaving the highway, the car turned into the yard of what appeared to be a deserted farmhouse. A door was opened even before they had come to a halt. The tall young man jumped out and led Connor into the house. He didn't acknowledge the cowering woman they passed as they marched in. Connor followed him up a flight of stairs to the first landing. The Russian opened a door, and Connor entered the room. The door was slammed behind him, and he heard another key turning in another lock.

He walked across the room and looked out of the only window. One of the bodyguards was standing in the yard, staring up at him. He moved away from the window, and noticed that a complete set of clothes and a black rabbit-skin hat had been laid out on a small, uncomfortable-looking bed.

Connor stripped off all his clothes and threw them over a chair by the bed. In a corner of the room was a plastic curtain, and behind it a rusty shower. With the aid of a rough bar of soap and a trickle of lukewarm water, Connor spent several minutes trying to remove the stench of the Crucifix from his body. He dried himself with two dishcloths. When he looked in the mirror he realised that it would be some time before the scars on his head would heal and his hair return to its natural length. But the number tattooed on his wrist would be with him for the rest of his life.

He dressed in the clothes that had been left on the bed. Although the trousers were a couple of inches too short, the shirt and jacket fitted quite well, even though he must have lost at least ten pounds while he was in prison.

There was a gentle knock on the door, and the key turned in the lock. The woman who had been in the hall when they'd arrived was standing there, holding a tray. She placed it on the side table and slipped back out before Connor could thank her. He looked down at the bowl of warm broth and the three bread rolls, and literally licked his lips. He sat down and began to attack the food, but after sipping a few spoonfuls of soup and devouring one of the rolls he felt full. Suddenly overcome by drowsiness, he slumped down on the bed.

'*This is the third call for Finnair Flight 821 to Frankfurt. Would all remaining passengers please board the aircraft.*'

Connor still remained in his place.

He must have fallen asleep, because the next thing he remembered was waking and finding the pale young man standing at the end of the bed, looking down at him.

'We leave for the airport in twenty minutes,' he had told him, and tossed a thick brown package onto the bed.

Connor sat up and tore open the envelope. It contained a first-class ticket to Dulles International, a thousand US dollars, and an American passport.

He flicked open the passport and read the name 'Christopher Andrew Jackson', above a photograph of himself. He looked up at the young Russian.

'What does this mean?'

'It means you're still alive,' said Alexei Romanov.

'*This is the final call for Flight 821 for Frankfurt. Would any remaining passengers please take their seats immediately.*'

Connor strolled across to the gate agent, handed over his boarding pass and made his way to the waiting plane. The steward checked his seat number and pointed to the front section of the aircraft. Connor didn't have to search for the window seat in the fifth row, because the tall young Russian was already strapped into the aisle seat. It was obviously his job not only to pick up the package, but also to deliver it and to make sure the contract was carried out. As Connor stepped over his escort's feet, a stewardess asked, 'Can I take your hat, Mr Jackson?'

'No, thank you.'

He leaned back in the comfortable seat, but didn't relax until the plane had taken off. Then it began to sink in for the first time that he really had escaped. But to what, he wondered. He glanced to his left: from now on someone would be with him night and day until he had carried out his side of the bargain.

During the flight to Germany, Romanov never once opened his mouth, except to eat a few morsels of the meal they put in front of him. Connor left an empty plate, and then passed the time by reading Finnair's in-flight magazine. By the time the plane landed in Frankfurt, he knew all about saunas, javelin throwers, and the Finns' dependence on the Russian economy.

As they walked into the transit lounge, Connor spotted the CIA agent immediately. He quickly detached himself from his escort, returning twenty minutes later, to Romanov's evident relief.

Connor knew it would be easy to shake off his minder once they were back on his own territory, but he also knew that if he tried to escape, they would carry out the threat the Chief had so vividly described. He shuddered at the thought of any of those thugs laying a finger on Maggie or Tara.

The United Airlines 777 took off for Dulles on schedule. Connor managed to eat most of the first and second courses of his lunch. The moment the stewardess removed his tray, he pressed the button in his armrest, reclined his seat and began to think about Maggie. How he envied the fact that she could always . . . A few moments later he fell asleep on a plane for the first time in twenty years.

When he woke, they were serving a snack. He must have been the only person on the flight to eat everything they put in front of him, including the two pots of marmalade.

In the final hour before they were due to land in Washington, his thoughts returned to Chris Jackson and the sacrifice he'd made. Connor knew he could never repay him, but he was determined not to let it be a worthless gesture.

His mind switched to Dexter and Gutenburg, who must now be assuming he was dead. First they had sent him to Russia to save their own skins. Next they had murdered Joan, because she just might have passed some information on to Maggie. How long would it be before they decided Maggie herself had become too great a risk, and that she also needed to be disposed of?

'*This is your captain speaking. We have been cleared to land at Dulles International Airport. Would the cabin crew please prepare for landing. On behalf of United Airlines, I'd like to welcome you to the United States.*'

Connor flicked open his passport. Christopher Andrew Jackson was back on his home soil.

CHAPTER TWENTY-FIVE

MAGGIE ARRIVED AT DULLES AIRPORT an hour early – a habit which used to drive Connor mad. She checked the arrivals screen, and was pleased to see that the flight from San Francisco was scheduled to land on time.

She picked up a copy of the *Washington Post* from the news-stand and wandered into the nearest coffee shop, perched herself on a stool at the counter and ordered a black coffee and a croissant. She didn't notice the two men occupying a table in the opposite corner, one of whom also had a copy of the *Washington Post* which he appeared to be reading. But however hard she'd looked, she wouldn't have seen the third man who was taking more interest in her than in the arrivals screen he was looking up at. He had already spotted the other two men in the corner.

Maggie read the *Post* from cover to cover, checking her watch every few minutes. By the time she had ordered her second coffee, she was delving into the supplement on Russia published in anticipation of President Zerimski's forthcoming visit to Washington. Maggie didn't like the sound of the Communist leader, who seemed to belong in the last century.

She had downed her third coffee twenty minutes before the plane was scheduled to land, so she slipped off the stool and headed for the nearest bank of phones. Two men followed her out of the restaurant, while a third slipped from one shadow into another.

She dialled a cellphone number. 'Good morning, Jackie,' she said when her deputy answered. 'I'm just checking to see if everything's OK.'

'Maggie,' said a voice trying not to sound too exasperated, 'it's seven o'clock in the morning, and I'm still in bed. You called yesterday, remember? The university is in recess, no one is due back until the fourteenth of January, and after three years of being your deputy, I am just about capable of running the office in your absence.'

'Sorry, Jackie,' said Maggie. 'I didn't mean to wake you. I forgot how early it was. I promise not to bother you again.'

'I hope Connor gets back soon, and that Tara and Stuart keep you fully occupied for the next few weeks,' said Jackie. 'Have a good Christmas, and I don't want to hear from you again before the end of January,' she added with feeling.

Maggie put the phone down, realising she had only been killing time, and shouldn't have bothered Jackie in the first place. She chastised herself, and decided she wouldn't call her again until the New Year.

She walked slowly over to the arrivals gate and joined the growing number of people peering through the windows at the runway, where early-morning flights were taking off and landing. Three men who weren't checking the insignia of every aircraft that arrived continued to watch Maggie as she waited for the board to confirm that United's Flight 50 from San Francisco had landed. When the message finally appeared, she smiled. One of the three men punched eleven numbers into his cellphone, and passed the information back to his superior at Langley.

Maggie smiled again when a man wearing a 49ers cap emerged from the jetway – the first passenger off the 'red-eye'. She had to wait for another ten minutes before Tara and Stuart came through the door. She had never seen her daughter looking more radiant. The moment Stuart spotted Maggie, he gave her the huge grin that had become so familiar during their holiday in Australia.

Maggie hugged them in turn. 'It's wonderful to see you both,' she said. She took one of Tara's bags and led them towards the subway which led to the main terminal.

One of the men who had been watching her was already waiting in the short-term parking lot, in the passenger seat of a Toyota transporter with a load of eleven new cars. The other two were running across the lot.

Maggie, Tara and Stuart stepped into the cold morning air and walked over to Maggie's car. 'Isn't it time you got yourself something more up to date than this old scrapheap, Mom?' Tara asked in mock horror. 'I was still in high school when you bought it, and it was second-hand then.'

'The Toyota is the safest car on the road,' said Maggie primly, 'as *Consumer Reports* regularly confirms.'

'No thirteen-year-old car is safe on the road,' replied Tara.

'In any case,' said Maggie, ignoring her daughter's jibe, 'your father thinks we should hold on to it until he begins his new job, when he'll be given a company car.'

The mention of Connor brought a moment of awkward silence.

'I'm looking forward to seeing your husband again, Mrs Fitzgerald,' said Stuart as he climbed into the back seat.

Maggie didn't say, 'And so am I,' but satisfied herself with, 'So this is your first visit to America.'

'That's right,' Stuart replied as Maggie switched on the ignition. 'And already I'm not sure I'll ever want to return to Oz.'

'We have enough overpaid lawyers in the States already, without adding another one from down under,' said Tara as they waited in line to pay the parking fee.

Maggie smiled at her, feeling happier than she had for weeks.

'When do you have to go home, Stuart?'

'If you feel he's already outstayed his welcome, we could just turn round and take the next flight back, Mom,' said Tara.

'No, I didn't mean that, it's just . . .'

'I know – you do love to plan ahead,' said Tara with a laugh. 'If she could, Stuart, Mom would make students register for Georgetown at conception.'

'Why didn't I think of that?' said Maggie.

'I'm not expected back at my desk until the fifth of January,' said Stuart. 'I hope you'll be able to tolerate me for that long.'

'She's not going to be given a lot of choice,' said Tara, squeezing his hand.

Maggie handed a ten-dollar bill to the cashier before pulling out of the parking lot and onto the highway. She glanced in the rear-view mirror, but didn't notice a nondescript blue Ford about a hundred yards behind her, travelling at roughly the same speed. The man in the passenger seat was reporting in to his superior at Langley that the subject had left 'Kerbside' at seven forty-three and was headed in the direction of Washington with the two packages she had picked up.

'Did you enjoy San Francisco, Stuart?'

'Every moment,' he replied. 'We're planning to spend a couple more days there on my way back.'

When Maggie glanced in her rear-view mirror again, she saw a Virginia State patrol car coming up behind her, its lights flashing.

'Is he following me, do you think? I certainly wasn't speeding,' said Maggie, looking down to check her speedometer.

'Mom, this car is practically an antique, and should have been towed away years ago. It could be anything,

from your brake lights to defective tyres. Just pull over.'
Tara looked out the back window. 'And when the traffic
cop speaks to you, be sure to flash that Irish smile of
yours.'

Maggie pulled over as the blue Ford drove by in the
centre lane.

'Shit,' said the driver, as he shot past them.

Maggie wound down her window as the two policemen
stepped out of their patrol car and walked slowly towards
them. The first officer smiled and said politely, 'May I
see your licence, ma'am?'

'Certainly, officer,' said Maggie, returning his smile.
She leaned over, opened her bag and began rummaging
around inside as the second patrolman indicated to
Stuart that he should also wind down his window. Stuart
thought this was an odd request, as he could hardly have
been guilty of any traffic offence, but as he wasn't in his
own country, he thought it wiser to comply. He wound
down the window just as Maggie located her driving
licence. As she turned to hand it over, the second policeman drew his gun and fired three shots into the car.

The two of them walked quickly back to their patrol
car. While one eased the car into the early-morning
traffic, the other phoned the man in the passenger seat
of the transporter. 'A Toyota has broken down, and is
in need of your immediate assistance.'

Soon after the patrol car accelerated away, the transporter carrying eleven brand-new Toyotas drew up and
stopped in front of the stationary vehicle. The man in
the passenger seat, wearing a Toyota cap and blue overalls, leapt out of the cab and ran towards the stationary
car. He opened the driver's door, lifted Maggie gently
across to the passenger seat and pulled the lever that
opened the car's bonnet, then leaned over to where
Stuart was slumped, removed his wallet and passport
from his jacket pocket and replaced them with another
passport and a slim paperback book.

The driver of the transporter opened the Toyota's bonnet and checked underneath. He swiftly deactivated the tracking device and slammed the bonnet closed. His companion was now seated behind the wheel of the Toyota. He turned on the ignition, put the car into first gear and slowly drove up the transporter's ramp, taking the one space left. He switched off the ignition, put on the handbrake, fastened the car's wheels to the ramp and rejoined the driver in the cab. The entire exercise had taken less than three minutes.

The transporter resumed its journey towards Washington, but after half a mile it took the air freight exit and drove back in the direction of the airport.

The CIA officers in the blue Ford had come off the highway at the next exit, then doubled back and rejoined the morning traffic heading into Washington. 'She must have committed some minor offence,' the driver was saying to his superior at Langley. 'It wouldn't be surprising with a car that old.'

The officer in the passenger seat was surprised to find that the Toyota was no longer registering on his screen. 'They're probably on their way back to Georgetown,' he suggested. 'We'll call in the moment we regain contact.'

As the two agents sped towards Washington, the transporter carrying the twelve Toyotas turned left off the Dulles service road at a sign marked 'Cargo Only'. After a few hundred yards it turned right, through a high wire gate held open by two men in airport overalls, and drove down an old runway towards an isolated hangar. A lone figure stood at the entrance to guide them in, as if the transporter was a recently-landed aircraft.

The driver brought the vehicle to a halt next to an unmarked van. Seven men in white overalls quickly emerged from the back. One of them undid the chains that secured the old car to the transporter. Another took his place behind the wheel, released the handbrake and allowed the Toyota to roll slowly back down the ramp to the ground. The moment it came to a halt, its doors were opened and the bodies inside were carefully lifted out.

The man in the Toyota cap jumped out of the transporter and took the wheel of the old car. He threw it into first gear, swung round in a circle and shot out of the hangar as if he had been driving it all his life. As he passed through the open gate the bodies were being gently placed in the rear of the van, where three coffins were waiting for them. One of the men in overalls said, 'Don't put the lids on until you're approaching the plane.'

'OK, doc,' came the reply.

'And once the hold's been closed, remove the bodies and strap them into their seats.'

As another man nodded, the transporter backed out of the hangar and retraced its route down the old runway and out of the gates. When the driver reached the highway he turned left and headed towards Leesburg, where he would deliver eleven new Toyotas to the local dealer. His fee for six hours' unscheduled work would allow him to buy one of them.

The wire gate had already been locked and bolted by the time the van drove out of the hangar and began heading slowly towards the cargo docking area. The driver passed rows of cargo planes, finally stopping at the back of a 747 marked 'Air Transport International'. The hold was open, and two customs officials stood waiting at the bottom of the ramp. They began checking the paperwork just as the two CIA officers in the blue Ford drove past 1648 Avon Place. After cautiously circling the block, the agents reported back to Langley that there was no sign either of the car or the three packages.

The old Toyota came off Route 66 and joined the highway into Washington. The driver put his foot down hard on the accelerator and sped towards the city. Over his earphone he listened to the two officers in the Ford being instructed to go to Mrs Fitzgerald's office to see if the car was in her usual parking space behind the Admissions building.

Once the customs officials had satisfied themselves that the coroner's documents were in order, one of them said, 'OK. Remove the lids.'

They carefully checked through the clothes, and in the mouths and other orifices of all three bodies, then countersigned the documents. The lids were replaced, and the men in white overalls carried the coffins one by one up the ramp and laid them side by side in the hold.

The ramp of the 747 was being raised as the old Toyota drove past Christ Church. It sped up the hill for another three blocks before screeching to a halt in the driveway of 1648 Avon Place.

The driver had already slipped around the side of the house and let himself in through the back door by the time the doctor began checking the pulses of his three patients. He ran upstairs to the master bedroom, and opened the chest of drawers by the side of the bed. He rummaged among the sports shirts, took out the brown envelope marked 'Not to be opened before 17 December', and slipped it into an inside pocket. He pulled down two suitcases from the top of the wardrobe and quickly filled them with clothes. Next he removed a small cellophane packet from his overalls and slipped it into a cosmetics bag which he threw into one of the cases. Before he left the bedroom he switched on the bathroom light, then the light at the bottom of the stairs, and finally, using the remote control, the television in the kitchen, setting the volume to high.

He left the suitcases by the back door and returned to the Toyota, raised the bonnet and reactivated the tracking device.

The CIA officers had begun slowly circling the university parking lot for a second time when a blip reappeared on their screen. The driver quickly turned round and headed back towards the Fitzgeralds' home.

The man in the Toyota cap returned to the rear of the house, grabbed the suitcases and let himself out by the back gate. He spotted the taxi parked in front of Tudor Place, and jumped into the back just as the two agents returned to Avon Place. A relieved young man called Langley to report that the Toyota was parked in its usual place, and that he could see and hear a television on in the kitchen. No, he couldn't explain how the tracking device had been out of action for nearly an hour.

The taxi driver didn't even turn his head when the man jumped in the back of his cab carrying two suitcases. But then, he knew exactly where Mr Fitzgerald wanted to be taken.

CHAPTER TWENTY-SIX

'ARE YOU TELLING ME that all three of them have disappeared off the face of the earth?' said the Director.

'It looks that way,' replied Gutenburg. 'It was such a professional operation that if I didn't know he was dead, I would have said it had all the hallmarks of Connor Fitzgerald.'

'As we know that's impossible, who do you think it was?'

'My bet is still Jackson,' replied the Deputy Director.

'Well, if he's back in the country, Mrs Fitzgerald will know her husband is dead. So we can expect to see her home video on the early-evening news any day now.'

Gutenburg grinned complacently. 'Not a chance,' he said, passing a sealed package across the table to his boss. 'One of my agents finally found the tape, a few minutes before the university library closed last night.'

'That's one problem dealt with,' said the Director, tearing open the package. 'But what's to stop Jackson telling Lloyd who's really buried in the Crucifix?'

Gutenburg shrugged his shoulders. 'Even if he does, what use is the information to Lawrence? He's hardly going to phone up his pal Zerimski, a few days before he's due to arrive in Washington on a goodwill visit, to let him know that the man they hanged for planning his assassination wasn't a South African terrorist hired by

the Mafya after all, but a CIA agent carrying out orders
that had come directly from the White House.'

'Maybe not,' said Dexter. 'But as long as Jackson and
the Fitzgerald women are out there, we still have a problem. So I suggest you deploy the best dozen agents we've
got to track them down, and as quickly as possible – I
don't care what sector they're working in or who they're
assigned to. If Lawrence can prove what really happened
in St Petersburg, he'll have more than enough excuse
to call for someone's resignation.'

Gutenburg was unusually silent.

'And as it's your signature at the bottom of every relevant document,' continued the Director, 'I would, alas,
be left with no choice but to let you go.'

Small beads of sweat appeared on Gutenburg's
forehead.

Stuart thought he was coming out of a bad dream. He
tried to recall what had happened. They had been picked
up at the airport by Tara's mother, who had been driving
them towards Washington. But the car had been stopped
by a traffic cop, and he had been asked to wind down
his window. And then . . . ?

He looked around. He was on another plane, but
where was it going? Tara's head was resting on his shoulder; on her other side was her mother, also fast asleep.
All the other seats were empty.

He began to go over the facts again, as he always did
when preparing for a case. He and Tara had landed at
Dulles. Maggie had been waiting for them at the gate . . .

His concentration was broken when a smartly dressed
middle-aged man appeared by his side and leaned over
to check his pulse.

'Where are we going?' asked Stuart quietly, but the
doctor didn't reply. He carried out the same cursory
examination on Tara and Maggie, then disappeared back
up to the front of the plane.

Stuart unfastened his seatbelt, but hadn't enough strength to stand up. Tara had begun stirring, while Maggie remained resolutely asleep. He checked his pockets. They had taken his wallet and passport. He tried desperately to make some sense of it. Why should anyone go to these extremes for a few hundred dollars, some credit cards and an Australian passport? Even more strangely, they seemed to have replaced them with a slim volume of Yeats's poems. He had never read Yeats before he met Tara, but after she had returned to Stanford he had begun to enjoy his work. He opened the book at the first poem, 'A Dialogue of Self and Soul'. The words '*I am content to live it all again, and yet again*' were underlined. He flicked through the pages, and noticed that other lines had also been marked.

As he was considering the significance of this a tall, heavily built man appeared by his side, towering menacingly over him. Without a word, he snatched the book from Stuart's hands and returned to the front of the plane.

Tara touched his hand. He quickly turned to her and whispered in her ear, 'Say nothing.' She glanced across at her mother, who still hadn't stirred, seemingly at peace with the world.

Once Connor had placed the two suitcases in the hold and checked that all three passengers were alive and unharmed, he left the aircraft and climbed into the back of a BMW whose engine was already running.

'We continue to keep our side of the bargain,' said Alexei Romanov, who was sitting next to him. Connor nodded his agreement as the BMW drove out through the wire gates and began its journey to Ronald Reagan National Airport.

After his experience at Frankfurt, where the local CIA agent had nearly spotted him because Romanov and his two sidekicks did practically everything except publicly announce their arrival, Connor realised that if he was going to pull off his plan to rescue Maggie and Tara, he would have to run the operation himself. Romanov had finally accepted this when he had been reminded of the clause agreed by his father. Now Connor could only hope that Stuart was as resourceful as he had appeared to be when he had quizzed him on the beach in Australia. He prayed that Stuart would notice the words he'd underlined in the book he'd slipped into his pocket.

The BMW drew up outside the upper-level Departure entrance of Washington National Airport. Connor stepped out, with Romanov a pace behind. Two other men joined them and followed Connor as he strolled calmly into the airport and over to the ticket counter. He needed them all to relax before he made his next move.

When Connor handed over his ticket, the man behind the American Airlines desk said, 'I'm sorry, Mr Radford, but Flight 383 to Dallas is running a few minutes late, though we hope to make up the time *en route*. You'll be boarding at Gate 32.'

Connor walked casually in the direction of the lounge, but stopped when he reached a bank of telephones. He chose one with occupied booths on either side. Romanov and the two bodyguards hovered a few paces away, looking displeased. Connor smiled at them innocently, then slipped Stuart's international phone-card into the slot and dialled a Cape Town number.

The phone rang for some time before it was eventually answered.

'Yes?'

'It's Connor.'

There was a protracted silence. 'I thought it was only Jesus who could rise from the dead,' said Carl eventually.

'I spent some time in purgatory before I managed it,' Connor replied.

'Well, at least you're alive, my friend. What can I do for you?'

'First, as far as the Company is concerned, there will be no second coming.'

'Understood,' said Carl.

Connor was answering Carl's last question when he heard the final call for Flight 383 to Dallas. He put the phone down, smiled at Romanov again, and headed quickly for Gate 32.

When Maggie eventually opened her eyes, Stuart leaned across and warned her to say nothing until she was fully awake. A few moments later a stewardess appeared and asked them to lower their tray tables. An inedible selection of food appeared, as if they were on a normal first-class flight.

As he contemplated a fish that should have been left in the sea, Stuart whispered to Maggie and Tara, 'I haven't a clue why we're here or where we're going, but I have to believe that in some way it's connected with Connor.'

Maggie nodded, and quietly began to tell them everything she had found out since Joan's death.

'But I don't think the people holding us can be the CIA,' she said, 'because I told Gutenburg that if I was missing for more than seven days, that video would be released to the media.'

'Unless they've already found it,' said Stuart.

'That's not possible,' said Maggie emphatically.

'Then who the hell are they?' said Tara.

No one offered an opinion as the stewardess reappeared and silently removed their trays.

'Have we got anything else to go on?' Maggie asked after the stewardess had left them.

'Only that somebody put a book of Yeats's poems in my pocket,' said Stuart.

Tara noticed Maggie give a start.

'What's the matter?' she asked, looking anxiously at her mother, whose eyes were now filling with tears.

'Don't you understand what this means?'

'No,' said Tara, looking puzzled.

'Your father must still be alive. Let me see it,' said Maggie. 'He might have left a message in it.'

'I'm afraid I haven't got it any more. I'd hardly opened it before a heavy appeared from the front of the plane and snatched it away,' said Stuart. 'I did notice that a few words were underlined, though.'

'What were they?' asked Maggie urgently.

'I couldn't make much sense of them.'

'That doesn't matter. Can you remember any of them?'

Stuart closed his eyes and tried to concentrate. '"*Content*",' he said suddenly.

Maggie smiled. '"*I am content to live it all again, and yet again*".'

Flight 383 did land in Dallas on time, and when Connor and Romanov stepped out of the airport another white BMW was waiting for them. Had the Mafya placed a bulk order? Connor wondered. The latest pair of thugs to accompany them looked as if they had been hired from central casting – even their shoulder holsters were bulging under their jackets.

He could only hope that the Cape Town branch was a recent subsidiary, although he found it hard to believe that Carl Koeter, with over twenty years' experience as the CIA's senior operative in South Africa, wouldn't be able to handle the latest new kid on the block.

The trip into downtown Dallas took just over twenty minutes. Connor sat silently in the back of the car, aware that he might be about to come face to face with someone else who had worked for the CIA for almost thirty years. Although they'd never met, he knew this was the biggest risk he had taken since arriving back in America. But if the Russians expected him to honour the most demanding clause in their contract, he had to have the use of the only rifle ideal for carrying out such an assignment.

After another silent journey they pulled up outside Harding's Big Game Emporium. Connor slipped quickly into the shop, with Romanov and his two new shadows dogging his every step. He went up to the counter, while they pretended to take a keen interest in a rack of automatic pistols on the far side of the shop.

Connor glanced around. His search needed to be quick, unobtrusive but thorough. After a few moments he was convinced there were no security cameras in the shop.

'Good afternoon, sir,' said a young assistant dressed in a long brown coat. 'How can I help you?'

'I'm out here on a shooting trip, and I'd like to buy a rifle.'

'Do you have any particular model in mind?'

'Yes, a Remington 700.'

'That should be no problem, sir.'

'It may need a few modifications,' said Connor.

The assistant hesitated. 'Excuse me for a moment, sir.' He disappeared through a curtain into a back room.

A few moments later an older man, also dressed in a long brown coat, appeared through the curtain. Connor was annoyed: he had hoped to purchase the rifle without having to meet the legendary Jim Harding.

'Good afternoon,' the man said, looking closely at his customer. 'I understand you're interested in a Remington 700.' He paused. 'With modifications.'

'Yes. You were recommended by a friend,' said Connor.

'Your friend must be a professional,' said Harding.

As soon as the word 'professional' was mentioned, Connor knew he was being tested. If Harding hadn't been the Stradivarius of gunsmiths, he would have left the shop without another word.

'What modifications did you have in mind, sir?' asked Harding, his eyes never leaving the customer's.

Connor described in detail the gun he had left in Bogotá, watching carefully for any reaction.

Harding's face remained impassive. 'I might have something that would interest you, sir,' he said, then turned and disappeared behind the curtain.

Once again, Connor considered leaving, but within seconds Harding reappeared carrying a familiar leather case, which he placed on the counter.

'This model came into our possession after the owner's recent death,' he explained. He flicked up the catches, opened the lid and swivelled the case round so that Connor could inspect the rifle. 'Every part is hand-made, and I doubt if you'll find a finer piece of craftsmanship this side of the Mississippi.' Harding touched the rifle lovingly. 'The stock is fibreglass, for lightness and better balance. The barrel is imported from Germany – I'm afraid the Krauts still produce the best. The scope is a Leupold 10 Power with mil dots, so you don't even have to adjust for wind. With this rifle you could kill a mouse at four hundred paces, never mind a moose. If you're technically minded, you would be capable of a half-minute of angle at one hundred yards.' He looked up to see if his customer understood what he was talking about, but Connor's expression gave him no clue. 'A Remington 700 with such modifications is only sought after by the most discerning of customers,' he concluded.

Connor didn't remove any of the five pieces from their places, for fear Mr Harding would discover just how discerning a customer he was.

'How much?' he asked, realising for the first time that he had no idea of the price of a hand-crafted Remington 700.

'Twenty-one thousand dollars,' Harding said. 'Though we do have the standard model should you . . .'

'No,' said Connor. 'This one will be just fine.'

'And how will you be paying, sir?'

'Cash.'

'Then I will require some form of identification,' said Harding. 'I'm afraid there's even more paperwork since they passed the Instant ID and Registration Law to replace the Brady Bill.'

Connor took out a Virginia driver's licence he'd bought for a hundred dollars from a pickpocket in Washington the previous day.

Harding studied the licence and nodded. 'All we need now, Mr Radford, is for you to fill in these three forms.'

Connor wrote out the name, address and Social Security number of the assistant manager of a shoe store in Richmond.

As Harding entered the numbers into a computer, Connor tried to look bored, but he was silently praying that Mr Radford hadn't reported the loss of his driver's licence during the past twenty-four hours.

Suddenly Harding looked up from the screen. 'Is that a double-barrelled name?' he asked.

'No,' replied Connor, not missing a beat. 'Gregory is my first name. My mother had a thing about Gregory Peck.'

Harding smiled. 'Mine too.'

After a few more moments Harding said, 'That all seems to be in order, Mr Radford.'

Connor turned and nodded to Romanov, who strolled over and extracted a thick bundle of notes from an inside pocket. He spent some time ostentatiously peeling off hundred-dollar bills, counting out 210 of them before passing them across to Harding. What Connor had hoped would appear no more than a casual purchase, the Russian was fast turning into a pantomime. The sidekicks might as well have stood out on the street and sold tickets for the performance.

Harding wrote out a receipt for the cash and handed it to Connor, who left without another word. One of the hoodlums grabbed the rifle and ran out of the shop onto the sidewalk as if he had just robbed a bank. Connor climbed into the back of the BMW and wondered if it was possible to attract any more attention to themselves. The car screeched away from the kerb and cut into the fast-moving traffic, setting off a cacophony of horns. Yes, Connor thought, they obviously could. He remained speechless as the driver broke the speed limit all the way back to the airport. Even Romanov began to look a little apprehensive. Connor was quickly discovering that the new Mafia in the States were still amateurish compared with their cousins from Italy. But it wouldn't be long before they caught up, and when they did, God help the FBI.

Fifteen minutes later, the BMW drew up outside the entrance to the airport. Connor stepped out and began walking towards the revolving door as Romanov gave instructions to the two men in the car, finally peeling off several more hundred-dollar bills and handing them over. When he joined Connor at the check-in counter, he whispered confidently, 'The rifle will be in Washington within forty-eight hours.'

'I wouldn't bet on it,' said Connor as they headed towards the departure lounge.

'You know the whole of Yeats off by heart?' asked Stuart in disbelief.

'Um, most of it,' admitted Maggie. 'But then, I do reread a few poems almost every night before going to bed.'

'Darling Stuart, you've still got so much to learn about the Irish,' said Tara. 'Now, try to remember some more of the words.'

Stuart thought for a moment. '"*Hollow*"!' he said triumphantly.

'"*Through hollow lands and hilly lands*"?' asked Maggie. 'That's it.'

'So it can't be Holland we're headed for,' said Tara.

'Stop being facetious,' said Stuart.

'Then try to remember some more words,' said Tara.

Stuart began to concentrate once again. ' "*Friend*",' he said eventually.

' "*Always we'd have the new friend meet the old*",' said Maggie.

'So we're about to meet a new friend in a new country,' said Tara.

'But who? And where?' said Maggie, as the plane continued its journey through the night.

CHAPTER TWENTY-SEVEN

WITHIN MOMENTS OF READING the priority message, Gutenburg was dialling the number in Dallas. When Harding came on the line, the Deputy Director of the CIA simply said, 'Describe him.'

'Six foot, possibly six one. He was wearing a hat, so I couldn't see his hair colour.'

'Age?'

'Fifty. Could be a year or two either way.'

'Eyes?'

'Blue.'

'Dress?'

'Sports jacket, khaki pants, blue shirt, penny loafers, no tie. Smart but casual. I assumed he was one of ours, until I noticed that he was accompanied by a couple of well-known local hoodlums, who he tried to pretend weren't with him. There was also a tall young man who never once opened his mouth, but he was the one who paid for the gun – in cash.'

'And the first man made it clear he wanted those particular modifications?'

'Yes. I'm pretty sure he knew exactly what he was looking for.'

'Right – hold on to the cash. We may be able to identify a fingerprint from one of the bills.'

'You won't find any of his prints on them,' said Hard-

ing. 'The young man paid, and one of the hoodlums
carried the gun out of the shop.'

'Whoever it was obviously wasn't willing to risk taking
it through airport security,' said Gutenburg. 'The two
thugs must simply have been couriers. What name did
he sign the forms in?'

'Gregory Peck Radford.'

'Identification?'

'Virginia driver's licence. The address and date of
birth all tied in with the correct Social Security
number.'

'I'll have an agent with you in under an hour. He can
start by e-mailing me any details you have on the two
hoodlums, and I'll need a police artist's computerised
sketch of the main suspect.'

'That won't be necessary,' said Harding.

'Why not?'

'Because the whole transaction was recorded on video.'
Gutenburg couldn't see Harding's smile of satisfaction
as he added, 'Even you wouldn't have spotted the security
camera.'

Stuart continued to concentrate. '"*Find out*"!' he said
suddenly.

'"*I will find out where she has gone*",' said Maggie with
a smile.

'We're going to meet a new friend in a new country,
and he'll find us,' said Tara. 'Can you remember anything else, Stuart?'

'"*All things fall . . .*"'

'"*. . . and are built again*",' Maggie whispered as the
man who had snatched the book out of Stuart's hands
reappeared by their side.

'Now listen, and listen carefully,' he said, looking down
at them. 'If you hope to survive – and I don't give a
damn either way – you will follow my instructions to the
letter. Is that understood?' Stuart stared into the man's

eyes and didn't doubt that he looked upon the three of them as just another job. He nodded.

'Right,' the man continued. 'When the plane lands, you will go directly to the baggage area, pick up your luggage and pass through customs without attracting any attention to yourselves. You will not, I repeat not, use the rest rooms. Once you're through customs and in the arrivals area, you will be met by two of my men who will accompany you to the house where you'll be staying for the foreseeable future. I will meet up with you again later this evening. Is that clear?'

'Yes,' said Stuart firmly on behalf of the three of them.

'If any of you is stupid enough to make a run for it, or tries to enlist any help, Mrs Fitzgerald will be killed immediately. And if she's not available for any reason, I get to choose between you two.' He looked at Tara and Stuart. 'Those were the terms Mr Fitzgerald agreed.'

'That's not possible,' began Maggie. 'Connor would never . . .'

'I think it might be wise, Mrs Fitzgerald, to allow Mr Farnham to speak on behalf of all of you in future,' said the man. Maggie would have corrected him if Tara hadn't quickly kicked her leg. 'You'll need these,' he said, handing over three passports to Stuart. He checked them and passed one to Maggie and another to Tara, as the man returned to the cockpit.

Stuart looked down at the remaining passport, which like the other two bore the American eagle on its cover. When he flicked it open he found his own photograph above the name 'Daniel Farnham'. Profession: University law professor. Address: 75 Marina Boulevard, San Francisco, California. He passed it across to Tara, who looked puzzled.

'I do like dealing with professionals,' said Stuart. 'And I'm beginning to realise that your father is one of the best.'

'Are you sure you can't remember any more words?' asked Maggie.

'I'm afraid not,' said Stuart. 'No, wait a moment – "*anarchy*".'

Maggie smiled. 'Now I know where we're going.'

It's a long drive from Dallas to Washington. The two thugs who had dropped Connor and Romanov off at the airport had always planned to break the journey somewhere before continuing to the capital the following day. Just after nine o'clock that evening, having covered around four hundred miles, they pulled into a motel on the outskirts of Memphis.

The two senior CIA officers who watched them park their BMW reported back to Gutenburg forty-five minutes later. 'They've checked into the Memphis Marriott, rooms 107 and 108. They ordered room service at nine thirty-three, and are currently in Room 107 watching *Nash Bridges*.'

'Where's the rifle?' asked Gutenburg.

'It's handcuffed to the wrist of the man booked into Room 108.'

'Then you're going to need a waiter and a pass key,' said Gutenburg.

Just after ten o'clock, a waiter appeared in Room 107 and set up a table for dinner. He opened a bottle of red wine, poured two glasses and laid out the food. He told the guests he would return in about forty minutes to clear the table. One of them told him to cut up his steak into little pieces, as he only had the use of one hand. The waiter was happy to oblige. 'Enjoy,' he added, as he left the room.

The waiter then went straight to the carpark and reported to the senior officer, who thanked him, then made a further request. The waiter nodded, and the agent handed him a fifty-dollar bill.

'Obviously not willing to let go of it even when he's

eating,' said the other agent once the waiter was out of earshot.

The waiter returned to the carpark a few minutes after midnight, to report that both men had gone to bed in their own rooms. He handed over a pass-key, and in return was given another fifty-dollar bill. He left feeling he'd done a good night's work. What he didn't know was that the man in Room 107 had taken the keys of the handcuffs, so as to be sure that no one would try and steal the briefcase from his partner while he was asleep.

When the guest in 107 woke the following morning, he felt unusually drowsy. He checked his watch, and was surprised to find how late it was. He pulled on his jeans and hurried through the connecting door to wake his partner. He came to a sudden halt, fell on his knees and began to vomit. Lying on the carpet in a pool of blood was a severed hand.

As they stepped off the plane in Cape Town, Stuart was aware of the presence of two men watching their every move. An immigration officer stamped their passports, and they headed towards the baggage claim area. After only a few minutes, luggage began to appear on the carousel. Maggie was surprised to see two of her old suitcases coming down the chute. Stuart was starting to get used to the way Connor Fitzgerald operated.

Once they had retrieved their bags, Stuart put them all on a trolley and they walked towards the green customs exit. The two men filed in close behind them.

As Stuart was wheeling the trolley through customs, an officer stepped into his path, pointed to the red suitcase and asked if the owner would place it on the counter. Stuart helped Maggie lift it, as the two men following them reluctantly moved on. Once they had passed through the sliding doors they stationed themselves a few feet from the exit. Each time the doors opened, they could be seen peering back through. Within moments they were joined by two other men.

'Would you open the case, please, ma'am,' asked the customs officer.

Maggie flicked up the catches and smiled at the mess that greeted her. Only one person could have packed that case. The customs officer dug around among her clothes for a few moments, and eventually came out with a cosmetics bag. He unzipped it and removed a small cellophane packet which contained a white powdery substance.

'But that isn't . . .' began Maggie. This time it was Stuart who restrained her.

'I'm afraid we'll have to conduct a body search, ma'am,' said the officer. 'Perhaps, in the circumstances, your daughter would like to join you.'

Stuart wondered how the officer could possibly have known that Tara was Maggie's daughter, when he apparently didn't assume that he was her son.

'Would all three of you care to follow me,' said the officer. 'Please bring the case, and the rest of your luggage.' He lifted a section of the counter and ushered them through a door that led into a small, drab room with a table and two chairs. 'One of my colleagues will join you in a moment,' he said. He closed the door, and they heard the key turning in the lock.

'What's going on?' said Maggie. 'That bag wasn't . . .'

'I expect we're about to find out,' said Stuart.

A door on the far side of the room opened, and a tall, athletic-looking man, who didn't have a hair on his head although he couldn't have been a day over fifty, bounced into the room. He was dressed in blue jeans and a red sweater, and certainly didn't give the impression of being a customs officer. He went straight over to Maggie, took her right hand and kissed it.

'My name is Carl Koeter,' he said in a broad South African accent. 'This is a great honour for me, Mrs Fitzgerald. I've wanted for many years to meet the woman who was brave enough to marry Connor Fitzgerald. He called me yesterday afternoon and asked me to assure you that he's very much alive.'

Maggie would have said something, but the flow didn't stop.

'Of course I know far more about you than you do about me, but unhappily on this occasion we will not have time to remedy that.' He smiled at Stuart and Tara, and bowed slightly. 'Perhaps you would all be kind enough to follow me.'

He turned, and began to push the trolley through the door.

' "*Always we'd have the new friend meet the old*",' Maggie whispered. Stuart smiled.

The South African led them down a steep ramp and along a dark, empty passageway. Maggie quickly caught up with him, and immediately began to question him about his phone conversation with Connor. At the end of the tunnel they climbed up another ramp, and emerged on the far side of the airport. Koeter guided them quickly through security, where they were met with only the most cursory of checks. After another long trek they arrived in an empty departure lounge, where Koeter handed over three tickets to a gate agent and received three boarding passes for a Qantas flight to Sydney that had been mysteriously held up for fifteen minutes.

'How can we begin to thank you?' asked Maggie.

Koeter took her hand and kissed it again. 'Ma'am,' he replied, 'you will find people all over the world who will never be able to fully repay Connor Fitzgerald.'

They both sat watching the television. Neither of them spoke until the twelve-minute clip had come to an end.

'Could it be possible?' said the Director quietly.

'Only if he somehow changed places with him in the Crucifix,' replied Gutenburg.

Dexter was silent for some time before she said, 'Jackson would only have done that if he was willing to sacrifice his own life.'

Gutenburg nodded.

'And who's the man who paid for the rifle?'

'Alexei Romanov, the son of the Czar and the number two in the Russian Mafya. One of our agents spotted him at Frankfurt airport, and we suspect he and Fitzgerald are now working together.'

'So it must have been the Mafya who got him out of the Crucifix,' said Dexter. 'But if he needed a Remington 700, who's the target?'

'The President,' said Gutenburg.

'You could be right,' replied Dexter. 'But which one?'

CHAPTER TWENTY-EIGHT

THE PRESIDENT OF THE UNITED STATES and the Secretary of State were among the seventy-two officials lined up on the runway when the Russian Air Force Ilyushin 62 landed at Andrews Air Force Base just outside Washington DC. The red carpet had already been rolled out, a podium with a dozen microphones was in place, and a wide staircase was being towed towards the exact spot on the tarmac where the aircraft would taxi to a standstill.

As the door of the plane opened, Tom Lawrence shielded his eyes from the bright morning sun. A tall, slim stewardess was standing in the doorway. A moment later a short, squat man appeared next to her. Although Lawrence knew that Zerimski was only five foot four, standing next to the tall stewardess cruelly emphasised his lack of stature. Lawrence doubted if it would be possible for a man of Zerimski's height to become President of the United States.

As Zerimski slowly descended the steps, the massed ranks of photographers began clicking furiously. From behind their cordon, camera crews from every network focused on the man who would dominate the world's news for the next four days.

The US Chief of Protocol stepped forward to introduce the two Presidents, and Lawrence shook hands warmly with his guest. 'Welcome to the United States, Mr President.'

'Thank you, Tom,' said Zerimski, immediately wrong-footing him.

Lawrence turned to present the Secretary of State.

'Nice to meet you, Larry,' said Zerimski.

Zerimski appeared disarmingly affable and friendly as he was introduced to each new official: the Defense Secretary, the Commerce Secretary, the National Security Advisor. When he came to the end of the line, Lawrence touched his elbow and guided him towards the podium. As they walked across the runway, the American President leaned down and said, 'I'll just say a few words of welcome, Mr President, and then perhaps you'd like to reply.'

'Victor, please,' Zerimski insisted.

Lawrence stepped up onto the podium, extracted a single sheet of paper from an inside pocket and placed it on the lectern.

'Mr President,' he began; then, turning towards Zerimski, he smiled and said, 'Victor. May I begin by welcoming you to America. Today marks the opening of a new era in the special relationship between our two great countries. Your visit to the United States heralds . . .'

Connor sat in front of three television screens, watching the major networks' coverage of the ceremony. That night he would replay the tapes again and again. There was an even greater security presence on the ground than he had anticipated. The Secret Service seemed to have turned out a full Dignitary Protective Division for each President. But there was no sign of Gutenburg, or of any CIA operatives. Connor suspected that the Secret Service was unaware that a potential assassin was on the loose.

Connor wasn't at all surprised that the rifle he had bought in Dallas had never reached its destination. The two Mafya hoodlums had done everything to tip off the

CIA except call them on their toll-free number. Had he been Deputy Director, Connor would have allowed them to deliver the rifle, in the hope that they would lead him to the person who intended to use it. Gutenburg had obviously considered that removing the weapon was more important. Perhaps he was right. Connor couldn't risk being put through another débâcle like the one in Dallas. They had made it necessary for him to come up with an alternative plan.

After the episode in the Memphis Marriott, it had become clear that Alexei Romanov wasn't willing to take the blame if anything else went wrong, and Connor now had overall control of the preparations for the assassination. Those shadowing him kept a respectful distance, although they never let him out of their sight – otherwise he would have been at Andrews Air Force Base that morning. Although he could still have shaken them off whenever he chose, Connor was made aware of their attitude to failure when he learned that the local Mafya boss in Dallas had chopped off the hoodlum's other hand, so that he couldn't make the same mistake twice.

The President came to the end of his welcoming speech and received a round of applause that had little impact in such a large open space. He stepped aside to allow Zerimski to respond, but when the Russian President took his place, he couldn't be seen above the bank of microphones. Connor knew that the press would remind the six foot one American President of this public relations disaster again and again over the next four days, and that Zerimski would assume it had been done intentionally to upstage him. He wondered which White House advance man's head would roll later that day.

Shooting a six-foot man would be much easier than one who was only five foot four, Connor reflected. He studied the agents from the Dignitary Protective Division who had been assigned to protect Zerimski during his visit. He recognised four of them, all of whom were as good as any in their profession. Any one of them could have brought a man down with a single shot at three hundred paces, and disarmed an attacker with one blow. Behind their dark glasses, Connor knew that their eyes were darting ceaselessly in every direction.

Although Zerimski could not be seen by those standing on the runway, his words could be heard clearly. Connor was surprised to find that the hectoring, bullying manner he had employed in Moscow and St Petersburg had been replaced by a far more conciliatory tone. He thanked 'Tom' for his warm welcome, and said that he was confident the visit would prove fruitful for both nations.

Connor was sure that Lawrence wouldn't be fooled by this outward display of warmth. This obviously wasn't the time or place for the Russian President to allow the Americans to discover his real agenda.

As Zerimski continued to read from his script, Connor glanced down at the four-day itinerary prepared by the White House and so conveniently catalogued minute by minute in the *Washington Post*. He knew from years of experience that even with the best-laid plans, such programmes rarely managed to keep to their original timetables. At some time during the visit, he had to assume that the unexpected would happen; and he had to be sure that it wasn't at the moment when he was lining up his rifle.

The two Presidents would be flown by helicopter from the Air Force base to the White House, where they would immediately go into a session of private talks, which would continue over lunch. After lunch, Zerimski would be taken to the Russian Embassy to rest, before returning to the White House in the evening for a black-tie dinner in his honour.

The following morning, he would travel to New York to address the United Nations and have lunch with the Secretary-General, followed by a visit to the Metropolitan Museum in the afternoon. Connor had laughed out loud when he read that morning in the style section of the *Post* that Tom Lawrence had become aware of his guest's great love of the arts during the recent presidential campaign, in the course of which Zerimski had found time in his busy schedule to visit not only the Bolshoi, but also the Pushkin and the Hermitage Museums.

After the Russian President returned to Washington on Thursday night, he would have just enough time to rush to the Embassy and change into a dinner jacket before attending a performance of *Swan Lake* by the Washington Ballet at the Kennedy Center. The *Post* tactlessly reminded its readers that over half the *corps de ballet* were Russian immigrants.

On the Friday morning there would be extended talks at the White House, followed by lunch at the State Department. In the afternoon Zerimski would deliver an address to a joint session of Congress, which would be the high point of his four-day visit. Lawrence hoped that the legislators would be convinced that the Russian leader was a man of peace, and agree to back his Arms Reduction Bill. An editorial in the *New York Times* warned that this might be the occasion at which Zerimski would outline Russia's defence strategy for the next decade. The paper's diplomatic correspondent had contacted the press office at the Russian Embassy, only to be informed curtly that there would be no advance copies of that particular speech.

In the evening Zerimski would be the guest of honour at a US–Russia Business Council dinner. Copies of that speech had already been widely circulated, with a casual indifference to any embargo. Connor had been through every sentence, and knew that no self-respecting journalist would bother to print a word of it.

On the Saturday Zerimski and Tom Lawrence would go to Cooke Stadium in Maryland to watch the football game between the Washington Redskins and the Green Bay Packers, the team that Lawrence, who had been the senior Senator for Wisconsin, had supported all his life.

In the evening Zerimski would host a dinner at the Russian Embassy to return the hospitality of all those whose guest he had been during his visit.

The following morning he would fly back to Moscow – but only if Connor had failed to carry out the contract.

Nine venues for Connor to consider. But he had already dismissed seven of them before Zerimski's plane had touched down. Of the remaining two, the banquet on the Saturday night looked the most promising, especially after he'd been told by Romanov that the Mafya had the catering concession for all functions held at the Russian Embassy.

A smattering of applause brought Connor's attention back to the welcoming ceremony. Some of the people standing on the runway were unaware that Zerimski had completed his speech until he stepped down from the podium, so the reception he received was not quite as enthusiastic as Lawrence had hoped.

The two leaders walked across the tarmac to a waiting helicopter. Normally no Russian President would fly in a US military aircraft, but Zerimski had brushed aside any objections, telling his advisors he wanted to take every opportunity of wrong-footing Lawrence. They climbed on board and waved to the crowd. Moments later Marine One rose, hovered above the ground for a few seconds, then lifted away. Those women who had not attended a welcoming ceremony before were unsure whether to cling on to their hats or hold down their dresses.

In seven minutes Marine One would land on the South Lawn of the White House, to be met by Andy Lloyd and the White House senior staff.

Connor flicked off the three televisions, rewound the tapes and began considering the alternatives. He had already decided not to go to New York. The United Nations and the Metropolitan Museum offered virtually no possibility of escape. And he was aware that the Secret Service were trained to spot anyone who appeared on more than one occasion during a visit such as this one, including journalists and television crews. Added to that, at least three thousand of New York's finest would be guarding Zerimski every second of his visit.

He would use the time while Zerimski was out of town to check out the two most promising venues. The Mafya had already arranged for him to be a member of the catering team that would visit the Russian Embassy that afternoon so he could be taken through the details of Saturday night's banquet. The Ambassador had made it clear that he wanted it to be an occasion that neither President would ever forget.

Connor checked his watch, put on a coat and went downstairs. The BMW was waiting for him. He climbed into the back seat.

'Cooke Stadium,' was all he said.

No one in the car commented as the driver eased the car into the centre lane.

As a transporter laden with new cars passed on the other side of the road, Connor thought of Maggie and smiled. He had spoken to Carl Koeter earlier that morning, and had been reassured that all three of the kangaroos were safely in their pouches.

'By the way, the Mafya are under the impression that they were sent straight back to America,' Koeter had told him.

'How did you manage to pull that one off?' asked Connor.

'One of their guards tried to bribe a customs officer. He took the money and informed him they'd been caught with drugs, and had been "returned to their port of embarkation".'

'Do you think they fell for it?'

'Oh yes,' said Koeter. 'They were made to pay a lot of money for that piece of information.'

Connor laughed. 'I'll always be in your debt, Carl. Just let me know how I can repay you.'

'That won't be necessary, my friend,' Koeter had replied. 'I will simply look forward to meeting your wife again in more agreeable circumstances.'

Connor's watchdogs had made no mention of Maggie's disappearance, so he couldn't be certain whether they were too proud to admit that they'd lost her, Stuart and Tara, or whether they were still hoping to catch up with them before he found out the truth. Perhaps they were afraid he wouldn't carry out the job if he knew his wife and daughter were no longer in their hands. But Connor never doubted that if he failed to honour the agreement, Alexei Romanov would eventually track down Maggie and kill her, and if not Maggie, Tara. Bolchenkov had warned him that until the contract had been completed – one way or the other – Romanov wouldn't be allowed to return to his homeland.

As the driver swung onto the beltway, Connor thought about Joan, whose only crime was to have been his secretary. He clenched his fist, and wished that his contract with the Mafya had been to take out Dexter and her conniving Deputy. That was an assignment he would have carried out with relish.

The BMW passed the Washington city limits, and Connor sat back, thinking about just how much preparation still needed to be done. He would have to circle the stadium several times, checking every exit, before deciding if he would even enter it.

Marine One landed gently on the South Lawn. The two Presidents stepped out of the helicopter, and were greeted by warm applause from the six hundred assembled White House members of staff.

When Lawrence introduced Zerimski to his Chief of Staff, he couldn't help noticing that Andy seemed preoccupied. The two leaders spent an unusually long time posing for the photographers before retiring to the Oval Office with their advisers to confirm the subjects that would be covered at the later meetings. Zerimski put forward no objections to the timetable Andy Lloyd had prepared, and seemed relaxed about the topics that would come under consideration.

When they broke for lunch, Lawrence felt the preliminary discussions had gone well. They moved into the Cabinet Room, and Lawrence told the story of when President Kennedy had dined there with eight Nobel Laureates, and had remarked that it was the greatest gathering of intellect there since Jefferson had dined alone. Larry Harrington laughed dutifully, although he had heard the President tell the story a dozen times before. Andy Lloyd didn't even attempt a smile.

After lunch Lawrence accompanied Zerimski to his limousine, which was waiting at the diplomatic entrance. As soon as the last car of the motorcade was out of sight – once again Zerimski had insisted he should have one more vehicle than any past Russian President – Lawrence hurried back to the Oval Office. A grim-faced Andy Lloyd was standing by his desk.

'I thought that went as well as could be expected,' said the President.

'Possibly,' said Lloyd. 'Although I wouldn't trust that man to tell the truth even to himself. He was far too cooperative for my liking. I just get the feeling that we're being set up.'

'Was that the reason you were so uncommunicative during lunch?'

'No. I think we've got a far bigger problem on our hands,' said Lloyd. 'Have you seen Dexter's latest report? I left it on your desk yesterday afternoon.'

'No, I haven't,' the President replied. 'I spent most of yesterday holed up with Larry Harrington in the State Department.' He flicked open a file bearing the CIA emblem, and began reading.

He had sworn out loud on three occasions before he had reached the second page. By the time he'd come to the final paragraph, his face was drained of colour. He looked up at his oldest friend. 'I thought Jackson was supposed to be on our side.'

'He is, Mr President.'

'Then how come Dexter claims she can prove that he was responsible for the assassination in Colombia, then went to St Petersburg intending to kill Zerimski?'

'Because that way she clears herself of any involvement, and leaves us to explain why we hired Jackson in the first place. By now she'll have a cabinet full of files to prove that it was Jackson who killed Guzman, and anything else she wants the world to believe about him. Just look at these pictures she's supplied of Jackson in a Bogotá bar handing money over to the Chief of Police. What they don't show is that the meeting took place almost two weeks after the assassination. Never forget, sir, that the CIA are unrivalled when it comes to covering their asses.'

'It's not their asses I'm worried about,' said the President. 'What about Dexter's story that Jackson's back in America, and is working with the Russian Mafya?'

'Isn't that convenient,' said Lloyd. 'If anything goes wrong during Zerimski's visit, she already has someone lined up to take the rap.'

'Then how do you explain the fact that Jackson was recorded by a security camera in Dallas a few days ago buying a high-powered rifle of near-identical specifications to the one used to kill Guzman?'

'Simple,' said Lloyd. 'Once you realise it wasn't actually Jackson, everything else falls into place.'

'If it wasn't Jackson, then who the hell was it?'

'It was Connor Fitzgerald,' said Lloyd quietly.

'But you told me Fitzgerald was arrested in St Petersburg, and then hanged. We'd even discussed how we might get him out.'

'I know, sir, but that was never going to be a possibility once Zerimski had been elected. Unless . . .'

'Unless?'

'Unless Jackson took his place.'

'Why on earth would he do that?'

'Remember that Fitzgerald saved Jackson's life in Vietnam, and has the Medal of Honor to prove it. When Fitzgerald returned from the war, it was Jackson who recruited him as an NOC. For the next twenty-eight years he served the CIA, and gained the reputation of being their most respected officer. Then, overnight, he disappears and can't be traced on their books. His secretary, Joan Bennett, who worked for him for nineteen years, suddenly dies in a mysterious car accident while she's on the way to see Fitzgerald's wife. Then his wife and daughter also vanish off the face of the earth. Meanwhile, the man we appoint to find out what's going on is accused of being an assassin and double-crossing his closest friend. But however carefully you search through Helen Dexter's numerous reports, you'll never find a single reference to Connor Fitzgerald.'

'How do you know all this, Andy?' asked Lawrence.

'Because Jackson called me from St Petersburg just after Fitzgerald had been arrested.'

'Do you have a recording of that conversation?'

'Yes, sir, I do.'

'Goddamn it,' said Lawrence. 'Dexter makes J. Edgar Hoover look like a Girl Scout.'

'If we accept that it was Jackson who was hanged in Russia, we have to assume it was Fitzgerald who flew to Dallas, with the intention of buying that rifle so he could carry out his present assignment.'

'Am I the target this time?' asked Lawrence quietly.

'I don't think so, Mr President. That's the one thing I think Dexter's being straight about – I still believe the target's Zerimski.'

'Oh my God,' said Lawrence, slumping into his chair.

'But why would an honourable man with a background and reputation as good as Fitzgerald's get involved in a mission like this? It just doesn't add up.'

'It does if that honourable man believes that the original order to assassinate Zerimski came from you.'

Zerimski was running late when his plane took off from New York to fly him back to Washington, but he was in a good mood. His speech to the United Nations had been well received, and his lunch with the Secretary-General had been described in a communiqué issued by the Secretariat as 'wide-ranging and productive'.

During his visit to the Metropolitan Museum that afternoon, not only had Zerimski been able to name the Russian artist who had been given an exhibition in one of the upper galleries, but when he left the museum he had abandoned his itinerary and, to the consternation of his Secret Service minders, walked down to Fifth Avenue to shake hands with Christmas shoppers.

Zerimski had fallen an hour behind schedule by the time his plane touched down in Washington, and he had to change into his dinner jacket in the back of the limousine so that he didn't hold up the performance of *Swan Lake* at the Kennedy Center by more than fifteen minutes. After the dancers had taken their final bow, he returned to spend a second night at the Russian Embassy.

While Zerimski slept, Connor remained awake. He could rarely sleep for more than a few minutes at a time during the build-up to an operation. He had cursed out loud when he'd seen the early evening news coverage of the walkabout on Fifth Avenue. It had reminded him that he should always be prepared for the unexpected: from an apartment on Fifth Avenue, Zerimski would have been an easy target, and the crowd would have been so large and out of control that he could have disappeared within moments.

He dismissed New York from his mind. As far as he was concerned, there were still only two serious venues to consider.

At the first, there was the problem that he wouldn't have the rifle he felt most at ease with, although with a crowd that large the getaway would be easier.

As for the second, if Romanov could supply a modified Remington 700 by the morning of the banquet and guarantee his getaway, it seemed the obvious choice. Or was it a little too obvious?

He began to write out lists of pros and cons for each site. By two o'clock the next morning, exhausted, he realised he would have to visit both venues again before he could make his final decision.

But even then he had no intention of letting Romanov know which one he'd chosen.

CHAPTER TWENTY-NINE

'PUG' WASHER – no one knew his real name – was one of those characters who is an expert on one subject. In his case it was the Washington Redskins.

Pug had worked for the Redskins, man and boy, for fifty years. He had joined the ground staff at the age of fifteen, when the team was still playing at Griffith Stadium. He had started life as a waterboy and had later taken over as the team's masseur, becoming the trusted friend and confidant of generations of Redskins players.

Pug had spent the year before his retirement in 1997 working alongside the contractor who was building the new Jack Kent Cooke Stadium. His brief was simple: to make sure that the Redskins' fans and players had every facility they would expect of the greatest team in the country.

At the opening ceremony, the senior architect told the assembled gathering that he would be forever indebted to Pug for the role he had played in the building of the new stadium. During his closing speech John Kent Cooke, the Redskins' President, announced that Pug had been elected to the team's Hall of Fame, a mark of distinction normally reserved only for the greatest players. Pug told the journalists, 'It doesn't get any better than this.' Despite his retirement, he never missed a Redskins game – home or away.

It took Connor two phone calls to track Pug down at his little apartment in Arlington, Virginia. When he explained to the old man that he had been commissioned to write an article for *Sports Illustrated* on the significance of the new stadium to Skins fans, it was like turning on a tap.

'Perhaps you could spare an hour or two to show me around "the Big Jack",' suggested Connor. Pug's monologue dried up for the first time, and he remained silent until Connor suggested an honorarium of $100. He had already found out that Pug's usual fee for guided tours was fifty.

They agreed to meet at eleven o'clock the following morning.

When Connor arrived at one minute to eleven, Pug ushered him into the stadium as if he were the owner of the club. For the next three hours he regaled his guest with the complete history of the Redskins and answered every one of Connor's questions – from why the stadium had not been completed in time for the opening ceremony to how the management went about employing temporary labour on the day of a game. Connor learned that the Sony JumboTrons behind the end zones made up the largest video-screen system in the world, and that the front row of seats had been raised nine feet above the field of play so the fans could see over the television cameras and the bulky players roaming restlessly up and down the sidelines in front of them.

Connor had been a Redskins fan for almost thirty years, so he already knew that all the season tickets had been sold out since 1966, and that there was currently a waiting list of fifty thousand. He knew because he was one of them. He also knew that the *Washington Post* sold an extra twenty-five thousand copies whenever the Skins won a game. But he didn't know that there were thirty-five miles of steam-heated pipes under the field of play, that there was parking space for twenty-three thousand vehicles, and that a local band would be playing the national anthems of Russia and the United States before tomorrow's kick-off. Most of the information Pug came up with would be of no practical use to Connor, but he still produced a gem every few minutes.

As they strolled around the stadium, Connor could see the tight security checks that the White House advance staff were carrying out for the following day's game. The magnetometers through which everyone who entered the ground would have to pass, and which would detect if they were carrying anything that could be used as a weapon, were already in place. The nearer they got to the owner's box – from where the two Presidents would be watching the game – the more intense the checks became.

Pug was irate when he was stopped by a Secret Service agent guarding the entrance to the executive boxes. He explained forcefully that he was a member of the Redskins Hall of Fame, and that he would be among the guests who would meet the two Presidents the next day, but the agent still refused to let him in without a security pass. Connor tried to assure the furious Pug that it wasn't that important.

As they walked away, Pug muttered under his breath, 'Do I look like the sort of person who would want to assassinate the President?'

When the two men parted at two o'clock, Connor handed his guide $120. The old man had told him more in three hours than an entire Secret Service detail would have divulged in a lifetime. He would have given him $200, but that might have aroused Pug's suspicions.

Connor checked his watch, to find he was running a few minutes late for his appointment with Alexei Romanov at the Russian Embassy. As he was driven away from the stadium he switched on the radio, tuning in to C-SPAN, a station he rarely listened to.

A commentator was describing the atmosphere on the

floor of the House, as the members waited for the Russian President to arrive. No one had any idea what Zerimski was going to say, as the press had not been issued with advance copies of the speech, and had been advised to check against delivery.

Five minutes before the speech was due to begin, Zerimski walked out onto the floor of the House, accompanied by his escort committee.

'Everyone present,' announced the commentator, 'has risen from their seats and is applauding the guest from Russia. President Zerimski is smiling and waving as he makes his way down the aisle through the packed House chamber to the dais, shaking outstretched hands.' The commentator went on to describe the applause as 'warm rather than rapturous'.

When Zerimski reached the podium he carefully placed his papers on the lectern, took out his spectacle case and put on his glasses. Kremlin-watchers immediately knew that the speech would be delivered word for word from a prepared text, and there would be none of the off-the-cuff remarks for which Zerimski had become notorious during his election campaign.

The Members of Congress, the Supreme Court and the Diplomatic Corps resumed their seats, unaware of the bombshell that was about to be dropped.

'Mr Speaker, Mr Vice-President and Mr Chief Justice,' Zerimski began. 'Let me begin by thanking you and your countrymen for the kind welcome and generous hospitality I have received on this, my first visit to the United States. Let me assure you that I look forward to returning again and again.' At this point Titov had written 'PAUSE' in the margin – rightly, because there followed a round of applause.

Zerimski then delivered several flattering homilies concerning America's historic achievements, reminding his listeners that three times in the past century their two nations had fought together against a common enemy. He went on to describe 'the excellent relationship currently enjoyed by our two countries'. Tom Lawrence, who was watching the speech with Andy Lloyd on C-SPAN in the Oval Office, began to relax a little. After another few minutes, he even allowed a flicker of a smile to cross his lips.

That smile was wiped off his face as Zerimski delivered the next seventy-one words of his speech.

'I am the last person on earth who would want our two great nations to become embroiled in another pointless war.' Zerimski paused. 'Especially if we were not on the same side.' He looked up and beamed at the assembled gathering, although nobody present appeared to find his comment particularly funny. 'To be sure that such a calamity can never befall us again, it will be necessary for Russia to remain as powerful as the United States on the battlefield if it is to carry the same weight at the conference table.'

In the Oval Office, Lawrence watched as the television cameras scanned the sullen faces of the members of both Houses, and knew that it had taken Zerimski about forty seconds to destroy any chance of his Arms Reduction Bill becoming law.

The rest of Zerimski's speech was received in silence. When he stepped down from the podium there were no outstretched hands, and the applause was distinctly cool.

As the white BMW drove up Wisconsin Avenue, Connor switched off the radio. When they reached the gates of the Russian Embassy, one of Romanov's henchmen checked them through security.

Connor was escorted into the white marble reception area for the second time in three days. He could immediately see what Romanov had meant when he said the Embassy's internal security was lax. 'After all, who would want to murder Russia's beloved President in his own Embassy?' he had remarked with a smile.

As they walked down a long corridor, Connor said to Romanov, 'You seem to have the run of the building.'

'So would you have, if you'd paid enough into the Ambassador's Swiss bank account to ensure that he never had to return to the motherland again.'

Romanov continued to treat the Embassy as if it were his own home, even unlocking the door to the Ambassador's study and letting himself in. As they entered the ornately furnished room, Connor was surprised to see a customised Remington 700 resting on the Ambassador's desk. He picked it up and studied it closely. He would have asked Romanov how he'd got his hands on it, if he thought there was any chance of being told the truth.

Connor gripped the stock and broke the breech. There was a single boat-tailed bullet in the chamber. He raised an eyebrow and glanced at Romanov.

'I assume that from that range you will only need one bullet,' said the Russian. He led Connor to the far corner of the room, and drew back a curtain to reveal the Ambassador's private lift. They stepped inside, pulled the gate shut and travelled slowly up to the gallery above the ballroom on the second floor.

Connor checked every inch of the gallery several times, then squeezed in behind the vast statue of Lenin. He looked through its cocked arm to check the sightline to the spot from which Zerimski would deliver his farewell speech, making sure that he would be able to see without being seen. He was thinking how easy it all seemed when Romanov touched him on the arm and ushered him back towards the lift.

'You will have to arrive several hours early, and work with the catering staff before the banquet begins,' Romanov said.

'Why?'

'We don't want anyone to become suspicious when you disappear just before Zerimski begins his speech.'

Romanov checked his watch. 'We should go. Zerimski is due back in a few minutes.'

Connor nodded, and they walked towards the rear entrance. As he climbed back into the BMW, he said, 'I'll let you know when I've decided which venue I've chosen.'

Romanov looked surprised, but said nothing.

Connor was driven out through the Embassy gates minutes before Zerimski was due to return from the Capitol. He switched the radio on in time to catch the early-evening news: 'Senators and Congressmen were falling over each other to grab the microphones and assure their constituents that after hearing President Zerimski's speech, they would not be voting for the Nuclear, Biological, Chemical and Conventional Arms Reduction Bill.'

In the Oval Office, Tom Lawrence was watching CNN's reporter speaking from the Senate press gallery: 'No statement has yet come from the White House,' he was saying, 'and the President . . .'

'And don't hang around waiting for one,' Lawrence said angrily as he switched off the television. He turned to his Chief of Staff. 'Andy, I'm not even sure I can face sitting next to that man for four hours tomorrow afternoon, let alone respond to his farewell speech in the evening.'

Lloyd didn't comment.

'I am looking forward to sitting next to my dear friend Tom and watching him have to squirm in front of an audience of millions,' said Zerimski as his limousine entered the grounds of the Russian Embassy. Dmitri Titov remained impassive.

'I think I shall cheer for the Redskins. It would be an added bonus if Lawrence's team lost,' Zerimski smirked. 'A fitting prelude to the humiliation I have planned for him in the evening. Make sure you prepare a speech so flattering that it will appear all the more tragic in retrospect.' He smiled again. 'I have ordered the beef to be served cold. And even you will be surprised by what I have in mind for dessert.'

Connor spent several hours that evening wondering if he could risk breaking the rule of a lifetime. He phoned Romanov a few minutes after midnight.

The Russian seemed delighted that they had both come to the same conclusion. 'I'll arrange for a driver to pick you up at three thirty so you can be at the Embassy by four.'

Connor put the phone down. If everything went to plan, the President would be dead by four.

'Wake him up.'

'But it's four o'clock in the morning,' said the First Secretary.

'If you value your life, wake him up.'

The First Secretary threw on a dressing gown, ran out of his bedroom and down the corridor. He knocked on the door. There was no response, so he knocked again. A few moments later, a light appeared under the door.

'Come in,' said a sleepy voice. The First Secretary turned the handle and entered the Ambassador's bedroom.

'I am sorry to disturb you, Your Excellency, but there's a Mr Stefan Ivanitsky on the line from St Petersburg. He insists that we wake the President. He says he has an urgent message for him.'

'I'll take the call in my study,' said Pietrovski. He threw back the blanket, ignoring the groans of his wife, ran downstairs and told the night porter to transfer the call to his study.

The phone rang several times before it was eventually picked up by a slightly breathless Ambassador. 'Pietrovski speaking.'

'Good morning, Your Excellency,' said Ivanitsky.

'I asked to be put through to the President, not to you.'

'But it's four o'clock in the morning. Can't it wait?'

'Ambassador, I don't pay you to tell me the time. The next voice I want to hear is the President's. Do I make myself clear?'

The Ambassador put the receiver down on his desk and walked slowly back up the wide staircase to the first floor, trying to decide which of the two men he was more frightened of. He stood outside the door of the President's suite for some time, but the sight of the First Secretary hovering at the top of the stairs stiffened his resolve. He tapped gently on the door, but there was no response. He knocked a little louder, and tentatively opened it.

In the light from the landing the Ambassador and the First Secretary could see Zerimski stirring in his bed. What they didn't see was the President's hand slipping under the pillow, where a pistol was concealed.

'Mr President,' whispered Pietrovski as Zerimski switched on the light by the side of his bed.

'This had better be important,' said Zerimski, 'unless you want to spend the rest of your days as refrigerator inspectors in Siberia.'

'We have a call for you from St Petersburg,' said the Ambassador, almost in a whisper. 'A Mr Stefan Ivanitsky. He says it's urgent.'

'Get out of my room,' said Zerimski as he picked up the phone by his bed.

The two men stepped backwards into the corridor and the Ambassador quietly closed the door.

'Stefan,' said Zerimski. 'Why are you calling at this hour? Has Borodin staged a coup in my absence?'

'No, Mr President. The Czar is dead.' Ivanitsky spoke without emotion.

'When? Where? How?'

'About an hour ago, at the Winter Palace. The colourless liquid finally got him.' Ivanitsky paused. 'The butler has been on my payroll for almost a year.'

The President was silent for a few moments before saying, 'Good. It couldn't have worked out better for us.'

'I would agree, Mr President, were it not for the fact that his son is in Washington. There's very little I can do from this end until he returns.'

'That problem may resolve itself this evening,' said Zerimski.

'Why? Have they fallen into our little trap?'

'Yes,' said Zerimski. 'By tonight I shall have disposed of both of them.'

'Both of them?'

'Yes,' the President replied. 'I have learned an appropriate new expression since I've been over here – "killing two birds with one stone". After all, how many times does one have the chance to see the same man die twice?'

'I wish I was there to witness it.'

'I'm going to enjoy it even more than I did watching his friend dangling from a rope. All things considered, Stefan, this will have been a most successful trip, especially if . . .'

'It's all been taken care of, Mr President,' said Ivanitsky. 'I arranged yesterday for the income from the Yeltsin and Chernopov oil and uranium contracts to be diverted to your Zurich account. That is, unless Alexei countermands my orders when he returns.'

'If he doesn't return, he won't be able to, will he?' Zerimski put the phone down, switched off the light, and fell asleep again within moments.

At five o'clock that morning Connor was lying motionless on his bed, fully dressed. He was going over his escape route when the wake-up call came through at six. He rose, pulled back a corner of the curtain and checked that they were still there. They were: two white BMWs parked on the far side of the street, as they had been since midnight the previous evening. By now their occupants would be drowsy. He knew they changed shifts at eight, so he planned to leave ten minutes before the hour. He spent the next thirty minutes carrying out some light stretching exercises to get rid of his stiffness, then stripped off his clothes. He allowed the cold jets of the shower to needle his body for some time before he turned it off and grabbed a towel. Then he dressed in a blue shirt, a pair of jeans, a thick sweater, a blue tie, black socks and a pair of black Nikes with the logo painted out.

He went into the small kitchenette, poured himself a glass of grapefruit juice and filled a bowl with cornflakes and milk. He always ate the same meal on the day of an operation. He liked routine. It helped him believe everything else would run smoothly. As he ate, he read over the seven pages of notes he had made following his meeting with Pug, and once again minutely studied an architect's plan of the stadium. He measured the girder with a ruler, and estimated that it was forty-two feet to the trapdoor. He mustn't look down. He felt the calm come over him that a finely-tuned athlete experiences when called to the starting line.

He checked his watch and returned to the bedroom. They had to be at the intersection of Twenty-First Street and DuPont Circle just as the traffic was building up. He waited a few more minutes, then put three hundred-dollar bills, a quarter and a thirty-minute audiocassette in the back pocket of his jeans. He then left the anonymous apartment for the last time. His account had already been settled.

CHAPTER THIRTY

ZERIMSKI SAT ALONE IN the Embassy dining room reading the *Washington Post* as a butler served him breakfast. He smiled when he saw the banner headline:

RETURN OF THE COLD WAR?

As he sipped his coffee, he mused for a moment on what the *Post* might lead with the following morning.

ATTEMPT TO ASSASSINATE RUSSIAN
PRESIDENT FAILS
Former CIA Agent Gunned Down in Embassy
Grounds

He smiled again, and turned to the editorial, which confirmed that Lawrence's Nuclear, Biological, Chemical and Conventional Arms Reduction Bill was now considered by all the leading commentators to be 'dead in the water'. Another useful expression he had picked up on this trip.

At a few minutes past seven he rang the silver bell by his side and asked the butler to fetch the Ambassador and the First Secretary. The butler hurried away. Zerimski knew both men were already standing anxiously outside the door.

The Ambassador and the First Secretary thought they should wait for a minute or two before joining the President. They were still uncertain if he was pleased to have been woken at four in the morning, but as neither of them had yet been fired, they assumed that they must have made the right decision.

'Good morning, Mr President,' said Pietrovski as he entered the dining room.

Zerimski nodded, folded the paper and placed it on the table in front of him. 'Has Romanov arrived yet?' he asked.

'Yes, Mr President,' said the First Secretary. 'He has been in the kitchen since six o'clock this morning, personally checking the food that's being delivered for tonight's banquet.'

'Good. Ask him to join us in your study, Mr Ambassador. I will be along shortly.'

'Yes, sir,' said Pietrovski, retreating backwards out of the room.

Zerimski wiped his mouth with a napkin. He decided to keep the three of them waiting for a few more minutes. That would make them even more nervous.

He returned to the *Washington Post*, smiling as he read the editorial's conclusion for a second time: 'Zerimski is the natural successor to Stalin and Brezhnev, rather than Gorbachev or Yeltsin.' He had no quarrel with that; in fact he hoped that before the day was out he would have reinforced that image. He rose from his chair and strolled out of the room. As he walked down the corridor towards the Ambassador's study, a young man coming from the opposite direction stopped in his tracks, rushed over to the door and opened it for him. A grandfather clock chimed as he entered the room. He instinctively checked his watch. It was exactly seven forty-five.

At ten minutes to eight, Connor appeared at the entrance of the apartment building and walked slowly across the street to the first of the two BMWs. He climbed in beside a driver who looked a little surprised to see him so early – he'd been told that Fitzgerald wasn't expected at the Embassy until four o'clock that afternoon.

'I need to go downtown to pick up a couple of things,' said Connor. The man in the back nodded, so the driver put the car into first and joined the traffic on Wisconsin Avenue. The second car followed closely behind them as they turned left into P Street, which was thickly congested as a result of the construction work that plagued Georgetown.

As each day passed, Connor had noticed that his minders had become more and more relaxed. At roughly the same time every morning he had jumped out of the BMW at the corner of Twenty-First Street and DuPont Circle, bought a copy of the *Post* from a newsvendor and returned to the car. Yesterday the man in the back seat hadn't even bothered to accompany him.

They crossed Twenty-Third Street, and Connor could see DuPont Circle in the distance. The cars were now bumper to bumper, and had almost ground to a halt. On the other side of the street the traffic heading west was moving far more smoothly. He would need to judge exactly when to make his move.

Connor knew that the lights on P Street approaching the Circle changed every thirty seconds, and on average twelve cars managed to get across during that time. The most he'd counted during the week was sixteen.

When the light turned red, Connor counted seventeen cars ahead of them. He didn't move a muscle. The light switched to green and the driver changed into first gear, but the traffic was so heavy that it was some time before he was able to edge forward. Only eight cars crawled through the light.

He had thirty seconds.

He turned and smiled at his minder in the back, and pointed to the newsvendor. The man nodded. Connor stepped out onto the sidewalk and started walking slowly towards the old man wearing a fluorescent orange vest. He didn't once look back, so he had no idea if anyone from the second car was following him. He concentrated on the traffic moving in the opposite direction on the other side of the street, trying to estimate how long the line of cars would be when the light turned red again. When he reached the news-vendor, he already had a quarter in his hand. He gave it to the old man, who handed him a copy of the *Post*. As he turned and began to walk back towards the first BMW, the light turned red and the traffic came to a halt.

Connor spotted the vehicle he needed. He suddenly switched direction and started sprinting, darting in and out of the stationary traffic on the westbound side of the street until he reached an empty taxi, six cars away from the lights. The two men in the second BMW leaped out of the car and began running after him just as the light at DuPont Circle turned green.

Connor pulled open the door and threw himself into the back of the taxi. 'Straight ahead,' he shouted. 'You get $100 if you beat that light.'

The driver pressed the palm of his hand onto his horn and kept it there as he ran the red light. The two white BMWs executed screeching U-turns, but the lights had already changed, and their path was blocked by three stationary cars.

So far everything had gone to plan.

The taxi swung left onto Twenty-Third Street, and Connor instructed the driver to pull over. When the car had come to a halt he passed him a hundred-dollar bill and said, 'I want you to drive straight to Dulles Airport. If you spot a white BMW coming up behind you, don't let it overtake you. When you get to the airport, stop for thirty seconds outside Departures, then drive slowly back into town.'

'OK, man, anything you say,' said the driver, pocketing the hundred-dollar bill. Connor slipped out of the cab,

THE HIRED ASSASSIN

darted across Twenty-Third Street and flagged down
another cab heading in the opposite direction.

He slammed the door shut as the two BMWs swept
past him in pursuit of the first taxi.

'And where would you like to go this fine morning?'

'Cooke Stadium.'

'I hope you got a ticket, man, otherwise I'll be bringing
you straight back.'

The three men stood as Zerimski entered the room. He
waved them down as if they were a large crowd, and
took the chair behind the Ambassador's desk. He was
surprised to see a rifle where the blotter would normally
be, but he ignored it and turned to Alexei Romanov,
who was looking rather pleased with himself.

'I have some sad news for you, Alexei,' said the President. Romanov's expression turned to apprehension,
and then to anxiety, during the long silence Zerimski
allowed to follow.

'I received a call earlier this morning from your cousin
Stefan. It appears that your father suffered a heart attack
during the night, and died on the way to hospital.'

Romanov bowed his head. The Ambassador and First
Secretary glanced towards the President to see how they
should react.

Zerimski rose, walked slowly over to Romanov and
placed a consoling hand on his shoulder. The Ambassador and First Secretary looked suitably grief-stricken.

'I shall mourn him,' said Zerimski. 'He was a great
man.' The two diplomats nodded their agreement as
Romanov inclined his head to acknowledge the President's kind words.

'Now his mantle has passed on to you, Alexei; a most
worthy successor.'

The Ambassador and the Chief Secretary continued
to nod.

'And soon,' Zerimski said, 'you will be given an opportunity to demonstrate your authority in a way that will leave no one in Russia in any doubt who is the new Czar.'

Romanov raised his head and smiled, his brief period of mourning over.

'That is,' added Zerimski, 'assuming nothing goes wrong this evening.'

'Nothing can go wrong,' said Romanov emphatically. 'I spoke to Fitzgerald just after midnight. He's agreed to my plan. He will report to the Embassy at four o'clock this afternoon, while you are at the football game with Lawrence.'

'Why so early?' asked Zerimski.

'We need everyone to think he's simply another member of the catering team, so that when he slips out of the kitchen six hours later nobody will give it a second thought. He will remain in the kitchen under my supervision until a few minutes before you rise to make your farewell speech.'

'Excellent,' said Zerimski. 'And then what happens?'

'I will accompany him to this room, where he will collect the rifle. He will then take the private elevator to the gallery that overlooks the ballroom.'

Zerimski nodded.

'Once he is there, he will position himself behind the great statue of Lenin, where he will remain until you reach that section of your speech where you thank the American people for their hospitality and the warm welcome you have received everywhere, *et cetera, et cetera,* and particularly from President Lawrence. At that point, I have arranged for prolonged applause. Throughout it you must remain absolutely still.'

'Why?' demanded Zerimski.

'Because Fitzgerald won't squeeze the trigger if he thinks you're likely to make a sudden movement.'

'I understand.'

'Once he has fired, he will climb out onto the ledge by the cedar tree in the back garden. He made us repeat the whole exercise several times yesterday afternoon, but this evening he will discover there is a small difference.'

'And what is that?' asked Zerimski.

'Waiting under the tree will be six of my personal bodyguards,' said Romanov. 'They will have gunned him down long before his feet touch the ground.'

Zerimski was silent for a moment before saying, 'But surely your plan has a minor flaw?'

Romanov looked puzzled.

'How am I expected to survive a shot from a marksman of Fitzgerald's reputation from such close range?'

Romanov rose from his chair and picked up the rifle. He removed a small piece of metal and handed it to the President.

'What is this?' Zerimski asked.

'The firing pin,' Romanov replied.

CHAPTER THIRTY-ONE

THE TWO WHITE BMWs sped west on Route 66, pursuing an empty taxi that exceeded the speed limit all the way to Dulles Airport. A second cab was travelling east at a more leisurely pace towards Cooke Stadium in Maryland.

Connor thought again about his decision to choose the stadium, with all its risks, rather than the Embassy. He had been allowed in and out of that building far too easily: no one was that lax about security, especially when their President was in town.

When Connor was dropped at the stadium, he knew exactly where to go. He walked up the wide gravel path towards the north entrance and the two long lines of people who hung around before every home game in the hope of a day's work. Some of them just needed the cash, while others, Pug had explained, were such fanatical Skins fans that they would resort to anything, including bribery, to get into the stadium.

'Bribery?' Connor had asked innocently.

'Oh yes. Someone has to serve in the executive suites,' said Pug with a wink. 'And they end up with the best view of the game.'

'Fascinating material for my article,' Connor had assured him.

The first queue was for those who wanted to work

outside the stadium, organising the parking for the twenty-three thousand cars and buses or selling programmes, cushions and souvenirs to the seventy-eight thousand fans. The other was for those who hoped to work inside the stadium. Connor joined that queue, mostly made up of the young, the unemployed and what Pug had described as the early-retirement junkies, who simply enjoyed the regular outing. Pug had even described how this group dressed, so that no one would mistake them for the unemployed.

On this particular day, a handful of Secret Service men were eyeing the hopeful applicants. Connor kept reading the *Washington Post* as the line moved slowly forward. Most of the front page was devoted to Zerimski's speech to the joint session of Congress. The reaction from the members was universally hostile. When he turned to the editorial, he suspected Zerimski would be pleased with it.

He turned to the Metro section, and a wry smile crossed his face as he read of the premature death of a distinguished academic from his home town.

'Hi,' said a voice.

Connor glanced round at a smartly-dressed young man who had joined the queue behind him.

'Hi,' he responded briefly, before returning to his paper. He didn't want to get involved in an unnecessary conversation with someone who might later be called as a witness.

'My name's Brad,' the young man announced, thrusting out his right hand.

Connor shook it, but said nothing.

'I'm hoping to get a job on one of the lighting towers,' he added. 'How about you?'

'Why the lighting towers?' asked Connor, avoiding his question.

'Because that's where the Secret Service's Special Agent in Charge will be stationed, and I want to find out what the job's really like.'

'Why?' asked Connor, folding up his paper. This was clearly not a conversation he could easily cut short.

'I'm thinking about joining them when I leave college. I've already taken the graduate training course, but I want to see them working at close quarters. An agent told me the one job nobody wants is taking meals up to the guys on the lighting platforms behind the end zones. All those steps scare them off.'

All 172 of them, thought Connor, who had dismissed the idea of the lighting towers early on, not because of the steps, but because there was no escape route. Brad started to tell him his life story, and by the time Connor reached the front of the queue he knew which school the boy had been to, that he was now a senior at Georgetown studying criminology – that made him think of Maggie – and why he still couldn't decide whether to join the Secret Service or be a lawyer.

'Next,' said a voice. Connor turned round to the man seated behind a trestle table.

'What have you got left?' Connor asked.

'Not much,' said the man, looking down at a list covered with ticks.

'Anything in catering?' asked Connor. Like Brad, he knew exactly where he wanted to be.

'Washing dishes or serving meals to employees around the stadium is all I've got left.'

'That will be just fine.'

'Name?'

'Dave Krinkle,' said Connor.

'ID?'

Connor handed over a driver's licence. The man filled in a security pass and a photographer stepped forward and took a Polaroid of Connor, which seconds later was laminated onto the pass.

'OK, Dave,' the man said, handing it over. 'This pass will get you everywhere inside the stadium except the high-security area, which includes the executive suites, the club boxes and the VIP section. You won't need to go there anyway.' Connor nodded and clipped the pass onto his sweater. 'Report to Room 47, directly below Block H.' Connor moved off to the left. He knew exactly where Room 47 was.

'Next.'

It took him a lot longer to get through the three security checks, including the magnetometer, than it had the previous day, as they were now manned by Secret Service personnel rather than the usual rentacops. Once Connor was inside the stadium, he ambled slowly along the inner walkway, past the museum and under a red banner declaring 'HAIL VICTORY', until he came to a stairway with an arrow pointing down to 'Room 47, Private Catering'. Inside the small room at the foot of the stairs he found a dozen men lounging around. They all looked as if they were familiar with the routine. He recognised one or two who had been standing in the line in front of him. No one else in the room looked as if they didn't need the money.

He took a seat in a corner and returned to the *Post*, rereading a preview of the afternoon's game. Tony Kornheiser thought it would be nothing less than a miracle if the Redskins beat the Packers – the finest team in the country. In fact, he was predicting a twenty-point margin. Connor was hoping for a totally different outcome.

'OK,' said a voice, 'pay attention.' Connor looked up to see a huge man wearing a chef's uniform standing in front of them. He was about fifty, with an enormous double chin, and must have weighed over 250 pounds.

'I'm the catering manager,' he said, 'and as you can see, I represent the glamour end of the business.' One or two of the old hands laughed politely.

'I can offer you two choices. You either wash dishes or you serve stadium employees and security guys stationed around the stadium. Any volunteers for the dishes?' Most of the men in the room put their hands up. Dishwashing, Pug had explained, was always popular because not only did the washers get the full rate of $10 an hour, but for some of them the leftovers from the executive boxes were the best meal they had all week.

'Good,' he said, picking out five of them and writing down their names. When he had completed the list, he said, 'Now, waiting. You can either serve the senior staff or the security personnel. Senior staff?' he said, looking up from his clipboard. Almost all the remaining hands shot up. Again the catering manager wrote down five names. When he'd finished, he tapped his clipboard. 'OK,' he said. 'Everyone on the list can now report to work.' The old pros rose from their seats and shuffled past him, through a door that Connor knew led to the kitchens. Only he and Brad were still in the room.

'I've got two jobs left in Security,' said the catering manager. 'One great, one lousy. Which one of you is going to get lucky?' He looked hopefully at Connor, who nodded and placed a hand in his back pocket.

The catering manager walked up to him, not even glancing at Brad, and said, 'I have a feeling you'd prefer the comfort of the JumboTron.'

'Right first time,' said Connor, slipping him a hundred-dollar bill.

'Just as I thought,' said the catering manager, returning his smile.

Connor said nothing as the fat man pocketed the cash, exactly as Pug had predicted he would.

That man had been worth every cent of his fee.

'I should never have invited him in the first place,' Tom Lawrence growled as he boarded Marine One to take him from the White House to the Redskins' stadium.

'And I have a feeling that our problems aren't over yet,' said Andy Lloyd, strapping himself into his seat.

'Why? What else can go wrong?' asked Lawrence as the helicopter blades slowly began to rotate.

'There are still two public events before Zerimski returns to Russia, and my bet is that Fitzgerald will be waiting for us at one of them.'

'This evening shouldn't be a problem,' said Lawrence. 'Ambassador Pietrovski has told the Secret Service on countless occasions that his people are quite capable of protecting their own President. In any case, who would take that sort of risk with so much security around?'

'The normal rules don't apply to Fitzgerald,' said Lloyd. 'He doesn't work by the book.'

The President glanced down at the Russian Embassy. 'It would be hard enough just getting into that building,' he said, 'without having to worry about how you'd get out of it.'

'Fitzgerald wouldn't have the same trouble this afternoon, in a stadium holding nearly eighty thousand spectators,' replied Lloyd. 'That's one place he would find it easy to slip in and out of.'

'Don't forget, Andy, there's only a thirteen-minute window when any problem could arise. Even then, everybody in the stadium will have passed through the magnetometers, so there's no way anyone could get a penknife in, let alone a gun.'

'You think Fitzgerald doesn't know that?' said Lloyd as the helicopter swung east. 'It's not too late to cancel that part of the programme.'

'No,' said Lawrence firmly. 'If Clinton could stand in the middle of the Olympic Stadium in Atlanta for the opening ceremony, I can do the same in Washington for a football game. Damn it, Andy, we live in a democracy, and I'm not going to allow our lives to be dictated to in that way. And don't forget that I'll be out there, taking exactly the same risk as Zerimski.'

'I accept that, sir,' said Lloyd. 'But if Zerimski were to be assassinated, no one would praise you for standing by his side, least of all Helen Dexter. She'd be the first to point out . . .'

'Who do you think will win this afternoon, Andy?' asked the President.

Lloyd smiled at a ploy his boss often fell back on if he didn't wish to continue discussing an unpalatable subject. 'I don't know, sir,' he replied. 'But until I saw how many of my staff were trying to cram themselves into the advance cars this morning, I had no idea we had so many Skins fans working at the White House.'

'Some of them might just have been Packers fans,' said Lawrence. He opened the file on his lap and began to study the short profiles of the guests he would be meeting at the stadium.

'OK, pay attention,' said the catering manager. Connor gave the impression of listening intently.

'The first thing you do is collect a white coat and a Redskins cap, to show you're on the staff. Then you take the elevator to the seventh level and wait for me to put the food in the service elevator. The Secret Service agents have a snack at ten, and lunch – Coke, sandwiches, whatever else they want – at the start of the game. You press the button on the left-hand side,' he continued, as if he was addressing a ten-year-old, 'and it should be with you in about a minute.'

Connor could have told him that it took exactly forty-seven seconds for the service elevator to travel from the basement to the seventh level. But as there were two other levels – the second (club seats) and the fifth (executive suites) – which also had access to the service lift, he might have to wait until their orders were completed before the elevator reached him, in which case it could take as long as three minutes.

'Once your order arrives, you take the tray to the officer stationed inside the JumboTron at the eastern end of the ground. You'll find a door marked "Private" down the walkway to your left.' Thirty-seven paces, Connor recalled. 'Here's the key. You go through it, and down an enclosed walkway until you reach the back entrance of the JumboTron.' Seventy yards, thought Connor. In his footballing days he could have covered that distance in around seven seconds.

While the manager continued to tell him things he already knew, Connor studied the service elevator. It was two foot three by two foot seven, and inside were clearly printed the words: 'Maximum weight permitted 150 pounds'. Connor weighed 210 pounds, so he hoped the designer had allowed a bit of leeway. There were two other problems: he wouldn't be able to test it out, and there was nothing he could do to prevent it from being stopped at the fifth or second floors once he was on his way down.

'When you reach the door at the back of the JumboTron,' the catering manager was saying, 'you knock, and the agent on duty will unbolt it and let you in. Once you've handed him the tray, you can go to the back of the stadium and watch the first quarter. At the break you go and get the tray and take it to the service elevator. You press the green button and it will go back down to the basement. Then you can watch the rest of the game. Did you understand all that, Dave?'

Connor was tempted to say, No, sir. Would you be kind enough to run through it once again, but a little more slowly?

'Yes, sir.'

'Any questions?'

'No, sir.'

'OK. If the officer treats you good, I'll send him up a steak after full time. When he's finished that, report to me and collect your pay. Fifty dollars.' He winked.

Pug had explained that serious fans didn't bother to pick up their wages if they wanted to be offered the job again. 'Remember,' he had said, 'when the manager mentions the word "pay", just wink.'

Connor had no intention of collecting the $50, or of ever returning to the stadium. He winked.

CHAPTER THIRTY-TWO

'WHY IS LAWRENCE TRAVELLING to the game by helicopter when I'm stuck in the back of this car?' Zerimski asked as his nine-limousine motorcade swept out of the Embassy gates.

'He has to make sure he's there before you,' said Titov. 'He wants to be introduced to all the guests, so that by the time you arrive he can give the impression he's known them all his life.'

'What a way to run a country,' said Zerimski. 'Not that this afternoon is important.' He was silent for a moment. 'Do you know, I've even seen the rifle Fitzgerald plans to kill me with,' he said eventually. Titov looked surprised. 'He's using the same model the CIA planted on him in St Petersburg. But with a refinement.' He put a hand in his jacket pocket. 'What do you think this is?' he asked, holding up what looked like a bent nail.

Titov shook his head. 'I've no idea.'

'It's the firing pin of a Remington 700,' Zerimski replied. 'So we can even allow him to pull the trigger before the bodyguards begin to pump bullets into him.' He studied it closely. 'I think I'll have it mounted and keep it on my desk in the Kremlin.' He dropped it back in his pocket. 'Has the speech I'm meant to be giving tonight been released to the press?'

'Yes, Mr President,' replied Titov. 'It's full of the usual

platitudes. You can be confident that not a word of it will ever be printed.'

'And what about my spontaneous reaction after Fitzgerald has been killed?'

'I have it here, Mr President.'

'Good. Give me a taste of it,' said Zerimski, leaning back in his seat.

Titov removed a file from the case by his side and began reading from a handwritten script: 'On the day of my election, President Lawrence telephoned me at the Kremlin and gave me a personal invitation to visit his country. I accepted that offer in good faith. What happens when I take it up? My outstretched hand is met not with an olive branch, but with a rifle pointing directly at me. And where? In my own Embassy. And who pulled the trigger? An officer of the CIA. Had it not been for my good fortune . . .'

'A *former* officer,' interrupted Zerimski.

'I thought it prudent,' said Titov, looking up from his notes, 'for you to appear to make the occasional error, even to repeat yourself. That way no one will suggest you always knew what was going on. In America, they want to believe that everything is a conspiracy.'

'I shall be only too happy to fuel their paranoia,' said Zerimski. 'Long after Lawrence has been removed, I expect Americans will be writing copious volumes about how I was responsible for the complete breakdown in relations between the two countries. Lawrence's administration will end up as nothing more than a footnote in the history of the resurgence of the Russian empire under my Presidency.' He beamed at Titov. 'And after I have achieved that, there will be no more talk of elections. Because I shall remain in power until the day I die.'

Connor checked his watch. It was nine fifty-six. He pressed the button beside the service elevator and immediately heard the whirr of an engine as it began its slow journey up to the seventh level.

There were still thirty-four minutes before the stadium would be opened to the public, although Connor knew it would take some time for the crowd to pass through the thirty magnetometers and the personal security checks. But he was keeping to a far stricter timetable than anyone else in the stadium. Forty-seven seconds later he removed the tray and pressed the button to let the staff in the basement know he had received it.

He walked quickly along the seventh-floor concourse, past a concession stand, and up to the door marked 'Private'. He balanced the tray on one hand, turned the key in the lock with the other and slipped inside. Then he switched on the lights and strode down the covered walkway at the back of the JumboTron. He checked his watch again – eighty-three seconds. Too long, but as the final run would be without a tray, it should be possible to complete the whole exercise, from roof to basement, in under two minutes. If it all went to plan, he would be out of the stadium and on his way to the airport before they had time to set up any roadblocks.

Connor balanced the tray in one hand and knocked on the door with the other. A few seconds later it was opened by a tall, heavily-built man who stood silhouetted in an oblong of light.

'I've brought you a snack,' said Connor with a warm smile.

'Great,' said the sharpshooter. 'Why don't you come in and join me?' He removed a pastrami sandwich from the tray, and Connor followed him along a thin, galvanised steel platform behind a vast screen made up of 786 televisions. The Secret Service man sat down and dug his teeth into the sandwich. Connor tried not to let him see how closely he was studying his rifle.

The JumboTron was on three floors, one above the platform and one below. Connor put the tray down beside the officer, who was sitting in the middle of the flight of stairs that led to the lower ramp. He took more interest in his can of Diet Coke than in Connor's roaming eyes.

'By the way,' he said, between swigs, 'I'm Arnie Cooper.'

'Dave Krinkle,' Connor replied.

'So how much did you have to pay for the privilege of spending the afternoon with me?' asked Arnie with a grin.

Marine One landed at the heliport to the north-east of the stadium, and a limousine purred up even before the copter's steps had touched the ground. Lawrence and Lloyd emerged a moment later, and the President turned to wave to the large gathering of well-wishers before climbing into the back of the waiting car. They covered the quarter-mile to the stadium in under a minute, passing through every security check without hindrance. John Kent Cooke, the owner of the Redskins, was waiting at the stadium's entrance to greet them.

'This is a great honour, sir,' he said as Lawrence stepped out of the limousine.

'It's good to meet you, John,' replied the President, shaking the slim, grey-haired man by the hand.

Cooke guided his guest towards a private lift.

'Do you really believe the Skins can win, John?' Lawrence asked with a grin.

'Now that's the sort of loaded question I might have expected from a politician, Mr President,' Cooke replied as they stepped into the lift. 'Everyone knows you're the Packers' number one fan. But I'm bound to say the answer to your question is "Yes, sir." Fight for old DC. The Skins will win.'

'The *Washington Post* doesn't agree with you,' said the President as the doors opened at the press level.

'I'm sure you're the last person to believe everything

you read in the *Post*, Mr President,' said Cooke. Both men laughed as he led Lawrence into his box, a large, comfortable room positioned above the fifty-yard line, with a perfect view of the whole field. 'Mr President, I'd like to introduce you to one or two of the folks who have made the Redskins the greatest football team in America. Let me start with my wife, Rita.'

'Good to meet you, Rita,' Lawrence said, shaking her by the hand. 'And congratulations on your triumph at the National Symphony Ball. I'm told they raised a record amount under your chairmanship.'

Mrs Cooke beamed with pride.

Lawrence was able to recall an appropriate fact or anecdote about every person he was introduced to, including the little old man wearing a Redskins blazer who couldn't possibly have been a former player.

'This is Pug Washer,' said John Kent Cooke, placing a hand on the old man's shoulder. 'Now, he . . .'

'. . . is the only man in history to make the Redskins Hall of Fame without playing a single game for the team,' said the President.

A huge smile appeared on Pug's face.

'And I'm also told that you know more about the history of the team than any living person.'

Pug promised himself he would never vote Republican again.

'So tell me, Pug, in Packers versus Skins games, what were Vince Lombardi's regular-season points when he was coaching the Packers, compared to his year with the Skins?'

'Packers 459, Skins 435,' said Pug with a rueful smile.

'Just as I thought – he should never have left the Packers in the first place,' said the President, slapping Pug on the back.

'Do you know, Mr President,' said Cooke, 'I've never been able to come up with a question about the Redskins that Pug wasn't able to answer.'

'Has anyone ever stumped you, Pug?' asked the President, turning to the walking encyclopaedia again.

'They try all the time, Mr President,' Pug replied. 'Why, only yesterday a man . . .'

Before Pug could complete his sentence, Andy Lloyd touched Lawrence's elbow. 'I'm sorry to interrupt you, sir, but we've just been informed that President Zerimski is only five minutes away from the stadium. You and Mr Cooke should make your way to the north-east entrance now, so that you'll be in time to welcome him.'

'Yes, of course,' said Lawrence. He turned to Pug and said, 'Let's continue our conversation just as soon as I get back.'

Pug nodded as the President and his entourage left the room to go and greet Zerimski.

'It's a bit cramped in here,' Connor shouted above the noise of the large ventilation fan in the ceiling.

'Sure is,' said Arnie, finishing off his Diet Coke. 'But I guess it goes with the job.'

'Are you expecting any trouble today?'

'Nope, not really. Of course, we'll all be on full alert the moment the two Presidents walk out onto the field, but that only lasts for about eight minutes. Although if Special Agent Braithwaite had his way, neither of them would be allowed out of the owner's box until it was time for them to go home.'

Connor nodded and asked several more innocuous questions, listening carefully to Arnie's Brooklyn accent, and concentrating especially on any expressions he used regularly.

As Arnie dug his teeth into a slice of chocolate cake, Connor looked through a gap in the rotating advertising boards. Most of the Secret Service officers in the stadium were also taking a snack break. He focused on the lighting tower behind the western end zone. Brad was up there listening intently to an officer who was pointing towards the owner's box. Just the sort of young man the Service needed to recruit, thought Connor. He turned back to Arnie. 'I'll see you again at the start of the game. A plate of sandwiches, another slice of cake and some more Coke suit you?'

'Yep, sounds great. But go easy on the cake. I don't mind my wife telling me I've put on a few pounds, but lately the SAIC has begun to comment on it.'

A siren sounded to let all the staff in the stadium know it was ten thirty, and the gates were about to be opened. The fans began to flood into the stands, most of them heading straight for their usual seats. Connor gathered up the empty Coke can and the plastic container and placed them on the tray.

'I'll be back with your lunch when the game kicks off,' he said.

'Yep,' replied Arnie, his binoculars now focused on the crowd below. 'But don't come in until after the two Presidents are back in the owner's box. No one else is allowed in the JumboTron while they're out on the field.'

'OK, I understand,' said Connor, taking a last look at Arnie's rifle. As he turned to go, he heard a voice coming over a two-way radio.

'Hercules 3.'

Arnie unclipped the radio from the back of his belt, pressed a button and said, 'Hercules 3, go ahead.'

Connor hesitated by the door.

'Nothing to report, sir. I was just about to run an eye over the west stand.'

'Fine. Report in if you see anything suspicious.'

'Will do,' said Arnie, and clipped the receiver back onto his belt.

Connor quietly stepped out onto the covered walkway, closed the door behind him and placed the empty Coke can on the step.

He checked his watch, then walked quickly down the covered walkway, unlocked the door and turned off the lights. The concourse was swarming with fans heading for their seats. When he reached the lift shaft, he checked his watch again. Fifty-four seconds. On the final run it would have to take less than thirty-five. He pressed the button. Forty-seven seconds later the service elevator reappeared. Obviously no one on the second or fifth levels had been calling for it. He placed the tray inside and pressed the button once again. It immediately began its slow journey down to the basement.

No one gave Connor, dressed in a long white catering coat and a Redskins cap, a second glance as he strolled casually past the concession stand towards the door marked 'Private'. He slipped inside and locked the door behind him. In the darkness he walked noiselessly back along the narrow walkway until he was a few yards from the entrance to the JumboTron. He stood looking down at the vast steel girder that held the massive screen in place.

Connor gripped the handrail for a moment, then fell to his knees. He leaned forward, grabbed the girder with both hands, and eased himself off the walkway. He stared fixedly at the screen which, according to the architects' plans, was forty-two feet in front of him. It looked more like a mile.

He could see a small handle, but he still had no idea if the emergency trapdoor that had been clearly marked on the engineer's plans really existed. He began to crawl slowly along the girder, inch by inch, never once looking down at the 170-foot drop below him. It felt like two miles.

When he finally reached the end of the girder, he dropped his legs over the sides and gripped tightly, as if he was on horseback. The screen switched from a replay of a touchdown in the Skins' previous game to an advertisement for Modell's sporting goods store. Connor took a deep breath, gripped the handle, and pulled. The trapdoor slid back, revealing the promised twenty-two-and-a-half-inch-square hole. Connor slowly hauled himself inside and slid the door back in place.

Pressed in on all sides by steel, he began to wish that he had added a thick pair of gloves to his clothing. It was like being inside a refrigerator. Nevertheless, as each minute passed he became more confident that should it prove necessary to fall back on his contingency plan, no one would ever discover where he was hiding.

He lay suspended inside the hollow steel girder 170 feet above the ground for over an hour and a half, barely able to turn his wrist to check the time. But then, in Vietnam he'd once spent ten days' solitary confinement standing upright in a bamboo cage with water up to his chin.

Something he suspected Arnie had never experienced.

CHAPTER THIRTY-THREE

ZERIMSKI SHOOK HANDS WARMLY with everyone he was introduced to, and even laughed at John Kent Cooke's jokes. He remembered the names of all the guests, and answered every question that was put to him with a smile. 'What the Americans call a charm offensive,' Titov had told him: it would only add to the horror of what he had planned for them that evening.

He could already hear the guests telling the press, 'He couldn't have been more relaxed and at ease, especially with the President, whom he kept referring to as "my dear and close friend Tom".' Lawrence, the guests would recall, did not show quite the same degree of warmth, and was slightly frosty towards his Russian visitor.

After the introductions had been completed, John Kent Cooke banged on a table with a spoon. 'I'm sorry to interrupt such a pleasant occasion,' he began, 'but time is marching on, and this is probably going to be the only opportunity I have in my life to brief two Presidents at once.' A little laughter broke out. 'So here goes.' He put on a pair of glasses and began reading from a sheet of paper handed to him by his public affairs assistant.

'At eleven twenty I will accompany both Presidents to the south entrance of the stadium, and at eleven thirty-six

I will lead them out onto the field.' He looked up. 'I have arranged for the welcome to be deafening,' he said with a smile. Rita laughed just a little too loudly.

'When we reach the centre of the field, I will introduce the Presidents to the two team captains, and they in turn will introduce them to their co-captains and the coaches. Then the Presidents will be introduced to the match officials.

'At eleven forty, everyone will turn and face the west stand, where the Redskins band will play the Russian national anthem, followed after a short pause by "The Star-Spangled Banner".

'At precisely eleven forty-eight our honoured guest President Zerimski will flip a silver dollar. I shall then accompany both gentlemen off the field and bring them back here, where I hope everyone will enjoy watching the Redskins defeat the Packers.'

Both Presidents laughed.

Cooke looked up at his guests, smiling with relief that the first part of his ordeal was over, and asked, 'Any questions?'

'Yes, John, I have a question,' said Zerimski. 'You didn't explain why I have to flip the coin.'

'So that the captain who correctly guesses whether it's heads or tails can choose which team kicks off.'

'What an amusing idea,' said Zerimski.

As the minutes slipped by, Connor checked his watch more and more frequently. He didn't want to be inside the JumboTron for any longer than necessary, but he needed time to familiarise himself with a rifle he hadn't used for some years.

He checked his watch again. *Eleven ten.* He'd wait for another seven minutes. However impatient you become, never go early – it only adds to the risk.

Eleven twelve. He thought about Chris Jackson, and the sacrifice he had made just to give him this one chance.

Eleven fourteen. He thought about Joan, and the cruel and unnecessary death Gutenburg had ordered for no reason other than that she had been his secretary.

Eleven fifteen. He thought about Maggie and Tara. If he managed to pull this off, it might just give them a chance to live in peace. Either way, he doubted if he would ever see them again.

Eleven seventeen. Connor slid open the trapdoor and eased himself slowly out of the confined space. He gathered his strength for a moment before swinging his legs over the girder and gripping it firmly with his thighs. Again, he didn't look down as he began the slow forty-two-foot crawl back to the walkway.

Once he had reached the safety of the ledge, he pulled himself up onto the walkway. He held onto the rail for a few moments, steadied himself, and began a short series of stretching exercises.

Eleven twenty-seven. He breathed deeply as he went over his plan for the final time, then walked quickly towards the JumboTron, pausing only to pick up the empty Coke can he had left on the step.

He banged loudly on the door. Without waiting for a response, he opened it, marched in and shouted above the noise of the ventilation unit, 'It's only me.'

Arnie peered down from the ledge above, his right hand moving towards the trigger of his Armalite. 'Beat it!' he said. 'I told you not to come back till the Presidents were off the field. You're lucky I didn't put a bullet through you.'

'Sorry,' said Connor. 'It's just that I noticed how hot it gets in here, so I brought you another Coke.'

He passed the empty can up, and Arnie bent down to take it with his free hand. As his fingers touched the rim of the can, Connor let go of it, grabbed him by the wrist and, with all the strength he could muster, pulled him down from the ledge.

Arnie let out a terrible scream as he came crashing

over, landing head first on the galvanised walkway, his rifle skidding away across it.

Connor swung round and leapt on his adversary before he had a chance to get up. As Arnie raised his head, Connor landed a straight left to the chin that stunned him for a moment, then grabbed for the pair of handcuffs hanging from his belt. He only just caught sight of the knee flying towards his crotch, but deftly moved to his left and managed to avoid its full impact. As Arnie tried to rise to his feet, Connor landed another punch, this time full on his nose. Connor heard the break, and as blood began to flow down his face, Arnie's legs buckled and he sank to the ground. Connor sprang on him again, and as Arnie tried to get up he delivered a blow to his right shoulder that caused him to go into spasms. This time when he collapsed onto the walkway he finally lay still.

Connor tore off his long white coat, his shirt, tie, trousers, socks and cap. He threw them all in a pile in the corner, then unlocked Arnie's handcuffs and quickly stripped him of his uniform. As he put it on he found that the shoes were at least two sizes too small, and the trousers a couple of inches too short. He had no choice but to pull up his socks and stick with his trainers, which were at least black. He didn't think that in the mayhem he was about to cause anyone would recall that they had seen a Secret Service agent who wasn't wearing regulation shoes.

Connor retrieved his tie from the pile of clothes in the corner and bound Arnie's ankles tightly together. He then lifted up the unconscious man and held him against the wall, placed his arms around a steel beam which ran across the width of the JumboTron, and clamped the handcuffs on his wrists. Finally he took a handkerchief out of his pocket, rolled it up into a ball and forced it into Arnie's mouth. The poor bastard was going to be sore for several days. It wouldn't be much compensation that he would probably lose those extra pounds the SAIC had berated him about.

'Nothing personal,' said Connor. He placed Arnie's cap and dark glasses by the door, and picked up his rifle: as he'd thought, an M-16. It wouldn't have been his first choice, but it could do the job. He quickly climbed the steps to the second-floor landing where Arnie had been sitting, picked up his binoculars and, through the gap between the ad panel and the video screen, scanned the crowd below.

Eleven thirty-two. It had been three minutes and thirty-eight seconds since Connor had entered the JumboTron. He'd allowed four minutes for the take-over. He started breathing deeply and evenly.

Suddenly he heard a voice behind him.

'Hercules 3.'

At first he couldn't work out where the sound was coming from, but then he remembered the small two-way radio attached to Arnie's belt. He snatched it off. 'Hercules 3, go ahead.'

'Thought we'd lost you there for a moment, Arnie,' said the SAIC. 'Is everything OK?'

'Yep,' said Connor. 'Just needed to take a leak, and thought I'd better not do it over the crowd.'

'Affirmative,' said Braithwaite, breaking into a laugh. 'Keep scanning your section. It won't be long before Red Light and Waterfall come out on the field.'

'Will do,' said Connor, in an accent his mother would have chastised him for. The line went dead.

Eleven thirty-four. He looked around the stadium. Only a few of the red and yellow seats remained unoccupied. He tried not to be distracted by the scantily-clad Redskinettes kicking their legs high in the air directly below him.

A roar went up from the stands as the teams emerged from the tunnels at the south end of the stadium. They jogged slowly towards the centre of the field, as the crowd began to sing 'Hail to the Redskins'.

Connor raised Arnie's binoculars to his eyes and focused on the lighting towers high above the stadium. Almost all the agents were now scanning the crowd below, looking for any suggestion of trouble. None of them was showing any interest in the one location it was actually going to come from. Connor's gaze settled on young Brad, who was peering down into the north stand, checking it row by row. The boy looked as if this was the nearest he'd been to heaven.

Connor swung round and lined the binoculars up on the fifty-yard line. The two captains were now facing each other.

Eleven thirty-six. Another roar went up as John Kent Cooke proudly led the two Presidents out onto the field, accompanied by a dozen agents who were almost as big as the players. One look and Connor could tell that Zerimski and Lawrence were both wearing bulletproof vests.

He would have liked to line up his rifle on Zerimski and focus the mil dots on his head there and then, but he couldn't risk being spotted by one of the sharpshooters on the lighting towers, all of whom held their rifles in the crooks of their arms. He knew that they'd been trained to aim and fire in under three seconds.

As the Presidents were introduced to the players, Connor turned his attention to the Redskins flag which was fluttering in the breeze above the western end of the stadium. He cracked the rifle open to find, as he'd expected, that it was in 'gun-box' condition – fully loaded, off-safe, off-cocked. He chambered the first round and slammed the breech shut. The noise acted on him like the crack of a starting pistol, and he suddenly felt his heart rate almost double.

Eleven forty-one. The two Presidents were now chatting with the match officials. Through the binoculars, Connor could see John Kent Cooke nervously checking his watch. He leaned across and whispered something into Lawrence's ear. The American President nodded, touched

Zerimski's elbow and guided him to a space between the two teams. There were two little white circles on the grass, with a bear painted inside one and an eagle inside the other, so the two leaders would know exactly where to stand.

'Ladies and gentlemen,' said a voice over the loud-speaker. 'Will you please stand for the national anthem of the Russian Republic.'

There was a clattering of seats as the crowd rose from their places, many of them removing their Redskins caps as they turned to face the band and choir at the western end of the field. The bandleader raised his baton, paused, then suddenly lowered it with gusto. The crowd listened restlessly to a tune few of them had ever heard before.

Although Connor had stood through the Russian national anthem many times in the past, he had found that few bands outside the country knew either at what tempo it should be played or how many verses ought to be included. So he had decided to wait for 'The Star-Spangled Banner' before he took his one chance.

When the Russian anthem came to an end, the players began to stretch and jog on the spot in an attempt to calm their nerves. Connor waited for the bandleader to raise his baton once more, which would be his cue to line up Zerimski in his sights. He glanced at the flagpole on the far side of the stadium: the Redskins banner was now hanging limp, indicating that there was virtually no wind.

The bandmaster raised his baton a second time. Connor placed the rifle through the gap between the triangular ad panel and the video screen, using the wooden frame as a rest. He swept the telescopic sight across the field, then focused on the back of Zerimski's head, lining up the mil dots until it completely filled the centre of the rifle's sights.

The opening bars of the American anthem struck up,

and both Presidents visibly stiffened. Connor breathed out. Three ... two ... one. He gently squeezed the trigger just as Tom Lawrence's right arm swung across his chest, his hand coming to rest over his heart. Distracted by the sudden movement, Zerimski glanced to his left, and the bullet flew harmlessly past his right ear. Seventy-eight thousand out-of-tune voices ensured that no one heard the soft thud as the inch of metal embedded itself in the grass beyond the fifty-yard line.

Brad, lying flat on his stomach on the lighting platform high above the executive suite stared intently down at the crowd through a pair of binoculars. His eyes settled on the JumboTron. The vast screen was dominated by a larger than life President Lawrence, hand on heart, lustily singing the national anthem.

Brad's glasses swept on. Suddenly he jerked them back. He thought he'd seen something in the gap between the triangular ad panel and the screen. He double-checked ... it was the barrel of a rifle, pointing towards the centre of the field from the gap where he had earlier seen Arnie peering through his binoculars. He touched the fine focus and stared at a face he'd seen earlier that day. He didn't hesitate.

'Cover and evacuate. Gun.'

Brad spoke with such urgency and authority that Braithwaite and two of his counter-snipers instantly swung their binoculars round to the JumboTron. Within moments they had focused on Connor lining up his second shot.

'Relax,' Connor was murmuring to himself. 'Don't rush. You've got plenty of time.' Zerimski's head again filled the scope. Connor lined up the mil dots and breathed out again. Three ... two ...

Braithwaite's bullet hammered into his left shoulder, knocking him backwards. A second bullet whistled through the gap where his head had been an instant before.

The national anthem came to an end.

Twenty-eight years of training had prepared Connor for this moment. Everything in his body screamed out to him to make good his escape. He immediately began to carry out plan A, trying to ignore the excruciating pain in his shoulder. He struggled to the door, switched off the light and clambered out onto the walkway. He tried to run to the far door that led out onto the concourse, but found he needed every ounce of energy just to keep moving. Forty seconds later, just as the two Presidents were being escorted from the field, he reached the door. He heard a roar from the crowd as the Redskins prepared to kick off.

Connor unlocked the door, staggered to the service elevator and jabbed the button several times. He could hear the little engine whirr into action as it began its slow progress towards the seventh level. His eyes were darting right and left, searching for the slightest sign of danger. The pain in his shoulder was becoming more and more intense, but he knew there was nothing he could do about it. The first places every law enforcement agency would check were the local hospitals. He stuck his head into the shaft, and watched the top of the elevator heading towards him. It was about fifteen seconds away. But then it came to a sudden halt. Someone must be loading or unloading at the executive level.

Connor's instinctive reaction was to fall back on his contingency plan, something he had never had to do in the past. He knew he couldn't hang around – if he waited for more than a few more seconds, someone would spot him.

He moved as quickly as he could back towards the door that led to the JumboTron. The service elevator resumed its journey. A tray of sandwiches, a slice of Black Forest cake and the Coke that Arnie had been looking forward to appeared a few seconds later.

Connor slipped back through the door marked 'Private', leaving it unlocked. He had to summon up every ounce of willpower in his body to cover the seventy yards along the walkway, but he knew that agents from the Protective Intelligence Division mobile team would be swarming through that door within moments.

Twenty-four seconds later, Connor reached the massive girder that supported the video screen. He gripped the rail with his right hand and eased himself over the edge of the walkway and onto the ledge just as the door to the corridor swung open. He slipped under the walkway and heard two sets of feet run towards him, pass above him and stop outside the door to the JumboTron itself. Through a gap in the walkway he could see an officer clasping a hand gun pushing the door open. Without stepping inside, he fumbled for the light switch.

Connor waited until the lights went on and the two officers had disappeared inside the JumboTron before he began to crawl along the forty-two-foot girder for the third time that day. But now he could only hold on with his right arm, which meant that his progress was even slower. At the same time he had to be sure that the blood dripping from his left shoulder fell the 170 feet to the ground and not onto the girder for all to see.

When the leading Secret Service agent entered the JumboTron, the first thing he saw was Arnie handcuffed to the steel beam. He moved slowly towards him, constantly checking in every direction until he was standing by his side. His partner covered him while he unlocked Arnie's handcuffs and gently lowered him to the ground, then removed the handkerchief from his mouth and checked his pulse. He was alive.

Arnie raised his eyes to the ceiling, but didn't speak. The first Secret Service man immediately began to mount the steps to the second level, while the other officer covered him. The first man edged cautiously along the ledge behind the vast screen. A deafening roar went up around the stadium as the Redskins scored a touchdown, but he ignored it. Once he had reached the far wall, he turned back and nodded. The second officer began to climb to the top level, where he carried out a similar reconnaissance.

Both officers were back on the lower level, double-checking every possible hiding place, when a message came over the first agent's radio.

'Hercules 7.'

'Hercules 7, go ahead.'

'Any sign of him?' asked Braithwaite.

'There's nobody here except Arnie, who was cuffed to a beam in his underwear. Both doors were unlocked, and there's a trickle of blood all the way to the concourse, so you definitely winged him. He has to be out there somewhere. He's wearing Arnie's uniform, so he shouldn't be too hard to spot.'

'Don't count on it,' said Braithwaite. 'If it's who I think it is, he could be right under your nose.'

CHAPTER THIRTY-FOUR

THREE MEN SAT in the Oval Office listening to the tape. Two were in evening dress, the third in uniform.

'How did you find it?' asked Lawrence.

'It was among the pile of clothes Fitzgerald left in the JumboTron,' said Special Agent in Charge Braithwaite. 'In the back pocket of his jeans.'

'How many people have heard it?' asked Lloyd, trying not to sound anxious.

'Just the three of us in this room, sir,' said Braithwaite. 'As soon as I'd listened to it, I contacted you immediately. I haven't even briefed my boss.'

'I'm grateful for that, Bill,' said the President. 'But what about those who witnessed the incident in the stadium?'

'Apart from myself, only five other people were aware that anything happened, and you can be assured of their discretion,' said Braithwaite. 'Four of them have been on my personal staff for ten years or more, and between them they know enough secrets to sink the last four Presidents, not to mention half of Congress.'

'Did anyone actually see Fitzgerald?' asked Lloyd.

'No, sir. The two agents who searched the JumboTron immediately after the incident found no sign of him except a pile of clothes, a lot of blood and one of my men handcuffed to a beam. After I'd played the tape, I gave an order that there was to be no written or verbal report concerning the incident.'

'What about the man who was hanging from the beam?' asked the President.

'He just lost his footing and slipped off the ledge. I've put him on sick leave for a month.'

'You mentioned a fifth person,' said Lloyd.

'Yes, sir, a young trainee who was up on the lighting tower with us.'

'How can you be sure he won't talk?' asked Lloyd.

'His application to join the Secret Service is on my desk as we speak,' said Braithwaite. 'I think he's hoping to be assigned to my division as soon as he's completed his training.'

The President smiled. 'And the bullet?'

'I made a hell of a mess digging it out of the field after the stadium had been cleared,' said Braithwaite, passing a spent piece of flat metal across to the President.

Lawrence rose from his desk, turned round and stared out of the bay window. Dusk had fallen over the Capitol. He looked across the lawn while he thought about what he was going to say.

'It's important that you realise one thing, Bill,' he said eventually. 'It certainly sounds like my voice on that tape, but I have never suggested to anyone, at any time, that Zerimski or any other person should be the target of an assassin.'

'I accept that without question, Mr President, or I wouldn't be here now. But I must be equally candid with you. If anyone in the Secret Service had realised that it was Fitzgerald in the JumboTron, they would probably have helped him escape.'

'What kind of man can inspire such loyalty?' asked Lawrence.

'In your world, I suspect it's Abraham Lincoln,' said Braithwaite. 'In ours it's Connor Fitzgerald.'

'I would have liked to meet him.'

'That's going to be difficult, sir. Even if he's still alive, he seems to have disappeared off the face of the earth. I wouldn't want my career to depend on finding him.'

'Mr President,' interrupted Lloyd, 'you're already running seven minutes late for the dinner at the Russian Embassy.'

Lawrence smiled and shook hands with Braithwaite. 'Another good man I can't tell the American people about,' he said with a wry smile. 'I suppose you'll be on duty again tonight.'

'Yes, sir, I've been detailed to cover the whole of President Zerimski's visit.'

'I may see you later then, Bill. If you pick up any new information about Fitzgerald, I want to hear about it immediately.'

'Of course, sir,' said Braithwaite, turning to leave.

A few minutes later, Lawrence and Lloyd walked in silence to the south portico, where nine limousines with their engines running stood in line. As soon as the President was in the back of the sixth car, he turned to his Chief of Staff and asked, 'Where do you think he is, Andy?'

'I have no idea, sir. But if I did, I'd probably sign up with Braithwaite's team and help him escape.'

'Why can't we have someone like that as Director of the CIA?'

'We might have had, if Jackson had lived.'

Lawrence turned to look out of the window. Something had been nagging at him ever since he had left the stadium, but when the motorcycle escort drove through the gates of the Russian Embassy he was still no nearer to dragging it up from the recesses of his mind.

'What's he looking so angry about?' said Lawrence, spotting Zerimski pacing up and down outside the Embassy.

Lloyd glanced at his watch. 'You're seventeen minutes late, sir.'

'That's hardly a big deal, after what we've been through. Frankly, the damn man's lucky to be alive.'

'I don't think that's something you can use as an excuse, sir.'

The motorcade drew up at the feet of the Russian President. Lawrence stepped out of the car and said, 'Hi, Victor. Sorry we're a couple of minutes late.'

Zerimski made no attempt to hide his displeasure. After a cool handshake, he led his guest of honour silently into the Embassy and up the steps to the packed reception in the Green Room without uttering a word. Then he made a perfunctory excuse and dumped the President of the United States on the Egyptian Ambassador.

Lawrence's eyes circled the room as the Ambassador tried to interest him in an exhibition of Egyptian artefacts that had recently opened at the Smithsonian.

'Yes, I've been trying to find a gap in my schedule to see it,' said the President, on autopilot. 'Everybody who's been tells me it's quite magnificent.' The Egyptian Ambassador beamed, as Lawrence spotted the man he was looking for. It took him three Ambassadors, two wives and the political correspondent of *Pravda* before he managed to reach Harry Nourse without causing undue suspicion.

'Good evening, Mr President,' said the Attorney-General. 'You must have been pleased with the result of the game this afternoon.'

'Sure was, Harry,' said Lawrence expansively. 'Always said the Packers could whip the Redskins any time, any place.' He lowered his voice: 'I want to see you in my office at midnight tonight. I need your advice on a legal matter.'

'Of course, sir,' said the Attorney-General quietly.

'Rita,' said the President, turning to his right, 'it was such fun being with you this afternoon.'

Mrs Cooke returned the smile as a gong sounded in

the background and a butler announced that dinner was about to be served. The chatter subsided, and the guests made their way into the ballroom.

Lawrence had been placed between Mrs Pietrovski, the Ambassador's wife, and Yuri Olgivic, the newly appointed head of the Russian Trade Delegation. The President soon discovered that Olgivic didn't speak a word of English – another of Zerimski's subtle hints about his attitude to opening up trade between the two nations.

'You must have been pleased with the result of the game this afternoon,' said the Russian Ambassador's wife, as a bowl of borscht was placed in front of the President.

'Sure was,' said Lawrence. 'But I don't think most of the crowd was with me on that one, Olga.'

Mrs Pietrovski laughed.

'Were you able to follow what was going on?' asked Lawrence, picking up his soup spoon.

'Not really,' she replied. 'But I was fortunate enough to be placed next to a Mr Pug Washer, who didn't seem to mind answering the most simple questions I asked him.'

The President dropped his spoon before he'd taken a sip. He looked across the room at Andy Lloyd, and placed a clenched fist under his chin – the sign he always used when he needed to speak to his Chief of Staff urgently.

Lloyd murmured a few words to the woman on his right, then folded his napkin, placed it on the table and walked over to the President's side.

'I need to see Braithwaite immediately,' Lawrence whispered. 'I think I know how to find Fitzgerald.'

Lloyd slipped out of the room without saying a word as the President's soup bowl was whisked away.

Lawrence tried to concentrate on what the Russian Ambassador's wife was saying, but he couldn't get Fitzgerald out of his mind. Something about how much she would miss the States once her husband had retired.

'And when will that be?' asked the President, not at all interested in her reply.

'In about eighteen months,' Mrs Pietrovski replied, as a plate of cold beef was placed in front of the President. He continued the conversation as first one waiter served him some vegetables, and a moment later another brought some potatoes. He picked up his knife and fork just as Lloyd walked back into the room. He was at the President's side a moment later.

'Braithwaite's waiting for you in the back of "Stagecoach".'

'I hope there isn't a problem,' said Mrs Pietrovski as Lawrence began folding his napkin.

'Nothing important, Olga,' Lawrence assured her. 'They just can't find my speech. But don't worry, I know exactly where it is.' He rose from his place, and Zerimski followed his every step as he left the room.

Lawrence walked out of the ballroom, down the wooden staircase and through the front door of the Embassy before jogging down the steps and climbing into the back of the sixth car.

Lloyd and the driver stood by the limousine as a dozen Secret Service agents surrounded it, scanning in every direction.

'Bill, if Fitzgerald is still in the stadium, there's one man who'll know where he is. Find Pug Washer, and my bet is you'll find Fitzgerald.'

A few moments later the President opened the car door.

'OK, Andy,' he said, 'let's get back before they discover what we're up to.'

'What *are* we up to?' asked Lloyd as he chased the President up the stairs.

'I'll tell you later,' said Lawrence, striding into the ballroom.

'But sir,' said Lloyd, 'you'll still need . . .'

'Not now,' said Lawrence, as he took his seat next to the Ambassador's wife and smiled apologetically.

'Did you manage to find it?' she asked.

'Find what?'

'Your speech,' said Mrs Pietrovski, as Lloyd placed a file on the table between them.

'Of course,' said Lawrence, tapping the file. 'By the way, Olga, how's that daughter of yours? Natasha, isn't it? Is she still studying Fra Angelico in Florence?' He picked up his knife and fork.

The President glanced in Zerimski's direction as the waiters reappeared to remove the plates. He put his knife and fork back down, settling for a stale bread roll with a pat of butter and finding out what Natasha Pietrovski had been up to during her junior year in Florence. He couldn't help noticing that the Russian President appeared nervous, almost on edge, as the time drew nearer for him to make his speech. He immediately assumed that Zerimski was about to deliver another unexpected bombshell. The thought put him off his raspberry soufflé.

When Zerimski eventually rose to address his guests, even his most ardent admirers would have been hard pressed to describe his efforts as anything other than pedestrian. Some of those who watched him particularly closely wondered why he appeared to be directing so many of his remarks to the massive statue of Lenin in the gallery above the ballroom. Lawrence thought it must have been put there recently, as he didn't remember seeing it at Boris's farewell dinner.

He kept waiting for Zerimski to reinforce his message to Congress the previous day, but he said nothing controversial. To Lawrence's relief he stuck to the bland script that had been sent to the White House that afternoon. He glanced down at his own speech, which he should have gone over with Andy in the car. His Chief of Staff had scribbled a few suggestions in the margins, but there wasn't a witty phrase or memorable paragraph from page one to page seven. But then, Andy had also had a busy day.

'Let me end by thanking the American people for the generous hospitality and warm welcome I have experienced everywhere I have been during my visit to your great country, in particular from your President, Tom Lawrence.'

The applause that greeted this statement was so loud and prolonged that Lawrence looked up from his notes. Zerimski was once again standing motionless, staring up at the statue of Lenin. He waited until the applause had ended before he sat down. He didn't look at all pleased, which surprised Lawrence, as in his opinion the speech's reception had been far more generous than it deserved.

Lawrence rose to reply. His speech was received with courteous interest, but hardly with enthusiasm. He concluded with the words, 'Let us hope, Victor, that this will be the first of many visits you make to the United States. On behalf of all your guests, I wish you a safe flight home tomorrow.' Lawrence reflected that two lies in one sentence were a bit much, even for a politician, and wished he had had time to read the line before delivering it. He sat down to respectful applause, but it was nothing compared with the ovation Zerimski had received for an equally banal offering.

Once the coffee had been served, Zerimski rose from his place and walked over to the double doors at the far side of the room. He soon began saying 'Goodnight,' in a voice that carried across the room, making it abundantly clear that he wanted his guests off the premises as quickly as possible.

A few minutes after ten had struck on several clocks around the Embassy, Lawrence rose and began moving slowly in the direction of his host. But, like Caesar in the Capitol, he found he was continually stopped by different citizens wanting to touch the hem of the emperor's clothes. When he eventually reached the door, Zerimski gave him a curt nod before accompanying him down the stairs to the first floor. As Zerimski didn't speak, Lawrence took a long look at the Nzizvestni statue of Christ on the Cross that was still in its place on the first landing. Now that Lenin was back, he was surprised that Jesus had survived. At the foot of the stone steps he turned to wave to his host, but Zerimski had already disappeared back inside the Embassy. If he had taken the trouble to accompany Lawrence beyond the front door, he would have seen the SAIC waiting for him as he climbed into the back of his limousine.

Braithwaite didn't speak until the door had been closed.

'You were right, sir,' he said as they passed through the Embassy gates.

The first person Zerimski saw as he walked back into the Embassy was the Ambassador. His Excellency smiled hopefully.

'Is Romanov still in the building?' Zerimski bellowed, unable to hide his anger for a moment longer.

'Yes, Mr President,' the Ambassador said, chasing after his leader. 'He's been . . .'

'Bring him to me immediately.'

'Where will I find you?'

'In what used to be your study.'

Pietrovski scurried away in the opposite direction.

Zerimski marched down the long marble corridor, hardly breaking his stride as he shoved open the door of the Ambassador's study as if he was thumping a punchbag. The first thing he saw was the rifle, still lying on the desk. He sat down in the large leather chair normally occupied by the Ambassador.

While he waited impatiently for them to join him, he picked up the rifle and began to study it more closely. He looked down the barrel and saw that the single bullet was still in place. As he held it up to his shoulder he could feel its perfect balance, and he understood for the first time why Fitzgerald had been willing to fly halfway across America to find its twin.

It was then that he saw the firing pin had been replaced.

Zerimski could hear the two men hurrying down the marble corridor. Just before they reached the study, he lowered the rifle onto his lap.

They almost ran into the room. Zerimski pointed unceremoniously to the two seats on the other side of the desk.

'Where was Fitzgerald?' he demanded before Romanov had even sat down. 'You assured me in this room that he would be here by four o'clock this afternoon. "Nothing can go wrong," you boasted. "He's agreed to my plan." Your exact words.'

'That was our agreement when I spoke to him just after midnight, Mr President,' said Romanov.

'So what happened between midnight and four o'clock?'

'While my men were escorting him into the city early this morning, the driver was forced to stop at a set of traffic lights. Fitzgerald leaped out of the car, ran to the other side of the road and jumped into a passing taxi. We pursued it all the way to Dulles Airport, only to find when we caught up with it outside the terminal that Fitzgerald wasn't inside.'

'The truth is that you allowed him to escape,' said Zerimski. 'Isn't that what really happened?'

Romanov bowed his head and said nothing.

The President's voice lowered to a whisper. 'I understand you have a code in the Mafya,' he said, clicking the breech of the rifle shut, 'for those who fail to carry out contracts.'

Romanov looked up in horror as Zerimski raised the gun until it was pointing at the centre of his chest.

'Yes or no?' said Zerimski quietly.

Romanov nodded. Zerimski smiled at the man who had accepted the judgement of his own court, and gently squeezed the trigger. The boat-tailed bullet tore into Romanov's chest about an inch below the heart. The power of its impact hurled his lithe body back against the wall, where it remained for a second or two before slithering down onto the carpet. Fragments of muscle and bone were scattered in every direction. The walls, the carpet, the Ambassador's dress suit and white pleated shirt were drenched with blood.

Zerimski swung slowly round until he was facing his former representative in Washington. 'No, no!' cried Pietrovski, falling on his knees. 'I'll resign, I'll resign.'

Zerimski squeezed the trigger a second time. When he heard the click, he remembered that there had been only one bullet in the breech. He rose from his seat, a look of disappointment on his face.

'You'll have to send that suit to the cleaners,' he said, as if the Ambassador had done no more than spill some egg yolk on his sleeve. The President placed the rifle back on the desk. 'I accept your resignation. But before you clear your office, see that what's left of Romanov's body is patched together and sent back to St Petersburg.' He began walking towards the door. 'Make it quick – I'd like to be there when he's buried with his father.'

Pietrovski, still on his knees, didn't reply. He had been sick, and was too frightened to open his mouth.

As Zerimski reached the door, he turned back to face the cowering diplomat. 'In the circumstances, it might be wise to arrange for the body to be sent back in the diplomatic pouch.'

CHAPTER THIRTY-FIVE

THE SNOW WAS FALLING HEAVILY as Zerimski climbed the steps to the waiting Ilyushin 62, creating a thick white carpet around its wheels.

Tom Lawrence was standing on the tarmac, wearing a long black topcoat. An aide held a large umbrella above his head.

Zerimski disappeared through the door without even bothering to turn and give the traditional wave for the cameras. Any suggestion of this being the time of year for good will to all men was obviously lost on him.

The State Department had already issued a press release. It talked in broad terms of the success of the new Russian President's four-day visit, significant steps taken by both countries, and the hope for further cooperation at some time in the future. 'Useful and constructive' were the words Larry Harrington had settled on before the morning press conference, and, as an afterthought, 'a step forward'. The journalists who had just witnessed Zerimski's departure would translate Harrington's sentiments as 'useless and destructive, and without doubt a step backwards'.

Within moments of its grey door slamming shut the Ilyushin lurched forward, almost as if, like its master, it couldn't wait to get away.

Lawrence was the first to turn his back on the

departing aircraft as it lumbered towards the runway. He walked quickly over to his waiting helicopter, where he found Andy Lloyd, a phone already pressed against his ear. Once the rotor blades began to turn, Lloyd quickly concluded his call. As Marine One lifted off, he leaned across and briefed the President on the outcome of the emergency operation that had taken place early that morning at the Walter Reed Hospital. Lawrence nodded as his Chief of Staff outlined the course of action Agent Braithwaite was recommending. 'I'll ring Mrs Fitzgerald personally,' he said.

The two men spent the rest of the short journey preparing for the meeting that was about to take place in the Oval Office. The President's helicopter landed on the South Lawn, and neither of them spoke as they made their way towards the White House. Lawrence's secretary was waiting anxiously by the door.

'Good morning, Ruth,' the President said for the third time that day. Both of them had been up for most of the night.

At midnight the Attorney-General had arrived unannounced and told Ruth Preston that he had been summoned to attend a meeting with the President. It wasn't in his diary. At two a.m. the President, Mr Lloyd and the Attorney-General had left for the Walter Reed Hospital – but again, there was no mention of the visit in the diary, or of the name of the patient they would be seeing. They returned an hour later and spent another ninety minutes in the Oval Office, the President having left instructions that they were not to be disturbed. When Ruth arrived back at the White House at ten past eight that morning, the President was already on his way to Andrews air base to say farewell to Zerimski.

Although he was wearing a different suit, shirt and tie from when she had last seen him, Ruth wondered if her boss had gone to bed at all that night.

'What's next, Ruth?' he asked, knowing only too well.

'Your ten o'clock appointment has been waiting in the lobby for the past forty minutes.'

'Have they? Then you'd better send them in.'

The President walked into the Oval Office, opened a drawer in his desk and removed two sheets of paper and a cassette tape. He placed the paper on the blotter in front of him and inserted the cassette in the recorder on his desk. Andy Lloyd came in from his office, carrying two files under his arm. He took his usual seat by the side of the President.

'Have you got the affidavits?' asked Lawrence.

'Yes, sir,' Lloyd replied.

There was a knock on the door. Ruth opened it and announced, 'The Director and Deputy Director of the CIA.'

'Good morning, Mr President,' said Helen Dexter brightly, as she entered the Oval Office with her Deputy a pace behind. She too had a file under her arm.

Lawrence did not return her salutation.

'You'll be relieved to know,' continued Dexter, as she took a seat in one of the two vacant chairs opposite the President, 'that I was able to deal with that problem we feared might arise during the visit of the Russian President. In fact, we have every reason to believe that the person in question no longer represents a threat to this country.'

'Could that possibly be the same person I had a chat with on the phone a few weeks ago?' asked Lawrence, leaning back in his chair.

'I'm not quite sure I understand you, Mr President,' said Dexter.

'Then allow me to enlighten you,' said Lawrence. He leaned forward and pressed the 'Play' button of the tape recorder on his desk.

'I felt I had to call and let you know just how important I consider this assignment to be. Because I have no doubt that you're the right person to carry it out. So I hope you will agree to take on the responsibility.'

'*I appreciate your confidence in me, Mr President, and I'm grateful to you for taking the time to phone personally . . .*'

Lawrence pressed the 'Stop' button.

'No doubt you have a simple explanation as to how and why this conversation took place,' he said.

'I'm not sure I fully understand you, Mr President. The Agency is not privy to your personal telephone conversations.'

'That may or may not be true,' said the President. 'But that particular conversation, as you well know, did not emanate from this office.'

'Are you accusing the Agency of . . .'

'I'm not accusing the Agency of anything. The accusation is levelled at you personally.'

'Mr President, if this is your idea of a joke . . .'

'Do I look as if I'm laughing?' asked the President, before hitting the 'Play' button again.

'*I felt it was the least I could do in the circumstances.*'

'*Thank you, Mr President. Although Mr Gutenburg assured me of your involvement, and the Director herself called later that afternoon to confirm it, as you know, I still felt unable to take on the assignment unless I was certain that the order had come directly from you.*'

The President leaned forward and once again pressed the 'Stop' button.

'There's more, if you want to hear it.'

'I can assure you,' said Dexter, 'that the operation the agent in question was referring to was nothing more than a routine exercise.'

'Are you asking me to believe that the assassination of the Russian President is now considered by the CIA to be nothing more than a routine exercise?' said Lawrence in disbelief.

'It was never our intention that Zerimski should be killed,' said Dexter sharply.

'Only that an innocent man would hang for it,' the President retorted. A long silence followed before he added, 'And thus remove any proof that it was also you who ordered the assassination of Ricardo Guzman in Colombia.'

'Mr President, I can assure you that the CIA had nothing to do with . . .'

'That's not what Connor Fitzgerald told us earlier this morning,' said Lawrence.

Dexter was silent.

'Perhaps you'd care to read the affidavit he signed in the presence of the Attorney-General.'

Andy Lloyd opened the first of his two files and passed Dexter and Gutenburg copies of an affidavit signed by Connor Fitzgerald and witnessed by the Attorney-General. As the two of them began reading the statement, the President couldn't help noticing that Gutenburg was sweating slightly.

'Having taken advice from the Attorney-General, I have authorised the SAIC to arrest you both on a charge of treason. If you are found guilty, I am advised that there can only be one sentence.'

Dexter remained tight-lipped. Her Deputy was now visibly shaking. Lawrence turned to him.

'Of course it's possible, Nick, that you were unaware that the Director hadn't been given the necessary executive authority to issue such an order.'

'That is absolutely correct, sir,' Gutenburg blurted out. 'In fact she led me to believe that the instruction to assassinate Guzman had come directly from the White House.'

'I thought you'd say that, Nick,' said the President. 'And if you feel able to sign this document' – he pushed a sheet of paper across the desk – 'the Attorney-General has indicated to me that the death sentence would be commuted to life imprisonment.'

'Whatever it is, don't sign it,' ordered Dexter.

Gutenburg hesitated for a moment, then removed a pen from his pocket and signed his name between the two pencilled crosses below his one-sentence resignation as Deputy Director of the CIA, effective nine a.m. that day.

Dexter glared at him with undisguised contempt. 'If you'd refused to resign, they wouldn't have had the nerve to go through with it. Men are so spineless.' She turned back to face the President, who was pushing a second sheet of paper across the desk, and glanced down to read her own one-sentence resignation as Director of the CIA, also effective nine a.m. that day. She looked up at Lawrence and said defiantly, 'I won't be signing anything, Mr President. You ought to have worked out by now that I don't frighten that easily.'

'Well, Helen, if you feel unable to take the same honourable course of action as Nick,' said Lawrence, 'when you leave this room you'll find two Secret Service agents on the other side of the door, with instructions to arrest you.'

'You can't bluff me, Lawrence,' said Dexter, rising from her chair.

'Mr Gutenburg,' said Lloyd, as she began walking towards the door, leaving the unsigned sheet of paper on the desk, 'I consider life imprisonment, with no hope of parole, too high a price to pay in the circumstances. Especially if you were being set up, and didn't even know what was going on.'

Gutenburg nodded as Dexter reached the door.

'I would have thought a sentence of six, perhaps seven years at the most, would be more appropriate in your case. And with a little assistance from the White House, you need only end up serving three to four.'

Dexter stopped dead in her tracks.

'But that would of course mean your agreeing to . . .'

'I'll agree to anything. Anything,' Gutenburg spluttered.

'. . . to testifying on behalf of the prosecution.'

Gutenburg nodded again, and Lloyd extracted a two-page affidavit from the other file resting on his lap. The former Deputy Director spent only a few moments reading the document before scribbling his signature across the bottom of the second page.

The Director rested a hand on the doorknob, hesitated for some time, then turned and walked slowly back to the desk. She gave her former Deputy one last look of disgust before picking up the pen and scrawling her signature between the pencilled crosses.

'You're a fool, Gutenburg,' she said. 'They would never have risked putting Fitzgerald on the stand. Any half-decent lawyer would have torn him to shreds. And without Fitzgerald, they don't have a case. As I'm sure the Attorney-General has already explained to them.' She turned again to leave the room.

'Helen's quite right,' said Lawrence, retrieving the three documents and handing them to Lloyd. 'If the case had ever reached the courts, we could never have put Fitzgerald on the stand.'

Dexter stopped in her tracks for a second time, the ink not yet dry on her resignation.

'Sadly,' said the President, 'I have to inform you that Connor Fitzgerald died at seven forty-three this morning.'

BOOK FOUR

The Quick and the Dead

CHAPTER THIRTY-SIX

THE CORTÈGE continued its slow progress over the brow of the hill.

Arlington National Cemetery was packed for a man who had never sought public recognition. The President of the United States stood on one side of the grave, flanked by the White House Chief of Staff and the Attorney-General. Facing them was a woman who hadn't raised her head for the past forty minutes. On her right stood her daughter; on her left her future son-in-law.

The three of them had flown over from Sydney two days after receiving a personal telephone call from the President. The large crowd assembled at the graveside could not have left Maggie Fitzgerald in any doubt how many friends and admirers Connor had left behind.

At a meeting the previous day at the White House, Tom Lawrence had told the widow that Connor's last words had been of his love for her and his daughter. The President went on to say that although he had only met her husband once, he would remember him for the rest of his life. 'This from a man who meets a hundred people a day,' Tara had written in her diary that evening.

A few paces behind the President stood the newly appointed Director of the CIA and a group of men and women who had no intention of reporting to work that day. They had travelled from the four corners of the earth to be there.

A tall, heavily-built man without a hair on his head stood slightly to one side of the other mourners, weeping uncontrollably. No one present would have believed that the most ruthless gangsters in South Africa would have been delighted to know that Carl Koeter was out of the country, if only for a couple of days.

The FBI and the Secret Service were also present in large numbers. Special Agent William Braithwaite stood at the head of a dozen sharpshooters, any one of whom would have been satisfied to end their careers regarded as the successor to Connor Fitzgerald.

Higher up the slope of the hill, filling the cemetery as far as the eye could see, were relatives from Chicago, academics from Georgetown, bridge players, Irish dancers, poets and people from every walk of life. They stood with their heads bowed in memory of a man they had loved and respected.

The cortège came to a halt on Sheridan Drive, a few yards from the graveside. The eight-man honour guard lifted the coffin from the gun carriage, raised it onto their shoulders and began the slow march towards the grave. The coffin was draped in the American flag, and resting on top were Connor's battle ribbons. The Medal of Honor lay in the centre. When the pallbearers reached the graveside they lowered the coffin gently to the ground, and joined the other mourners.

Father Graham, who had been the Fitzgeralds' family priest for over thirty years, raised his arms in the air.

'My friends,' he began. 'Priests are often called upon to sing the praises of parishioners who have passed away, with whom they were barely acquainted and whose achievements were not always apparent. But this cannot be said of Connor Fitzgerald. As a student, he will be remembered as one of the finest quarterbacks the University of Notre Dame has ever produced. As a soldier, no feeble words of mine could possibly match the citation written by Captain Christopher Jackson, his platoon commander: "A fearless officer in the face of danger, who always placed his men's lives before his own." As a professional he gave almost three decades' service to his country; you only have to look around to see the high regard in which he was held by his peers. But most of all, as a husband to Maggie and a father to Tara, we will remember him. Our hearts go out to both of them.'

Father Graham lowered his voice. 'I was lucky enough to count myself among his friends. I had been looking forward to playing bridge with him again over the Christmas holiday – in fact, I was rather hoping to win back the $10 I lost to him in a rubber just before he went away on his last assignment. Dear God, I would happily give everything I possess just to be able once again to lose a game of bridge to him.

'Sportsman, soldier, professional, lover, father, friend, and for me – although I would never have had the courage to mention it in his presence, simply because he would have laughed at me – hero.

'Buried not far from you, Connor, is another American hero.' The elderly priest raised his head. 'If I were John Fitzgerald Kennedy, I would be proud to be buried in the same cemetery as Connor Fitzgerald.'

The pallbearers stepped forward and lowered the coffin into the grave. Father Graham made the sign of the cross, bent down, picked up a handful of earth and scattered it on the coffin.

'Ashes to ashes, dust to dust,' intoned the priest as a lone Marine bugler played Taps. The honour guard folded the flag from the coffin until it ended as a neat triangle in the hands of the youngest cadet, a boy of eighteen who, like Connor, had been born in Chicago. Normally he would have presented it to the widow with the words, 'Ma'am, on behalf of the President of the United States.' But not today. Today he marched in a different direction. Seven Marines raised their rifles in the air and fired a twenty-one-gun salute as the young cadet stood to attention in front of the President of the United States, and surrendered the flag.

Tom Lawrence received it, walked slowly around to the other side of the grave and stood before the widow. Maggie raised her head and tried to smile as the President presented her with the standard of the nation.

'On behalf of a grateful country, I pass to you the flag of the Republic. You are surrounded by friends who knew your husband well. I only wish I'd had that privilege.' The President bowed his head and returned to the other side of the grave. As the Marine band struck up the national anthem, he placed his right hand over his heart.

No one moved until Maggie had been escorted by Stuart and Tara to the entrance of the cemetery. She stood there for almost an hour, shaking hands with every mourner who had attended the ceremony.

Two men who had remained on the top of the hill throughout the service had flown in from Russia the previous day. They had not come to mourn. They would return to St Petersburg on the evening flight, and report that their services were no longer required.

CHAPTER THIRTY-SEVEN

AIR FORCE ONE was surrounded by tanks when the President of the United States landed at Moscow airport.

President Zerimski left us in no doubt that he had little interest in giving Tom Lawrence a photo opportunity for the folks back home. Nor were there the usual 'Welcome to Russia' speeches delivered from a podium on the runway.

As a grim-faced Lawrence descended the aircraft's steps, he was greeted by the sight of Marshal Borodin standing in the turret of a tank.

When the two Presidents eventually met at the Kremlin later this morning, the first item on the agenda was President Zerimski's demand that the NATO forces which patrol Russia's western borders be immediately withdrawn. Following the heavy defeat of his Nuclear, Biological, Chemical and Conventional Arms Reduction Bill in the Senate, and the Ukraine's voluntary return to the Soviet Union, President Lawrence knows that he is not in a position to give an inch on NATO's role in Europe, especially since the newly elected Senator Helen Dexter keeps describing him as 'the red stooge'.

Since Senator Dexter's resignation as Director of the CIA last year, in order to 'more openly oppose the Presi-

*dent's misguided foreign policy', there is already talk
on the Hill of her becoming the first woman President.
At this morning's preliminary talks in the Kremlin,
President Zerimski made no pretence of . . .*

Stuart looked up from the front page of the *Sydney Morning Herald* as Maggie walked into the kitchen, dressed in jeans and a sweater. They had been living in the same house for over six months, and he had never seen her with a hair out of place.

'Good morning, Stuart,' she said. 'Anything interesting in the paper?'

'Zerimski's still flexing his muscles at the slightest opportunity,' Stuart replied. 'And your President is having to put a brave face on it. At least, that's the view of the Russian correspondent of the *Herald.*'

'Zerimski would drop a nuclear bomb on the White House if he thought he could get away with it,' said Maggie. 'Isn't there any brighter news to tell me on a Saturday morning?'

'The Prime Minister has announced the date for the election of our first President.'

'You're so slow in this country,' said Maggie, filling a bowl with cornflakes. 'We got rid of the British over two hundred years ago.'

'It won't take us much longer,' said Stuart with a laugh as his wife strolled into the room in her dressing gown.

'Good morning,' she said sleepily. Maggie slid off her stool and gave her a kiss on the cheek.

'You sit there and have these cornflakes while I make you an omelette. You really mustn't . . .'

'Mother, I'm pregnant, not dying of consumption,' said Tara. 'I'll be just fine with a bowl of cornflakes.'

'I know, it's just that . . .'

'. . . you'll never stop worrying,' said Tara, putting her arms around her mother's shoulders. 'I'll let you in on a secret. There is no medical evidence that miscarriages are hereditary; only fussing mothers. What's the big story this morning?' she asked, looking across at Stuart.

'My case in the criminal court has made the headlines – on page sixteen,' he said, pointing to three short paragraphs tucked away in the bottom left-hand corner.

Tara read the report through twice before saying, 'But they don't even mention your name.'

'No. They seem to be more interested in my client at the moment,' admitted Stuart. 'But if I get him off, that could change.'

'I hope you don't get him off,' said Maggie as she broke a second egg. 'I think your client is a little creep, and ought to spend the rest of his life in jail.'

'For stealing $73?' said Stuart in disbelief.

'From a defenceless old woman.'

'But it was the first time.'

'The first time he was caught, I think you mean,' said Maggie.

'You know, Maggie, you would have made a first-class prosecuting counsel,' said Stuart. 'You should never have agreed to taking a sabbatical this year – you should have enrolled in law school instead. Mind you, I suspect life imprisonment for stealing $73 might not go down that big with everyone.'

'You'd be surprised, young man,' retorted Maggie.

There was a thud on the doormat. 'I'll get it,' said Stuart, rising from the table.

'Stuart's right,' said Tara, as her mother placed an omelette in front of her. 'You shouldn't waste your time being an unpaid housekeeper. You're far too good for that.'

'Thank you, my darling,' said Maggie. She returned to the stove and cracked another egg. 'But I enjoy being with you both. I only hope I'm not outstaying my welcome.'

'Of course you're not,' said Tara. 'But it's been over six months since . . .'

'I know, darling, but I still need a little longer before I can face going back to Washington. I'll be fine by the time the fall semester begins.'

'But you don't even accept invitations to things you'd enjoy.'

'Such as?'

'Last week Mr Moore invited you to *Fidelio* at the Opera House, and you told him you were already going out that evening.'

'To be honest, I can't remember what I was doing,' said Maggie.

'I can. You sat in your room reading *Ulysses.*'

'Tara, Ronnie Moore is a sweet man, and I have no doubt that whatever it is he does at the bank, he does very well. But what he doesn't need is to spend an evening with me being reminded how much I miss your father. And I certainly don't need to spend an evening with him being told how much he adored his late wife, whatever her name was.'

'Elizabeth,' said Stuart, as he returned clutching the morning post. 'Ronnie's rather nice actually.'

'Not you as well,' said Maggie. 'The time has come for you both to stop worrying about my social life.' She placed an even larger omelette in front of Stuart.

'I should have married you, Maggie,' he said with a grin.

'You'd have been far more suitable than most of the men you've been trying to fix me up with,' she said, patting her son-in-law on the head.

Stuart laughed and started sorting out the letters, the bulk of which were for him. He passed a couple over to Tara and three to Maggie, and pushed his own little pile to one side in favour of the sports section of the *Herald.*

Maggie poured herself a second cup of coffee before she turned to her post. As always, she studied the stamps before deciding in which order she would open them.

Two of them carried the same portrait of George Washington. The third displayed a colourful picture of a kookaburra. She tore open the Australian letter first. When she had finished reading it, she passed it across the table to Tara, whose smile became broader with each paragraph she read.

'Very flattering,' said Tara, handing the letter to Stuart.

Stuart read it through quickly. 'Yes, very. How will you respond?'

'I'll write back explaining that I'm not in the job market,' said Maggie. 'But not until I discover which one of you I have to thank for it.' She waved the letter in the air.

'Not guilty,' said Tara.

'*Mea culpa*,' admitted Stuart. He had learned early on that it wasn't worth trying to fool Maggie. She always found you out in the end.

'I saw the job advertised in the *Herald*, and I thought you were ideally qualified for it. Overqualified, if anything.'

'There's a rumour that the Head of Admissions will be retiring at the end of the academic year,' said Tara. 'So they'll be looking for a replacement in the near future. Whoever gets this job . . .'

'Now listen to me, you two,' said Maggie, starting to clear away the plates. 'I'm on a sabbatical, and come August I intend to return to Washington and continue my job as Dean of Admissions at Georgetown. Sydney University will just have to find someone else.' She sat down to open her second letter.

Neither Tara nor Stuart made any further comment as she extracted a cheque for $277,000, signed by the Treasury Secretary. 'Benefit in full', the attached letter explained, for the loss of her husband while serving as an officer with the CIA. How could they begin to understand what the words 'benefit in full' meant?

She quickly opened the third letter. She had saved it

till last, recognising the ancient typeface and knowing exactly who had sent it.

Tara nudged Stuart. 'The annual love letter from Dr O'Casey, if I'm not mistaken,' she said in a stage whisper. 'I must admit, I'm impressed that he managed to track you down.'

'So am I,' said Maggie with a smile. 'At least with him I don't have to pretend.' She tore open the envelope

'See you both outside and ready to leave in one hour,' Stuart said, checking his watch. Maggie glanced over the top of her reading glasses and smiled. 'I've booked a table at the beach café for one o'clock.'

'Oh, you're so masterful,' said Tara with an adoring sigh. Stuart was just about to hit her on the head with his newspaper when Maggie said, 'Good h------ ----y both look-- -- --- --- amazement. It was the nearest they'd ever heard her get to blasphemy.

'What is it, Mother?' asked Tara. 'Is he still proposing, or after all these years has he finally married someone else?'

'Neither. He's been offered a job as head of the Mathematics Department at the University of New South Wales, and he's coming over to meet the Vice-Chancellor before he makes a final decision.'

'Couldn't be better,' said Tara. 'After all, he's Irish, handsome, and has always adored you. And as you regularly remind us, Dad only just managed to beat him off in the first place. What more could you ask for?'

There was a long silence before Maggie said, 'I'm afraid that's not altogether accurate.'

'What do you mean?' said Tara.

'Well, the truth is that although he *was* handsome, and a magnificent dancer, he was also a bit of a bore.'

'But you always told me . . .'

'I know what I told you,' said Maggie. 'And you needn't look at me like that, young lady. I'm sure you occasionally tease Stuart about that young waiter from Dublin who . . .'

'Mother! In any case, he's now a . . .'

'A what?' asked Stuart.

'. . . a lecturer at Trinity College, Dublin,' said Tara. 'And what's more, he's happily married with three children. Which is more than can be said for most of your ex-girlfriends.'

'True,' admitted Stuart. 'So tell me,' he said, turning his attention back to Maggie, 'when does Dr O'Casey arrive in Oz?'

Maggie unfolded the letter again and read out:

> 'I'm flying from Chicago on the fourteenth, arriving on the fifteenth.'

'But that's today,' said Stuart.

Maggie nodded before continuing:

> 'I'll be staying in Sydney overnight and then meeting the Vice-Chancellor the following day before returning to Chicago.'

She looked up. 'He'll be on his way home before we get back from the weekend.'

'That's a shame,' said Tara. 'After all these years, I would have liked to meet the faithful Dr Declan O'Casey.'

'And you still could, just,' said Stuart, glancing at his watch. 'What time does his plane land?'

'Eleven twenty this morning,' said Maggie. 'I'm afraid we're going to miss him. And he doesn't say where he'll be staying, so there's no way I can get in touch with him before he flies home.'

'Don't be so feeble,' said Stuart. 'If we leave in ten minutes, we might still get to the airport in time to meet his plane. You could invite him to join us for lunch.'

Tara looked across at her mother, who didn't appear at all enthusiastic about the idea. 'Even if we do make it, he'll probably say no,' said Maggie. 'He'll be jetlagged, and he'll want to prepare for his meeting tomorrow.'

'But at least you'll have made the effort,' said Tara.

Maggie folded the letter, took off her apron and said, 'You're right, Tara. After all these years it's the least I can do.' She smiled at her daughter, quickly left the kitchen and disappeared upstairs.

In her room she opened her wardrobe and picked out her favourite dress. She didn't want Declan to think of her as middle-aged – though that was rather silly, because she was, and so was he. She inspected herself in the mirror. Passable, she decided, for fifty-one. She hadn't put on any weight, but one or two new lines had appeared on her forehead during the last six months.

Maggie came back downstairs to find Stuart pacing up and down in the hall. She knew the car would already be loaded, probably with the engine running.

'Come on, Tara,' he shouted up the stairs for the third time.

Tara appeared a few minutes later, and Stuart's impatience evaporated the moment she smiled.

As she climbed into the car Tara said, 'I can't wait to meet Declan. Even his name has a romantic ring to it.'

'That's exactly the way I felt at the time,' said Maggie.

'What's in a name?' said Stuart with a grin as he manoeuvred the car down the drive and out onto the road. .

'Quite a lot when you're born Margaret Deirdre Burke,' replied Maggie. Stuart burst out laughing. 'When I was at school I once wrote a letter to myself addressed to "Dr and Mrs Declan O'Casey". But it didn't make him any more interesting.' She touched her hair nervously.

'Isn't it just possible,' said Tara, 'that after all these years, Dr O'Casey might turn out to have become amusing, rugged and worldly?'

'I doubt it,' said Maggie. 'I think it's more likely he'll be pompous, wrinkled, and still a virgin.'

'How could you possibly have known that he was a virgin?' asked Stuart.

'Because he never stopped telling everybody,' Maggie replied. 'Declan's idea of a romantic weekend was to deliver a trigonometry paper at a math conference.'

Tara burst out laughing.

'Though, to be fair, your father wasn't a lot more experienced than he was. We spent our first night together on a park bench, and the only thing I lost was my slippers.'

Stuart was laughing so much he nearly hit the kerb.

'I even found out how Connor lost *his* virginity,' Maggie continued. 'It was to a girl known as "Never Say No Nancy",' she whispered, in mock confidentiality.

'He can't have told you that,' said Stuart in disbelief.

'No, he didn't. I would never have found out if he hadn't been late back from football training one night. I decided to leave a message in his locker, and I found Nancy's name scratched inside the door. But I couldn't really complain. When I checked his team-mates' lockers, Connor had by far the lowest score.'

Tara was now bent double with laughter, and was begging her mother to stop.

'When your father finally . . .'

By the time they reached the airport Maggie had exhausted all her stories of the rivalry between Declan and Connor, and was beginning to feel rather apprehensive about meeting up with her old dancing partner after so many years.

Stuart pulled into the kerb, jumped out of the car and opened the back door for her. 'Better hurry,' he said, checking his watch.

'Do you want me to come with you, Mom?' Tara asked.

'No, thank you,' Maggie replied, and walked quickly towards the automatic doors before she had time to change her mind.

She checked the arrivals board. United's Flight 815 from Chicago had landed on time, at eleven twenty. It was now nearly eleven forty. She had never been so late to meet someone off a plane in her life.

The nearer she got to the arrivals area, the slower she walked, in the hope that Declan would have time to slip away. She decided to hang around dutifully for fifteen minutes, then return to the car. She began studying the arriving passengers as they came through the gate. The young, bright and enthusiastic, carrying surfboards under their arms; the middle-aged, bustling and attentive, clutching their children; the old, slow-moving and thoughtful, bringing up the rear. She began to wonder if she would even recognise Declan. Had he already walked past her? After all, it had been over thirty years since they had last met, and he wasn't expecting anyone to be there to greet him.

She checked her watch again – the fifteen minutes were almost up. She began to think about a plate of gnocchi and a glass of Chardonnay over lunch at Cronulla, and then dozing in the afternoon sun while Stuart and Tara surfed. Then her eyes settled on a one-armed man who was striding through the arrivals gate.

Maggie's legs felt weak. She stared at the man she had never stopped loving, and thought she might collapse. Tears welled up in her eyes. She demanded no explanation. That could come later, much later. She ran towards him, oblivious of anyone around her.

The moment he saw her, he gave that familiar smile which showed he knew he'd been found out.

'Oh my God, Connor,' she said, flinging out her arms. 'Tell me it's true. Dear God, tell me it's true.'

Connor held her tightly with his right arm, his left sleeve dangling by his side. 'It's true enough, my darling Maggie,' he said in a broad Irish accent. 'Unfortunately, although Presidents can fix almost anything, once they've killed you off you have no choice but to disappear for a little while and take on another identity.' He released her and looked down at the woman he had wanted to hold every hour of the past six months. 'I decided on Dr Declan O'Casey, an academic considering taking up a new appointment in Australia, because I remembered your once telling me that you'd wanted nothing more from life than to be Mrs Declan O'Casey. I was also confident that I wouldn't be unduly troubled by too many Australians testing me on my mathematical prowess.'

Maggie looked up at him, the tears streaming down her cheeks, not sure whether to laugh or cry.

'But the letter, my darling,' she said. 'The crooked "e". How did you . . . ?'

'Yes, I thought you'd enjoy that touch,' said Connor. 'It was after I saw the picture of you in the *Washington Post*, standing by the grave opposite the President, and then read the glowing tributes to your late husband that I thought, Declan, my boy, this could be your last chance to marry that young Margaret Burke from the East Side.' He smiled. 'So how about it, Maggie?' he said. 'Will you marry me?'

'Connor Fitzgerald, you've got a lot of explaining to do,' said Maggie.

'I have indeed, Mrs O'Casey. And the rest of our lives to do it.'